SHELTER

Lost and Found

R.A. CONROY

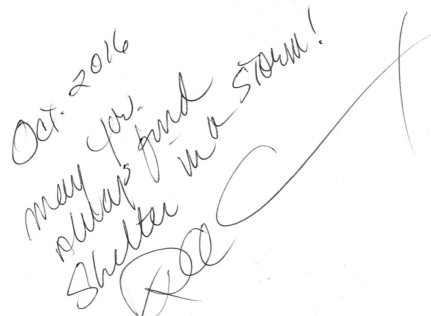

SHELTER
Lost and Found

R.A. CONROY

Brass Frog Bookworks ™
Independent Publishers
2764 Compass Drive Suite 201-2
Grand Junction, CO 81506
www.BrassFrogBookworks.com

Published by BRASS FROG BOOKWORKS™ Independent Publishers
2764 Compass Drive Suite 201-2 | Grand Junction, CO 81506
909-239-0344 | www.BrassFrogBookworks.com

Brass Frog Bookworks is dedicated to excellence and integrity in the publishing industry. The company was founded on the belief in the power of language and the spiritual nature of human creativity. *"In the beginning was the Word…"* John 1:1

Book design copyright © 2014 by Brass Frog Bookworks™ All rights reserved.
Cover & Interior Design – Laurie Goralka Design
Illustrations & Cover Image – R.A. Conroy

Inquiries should be addressed to:
R.A. Conroy
c/o Brass Frog Bookworks
2764 Compass Drive, Suite 201-2
Grand Junction, CO 81506
raconroy.query@yahoo.com

Printed in the United States of America | First Printing 2014

Library of Congress Control Number: 2013958141

ISBN: 978-0-9857191-7-3

1. Fiction/General   2. Fiction/Animals   3. Fiction/Family

DEDICATION

This story is dedicated to the selfless, heroic souls who speak up, and stand up, for our four-legged and winged brethren; who have no voice and no choice, when it comes to the affairs of mankind.

It is based on a snippet from my own life. To weave the story, I have taken heaps of creative liberties. I've dabbled with time, changed names, created characters and situations, as well as conjured particulars, in order to shine a light on the brave, protect the innocent–as well as the guilty–prowling within these pages.

R.A. Conroy

PREFACE

When the New Jersey State Commission for Investigation was formed in 1969, it was dubbed 'the watch dog' for the entire New Jersey legal system. Granted the ability to recommend new laws and remedies, the Commission began to examine the state's civil infrastructure with the specific intent to ferret out corruption and governmental laxity via fact-finding investigations. Many important, long overdue changes to the social system were the result of these investigations, often through such sponsored bills as Senator Frank J. Dodd's S-1217; a bill that broadened the power of the woefully overburdened Juvenile and Domestic Relations Court in dealing with child abuse cases, signed into law by then Governor Brendan Byrne, five years later in October of 1974.

It would be another thirty-one years, however, before the Commission turned its investigative attention to one of the most overlooked, fractured and miserably ineffective branches of civil service in the state; the hundred-year-old SPCA system. Despite decades rife with complaints and requests for reform, and numerous studies showing the direct correlation between child abuse and the subsequent abuse of animals, animal welfare was routinely relegated to back burner status.

For those New Jersey counties lacking one of the state chapter's sanctioned, independent SPCA charters (there were only seventeen), responsibility for animal welfare fell to the police, the town pound, or if a community was lucky enough to have one, a local volunteer group. Those animal control officers and volunteers willing to wrestle with poverty and ignorance did their best to give hope and a second chance to the neglected, abused and unwanted animals that crossed their paths, in spite of the tangled and ineffective bureaucracy that offered little in the way of legal recourse at the time.

Essex County never had an organized SPCA charter. All animal welfare issues were dealt with at the local level. This is the story of just one of those forgotten 'town pounds', its dedicated, eccentric crew, and one lost and lonely girl who walked in out of the cold to save one dog, and ended up saving them all, including herself.

ACKNOWLEDGMENTS

First and foremost, I would like to thank Patti Hoff of Brass Frog Bookworks, my publisher. The day I trudged through crowds at the L.A. Times Book Fair, hauling a heavy cart filled with 50 copies of chapter samples from *SHELTER*, turned out to be my lucky day. There were plenty of self-publishing firms more than willing to take my money and hand me back a book, whether it was good or not. No one was interested to even read it!

Seven hours later, disillusioned and about to give up, I spotted a fat frog on a placard beside a modest tent across the lawns. I dragged my cart over to the tent, where I was greeted by Ms. Hoff, who offered me water and asked if she could help me. I blurted out my frustration and disappointment, and instead of trying to sell me something, she sat me down and listened to my hopes and dreams for well on an hour. She offered me a great deal of information about the publishing world, including the pitfalls. I was impressed with Brass Frog's commitment to publishing good work they believe in, and their dedication to their authors.

I submitted sample chapters from my novel for review and consideration by the team at Brass Frog. After a few weeks, BFB called to inform me they would love to publish *SHELTER*. At the same time, she unselfishly gave me even more advice and told me to do my homework. For eight months, I did just that. During that time, BFB continued to answered my questions about what I could and would need to do with this novel as well as the challenges a new author faces.

I chose to publish with Brass Frog for a number of reasons. The most important being Ms. Hoff's generous giving of her time and expertise, without asking for a penny, while taking this fledgling author under wing, treating me and my work with the respect of a Pulitzer Prize winner, and giving my story a chance to be told. All the other reasons can be wrapped up in my mission to support those who "walk the talk", those who embody all those "corny" virtues like honesty, loyalty, and kindness, and whenever possible, to give back ten-fold for the honor shown me.

My thanks to D.A. Brockett, a talented award-winning editor and author with whom I was paired for this project. Together we plowed through my manuscript and she helped me massage it into shape. Debbie taught me so much, without ever making me feel like the dunce that I was, more than once!

Great heartfelt thanks to Poet Laureate Charles Simic, for his permission to reprint one of his heart-wrenchingly beautiful poems, *Dog On a Chain*. I have carried that poem around with me for decades. I even put a copy in a few mailboxes with the hope that the residents might reconsider the lonely soul attached to the chain in their backyard.

Special thanks to Laurie Goralka, my talented graphic designer for her patience in working with me while I tweaked and changed the artwork. Thank you for the great job.

Thank you to my family members, who have seen me through so many incarnations as I seek my way. To my departed father, my undying love and gratitude for believing in me - and the magic we can create when we do believe. To my beautiful, talented mother, who instilled the sense of "can do!" in her daughters, ever supportive of her first born dreamer. To my remarkable sisters, Faith and Laura for their encouragement, love and cheerleading through it all. To Jim Wilson for his kind respect, personally and professionally, and to his family for their generosity of spirit, and a place to land when the rug was pulled out from underneath me for the umpteenth time! To my extended family, Al (R.I.P.) and Rita, my aunts, uncles and cousins; you have figured more importantly in the development of who I am as an artist and a person, than you know.

Lastly, I would like to acknowledge a few special people who hold a very special place in my heart, and always will. With the utmost respect and love, this book is for you: Kerry Rasp, Rob Arms, Azalena, Ann & Louie Kraus (R.I.P. dear ones), Dr. George Cameron DVM, Dr. Kurt Blaicher DVM, Dr. Jay Jasan DVM (R.I.P.) - Jay, I carry at least one of your torches forward for you - Chip, Marcy, Sue, Sue Blaicher, Lil' Sue, Agnes, Kathy F., Katherine & Edith P., Mary Jean—and Rufus, the first of the "lucky" dogs—and cats, birds, squirrels, raccoons—all the creatures big and small, who taught me more about the power of love when it comes to healing wounds than can ever be found between the covers of a book.

DOG ON A CHAIN

So that's how it's going to be,
A cold day smelling of snow.
Step around the bare oak tree
And see how quickly you get
Yourself entangled for good.
Your bad luck was being friendly
With people who love their new couch
More than they love you.

Fred, you poor mutt, the night
Is falling.
The children playing
Across the road were cold,
So they ran in.
Watch the smoke
Swirl out of their chimney
In the windy sky as long as you can.
Soon, no one will see you there.
You'll have to bark even if
There's no moon, bark and growl
To keep yourself company.

By Charles Simic
Used by permission
© Charles Simic

shelter (shel'tr) n.: Something that covers, protects or defends; a place affording protection from the elements, danger, etc.

- Webster's Dictionary

Chapter 1

"You lost?"

Peggy slammed back against the tunnel wall, dropping her tattered, duct-taped suitcase. She couldn't see the man's face. The flashing lights behind him were too bright, the screeching of metal on metal deafening. She cowered as subway cars bulleted past and harried forms pushed her aside.

What are you doing? The question wailed in her mind unanswered.

Don't stop! Keep running! The wave of voices echoed their warning inside her head, shouting at her. *Run! If they catch you, you'll be sorry!*

She tried to dam the torrent of their threats above the screaming rails, but she could no longer tell the difference between the two. Why in hell should she listen now? What stinking good had they ever been to her? The crowd parted, and a shiver ripped down her spine when she saw that the man was still there. Unable to loosen her tongue, she could only stare at him.

"One way out, miss," the man shouted, pointing ahead. "Keep moving forward."

Snatching up her suitcase, Peggy dove into the throng of winter coats. Between briefcases, newspapers, and shoulders hunched against the cold, she spotted a damp stairway and stumbled to a stop at the bottom. Her breath caught in her throat. *Oh no!*

Go back! You know what happens! Go back! Hide! The taunting voices continued to shriek from inside her head

Trembling, Peggy backed away from the stairs, but was pushed around by the heedless crowd. She struggled to break free but was spun around like a loose penny. Catching sight of the stairs again, she realized that people were racing up the stairs. Not down, but *up!*

This was her chance! She threw herself forward, grasping the cold handrail and hauling herself upwards, hand over hand. She held her breath against the acrid stench of urine burning her nose.

What do you think you're doing? Get back down there!

As if possessed, Peggy ignored the angry voices in her head. Swept along with the crowd, she climbed up and up until the stairwell walls brightened from sooty gray to dingy yellow. Just to her left she spotted a mosaic of blue inlaid tiles that read: NEWARK - NEW JERSEY.

Propelled by a sudden surge of adrenaline, she climbed faster and faster. *Almost there,* she panted, *soon I'll be free!* She pushed forward blindly but was jarred with a painful smack of her toes against an enclosed turnstile. Her shabby suitcase jammed inside and held her fast. *No! No-o-o…*

"Hey! Move it, stupid! Get outta there!" The growing cluster of impatient people peered over each other's shoulders, muttering, complaining and hurling obscenities. She gyrated around in confusion trying to escape the jammed turnstile.

Thought you could get away? Now you're gonna get it, you filthy piece of…

Ignoring the taunting voices, Peggy pounded the suitcase until it popped from the rungs, mercifully spitting them both out. She raced past the mob, tore up the last volley of stairs and burst up onto the open street.

Pigeons exploded into the air as a cold gust of wind slapped her face. She peered through the drizzling rain and caught her breath. Buses roared past and sirens wailed in the distance. Tall, brick buildings scarred with graffiti and boarded-up windows loomed above her, their shadows slicing the daylight into slivers. Peggy looked around cold, confused and her teeth chattering. *This was New Jersey? The Garden State?* It was hardly better than where she had just escaped.

Another tidal wave of coats rushed towards her, and she froze. *Run! Hide! They'll take you back!*

Peggy couldn't move and squeezed her eyes shut. At the last second, the crowd fanned out around her like a stampede and poured down the dank stairwell into the bowels of the subway system. Quickly, Peggy scanned the crowded streets and wondered which way to go. Just across the street, buses lumbered in and out of a dingy station. Her mind raced. Buses go somewhere. Did it really matter where, as long as it was far away?

Peggy hoisted her suitcase and launched herself into the traffic, darting between cars like a skittish squirrel. Once she reached the platform, her eyes zeroed in on placards of route maps. She scoured them for a reference point but kept her face averted, lest someone ask questions.

"Where you goin'?"

Peggy felt her stomach tighten like a clenched fist and whirled around. A burly black bus driver regarded her from under the brim of his hat. He zipped his winter parka up to his chin, and pulled oil-stained gloves on, as he looked her up and down.

Peggy stammered. "I-I don't know. I mean I…"

He raised a brow. "Put it diss way; where you *wanna* go?"

Buses engines revved, and air brakes hissed on either side of them. Peggy bit her lip. "I-I'm not sure."

"What?" the driver shouted over the rumbling buses, cocking his head toward her.

"F-far away!"

"What? You say Farroway?" He pointed past her shoulder. "Numbah twenty-one, lane seven. You got five minutes before last call."

For a split second, Peggy didn't move, and then as if kicked from behind, she bolted toward the #21 bus. As she waited in line, the people in front of her boarded and dropped change into a glass canister on a stand. Below it, a metal box swallowed the coins. Suddenly it was her turn.

"Where to?" The driver blew his nose distractedly, then jammed his soiled handkerchief into his pocket.

"F-far-o-way?"

"You sure 'bout dat?"

She looked behind her at the subway stairs across the road, then back at the driver, and nodded.

"Dollah fifty," he coughed.

Peggy stuck numb fingers into her pockets for change, but coins cascaded to the floor as she pulled them out. "S-sorry! So s-sorry!" Burrowing around the feet of strapholders, she snatched as many coins as she could find.

"Leave it," the driver sighed. "Sit down. I said *sit!*"

"Sorry!" Grabbing her suitcase, Peggy stumbled into the first empty seat she could find and peered out the grimy window. Her reflection startled her. Staring back at her was a pale, skinny girl, maybe in her early twenties. In a worn cloth coat several sizes too big for her, she looked both waifish and weary. Under a tangle of auburn hair, dark, haunted eyes stared back at her. Her chapped lips were bracketed by worry.

Ashamed, she dragged her eyes away from the reflection, swallowing a lump in her throat.

Maybe the coast was clear, she thought, trying to distract herself. Maybe. Looking out another window, she perused the passing sprawl of urban decay, accelerated by an unglued economy still crashing down around everyone's ears, courtesy of the Vietnam War. Watergate had stripped America of its innocence, forcing the resignation of Richard Nixon, a once popular president. A runaway inflation had chased double digit unemployment until it had driven everyone to their knees. For most Americans, things were worse instead of better, but to Peggy, it was as if the whole world had fallen from grace. The only thing left to look forward to, was finally bidding 1974 *adieu*.

Peggy rested her forehead against the cold glass and closed her eyes. We made it. *You'll never make it. You know what happens.* The voices continued to taunt her, but she frowned, determined.

Not this time. We'll get far away now. Far, far away from...from...

Then the bus engine revved, lurching Peggy forward and her eyes popped open with a start. *No! I won't go back!*

For a split second, she wasn't sure if she'd blurted it out loud. Shaking her head, she realized she must have dozed off. Where was she? It took a moment before her heart stopped hammering in her ears and then she remembered. She was on her way to somewhere called Farroway. In cold silence, she prayed that Farroway would be far enough away.

"Tory Corner," the driver called out, coughing into his handkerchief.

Perched on the edge of her seat, Peggy had been straining to hear him for nearly half an hour. He'd sneezed through almost every stop and was losing his voice. What if she'd missed the stop? More than anything, she wanted to ask the driver if she had, but his gruffness strapped her to her seat. Her fear that they may be heading back to those stairs, however, propelled her up and wobbling towards the front of the bus.

Just as she reached the driver, he stomped on the brakes, pitching her into the safety bar. Punching the window open, he bellowed at a truck ahead.

"What the hell wrong witchoo? Git yo' ass in gear, mo'fo!"

Peggy clung to the safety bar, sure the driver was going to get out and beat the crap out of the offending truck driver. Peering out through the windshield, she saw that the truck had stopped in the middle of an intersection. She spotted a skinny dog slink past the truck's bumper. She watched it dart between the cars and silently called out to it. *Oh! Watch out! Get off the street. Hurry! Run! Hide!*

The bus driver snorted a wet sneeze and thrust the bus in gear. Traffic resumed its sluggish pace. Soon, the bus eased up to a curb. The door whooshed open.

"You gittin' off or what?" he muttered, impatiently.

"I'm-I'm going to F-far-o-way?"

"This is it!"

"But you-you said Tory Corner."

The driver yanked his window shut. "This be yo' stop girl, now either sit or git!"

Peggy descended the steps slowly, her knees shaking. When she reached the sidewalk, she looked around. As the bus rumbled away, a belch of blue exhaust engulfed her. She coughed, waving the fumes away from her face. When she could breathe again, she found herself standing in a traffic roundabout where four streets intersected. The street signs read Main, Washington, Franklin and Valley Roads. Under a naked flag pole, she spied a bronze plaque affixed to a rock. She walked over and read:

Tory Corner - The Farroways
George Washington stopped here too!
American Revolution 1776

Given the bleak surroundings, Peggy couldn't fathom why George Washington would have bothered stopping here at all. The town looked about as depressed as she felt. A row of three-story boarding houses butted up against a few forlorn shops. Paddy's Diner, a long chrome trailer, dominated the middle of the block. Her stomach growled at the smell of bacon grease. She had to drag her eyes away from its inviting lights. On the east side of Washington Street sat a dowdy church, perched atop a slight slope. A cemetery, whose grounds had gone to seed, flanked one side.

Peggy spotted a newspaper dispenser on the corner, trotted over to it, and inserted a dime. She pulled out a paper and opened it to the classified section. Oh No! According to the listings, there were four

Farroways! West Farroway, East Farroway, South Farroway and just plain Farroway. Which one was this?

Shouts and yelling erupted behind her. Peggy ducked behind the church's cemetery wall and peeked over the ledge. She saw three boys, their greased-back hair gleaming in the setting sun. They were taunting and throwing garbage at the stray dog she'd seen from the bus. The pitiful animal was cowering behind some trash cans.

As if the voices within her sensed her outrage, they hissed at her. *Keep your mouth shut! They won't see you. Just keep quiet!*

Being outnumbered by both the rowdy boys and the voices, Peggy scrunched down behind the wall, watching, silently begging the dog to run.

It didn't, though. As each piece of garbage hit the whimpering dog, she cringed, too. Shame burned her cheeks. Here she was hiding behind a wall, and there was the mutt, cowering behind trash cans; both trapped by fear, but only one of them able to do something about it.

A grapefruit knocked the dog sideways, and he yelped. Peggy clambered out from behind the wall and opened her mouth to holler at the boys, but all that came out was a plume of frosty air.

What are you doing? Get back!

The dog cried out again, and Peggy snatched up a rock. She threw it as hard as she could towards the boys, hitting the rusted dumpster with a loud clang.

The surprised boys spun around, staring. Peggy tried to steady her shaking knees, which threatened to spill her to the ground. She lifted her chin, trying to look taller, and pinned them with an angry glare.

The tallest of the boys regained his composure and threw his shoulders back, pushing out his chest in a menacing posture. He strutted towards her, his buddies tailing him closely. "You cruisin' for a bruisin'?"

"Leave-leave him alone."

"Beat it, bitch. Or are you lookin' for a piece of me, too?" The boys behind him chuckled.

Peggy held her ground. *Are you crazy? Run, stupid!* Peggy didn't move.

The boy's cocky grin vanished. He tore across the street towards her. Peggy waited until the boys were far enough away from the dog, then snatched up her suitcase. She dashed around the corner and skidded to a stop. Fear rose in the back of her throat nearly choking her as she realized she had run into a dead end alley.

Too late! Give up. It won't take long.

No! Peggy ran to the chain-link fence at the end of the alley. Trapped, she pressed her body into it and pulled her suitcase up as a shield. Just as the boys bore down on her, she heard a man's voice boom.

"Hey! Stop it right der!" the deep voice barked.

The cocky kid stopped, midstride, and his cohorts collided into each other's backs. "The fuzz!" he shouted. "Scatter!" The boys immediately took off running.

Peggy peeked around her suitcase. A uniformed cop stood with his hands on his hips, watching the boys go, making no attempt to stop them.

"Y'all right, miss?" he asked in a worn, Irish accent.

Peggy sagged against the fence. "Yes. Thank you." Tears welled in her eyes, but she blinked them away.

"Y'sure, now? Saw the whole ting from Paddy's. Want to file a repart?"

"No!" Peggy blurted out. "No-no. I'm okay, really."

"Aye, well it's a waste o' time, to be sure. Buncha greasers playin' hooky." The officer picked up her suitcase, looking at it as if it might be suspect. He cocked a bushy eyebrow at her. "This yours? Where ye be goin', if y'don't mind me askin'?"

Peggy took a measured breath. "F-far-o-way?"

"Oh! Well, I wager you be wantin' the college, den."

Eyes downcast, Peggy risked a nod.

"'Aye, dat's what we t'awt. You'll be wantin' Uppah Farroway, den. No college down here. Everybody makes dat mistake." He led the way through the garbage-lined alley and back to the street. "Der's another bus along in a while. T'eighty-eight, runs past da campus. Dem little wops won't be back anytime soon, mark me. If dey show, git yerself inta Paddy's. He'll put 'em to straights, right quick."

The cop whistled and a squad car pulled away from a curb across the street and headed towards them. "Now, if y'don't mind, I'm goin' t'give ya little piece of advice. Next time, leave well enough alone. No dog is worth dat kind o' trouble." He handed her the suitcase and, with a wink to her, climbed into the squad car.

Walking towards the bus stop, Peggy kept an eye on the police car until it disappeared. She exhaled with relief and then crossed the street to look for the dog.

The voices echoed in her head. *What's the matter with you? Go. Now! Run!*

But, what if he's hurt? The wind had picked up, and Peggy knew if she was cold, the dog was cold, too. She ignored the warnings and scanned the garbage-strewn lot. She looked behind boxes and empty trash cans rolling around in the gusts, and then peered around the last rusty receptacle.

"Oh! Hello."

The skinny dog shivered against the fence. At first glance, it was ugly, a big dog with a lopsided face and drooping jowls. His eyes, framed by rust patches, had a sweet sorrow about them. He looked at her with fear in his eyes, but there was a glimmer of trust, too. When she inspected him more closely, she saw that he wasn't gray as she thought. There were white patches showing through the sooty dirt that coated him from snout to tail. She reached out a hand. The dog backed up warily, peeing on itself.

"Shhhh...it's all right, I-I won't hurt you," Peggy soothed. She reached out again. This time, the dog allowed her to pet him. He leaned his weary head into her hands, and that's when she saw the welt marks across his boney back.

She felt fresh tears spring to her eyes. She knew right away those bully kids didn't do it. These were old wounds. Two looked infected.

Peggy glanced around. It would be dark soon. Rummaging around in the trash, she made a crude leash from newspaper twine and carefully knotted it around the dog's neck. She uncovered a discarded jar of peanut butter and used it to coax the hungry dog out from its hiding place, and then led it across the street towards the boarding houses.

Chapter 2

"NO PETS! OUT!"

"P-please; he's hurt!" Peggy stood in a chilly foyer, just inside the boarding house entrance. To the right, wooden stairs led up to a second floor, where she could see a landing, and several closed doors. Pan-fried dinner smells and cranky baby cries emanated from behind them.

"No, I donta care! Filthy, dirty…*out*!" The squat building manager, bound tight in a soiled apron, wagged a finger at Peggy and the dog, her Sicilian accent thick and testy.

Above her, Peggy noticed tenants had emerged from their rooms and peered over the railing at her. One woman, clad in a thread-bare robe, grabbed a fluffy cat as it sauntered into view, and covered its mouth to stifle its indignation. Catching Peggy's eye, she put her finger to her lips, begging her to keep quiet, then hurried away. Peggy heard a door slam shut.

"Please." Peggy dug into her coat pockets. "I have money!"

"Money! Yeah! You gotta job?" The woman scrutinized Peggy's frayed coat and taped suitcase.

"Well-uh, not yet, but…"

"Notta yet! Marone! No job, no rent! Thissa no charity! Come back with a job and no dog!" The woman lumbered toward the door and pushed it open. "Dogs belong outside! Notta inside!"

Deflated, Peggy led the dog back outside, the whipping cold sucking the breath out of her. Biting her lip, she kneeled down to pet the dog. "I didn't figure on needing a job," she admitted to him. "Or you." The dog licked her hand, and she had a hard time swallowing the lump in her throat. Pulling him close, she whispered. "Don't worry, I won't leave you."

Nudging the dog down the street, she looked for other vacancy signs. There were none. She noticed the dog shiver and hurried him into a glass phone booth, out of the wind. Its fractured glass panels and squeaky broken door offered little shelter, but it was better than nothing. The phone receiver had been ripped out, but a chained phone book hung below it. Peggy grabbed it and thumbed through the pages. Stymied, she was unsure what she was even looking for. "What about a pet shop?" she asked the dog.

The mutt looked up and cocked his misshapen face at her as if considering her question. Despite their predicament, it made her laugh.

"Maybe not," she decided. Starting over, she leafed through the phone book from the beginning, and after a few pages, paused as her finger perched on a listing. Farroway Animal Shelter. 95 Walnut Street. She exhaled in relief. She remembered the driver calling out Walnut Street. It was by some railroad tracks. She kneeled down and cupped the dog's head in her hands. "It's gonna be okay! C'mon."

Peggy hurried the dog towards the bus stop. Fifteen toe-numbing minutes later, a bus pulled up to the curb. The bus door whooshed open, and she looked up to see the very same driver as before, looking even more bleary-eyed and miserable. His eyes bounced from her to the dog, and then he pointed to a sign hanging above the windshield. NO PETS.

Peggy opened her mouth to plead, but he closed the door on her. She nearly burst into tears, watching the bus leave in a belch of exhaust. The dog whimpered, as if sensing her disappointment.

"Well," she sighed. "Wanna go for a walk? It'll keep us warm."

He wagged his tail. Peggy led the dog back down the hill in search of Walnut Street. The railroad tracks were at least a half-hour away, by bus. On foot, she was afraid to guess. Either way, she was grateful for one thing; there was a place that would take the dog in out of the cold. That was all that mattered.

An hour later, Peggy passed the boarded up train station for the third time, and stopped. She was lost. There were no street signs, and she felt sure that she'd crossed Walnut Street a dozen times already without knowing it. With the cold knifing through her coat, she was afraid that she and the dog would freeze to death before they found it.

Screeeech! A souped-up caddy crammed with black teens skidded around the corner. They spotted Peggy and rolled down windows, hooting at her over thumping Motown.

"Yo, dawg! Ahhooooooooo!"

Pulling the dog into a doorway, Peggy hunkered down in the shadows, until the car fishtailed around the corner. The thumping faded in the distance. Peggy waited, petting the dog as much to calm her own pounding heart. That's when she heard it. Her companion's ears pricked forward. He'd heard it, too. A dog barked, then another. Poking her head out of her hiding place, she checked both ways before emerging from the shadows. Peggy trotted the dog towards the barking. She passed a lone sign reading simply —SHELTER— a bullet hole piercing its center, then followed a narrow driveway between an empty mill and a brick fire house. Glancing up, she caught sight of two firemen in a brightly lit window, sipping coffee. Had they been watching her the whole time? Why didn't they come to her rescue? She kept running. The narrow corridor finally opened into a small parking lot. She stopped and looked around.

Surrounded by abandoned warehouses, she faced what looked like a long shed that stretched across the width of the enclosed lot. It was a dilapidated structure that reminded her of a covered bridge, hanging precariously over the end of the driveway. The driveway dipped down under the left half of the overhang, ending at a back gate. Capped with a tin roof and fronted by rusted dog runs, the place looked like an ancient prison yard. The front gate creaked in the wind, displaying a cardboard sign dangling from the latch that read: Open.

Peggy considered leaving, but then she noticed two black boys playing tug-of-war with a yappy little brown dog in a run. They saw her at the same time.

"Yo! That yo' dog?" the younger boy called out.

Shoring up her courage, Peggy hurried the dog past them, up a narrow walkway between the runs that ended at a massive, green front door. She rapped on it. An explosion of barking sounded from within, causing her to shy back.

"They ain't gonna hearken you," the older boy said.

She knocked again, this time more insistently. When no one answered, she shoved on it until it opened. Peggy stumbled inside, the dog right behind her. Barking reverberated off of cinderblock walls. She clapped her hands over her ears. Spotting a door at the end of the kennel, she ran the dog toward it and wrenched it open.

"Shut the bloody door!" a woman's guttural English accent hollered.

The dog pulled Peggy inside and she slammed the door shut. The next instant she ducked, as a ferret leaped over her head to a shelf, knocking books to the floor. A petite, wrinkled old woman tottered after it, swinging a fishing net. Her ash-blonde wig hung askew, and as she bustled past Peggy, she sang *Pop Goes The Weasel!*

"There he goes!" A buxom black woman popped up from behind a chair, a phone receiver in each hand. "Sheltah," she snapped as one of the phones jangled. She paused to listen, then she exclaimed, "Say what?! Well, what you want us to do 'bout it? Excuse me, I said '*scuse* me! Why ain't you spayed that bitch yet? Un-natural? I tell you what be *un*-natural! Them thousand bastard puppies put to sleep every year insteada you!" She banged the phone down muttering under her breath.

"'Ang 'em by the bollocks, Betty!" cried the old English woman, thrusting the fishing net at Peggy. "You there! Get 'im or get out the way!"

"W-what?" Sure that she'd stumbled into a loony bin, Peggy's first impulse was to flee. She yanked on the door, but the doorknob popped off in her hand. She just stood there staring at the doorknob, when the ferret used her head as a springboard and, in one rapid blur, dove to the floor at her feet. Two big hands grabbed her ankles from under the counter and Peggy yelped, falling backwards into the waste basket.

"Oh!" From over her knees Peggy saw her attacker was a middle-aged man in a uniform with the word Warden sewn in big yellow letters on the pocket.

"Oh!" he exclaimed, like an echo, looking just as surprised. Trying to extricate himself, he smacked his forehead smartly under the counter top. "Blast it! So sorry! Which way did he go?" His English accent had a more refined sound to it, unlike the old woman's colloquial dialect.

Stuck like a cork in the waste basket, Peggy gulped and pointed past his shoulder.

The ferret dashed across the counter, just ahead of the old woman, who slapped the fishing net down, catching nothing but frigid air.

"Bloody, buggery bollocks!" she cried and took off after the escapee.

"Clara?" the warden beseeched her, "The prisoner's to be taken *alive*!"

"I've got you now!" The old woman stalked past Peggy, her eyes fixed on a jacket hung on the coat rack. As she passed an open cage door, her wig was snagged and lifted right off of her head. The missing wig revealed cotton white wisps of hair projecting haphazardly from her pink scalp. Intent on her mission, the old woman didn't even notice. She cooed, "Here kitty kitty kitty...."

By now, Betty had joined the hunt. Peggy watched the three people bumble about, colliding with each other. Meanwhile, the ferret tore about, snatching crumbs off what appeared to be breakfast plates. Squeezing herself out of the waste basket, she pulled the half-eaten peanut butter jar from her pocket, and while the crew inadvertently chased another cat under the counter, she lured the ferret into a cage, latching the door behind it. Turning, she found the trio cornering the old woman's wig which had fallen onto the floor. Peggy cleared her throat.

"Ex-excuse me?" She stood aside to reveal the captured ferret.

The warden blustered. "Hello, how did you do that? We've been at it all morning and you show up, and in one two three, you nobbled him!" He grinned at the ferret behind bars. "Houdini here gives us a go at least once a fortnight." He lowered his voice, glancing towards the old woman. "Clara forgets, you see. She thinks he's a cat and you can imagine the confusion." He threw up his hands and shook his head. "But, never mind, here you are, just in the nick of time!"

He handed her a cat. "Would you be so good as to find a cage for George here and…" he handed her a second cat, "…another for Tiger?"

"Oh!" Peggy juggled the two squirming cats in her arms. "But I-I—"

"Anywhere you find room. I dare say it won't make a tinker's dither at this point!"

"But, I—" It was all she could do not to drop the cats, so Peggy wandered about the cramped office after the warden. The dog dutifully followed along behind her.

Two phones rang nonstop. Before answering either one, Betty rummaged around the countertop that seemed to serve as a desk, and finally held up an inhaler. She put it to her nostril, inhaled deeply and then snatched up a phone receiver. "Sheltah!" She sneezed and searched again for a tissue, gave up and blew her nose on a pink invoice. "Hold on—I said *hold on!*" Cupping her hand over the receiver, she hollered to the warden. "Mistah Riley say he ain't gonna touch the boilah 'til we done paid up from last time."

Peggy noticed that it was nearly as cold in the office as it had been outside, and everyone wore heavy coats and hats.

The warden handed Betty a box of tissues. "What say we give friendly persuasion a go?" His eyebrows did an impish dance.

"Friendly whoozit? On what planet do that work? Which die-mention?" Blowing her nose, she returned to the phone. "Mistah Riley? We

go troo this every damn wintah. You fix the boilah, we write you a check, the boilah break down, we stop the check. What? Oh please! When hell freeze ovah and done thawed out, again, maybe we'll pay that bill. Git yo' butt ovah here!" Slamming the receiver down, she picked up the other one and sneezed into it. "Sheltah. Make it quick, it be closin' time."

The warden confided to Peggy, "Betty is our P.R. point person, our ambassador of good will, if you will."

"Say what?" Betty exclaimed to the caller. "You want *us* to sell yo' eight bastard puppies? This ain't no pet shop! Ain't 'nuff homes fo' half what we got now 'cause of nimrods like you!"

Peggy darted a dubious glance to the warden.

He merely smiled at her. "Dear me, here we are, taking advantage of your time and we never even asked—how may we help you?"

Peggy coaxed the dog out from behind her legs. "I found this-this dog."

"Dog?!" the old English woman cried, shielding a tabby cat in her arms, "This here's the feline sanctuary! No dogs in here! Good for nothing, slobbering, cat chasin'…"

"He's hurt. Somebody beat him."

The old woman fell quiet, and the warden's easy smile caught at its corners. He kneeled beside the dog.

"Ah." A vague weariness clouded his gray eyes. "Hello Lucky," he murmured, scratching the dog's ears.

"You know him?"

"His name's Boy, of all things, but we call him Lucky. Betty? Any word from Harrison?"

"Do you not see me on this here phone?" Betty shot back, but on seeing the dog, a similar shadow passed over her face. "Hmph! Since when do that butt wipe give diddly-squat 'bout that dog? I am not callin' him, so don't axe me." She snatched up the other phone. "Sheltah. Ten to six. I said, read my lips—six o'clock!"

The warden turned to Peggy with an apologetic smile. "Bit of a hectic day. Why don't we settle Lucky into a run?" Reaching to open the door for her, he stared at the hole where the knob should be.

Sheepishly, Peggy pulled the doorknob out of her pocket and handed it to him. "Sorry."

"Oh! Not to worry!" He wrenched the knob back into the door. "Been meaning to fix that." Pulling a Polaroid camera down from a shelf, he gestured her out into the kennel. "After you."

Chapter 3

"Oops!" The warden tripped just outside the door.

"Oh! S-so sorry!" Peggy exclaimed.

"My fault entirely, I should have seen the, er, the suitcase?" He looked between it and her.

For a split second, Peggy considered pretending it wasn't hers, but since there was only the two of them standing there, she ditched that idea. She shoved it out of sight, behind the nearby radiator.

The warden released Lucky into the run beside the office door. The dog looked back at Peggy, his tail drooping. She watched the warden raise the camera to take a picture of him, and click. Nothing happened. Sighing, the warden pulled a small tape recorder from his jacket pocket and, fumbling with buttons, spoke into it.

"Have Joe pick up more film." He fiddled some more with the buttons, then tapped it against his palm. "Can't shut the thing off." He held it up to Peggy. "Brand new. Haven't quite got the hang of it, yet. The crew got tired of my napkin scribbles everywhere. I don't know about you, but give me a fountain pen any day, except when they leak in your pocket. And I forget, is it lemon juice or rubbing alcohol gets it out?"

"I-I don't know," Peggy stammered. She wasn't sure what to make of his rambling, but she smiled, in hopes he would help the dog.

"What made you bring Lucky here?"

"The apartment house w-wouldn't let me have him."

"Ah. What I meant was, how did you hear about us? Most people are locals." He glanced towards the radiator and her duct-taped suitcase.

"In...in the phone book." Peggy dragged her eyes away from his and looked around at all the barking dogs. "You...you find homes for all these animals?"

"We do our best." He walked down to a standing sink at the other end of the kennel. "As Betty said, there are only so many homes and, well, we push on."

While he filled a steel bowl with water, the dogs quieted. Peggy noted that with nearly two to every run, the damp and drafty place held around fifty scruffy, smelly canines.

As if reading her mind, the warden said, "I know we may not look like much, but we've got what it takes where it counts, as they say."

Peggy knelt to pet Lucky through the fencing, wondering just what exactly *did* they have, and how it counted when the place looked this dilapidated.

"Happy Thanksgiving, by the way." The warden set the water bowl into Lucky's run. "Home for the weekend?"

Be careful!

Peggy pulled her coat closer around her. She didn't need the warning. She knew what he must be thinking of her, the hand-me-downs, her tangled hair, scraped knees—and the suitcase. But, when she met his eyes, she found kindness reflected back at her, not judgment.

"Forgive me," he said. "None of my business. I just assumed...your suitcase...the holiday."

"I-I just got off the bus, when I-I found him. I-I'm moving to-to a new place."

"Moving, ah! Well, my condolences. Moving can be so...unsettling, eh? The upheaval, and the strangeness of a new place. Found a flat, then? To stay?"

Peggy shrugged. She tried to match his nonchalant tone. "Not yet. The dog...they wouldn't let me..."

"Ah, yes. New Jersey tends to be a bit rigid with the no pets policy. I suspect half this lot here is the result of foreclosures all over town."

Peggy perused the pens. "What happens when...I mean if-if..." She encompassed the dogs with a tentative sweep of her arm.

"If we don't find them homes? Well, depending on available space, time and money, if we run out of options, then we have no choice but to have a veterinarian humanely euthanize them. Put them to sleep."

He had said it plainly, without trying to dodge or sugar-coat his answer. Peggy noted a genuine sadness in his tone. "How-how often do you...do you have to..."

"It can be as often as every Friday."

She blinked at him. It was Friday, the day after Thanksgiving.

He seemed to read her mind. "With us it's not a hard and fast rule. As you can see, we do what we can to keep them for as long as we can. Having said that, we take in between sixteen-hundred and two thousand dogs and cats per year. And as Betty said, it boils down to numbers."

"But...but...what if they're just lost?"

He closed and latched a gate, and then turned to her. "Trust me. Ending up here is better than starving or freezing to death out there, all alone on the street or worse. Wouldn't you agree?"

She grew uncomfortable under his scrutiny.

A squeal of car brakes sent the dogs dashing through open chutes to the outside runs, barking wildly. The warden unhooked cables, releasing the metal doors above the chutes, one by one, shutting out the frigid air and noise.

"Be right back." He trotted out the front door, leaving Peggy alone.

Above the muffled barking from outside, she heard a whine, and found Lucky cringing in the corner of the run. She dropped to her knees and reached through the fencing. "Shhh...it's okay, Lucky."

BAM! The front door burst open, bouncing off the wall. Startled, Peggy ducked down in the shadows. She felt a broom at her back and grasped hold of it, like a club.

A young man stomped in, his arms loaded with Hav-A-Hart, humane animal-traps. "SHAAAADAAAAAP!!" he hollered at the dogs.

The warden followed him inside, his fingers in his ears. "Joe, why must we go through this little ritual every day?"

Joe kicked the door shut, tossed the traps down to the floor, and whipped off his aviator shades. "I *hate* people! I *hate* this job! *What* is the friggin' point, huh?!"

"This a rhetorical question?" The warden calmly picked up a trap and set it on a free-standing cage, in the middle of the room.

Seeing the warden wasn't afraid of this blustery guy, Peggy set the broom aside. She reckoned he was in his mid-twenties. With the highly polished badge pinned to his bomber jacket, a walkie-talkie hung from his belt along with a holster, he looked like a cop, except for the beaut of a shiner encircling his left eye.

He strode past her to the fenced run, and Lucky. "Motherluvin' Friggitoid! *Again*?! I don't freakin' bullleeeeeeve it! That's it!" He drew a gun from the holster. "We nail the effin' S.O.B. this time!"

Peggy yelped and ducked, as the warden wrestled the pistol out of the young man's hand—and then broke it in half.

"Hey that's my best water pistol!" the young man wailed.

"And to be considered illegal in this contentious neck of the contiguous forty-eight states!"

"Fifty. There's fifty states, Ter."

"I wasn't including Canada or Mexico."

"Oh. Hey! Don't go changin' the subject! What're we gonna do about Lucky, huh? This is bogus, man!"

"Joe, we've been through this," the warden said, as he picked up two traps and handed them back to the irritated young man. "Stack these on the cage, if you please, that is until you return them below, where they belong?"

"C'mon, lookit him! How long's Harrison gonna get away with usin' his own dog for a freakin' punchin' bag?"

Peggy stepped out of her corner. "His-his owner did this?"

"Well now, we don't know that," the warden admonished.

"Ha!" Joe exclaimed, and then looked at her. "Uh, Ter? Who the frig is she?"

"She is the Good Samaritan who found Lucky running stray, again."

"Ya mean runnin' for his life, again!"

"Now, we don't know that, either."

Peggy stood between the men and Lucky, wringing her hands. As the warden and his officer spoke in hushed tones, she unlatched the run gate. Her trembling fingers made the task more difficult than it should have been. She leashed Lucky and then ushered him to the front door.

"Miss? What are you doing?" The warden stepped between her and the door. Startled, Peggy backed up into the fencing.

"I-I made a mistake!"

"Mistake? Well, you'd be making a bigger one and breaking the law, if you were to leave with Lucky right now. I'm sure that's not what you want to do."

"It should be against the law to-to beat a poor, help-helpless dog!" Peggy blurted out.

"It is. Title four, Chapter twenty-two, to be exact."

This is your chance! Run! Go! Now!

Peggy looked around wildly for an escape.

"Believe me," he continued, "I know how you feel, I do, but what we know, and what we can prove is often a horse of a different color. What we need more than anything else at the moment is evidence. If you walk out that door with Lucky now, you'll only be giving the man cause against us. Besides, I'm sure you don't need any more trouble on your shoulders than you have at the moment, what with your move and such."

It's a trick! Don't believe him! Run!

Peggy waffled, unable to let go of the doorknob.

"Joe," the warden called out, "do us a favor. Postdate Lucky's record a couple of days. We don't have him, yet."

"Ter, you can't do that!"

"Thank you, Joe."

The young man slouched past them into the office. The warden held out his hand, and Peggy struggled to decide whether to hand him the leash or not.

Her vacillation seemed to give the warden the encouragement he needed. "I know you've no reason to, but I'm asking you to trust me. Give us a chance to help him. I'm sure you know better than anyone else what he's been through."

Peggy looked up at him. He returned her gaze with gentle eyes. What should she do? *Run!*

But, it's already dark, she fretted. She could feel the cold draft wafting in from under the door. Lucky nosed her hand. Reluctantly, she handed the leash over to the warden.

"Thank you," he said. "You're doing the right thing."

Peggy watched him lead Lucky back to the run. The dog looked back to her. She hung her head and followed after them.

The front door burst open again, and the two black boys traipsed in. The smaller one hauled on a cable, which raised a chute and allowed a shaggy mutt in. The boy teased it into playing with a stick, while the taller boy continued lifting the rest of the chutes. Soon, the dogs were back inside.

"Let's leave the fetch stick outside, shall we, gentlemen?" the warden tempered his order with a smile.

"Yo' Stretch! Got you any mean ones in yet?" asked the smaller boy, "Want me a bad watchdog."

"You know we only have family dogs here."

"Aw, three-six-nine, man!"

"Mind your language, please. Ladies present."

The taller boy knelt beside an old German shepherd. "How come y'all ain't got ol' Prince a domicile yet? Y'oughta bestow him to me."

"Curtis, your mother would skin me alive, if I gave you a dog."

The smaller boy laughed out loud. "Won't neither. Scotty's got her!"

"Shutup!" Curtis hissed and smacked his buddy on the shoulder.

"Crackin' but fackin'! She so wasted, man, she don't know a diff! Thissun ain't bad 'nuff, anyhow. Need yo'seff a mean one, go fo' yo' throat."

"Nah." The warden had joined Curtis and scratched Prince's ears. "Get a nice dog, treat him well, you've a friend forever, right Curtis? Better deal."

"An' all that," the other boy snorted, pulling Curtis out the door. "Let's go, bro'. Stinks in here."

"I'm still waiting for you fellas to volunteer!" the warden called after them. Shutting the door, he turned and looked at Peggy. "How about you?" he asked. "Perhaps a few hours here and there, once or twice a week? Might be just the thing to help get your bearings in a new place."

"How-how much do you pay?"

"Pay?" the warden repeated. "You mean, as in a job? Well, volunteers don't usually, that is to say, times being what they are, the economy, and the cutbacks…it's not that we couldn't use someone who cares, but…"

Peggy held her breath. He glanced at her suitcase then something shifted on his face.

"When could you start?"

"To-today?"

"Today? Oh." He glanced at his watch. "Well, all right, then. Today, it is. Splendid! Shall we go break the good news?"

He sounded cheerful, but as they walked towards the office, Peggy sensed that he was just a tad nervous.

Chapter 4

"Folks?" the warden called out over Frankie Valli and The Four Seasons blaring over a radio on the shelf. "Joe? Joe! might you lower that a decibel or three, please?"

Heaving a heavy sigh, Joe made a show of turning the volume down. Peggy remained by the door, wringing her hands.

"Let's wait for Betty to finish up with her call," the warden said.

"No, ain't no such thing as a vaccine to stop shedding." Betty sneezed three times in a row, then snapped, "Uh, yeah, I'm sure."

"Stupid shits," the elderly Clara scoffed. She sat on a stool, lovingly combing her wig. Hairpins hung loosely in her thin hair, one jostle away from falling out.

At last Betty slammed the phone down. "Vaccine to stop shedding. I wish!"

"Gather round, will you?" the warden said. "I've wonderful news. After much consideration I've asked..." he paused, and then turned to Peggy with an apologetic look. "Do forgive me, but what is your name?"

"P-peggy," she whispered.

"What's that? Peggy you say? Short for Margaret?"

Peggy gulped, thinking about that for a second, then shook her head no.

"Well, then, Peggy it is!" He turned back to his crew. "I've asked Peggy..." he paused again. Turning to her, he asked, "Your last name?"

"Dil-Dillan."

"Dildillan?"

"N-no, just-just Dillan."

"Ah. Very good! I've asked Peggy Dillan, here, if she'd like to join the ranks as our new third assistant manager!" Startled, Peggy's head jerked up. The crew stared at him too, slack-jawed. The warden continued cheerfully. "And you'll never guess. She agreed. Isn't that good news?"

Silence.

Unabashed, the warden introduced Peggy to each of them. "Joe here is our first assistant manager, Betty's our second assistant manager, and Clara is..." The old woman narrowed her eyes at him, which caused him to pause. "...she's in a class by herself. Our expert on all issues feline."

Peggy's toes cramped in her shoes from tension. There was not a happy face amongst them.

"Oh!" the warden tapped his own forehead. "I nearly forgot. I'm Terry Brannan." He grasped her hand before she could shy away, shaking it up and down with vigor. "I sort of manage things. Oh! You'll need..." He rummaged through some boxes under the counter. "...I'm almost certain we have an extra...what do you call it?"

As he struggled to remember whatever it was he couldn't think of, Peggy risked another peek at her new coworkers. They were still stone faced.

"Uniform!" Terry held up the word like a hard-won prize. "Every day they say ten-thousand brain cells take the slow boat over the falls? Must be thrice that when you get to my...ah! Here we go!" Pulling a dusty package out from under the cage banks, he smacked cat hair off of the yellowed plastic before handing it to her. "It's a little big. They all are. Oh, and badge...badge..." He dumped out several more boxes onto the counter, searching, but then gave up. He removed his own badge and, gesturing his need to approach her, he leaned in to pin it to her coat.

Unsure what he meant to do to her, Peggy backed away from him and bumped into the door.

"Well, you can..." he held out the badge, "...just anywhere on your person," he said with a flutter of his hand.

Peggy stared at it. Did he really mean for her to wear it? Now?

"Not to worry," he assured her. "I can always find another one. Crackerjacks still has a prize in every box!" He chuckled. "It seems a bit of a laugh that, eh? But, certainly not what it represents, of course. This badge identifies you as an Officer of the Court. Authority figure and such."

Peggy plucked the badge from his outstretched hand and quickly withdrew.

Terry seemed satisfied and smacked dust off of his hands. "Very well, then! We'll be putting you through your paces, so to speak. You don't mind Sunday as training day?"

"N-no."

"Splendid! So. This is splendid. Any questions?"

The crew exploded, voicing objections all at once. Peggy shrank even further into the door, unable to hear one for the other. Apparently, neither could the warden.

"Hold on a tic! I say hold on!" He whistled, quieting them.

Betty spoke up first. "Gee mo nitty! How we gonna make this place jive on paper if you keep raisin' overhead, 'steada fixin' what's broke?"

"Specifics, please?" he demanded.

"Hello? That antichrist you call a boilah? Can't heat a can of beans worth a damn!" At that, she sneezed so hard she fell back into her chair.

"How's about the van overhaul you promised?" Joe whined. "The brakes're shot, the axle's gone pretzel and the muffler farts like a friggin' Hog, without the coolness factor! And th' inspection station won't take our bribes no more!"

"Bugger it," Clara snarled, "we been wantin' our own vetinary for a dog's age!"

Betty sucked deeply on an inhaler, wagging her finger at him. "We be on E, mistah! Tank be empty! Can't afford anothah mouff to feed!"

Peggy cringed with embarrassment, glancing at her benefactor.

"You know," he said, "if I had a penny for every moan and groan about the lack of help around here, we'd not only be out of debt, we'd have a new building, by now. Let's count our blessings, shall we, that..." he glanced at Peggy, his face pinched with forgetfulness again.

"P-Peggy," she whispered.

"Peggy! That Peggy here came along! Someone who cares! And someone who wants to get involved. Isn't that what you're always griping about? Apathy? Lack of support? Now, I have *not* forgotten about the boiler, the budget, the van, *or* the need for our own vet, but these things, like progress and change, do not happen overnight. One corner at a time, remember?"

From his crew's tightlipped expressions, it was clear to Peggy that they'd heard this speech many times before. Still, she sensed that the warden had won this round.

Terry stole a look at the clock. "All right, then, what say I catch two budgies with one cuttlefish bone, and stop by the EVC with Lucky. Might help us with the case, and I'll hit the doc up for our half-term extern, come the new year."

The crew groaned in unison.

"Aw, jeeze, Ter!" Joe whined. "Beggin' for an Ivy-Leaguer who snot-noses us and never stays the term? What's the point?"

"As Clara so passionately reminds us, we are in need of a vet."

"They're green peas, Ter! They only show up when we havta nuke our animals! And they treat us like second-class mopes!"

"Very well, then," the warden challenged, "floor's open. Answers on a postcard? Anyone?"

The crew drew a collective, if not resigned sigh.

He looked among them. "I take it then, we're unanimous?" Silence. "Splendid!" He smiled. "Then we're adjourned. Carry on."

They exchanged glances, then each turned their back on Peggy, suddenly finding something with which to busy themselves. It was all she could do not to shrivel up and sink into the cracks in the floor. The warden's shadow fell over her.

"Since you're the one who found Lucky," he said, "what say you come with me, and we'll fetch an expert opinion?"

Peggy managed a nod. "Oh-okay." She was more than happy to leave. The temperature in the office had dropped to arctic, and it had nothing to do with the busted boiler.

"Hold the fort," the warden called out, cheerfully. He opened the door, and Peggy hurried after her new boss.

"Pfft!" Clara exclaimed after the door closed. "'Ow's *that* for a midden game o'soldiers!"

"Just what we need," Joe whined loudly, "another friggin' charity case."

"You evah see such a gumby-girl?" Betty bellowed. "How is that white-on-white stick gonna be any help 'round here?"

"Bah!" Clara chuckled and tossed a dollar on the counter. "She won't last to day's finish."

Betty and Joe considered this, then each slapped down a dollar. They all laughed.

Just outside the office door, Peggy overheard the exchange. Terry leashed Lucky and handed her the reins.

"Don't let them fool you," he said. "They like to play the part, but they're good folk. Perfectly harmless. Except perhaps for Clara, but when she gets out of hand we just lock her in the closet."

His laugh was a little late in coming, and Peggy wondered if he was only half-joking. He opened the front door, and held it open for her.

"After you."

Clutching the leash tightly, Peggy led Lucky down the walk into the bracing cold, past the barking dogs. As the warden ambled ahead to open the gate, Peggy studied him. Slender, about six feet tall, he was a rather nice looking man for his age. He wore an old barn jacket over his slightly rumpled, khaki uniform. His geniality was infectious, and nothing seemed to betray his easy-going smile.

Still, watch your back!

She nearly gasped aloud. Where had her voices been when she was facing the warden's firing squad? Abandoned her to her own devices, as usual!

Penetrating her cloth coat, the cold had reached her bones swiftly. She shivered as she followed the warden to a battered, tan and orange Ford Pinto parked beside the sagging fence. Keying the passenger side door first, he grimaced when it wouldn't open.

"Gets stuck," he said, as he wrestled with the door handle. He tried jiggling the key, lifting up on the door frame while pressing the handle down, pushing in, pulling out, all to no avail. With a little sigh, he gave the door a sharp kick just under the handle. The door popped open with a creak. He grinned at her. "It's all in the wrist, you see."

"Y-yes." Peggy couldn't help but smile.

Assisting Lucky into the back seat was no mean feat, since it appeared that the warden had been using the car as a filing cabinet. She carefully pushed boxes of files aside to make room for the dog.

"So sorry about the mess," he said, "just toss it all aside. I'm at least a month behind with more than half of it, anyway." Shoving her door closed, he enunciated through the glass, "Whatever you do, don't lock it! You'll never get out."

Peggy watched as he trotted around to his side. That's when he found out that his door had been unlocked the whole time. With a philosophical shrug he climbed in.

"Bit of a trickster, is our Ethel," he said and turned the key in the ignition. The engine sputtered. "I call her Ethel, like the fuel she would probably prefer. She's a bit peckish in the cold."

It took three tries, but Ethel's engine finally kicked over. When a puff of gray smoke eeked out from under the floor, Peggy reached out a hand

to roll down the window, only to find the hand crank missing. There were no seat belts, either. They'd been chewed off.

"Terribly sorry, but there's no heat," he added, and then pulled the recorder from his pocket, fumbling with the buttons. "Have Fegetti take another look-see at Ethel's heater. And the doors. Again." He twisted in his seat to see over his shoulder as he backed the car out. "If you feel the floor give way, jump into the back."

Peggy was unsure if he was kidding or not. He began to whistle, possibly to offset the little car's backfiring. They bucked out of the parking lot, barely missing an oncoming bus, which blared its horn at them.

With a start, Peggy spotted the same flu-ridden bus driver behind the wheel! The driver punched the side window open and opened his mouth to shout at them. When he saw her, he faltered and then clamped his mouth shut. As he drove by, he glared at her.

Gripping the dashboard as the warden careened up the hill, her mind raced. What in heaven's name have we gotten ourselves into? Please God, please let it be a short ride, and no time for Twenty Questions!

Chapter 5

"So. Tell me about yourself."

Peggy's stomach cinched into a tight double knot. *Careful.* "There's-there's not much to tell."

"Everyone has a story."

Peggy turned to the window, wondering the odds of her survival if she jumped out of the car. She weighed being trapped with this talkative stranger versus a night in the cold, possibly with a broken leg, and ditched the idea. At least until the next stop light. The passing scenery paraded derelict buildings and railroad tracks, all the way up the hill through working-class neighborhoods of diners, roundabouts and boarding houses. All of a sudden she recognized the area.

"Th-there! Th-that's where I found him."

"Tory Corner. Lucky traveled a ways, this time," the warden remarked. "You from around here?"

"N-no, I told you. I-I moved."

"Ah, yes, so you did. Just off the bus, then? I should have guessed."

Wary, Peggy stole a glance at him.

"Your suitcase," he confessed. "Tory Corner is still immigrant central, around here. Not to imply that you're...are you?"

"Um, no."

"Dillan." He seemed to mull over her name. "That's Irish, isn't it? You wouldn't be a Tory, then. I take it from your expression that you haven't a feather what I'm going on about. You're American born. Don't they teach you your side of the story anymore?"

"I-I don't know. I mean, I-I don't-I don't remember."

"Well, Farroway's Tory Corner dates back to Tea Party days, much like Tory Corner in West Orange a few townships over. Similar history, more or less, except that West Orange was given the official historic marker. Politics. What can one do?

"Back to brass tacks, then. A Tory was a loyalist to the crown. During your upstart revolution, if you will, living around here meant you were a supporter of the King of England, thus a Tory. The area fell into disfavor after they sent us back over the pond. Ironic, really. Two hundred years ago in Ireland, a Tory was an Irish outlaw who favored skewering an English settler. Exact opposite, you see!"

Peggy didn't see, but smiled anyway. She had no interest in a history lesson at the moment, but his kindness and generosity tugged at her. The least she could do was to feign interest.

"During the famine," Terry continued, "once again, Tory Corner became a popular landing place, for the Sons of Eire. Now, sadly, we're seeing a whole new wave of immigration due to the violence in Belfast. Bloody Fools." He looked her way. "Don't misunderstand. I tend to see both sides of the coin. I've the blessing of being Irish born and British educated. I say the Irish are fools for killing one another in the name of God, but the English are no better for goading them into it, which might be the gist of the problem. If you ask me, the poofters have some nerve being they're merely what's left over after the French got through with them."

Peggy laughed lightly along with him, even though she had no idea what he'd just said.

"It's true!" He went on, "Now, the Irish on the other hand, they're what I call the Texans of Europe. They're a brash, tough lot. God's truth, they're not afraid to get in there, get their mitts dirty. And they've got the best pubs anywhere. We happen to have a transplant right down Valley Road there." He peered out the frosty windshield. "Oops. Can't see it from here. Kierney's. Ever been? Good craic there, as they say. Today, most immigrants come to Tory Corner first. Thirty years ago I did, as well. I was fortunate enough to avoid the factories, finding work in that magnificent city across the river. I worked my way up the corporate ladder, but then Lorraine died. That was my wife. Lost her five years ago, Christmas..."

The warden's rambling stopped, and the quiet hung thick in the chilly car. Peggy glanced at his face. His eyes were sad and he seemed far away. After a moment, he shifted in his seat, as if shrugging a weight off of his shoulders.

"We never had children, so we decided that after I retired, we'd travel. She always wanted to see this country. So did I. She collected maps and atlases for as long as I'd known her. We'd talk about just chucking it all, and beetle off down the road, willy-nilly, towards the sunset, casting our fates to the wind. Every fortnight, she'd spread those maps in her hand like a deck of cards and tell me to pick a latitude, any latitude." He sighed, the smile on his face slowly ebbing.

"But, life has a funny habit of getting in the way of it, doesn't it? After she passed, things changed. Perhaps I did, as well. When the bottom fell out of the market, I was informed by management that I'd lost my edge." He laughed to himself, but it sounded hollow to Peggy.

"My edge! Suffice it to say that at age forty-six, besides finding myself without my life's companion, I was also without work. Without a feather as to how to bloody well start over, pardon my French. However! What they say is true enough. When one door closes another opens. I ended up selling our house to a vet up at the EVC. Turns out, the head sawbones, Doc Caldwell, had been involved in a contentious debate with our proud town over the condition of the pound. Long story short, he suggested that with my managerial background, I take over and turn it into a shelter. To my surprise, I accepted. I didn't know the first thing about managing an animal shelter, and convinced myself it was only temporary. Four years later, I'm still here." He shrugged and glanced at her. "There you have it. Now, it's your turn. What's your story?"

Peggy pressed her lips together. The man seemed intent on hearing about her life. Just then, Lucky whined in the back seat, and she turned around to him. "It's okay. S-sit," she whispered. Lucky licked her hand and offered her his paw. She felt another tug on her heart, as she shook it. "Good boy."

"Something, isn't it?" mused the warden. "The way they trust? Despite everything that they've been through. Braver than most people, eh?"

Peggy scratched Lucky's ears but kept silent. The radio sputtered to life, in the middle of Les Anderson's *Sleigh Ride*. The warden began to hum along, off key.

Peggy faced front. Well, at least there were no more questions. Still, she couldn't get his comment out of her head; braver than most people. She looked out the window. Tied to trees and lamp posts up and down the streets, yellow ribbons flapped in the wind. Some were old and tattered, some were new. Many of the neighborhood boys were missing in action in Vietnam. A few miles later, oak trees canopied the streets, their bare branches barely shielding the austere homes perched high above expansive grounds. They were impressive, even in the stark grayed wash of early winter. No ribbons here, Peggy noted.

"This is Upper Farroway," Terry spoke again, startling her. "And, just so you know, there's no such place on any map. To the folks who live up here, however, there is most certainly a distinction, thank you very much, and they have the separate zip code to prove it. In retaliation, the Irish residents of the valley have been mocking the snobbish affectations, if you will, of the wealthier, predominantly British, Upper Farroway residents for generations, pronouncing "Upper" as "Uppah". It's been pronounced this way for so long that it's become part of the local vernacular. Still, mock it as one might, *Uppah* Farroway is where everyone secretly wants to live." He pointed out the window. "Clara lives up that road there."

Peggy followed where he pointed, and caught sight of stately Victorian homes situated along a winding road. It was flanked by towering oaks and pines. She thought of the elderly cat lady back at the pound. Why would she choose to leave this beautiful sanctuary and work in such a depressing place?

A few miles beyond, the warden turned the Pinto into a driveway alongside a colonial-style house. Peggy spotted a modest sign framed in the ivy: Emergency Veterinary Clinic.

Pulling hard on the parking brake, the warden opened the glove compartment and extracted a pre-knotted tie. He slipped it over his head and tightened it under his collar. With a sheepish grin, he said, "For special occasions."

He shouldered his door open and hurried around to her side. He tried yanking the door open, to no avail. After trying three different combinations of pushes and pulls, he directed Peggy to jiggle the handle along with him. Nothing worked. Finally, he gestured her to lean back and gave the door a swift kick. It popped open with a creak. With the bow of a gentleman, he held out his hand to her.

"Th-thank you, I-I'm okay." Peggy avoided his outstretched hand, and helped Lucky out from the back. They walked alongside a brook bordering the wooded acreage leading to the clinic's entrance. It was draped in festive garland and twinkling Christmas lights.

The warden opened the wreathed door like a proud investor about to show off his own company. "Welcome to the twentieth century."

Peggy walked Lucky into an open, modern waiting room with no windows. The walls were divided by two colors, the top portion in peach, and the bottom in a warm java. Dark brown benches jutted from the walls, over a recently mopped, shiny linoleum floor. Recessed lighting cast a warm glow over the room and soft, classical music played through hidden ceiling speakers. It all had a calming effect, and Peggy assumed it was for the sake of both two-legged and four-legged visitors. A monolithic desk rose up from the floor at the end of the room. It was clearly a barrier between the waiting area and the hospital beyond.

The desk was staffed by a middle-aged receptionist whose crisp hospital whites and stern mouth gave Peggy the impression that no one got past her without a fight. The woman busily wrote in a ledger, and didn't acknowledge them when they arrived at the desk in front of her.

"Back again." The warden spoke to the top of her perfectly coiffed salt and pepper hair. "That's thrice in one week. People will think we're in love."

The receptionist apparently had no sense of humor. Without looking up, she slid a clipboard of forms to him.

"Ah," Terry smiled pleasantly. "Thank you, Nan. The doc in today?"

"I'll let him know you're here," Nan replied, in a clipped tone. She continued to scribble in the ledger, then tapped keys on an adding machine.

"Splendid. Appreciate it, as always."

After filling out the paperwork, he slid the clipboard back to her. The woman made no move to take it. Peggy and Lucky watched Terry peruse medical pamphlets displayed on the desktop. He hummed tunelessly and rather loudly. Peggy cringed with embarrassment for him, but his off-key warbling worked wonders in moving the receptionist. She finally snatched the clipboard off of the counter and pushed through swinging doors. Terry took a seat next to Peggy, with an innocent smile.

A few minutes later, the receptionist returned and barked, "The doctor will see you, now."

The trio entered a large, pristine room. Fluorescent lights reflected off of white walls, a white ceiling, white flooring, white cabinets, and a crowd of young, white men in white lab coats. The effect was blinding. Gleaming, stainless steel tables abutted the walls. The tables were draped with hoses, spigots and nozzles of every size and description. Steaming autoclaves stuffed with instrument packs shared crowded counter

space with electron microscopes and whirling centrifuges spinning what looked like vials of blood. This might have been a human hospital, for all its cutting edge paraphernalia. The only difference was the bank of cages stacked against the wall, holding dogs and cats hooked up to slow-dripping bottles hanging upside down from metal stands.

Peggy looked around trying to take it all in. Behind her extended a long, narrow hallway of fifteen-foot high cabinets, sloping downward to-wards the back door, and a rear room where she could see additional cage banks.

In front of her, just past the warden's shoulder, she saw a small win-dow that lent a view into another room. A sandy-haired, masked surgeon labored over a draped animal. She couldn't see whether it was a cat or a dog. As she watched, he yanked down his surgical mask and spoke briefly into a phone held to his ear by a masked nurse. Strikingly good-looking, the young vet exuded cool and intense concentration. Peggy couldn't help but feel impressed, watching him.

All at once a rowdy rendition of *Happy Birthday* erupted around her and champagne glasses were raised. Lucky pressed close to Peggy, apparently nervous at all the noise. She reached down and gently stroked him, then peered through the crowd to the source of the celebration.

Bent over a steel gurney, an elderly man dressed in surgical greens stood up into view. A foil birthday hat was ceremoniously placed atop his silver head by a uniformed nurse, who then kissed his cheek.

"That's Doc Caldwell," Terry shouted. "He owns this place and is a damn fine vet. He's known all over the state."

Peggy observed the doctor. Tall and big-boned, Dr. Caldwell possessed the largest hands she had ever seen. She marveled at their fine dexterity as he deftly wielded scissors, snipping wrapping paper into a paper-chain of cats and mice. Delighted, his staff applauded. After bestowing the chain on his nurse, he opened his gift. His laugh resounded around the room, as he held up a plush toy cat. Then Peggy saw tire tread marks stitched across its back. Dr. Caldwell panned the accompanying death certificate around, eliciting raucous laughter from everyone, including the warden.

Peggy swiveled her astonished gaze to him. He sheepishly stifled his mirth.

"Terry!" Dr. Caldwell's voice called out above the laughter. The senior vet maneuvered through the party to them and held up the toy cat to Terry.

Despite his struggle for decorum in front of her, Terry snickered along with Dr. Caldwell, the two grown men acting like a pair of school boys caught in a mischievous prank.

"Tsk Tsk!" Terry admonished him, for Peggy's benefit. "Amazing what people find funny these days!"

"Just awful!" Caldwell agreed, with mock indignation. "But, since a percentage of the proceeds go to the Humane Society, all for a good cause!"

"Not a word to Clara about it, though!" Terry warned him.

"Oh, no!" Caldwell hid the toy cat behind his back. "She'll have us both in irons and hoards of protest signs at my door by sunup!"

"Lord Forbid!"

Caldwell laughed. "Good to see you, Terry." He pumped the warden's hand.

"I'd like you to meet my new assistant, Peggy Dillan."

"Nice to meet you."

"Hello," Peggy said, shyly.

"For a second, I thought this might be a retirement party," Terry said.

"Next year, next year!" Caldwell said.

"I seem to remember that's what you said last year."

"Well, what do you think; time for a changing of the guard?"

"Not unless you've a clone of yourself to carry the torch."

Caldwell clapped Terry on the back, gesturing him toward the surgical suite. "Well, since you mention it, do come in. It's all right; he'll be finished closing by now."

Chapter 6

"Excuse the intrusion, Paul," Caldwell announced. "Wanted to trot you out here. Terry, this is Dr. Paul Hayward, VMD-PhD. Graduated Summa Cum Laude out of Penn Vet's double major program. He finished a full year early, no less. Paul, this is Terry Brannan. He manages the animal shelter below."

"Hello," Paul said through his mask. "Is that one of your strays?"

Terry turned around and looked at Peggy, who huddled by the door. "Ah, there you are! Well, yes and no. This is Peggy Dillan, my new—"

"Oh, who's that behind you there?" Caldwell pointed to Lucky, half-hidden behind Peggy's coat. "Sorry Paul; didn't notice him in the crowd."

"My fault," Terry said. "I wasn't thinking."

"No fault." Caldwell jerked his thumb towards the young vet. "By the book, this one. Phi Zeta. Knows his P's and Q's. Keeps me on my toes." He clapped his protégé on the shoulder. "I think we can safely table a sterility breach, Paul. You've closed. Send her to the back."

"Put her on a warming pad, low, three cc's penn," The young vet instructed his technicians. "I'll call the owner later with an OS update."

Caldwell knelt beside the dog trembling against Peggy's legs. "You look familiar, fella."

"It's Lucky, again," Terry said. "Wondering if you can confirm those sores were inflicted or..."

Caldwell ran his hands over the dog, gentle and probing. When he was done, he stood up. "Paul, let your assistant clean up. Give us a look-see here, will you? This is a stickler of a case."

Peggy watched Dr. Hayward scrub his hands in the sink twice, then hold them out, waiting for the pretty nurse to rip open a fresh towel from its package. She dried them, working each finger as if it was a sterile instrument. Once his hands were dried, the nurse stretched a fresh pair of latex gloves over them, and then helped him into a fresh lab coat. The ritual reminded Peggy of the coronation of a prince–or the Pope!

As she draped a stethoscope around his neck, the nurse flashed him a coquettish smile before wheeling the instrument tray out of the room. Dr. Hayward checked his watch against the clock over the cabinets, and then knelt down beside Lucky. He plugged the stethoscope into his ears and placed the diaphragm to Lucky's chest. He rested his other hand on the inside of Lucky's hind leg for a moment, and then checked his watch again.

"Respiration's normal at twenty five resps per, normal heart rate at one-thirty. There is a minor murmur, but for a dog this size…" he lifted Lucky's lips and examined his teeth, "…and age, it's not uncommon." He pressed against Lucky's gums repeatedly with his gloved finger. "Mucus membrane is pink. Cap refill at three seconds may indicate possible de-hydration." He scrunched Lucky's neck skin between his fingers twice, and then nodded. "Yes," the doctor concurred with himself. "Moderate need of fluids."

Peggy frowned. When was he going to get around to the scars on Lucky's back? They were smack in front of his face!

He flicked a thermometer in the air a few times, squirted KY jelly on the end, and then deftly inserted it into Lucky's rectum. Peggy acceded the young vet's skill was expert enough that Lucky didn't even flinch.

"Protruding ribs, dull, dry coat indicate malnutrition…" When he came to the welts across the dog's back, Dr. Hayward paused.

Finally, Peggy thought! She tried to read his expression, but his handsome face was blank. He briefly prodded the scars, and followed it with an emotionless summary, as if reading a weather report.

"Recent sub-Q bruising, and external trauma over the lumbar region. Scabbing and possible marginal infection of lacerations two and four." He removed and read the thermometer. "Temp is ninety-seven point nine. Possible hypothermia." He pulled out a tweezers from his pocket and lifted each one of Lucky's paws in turn. "See his pads here? They're scraped, with bits of macadam embedded in the lacerations."

He tweezed debris onto tissue paper and wiped Lucky's toe pads with hydrogen peroxide. Then, he massaged the dog's abdominal area. "Neutered. No mass or growths on palpation, stomach is empty." He pulled a metal scope from his lab coat pocket and peered into Lucky's ears. Then he shone a light into his eyes with another metal scope. "Ears clear, no sign of infection; eyes clear." He gently kneaded Lucky's neck and jaw. "Lymph glands are normal."

Peggy fidgeted Lucky's leash between her fingers with mounting frustration. He'd passed over Lucky's welts as if they were nothing to worry about! For all his fancy education, he sure lacked common sense! Couldn't he see that Lucky was abused?

Dr. Hayward stood up. "The dog appears to be responsive, no immediate indication of internal injury or fractures of the skeletal system. With a below-average temp, poor cap refill, indications of malnutrition, and the extent of scabbing on the toe pads, I'd say he's been running stray for at least two weeks. That alone precludes me from citing this as a definitive case of abuse."

Caldwell turned to Terry. "That's your problem, isn't it?" Terry nodded.

Dr. Caldwell sighed and filled out a form on the counter.

Peggy glanced from one to the other, incredulous. Was that *it*? Nothing more to be said about the scars and welts? She wrestled with a tremor that began in her hands, ran up her arms and cascaded down her back. At last, she couldn't bear it any longer.

"Being beat-beaten with a belt, isn't that abuse?" Her voice croaked hoarsely in her throat.

The men turned to her.

"Belt?" The young vet repeated.

Peggy pointed to Lucky's back, her hand trembling. "You can-you can see the marks!"

"As I stated, the Sub-Q bruising, coupled with road macadam in his pads might also suggest that he's been side-swiped by a car. Without further evidence, there's no way to know for certain if that dog was hit by a belt or a steel-belted radial." He snapped a glove off, dismissing her.

"All-all you have to do is look at him."

"Excuse me? I think I did just that."

"Ah, you see Doctor," the warden interrupted, "we suspect the owner beats him, but we haven't been able to prove that, as yet."

"This dog has an owner?" Dr. Hayward turned to the elder veterinarian. "What's it doing here without its owner?"

"Yes well," Terry shifted on his feet. "We haven't exactly rung him yet."

"And we didn't hear that," Caldwell said, filling a syringe from a white bottle.

Dr. Hayward sidled up to Caldwell. "You're going to treat this dog without the owner's permission?"

"What dog?" Caldwell countered.

Whistling softly, Terry rocked back and forth on his heels. He glanced over to Peggy and shrugged.

"Give them a tube a Bacitracin, will you, Paul?" Caldwell said and injected Lucky's thigh. Dr. Hayward didn't react immediately but finally handed a tube of ointment to Peggy.

"Use a dab three times a day, after flushing out and drying the wounds thoroughly. You'll give the instructions to the owner?"

Glowering at him, Peggy snatched the tube from his hands, and pulled Lucky close, protectively.

"Thanks, Doc," Terry shook Dr. Caldwell's hand. "What do we owe you?"

"Thought you'd never ask." Caldwell stepped out the door and returned shortly with a box of kittens. Several sneezed. "How about a trade?"

The warden peered into the box. "URI?"

"Mmn-hmn. The big nasty. FVR. The Good Samaritan never came back when he heard how much it was going to cost to get them healthy again. They'll be up to snuff in about three weeks."

"Deal."

"Excellent!" Caldwell called out into the main arena, "Dr. Miller?"

A short, energetic intern skidded to a stop in the doorway and quickly drained his champagne glass.

"Dr. Miller," Caldwell instructed, "let's start this litter on Gentocin and Lactated Ringers. I'd also like a fecal, urinalysis, and do a bacterial smear on the nasal mucus by six o'clock, will you?"

Dr. Miller hesitated. "You're going to treat them?"

"No, you are." The vet handed him the box of kittens.

"But, I thought it was policy to euth all stray URI."

"Lesson number one-o-one: There's an exception to every rule. With a promise of good homes, I think it's a sound investment, don't you? Quarantine them in the back, usual disinfect protocol. After you disinfect the surgery, that is. Dr. Hayward needs to take a well-deserved break before his next pyo. Thank you."

"Ah, Doc?" the warden piped up. "There's just—well, there's just one more thing. Can you spare a moment?"

"Sure, sure," Caldwell led Terry past Miller, into a side office.

Miller sauntered past Peggy, as if she wasn't there, and set the box of kittens on the counter. "So," he addressed Paul's back. "It's rookie time at the pound, again. Not that you give a rat's ass, you privileged schmuck, but who is it this time? My money's on Benson. You remember. He removed a bitch's spleen instead of its ovaries, last term? C'mon, teacher's pet, it's not me, right? Who covers your ass when you forget to send your x-rays to the AMC? Fess up. Who's the poor dick, this term?"

Paul swung around and folded his arms across his chest. He lifted his chin to the doorway, where Peggy and Lucky stood. Miller followed his eyes.

Peggy leveled them both with a frosty glare and led Lucky out of the room.

Miller exhaled in a sputter of laughter. "Holy shit! You see the puss on her?" While Miller laughed, Paul cooly filled a twenty-cc hypo from a brown bottle. "What are you doing?"

"Vaxing for hoof and mouth." Paul reached out for Miller's arm, but the intern wrenched free.

"You serious? When you're this close to wiping the slate clean?"

Paul depressed the plunger on the hypo, sending a spurt of liquid in the air. Miller stood his ground, but only for a second. Flipping Paul the finger, he backed out of the room and returned to the party.

Paul caught sight of the girl, who shot him a smoldering look. He squirted the syringe's contents down the drain, and then washed his hands. Twice.

Peggy didn't see Terry and Dr. Caldwell as they exited the office, and she bumped into them. "Oh!"

"Hello!" Terry chortled, catching her.

"Sorry!" Peggy backed up, pulling her coat collar tight against her neck.

"I'll give you a call later," Dr. Caldwell told Terry. A chart was thrust into his hands by a nurse. He scanned the papers, and then said, "Let me know what you think."

"Will do," Terry replied, and then peered at Peggy. "Everything all right?" Peggy nodded briskly. "Ready to go?"

She nodded again, and ushered Lucky towards the exit.

Terry shook Caldwell's hand. "Thanks George, thanks again."

"Be well." Caldwell waved to him and rejoined his staff. "Okay, queue for review! Who's first? Dr. Miller?"

Groans went up, as Terry hurried after Peggy.

Outside, the cold air was refreshing, but Peggy felt sick. Her head had begun to ache, and her stomach churned with nausea. All at once, the parking lot began to spin, and she felt herself falling sideways.

"Oh dear!" The warden reached out to catch her, but she stumbled back away from him, falling against the Pinto.

"I'm-I'm all right."

"I beg to differ. What say we put our head between our knees, shall we?"

Too dizzy to argue with him, Peggy bent over, bracing herself against the car.

"That's a girl." The warden's voice was soothing. "Breathe slowly. You're not used to the anesthetic, that's all. Between the halothane, ether, and chloroform and all that blood…oh dear." He cocked his mouth to one side and frowned. "Pretend I didn't say that. Suffice it to say, more than one strapping intern has hit the deck in there, I assure you!"

Peggy wanted to tell the warden that it wasn't the hospital fumes that had turned her stomach, but she didn't. "S-sorry."

"No need to apologize!" Terry assured her. "It can be a bit over-whelming."

Peggy felt a wet nose against her cheek and found Lucky peering at her, too. She reached out a shaking hand and stroked his ears.

"How are we getting on, then?" Terry asked. "Better? Let's take a few more breaths. That's it. Splendid. You have to admit, though, it is quite the place!"

Peggy remained quiet.

"Ah, that impressed, are we?" the warden mused. "Well, believe me, like my rather standoffish crew, once you get to know them, they're–well, in terms of veterinary staff, they are the best. The top of the food chain, as it were. And *we* represent the not so pretty half, the down and dirty nitty-gritty. What we deal with day to day is a very different kettle of fish. Our side of the tracks can put some people off, especially when they've set their sights on another prize."

He pulled a lollipop from his pocket, offering it to her. "Thank you for being a good girl and not clobbering the snot-nose."

Peggy laughed and took the lollipop. "It-it was hard not to." She stuffed the candy into her mouth, trying not to swallow it down in one hungry gulp. As glad as she was that the warden was on her side, still, something bothered her. She frowned.

"You have a question," Terry noted.

"If-if he couldn't see Lucky was abused, how-how good can he really be?"

Unwrapping a lollipop for himself, the warden mulled that over. "As good as the law will allow him to be."

Peggy sagged against the car.

"I promise you," he assured her, "this isn't over. We're going to make sure that Lucky gets his due, all right?"

Despite her disappointment, Peggy felt her heart lift with his promise. She nodded.

"Splendid." Terry pulled out his keys. "Now, what say we work together on this pesky door? You bear down, and I'll pull up."

It only took about four minutes to wrestle her door open, without the need for a kick. Peggy couldn't help but think that even the little car noticed the rapport between her and the warden, at least where Lucky and the cocky Dr. Paul Hayward, VMD-PhD, were concerned.

Chapter 7

Peggy had a difficult time coaxing Lucky through the gate and back into the shelter full of barking dogs, but she did it. She knew if anyone could help the dog, it would be the warden. The young vet may have doubted her, but Peggy had no doubt whatsoever that Lucky had been beaten by his owner. She felt that the warden knew it, too.

Entering the kennel, she shivered. The chill factor inside still matched the temperature outside. "Do they-do they get blankets at night?"

"Hmm? Blankets? Oh, not to worry!" The warden placed his hand on the radiator rungs, rather doubtfully. "We will have heat soon." He wiped a large, plastic dog bed down with a rag and set it in the run closest to the radiator. "Why don't you let him in?"

Lucky's tail drooped when Peggy shut the run gate after him. She would have apologized to him, if the warden hadn't been standing right behind her.

"Yo, Ter!" Joe strutted out of the office, his jacket zipped to his chin. "Ya want the good news or the bad news, first?"

"Are they very much different?"

"You're kiddin', right?"

"Let me venture a guess. Beula's out."

"Yeah well, that's the good news." One by one, Joe hoisted the guillotine doors up to let the dogs back inside.

"Beula is our rather eccentric boiler," Terry began to explain to Peggy.

"Yeah, right!" Joe snorted.

"And the bad news?"

"Riley's downstairs tryin' to fix her."

"Mr. Riley is our handyman—"

"Ha!"

"—and local bird expert."

"Don't let Brunhilda hear that, or you're gonna have one humdinger of a hoo-ha on your hands."

Terry turned to Peggy. "Clara and Mr. Riley have a bit of a tiff going on between them."

"It's called hate, Ter."

"A differing philosophy," the warden clarified. "Mr. Riley is a bird fancier, you see, and thinks cats ought not to be allowed out loose. I agree, but for different reasons. The feral cat population is rising at an alarming rate in this state. Clara plays for the cats' side naturally and thinks their birding is natural."

"Baloney! He's a Catholic shamrock and she's a Protestant limey. End of story!"

The warden passed a weary hand over his eyes, as Joe continued to regale them.

"It's true! You people are still chuckin' Molotov cocktails at each other over there! Riley and Croft are just carryin' on tradition; you know what I'm sayin'?" Joe pointed at Lucky. "What'd the doc say? Wait, don't tell me. Lemme guess! They can't do nuthin', right? Told ya! Want me to buzz Harrison now, get it over with? Y'know Betty won't do it." He opened the office door.

"Hold on there, Joe. Let's wait a week or so. Teach Harrison a lesson."

"Yeah, right!" Joe sneered then looked at the warden, incredulously. "Ter, you can't do that!"

"I'm the manager. I can do whatever I want. And, I say we need to hold Lucky; see if we can heal up his sores, fatten him up a bit."

"But, where we gonna keep him? We're doubled-up, and what about the others lookin' for reprieve! No fair!"

"Right again," Terry looked around the kennel, frowning. "So, what do we do? It's Friday, remember?"

Peggy looked up at the warden with alarm, remembering well what happened nearly every Friday. "You-you're not going to put them to sleep because-because of Lucky, are you?"

"It wouldn't be because of Lucky," he assured her, then turned to Joe. "What say we delay that, too, to be fair to all of them."

"That's cool, but Ter, we're full up!"

"We'll work it out."

Joe raised his brow. Terry raised his own. Joe seemed to know he was beat and trudged inside the office, kicking the door closed behind him.

The warden strolled up and down the rows of dogs, reading their cage cards. Peggy couldn't imagine that he'd made the decision just for her. She felt relief but struggled with a nagging question. "After-after the week is up, wh-what happens then?"

The warden leaned against the fencing. He seemed reluctant to answer her question, but she waited. "Well, with no evidence of wrong-doing, we'll have to return him to his owner. We'll book him for medical and boarding fees, plus a fine, but outside of that, there's not much else we can do."

Peggy reached through the fencing and rubbed Lucky's muzzle. "He's only going to do it again." It was quiet for so long, that she looked up and found the warden regarding her.

"What makes you so sure?" he asked.

It took a moment before she could get the words out. "I just am."

"Peggy," he said finally, "one thing you must understand; Lucky isn't the first case like this we've had and, unfortunately, he's not going to be the last. It's easy to forget that, sometimes."

Peggy remained quiet.

"Let's call it a day," he suggested, "and tomorrow I'll give you the grand tour."

Peggy stood up, and Lucky pawed the fencing, wanting more attention. She obliged by scratching his ears. He acted more like a pet now, rather than a dog who'd been cruelly whipped.

In spite of her growing feelings for the dog, she felt a rising uneasiness, too. There was still time. She could still walk away from him, this place, these people, and all the rest of the animals that may or may not be there in the morning, despite what the warden had said earlier.

People make promises they don't keep, you know that.

But, who'll put the ointment on Lucky's sores?

Save yourself! Run!

"Peggy?"

Flinching, she faced the warden. "Th-thank you for helping him." She picked up her suitcase and headed for the door.

"Ah, hold on there a tic!" The warden trotted into the office, but was back in a moment. He held the uniform package and a piece of paper. "You might need this Promise of Employment, too. The boarding houses tend to waive formalities at the sight of the town seal. Oh!" He held up a finger and then unhooked a key from his belt. "You'll need this in the morning. Joe and I often have early calls. Everyone has their own key. I'll copy Joe's."

Peggy's hand was frozen on the doorknob. She stared at the uniform package, the paper, and the key in his hands.

Don't fall for it! Run! Before it's too late!

The warden glanced at his watch. "The twenty-one bus will be stopping right across from the firehouse in five minutes. It runs roughly every half-hour up through Tory Corner. You couldn't ask for an easier commute!"

Peggy heard Lucky whine, as if putting his two cents in, too.

"I know Lucky here will be looking forward to seeing you, tomorrow!"

No! Go!

Peggy pressed her eyes closed. Go where? Please, I'm tired. I'm hungry and cold and…she heard Lucky whine again and opened her eyes. Lucky wagged his tail at her. Trembling, she reached for the key in the warden's hand. The moment she grasped it, her voices wailed and fled, abandoning her.

"'Til tomorrow, then!" The warden opened the door for her. "And it is we who need to thank *you* for coming to us for help. You came to the right place, trust me."

Something in his tone stopped her. His searching eyes conveyed far more than his words. She had trouble dragging hers away. "Th-thank you."

She felt his gaze on her even after she turned the corner and passed the firehouse.

"Where's Miss Diddicoy off to, then?" Clara queried the warden. "Flown the coop already, has she?"

"Aha!" Joe swiveled around in his chair. "You told her, and she quit! I knew it! Civvies always high-tail it when they find out we nuke 'em." He turned to Clara and Betty. "Ante up, ladies."

"I didn't hear nuthin' bout Ghost Girl quittin', yet!" Betty challenged. "Maybe she done be sent on her way, 'cause she ain't got no experience, and we ain't no half-way house."

"Her name is Peggy," Terry admonished. "She didn't quit, I didn't fire her, and like any one of you at your start, with time and a little TLC, I daresay she will be a nice addition to the fort, here."

"She's a spaz!" Joe argued.

"She's shy."

"What's the diff?"

"Look it up in the dictionary. Second shelf. On the subject of nuking, I wish you'd all devise another way to draw up the euth list," he added, as Clara flipped cage cards across the room into a bucket.

"'Eeny, meeny, miny moe' gets old," retorted Clara.

"Amen," Betty said, blowing into a tissue.

"We're fair, and you know it," Joe chided him. "This way is more democrat-like. Nobody can play faves. Back to what's-her-face. So, she didn't quit–yet. And you didn't eighty-six her–yet. She just don't seem like the kinda chippie that's gonna cut it, y'know what I'm sayin'? I mean, c'mon, it's just us now. You can talk turkey. You really figure she's gonna come back tomorrow?"

Terry turned toward the window, the long, empty driveway framed by chipping paint. "I hope so." Behind his back, he heard his crew slap down another bet.

Chapter 8

Scrutinizing the Promise of Employment form, the super's meaty lips mouthed the words silently as she combed over each line.

Peggy felt faint as she watched, the uniform package trembling in her hands. She'd been relieved that the form did not list the animal shelter as employer, but rather the more auspicious "Town of Farroway". Town Hall was listed as the legal address, and under occupation, someone had typed "Officer of the Court".

You'll never get away with it! You'll never get away!

Peggy clamped her lips shut before the warning whispers slipped out.

The super glanced up at her. Whether it was the town seal or the warden's badge that tipped the scale, Peggy wasn't sure, but the stubby woman held up a key, just out of reach.

"No pets, no parties, no *mens*, no noise! Rent is first of month. Late one day, anna out you go!" The woman raised a pencil-thin brow. "First anna lasta month in advance."

Peggy withdrew an envelope from inside her coat pocket. Pulling the rubber bands off, she doled out tens and twenties into the woman's waiting palm. The woman grunted as she thumbed through the bills, and then she stuffed them down her grease-splattered blouse. Grasping the bannister, she hauled herself up the marble stairs, her pink vinyl slippers clap-clapping on each step. Half-way up, she turned around.

"You comin' or what?"

"Oh. I'm sorry!"

Peggy snatched her suitcase and scrambled up the stairs. They climbed three flights, and then the super led her down a dim hallway to a door with a tarnished brass marker engraved with the room number 3-D. She slapped the key into Peggy's hand.

"Anythinga broke, donta call me, call management. Number is on posta box. Tell 'em Vida's house." She turned and headed to the stairs.

"Thank you," Peggy called after her. She waited until she could no longer hear the super's slippers, then peered first one way and then the other. Three doors shared the floor with her. One was open a crack. Just as she noticed it, it closed with a thud, and she heard a lock latch. Turning back to her own door, she was presented with half a dozen locks. She held up the lone key. It took a few tries before she matched it with the correct keyhole half-way up the door. Taking a deep breath, she slowly turned the knob and pushed it open. Beyond her loomed darkness. Her heart began to pound in her ears. She reached into the shadowy interior with a shaking hand and felt around the wall for a light switch. When her fingers connected with it, she flipped it on.

A single bulb dangled from the ceiling like a hanging victim on a slender wire. When it popped on, it illuminated a smallish room in a pool of yellow light. The entire flat was comprised of a kitchenette, living room, bedroom and bath. She closed and locked the door behind her and studied the place. The door was only one escape from the apartment that she could discern. There were three windows etched in frost. The smallest one hung in the kitchenette to her right. The other two shared the corner with a night stand and a small bed. The wind rattled the panes and whipped the naked tree branches in the yard below. If there was an emergency, the windows wouldn't be her first choice of escape, but in a pinch, they'd do.

The walls hadn't been painted, but they were clean. In the kitchenette, a small Formica table and matching chair sat under the window. To her surprise, there was a small stove and refrigerator tucked into the corner. The fridge was a squat, antiquated model that hummed noisily. The side next to the stove was caked with layers of grease. Tie an apron around it, she mused, you'd be hard-pressed to tell the difference between it and the super.

With a timid hand, she inspected every cabinet and drawer. The warped cupboard doors didn't shut all the way and the drawers stuck, but it didn't matter.

Peggy returned to the main room and peeked into a closet that was so tiny it wasn't even big enough to stand in. She propped the door open with her suitcase so that light shone into every corner. Behind her was the bathroom. Warily, she peered behind the door. The ancient fixtures were rusted and crusted with lime. The sink stood under a scratched, mirrored medicine chest. The cold water ran hot and the hot water ran cold. Pulling back a plastic shower curtain decorated with colorful fish, she saw the rusted shower head dripped steadily into the tub.

Peggy sat down on the bed. It creaked as she began to sink, until her knees were almost level with her chin. She smiled so big, her chapped lips cracked. Running her fingers over the soft mattress, she could have cried. It was heaven!

A gust of icy wind rattled the windows. Cold air drifted down from the frosty glass, and Peggy shivered. She spotted an ornate radiator in the corner and pried herself away from the bed. After a few stiff turns of the knob, she heard a far-off knocking in the walls. A few moments later, the rungs began to warm. She rested her hands on them in wonder. Running water and heat? She could not believe her good fortune.

Unpacking her suitcase took all of two minutes. She pulled out baggy pants, a moth-eaten sweater, two flannel shirts, two pair of cotton underpants, two pair of socks, a small wind-up alarm clock, and a cheap plastic radio, which she plugged into an outlet. The voices of an AM talk station host, and a caller, broke the quiet. She rested a hand on it, as if greeting an old friend.

"...always th'ones to save everybody else, huh?"

"I take it," the show host responded, "you have no sympathy for—"

"Why should I be payin' for losers on welfare when they could get up off their—" The radio bleeped.

"Hey! No foul language on the air, pal! Whattsa madda f'you? C'mon, look around, inflation's at twelve point two percent! It's not even a year after the war and we've got ourselves into, how many billion dollars in debt? Nice parting gift from Tricky Dick. Thanks a lot, DICK! You gotta ask what was missing in those eighteen minutes, huh? And hey, I hope you're savin' up, schmoe, because when they ship your job overseas, and they will, you'll be on the dole too, okay? Because we won't be makin' jack here in this country, and the only job you'll be getting is serving up fries with that burger! But, don't ask *me* how anybody's gonna be able to afford that rat burger when THERE'S NO WORK, PEOPLE! And in case you haven't noticed, food prices have doubled. And sixty-three cents a gallon for gas? Are they nuts? And you wait, the gas lines aren't over—you think the fifty-five mile per hour law those morons in Congress passed in January has made any difference? Please! How about solar energy? Is anybody looking into that? No, instead, they're pissing off OPEC and, hey, we just had the Franklin National Bank fail! What does that tell you? Big, fat failed, people! Biggest bank failure since—look, read the papers once a year, okay? I don't think it's a few down and outs caused this mess."

Peggy nearly knocked the radio over when she reached to change the station. She didn't want to hear the bad news. Not tonight. Maybe, not ever, again. She twisted the dial until she found Christmas music. It reminded her of her ride with the warden. Picking up the uniform package, she held it to her chest. She sank down into her bed and laid her head on the pillow. The music filled the room, and she felt her heart dive deep into the sentiment of the song.

"...in sad despair I bowed my head, there is no peace on earth, I said, for hate is strong and mocks the song of peace on earth, good will toward men... then the bells pealed loud and deep, God is not dead, nor doth he sleep, the wrong shall fail, the right prevail, with peace on earth, good will to men..."

Peggy wished she could snatch hold of the last notes before they faded and tuck them away for safe keeping.

Don't believe that crap. It isn't true, you know. You know. Peggy pressed her eyes closed. Please, not tonight. Please.

An announcer's voice broke in. "That was Frank Sinatra with *I Heard The Bells*. In the news tonight, there's been an increase in the number of bombings in Dublin, the violence once again suspected to be the work of the Irish Republican Army. The fallout from the Franklin National Bank continues to ripple through the economy as the recession deepens, with a call to Congress for legislation to prevent further collapse within the banking industry. With the recent passage of the Freedom of Information Act, over President Ford's veto, there are some experts who question whether the government should step in and take over other institutions on the brink of similar collapse. Massachusetts Governor Sargent has lifted the curfew in Roxbury as National Guard troops are pulled out of South Boston, following the race riots that erupted in September, over forced desegregation of the students between the predominately black Roxbury and white South Boston. The death toll has risen to one point five million in Ethiopia due to the famine, exacerbated by an influx of refugees fleeing the violence of military juntas. At the World Food Conference in Rome, The United States has declined to make any increases in food aid to developing nations, calling on those nations' leaders to take the lead instead, in matters of self-help, including utilizing advances available in population control. More after these messages."

Peggy listened absently, too tired to even lift her hand and turn the dial. She felt herself drifting away, her eyes losing the fight to remain open. She couldn't remember the last time she'd actually slept. Had she ever slept? Her fingers languished on the outline of the warden's badge. The raised letters, like Braille, spelled out the word Police. How odd. How ironic. She was going to wear a police badge.

Though still a little scared, for now she was safe. And for that, she was very, very grateful. It was so awfully cold out there.

Chapter 9

Bang, bang, bang!

Peggy jolted awake. Drenched in sweat, she yanked her blanket up to her chin, waiting for the ambush. She looked wildly around, but found no one lying in wait. She was alone.

The lights were still on, and so was the radio. She was still dressed and in her coat. Steadying herself with a few deep breaths, she finally recognized her surroundings. She was in a rental apartment. Her eyes darted to the door. It was shut and locked. The strains of *White Christmas* worked their way into her consciousness.

When the buzzing subsided in her arms and legs, she eased off of the bed and slunk to the bathroom door, making sure there was no one in there, either. All clear. She slumped against the doorjamb.

Somewhere below, she heard garbage cans fall over. Bang, bang, bang! She crept onto her bed and peeked out the window. The early morning stars glittered like broken glass on a deep blue sea. The wind howled, shaking the sumac branches, and the loose trash cans below.

All at once, a prickly heat began choking her under her collar. She threw off her coat and dashed into the bathroom. She splashed cold water on her face, over and over. As she hovered over the sink, she waited for the painful hammering of her heart to subside.

After one last deep breath, she looked into the mirror and gasped. She looked like a ghoul! Dark circles under her eyes made her look gaunt, much older than her years. Her hair was stringy and her skin was sallow. She barely recognized herself and felt the sting of shame burn a hole in her back.

What did you expect?

I don't know...not this ghost staring back at me. Peggy dragged herself away from her reflection and turned on the shower. Under the warm stream of clean water, she should have felt revived. She closed her eyes and hung her head. She just wanted to forget.

Thoughts of Lucky crept into her head. Did he wake up tonight in the shelter, confused and scared, too? She lathered her hair with a soap remnant, wishing that soap and water could scrub out the past as easily as it stripped sweat and dirt. But, those kinds of stains burrow under the skin and seep deep into bone. Once buried, nothing can reach it, let alone cleanse it.

Peggy stepped into the hallway, bundled in her coat and hat, and locked her door. She tried to sneak down the steps, but spotted Vida, the super, right away. In the lobby was a bank of renters' mail slots. The mailman was busy dispersing letters to individual boxes, and while his back was turned, Vida grabbed a letter and held it up to the light. She quickly put it back on the stack and picked up another one. Peggy tried to scoot by, but tripped over the mail cart, sending it squeaking across the floor.

Vida spun around. "Hey! That you screamin' in the middle of the night? I no wanta complaints, you hear?!"

Peggy flew out the lobby door.

Stamping her numb feet, Peggy waved to the number twenty-one bus. As it drew near, it swerved to the curb with a screech of brakes. When the door whooshed open, the same driver as before glared down at her. He was swathed in a thick scarf, and the bracing scent of vapor rub wafted down the steps to her nose.

"You waitin' fo' th'elevatah?" he croaked.

"S-sorry." Peggy stumbled aboard. "The-the shelter, please."

"Downtown? This bus don't go to Newark."

"Newark? No, Farroway. The-the animal shelter?"

"The who?"

"The animal shelter. B-by the firehouse and the railroad tracks?"

"You mean Walnut Street station. Fifty cents."

Peggy deposited her fare and stumbled into the only seat left on the front bench. She took off her hat, feeling somewhat confused. How was it that the bus driver not only didn't know where the animal shelter was located, he didn't even seem to know that it existed?

She began to sweat and removed her coat. The bus was so overheated she could barely breathe. In a moment, she noticed the people opposite her were staring at her—or rather, her baggy dogcatcher uniform and the warden's badge drooping over her breast pocket. She pulled her coat back on and turned her gaze out the windshield.

This time, she kept track of the route, counting out the minutes in her head, as the bus lumbered on. She had to be careful. She didn't want to end up at those stairs. Never again!

The stop and go traffic took longer than she'd thought, and she was glad that she'd started out so early. After about twenty minutes, she caught sight of the firehouse ahead and stood up, holding tightly onto the safety bar.

The driver steered the bus over to the curb and hauled the door open. "Thank you," said Peggy, and the driver grunted.

Descending the steps, she clutched her coat closed against the icy wind and hurried along the half block to the shelter.

Trotting down the narrow driveway leading to the shelter, Peggy felt a rush of relief. There were no cars in the lot, yet. She would have time to get her bearings in peace and quiet before anyone else showed up. The moment she latched the gate, she heard the dogs erupt into barking inside. In the early dawn, it sounded even louder than it had the day before. She inserted her key into the faded green front door, and shoved it open, having to use her whole weight. The din of barking assaulted her, and she held her breath against the thick, overnight stink that permeated the chilly air. She reached her hand inside and felt along the wall for a light switch. She flipped it up, and a single fluorescent fixture flickered on and off.

She clapped her hands over her ears and ran down the length of the runs to find Lucky. The dog shivered in the last run by the radiator. When he saw her, he wagged his tail but shrank back from the raucous noise. She decided to let the dogs out, just to quiet them.

She grasped hold of the wire cables over Lucky's gate, as she'd seen the warden do, and tried to haul the heavy steel chute door up. Screech! It jammed in its tracks, and no amount of yanking on the cable would dislodge it. Lucky circled the pen, whining. Peggy hauled on the next cable, but that door screeched to a halt only a third of the way up, leaving a rotund rottie-mix trapped, too. Frenzied with a desire to get out, the rottie-mix pounded on the chute door with its paws, like a boxer, making a booming racket.

Throwing off her coat, Peggy jumped at the next chute, and the next, one after another. Try as she might, twenty-two of the twenty-four chute doors jammed, which only incited the dogs to ever louder barking and howling!

Perspiration broke out across her face. What to do, what to do? Then, she remembered that the front runs had outer gates, too. She could just walk the dogs out through the kennel and into their outside runs! How hard could that be?

She snatched a leash off of the center beam and sprinted down to the loudest barker, a black shepherd-mix mutt. The dog's cage card read: "Zorro". Other than a red dot on the upper right hand corner, there was no other information.

"Hello, Zorro."

The dog wagged its fringed tail at her. Good enough. Peggy opened his run gate a crack to slip the leash around his neck, and the dog zipped right past her. "Wait! No, no, no!"

In a flash, the dog dashed down the length of the runs, and catapulted off of the rear wall, his paws barely connecting with the floor. Chasing him around and around, Peggy made a frantic leap for him, but missed, and collided into the trash cans with a crash!

That's when the warden walked in. A lollipop in his mouth, he looked down on her, calm as could be. "Good morning!"

Joe skidded to a stop behind him and dropped a box of doughnuts. "Awww, JEEZE!" He jumped over Peggy and chased Zorro up and down the room for a good two minutes until he finally lassoed the dog like a steer at the rodeo. Breathless, he hollered. "How the frig he get out?"

"S-sorry!" Peggy scrambled to her feet, near tears. "I-I couldn't get them open."

"You mean the chutes?" The warden gestured her to follow him to the radiator. He hefted what looked like an anvil up off of the rungs, and shouted an introduction over the barking. "Peggy, meet EL Kabong!"

With a roll of his eyes, Joe trudged over and lifted the anvil out of Terry's arms. With dramatic grunts, he smacked the corners of each chute door with it, then hoisted them up, one by one, with another show of effort. As the dogs dashed outside, it became easier for the three humans to hear one another.

"As you can see," the warden mused, "Joe and EL Kabong are old friends." Joe shot him a withering look and released a chute door so that it fell down hard. WHAM!

"The snag with the guillotines," he continued, "and I'll wager you can gather why we refer to them as such—"

"Duh!" Joe snapped. "Chop your friggin' foot off, you ain't sharp!"

"Yes, well, along with rest of the abode, they've aged, a bit. And, what with the summer heat and winter cold, they tend to warp and—"

"And ya havta whack the freakin' crap outta them!" Joe whacked a door frame with the anvil. Bang! Bang! Bang!

Peggy knelt down by Lucky, crouched in his pen.

The warden bent down beside her. "How's our patient, then?"

"The noise…he's scared."

"No doubt." He stood up and jimmied the cable over Lucky's 'guillotine door', and as if by magic, it un-jammed. He raised it up and Lucky skulked outside to relieve himself.

Both men made it look so easy. Peggy squirmed in her shoes with embarrassment.

"Not to worry," Terry gestured her to follow him. "Once you iron out the quirks of our chutes, it's easy. Number twelve here is a fussy lady. You have to haul her up slow and favor the right to avoid a bent left rail. Number four, ten and eight require a quick hoist or they'll crimp on your left. Number six, nine and fourteen want a sort of start-stop then a sharp jerk to the left—hold on a tic—I believe I have that backwards." He consulted a diagram on the wall. "No, see here, it's a right jerk or they'll stick to the left. Oh," he chuckled as if confiding about a favorite grandchild, "and nothing will do for number sixteen except a good swift—"

Bam!

Peggy flinched. Joe hauled off and kicked number sixteen again, for all it was worth. Bam! Bam!

"And FYI?" the junior officer chided her. "A red sticker on their run card means don't open their friggin' gate!"

"Zorro is our Houdini of the kennel," the warden concurred.

"I'm-I'm so sorry."

The warden waved her apology away. "Joe and I had ourselves a dickens of a time figuring out these chutes. Isn't that right, Joe?"

"Whoever built this dump was a freakin' monkey dick!" cried Joe, and kicked number nine. Bam! Bam!

"You'll get the gist of it," the warden assured her over Joe's commotion. "Worse come to worse, there's always the cheat sheet on the wall there."

Muttering under his breath, Joe returned El Kabong to the radiator with a clank then felt the rungs. "Beula's out again. Surprise, surprise."

"Apparently so. All right. Oh, when Beula's in good humor," he pointed out to Peggy, "we switch on this hot air blower, and it heats the place rather nicely." He flipped a switch on and off under a square metal box above the silent radiator. "Don't ask me how it works, I haven't a clue."

"It's 'cause Riley got it jerry-rigged that way," Joe shot back. "Crap forbid somethin's simple, he's gotta complicate it."

"Now, why would he do that?"

"'Cause he's a Mick, Ter. That's what they do. No offense."

"Joe, have you heard about the latest cultural concept circulating the globe these days, referred to as, political correctness?"

"I don't vote; what's your point?" The phone rang in the office.

"Why don't you man the phones until Betty arrives, then muck the back this morning, while I sort this out?"

Joe snatched the box of doughnuts up off of the floor. "Ten-four." He stalked past Peggy without so much as a glance to her and kicked the office door closed behind him.

Peggy wrung her hands red with worry, as the warden gazed around at the mess, a frown on his face. She couldn't believe it. Her first day, and she'd caused a catastrophe before the place even opened! Would he fire her? For that matter, why did he even hire her? It was brutally clear that she hadn't a clue as to what she was doing. To beat him to the punch, she began to unpin the badge from her shirt when he turned to her with a bemused smile.

"I daresay, this is as good a place as any to begin our orientation tour!"

Chapter 10

Terry opened his arms wide. "This is the kennel room. Fifty-some-odd years ago, it served as the railroad's tool shed. When the DOH—the Department Of Health—mandated the need for an animal control facility, rather than condemn the place, as it probably should have been, it was converted. However, contrary to Joe's notion, whoever saw to the work actually did a smart job of it. For example, you see this run-away here?"

Peggy looked where he was pointing toward a small, round grate in the center of the slate flooring.

"What you yanks call 'a drain'," he added. "It's perfectly situated. You'll find that the floor slopes down towards this point from every corner. It allows us to hose the entire room, ceiling to floor, which we do, twice daily." He pulled out a dark green glass bottle from the sink cabinet and unscrewed the lid. "It's crucial to keep the place clean, so we use this pine-scented disinfectant that doesn't so much smell like pine, but rather, turpentine."

He held the bottle under Peggy's nose. She took a polite whiff and grimaced. Her eyes watered instantly.

"Oh."

"Yes. Bit of an industrial flavor," he commented, arching his eyebrows. "However, it works."

Behind them, the office door opened and shut. Joe sauntered past them to the front door, zipping his jacket to his chin. "Riley's on the move. Betty just pulled up. I'll be out back." He held up his walkie-talkie. "Got my ears on."

"I could just as easily give you a shout from the back window."

"And I'd hear you how?" Joe opened the front door and paused, jerking a thumb to the dogs outside. As if on cue, they exploded into barking. He saluted Terry and then yelled, "SHADD…!" The slamming door cut off the rest of his bellow.

Terry sighed. "If you want to make Joe a happy camper, muck the kennel in the morning, so he doesn't have to."

Peggy nodded in earnest.

He picked up what looked like a mini-shovel and rake. "This is a poop scooper. We use it, thusly." He scraped feces off of the floor of the runs, one lump at a time. Peggy walked along with him, her hands tightly clasped behind her back. Whenever he looked at her, she searched his face. When was he going to do it, she wondered? When was he going to punish her for the mess she'd caused? She kept her eye on the front door, because she was convinced that, any second now, he'd drop the Mr. Nice Guy routine and turn on her in a rage.

He turned to her. Peggy gulped. "I hope you're not squeamish," he said, as if in apology. "Most of the dogs are not house-broken, you see. Even if they were, between confinement and the stress, whatever habits they knew once, they often lose. This is where we dump the poop."

He removed the lid to a plastic-lined garbage can. It was almost filled to the brim with fecal matter. Peggy's nose cinched up over the stench. He looked at her with a smile. She took a step backwards. Oh no! This was it. He was going to dunk her head into it!

"Bit of a stink, I fear," he said. "With time, you'll get used to it." He scraped the feces off of the scooper, replaced the lid and set the scooper aside. "Help me right the beds, will you?" He walked past her and began to set the plastic dog beds up against the wall.

It took her a second to follow suit. Had she misread him? Was he not going to punish her?

Watch your back! It's only a matter of time!

Peggy wasn't so sure, though, and unclenched her fists only to pick up a soiled bed and prop it against the fencing. She kept her back to the wall at all times and didn't take her eyes off of the warden.

"Very good," he said, after they'd finished. He extracted a plastic canister and a jug of liquid soap from the cupboard. "Next, we fill this with a capful of the pine disinfectant and a dollop of this liquid soap." He screwed the canister to the hose. "Attach it like so, then stand back because…" His fingers fumbled on the hose trigger.

Peggy ducked as a jet of steaming, sudsy water blasted the wall right over her shoulder. She wiped spray off of her cheek.

"So sorry!" Terry exclaimed. "Bit of a sensitive trigger! Better scoot behind me."

Peggy darted behind him and watched him thoroughly spray the walls, the dog beds and the fencing. Once the whole room had been soaped, he shut off the spigot. "While that sits for ten minutes, we wash their dishes. Any questions so far?"

"I-I don't think so." Peggy couldn't remember a thing he'd said before the soap blast. Did he put the soap in first or that nasty green stuff? Did it matter which was put in first? Did they do it every day? Did he say two times a day? Or three? She had only half-listened to his instructions, waiting for the inevitable shoe to drop. His calm, quiet manner had utterly confused her.

He unscrewed the soap sprayer from the hose. "This morning, we'll forego the ten minute soak, as I neglected to pick up their bowls. No harm done. We'll just give them a good rinsing before we collect them."

Taking careful aim this time, he pulled the hose trigger and swept the walls, fencing, the bowls and beds, sending suds and muck down the gutters, and across the floor to the central drain.

"See how nicely that works? We'll let the beds drain now, and set down fresh water for them. What say I rinse and you stack?"

"Okay."

"Splendid."

Terry worked the right side of the room, picking up food and water bowls out of the runs, so Peggy mirrored him on the left side, until her arms were loaded with bowls.

"Very good!" He took the bowls from her and dumped them in the sink, and then turned on the tap. "Found a flat, then?"

"S-sorry?"

"Accommodations? An apartment?"

"Oh. Y-yes. Thank you."

"Satisfactory, I trust? No issues?"

"Yes. I-I mean no. To the second part. Of-of your question."

"Very good. Tory Corner?"

"Yes."

"Quaint little neighborhood, isn't it?" He turned off the tap.

Peggy's stomach growled loudly above the dripping quiet of the room. "Paddy's makes a fine breakfast," he added. "Tried it yet?"

"I-I forgot breakfast."

"First day jitters? Well, we can't have you run off your feet on an empty stomach. I'm afraid there're not many shops left, this end of the tracks. Help yourself to the pastries in the office, before Joe scarfs them down. From here on, you must eat before coming in to work. Promise?"

Peggy felt her cheeks flush and she looked down at her shoes. "Yes."

"Very good. Go on, now, fetch a doughnut. Have two," he called after her.

Peggy walked swiftly to the office. She spotted the pink box on the counter and grabbed a sugared cruller. She wolfed it down, thinking nothing had ever tasted so good. As she ate, she perused the cats behind the cage bars, all meowing for attention. She spotted Houdini, the wayfaring ferret, who peeked at her from under shredded newspaper. How was she going to clean his cage without letting him out? She'd have to be extra careful with that one!

As her stomach settled, she wondered about the warden. Why hadn't he yelled at her, yet? Maybe he was used to this sort of thing. After all, she wasn't the only one who made mistakes! Look at Clara, who habitually mistook Houdini for a cat. She'd made a shambles of the office the other day, and Peggy had a sneaking suspicion that it might be a regular occurrence.

She licked sugar off of her lips and snatched up a fat cream doughnut dripping with vanilla icing. Stuffing it into her mouth, she reveled in the sweet, thick custard taste. It was sheer heaven.

Peering out the front window, she caught sight of Betty. The woman was bent inside the door of a vintage, powder-blue Buick. It looked like she was trying to help Clara out of the car, but she kept losing her grip on the old woman's hands. Clara's orthopedic shoes flipped up into the air, over and over. Peggy could almost hear Betty cussing a blue streak in the frosty air. She sputtered crumbs, stifling a giggle.

After she tossed the last bite into her mouth, she hurried back out into the kennel. Half way across the room, she realized she'd left the office door open and ran back to shut it.

"Good girl!"

She sprinted up to Terry and skidded on the wet slate.

"Easy there! It gets slippery! We don't want to fall and crack our noggin, now do we?"

"N-no. S-sorry."

"Filled up, are we?"

"Yes. Thank you."

"Jack's makes the best doughnuts in town. Ditto, the best Chinese tack for tiffen, or what you yanks refer to as, grub for lunch." He handed her bowls of fresh water. "To the left of the gates, if you please. The dogs are less apt to up-dump them on that side, when barking at Joe, twenty times a day. Speaking of lunch, did you bring yours?"

"I-I forgot that, too."

"Since it's your first day, we'll have Joe fetch lunch from Jack's. It's my shout, this time. Do you like Chinese?"

"I-I think so." Did this mean he would shout at her, first *then* give her Chinese food for lunch? She watched as he pulled out two enameled tubs from under the sink.

He set them on one of the two standing cages bookending the room. Lifting a lid from a second, plastic-lined garbage can, he scooped dog kibble from it and dumped it into the pans. Peggy made a mental note to keep the two garbage cans straight. She didn't want to dump poop into the kibble!

"This is how we make breakfast for the dogs," he said. "We order bulk from BJ's, a feed store located up near Wayne. It's run by BJ, a bearded young man who refuses to tell anyone his real name. You should know that he considers himself to be an animal expert. Although, I suspect his sum total knowledge is derived from subscriptions to dog and cat magazines. However, he's affordable and he delivers. Alternate Tuesdays every month at ten a.m., although not always on time, and not always on Tuesdays, and sometimes not every month. Just when we're about to tear up his phone card for good, he shows up and saves the day."

He handed Peggy a can opener and pulled six cans of beef dog food off of a shelf over the sink. "Open these, will you? Thank you."

He poured a bowl of hot water into each pan of kibble. "We let this soak for about ten minutes, then add the canned food for a bit of flavor. Otherwise, most of them won't eat it. I can't honestly blame them, can you?"

Peggy was not about to admit that it smelled pretty good to her. Worst case scenario, she'd gladly have a bowl of it for lunch!

The front door blew open and Betty bustled in, muttering under her breath. Clara toddled in after her, toting an overstuffed, carpet bag of knitting.

"Good morning, ladies!" Terry called out with a cheerful wave.

Spotting Peggy beside him, Betty stifled a sigh, dug into her purse and handed Clara a dollar. With a mischievous grin to Terry, Clara followed Betty into the office. Terry and Peggy watched until the door closed.

"I do believe our Clara missed her calling. She'd have made a first rate bookie. We can set the beds down, now."

Peggy stopped in front of the plastic beds. They were still damp. "What do you dry them off with?"

"Dry them? Oh. Well, we merely let them drain."

"Oh." Peggy continued looking at them.

"You've a question. It's all right! Ask away. We don't bite."

"It's just...well, won't the dogs get damp and then cold?"

"Ideally, we would make sure that the beds are dry, and that the whole place was dry after every hosing. However, using that many paper towels would prove much too pricey for our meager purse strings. We're saving for a new boiler, you see. Although, I dare say it'll be awhile before we can afford that, either. Dogs are remarkably adaptable, however, and thus far, we've managed to stay one step ahead of Old Man Winter. But, you're quite right. I'm certain we wouldn't have near the coughs and sneezes should we provide dry bedding, twice daily. Our crumbling walls don't help matters."

Peggy studied the aging cinder block walls and their many gaps. Her eyes fell on a stack of newspaper on the second standing cage. "That-that might help."

"Hmn?" Terry glanced up from stirring the kibble.

She bunched up a section of newspaper and stepped inside a run next to a wall. She stuffed it tightly into a gap in the wall.

Terry grinned. "Of course! It's the cheapest insulation one could ask for. Now, why didn't I think of that? The homeless use it, as a matter of course!"

Peggy averted her eyes and continued to stuff wads of newspaper into cracks in the wall.

Outside, the dogs erupted into barking, and in a moment, Joe kicked the door open. He hollered over his shoulder. "SHAAADDAAAAP!" He slammed the door. "Jeeze Louise! It's the same friggin' thing every mornin'!"

"So I've noticed," Terry said.

"Back runs're ten-ninety-nine. Riley's down below deck."

"Jolly good."

"He's gonna blow us all to Kingdom Come one of these days, y'know."

Terry handed Joe a sheet of newspaper. "Let's hope not."

"Luck of the Irish, Ter. No offense. He don't never fix nuthin' right, so the odds ain't jake, catch my drift?" Absently, he followed the warden's lead and balled up wads of newspaper. "So, why we keep usin' him?"

"Because no one else will come within a stone's throw of Beula without hazard insurance."

"Insurance? Ha! He don't even got a license! And he's goin' soft in the head. Half the time I don't think he even knows what day it is."

"Neither do I."

"And ya can't tell him nuthin', 'cause he's stubborn as a goat."

"Set in his ways," Terry corrected and knelt down to stuff a gap near the floor.

"What I said! Like the time he tried to jump-start the Pinto offa the power pole?" Joe knelt down and shoved a ball of newspaper into a hole. "He coulda 'lectrocuted the whole friggin' place, y'know!"

"Yes, well, it's the thought that counts."

"Ter, he needs a check-up from the neck up!"

"Don't we all?"

Joe sat back on his heels then and looked at the newspaper balls in his hands. "Ter, what the frig we doin'?"

"Brilliant, isn't it? Peggy's idea. It's insulation."

"Against what? Mind control beams from Mars?"

"The cold, Joe. It's winter."

"Aha! You don't got no faith in Riley neither!"

"We're going to need more newspaper. Be a good lad and snitch some more tonight from Town Hall's dumpster, will you?"

"Without a form from Hackensack? I get caught, you gonna bail me out?"

"Don't I always? Do us another favor, and help feed the dogs? We're running a tad behind this morning."

"Wonder why..." Joe muttered.

Peggy caught his irritated glance. Heaving a sigh, he got up, flipped the lid off of the feed can and popped a handful of dry kibble in his mouth. "We're gonna need more chow. BJ is three days late again."

"If you'd quit snacking on it, perhaps we wouldn't run out as quickly."

Terry took full bowls from Joe, as he filled them. He set one in Lucky's run, before hefting the cable and raising the chute. Lucky nosed the opening, and when Peggy called him, he trotted over to her. He licked her hand then sniffed the bowl of food. He gulped it down noisily.

"He wants more," Peggy said.

"I'm sure he does. But, we need to err on the side of caution. Gradually increasing portions will ensure he can handle the new food. Stress plus malnutrition can equal diarrhea, and that can turn deadly, rather quickly. He'll get a bit more for supper if he holds it all right. Are you ready for more? Peggy?"

"Me? I-I had two. Doughnuts."

"I meant more in the way of *orientation*."

"Oh! Y-yes."

"Splendid. All right. Of all the dogs we take in, in contrast to the cats, only one or two of them, in most any shelter for that matter, are ever true strays. They're just…"

"Dumped!" Joe interjected, slopping more kibble into bowls.

"Unwanted," Terry clarified. "I never knew that before. Did you?"

Peggy shook her head.

"I wager you wonder why."

She nodded.

"Well, it's due most often to behavioral problems. People get a puppy or a dog, and they either don't know how, or simply don't take the time to train it. This leads to a ruined house or yard, and that shiny new pet ends up here. By law, we can't turn anyone away from our contracted towns and we are contracted with three; Farroway, both Uppah and Lower, Verona, and Claremont. Residents of other towns tend to figure out ways around it. They'll tell you, 'I found this dog on such and such street', or they say they found it wandering the railroad tracks. That's the most popular ruse, since the tracks run through all three towns. They come to us because we have a reputation for going the extra innings to find homes for the animals, you see. Most places don't have the luxury of trying beyond the legal hold time, due to even bleaker circumstances than ours."

"Like Newark," Joe said.

"Like Newark," Terry echoed.

"And Sacred Heart," Joe chided, raising a brow at him.

"Well, Sacred Heart is a special case."

"Yeah, right! Gimme a break!"

"Sacred Heart," Terry explained, "is a shelter run by the nuns of Our Lady of the Valley, and they're forced to farm out their euthanasia in order to maintain the claim that they don't put animals to sleep. They are subsequently deluged with donations and animals. It's a bit of a vicious cycle. They're half our size and currently serve ten towns."

Peggy's eyes widened. Even she could do the math. "You see the dilemma," Terry nodded.

"Dilemma Schlamemma, it's a friggin' lie," Joe argued, "and hey, ain't that like, a sin?"

"A fuzzy line."

"Fuzzy? Fuzzy like shark skin!"

"Their hearts are in the right place."

"Yeah, right next to their coffers. Y'know how much moola they haul in? Ya think they'd at least build a bigger place."

"Perhaps, they have more pressing priorities?"

"They're nuns, Ter. What do they do all day but count beads and cash, and say 'Hail Mary, ain't this some racket!'"

"Whatever their reasons," Terry handed bowls of dog food to Peggy, indicating she should set them in the back runs, "they have not, as yet, admitted to their arrangement, shall we say, despite our pleas to do so. I believe that it's in everyone's best interest to know the truth about pet overpopulation, the problem is that serious."

"It's a friggin' joke," Joe countered.

Setting bowls in runs, Peggy watched the warden and Joe raise the remaining chutes. Not a single door jammed on them. Most of the dogs rushed in, eager to eat, but not all of them. Joe paused by a run. A chocolate lab mix had ambled in and lay down in his bed, looking disinterested in the food.

"Ter, he's off his grub again."

Terry knelt before the dog's run. "This is Digger," he told Peggy. "Couple brought him in, an eleven-year-old family dog, and said he didn't fit in with their lifestyle, anymore. He sat at the end of his run all month waiting for them to come back. We keep hoping someone will adopt him. But so far, no one seems interested in an eleven-year-old dog. Sometimes the dogs...they give up."

Peggy's throat tightened and her eyes welled up.

"They're not all sad stories, I promise!" Terry assured her. "We have our fair share of happy endings."

"Yeah, right," Joe grumbled. "Don't get me started."

"Yes, well, what Digger needs is what we don't always have time for. And that's out-back time. You know, one-on-one. Perhaps that's something that you could do, Peggy?"

Peggy rubbed her eyes with the back of her hand. "Yes. I-I could do that."

"Splendid! Why don't I show you the back yard then!"

The office door opened, and Betty leaned out. "Mrs. Cruikshank called again. Goblins in the chimney."

Terry clapped a hand to his forehead. "That's right. I forgot. Very good. I'll sort it out."

Betty slapped an unbelieving fist on her hip.

"I'll take care of it, I promise. Soon as I finish giving Peggy the tour." He opened the front door and gestured Peggy to follow him outside.

"Goblins?" Peggy stepped past Terry and waited for him to shut the door.

"Mmn-hmn."

"Tour?" Betty said to the closed door. "What tour?"

Joe dropped a guillotine door down with a crash. "He never gave *me* no tour!"

Chapter 11

"G-goblins?" Peggy ventured again.

"Oh yes." Terry led the way past the runs, down the slope of gravel that ran under the office overhang. "We go through this twice yearly with Mrs. Cruikshank. Mind your head."

They ducked under the low clearance.

"Ninety years if she's a day, bless her soul. Come March and November, the police get a call about goblins ransacking her house. It seems the buggers come down the chimney and help themselves to the brandied fruit compote she cooks up for Bingo Sweeps at her church. She claims they are an evil handed down through an old family curse, all the way from the Emerald Isle.

"Now, I must say, we get reports every so often about the Jersey Devil, but this was a new one for us. Took Joe and I staking out her roof," he shuddered, "for two weeks to see that she wasn't merely a bit tipsy on her own hard sauce. One night, we caught the rabble-rousers in the act! We were perched on that roof and could hear the trash cans being upturned as they made their way up the street. Quick as you please, the masked thieves clambered up to the roof, and then climbed down her chimney. We were told they helped themselves to her eighty-proof desserts, as well as stole some knick-knacks, before they made their exit out the chimney in the wee hours of the morning. We watched them retreat to a hollow tree in her yard to sleep off their drunken stupor! Case solved.

"Dear Mrs. Cruikshank forgets to close the flue, you see. Her chimney ought to be capped, too. We use Hav-A-Hart humane traps to catch and then relocate them to Eagle Rock Reservation, South Mountain, or better yet, to a refuge down south Jersey in the Barrens where they've a lovely rehab program. Pun intended."

He stopped before a massive water pipe painted with yellow stripes and a cardboard sign dangling at eye level that read: LOW — DUCK HEAD.

"So they-they're real?" Peggy asked.

"Hmn? Real? Oh, you mean the goblins? Didn't I say? The goblins were a family of raccoons. But you won't convince Mrs. Cruikshank of that. This way," he said, indicating she should follow him. "We keep the traps down in the cellar."

The warden bent under the water pipe and jiggled the doorknob on a warped yellow door behind it.

Peggy felt all the blood drain from her face. "C-cellar?"

"It's warped." The warden twisted the knob and pushed against the door, but it wouldn't budge. "Must get this fixed. Hold on. Do you smell gas?" He sniffed at the keyhole and called through the door. "Mr. Riley?"

Peggy didn't smell any gas. She couldn't smell anything. Her throat tightened, as if gripped by a clamp, choking off her breath. Her knees locked and she couldn't move.

Stupid piece of filth! You wouldn't listen, would you? Now you're going to pay!

The voices shrieked in Peggy's head so loudly, she could barely hear the warden.

"Mr. Riley?" The warden shouldered the door hard and it burst open, spewing a cloud of smokey ash at him. "Mr. Riley, are you all right?"

Her heart pounding, Peggy watched helplessly as the warden disappeared into the smoke and descended down the staircase into darkness. The sounds around her muffled. The warden's voice faded into a sonorous hum inside her head—a drone of such intensity, it drowned out all thought. The shelter grounds no longer existed. A gaping, pitchy void writhed beneath her feet, threatening to swallow her whole. Dizzy, she clutched at the door frame.

Coughing, Terry descended the rickety steps through the smoke toward the sound of clanking pipes and testy cussing. "Mr. Riley, where are you?"

Fanning the smoke with his jacket, he caught sight of the wiry, eighty-year-old fixit man whacking the boiler over and over with a wrench. Clad in oil-stained overalls, his thin white hair had been blasted upright into dusty charcoal spikes. The old man shook his fist at the furnace and wailed.

"Die ye frost bitten, waffle iron! Rust an' die! I'm done wit ye!"

"Good heavens, Mr. Riley, what happened?"

"'Tis the devil itself, it is! Kill it while ye got a chance!" Mr. Riley implored him. Then he snatched up a heavy mallet, and hoisting it over his head, he took aim. "May the devil swallow ye sideways and choke on ye, ye banjaxed twat!"

"Ho there!" Terry caught hold of the old man before he crashed into the boiler. "You'll bring the house down, Mr. Riley!"

"Ye kin hammer her evil heart to kingdom come, I tell ye! Won't make no naboc'lesh!" Riley shook his bony fist at it. "Go out, burn out, *die*, ye protestant herring!"

Terry struggled to avoid the mallet. "Mr. Riley, Beula holds a grudge, so let's remember ourselves, shall we? Now, I would like to let go of you, but I will do so only if you promise to be a good lad and drop the mallet."

With a pitiful whine, Mr. Riley dropped his weapon and plopped himself down on an upturned bucket, long-faced and miserable.

Taking a deep breath, Terry set the mallet out of Riley's reach, and then looked around for Peggy. Not seeing her, he turned back to the stairs and spotted her hanging on to the door frame. Even in the dim light, he could see that she was pale.

"Peggy?"

He watched her sway, stumble backwards, and then collapse on the gravel. He took the stairs two at a time. As he crested the threshold, he smacked his head on the water pipe.

"Bloody hell!" Rubbing his forehead, he staggered over to Peggy. "Are you all right? What happened?"

Peggy gasped for air, and Terry became alarmed. Tears streamed down her cheeks, but she managed to croak, "S-sorry...sorry..."

Peggy heard, from far, far away, the warden's soothing voice, but she couldn't understand the words. Her heart had begun to slow down to a normal rhythm when she was hit by a stream of icy water. Instantly, she was wide awake.

"Blast it!" the warden exclaimed.

Peggy opened her eyes to find him, soaking wet, wrestling with a spewing hose. He kicked at a valve, and the water fizzled to a trickle. Grabbing a dirty rag, he knelt down and dabbed at her ice-drenched hair.

"Terribly sorry! Need to fix that. Steady on, take slow deep breaths. There we are. Feeling better?"

Peggy's teeth began to chatter and he removed his parka. Draping it across her shoulders, he said, "Did you bump your head on the pipe, like I did? No? What happened?"

Keep your mouth shut!

"N-nothing."

Liar!

"Nothing?" Terry repeated. "It had to have been *something.*"

Peggy wished he'd just let it go. It hurt her insides to push the words out of her mouth. "Please...it was nothing." The words escaped her lips like vapor, barely audible, even to her.

"Can you sit up?"

Peggy backed herself against the stone wall and stared at the open cellar door.

"Ah." Terry walked over and eased the cellar door closed. "Let me fetch some water. To drink, this time." He returned with a full Dixie cup. "It's clean, I assure you. We have a dispenser behind the rear stairs, there."

Peggy's eyes followed where the warden pointed, and she spied a set of stairs that rose out of sight, behind the overhang. They didn't descend anywhere that she could see. She took the cup and sipped.

"Do you mind if I ask a personal question?" he asked. "Are you... claustrophobic? It's all right, it's just, as your employer I need to be aware of any, er-uh, *conditions*, in case of emergency."

Feeling ashamed, Peggy averted her eyes. Claustrophobic? It sounded plausible, enough.

Yes! Say yes!

Her mind raced. If she said yes, then maybe he'd let the whole thing drop. Maybe she was claustrophobic. "Sorry," she murmured, and handed her empty cup back to him.

Coward!

"It's not your fault," the warden said, and looking around, found the trash can full. He crushed the cup and stuffed it in his pants pocket. "I'm afraid of heights."

Peggy risked a sidelong look up at him. His expression held no pity, but rather, understanding.

"Have been all my life," he admitted. "Good, old-fashioned vertigo. Bit of a handicap when you're thirty meters up a ladder wrangling goblins from a chimney! Gives me the willies just thinking about it. So, it's all right, is what I'm getting at. We all come into this world with only so many tools in the old toolbox, eh?"

They both turned towards the cellar, hearing stomping on the steps. Mr. Riley flung open the door, hefting his metal tool box. He leaned against the threshold, wheezing, and then wagged a finger at them.

> *"Said a foolish householder of Wales,*
> *An odor of coal gas prevails,*
> *She then struck a light, and later that night,*
> *Was collected in seventeen pails!"*

It took a moment for Peggy to realize that this strange old man was reciting a poem.

Mr. Riley tossed his tool box into a little red wagon parked by the back gate, picked up the handle, and scolded Terry. "Now, I'll check 'er whistle, you check 'er water." He staggered away, pulling the red wagon behind him.

"I rest my case," Terry sighed. "I'd have introduced you, but he won't remember. Besides, to Mr. Riley, every man under fifty is 'Harry', and every young lady is 'Colleen'. Well, got your sea legs yet?"

Peggy nodded.

"Splendid. Get yourself into the office and get dried off, while I 'check 'er water.'"

Peggy hesitated, though she was getting colder by the minute. She wanted to tell this kind man the truth.

Are you crazy? Keep your mouth shut! Go. Run! Now!

Shaking, she handed him the soaked rag. "Thank you."

"For what, triggering a phobia, and then dousing you with freezing water?"

Peggy began to remove his parka from around her shoulders when he held up a hand. "Hold onto it, before we can add causing you pneumonia to the list."

Managing a smile, Peggy nodded and ducked under the overhang. She trotted up toward the front of the building, following after Mr. Riley.

Terry watched her go then gave a long, appraising look to the cellar door creaking open in the wind.

Chapter 12

Crouched in Lucky's run, Peggy pulled the tube of Bacitracin from her pocket and dabbed it onto the dog's welts. She was still shaky, and Lucky licked her hand. Fresh tears welled up in her eyes and she put her arm around his neck, holding him close. That was a close call.

It's your own fault!

But what else could I do? Peggy bit her lip. She felt a rotten sourness churn in her gut over the incident, but most especially, she felt ashamed for having deceived the warden.

RRRRRIIIIIP!

Peggy ducked, with a start. Mr. Riley sat hunched in the broom closet, right across from her, wrapping a pipe. He ripped another length of duct tape, muttering to himself.

"Pissin' pillbox!" He leaned out of the doorway. "Get me a pan then, lass, I'm goin' to hafta bleed 'er."

"Wh-what?"

"Fetch me a pan, I say! Scoot, now!"

Pocketing the ointment, Peggy kissed Lucky's ear and backed out of his run. She made sure to latch the gate securely. Opening the cabinets beside the little sink, she found an enameled basin and hurried it back to the elderly handyman.

"Wrench," he said, holding his hand out to her like a surgeon waiting for a scalpel. Peggy rummaged in his tool box. "No, no, no!" he scolded. "Dem's pliers! Look to d'one north o' d'hammer der!"

"S-sorry? North? You mean here?"

"Och! Are ye blind as well as deef, Colleen?"

"My-my name's Peggy."

"What's dat? Look there! If it had teeth itta bit y'hand clean off at t'elbow! There! There!"

"S-sorry." Peggy handed him the Phillips head screw driver.

"That's it. None's the worse for it. Thank ye."

Tapping one pipe then the other, Mr. Riley wedged the washbasin under the radiator's whistle spout, then twisted the whistle round and round until, squeaking, it came off in his hands. Out of the thin tubing trickled a rusty stream of water.

"Ahhhhh....dat's better, isn't it, y'old turn-spit?" He patted the rungs with affection and winked at Peggy. "She'll be right as rain now, she will. Bit o' bad blood was all." He leaned back and puffed on his pipe, and recited.

"'Round the time they call Easter,
there blew in a fearsome Nor'easter.
They shuttered the winders,
they billowed the cinders,
but it still knocked 'em clean on their keisters!"

Peggy stifled a sputter of laughter. The old man crooned with such devotion, he might have been belting out a hymn. Just past Mr. Riley, Peggy noticed old Digger, still staring at the front door, his morning bowl untouched. She walked over to him. The dog's eyes dodged to her for a second and then swung back to the door, waiting. Crouching down, she reached through the fencing and stroked his head. Undeterred, he kept his vigil.

"Maybe after lunch we can go out back with Lucky," she whispered to him. If the warden doesn't fire me, she thought with a jab of worry.

It took concerted effort to stuff down the reminder of that big yellow cellar door. Seeing Digger was not responding to her affections, she withdrew and collected the rest of dogs' food bowls, empty and licked clean. So as not to feel completely useless, she filled the sink with soapy water and began washing them.

The dogs burst into barking outside, and soon, the front door opened. The warden butted it closed, his arms weighted down with a case of dog food.

"Good heavens, what are you doing there?"

"Oh!" Peggy jumped in fright and knocked bowls all over the floor. "I'm-I'm sorry!"

"You should be in the office. It's much too cold in here! You'll catch your death!"

"Catch 'er death?" Mr. Riley popped into view beside the radiator. "Ye may well say dat now sir, but never fear! Won't be for longer than a candlewick, now, ye'll be tinkin' yer in d'tropics, ye will. Steamy an' swelterin', it'll be!"

"I'll settle for sixty-five degrees, Mr. Riley," Terry thumped his burden down and patted the old man's shoulder. He gestured Peggy to the office. "Come on, then. I'm sure Betty's got the milk-house heater on roast, by now."

"Digger didn't eat," Peggy said, pointing to the lab's full bowl.

"Hmn. No, he didn't, did he? Perhaps we'd better—"

Joe opened the office door and hailed him. "Yo' Ter!" When he reached the warden, he handed him a bucket full of cage cards. "Not to be pessimissick, but we got three dogs and four cats comin' in. Here's the lottery pick for today. If we want th'EVC for a doc drive-by, we better call 'em, now."

Terry took the bucket with a sigh. "Peggy, I was hoping to spare you another week or so, but it seems circumstances are, once again, beyond our control." He gestured her inside the office. "After you."

Once inside, he sat down in his chair by the front window and perused the cards in the bucket. "I do believe I've requested that we devise another way to draw up the euth list?"

"We did," Joe said. "This time we went by age." He swiveled around in his chair to Clara. "How'd *you* get past the first cut?" The old woman flipped Joe the finger, and he spun around to Terry. "Did you see that?!"

"I'm sure that whatever it was, you asked for it," Terry murmured, reading a cage card.

"How's come you never yell at her?"

"Do the phrase respect yo' eldahs ring a bell?" Betty remarked from under a towel. She hovered over a pot of steaming water simmering on the hot plate.

"What about her?! She don't respect nobody!"

"She don't have to; she be old!"

"You guys always take her side!"

"One of these days, Joe," Terry said, "you will learn that with age comes wisdom, and with wisdom comes..." His face went blank. Clara eyed him like a cat. He cleared his throat. "...well, comes all the rest of it. So, Joe? Let's just mind our manners, shall we?"

Peggy hadn't ventured any farther into the office than the doorway. Biting her lip, she shifted uncomfortably on her feet, when she noticed Joe's eyes flick in her direction. She averted hers from his calculating scrutiny.

"And while contemplating the meaning of respect, Joe, let's find Peggy a chair, shall we?"

Peggy heard Joe stifle a sigh. He scraped his metal chair back and approached her, leaning a chair against the door beside her. He started to walk away.

"And set it up for her?"

Joe rolled his eyes and then unhinged the chair, pushing it in front of her. Then he flopped back into his own seat, popping open a soda can.

Peggy sat down, stiffly. The warden gestured her to scoot closer. She could feel everyone watching her, as she scuttled her chair up beside him. Terry pulled a notebook down from the shelf and opened it between them on the counter.

"What I'm doing here," he explained, "is looking up each of our animals in the Record Book, to determine which ones we might have to euthanize due to...Peggy, are you going to be all right with this?"

Over his shoulder, Peggy witnessed the exchange of dollar bills between crew members. Oh no, you don't, she thought to herself. Not this time! Sitting up a little straighter, she replied a little too loudly, "Yes. I-I am!"

"Good girl. Fortunately, we have a choice as to which animals we place on the list. We try to be as objective as we can, and we discuss each one, as a group, to be fair. Why don't I start?" He pulled a card from the bucket. "Number eleven. That's Scooter, isn't it?"

"Yup." Joe took a long swig of his soda.

Terry leafed through the notebook. "Here we go, number eleven. Scooter, yes, our ten year-old schnauzer. He's been here four weeks, already?"

"He's got gi-huge-ick skin probs," Joe reminded him. "They're just doohiggies, whatchamacallits—cysts—but nobody wants to mess with him 'cause it's gonna cost big bucks. And, he don't like kids, neither. Record of nippin'."

"Ah, yes..." Terry tapped his pencil on the notebook, thinking. At last, he looked up and surveyed the room. "I take it, by your silence, that we are unhappily unanimous about Scooter?"

Betty peered out from underneath the towel. "Who gonna flush they paycheck down the crapper to fix a ten-year old, carbunkle gimp who bites babies?"

"Eighty-six number eleven," Terry noted, then handed the bucket to Joe.

Joe closed his eyes, pulled a card out, and balked. "Aw, double-dip no fair! Jasper?! Who sneaked that one in there? He's a cool cat!"

"You can't be keepin' toothless, bald old cats what do nuthin' but piss on themselves all day long, it's inhumane!" declared Clara.

"Why not? We keep you around."

Terry tapped his pencil on the counter. "Shall we keep to the task at hand, ladies and gentleman?"

"I agree wiff Clara." Betty shut off the hot plate and opened what looked like a pack of cigarettes.

"Traitor!" Joe hissed.

"Be-*cause*," Betty pulled out a cigarette from the pack with her teeth, "he done been here fo' three month in that damn cage. Can't hold his water, got a skin disease, got allergies, can't eat right 'cause he got no teef left in his head, nevermind he be so god-forsook ugly. That cat be miserable! C'mon. Fair? Walk it like you talk it, baby."

To Peggy's astonishment, Betty then crunched the cigarette in her mouth, chewed it up and swallowed it. It was candy.

"But, he's the sweetest cat in the world!" Joe argued.

"Then you take him home! Spend every last dime you got on him! We be full up."

Gripping the edge of her chair, Peggy wondered what the warden thought about all this. She was amazed at his rectitude. He did not offer his opinion nor admonishment, but simply sat there and patiently allowed his crew to work it out between themselves.

"Okay! Okay!" Joe threw his arms in the air. "But I wannit on record I hate this place."

"Duly noted," Terry said and jotted Jasper's name down on a pad of paper.

Joe thrust the bucket at Clara. She rifled through the cards, studying each one. "Hey hey hey! No fair peeking! She's cheatin', Ter!"

"Am not!" The old woman sniffed. "Can't read your chicken scratch!" She pulled a card and read it, her lips moving silently.

"Hullo! Out loud, wouldja?"

"Number twenty!" Clara shouted at him.

"Not Cuddles!" Betty gasped, whirling around in her chair, two candy cigarettes between her lips.

"Aha!" Joe chortled, "shoe's on th'other foot, now, huh? Well, FYI, the dog's bit the gas man, the milkman, the mailman, barks all night long, and craps everywhere except outside. Who's gonna diaper her, *you*?"

Betty looked like she was considering it.

"I seem to have heard a rumor," Terry interjected, "about a certain person concealing six to ten animals in a rental that doesn't allow pets."

Betty wriggled in her seat, like a school girl in the principal's office.

"And," continued the warden, not looking up from the notebook, "if this certain Good Samaritan gets caught, instead of one animal being put down, it will be six, and she will be put out of her living quarters."

"All right, all right!" Betty reached into her bosom and pulled out a crucifix on a chain. Kissing the cross, she snapped, "Fine! Numbah twenty, dammit to hell!"

Peggy was taken aback. They had all seemed so flippant, hard-bitten and detached when she first met them. Clearly, this was not the case, at least, not where the animals were concerned. All at once, the bucket was tossed into her lap. Catching hold of it before it spilled on the floor, Peggy caught Clara eyeing her. Challenge seemed etched on her face. She saw the same look on Betty and Joe's countenances, too.

Terry eased the bucket out of Peggy's hands, addressing the others. "Let's give our new recruit at least a day before sending her running for the hills, shall we?"

Outside, the dogs erupted into barking. In unison, the crew looked out the window. Peggy strained her neck to peek over their shoulders and saw a group of nuns exit a long station wagon. They headed towards the front gate, their flowing, black habits flapping like a fleet of ships sailing into port.

"Cor!" Clara exclaimed. "It's the inquisition!"

Terry clapped a hand over his eyes. "Sacred Heart. My fault. I forgot. I invited them down."

"Ter, they're the enemy!" Joe said.

"They are colleagues, and I invited them in to discuss our differing policies."

"Amen!" Betty exhaled and broke open a fresh pack of candy cigarettes.

"What're we gonna do 'bout bein' full up? We got the weekend to get through," Joe reminded the warden.

"I'll sort it out," Terry said, rifling through a pile of papers.

Peggy's eyes widened, as Clara climbed her milk stool at the window. She made the sign of the cross with spoons and hissed at the nuns.

"Clara?" Terry said calmly, "Clara, these are women of the cloth, not vampires. Let's try and be civil, shall we? Oh! Speaking of which …" He grabbed some forms and thrust them at Peggy. "Being you're now a civil servant, when you have a moment, you'll need to fill these out: W-two, social, for taxes, red-tape, etcetera. All right?"

Peggy stared at the papers in his hands, making no move to take them.

"You do want to get paid, I take it?"

She took the papers from him. "Yes, sorry."

"Very good. Hold the fort."

As he hurried out the door, Peggy looked over the papers, the words hard to read because of her trembling. The rest of the crew were straightening up the office for company, so she folded the papers and tucked them into her coat pocket, then slipped out the door, following after the warden.

Chapter 13

"If only people knew the truth about what really happens to innocent souls like this. It's a sin, isn't it?" The warden sighed and leaned against Lucky's run.

Lifting their skirts above the wet floor, the six devout sisters from Sacred Heart gaped at the woebegone dog. He looked up at them with sorrowful eyes and shivered.

"I do apologize for the lack of heat," Terry added. "You know how dear the oil prices have been and, without the help of sorely needed donations, well, it forces us..." he paused, hand over his heart. "...to make difficult decisions."

The nuns tsk-tsked with what seemed like great concern. Their pity encompassed all of the other dogs that Terry had let in.

At the sink, soap suds up to her elbows, Peggy peeked over her shoulder at the warden. She hardly knew the man, but even she could tell he was playing it a bit melodramatically.

"Still, how in good conscience can one turn any of them away? There but for the grace of..." he cast his eyes heavenward and bowed his head. Then, with a dramatic sweep of his arms around the kennel, he beseeched them. "Surely, this is not the sort of fate that the Good Lord intended for his four-legged children? But alas, what can one do, when barely able to provide basic humane care, like food and..." he zipped up his jacket to his chin. "...heat?"

Abruptly, a small pipe snapped under the hot air blower, and steam hissed up the wall. Mr. Riley burst out of the broom closet, hopping mad and shook a wrench at the radiator.

"You foul bitch! May d'curse o' Mary Malone and her seven stillborn bastard sons hound ye inta d'black pit o'hell so deep dat Jaysus Christ, himself, can't find ye wit a tellyscope!"

Peggy clapped a hand over her mouth. The nuns' jaws dropped open, and the dogs were startled into barking.

Terry winced. "Oh, dear."

Joe kicked the office door open. "What the friggin' hell's goin' on out here now?!" He spotted the nuns and clapped a hand over his mouth. "Shit—I mean—shoot!"

"You boys busted her again, that's what! I told ye t'check 'er water!" Mr. Riley hollered.

Clara appeared in the doorway, broom in hand. "Who's stirrin' it up out here? Me cats're fit to be tied!" She grimaced when she saw the nuns. "Cor', I thought so!" She shook the broom at them. "Back from whence you came, dark mistresses! We'll have none of your druids here! This is an orange house."

"Orange house?!" Mr. Riley whirled around to face her. "Why, ye blasphemin' ol' pishogue! A curse upon yer heathen Protestant cat house!"

"Oh Jooooe…" Terry sang out and gestured to Clara.

"Ten-three, Brunhilda!" Joe grabbed Clara around the waist and dragged her, kicking and snarling, back into the office, and slammed the door behind him.

By this time, the nuns had fluttered to the exit like a flock of frightened crows. "Sisters?" Terry entreated them. "We haven't discussed euthanasia, yet."

"Sisters?!" Mr. Riley exclaimed and whirled around. "Och! Savin' yer presence, Sisters! Please forgive me!"

Peggy craned her neck to watch the nuns fly down the walkway with Mr. Riley in hot pursuit, pleading for forgiveness from the Holy Father, Archbishop Gerety and the Pope. She tried to hush the dogs, but their barking was relentless, all but drowning out another ruckus emanating from behind the office door. Thuds and crashes, punctuated by Clara's shrieks of "Let me out of here!" kept Peggy rooted to her spot at the sink. Criminey! The warden had said they often locked Clara up in the closet when she got out of hand. Apparently, they were dead serious! At the other end of the kennel, in his run beside the office door, Peggy saw Lucky raise his head up and look at her with wide eyes. She shrugged at him.

Just then, she felt a splash of water on her shoe. "Oh no!" She'd left the tap water running, and now suds gushed over the edge of the sink onto the floor. She grabbed the knob and twisted, but it popped off in her hand. A jet of water hit the ceiling, raining on her.

Squealing, Peggy raced down the room to Lucky and threw a leash on him. Sprinting to the front door, she wrenched it open and slammed it shut behind them. Wham!

Joe charged out of the office. "Hey!" He slipped on the soapy water flowing across the slate floor, fell on his behind and slid into the cabinets with a crash. Stacks of food bowls cascaded over him.

"*Jeeze Louise!*" He pounded his fist on the cabinet doors to pop them open. Under the waterfall, he fumbled inside to wrestle with the water valve, trying to shut it off. The closer the flood got to the hot blower box, the more furious his efforts.

"Shall we reschedule then, Sisters?" Terry held a passenger door open for a last nun, who couldn't get into the station wagon quick enough. She yanked the door from him, slammed it shut and immediately locked it.

Mr. Riley was on his knees, weeping and begging, even as the vehicle shot past him, up the driveway, backwards. "Forgive an old man de salt of his tongue, Sisters! Sinner dat I am, it's got a mind of its own, it does!"

"Thank you so much for stopping in!" Terry waved and then helped the handyman to his feet. "It's all right, Mr. Riley, Sunday confessional is only three rosaries away."

Peggy reached the gate, just as Joe burst out the front door. "Hey! Who's the frickin' feeb started the flood?!"

Terry dusted Riley off and looked up to Joe. "Is the main water shut off?"

"It is *now*!"

"Jolly good." Terry walked over to Peggy and Lucky at the gate. She was sopping wet and held out the faucet knob to him.

"Sorry."

Mr. Riley tottered up behind them. "What was that ye said jest now, 'bout shuttin' de water off?"

Terry clapped a hand over his eyes. "Oh, dear."

Joe paled. "Awwwww, shhh…"

A muffled roar from inside shook the walls, then steam and water shot past the front door behind Joe. Even the dogs were startled into silence, but only for a second. As Joe dashed back inside the building, they jumped up and down, barking and howling wildly.

Peggy saw a congregation of firemen emerge on their back stoop, looking none too amused at the ruckus. Riley staggered down the gravel path towards the cellar, but Terry remained at the gate.

"Well," he mused to her, "you can't tell me God doesn't have a sense of humor."

"I'm so sorry."

"It's not your fault," he said, and pocketed the faucet knob. "Been meaning to fix that." He saw her shivering, and once again removed his jacket, draping it over her shoulders. "Why don't you take Lucky for a little walk while I..." he looked between the kennel, the cellar, and the none-too-happy firemen. "...while I try and delay DEFCON Four. If I'm not right up in fifteen minutes," he said, striding to the cellar, "hail the firemen there, will you? They'll be pleased as punch to call the cops." With a small wave, he ducked under the overhang and descended the stairs.

Walking around the block, Peggy tried to keep sight of the shelter between the buildings. The layout of the century-old, abandoned factory compound was such that she couldn't see past the many walls, fences and rooftops. What she really wanted to do was run away, in the worst way. She couldn't very well abscond with the warden's jacket, and so she snuggled into its merciful warmth. It smelled nice, too. Outdoorsy, like wood-smoke and apples.

Mulling over this latest escapade, she realized that she didn't have to run away. Surely the warden would fire her, now. She bit her lip. She really needed that first paycheck. She'd spent all of her money renting the apartment, with only enough left over to buy food for a couple of days.

As Lucky sniffed around, Peggy took in the abandoned street. Barren empty lots across the road were strewn with crumbling foundations overgrown with frostbit ivy, browned Queen Anne's Lace, rusty goldenrod, and prickly, grayed thistles. Blue jays quarreled with squirrels and starlings in the bare branches of straggly horse-chestnut trees. Despite the desertion, Peggy found it peaceful, and not nearly as sinister a neighborhood as she had first imagined. A number of the neglected factory buildings were actually attractive. Their art deco, brick and tile architecture harked back to the heyday of the industrial revolution. Sparrows flitting in and out of broken windows betrayed their decline. Looking at them in the cold light of day, the once stately edifices seemed almost embarrassed to be caught looking their age. Peggy felt sorry for them.

Lucky nosed her hand, and she mustered a smile. "I'm sorry. I think I blew it this time." She paused, waiting...listening. There was no concurring voice of criticism echoing within.

She held her breath, but it never came. She frowned. When the going gets tough, you get abandoned again. Just like these poor buildings, she thought and kicked a stone across the broken sidewalk. Heaving a sigh, she realized she'd forgotten to count out fifteen minutes in her head. Not that it mattered. Not anymore. She was sure as sacked, now.

"Well, may as well face the firing squad."

Lucky wagged his tail. With a sigh, she walked him around the next corner onto Walnut Crescent. She skirted the railroad tracks, her spirit sinking with every step. She spotted the sign for the shelter with the bullet hole in the center and reluctantly, led Lucky down the driveway back to the shelter.

Just then, Mr. Riley stomped up from the cellar, turned and hollered back down the stairs. "Nivver shut the water off widdout openin' 'er pressure valve! How many times I hafta tell ye?!" He shuffled up the slope and back into the building.

Peggy's heart thudded in her chest when Terry came up into view at the top of the cellar steps. He looked grim. She couldn't afford to pay for the damage. How far would she have to run before she crossed the state line? The warden looked up and waved to her, and headed up the slope. Taking a last, steadying breath, Peggy walked Lucky towards an almost certain, public flogging.

Terry held the gate open for her and gestured her into the building.

Once inside, Peggy hung by the doorway wringing her hands. Riley was nowhere to be seen, but Joe was sweeping water down the drain, with a scowl on his face.

"Joe?" the warden called out. "The scuttlebutt, if you please?"

"Blower pipe just needs soldering, but Riley's gonna hafta replace the whole sink works."

"Right," the warden murmured, then pursed his lips. Hands in his pockets, he stood rocking gently back and forth on his heels, thinking.

Peggy held out Lucky's leash to him, but he didn't take it. He smiled as he said, "Why don't you take Lucky inside to the office 'til the heat comes up. I need to set goblin traps for Mrs. Cruikshank, call by the EVC, and run a few errands. When I get back, we'll finish the tour, all right?"

For a second Peggy didn't think she'd heard right. When it dawned on her that he was not going to flog, fire or incarcerate her, she nearly cried. Unable to speak, she removed his jacket, folded it carefully and handed it to him. Then, she led Lucky into his run and latched the door.

"Joe? I'm off. Until I get back, show Peggy the ropes, will you?"

"What ropes?"

"Start with the back yard, then have Bet catch her up to speed in the office."

"But Ter—"

"Thank you, Joe."

Peggy followed after him down the walkway to the Pinto, and when he climbed in, he seemed surprised to see her there at the door. "Question?"

Peggy shook her head, then finally stammered. "Th-thank you."

He smiled. "Go back inside and get warm. I won't be long. Hold the fort."

It was all she could do not to tug on his sleeve and beg him to take her along. She watched him steer the Pinto up the driveway. After it backfired around the corner, she heard Joe sigh loudly behind her. She turned around, and he kicked the gate open for her.

"Th-thank you," she said.

He rolled his eyes at her, and she hurried past him, back into the shelter.

Chapter 14

"'Ello!" Clara snarled. "What's that cur doing in 'ere!"

Betty swiveled around in her chair. "Hey! This here be the cat room!"

"He-he told me to," Peggy stammered, holding Lucky close by her side.

"He who, told you, say what?"

"Who ya think?" replied Joe. "Ter said to show her the ropes."

"Ropes? What ropes?"

"Beats me. I gotta show her the back, then you gotta catch her up to speed in here."

"Wiff what?"

"How do I know?! With whatever!"

Peggy laid her coat down on the floor beside the radiator for Lucky. The dog flopped down on it and settled his head on his paws. "Stay," she whispered and stroked his ears. He thumped his tail and licked her hand.

"Uh...like, we ain't got all day, here!"

"S-sorry." Peggy scurried out from under the counter and swept out the door. Behind her, she heard Joe exclaim, "Jeeze!" before he shadowed her out.

Her arms wrapped around herself against the cold, Peggy waited by the front door.

Joe brushed past Mr. Riley as the old man swore again, rewrapping a pipe with duct tape. "Yo', Mr. Riley, what're the odds on heat by New Year's?"

"Me hand to ye, by closin', lad."

"I got a deuce on ya."

"Woort its weight in gold, it is."

"Not in this frickin' economy, it ain't." At the door, Joe raised a brow to Peggy. "You're gonna freeze, y'know."

"I'm-I'm okay."

"Live n' learn." Joe zipped his jacket to his ears and strutted down the walkway to the van. He slid open the side door, reached inside and yanked out a pendulous, black plastic bag. He held it up to her. "This is Pepe le Pee-Eeew, a.k.a. today's road kill."

Peggy recoiled at the stench wafting out from it.

"Friggin' skunks!" he snorted, and led the way down the gravel slope. "Ya think after a jillion years, they'd figger it out. Darwin my butt! Only reason they ain't extinct is 'cause they stink so bad, their only enemy is a semi doin' sixty mph, at two in the mornin'. Dumb little effers stand in the middle of the road stampin' their feet, and when the Mack don't stop, they turn their backs, lift their tails and—splat! Skunk succotash!"

They ducked under the office overhang, and Peggy felt a prickling fear crawl up her spine as they approached the cellar door. Did the warden tell the crew yet? Surely, he wouldn't have deliberately sent her down there, again. Would he? To her profound relief, Joe trudged right past the looming, yellow door. She nearly ran right up his back, darting past it.

Joe kicked open the back gate, and led her into a narrow, barren yard of packed dirt. Her teeth chattering, Peggy looked around. A lone maple tree wearing a skirt of fallen and faded yellow leaves stood in the corner. Its bare branches reached skyward, scratching the colorless sky. Surrounded on all sides by empty warehouses and fencing, the yard was completely enclosed.

Joe walked past a steep cement staircase. Peggy glanced up the steps. They led up to the rear outdoor runs, set on a platform fifteen feet in the air. She hurried past the stairs to follow Joe, as he ducked under the runs, into a door-less storage room. Inside, a long, white freezer hummed against the wall. He took a few short breaths, then held his breath, and lifted the lid.

"Oh!" Peggy shrank back from the nauseating odor that engulfed the small room.

"Yup, Stink City, man!" Joe grimaced. "One skunk and the sucker reeks 'til we bleach her out." He shoved and tossed similar black bags around inside the freezer.

Peggy's stomach churned when she realized that the freezer was full of black bags! 'Pepe le Pee-Eeew' was about to become one of many frozen carcasses!

Joe flipped the stinky bag inside and thumped the lid down. It didn't quite shut, due to overcrowding, and he slammed it, over and over.

Horrified, Peggy gasped. Joe looked up. "Whattsa matter?"

"Noth-nothing. I just-I mean, I thought-I thought when the animals..."

"Wait! Don't tell me!" Joe smirked. "Ter didn't explain the freezer! Welp, this is where they all go when they bite it!" He opened the lid and elbowed the bags down further. "Road kill, euths, DOA's, all of 'em."

"But-but what do you do when...when it's full?"

"Garbage truck comes down every Friday morn t'unload the dumpster and we use this." He pulled a rusted, Acme shopping cart out from behind the wall. "Ya pile 'em in, then wheelie up to their truck. Ya havta toss 'em in yourself, 'cause they won't. They don't touch nuthin' from the freezer. They got it in their contracts."

"Contracts?"

"Yup." He jumped up and sat down on the lid. Whump! "Every friggin' week they try to book it outta here without the frozen food section here, so, when you hear them coming, don't fart around. Haul butt for real, or we'll be sending 'em home with you to store in your fridge 'til the next pickup." He pulled a bag of peanuts from his pocket and began cracking shells. Popping a peanut in his mouth, he grinned at her. "Betcha thought they all went to the pet cemetery."

Peggy wasn't about to confess she thought the back yard was the pet cemetery.

He cracked another shell. "Nope. Garbage truck's the end of the line. Bulleeve me, land fill's a better place than where they go after they cash in at most other joints."

"What do you mean?"

"Lemme guess. Ter didn't tell you 'bout that neither. Okay, except for our place and maybe a hand fulla dives that give a crap, dead pets get ground up at rendering factories, then dumped into the pet chow you buy."

Peggy gaped at him.

He held a hand over his heart. "Swear. Ask Ter. They call it protein. Or like when they add sawdust and wood chips? Then they call it filler. And what they hawk as real beef? That's really cow brains, tongues, rotten guts, and cancer-eaten bones. Then, they spray the whole mess with spoiled corn oil to make it taste better to 'em. Almost all the big boys do it. Chow chow chow? Meow meow meow?"

Peggy felt repulsed to the point of gagging. "But-but, isn't that...do people know?"

Joe laughed out loud. "Ya kiddin'? If you knew, would you buy it? They keep that under wraps from John Q. Public, but you better bulleeve the FDA knows about it! It's big business, man! Only those new whatchamacallits—those new—organic, that's it, they're the only ones don't do it. And maybe one or two outfits that still got a conscience. But, forget about findin' that hoity-toity organic stuff in the Acme, right? Who's gonna fork over fifty bucks for dog chow, when you can pinch horse meat for a nickel a pound?"

He shoved himself off of the freezer and strolled away, whistling *How Much Is That Doggie In The Window?*

With one last look of disbelief at the freezer, Peggy hurried after him, grateful to leave the stench behind.

Lucky was sound asleep on Peggy's coat when she and Joe returned to the office. The little milk-house heater had warmed the room to toasty, and Peggy knelt beside the dog, grateful to be back inside, out of the cold.

Betty untangled herself from coils of adding machine paper and muttered under her breath. "Show her the ropes..." She dragged a box of files out from underneath the counter and shoved it over to Peggy. "Start wiff those. Th'info oughta match what be on the cage cards. Update whatever look like it be needin' updatin'."

"But...but how will I know what it should say?"

"Don't take brain surgery! Just lookit th'animals and figger it out. Old ones, put they records to the front, bein' they git picked first. Any of 'em got anythang wrong wiff 'em, ditto."

"Oh, you mean...this is for..."

"Th'euth list, that's right." Betty broke open a pack of candy cigarettes. "Rule numbah one. We git too many to cry ovah one."

Peggy looked up at the many unwanted cats mewing in the cages above her. How long before they became black bags in the freezer out back? She pulled the tube of ointment out of her pocket and dabbed the cream on Lucky's sores. Finished, she turned and saw Clara eyeing her from the corner where she sat knitting.

"Rule number two," the old woman said with a raised brow, "don't get attached."

"And just how much that cream cost us?" asked Betty, thumbing through a fistful of receipts.

"Oh, well the vet he-he didn't charge us. I mean, the warden...it was free."

"Free?" Clara chortled. "T'isn't anything free in this world, Saint Francis."

Peggy felt her cheeks blush when Joe and Betty stifled laughs, repeating the new nickname for her, under their breaths. She cleared her throat. "Um, well, in-in exchange for…"

"Uh oh," Joe swiveled around in his chair. "In exchange for *what*?"

"For some kittens."

"Aw, Jeeze. Don't tell me. Sick kittens?"

"Um, well, Dr. Caldwell said they had...URI?"

"Ha! I knew it!" He rounded on the ladies. "As if we don't got enough charity cases!"

"Why is Terry always lettin' people dump they problems on us?" Betty griped.

"'Cause he's a soft soap!" Clara reminded them.

Peggy squirmed in her shoes. They might have been referring to her, as well. To her relief, the phones rang, and the crew turned their backs on her. With no further tutorial forthcoming, she picked through the contents of the file box, trying to familiarize herself with the shelter's animals. She decided to start with the office cats. Quite a few of the cats had been turned in over allergy issues. Due to the economy, more and more people decided to cohabitate, and often, one or the other roomate/fiancé/spouse was allergic to cat dander. The reasons for other turn-ins were more bothersome. Peggy pulled a file on Burnett; a ten-year-old spayed house cat. Burnished brown with slate gray stripes, Burnett was a pretty and rather stout cat. Peggy read the reason for her turn-in, unable to quite believe what the card said.

"My new wife redecorated and the cat clashes with the drapes."

Peggy reached her fingers through the cage bars. The fat, purring cat rubbed against her hand, over and over, and Peggy swallowed a lump in her throat. How could anyone prefer a set of drapes over their own cat?

Checking the cage card in the slot, Peggy found that Burnett was sitting in Oreo's cage. Pulling Oreo's file, she read that Oreo was a black and white, two year-old neutered male with green eyes. She found Oreo in the cage below Burnett. The lanky cat reached for her through the bars, wanting to play. He kept his claws sheathed so as not to scratch her. According to the comments line on his form, Oreo was turned in because the young wife was due to have a baby and was afraid that Oreo would attempt to smother their newborn. Peggy paused. Gee whiz. She'd never heard that, before. Could it be true?

"Ex-excuse me, Clara? I-I didn't know cats smothered babies. Why do they do that?" The old woman turned three shades of purple and then shook her fist to high heaven.

"Two thousand years and we're still cowerin' in the Dark Ages!"

"Hey! Hey! Hey! What's she flippin' out about now?!" Joe snatched the file out of Peggy's hands and read it. "Awww, Jeeze, ya kiddin' me?"

"I'm-I'm sorry. I didn't know. So-so it's not true? Cats don't smother babies?"

"If *only!*" snapped Clara. "There'd be that many less ankle-biters growin' up trashing the planet!"

"Down girl!" Joe said. "There's some pork-choppers in D.C. wanna cull your gray-panther numbers, too!" He tossed Peggy the file. "Don't go stirrin' up a hornet's nest by askin' questions, okay?"

"That's precisely why this country's in the state it's in, now!" Clara rebuked him. "Your generation's answer to everything! Just stick your 'eads in the sand!"

"Y'see?" Joe regaled Peggy. "See how she gets started?"

"I…I'm sorry," Peggy stammered, wringing her hands.

"You listen to me, missy," Clara cornered her. "You go on asking your questions and to 'ell with the ostriches! Now, take note! Before the so-called experts decided SIDS was a real thing, coppers blamed the parents. Left to their own superstitions, the parents went and blamed the family cat, what likes to curl up next to somethin' warm! Stupid hat stands, the lot of them!"

"S-s-SIDS?"

"Look it up! Educate yourself! Or they'll pull the wool over yer eyes and sell ya a pig in a poke! Cats been blamed for everything from witchery to the plague, since the dawn of time!"

"Hey, those mummies in Egypt worshipped cats, so don't gimme that!" Joe shot back. "For a dog's age, they had it better n' all of us!"

As they argued about the history of the maligned feline race, Peggy tried her best to make sense of the cage mixups, as well as the scraps of information the crew bandied back and forth in debate. After an hour, she had only managed to put the cats back into their proper cages, but at last she'd accomplished a task without causing a major catastrophe.

Then the public began to arrive.

Chapter 15

"I'd like to borrow a cat to kill a squirrel."

Peggy blinked at the well-dressed woman, unsure if she'd heard her correctly. "P-pardon?"

"It eats all the bird seed in every feeder I've tried!"

"Yes, but...wouldn't the cat kill the birds, too?"

"Not if I tie it to the tree."

The shelter officially opened to the public at ten a.m., seven days a week, and three hundred and sixty-five days a year. How they managed that, with just the four of them, she was afraid to ask. Being new, Peggy assumed she'd be excused from dealing with the public, whom Clara repeatedly referred to as "one immense arse". However, despite keeping her head buried in the files, wearing a uniform equated to having a bulls-eye pinned to her person. People harangued her with questions and problems that she couldn't understand, let alone answer. So, she did the next best thing.

"Ex-excuse me, Betty? This woman has a question?"

Juggling two phones and an ice pack against her forehead, Betty swiveled around in her chair for the umpteenth time that morning. "Just handle it!"

Cringing, Peggy turned back to the squirrel woman. "I-I don't think we have any squirrel killers, today. I'm sorry."

As it turned out, Clara had been out of ear shot for the whole exchange. Peggy wasn't so lucky the next time. A couple with six children entered, looking to adopt a female cat, with very specific attributes. After listening to their want list, Peggy turned to their feline expert.

"Ex-excuse me, Clara? Which cats are unspayed?"

"Why?" asked Clara, her eyes narrowed.

"These nice people want to have kittens, so they can share the miracle of birth with-with their children!"

"Miracle of birth?! Y'off your box? How 'bout this family snapshot!" Clara shoved the coat rack aside, to reveal a poster. In a graphic photo,

dead puppies and kittens lay heaped in a pile on the floor and the caption read *Stop Pet Overpopulation.*

"Oh!" Peggy gasped, along with the family behind her.

"It's hardly the same thing!" the young wife declared. "We want to bring life into the world, not take it away!"

"Looks to me like you might need a spay of your own, missus!" Clara gestured to the woman's own brood of six.

The woman's husband went red in the face. "How dare you!"

"You might want to get 'is dandies clipped too, while you're at it," Clara remarked to the woman. "He looks like a rum'un."

The husband ushered his family to the door. "We're going to report you to the town!"

"I'm reporting you to Zero Population Growth!" Clara shouted after them.

Slamming down a phone, Joe whirled around in his chair. "Hey! Do we have to lock you in the closet, again?" Then, he turned on Peggy. "What'd I tell you 'bout askin' questions?!"

Peggy sneaked Lucky out of the crowded office to hide in the kennel room. She hated to put the dog back into the run, but she felt he might be safer there, than underfoot. She certainly felt safer surrounded by the dogs, as opposed to people. Very few dallied long in the noisy kennel.

Once the dogs had quieted, Peggy found the kennel peaceful. She began reading the dogs' cage cards to learn about their histories. Right away, she noticed a pattern that the warden had alluded to, earlier. Nearly all of the dogs were turned in due to behavioral problems, and of those dogs, most were two years of age or younger. The reasons for turn-in varied:

— pees in house
— digs holes in yard
— barks all day
— chews furniture
— chases the cat
— ate the cat

After observing the dogs awhile, it didn't take Peggy long to decide that they weren't bad dogs, they were just full of puppy energy. Maybe all they needed was one-on-one time—someone to teach them. Then, she studied the older dogs. Out-numbering the younger dogs, most had been turned in due to owners losing their homes, as Terry had said. Others had medical issues that had become financially burdensome; a two strike blow. The American family dog had suddenly become a luxury that many could no longer afford.

Peggy regarded the old dogs lying in their runs, often beside an un-touched bowl of food, like Digger. To her, theirs was the sadder story. She pet them through the fencing, wondering if their owners had any idea what their dog was going through, having been abandoned and then forgotten. Her throat tightened and her eyes welled up. She wiped her cheeks roughly. In a moment, the wave of hurt ebbed, and she could breathe again.

She returned her attention to the dogs. One thing she noticed about all of them was that they were all unkempt. Due to the shelter's work-load, it was easy to understand how grooming might have been relegated to the back burner. Still, Peggy reasoned that if the dogs looked better, maybe people would be more inclined to want to take one home.

She rummaged in the cabinet under the sink, and found an as-sortment of brushes, a pair of scissors and a box of stale dog biscuits. She began at the rear of the kennel and squeezed into each dog run, armed with a brush and a biscuit. Combing the dirt and tangles from the dogs' fur, she whispered soothing words, in a feeble attempt to comfort them.

"As God is mah secret judge," Betty declared and glared at the clock, "I'm gonna blow a fuse! That man be late, again! And where be ghost girl? She could leastwise be helpin' to ansah the damn phones!"

"If she's smart, she quit!" Joe retorted, snatching up a phone. "Yel-lo, Shelter."

But no sooner had he hung up one phone, another rang. All the while, people continued to stream into the office. They all wanted ser-vice and they all complained about the lack of it.

"Well don't just stand there!" Betty snapped at Joe. "Go git her!"

"Aw, whyzzit always up to me?" He squeezed through the throng of complaining people. "Just a sec! Hold on; be right with ya!"

Yanking open the office door, he called out, "YO! Saint Francis! You gonna give us a hand or what?"

Peggy looked up from brushing Zorro. She whispered, "Be a good boy. Stay."

"Now?!" Joe shouted over the barking.

"Okay! Sorry!" She stumbled out of Zorro's run, hastily shut his gate, and dashed past the barking dogs into the office, closing the door behind her.

Zorro watched his gate latch bounce off the clip that Peggy forgot to affix to it. He cocked his head as the gate slowly swung back open. He sauntered out, and the rest of the dogs launched into wild barking, as he happily nosed at their unclipped gate latches.

Amidst jangling phones and a crush of impatient people, Peggy chewed on a twisted strand of her hair in the corner of the room, feeling claustrophobic for the first time.

"Here," Clara dropped Burnett, the cat, into her arms. "Put 'er back in that cage there before some mutton-head steps on 'er!"

Peggy clutched the cat like a life preserver and maneuvered her way through the crowd to the cage Clara had pointed to. It was already occupied by Oreo. According to the I.D. card, the cage didn't belong to Oreo either, but to Tom, the orange tabby three cages down. Peggy couldn't believe it. She'd just sorted out the cats, and now they were all mixed up, again! She opened the only empty cage she could find and instantly realized her mistake. "Oh no!"

Streaking out from under shredded newspaper, Houdini, the ferret, vaulted over her head and scampered across patrons' shoulders, quick as you please, around the room.

"A rat! a rat!" A woman shrieked, plowing backwards into the medicine cabinet, taking down half the shelves with a crash!

Tangled in phone cords, Joe whirled around. "What the…" The ferret used Joe's head as a spring board, and dove onto shelves, scattering books. "Awww, JEEZE!"

Panicked, patrons pushed and shoved each other, and Peggy, smack into the office door. "You!" Joe railed at Peggy, himself pinned against the cages by the crowd. "I shoulda figgered! This is your fault! Go get a trap in the cellar!"

Peggy gawked at him. "C-c-cellar? But-but I…"

"Go! *Now*!"

Yanking open the door, Peggy froze.

Zorro raced a dozen loose dogs around the kennel, all of them sopping wet and scattering food and water everywhere. Spotting Peggy, they barreled happily toward her and the open office door, barking. People screamed, pushing back into the office. Frantic, Peggy squeezed through them and ran past the oncoming dogs, right out the front door.

"Holy shhhh…" Joe pulled people back into the office, and threw his weight against the door.

Slam! He heard the dogs collide with it on the other side. Bump! Thud! Whump!

Pushed by the wind, Peggy skidded to a stop on the loose gravel, right before the cellar door.

Get down there! You heard him!

I can't! Peggy paced back and forth. I can't go down there! Muffled shouts of hysteria could be heard through the floor above her head. She clapped her hands over her ears.

Do it!

Please don't make me!

Do as you're told! This is your fault!

I'm sorry! I'm sorry! She heard more screams above her head. Panting, she grasped hold of the doorknob, and steeling herself, she yanked the door open. A dark and ominous void gaped below her. Peggy felt along the inside wall, and her trembling fingers connected with a light switch. She flipped it up. Pop! The light bulb shorted and blew out. She winced and swallowed a dry lump in her throat. Then she spotted the glint of a trap below, just at the bottom of the stairs.

What are you afraid of!

Gripping the door jamb, Peggy stared at the trap, down below. It's right there! I have to get it! If I don't, he'll get upset! She grasped the hand rail, her eyes fixed on the trap, instead of the steps. Her shoe caught the lip of the third plank, and in a tumble she fell down the stairs, landing in a heap at the bottom. The wind slammed the door shut above.

Engulfed in the dark mustiness, Peggy was instantly blind. "*No!*" she wailed into the dense gloom.

You're going to get it now!

Peggy groped the dark steps on her hands and knees, scrambling upwards, until she plowed headlong into the door. Ignoring the pain, she grabbed the doorknob and twisted, but it didn't open. Pounding on it with all her strength, Peggy screamed, "Help!"

Shutup!

"No! Please! Let me out! Please!"

Thought you could hide? Thought you could get away?

Peggy yanked and yanked on the door knob, screaming. "Let me go! Open the door! *Ple-e-e-ase!*"

The inky black of the clammy cellar below welled up behind her, while voices assaulted her, pressing her up against the door until there was no room left for her chest to expand. Blood roaring in her ears, she couldn't hear her own shrieking, nor feel her fists bruising as she banged on the door in cold, raw terror.

"Help! Please somebody! Help!"

Abruptly, the door was yanked open from the other side, a dark shadow looming above her on the threshold. She screamed wildly.

"Ahhhhhhhhhhhhhhhh!"

"Ahhhhhhhhhhhhhhhh!" The shadow screamed back, in terror. It was Joe.

Chapter 16

Terry secured the last Hav-A-Hart trap, just in time. He couldn't feel his fingers, anymore. He never wore gloves when securing traps, because he was unable to feel the tension in the ropes. And, if there was anywhere he needed to feel confident in his grip, it was a hundred feet in the air on one of 'Uppah' Farroway's historic Victorian roofs.

Mrs. Cruikshank's three-story manor held the dubious honor of being one of the oldest registered historic homes in Essex County. A frail, petite woman of ninety, Mrs. Cruikshank lived alone. Her two grown sons lived in California with their families, coming home only for Thanksgiving and Christmas. Having outlived most everyone she knew, she had nothing much else to do between the holidays, except dote on her only visitors: the mailman, the gardener, the grocer's delivery boy, and Terry Brannan.

Despite the need to climb dizzying heights twice a year to deal with her drunken raccoons, Mrs. Cruikshank's home became one of Terry's favorite stops. Once a month, she set out bundled newspapers for the shelter, on the very same day that she tested a new recipe. Terry not only picked up her newspapers, he became a test-taster for her latest batch of brandied fruit and liqueur cakes. The old woman took his opinion quite seriously. Summer time found them on her wrap-around porch sipping mint juleps and winter time they shared spiced hot toddies. They discussed the virtues of each recipe. Terry would listen as the wispy-haired little woman told stories of her sons, her brothers and sisters, parents, grandparents, and pets, all long gone. Although the stories were often repeated, Terry never minded. The stories had become, in and of themselves, old friends. And every Christmas, he was rewarded for his friendship with a basket brimming with her prize-winning brandied fruits and rum cakes.

High up on that peaked roof in the gusty wind, however, Terry wasn't reminiscing, nor anticipating the spiked hot cocoa that would surely be waiting for him below. He checked his watch for the third time in ten minutes. He'd been away from the shelter nearly two hours longer than he'd planned. He had never worried about leaving his crew alone, before. However, this time was different. There was a wild card in the deck. A girl named Peggy Dillan.

Yanking the knots of rope tighter around the cages, Terry wondered if it hadn't been an impulsive mistake to hire her. What worried him most was the way she'd bonded so quickly with the dog. Sooner or later, they would have to deal with Lucky's owner. How would this fragile girl react when she had to turn Lucky back over to the man who had quite probably beaten him?

He hunched deeper into his jacket against a gust of wind and pulled the recorder from his pocket. "Call the mayor's office, re: Title four-Chapter Twenty-Two and the impound statute."

He fumbled with the off switch, and in so doing, dropped the recorder. Snatching at the air for it, his boot heels slipped on the wet shingles, and he fell back against the roof. He rolled over as he slid, grabbing for a hand hold, but stopped only when he butted up against an exhaust pipe. For a couple of seconds he lay there, breathless and perspiring, despite the icy wind whipping the trees branches above him. Adrenaline surged in his bloodstream. He stretched out an arm and grasped hold of a cable rope, then dug his toes into the splintering shingles. With a grunt and a few shoves, he shifted himself over the roof to the ladder, and rested against the rain gutters.

He reached out and plucked the recorder from the gutter, then sat up carefully, pocketing it. Running a shaking hand through his hair, he took a few moments to collect himself. When his hands finally stopped trembling, he turned his back to the dizzying drop below and methodically, rung by rung, descended back down the ladder.

Once his boots touched the ground, Terry exhaled and leaned his forehead against the aluminum ladder. He breathed in the cold, sobering air a good few minutes.

"We're getting too old for this."

When the sparks stopped dancing before his eyes, he shook out his hands then ratcheted the ladder down. Hefting it to a shed in the back yard, he stowed it before checking his watch, then hurried down the side driveway towards the Pinto.

As he rounded the burlap-wrapped rose garden, he spotted Mrs. Cruikshank, bundled in a heavy coat, thick wool scarf and furry hat. She tottered across her wrap-around porch, a tea tray in gloved hands.

"Oh dear," he lamented. "Mrs. C., I'm afraid I'm running rather late, today, and..."

One look at the rum cakes piled high upon her finest china told him that she'd been baking all morning. Looking up into her softly creased face, he smiled.

"And wild goblins couldn't drag me away." He climbed the porch steps and eased the heavy tray from her grasp. She beamed, took his arm and let him escort her into the enclosed sun porch.

An hour later, Terry finally arrived back at the shelter. He was surprised to see so many empty runs in the kennel. Heartened, he entered the office about to congratulate his crew for a splendid adoption day but stopped short. Joe, Betty and Clara looked up at him sourly, cleaning up a thoroughly disheveled office.

"So sorry I'm late..." he began.

Joe peeled a smashed sandwich up off of the floor and glared at him. Betty folded her arms across her bosom in front of unplugged phones. Clara tossed her wig into the trash.

"Ah," Terry nodded. "Bit of a hullaballoo, I see. So...where's Peggy, then?"

Under the bare maple tree in the back yard, with Lucky by her side, Peggy sat and groomed the dogs. She'd heard the Pinto backfire into the lot up front. Counting out the minutes in her head, she knew that any moment now, the warden was going to come out and fire her.

It's your fault! You should have run when you had the chance!

Where? Where was I supposed to run to? She pressed her eyes closed, tightly. Last night, she'd intended to at least walk, if not run, away from the place. She'd thought about it on the bus. What had changed? One warm night under a roof? A locked door? A stomach full of sugared doughnuts? She stroked Lucky's floppy ears and blinked back tears. What would happen to him, if she wasn't there to look after him? Nobody else would take him out there to the back yard. The crew was too busy. There was no time. Would the warden even keep his promise?

People never do.

No, they don't. She watched the other dogs playing tug of war with a dirty rag. What about them? How long before they ended up in the freezer, over there? She felt as if she'd failed them, without knowing why.

She heard the warden's boots crunch over the gravel, down under the office overhang and up to the back gate just behind her. Then, it was quiet. Above her, the clacking of the brittle branches in the wind sounded like rulers clapping across knuckles. The silence weighed down on her until she couldn't stand it any longer. She turned to face him, clutching the dog brush against her chest like a crucifix.

"I'll s-stay late. I'll c-come in early. I'll-I'll work harder-please. I-I need this job!"

The warden leaned on the back gate, his arms folded across his chest. But, he wasn't looking at her. He gazed past her. "Are those the dogs on the euth list?"

"It-it wasn't their fault. Please don't punish them for…"

"They don't even look like the same dogs!"

"It was my fault."

"That one there, is that Barney? And that can't be Digger playing there?"

Peggy was taken aback. He didn't seem angry. He didn't mention the calamity up in the office. He didn't even seem to be listening to her. He just kept gazing at the dogs.

"L-like you said, he just n-needs some one-on-one time. They all do."

Terry nodded absently, his expression pensive, as if he was deep in thought.

"Th-there's nothing wrong with any of them," Peggy ventured. "I was…I was thinking, if you, m-maybe if you put an ad in the paper, y'know, maybe ad-advertise about them. It's almost Christmas and…"

"Sold. But only if *you* see it through, start to finish. That means the grooming, the training, the ad, the adoption interviews, everything. Deal?"

Peggy gawked at him. Was he serious? He extended his hand over the fence to her. Apparently so. Standing up on shaky knees, she extended a trembling hand over the gate, and he gently shook it. Then, he grinned.

"I have some more good news."

Congratulatory handshakes and much back-slapping filled the hall of the EVC. After a nerve-wracking morning, the roster had finally been posted for the interns and externs, their assignments now a matter of record.

Miller re-read the list with a bespectacled first year intern. "I don't get it. Benson, if it wasn't you posted to the pound, then who?"

Slam!

Everyone whirled around. Paul Hayward stormed out of Caldwell's office and strode down to the rear ward, and out the back door. He slammed that door, too.

"But, he's not an intern," Benson said. "He's not even an extern, he's--he's..."

Miller cocked his head to one side and whistled low. "He's screwed."

Dr. Caldwell opened his office door and stepped into the hallway. Technicians and vets scattered, bumping into each other as they scrambled to busy themselves. Caldwell gazed at the back door a moment, but then turned and headed for the surgery. The young vets exchanged shocked glances, not one of them uttering another word. Not even Miller.

Paul paced by a tree overlooking the frigid, rushing brook. He didn't feel the cold, the wind, or the snow in the air. He didn't feel a thing; except absolute, utter incredulity. How was it that he, Dr. Paul J. Hayward, fully qualified, multiple-honored VMD-PhD, had been dumped at the town pound for six goddamn months? And full time no less? As terms of his contract and any future partnership offers from the Emergency Veterinary Clinic? What in hell could have seized up the old man's mind to do this to him?

No matter which way he dissected it, it just didn't add up. Hyperventilating, he stopped his pacing and leaned against the tree. Then, he shoved it. Then, he kicked it. If he could have yanked it out of the ground, he would have thrust it like a lance, right through the windows of the damn place. Christ, he wanted to beat the living shit out of something! He realized he might have beaten the shit out of his right hand. He massaged it and half-laughed out loud. Miller would love it if he broke his hand. Miller would be first to lead the charge over his still-warm corpse for a shot at heading the surgical team. It took several minutes of deep breathing, to finally ease the pounding in his temples. He rested his forehead against the tree and exhaled a bitter laugh.

"Dr. Hay-Hayward?" Peggy repeated.

"He's the finest vet to ever enter their doors. We're lucky to get him." Terry said, and then smiled. "Pun intended." Peggy didn't smile. "He's the one looked at Lucky for us, remember?"

Peggy put her arm around Lucky's thick neck. The dog licked her cheek. She mustered a wan smile for the warden. Oh, she remembered Dr. Hayward, all right. Under the circumstances, she couldn't afford to look any gift horse in the mouth, so she said nothing more about it. If anything, she was determined to not only make good on her deal with the warden, but to prove him right and prove the crew wrong when it came to her hire. It was the least she could do, she told herself, in return for his bending the rules for Lucky. More than anything, however, she was secretly determined to prove the arrogant Dr. Hayward wrong. She ruffled Lucky's ears and threw a stick for him to fetch.

Dusk crept over the shelter grounds, plunging the compound into darkness as Peggy and the warden walked the dogs up to the front.

Joe, Betty and Clara had gathered at the front gate, ready to leave for the day. They averted their eyes, as Peggy hurried past them with Lucky and ten other dogs in tow.

Terry hung back at the front gate with them, too and watched her. He smiled broadly. Once she went inside with the dogs and closed the door, he turned to the crew.

"Have you ever seen those dogs looking so splendid?" The trio gawked at him.

"You copped out," said Joe at last.

Terry clapped his hands together. "Picture this: a Christmas advert in the *Recycler*, with photos of the animals in Christmas hats. We deck the halls like a Currier and Ives Christmas card, dress up like elves and offer the public biscuits and cocoa!"

"You copped out!"

"How long have we all been here, and not a one of us ever thought of having a Christmas adoption slash open house party? Did I mention it was all Peggy's idea? I'll wager we adopt out the entire hold before Christmas Eve!"

"I don't friggin' bulleeeeve it!" Joe threw his arms up in the air and stomped away.

"Hey, Dimple Cheeks!" Clara chased after him. "That's a fiver y'owe me now! Ante up!"

Betty eyed Terry and took a long swig from a bottle of antacid before walking away.

"It'll be splendid!" he called out after them, "Just wait! You'll see! Christmas! Trust me!"

Chapter 17

In a cold, light rain, Joe zigzagged a scrawny Christmas spruce to the end of the runs where it could be seen from the street. The dogs barked wildly at him, jumping up and down.

"Shadaaap!" he yelled. He held the spindly tree at arm's length to get a better look at it. Then, he heard a tinkling sound. Through the fence, two dogs peed on the tree, and then on his boots. He sighed. "Aw, Jeeze..."

"...information from Pioneer Eleven seems to substantiate scientists' theories about the great red spot. NASA is hoping that a few other riddles about Jupiter will be answered, questions that have been plaguing scientists for centuries. Remarkable," the news caster commented, "since only two weeks ago, they discovered Lucy, evidence of the first human in the African desert. What was it, a million years plus, and here we are, nineteen seventy-four, orbiting Jupiter. Whew! We'll be back with more news and the weather after these messages. Shoppers! Just eight more shopping days 'til Christmas!"

A jaunty commercial jingle faded in and out of static over the radio, as Clara, Betty and Terry hung green plastic garland around the windows.

"A million years, and they're braggin' like it's something to be proud of?" remarked Clara. "It's a wonder we're not extinct by now, too!"

"You be preachin' to the choir, honey." Betty crunched a candy cigarette. "Why they all hepped up ovah Lucy? Done got a barrel full o'monkeys been runnin' Washington fo' years."

"When you look at Earth's four-billion year timeline," Terry hung a green, glass ball on the garland, "then we've barely just come down from the trees. Civilization followed in a mere forty-thousand years. You must admit, that's awfully impressive." He held out his hand. "Red, please."

"God made the world in seven days, mistah!"

"Pfft! And look how well that's turned out," scoffed Clara.

"From Lucy to I love Lucy, to Lucy in the Sky with Diamonds," Terry countered, "it's all a process. The human being of today, whether of divine creation or not, you must agree, is at the very least, a prime example of wondrous social evolution."

"Yeah. Look how well that done turned out!" Betty retorted.

"You of all people. How can you be so pessimistic? It's Christmas!"

The radio announcer's voice wavered in "...with no end in sight to the famine in Ethiopia, the U.S. is being criticized for its refusal to send aid to the stricken nation, citing that…"

Terry twisted the radio dial. "Ladies, what say we find some music of the season?"

"Uh-huh." Betty raised a brow at him.

Turning the dial from doo-whop to heavy metal, to disco, then to more bad news, Terry searched the frequencies in vain. "Good heavens, where is Bing Crosby and White Christmas?"

"Jupiter."

He settled on a station blaring *Jingle Bell Rock*. "Close enough." He glanced at the clock, and then at the kennel room door.

Betty eyed him from over the ornament box. "Go take a gander! You know you want to!"

"Oh, I'm sure she's fine." He climbed down the chair, however, and inched the office door open a crack.

Peeking out into the kennel room, his eyes widened.

Vaguely discernible in the steam, a sopping-wet Peggy wrestled with a shaggy dog in a small, wading pool in the center of the room. The dog tried to leap out of the bath, but she grabbed hold of its collar and quickly doused it with a pot of water.

"Gotcha!" she laughed, then waved her hands. "No! No! No!"

Too late. The dog shook itself from nose to tail, spraying her with water. Terry eased the office door closed.

"What's the score?" asked Betty.

"Looks like a tie."

She offered Terry a candy cigarette. He took it.

By noon, Peggy had managed to bathe only one and a half dogs. Between her and the dogs, she wasn't sure which of them got the better bath, either. Drenched, Peggy sat on an upturned bucket and shivered. For a pre-Christmas Eve trial run, things weren't exactly running smoothly.

From the moment she had shaken hands with the warden over the back gate, her days had blurred together in a race against the calendar. Attempting to learn the ins and outs of the shelter was workload enough. Coupled with the responsibility of hatching an event that she knew nothing about, left her little better than sleepless at night. On the positive side, at least without sleep, she didn't have the nightmares. Plus, stuffing her head with so much new information had squeezed out most of the nagging voices that needled her, day in and day out. That alone encouraged her to work even harder!

The sheer volume of information regarding animal welfare was staggering. The questions raised seemed endless. At times, it was all Peggy could do just to take it one day, one hour, and often, just one chore at a time. Of course, the frosty attitude of the crew did not help matters. Although they were not disrespectful, nor unpleasant to her—outside of calling her "Saint Francis" whenever the warden wasn't around—they did not welcome her into the fold, except as a handicap in numerous bets placed behind the warden's back.

There was one perk in having a special project that Peggy found to her liking, the permission to spend half the day on her own doing research. The warden's only request had been that she do all of it in the office. She wondered if he might have insisted on that in order to force her presence on the crew, and vice versa. However, it tended to have the reverse effect in that they grew so used to her being there with her nose in a book, she seemed invisible to them. This gave Peggy just the right amount of distance to comfortably observe them, much like they were animals, too. And, they were a curious pack.

Joe Wozniak served as the shelter's town crier. Not an hour went by without a comment or complaint from Joe about everything and anything that irked him, or that he thought should irk everybody else. He lived with his father in Bloomfield, the next town over. It was intimated, but never actually brought out into the open, that theirs was a rocky relationship, due to the father's drinking. The fading shiner over Joe's eye spoke volumes to Peggy. Six years earlier, Joe's older brother Christopher had been killed in action in Vietnam, devastating his father. Whether or not his father's heartbreak had anything to do with his drinking, Peggy didn't know. Joe never spoke about either one of them.

Without a car of his own, Joe used the shelter van as his vehicle; a perk for being on call twenty-four/seven. Except for holidays. That's when Terry took over. It seemed to Peggy, that Joe lived for patrol duty. Starting his day at seven a.m., she knew he cruised around town on the lookout for stray dogs, or those not on a leash. Citing the New Jersey State SPCA statutes to the letter, Joe enforced the law at every turn. To Joe, off-leash/stray violations were a serious offense, and he never hesitated to pick up both dogs and cats, with or without ID tags, and often when the animals were headed back towards their own yards!

"Hey, a leash law means they gotta be ON leash, not just thinkin' about it!" Joe insisted. "If I had a nickel for every HBC I hauled up to th' EVC, I wouldn't be wastin' tax dollars by handin' out summonses!"

When Terry told Peggy that HBC stood for Hit By Car, she understood why Joe was so adamant about picking up strays. He was the one that rushed all HBCs up to the EVC. And every one of them brought Joe back to the shelter both swearing and surreptitiously wiping tears off of his face.

After every stray pickup, Joe dutifully called the owner if the dog had an ID tag. Often there were no collars, let alone tags. If an owner was found, Joe fined them ten dollars for breaking penal code 74-13 section B. If the dog was not licensed, he'd double the fine.

Even though he was just doing his job, the townspeople held a very narrow view of "the pound", partly due to Officer Wozniak's summonses. Peggy could well understand their indignation. She'd never heard of ordinance 74-13, section B, either. With no signs on the streets or in the parks, how were people supposed to know about it? Joe argued that people did know about it, his evidence being the percentage of repeat offenders!

"Perhaps," the warden had suggested, one day, "it might be helpful if you explained to people the reasons behind the law."

"Ya kiddin'?" retorted Joe. "The only thing worse than tellin' people they're wrong is telling 'em why they're wrong. Bein' stupid's one thing, bein' proved stupid only pisses 'em off."

To his credit, Joe did explain the reason behind the rules to people with their first offense. After that, he said, they were asking for it. When it came to animal welfare, by virtue of the badge gleaming on his chest, Joe was The Man, THE LAW. Well, doggie law, anyway, but by authority of the Municipal Court of Farroway, he was a bona-fide officer of that law and never forgot it for a second. He didn't let anyone else forget it, either.

At first, Peggy assumed that Joe aspired to be a cop. He regaled the crew endlessly with police reports he'd read in the newspaper, or heard over the scanner that he'd installed in the van. Slung low on Joe's hip hung a utility belt sporting a flash light, the walkie-talkie, and a new water pistol that could have passed for a real Baretta. He only wore it around the shelter, tossing it in a drawer when he patrolled, because Terry wouldn't let him out of the door with it on. He swore up and down that it was to deter vicious dogs from jumping him out on the streets, but Terry didn't buy it for a second.

"Ter, it's a water pistol!" Joe argued.

"Yes, and in your hands, to be considered a deadly weapon."

"C'mon, Ter! Bergen County's badges pack heat!"

"They are an official SPCA chapter, and their law enforcement arm is sanctioned by the New Jersey State SPCA. If you recall, we are not so officially sanctioned. Our municipality said no to arms for its animal control officers."

"Then what's the point of this badge?"

"Free coffee at the Seven Eleven."

Peggy wondered if Joe's weapons obsession had more to do with appearances than anything else. He checked his Brylcreem look in every reflective surface upon entering a room; his boots were spit polished, his bomber jacket oiled, and he didn't walk into a room, he strutted.

On quiet days, he tinkered with a CB unit that he'd built himself with junk yard refuse. His intent was to install it in the Pinto, so that the warden could be reached for emergencies while out on the road. Peggy got the distinct impression, however, that Terry was in no hurry for Joe to figure it all out. Joe had only just reached the point where he could possibly electrocute himself with it, when one morning a crackling static sounded from the half-gutted unit.

Joe slammed his hand down on the microphone lever, and shouted excitedly, "Ten-four good buddy, hang it low and left, come back with your twenty!" There was no response except for more annoying static, but Joe persisted, repeating his message over and over.

"Joe, squelch it, will you?" Terry sighed.

"C'mon, Ter, one of these days this puppy's gonna work, and you're gonna need to pick out a handle."

"A what?"

"Your CB name! C'mon, guess mine."

"He-Who-Tries-The-Patience-Of-Saints?"

Joe laughed. "Nah, it's Napper. Get it? Dog? Napper? Cool, huh?"

"As a cuke."

"No joke! Once I install it in Ethel, you'll never be outta earshot."

"That's the day I retire."

In the meantime, Joe continued to tinker with the CB unit, in between patrols and handing out summonses, which is all he seemed to really want to do in the first place. It wasn't that he wanted to be a real cop, Peggy decided. He just wanted to play hero; a cop on the beat for dogs and cats.

Betty Shepherd was the warden's no-nonsense Gal Friday. She lived in a world of absolutes. There were no slippery slopes for Betty. There were no ifs, ands, or buts. Facts were facts, true or false. There were no free lunches, no unpaid debts forgotten, and no good deed that went unpunished.

A big-boned woman, Betty wore stylish, smart outfits to work rather than the shelter uniform. Peggy figured it must be because Betty represented management, or the Lord himself, as she also sported quite a collection of crucifixes. Peggy found this aspect of Betty most paradoxical. As devout and moralistic as she was, she spent the better part of every day, damning people to hell and back again, in some of the most colorful language Peggy had ever heard!

Betty was also dedicated. Once she sat down in her chair in the morning, she never got up until closing. Lunch times were spent hunched over a steaming pot of water on the hot plate, a towel draped over her head; sneezing, coughing, and groaning. At first Peggy thought Betty was suffering from the nasty flu that had plagued her bus driver for over two weeks, and she asked Terry if the woman might need a doctor.

"Oh, it's merely her allergies," he assured her. "Began sniffling her first day, and she's been sneezing ever since."

"She's allergic to the animals?"

"Not the animals—just people. It takes its toll on her, you know, being such a soft touch."

"Say what?!" Betty barked into the phone. "*Don't* you make me come ovah there and spay that bitch, myself! You let her out one mo' time off leash you just see if I don't!" She slammed the phone down and sneezed so loudly, the caged cats hissed in unison.

"It's positively sinful the way she suffers," Terry lamented. "Her allergies actually worsened the day she quit smoking."

Armed with bronchial inhalers, antacids, nose drops, eye drops and a five-pack a day candy Camel habit, Betty battled her agonizing sinus condition, valiantly. Miraculously, at five p.m., the moment the phones stopped ringing, Betty's symptoms all but disappeared, that is, until eight a.m. the following morning.

Despite Terry's insistence that Betty was not allergic to animals, she never touched a single one of them. Peggy watched her clean litter pans, coo and give them treats, but she never touched them. Ever.

"Oh goodness no, she can't!" Terry had explained. "Not without instantly bonding with it and having to take it home!"

Betty belonged to every animal cause advertised in the pages of every animal magazine in publication. She donated chunks of her paycheck to them, too. Unable to visit zoos or aquariums without breaking down into tears, she had also become a vegetarian. Even that was to be a short-lived solace, however. After reading *The Secret Life of Plants*, the woman couldn't slice a tomato without wearing ear plugs, for she swore up and down on her New Testament that she could hear them scream.

Clara Croft ruled the roost in a class by herself. Holding title to being older and more cantankerous than Beula, the boiler, she had voted herself in charge of the cats from day one. A staunch animal activist, she identified with cats and their feisty, intelligent independence. Her anti-dog posture sprang from the shocking stats on cat abuse in predominately Rin-Tin-Tin Happy, USA. Dogs chased cats. Dogs killed cats. End of discussion.

Only one species ranked lower than dogs on Clara's totem pole of respect: humans. It's probably why she and Betty got along so well. Unlike Betty, however, Clara refused to belong to any club or organization, referring to them as "Penance-For-The-Mess-We-Caused-To-Begin-With" clubs. Despite her disregard for charities, she founded one of her own, adamantly referring to it as an "information clearing house". She dubbed it Cat Owners and Cat Owner's Aid, or COACOA for short.

On bi-monthly Sunday afternoons, Clara and her COACOA members met to share catnip tea and readings from their handmade newsletter called "Kitty Corner". Filled with anecdotes, essays, recipes and poems for, from, to and about cats, Joe referred to it as Kitty Coroner.

Every member of COACOA was an activist for animal welfare reform and over sixty-five years old. More than once, the warden had been summoned down to the court house to set bail for Clara and her geriatric cohorts. A typical call had them hauled in for laying prostrate across the railroad tracks, trying to stop the Erie Lackawanna from transporting pigs' knuckles into Manhattan. The police had no choice but to arrest the seniors, if just to protect them, as every train conductor on the line was fed up and wanted to run them down.

"They mean well," Terry explained to Peggy one day. "And half of the time I rather think they're ahead of their time. Of course, the other half of the time, they set us all back a good fifty years in the credibility department. I suspect the FBI has a file on her, too."

A self-proclaimed anarchist, Clara became a U.S. citizen in 1948 just so that she could vote to impeach Congress. Of course, she refused to join either the Democratic or Republican party, claiming that a two party system was nothing but a fifty-fifty bet against the House, and she didn't like the odds. Every voting day she caused traffic jams by reciting the Bill of Rights and the Constitution through a megaphone in front of Town Hall. The only thing that kept her out of jail for disturbing the peace was reluctance on the part of the judge to incarcerate a woman older than his grandmother.

Clara rode to the shelter every day with Betty, because she was unable to drive. The police had revoked her license. It was not due to any infirmity, at least none that anyone could prove. It had to do with her car. The 1930 Rolls Royce was missing the driver's side door, having been wrenched off one day when, in aiming for her garage, she side-swiped her porch, instead. Clara was also so petite, she had to sit on two phone books to reach the steering wheel, and in the winter, the snow tended to drift inside the car in such a way, that the old woman couldn't find the brake pedal.

Once Clara arrived for the day, all bets were off. Routine chores switched from trying to open up for the public, to trying to keep the public from suing. Clara's proclivity for debate drove her, the crew, and the public to distraction. In less than an hour after her arrival, utter chaos erupted.

Still, no one that Peggy had ever met cared as much about cats, as did the shelter's fiery English rose. The cats in her care reflected this devotion. For living behind bars as long as they had been, the shelter's felines were remarkably well-adjusted and seemed content to spend their days watching the humans bumble about like silly fools.

Then, there was Terry. Ordinarily, the warden could be found hunched over a mountain of paperwork in front of the office window. He wore tortoiseshell glasses when reading. This lent him a distinguished, if a bit tousled, air. He looked like a college professor, Peggy mused. He embodied patience. No matter how many times Peggy forgot how or why to do something, he kindly explained it all to her as if she were hearing it for the very first time.

A consummate diplomat, he was not a push over, either. When challenged, he could stand firm on principle. He could also bend over backwards for a greater good, too. He was flexible, yet rock solid, with an uncanny feel for the big picture.

It was not hard to see why the crew respected him the way they did. Outside of an occasional verbal Ping-Pong match over this, that, or another gripe, his was more than just the last word. It was gold. Peggy felt that their loyalty to him might have to do with the way that he not only accepted them for who they were, he genuinely liked them, warts and all.

Along with his perpetual smile, if there was one thing that stood out about the warden more than anything else, it was his unshakable optimism. No matter what sort of curve ball he'd been thrown, he always managed to spin it into a silver lining, nearly to the point of silliness.

In the midst of a spirited debate one morning about positive versus negative thinking, Betty had challenged him by asking what possible good anyone could find in disease.

Without missing a beat, he said, "It keeps doctors and nurses employed, doesn't it? And it's led to remarkable advances in medicine, vaccines, and coca cola, you know!"

"And insurance companies bilkin' everybody wiff sky-high premiums!"

"Yes, well, progress comes at a cost, does it not?"

"You just playin' devil's advocate!"

Peggy wasn't so sure. The warden truly seemed able to understand both sides to every argument. He sometimes played the buffoon, too, just to settle an argument! One late afternoon in the kennel room, Peggy watched as Betty and a woman had nearly come to blows over the turn-in of a dog in Joe's absence. With no proof of residence, the woman claimed she'd found the little terrier mix within the township's borders. Betty didn't buy it. As the argument escalated into raised voices, the warden returned from his errands and politely interrupted.

"Excuse me. Do you believe animals can think?"

The question in and of itself was enough to make anyone pause. Tossed into the middle of an argument, it was like yanking the emergency brake while bouncing downhill at sixty mph. Derailed, both women gaped at him.

"That is to say," he shrugged, "do you believe they can reason as most liberals claim they can?"

"Say what?" Betty raised a brow.

The other woman adjusted her glasses, as if to see Terry and his question more clearly.

"I was wondering," he continued, "is a whale really smarter than a dog? And by what standard do we measure that: the dog's standard, the whale's, or ours? Can you honestly say without a shadow of a doubt, that they even know the difference between having it good or not?"

Peggy couldn't believe what she was hearing. Neither could Betty. "You been drinkin'?" she asked him, low.

The other woman frowned. "Leave it to a man to make such a dumb statement! Of course they can think! And if you ask me, they're a lot smarter than most people!"

"Really? You think so?" Terry asked with seemingly genuine interest.

"This is exactly what's wrong with the world. Simpletons like you in charge!"

"I'm so sorry, have I said something to offend?"

The woman turned her back on him and apologized to Betty. "I had no idea what you had to deal with here. I was just trying to do the right thing, but I can see now, that this is not the place for a smart, feeling creature!"

To Peggy's surprise, the woman adopted the dog, as well as Tatum, a sweet shepherd mix who'd been abandoned by his family when they moved. When the woman left, she invited Betty to bingo night at her church.

Peggy watched Terry wave goodbye to the woman, while Betty helped her into the car with her pets. The woman shot him a withering look as she drove away.

Trotting back to the gate, Betty eyed him. "You did that on purpose."

"Did what?"

"Don't you dance me!"

"I was merely curious as to her opinion on the subject."

"Uh-huh." Betty sashayed past him into the building.

Terry turned to Peggy. "What do *you* think?"

Peggy pulled out the tube of ointment from her pocket and squeezed inside Lucky's run. She rubbed some of the cream into the welt marks on his shoulder. "I-I think they understand a lot more than people think they do."

"So do I. How anyone could believe that they don't is beyond me!"

"B-but you said..." Peggy watched a grin spread across his face. It took her a moment to realize that he'd said nothing, really. He'd merely posed a question to the woman!

"Penny in the slot!" he chuckled. "Got you too, didn't I? You see, when attempting to solve problems with those sorts who may be, shall we say, a bit overwrought? I've found it helpful to engage them in a wee debate. Sometimes all it takes is a little nudge to...jog the skip in their record, as it were. Any sort of monkey wrench will do. Often, it's enough to simply call their bluff."

"Bluff? You just made her mad."

"Let's just say I made her weigh what was important to her."

Peggy had to think about that. Bluffing seemed rather risky. What if they threw the monkey wrench right back at you? According to Terry, it didn't even matter if your adversary was aware that he/she had been taught a lesson. He seemed satisfied that the end justified the means. She found his faith in this, nothing short of astounding.

Despite Terry's laconic nature, Peggy sensed a rebellious streak lurking underneath the smooth veneer, and that made him difficult to read. She could never quite tell when he might be kidding her. About the shelter, he was an open book. His involvement seemed to spring from a real commitment to forge change in animal welfare. He truly believed in his "one corner at a time" mantra.

The only personal aspect of his life that Peggy knew about, outside of the loss of his wife, revolved around the weekly calls from his sister Irene, the RN living in Chicago. It was the only time he ever took a break without once looking at the clock. For Irene, he'd push his papers aside, sit back with a cup of cocoa, chat and laugh, but most of all, listen. There was always a smile in his eyes.

Peggy found herself wondering what he might do with his time outside of the shelter. He wasn't the sort that talked about himself the way most people did, eagerly spilling their guts to be seen and heard. Terry kept his cards close to the vest.

Still, every once and again, Peggy felt certain that she caught sight of the man behind the mask. It usually happened when he gazed out of the back window, apparently lost in thought. Even though the warehouses blocked any view beyond the dirt patch below, Terry looked right through them, as if to a horizon that only he could see. Those were the moments that Peggy felt the real Terry stood before them. As it so often happened, it occurred when the crew was preoccupied, leaving Peggy as the only one privy to the moment. She wondered every time she found him at that window, where he and his wife might be traveling, in his mind's eye.

It worried her, too. More than once, she woke in the morning from a bad dream, terrified that she might arrive at the shelter to find him gone. She didn't know why, since she was the one who fought the urge to turn tail and run away, every day.

As the days turned to weeks, it was no longer just for Lucky that Peggy worked so hard for, now. She hoped that one day things might improve so much, that this contemplative, far away Terry Brannan might abandon his lonely vigil at the window.

Chapter 18

"How would you like to escape this afternoon?"

Before Peggy could respond, Terry helped her on with her coat. It had been a topsy-turvy morning. Clara accidentally set Houdini loose, again, and mixed up all the cats that Peggy tried to sort back into their cages. Barely half of the chores had been finished, the other half not even begun. Joe was still out chasing down two stray dogs up-dumping trash cans across town, and in fifteen minutes they opened to the public.

"But-but what about…"

"Perfect day for a little field trip. Do us a world of good. New perspective and all that!"

Both phones in hand, Betty whirled around to Terry. "Just where you think you goin'?"

"Charlie's place." He peeked in boxes and jars, and under piles of papers on the counter.

"And just when you figger bein' back?"

"Oh…sooner than later." He ducked Betty's hard glare. "I promised Charlie I'd call by, over a week past, and Peggy needs to see how other facilities manage. Have you seen my keys?"

Betty shook a phone receiver at him. "Don't you be leavin' me here alone wiff all diss hullaballoo!"

"Joe'll be back in a tic," Terry glanced at his watch, which was not on his wrist, and began searching for that, too.

Betty watched until she couldn't stand it, anymore. "Keys in the drawer, watch in the cash box! If you'd put things back where you—"

"Who's that on the phone there? Anyone I need to…"

"Don't you Step 'n Fetchit wiff me!"

"Not to worry, it'll be quiet today. I promise."

"You promise. It be on your head, mistah!"

"Two hours, tops."

"Five-fifty nine, I be lockin' them doors!"

Terry checked his watch against the clock. "What would I ever do without you, Betty?"

"Hmph. I should think it be obvious."

Following Terry out the door, Peggy glanced back over her shoulder just in time to see Clara slap a dollar bill on the counter, and Betty up the ante by a quarter.

Outside, Peggy pet Lucky through the fencing, and they both watched the warden use a state inspection flyer to wipe the Pinto's grimy windshield clean.

"Pick up a roll of paper towels," he dictated into his pocket recorder. He squeezed into the car and kicked the passenger door open from the inside, this time. "...and call Fegetti about Ethel's doors. Again."

Thankfully, it wasn't nearly as cold as it had been earlier in the week, so Peggy didn't mind the idea of a drive in the drafty car. She didn't even mind being alone with the warden. It was the idea of leaving Lucky for very long that worried her, now.

Day by day, Lucky had grown accustomed to life in the shelter. He had put on a couple of pounds and his sores had begun to heal nicely. He cowered less and wagged his tail a lot more. Peggy worried, though, because it had been not one, but nearly three weeks since the warden had 'postdated' Lucky's arrival. Not a word had been said with regards to the situation. Peggy was afraid to bring it up, lest the warden remember and call the owner. She had secretly hoped that with the passing time, they'd all forget about it. Then, Lucky could stay safe in the shelter, until she could figure out how to adopt him, herself. So far, so good, she thought.

"How is Lucky getting on?" asked the warden, turning the Pinto onto the Garden State Parkway.

"Oh! He's...the sores are...well, they're..."

"They've scabbed up nicely under your care. He's certainly faring well."

"But, he-he might, he prob-probably needs more time. To-to get even better."

It was quiet in the car. Peggy bit her lip and tried to think of what sort of red herring she might toss at him, like he did to other people, to deflect his thoughts away from Lucky.

"How's your Christmas adoption advert coming along?" he asked.

Peggy felt her heart thud loudly. "The ad? Oh...g-good. Fine."

Liar liar, pants on fire!

She shifted in her seat, sure that he could hear her stomach flip flop. She'd been sleepless for nights now, unable to come up with one. How could she distill all that she thought it should say, in eight words or less? Especially, when her sole motivation was to prevent an animal from being put to sleep. Adopt today or they'll be dead tomorrow! Not exactly cheerful. Try as she might, she hadn't come up with a single idea, yet. She needed more time.

"You'll need to get it in tonight for Thursday's press," Terry said. "Only seven more shopping days and such."

"Oh. Y-yes, of course." Peggy gulped. Great. Not only was she stymied, she had less than eight hours to do it, while on a field trip. To her relief, Terry turned on the radio. She listened absently to the Christmas songs of Andy Williams, Perry Como, Johnny Mathis, The Ray Conniff Singers and Barbra Streisand. It should have been comforting. It needled her, now. Her first holiday event loomed just ahead, and she didn't know what she was doing.

The news was mercifully short. Peggy tried not to listen. When people were losing their jobs and houses, how could she convince them, in eight words or less, to take on another mouth to feed? Chin in hand, she gazed out at the passing towns of Passaic, East Rutherford and Carlstadt. They blurred together in the fog and fanned out into a tangle of half-finished, crisscrossing highways. Peggy caught sight of Manhattan's skyline, and she shuddered. It's okay, she reminded herself. There's a deep cold river between here and there.

Bouncing down Moonachie road, the Pinto hugged the New Jersey Turnpike. It sputtered past factories spewing corrosive, sulfur-yellow smoke along the banks of the Passaic and Hackensack rivers. Peggy's nose wrinkled in protest of the noxious odor.

"Wretched, isn't it?" Terry said, and Peggy jerked her head up, startled. How long had he been watching her?

"It's called the Secaucus Breeze," he added. "People blamed the pig farms in Secaucus. Even though the EPA folks proved the source to be these factories, and not the pigs, the reports ended up buried in the back pages of papers, and nothing ever came of it. A crime, really. Their inaction has led to wholesale disregard for one of the greatest watersheds on the east coast. You're looking at what's left of The Meadowlands."

Peggy peered out over corrupted landfills. Winter-shucked cat-tails thrust bravely up through rusted cars that had been dumped in greenish pools of slime beside the service road. Refineries erected dirty steam along jig-saw railroad tracks, scratching up the tributaries like the scarred arms of a wasted junkie.

"Believe it or not, it's still home to migratory birds. But, not for much longer, thanks to commerce and politics. See that over there?"

Peggy followed his pointed finger and spotted acreage crowded with bulldozers and towering cranes hoisting enormous concrete pillars. They rumbled through what looked like a monstrous carcass of concrete bones, scattered in the distance. "What are they doing?"

"Building a sports stadium. Football, I believe, and a racetrack. They've been working on it the past two years. The environmental boys and developers are still duking it out in court. I think it's a bit daft to build anything on top of a swamp, but the Governor said it will bring jobs to Jersey, so...I daresay, the birds look to lose this round."

To Peggy, it looked like the birds lost the battle, long ago. She tried to imagine what the brutalized area might have looked like before people bought a bill of goods called progress.

"Here we are!"

Terry turned the Pinto onto a sandy path cleaved through deep rock outcroppings, alongside the banks of the sluggish, reed-choked Hackensack River. They came to a stop in a dead-end dirt patch, where tufts of immigrant pampas grass waved stiffly in the smog. Screeching gulls circled over a two-story brick building that punctuated the other end of the clearing. A rusted, '57 Ford pickup listed against a crumbling rock wall, its front tire flat.

"Shall we?" Terry shouldered his door open, stretched, then came around to her side. "Perhaps if you pull up on the handle this time when I push down?"

Peggy did her utmost to synchronize her handle flips with Terry's tug of war on the other side. Alternating his up to her down, jiggling it left to his right, they spent a good few minutes trying to open the door. At last, he gestured her to lean back, and he kicked the door smartly. It creaked open.

"All in the wrist, you see!"

"Yes." Peggy stepped out of the car then paused. The sound of dog barking came from the two-story tenement.

Pulling two lollipops from his coat pocket, he offered one to her. "Welcome to the Hackensack River Shelter."

Peggy gaped. "This...is a shelter?"

"Charlie?" Terry rapped on the wooden door. Flakes of paint fluttered to the stone stoop. "Yo ho, Charlie. You have company!"

Shoving the door open, Terry pressed on ahead into the dank interior. *Wait! Be careful!*

Peggy hesitated on the stoop, enveloped by a musty odor of wet wood, sawdust and damp fur. She could hear Terry walking across what sounded like a stone floor. He did not descend any stairs.

Once her eyes adjusted to the dim light, she observed what looked to be one big room with four floor-to-ceiling posts holding up the ceiling to the second floor. She stepped inside and pulled the door closed behind her. The entire place had been cordoned off into holding pens five feet high. Crude wooden planks served as doors to the pens. Inside each pen were dogs of every description, sometimes five to a pen, and often shared with a couple of cats! To her amazement, the cats didn't seem mind the dogs. Still, she couldn't help but think how Clara would hit the ceiling over it!

How had a place like this not been condemned? It was worse than the Farroway shelter. Peggy picked out Terry's silhouette in the pall of milky light spilling in from thick, bottle-glass windows. He was talking with a young man in overalls. As she approached, she couldn't believe her ears.

"You've done an amazing job here, Charlie," Terry shouted above the barking. "Only a year and...ah, there you are! Charlie, this is Peggy Dillan, my new assistant manager."

"Nice to meet ya." Charlie grasped her hand before she could shy away, and she felt the rough calluses and earnest grasp of a hard-working man. "So, how'd ya score the dough for more help?" His street-wise Jersey cadence was thicker than Joe's.

"Well, we didn't exactly," Terry admitted, "but it'll all pan out."

Charlie leaned in to Peggy, with a wink. "Always got an ace up his sleeve, this guy."

Peggy studied him. He looked around thirty years old. Wavy black hair and heavy-lidded brown eyes suggested he was Italian. He had a nicely-chiseled face, except that only the right half of it moved. His smile was crooked, like his teeth.

"You should have seen this place before Charlie took over," Terry told her. "It was a pig sty."

"Tell me about it!" Charlie laughed. "Yeah, some biz we're in, huh?" He shifted his body weight onto a shovel, and Peggy noticed he wore what looked like a metal brace fitted to a thick, corrective shoe-boot. The left side of his body was thinner, and shorter than his right side.

"One year ago," Terry said, "these animals had nothing at all. They were tied with rope and twine to hooks on walls. Even the cats. Euthanasia was a weighted bag into the drink out there."

Peggy gasped. "But-but isn't that...against the law?"

Charlie and Terry exchanged what looked like a knowing look, and Charlie shook off a sad laugh.

"Not if nobody don't know about it!"

"Well, Charlie here changed all that." Terry clapped the young man on the shoulder. "Built these pens himself, manages the place, handles the adoptions...how much did the township give you again?"

"'Bout five thou, give or take. Mostly take! On my mudda's life, every month I says, that's it, I'm done! Whadda they want, blood? And then, don't ask me how, man, but we skate by, by an ass hair—oh, 'scuse the mouth, miss!"

"It's all right," Peggy half-laughed. Charlie's language was mild in comparison to the crew's daily dialect!

"It's just I get so goddamn pissed about it, oops! 'Scuse me again!"

"Rightfully so," Terry interjected. "You see, the difference between our place and Charlie's, is that most of the animals here are strays, not turn-ins, like at our place."

"Mostly dumped up there by the turnpike," Charlie concurred.

Peggy's hand fluttered to her mouth. "You-you mean people just..."

"Sometimes they don't even slow down, the sons of bitches! Oops, 'scuse me again! Sorry, but it balls, me, y'know? Gets me goin'! But, hey, we're workin' on it, right? We don't look like much miss, but we got what it takes, yeah? One corner at a time, right man?"

Peggy glanced at Terry. There it was again. One corner at a time. Even here by the river, they believed it. As Charlie walked them around, she marveled at just how difficult the chores must be for the man. He had to swing his body forward at an angle to walk and his withered left arm looked almost useless.

She was impressed with the animals, too. They were all very friendly and Charlie was clearly fond of them, talking to them as if they were his own children.

"Oh!" Terry clapped his forehead. "I have something for you. Be right back." He hurried out the front door.

Charlie leaned against a pen and gestured to a little mutt that hopped about on three legs. "I call him Chester. Lost a leg to one of them leg-hold traps. Not even in the woods. In town! Flat out illegal, okay? Never caught the S.O.B. neither. Effin' shits. Oops, sorry! Anyhow, Doc Hayward up at the EVC fixed him up and now it's like nuthin' ever happened."

Peggy was surprised to hear the young vet's name.

"Yeah, your boss helped me get it all square with them. But man, it was like pullin' teeth. First, they say I should put him down, on accounta adopting him out would be a bitch," he clapped a hand over his mouth. "Damn! Sorry. But man, I couldn't do it! I mean, lookit him." He scratched the dog's ears. "I had no bread, but Terry, he worked it out, and I gotta say, the doc did a helluva job. I go, Terry, how am I ever gonna pay ya back? And he goes ta me, 'find him a good home, Charlie, that's payment enough!' Man, does he know me like yestaday's news, or what? So, I take Chester home and nurse him, but, c'mon! I got four already. Y'know how it is. I'd keep 'em all, but...anyhow, he got me this job, too. Heard some grapevine 'bout the place, so he goes to bat for me. And Terry, he's talkin' his English to these schmoes don't got shit between their ears, ya know? But whatever, he and Doc Caldwell twisted some arms and it worked out, right? They gimme the job. Yeah...he's okay, your boss."

The door burst open and Terry butted backwards across the threshold, straight-arming a box at his waist. He thumped it down on a plank table with a grunt. "There we are!"

"Oh man! You're shittin' me! Damn, miss, sorry! But this is—oh man!"

Terry pulled out bottles of pine disinfectant, flea spray, and a dozen cans of dog and cat food out of the big box.

"You sure you can spare it?" Charlie asked, his eyes lusting over the box of supplies.

"No sense it collecting dust on shelves, right?"

Peggy stole a glance at Terry, wondering just how he'd managed to pilfer supplies on Betty's watch.

"Merry Goddamn Christmas, man!" Charlie pumped Terry's hand then winced at Peggy. "'Scuse the mouth, babe, but this is bitchin'!"

Chapter 19

The thin afternoon sun had burned a ferruginous haze over the Hackensack River, by the time they waved goodbye to Charlie. Ethel, the Pinto, as if in a more generous mood, too, opened her doors on the very first yank of her handles. Her engine sputtered to life with Terry's first crank of the ignition.

Tapping the horn in farewell to Charlie, Terry steered Ethel onto the bumpy service road. "So?" he prompted.

"It's-it's...and he's so-so..." Peggy gushed.

"Indeed!" Terry agreed. "He's a special chap."

They passed the entrance for the Turnpike, and Terry zipped the car north back onto the Garden State Parkway, instead of west, towards Farroway.

Peggy glanced at him. "Um...wasn't that the exit for..."

"Have you ever been to the Great Falls shelter?"

"No. But, Betty said..."

"Oh, you're in for a treat! You're about to see what happens when six townships get together and set up a Cadillac!"

"Yes, but what about what Betty said? Isn't it getting late?"

"You're going to love it! Trust me!"

Exiting the Parkway, they drove through countrified, upscale Bergen County. It reminded Peggy of the well-to-do neighborhood of West Hills, where the EVC held court. Following official signs down a tree-lined road, they pulled up to a brand new building on a brand new parking lot. Colorful flags flapped along its entire roof line. Evergreen hedges along the walkway had been clipped artfully into the shapes of dogs and cats. Festooned with bouquets of balloons, the entrance to the glass-fronted facility was obscured with families streaming in and out. For a moment Peggy thought they'd arrived at an amusement park.

Peggy followed Terry into the building and paused in the wide lobby. Underfoot, a circular mosaic artfully depicted a happy family, surrounded with companion animals of every description: cats, dogs, rabbits, guinea pigs, canaries, parrots, even a ferret that looked like Houdini. Wood paneling rose like trees from the floor to the open-beamed ceiling above their heads. An art gallery and a gift shop flanked a bright, busy office under a cheerful banner: Welcome to the Great Falls Shelter!

Directly across from the office, families crowded around two picture windows. Behind the glass, kittens and puppies played in confetti-paper. A wall speaker allowed children to listen to their yapping and mewing.

Peggy felt a nudge at her elbow. She looked up at Terry, who was grinning at her. Duly impressed, she shook her head, and smiled, too. She followed him to a door with a brass nameplate that read: Director. Terry knocked, and the door opened.

A well-heeled secretary greeted him with polished, business-like aplomb. "Come in, Mr. Brannan, he's been expecting you."

"Terry!" A man in a crisp, tailored suit stood up from behind a mahogany desk and extended his hand. "Good to see you again!"

"Likewise. Dave, this is my new assistant, Peggy Dillan. Thought I'd show her how the other half lives."

"Terrific! Though, I'm afraid I'm just on my way out to tape a public spot, but I've told Connie here to roll out the red carpet for you, and if we can help you with anything, don't hesitate to..." he mimicked picking up a phone, while briskly walking them right back out of his office. "How've you been? We'll have to catch up. Don't be such a stranger!"

In a flurry of doors and coats, he was gone. It had all passed by so quickly, Peggy wasn't sure the man had really been there at all.

The brisk and efficient Connie led them down a corridor to a door that read "Employees Only Beyond This Point." She pressed a button beside the door, and a young woman opened it. Dressed in an aqua smock, with the Great Falls Shelter logo embroidered on the chest pocket, her name tag read: Your Hostess: Vicki.

"Vicki, this is Terry Brannan, he's here for a tour," Connie instructed and then turned to Terry. "If you have any questions, Vicki will be happy to answer them. So nice to have met you." She then brushed past them, her heels clacking briskly down the freshly-waxed hallway.

"I see we have professionals here today," Vicki bubbled, nodding to the patch on Terry's parka. "And you're from?"

"The Farroway shelter, Essex County."

The name did not seem to register to her. "Well, there are so many aren't there?"

"Indeed."

"All righty, then! Ready to be bow-wowed?"

"We're looking forward to it." Terry gestured Peggy ahead of him. Vicki led them to another set of doors with yet another sign. It welcomed them to "The Dog House."

To Peggy's surprise, the doors whooshed open automatically, as they approached. They entered an enormous kennel, modern in every design and detail. There was simply no comparison to their own, and even less to Charlie's labor of love down by the river. Sky lights and state-of-the-art track lighting traversed the ceiling. Gleaming cream and beige tiles were laid from floor to ceiling. The surface was sparkling and squeaky clean above row upon row of spotless runs. One could have eaten off of the floor.

Peggy glanced at Terry, who was apparently getting a big kick out of watching her expression. A dozen matronly women and men in yellow smocks doled out food and water to at least one hundred and fifty dogs.

"Our volunteers have three shifts to choose from," Vicki said with chipper pride. "Morning, afternoon, or evening. As you can see, our dogs have automated access to their outdoor runs. A sensor above the run can also be activated by a panel in the main control area. Grates on each run allow for easy access to food and water bowls, negating the necessity for actual physical contact, so we rarely have any..." she finger quoted in the air, "'mishaps'. Liability and all that."

Peggy watched in wonder as the rear chute doors lifted whenever a dog wandered near the red sensors. No jamming chutes and no chopping off of toes, here! Still, the woman's words echoed in her head. No contact? Surely, the dogs must have some contact? Peggy noticed then, that the volunteers' smocks were very clean. The only time Peggy's uniform was clean was on the bus ride down to the shelter in the morning. Perusing the cage cards, she found little information beyond age, sex, and breed. No names. The dogs were identified only with a number.

"As you can see," their hostess pointed out, "our animals are cross-referenced by row and run number. It's a new identification system we've implemented both for security and the ease of record keeping. If you'll follow me," she led them towards another set of double doors painted like two cats. The placard there said, "Welcome to our Cat Haven."

With a last look back at the nameless dogs, Peggy walked into Cat Haven and stopped in her tracks. It was huge. Wall-papered with dancing mice and birds, at least fifty split-level cages were built into the walls. Cats lounged on soft beds, where they watched fish in tanks, or cartoons on three television sets.

"Our felines have their own eco-air system," the hostess bragged, "the walls are soundproofed, with a separate lobby entrance so they never have to see the dogs, let alone hear them."

All Peggy could think of at that moment was Clara. She turned to Terry, her eyes wide. He was still grinning at her.

"If you'll come with me," their guide led them across a short passageway, where they came to a large picture window and the *coup de grâce*.

"This is our in-house surgical suite. Our facilities are up to AAHA standards, and we have our own x-ray room, mini-lab and post-op care!"

Peggy peered through the glass partition to a small, but well-appointed veterinary space. A woman veterinarian examined a dog, with help from two assistants in white lab coats.

Terry nudged Peggy. "They just instituted their own spay and neuter program."

"Oh yes!" the hostess declared. "Here at Great Falls, as part of our campaign against over-population, we now spay and neuter all of our guests."

"How utilitarian," Terry grinned impishly.

"Yes," the hostess went on, blithely, "As far as Great Falls is concerned, every town ought to have an ordinance making it a requirement of residence. The problem is that serious."

"Our own cat expert sent a petition to Rome."

"Oh absolutely, it's a global problem!"

"Indeed."

Peggy pressed her lips together hard to keep from laughing. Terry nudged her again, in mock chastisement.

The hostess led them back into the kennel.

"What about your education program?" Terry asked.

"Hmn?" The woman checked her clip-board schedule. "Edu...oh, we don't have an education program, per se. Our funding is strictly slated for operational, being we serve six towns, so we have the tour, instead. There are brochures available at the front desk, if you like.'

"Thank you. I do have a question about your funding."

While Terry chatted business with the woman, Peggy wandered away to look at the dogs. She listened to the volunteers as they talked to prospective adopters about the dogs. It was curious, but they didn't formally interview people, not like Terry did, with questions about their family situation, jobs, their knowledge of this or that breed. Peggy was surprised to learn that nearly every dog in their kennel had been adopted out at least once. For some of them, it was half a dozen times in just one month!

Peggy wondered what it must be like for the dogs to be adopted, get attached to a family, only to be brought back again to watch that family walk away over and over. One volunteer encouraged a family into adopting a rowdy, loud young shepherd mix; his run littered with shredded toweling. He reminded Peggy of Zorro. The family seemed to like the fact that he was young, and a shepherd. A good guard dog, no doubt. Since they had a yard, and the kids wanted him, that was that.

The volunteer took the dog's card to a podium and a big IBM typewriter. In less than a minute, a tally sign above the doorway ran the message like a ticker tape: Adoption for # 25...thank you Armstrong family!

The family cheered, volunteers applauded, then Vicki, the hostess, gave the family a doggie bag of peanut-butter cookies, while they filled out the paperwork. In less than five minutes, the family was dragged out of the building by the dog.

Their tour concluded, Peggy and Terry headed for the exit. Peggy's one parting thought lay in wondering how long it might be before the Armstrong family brought their newly adopted, nameless dog back for an exchange, and whether or not anyone back at the shelter had thought to bring Lucky inside before it got dark.

"Where the coal crap you been?!" Betty hollered from the stoop.

With a deft little kick to open Peggy's door, Terry checked his watch. "I have five fifty-eight." He raised his arm to show Betty his watch.

"You on colored people's time?"

"I'll sit gunshot tomorrow, I promise."

"Don't you buffalo me! We had a house fulla fools today. I ain't in no mood!"

Traipsing up the walkway, Terry offered her a box of cat-shaped cookies. "Just for you."

"Don't think this gets you off the hook!"

"Of course not. Any messages?"

"Would it mattah? It be aftah closin'!"

Terry checked his watch again. "I have five fifty-nine..."

"Yo' watch is ten minutes bee-hind and you know it."

Peggy hurried inside, leaving Terry to smooth things over with Betty. Relieved, she found Lucky curled up in his bed, the radiator beside the office door hissing steam. Seeing her, he thumped his tail. She squeezed into his run and pulled the nearly empty tube of ointment from her pocket. It was a struggle to squeeze the last glob out.

"And about that dog," Betty said, shutting the front door after Terry. Rubbing ointment onto Lucky's scabs, Peggy held her breath.

"Ah yes. Well, we're looking into how best to handle it," said the warden.

"You know what I be sayin'!"

"Yes, well, let's give those scabs a chance to fur out, shall we?"

"I ain't th'one gonna git hung out to dry."

"I'll sort it out."

"I ain't gonna argue witchoo."

"I appreciate that."

Terry escorted Betty into the office, closing the door behind them. There followed the muffled sound of the crew's raised voices, but after a moment, it got quiet again. Peggy knew that somehow, Terry had once again won the bout with his "friendly persuasion".

"Alls I'm sayin' is," Joe said later, soldering wires in the CB unit, "they got it made in the shade up there at Great Falls. Big bucks from all those Fifth-ave broker-babes livin' it up in Saddle River, catch my drift? You catch their ad in the paper? Gimme a break! 'Great Falls - a great place for pets?' A pound ain't about bein' a great place for pets! Jeeze!"

Terry glanced over at Peggy. She hadn't said a word for the last hour. Hovered over her ad mock-up, she wiped glue off of her hands and seemed deep in thought.

"Whadoo you expect?" Betty broke open a pack of candy cigarettes. "Any doofus go there, see a crazy-fine place like that, 'course they gonna think it fresh!"

"Exactamundo! It's slick. So what?"

"Slick sells, baby."

"Yeah but, there ain't nuthin' under the wrappin'. It's like, a gimmick. All slick n' schtick."

"They're merely giving the public what they want," Terry said, sorting the mail. "And they do it with the best of intention."

"Yeah, so? What's your point?"

"No point. You're right, and so is Betty. We're all doing our best with what we've got."

"Yeah, but peeps think that just 'cause Great Falls puts on a dog 'n pony show, they're jake. Their dogs ain't any cooler just 'cause ya get a dorky balloon when y'adopt one."

"What matters is that an animal gets adopted."

"Their mutts don't even got names! Where's the love is all I'm sayin'! At least we know all our animals' names."

"That's love, man."

"I'm serious," Joe popped a handful of cat kibble in his mouth.

"So am I. Love is about what people do, not what they say."

"Exactamundo! It's easy to fool people with all the glitter. Like this new disco crap," Joe switched the radio off. "Jeeze, what's happening t'all the good stuff, huh? Everybody's sold out. Hippies sold out. Nixon sold out. All those Watergate mopes, they sold out. All our heroes are dead. American Dream's dead. Music's dead. God is—"

Whap! Betty smacked him over the head with a rolled up newspaper.

"Owww!"

"Catch yo'self a real beat down, Clara catch you!"

"Terrrrrr!"

"Joe, stop eating the cat food..."

The office door opened and Clara wobbled into the office. She shook out her wet umbrella over Joe, who squealed like a five-year old.

"*Hey!*"

"...or I'll tell Clara," added Terry with a raise of his brow.

"Tell me what?" Clara fastened her narrowed eyes on Joe.

"Oh...go knit yourself a muzzle!" Joe swiveled back to the CB unit.

"Clara? New cats all right down in the...downstairs?" Terry asked.

"Not dead, yet."

"Splendid. All right, folks, let's call it a day, shall we?" Terry glanced again to Peggy. She scribbled madly, crossing out lines, re-writing, deep in concentration.

Joe whispered none-too-softly to Betty. "She lookin' to be promoted now?" Whap! "Oww!" Joe whirled around in surprise.

Terry handed him the rolled up newspaper. "Recycle that, will you?"

Joe snatched it from him and opened the door for Betty and Clara. "I could file a report with social, y'know."

"Yes, and after five minutes talking with you, they'd probably ask for a whack at you themselves."

"That's cold, Ter."

"Yes it is, so close the door, will you?"

"Night," Betty laughed.

"Nobody understands me." Joe sighed and followed the ladies out the door.

Terry swiveled around to find Peggy already in her hat and coat too, holding out a sheet of paper to him.

"If-if it's not good enough, maybe someone else can…" she stammered.

"Is this the ad for the paper? Splendid!"

Sidestepping him, Peggy made a move for the door. "One moment please," he murmured, reading the paper.

Peggy listened to the clock ticking loudly on the wall for what felt like an eternity, her heart thudding in her chest so hard, her whole body shook. She didn't understand what was taking him so long. It was only eight words long.

Finally, Terry looked up at her. "It's perfect."

Peggy frowned and hung her head. "It's not…it's not very slick." Terry slid her chair towards her and gestured her to sit.

Unable to look at him, Peggy sat down.

"I know people look at Great Falls and think, now there's a winner!" Terry said. "And granted, if we had that sort of funding, I'd see to some changes around here, too. But, are you going to tell me that Great Falls is a better outfit than Charlie's place?"

Peggy raised her brows.

Terry nodded. "All right, in some respects, perhaps so, but setting aside bells and whistles, what about under the wrapping, like Joe intimated? Did you know that Charlie's adoption rate is eighty percent? Great Falls barely reaches forty percent in a given month, figuring in all the returns. What's so slick about that?"

"Not much, I guess."

"I think what's important to remember, is exactly what you wrote here," he adjusted his glasses, reading her ad aloud. "This Christmas, give the gift of love. Adopt." He smiled at her. "Madison Avenue should be so slick. Well done."

Peggy shrugged. "I just wrote down what you were all talking about, before."

"But, you put it together. Give yourself some credit."

Peggy searched his eyes and saw that he meant it. "Th-thank you."

"That's better. Now, how about I swing you by the press desk," he donned his parka and opened the door for her, "on our way up to the EVC Christmas party?"

Peggy looked up sharply. "P-party?"

"Oh, didn't I mention? The kittens are ready for pick up, and I see that you need another tube of ointment for Lucky there."

"Yes, but—"

"Splendid. I don't know about you, but I'm ravenous. They cater, so we're in for a treat."

"But-but I— "

"Consider it good P.R.," Terry fished around the counter for his keys, "you being in charge of adoptions, advertising, and such. We need to introduce you around. They call it networking, these days." He bent over the goldfish bowl. "I say, how did they end up in there?" He netted his keys out and dried them off with his hankie. "It's important to get out there and mingle. Now, what say we go fetch those lucky kittens for your big adoption day next week!"

Ushered to the door before she could even get a word in edgewise, Peggy realized she, too, had been finessed by the warden's friendly persuasion.

Chapter 20

Christmas lights twinkled through the garlands of holly and ivy draped over the windows and doors of the EVC. Terry steered the Pinto through the drizzling rain and sputtered into one of the last spaces in the crammed parking lot. Even through closed windows, Peggy could hear the jazzy holiday music, along with the kind of ribald laughter that free-flowing champagne elicits. Terry donned his pre-knotted tie from the glove compartment and caught her eye.

"I have another one if you'd like."

"Oh, no, thank you." Peggy buttoned her coat up to her collar.

When he hopped out of the car, she peeked at herself in the rear-view mirror. "Oh, no!" She tried to wipe the day's grime off of her face with her sleeve, but it only smeared. She couldn't believe it. Yet again, here she was at the upscale hospital, looking like road kill.

As she hastily detangled her hair, Terry unexpectedly yanked her door open on his first try, and out she tumbled onto the muddy lawn in a heap.

"Oh dear! You all right?" Terry reached to help her, but she managed to scramble to her feet. "Had our signals crossed there!"

"Sorry!" She tried to wipe the axle grease off of her coat, but only managed to smear it over her hands, too.

"My fault, entirely!" He handed her his handkerchief.

"No, I-I should have, uh..." She paused and sniffed the handkerchief. Too late. She now smelled like fish and algae.

"Ah, terribly sorry about that! Not to worry! Between the halothane and chloroform in there, they'll never notice, I promise. Come, I'll buy you a drink."

He gestured her ahead of him to the walkway.

"Oh," Peggy stammered, "that's nice, but you don't have to. I-I don't drink."

"Ah! Well, I meant it as bit of a joke. These soirees are catered. Hmn. Really? Not even wine? What sort of red-blooded Celt doesn't drink? I promise not to hold it against you. Surely, you must be a saint, or an orthodox Catholic."

"No, no, I...no."

"No? Well, aside from an ale at Kierney's now and again, neither do I. And I'm Protestant. We drink all the time!"

Despite her flip-flopping stomach, Peggy laughed lightly. He had the most disarming way of upending even the most embarrassing moment into a smile. As they approached the entrance to the clinic, she stuffed her smelly hands in her pockets and lifted her chin.

Terry moved through the crowd as if he himself had thrown the party. He introduced Peggy to everyone they encountered. Of course, everyone wanted to shake hands. Catching sight of herself in a reflective cage bank, Peggy suddenly wished she *had* been drinking. The dark interior of the Pinto had concealed more than she'd realized. She not only looked like road kill, she looked like she'd been dragged behind the car for at least a mile and half. She smelled like it, too.

Despite Terry's assurance that dress would be casual, all around her fresh-scrubbed men in tailored jackets, and chic women in slinky cocktail dresses mingled. Peggy kept her coat buttoned to the collar, despite the stuffy warmth of the coterie. The only saving grace had been that she hadn't run into the impeccable Dr. Hayward or the superior Dr. Miller in the crush.

After a perspiring hour and a half, Peggy's head began to ache. Dabbing at her brow with a napkin, she heard the warden's voice above the buzzing.

"How are we doing? We're not dizzy, are we?"

"No, no," she fibbed, and offered a brave smile.

"Well, we've made the rounds. Let's say our goodbyes, shall we?"

Relieved, Peggy trailed him through the wash of Sea Forth and sequins, catching sidelong looks and wrinkled noses as she passed.

"Merry Christmas, Doc!" Terry called out.

In the midst of a round robin of toasts, Caldwell waved. "Terry!" A Santa hat listed sideways on the elder vet's head at about the same angle he was listing. He clapped Terry on the back, spilling wine. "You're not leaving, already? Your assistant hasn't even taken off her coat!"

Clutching her collar, Peggy backed up into a cage. "I-I'm fine!"

"It's been super," Terry reiterated, "but we really must be off."

"Really? Well, thank you for finding homes for those kittens. They're down in the back. But, I won't hear of you running off before we share a Christmas toast."

"Here, let me pop this one," Terry took the bottle from the vet, with a wink to Peggy, "while Peggy gathers the kittens. Just down the hallway there in the back, all right?"

"Yes." With a smile of relief, Peggy retreated from the crowd and headed down the dim hallway. She slowed as she approached the shadowy rear of the building.

Don't go down there!

She paused. It was awfully dark at the end of the passage. Over her own thumping heart, she heard a low rumbling; a throaty, menacing sound from somewhere ahead, in the shadows. Sweat trickling down her neck, she glanced back to the party.

Go back!

I can't! Not without the kittens! How would I explain that?

Don't talk back! You'll be sorry!

Peggy's hands began to tremble, as she listened to the strange rumbling. This is a hospital, she told her voices. Nothing bad could be down there. Not with a party going on, right?

No answer.

Fine, she told herself. With a frown, she reached out and felt around the wall for a light switch, but couldn't find one. She glanced over her shoulder. The warden was within eyeshot. Her knees quaking, she turned and stared into the darkness until her eyes adjusted. She made out a swath of faint light spilling out into the hall from a room off to the right. On tip-toe, she eased one foot in front of the other, until she reached the room. She peered around the doorway. In the corner of the room sat a washing machine and a dryer, both rumbling with loads of laundry.

Peggy exhaled, but instead of relief, she felt a jab of irritation. See, she chastised her silent taskmasters. Nothing. No bogeyman. No monster. You scared me for nothing!

Without waiting for an argument, she unclenched her fists and stepped into the room. Two large runs flanked the opposite wall. The first run was occupied with a Saint Bernard, snoring loudly, the source of those menacing sounds. A Great Dane slept in the other run.

Peggy felt silly as she looked around for the kittens. They weren't there and it dawned on her she would have to go back into the gloomy hallway, and go farther. She immediately broke out in a sweat.

Serves you right, stupid!

Nothing's going to happen, not while the warden's here!

You can't trust anyone! You know that!

Peggy held her breath, inching her way down the hall in the darkness. Please, just let me do this, please, I promise I'll be good, I'll…

All at once, she sensed a shadowy presence in front of her and gasped. She clapped a hand over her mouth. The shadow gasped, too, and turned into the spill of the security light through the back door window. It was Dr. Hayward. The washing machine suddenly ended its cycle, sending a vibrant quiet into the hallway, the party sounds a distant intrusion.

"I-I'm sorry," Peggy stammered, "I didn't mean to…the kittens—Dr. Caldwell said they were back here."

"Kittens?" Dr. Hayward spoke brusquely, irritated either by her, or by her quest.

"Yes."

He turned towards the cages against the wall, searching.

Peggy wondered why the young vet seemed mad at her. It occurred to her that he probably wasn't very happy about his shelter assignment. Well, that made two of them.

He opened a cage door and carefully pulled out four tabby kittens, mewing at being awakened from their sleep. He placed them on a soft towel inside a pet carrier and then handed it to her.

"Their record is up front. No follow-up indicated."

Peggy wasn't sure what he meant, so she hesitated.

"Was there something else?" he asked.

"No-no. Th-thank you."

With a curt nod, he walked past her up the long corridor. Just before reaching the bright, raucous Christmas celebration, he veered through another darkened door, leading elsewhere. Peggy looked after him a long moment, and then headed to the party.

Chapter 21

"Splendid job!"

Ribboned fluffy kittens mewed in Peggy's arms. She beamed as Terry appraised her work. And why not? The entire shelter was spotless! She'd had the animals fed and groomed, their cages decorated in colorful paper garland, all before the eight a.m. arrival of the crew.

"I say, however did you manage it?" Terry asked, with just the right amount of marvel in his voice. "Not that I had any doubt, mind you! And what are all these?"

"Adoption kits!" Peggy handed him a packet wrapped in ribbon. "Each cat and dog comes with one, so that p-people can read all about them. It explains their history, if-if we know it, their likes and dislikes, and-and any medical needs. I added information about their breed mix, like George, the Rottweiler? You know how he likes to be the boss."

"Indeed!" Terry raised his brow at a wide-eyed Joe, Betty and Clara. They'd all traipsed in, while Peggy was sharing her handiwork with the warden. Their surprised gazes took in the spic n' span sparkle of the place. "Yes, remarkable what can be accomplished with sheer gumption, eh?"

The crew exchanged glances. Despite their reticent silence, Peggy felt herself standing a bit taller in their midst. The warden had recognized her hard work, and even though that's all that really mattered to her, she couldn't help but feel a bit smug, knowing that any and all bets made behind her back were now a wash.

"Well, I daresay, this is going to be the best Christmas Eve adoption event we've ever had!" Terry tossed an adoption kit to each crew member, in turn.

"It's the only one we ever had," Joe retorted.

"Then, we're off on the right foot!"

Peggy felt butterflies in her stomach. Maybe Terry was right. It might possibly turn out to be the most successful event the shelter had ever had. No, she was sure of it!

Jingle Bells, as barked out by dogs, crackled over the radio yet again.

Biting her lip, Peggy looked at the clock for the hundredth time. It was just five minutes to closing. She looked out the window again.

Under overcast skies, the parking lot was dark and empty. Except for the warden, who stood at the front gate, gazing up toward the street. He'd been standing there for nearly an hour, as if waiting for an overdue train. He kept checking his watch. The one he never wore—until today.

Peggy sagged inwardly. Not a soul had come down to the shelter, all day. It had rained earlier in the morning, but the rest of the day had been merely cloudy, and not even that cold, so she couldn't blame the weather.

Feeling a wet nose on her hand, Peggy looked down. Lucky wagged his tail at her and offered his paw. She scratched his ears and smiled feebly.

"Maybe we should have been slicker?" she whispered to him.

It had become routine to bring Lucky into the office every afternoon, at first with the excuse of ministering to his sores. He stayed out of the way and slept under the counter at Peggy's feet while she worked. Perhaps everyone simply got used to him being around, much like the new girl.

Peggy heard a long, drawn out sigh and snuck a glance over her shoulder. Chin in hand, Joe stared at the clock, tapping a pencil on the counter. Hunched under a towel over a pan of steaming water, Betty inhaled menthol-rub vapors. Half-asleep on her stool in the corner, Clara's head bobbed. The kittens fought over the knitting yarn wound around her ankles.

The radiator whistled and sputtered steam. It just wasn't fair, Peggy protested in silence. Even cranky old Beula was working! She eyed the trays of cookies and pitchers of eggnog she'd bought with her own money; enough for a dozen families. All of her work; the cleaning, grooming, the decorating, all of it, for nothing. There hadn't even been one adoption to offset the cost of the ad!

Joe's pencil tapping increased in tempo.

"Would you please stop that?" Betty croaked from under her towel.

"It's time to blow this friggin' hot-dog stand!" Joe griped.

"Watch yer mouth," Clara yawned, "it's Christmas!"

"What, like that changes nuthin'?"

A horn honk jerked everyone's attention to the window. Peggy cupped her hands over the fogged glass. A dark Mercedes Benz cruised down the driveway and pulled alongside the gate. Peggy could just make out Terry walking toward a man and a woman getting out of the car, helping two young children from the back.

"It's a family!" she exclaimed.

"Don't tell me," Joe retorted, "it's the Cratchets."

Peggy snatched an adoption form from the shelf, determined to make this one last shot a winner. Maybe the family would get swept up into the spirit of it all and adopt not only a dog, but a cat too, and all four kittens! Now, that would be a Christmas present!

She heard the front door open. The dogs burst into their barking chorus, and she scribbled in her name on the form as the officer in charge. Then, the office door swung open. Peggy smiled, as a well-dressed man in his mid-fifties, his attractive wife and two children, a girl and a boy, about six and eight years old, walked into the office.

Almost at once, it felt as if the air had been sucked out of the room. The chilled silence was so pervasive it compelled her to glance back at the crew. They stared at the man, mute. Her eyes flicked to Terry. Why did he look so solemn?

"Is that him, Mr. Harrison?" the warden asked.

It took a moment for the name to register with Peggy. When Lucky ducked behind her legs, her heart froze. She looked up at the man. Harrison. Her throat constricted.

Keep quiet! Just keep your mouth shut!

"I should have known!" Mr. Harrison laughed, affably. "We were passing by and I thought, what are the odds; should we stop in?"

Her heart pounded over the hum in her head, as Peggy guardedly measured the family. Mrs. Harrison's eyes pierced Peggy, belying her husband's gregariousness. Suddenly, Peggy was very afraid. The children acted like skittish rabbits, sensing danger and tensed to flee in an instant. Peggy couldn't run if she wanted to. She couldn't feel her legs.

Mr. Harrison swept past her to Lucky, and the dog cowered further under the counter. Glancing helplessly up to Terry, Peggy searched his face. Surely, any moment now he was going to say or do something to intervene?

Keep quiet, if you know what's good for you!

The warden bent over the desk and filled out a release form. Peggy stared at his back, her hands trembling. He wasn't going to sign Lucky over to the man, was he?

Keep your mouth shut!

"How much is it this time?" Mr. Harrison asked, pulling a checkbook from the pocket of his camel-hair coat.

"Seventy-five dollars, Mr. Harrison."

"Seventy-five? Where's your Christmas spirit?"

"In the medication used for the sores across his back. Any idea as to how he might have acquired them?"

"Sores?" Mr. Harrison exchanged a surprised look with his wife and then bent down to look at Lucky, still huddling under the counter. "How long has he had those?"

"Was rather hoping you could tell us."

"Well, let me see now, he's been missing for what, two-three weeks, is it, honey? We called every week; you must have it on record."

Peggy dragged her eyes to Betty. She didn't flinch.

Mr. Harrison turned to Joe. "How long have you had him?"

"I dunno. How long we had him, Ter?" Joe countered smoothly.

"I'd have to look it up," Terry said, "we've been so busy, as you can imagine, what with the holidays. With no I.D. tags, his condition, the weight loss—you must admit, he barely looks like the same dog."

Mr. Harrison acquiesced with a shrug. "Could have been anything, right? They get out, they get into trouble. No way to really know, is there?"

His eyes rested on Peggy, and he cocked his head at her, as if trying to place her. Peggy thought her heart would hammer her ribs to splinters. She felt sure she'd fall down from the force of it.

"You'll want to have your vet check him over, right away," the warden's voice sounded calm, but firm. "Sign here, please."

Harrison's gaze lingered on Peggy, as he pulled a pen from his pocket. Rather than take the clipboard from Terry, he leaned on it to write his check, forcing Terry to steady it for him.

"Where do I sign?"

"Same place; bottom of the form by the X."

Harrison signed the form and then leaned past Peggy to leash Lucky. The smell of his aftershave burned her nose. The dog shrank back against the wall.

"C'mon, Boy," Harrison jerked the lead and pulled Lucky out from under the counter. Peggy watched, helpless. Her voice froze in her throat, and she couldn't even lie to Lucky, and tell him everything would all right.

"Ah, Mr. Harrison?" Terry's voice sounded far away. "So that there are no misunderstandings, fines will be exponential from here on."

Harrison's smug smile caught on his lips. "Really? Maybe I should talk to the mayor about the way fines are levied in the county? There really ought to be some consistency, don't you agree? Just so there're no... *misunderstandings.*"

Terry didn't reply.

"Merry Christmas." Harrison's family followed him closely, as they exited the office. Lucky looked back at Peggy with a whimper, before being tugged out the door.

Peggy listened for the car doors slamming shut and then she inhaled what felt like her first breath in hours. She couldn't feel her limbs. They were numb. Behind her, she heard the crew shuffle around, pulling on coats and hats. If the earth had opened up just then beneath her feet and flung her into oblivion, it would have been a welcome relief.

"Speakin' of the mayor," Betty sighed, "his office sent ovah these budget cut thingees, and you supposed to go ovah them, then sign it."

"Yeah, and Happy Friggin' New Year to him, too," Joe muttered.

"I'll take care of it," Terry murmured.

The office door opened. Terry and the crew looked around and watched Peggy walk stiffly, unsteadily, towards the front door. She struggled to open it and then stood on the threshold, staring into the night.

Terry was the first to find his voice. "Thank you for your help today, folks. Go home. Make Merry."

Joe, Betty and Clara exchanged glances, and with clumsy attempts at hugs, mumbled "Merry Christmas" and filed out. By then, Peggy had moved to the sink, and with her back to them, was washing bowls. They closed the front door, quietly.

Terry watched Peggy at the sink. He reached for two mugs on the shelf, set the kettle on the hot plate, and opened two packets of instant cocoa.

"Believe me, I understand how you feel, but we must play by the rules. With no proof, we have to give Lucky back."

Peggy cradled a cup of cold cocoa in her hands. "He's only going to do it, again."

"I don't think he's stupid enough to do it again. Not after tonight."

"No, h-he's smart enough to hide it better, next time."

Terry peered at her over his cup. He was slightly taken aback by how matter-of-fact her comment had been. "Well, we'll be keeping an eye on him. He knows that, now. Perhaps that's enough to make a difference."

Peggy said nothing, but a tear coursed down her cheek. Terry handed her a tissue.

The Pinto sputtered up to the curb and stalled out with a little fart of blue exhaust. Except for the rattling of the loose windows and Christmas tunes on the radio, the ride to Tory Corner had been one ridden in silence.

Too spent after the day for their usual tug of war with the car door, Peggy leaned back, while Terry went straight for the kick. Even Ethel seemed to be smarting from the day's disappointments. The dented door creaked open with a groan.

As usual, Terry extended his hand to help Peggy. As usual, she demurred and helped herself out of the broken seat. In quiet contemplation, they walked to the entrance of the boarding house, their breath foggy in the damp night air.

"We didn't discuss the turn out today," Terry said, finally.

"I'm-I'm sorry it didn't..."

"No need to apologize. Christmas Eve tends to be hit or miss. The new malls have nicked business away from the local pet shops, too. Your ideas and your work were exemplary. You must know that."

Reaching the lobby doors, Peggy stared at her shoes, unsure how to answer his kindness.

"So...what are your plans?" Terry asked. "For tomorrow, I mean. Or don't you believe in Father Christmas, either?"

"Do you?"

"Jury's still out, but I hang a stocking, just in case. Family?"

Peggy averted her eyes. "N-no."

"Ah. Well then...why don't you come in, tomorrow? Keep the dogs and I company? That is, if you don't have other plans."

"But, what about you-your family? Oh, I mean, I'm sorry!"

"It's all right! I know what you meant. Snow, ice and air travel don't sit all that well with my sister, or myself, for that matter. I made the trek last year and ended up stranded along with half the country at O'Hare for the better part of a week. Not my idea of Ho, ho, ho. And with her being an emergency RN, holidays tend to be overtime shifts for her, anyway. I take holiday there every Memorial Day, and we celebrate a year's worth then! Christmas Day is merely another day to me...with one exception. It's the one day of the year that the fort is blessedly quiet! No phones, no crises, no Joe yelling at the dogs to 'shaddap'. Sheer heaven!"

Peggy laughed, lightly. "What time?"

"Splendid! Seven-thirty, all right? Let me fetch you. Buses tend to be hit or miss on Christmas, too."

"Thank you."

"'Til tomorrow, then."

Peggy paused in the doorway to watch Terry and the Pinto disappear down the street. She pulled a bag of dog treats from her pocket, wrapped in red ribbon. She wished now, that she'd given them to Lucky when she'd had the chance. Gazing out over all the Christmas lights blinking down the street, she was suddenly glad that she didn't have to spend Christmas day alone, crying about Lucky and things she could not change.

 Chapter 22

"Nooooo!"

With a scream, Peggy woke and bumped her head smartly on something hard above her. She groped around, disoriented, until she realized that she was underneath a bed. Trembling, she peered out from under her hiding place.

With all of the lights still on, she could see that there was no one else within striking distance. It took a few moments for her to recognize she was in her own apartment.

She lay back on the hard floor, catching her breath. Finally, she crawled out from under the bed. The first thing she saw was her ghostly reflection in the window, and she gasped. Snatches of memory assaulted her. Lucky. Harrison. She'd done nothing to stop that horrible man!

Coward!

I'm sorry! I'm sorry! Peggy folded up like a fetus on the floor. Hot tears burned the back of her throat.

Be quiet! Or you'll get something to cry about!

She roughly wiped her wet face, reached up and yanked the window shade down, obliterating her reflection.

Frosty the Snow Man crackled over the radio. The candy-sweet music sounded almost perverse to Peggy, especially in contrast to the files of animal abuse that she'd been leafing through, all morning. Inwardly, she recoiled at the grisly photos, and yet she couldn't look away.

Hunched over a mountain of paperwork, Terry had been preoccupied for most of the day. Christmas had unfolded at the shelter just as he'd said it would, uneventful, quiet. Despite the foggy rain and the threat of snow, Beula, the boiler, kept the radiators hot and clanking. Treated to biscuits, the dogs dozed the day away. The cats had played themselves out with the hand-sewn catnip mice Clara had left for them and were slumbering cozily.

Peggy's Christmas Eve slumber had been anything but cozy, and when Terry picked her up that morning, she'd kept her bloodshot eyes averted. She was sure he'd noticed, but being the gentleman he was, he never said a word about it.

Without the constant interruptions of a typical shelter day, he and Peggy completed the day's chores in record time. Keeping busy, they'd managed to skirt around the topic of Lucky all day.

Pouring over SPCA manuals and casebooks, Peggy searched for anything in the files that could be used against Lucky's owner. She surmised that the warden would have cited the man already, if there had been a way to do so. Still, burying herself in study seemed to be the only antidote against the haunting look in the dog's eyes as he was taken away.

Terry leaned back in his chair with a prolonged yawn and startled her out of her reverie. She'd almost forgotten he was there. He switched on the hot plate under the kettle and swiveled around to her.

"How about a nice cup of cocoa?"

"Thank you, yes."

Stretching to his feet, he leaned against the window and looked out at the rain. Peggy felt a tug on her heart, when she saw that faraway look on his face, again. She didn't want to disturb him, and yet, what if he was sad, thinking about his dead wife?

"Mr. Brannan? What is the worst penalty f-for abuse?"

He seemed surprised at the question and peered over her shoulder to the book in her hands.

"Oh dear! Not exactly merry reading, there. Are you sure you want to fill your head with all this? Might give you nightmares."

"It's all right. I'm used to that."

He faced her. "Oh...well, then. By the by...that will be the last of 'Mr. Brannan.' It's Terry, all right?"

Peggy shyly averted her eyes. "Yes."

"The worst penalty, you say...hmn." He tore open two packets of cocoa. "Funny you should mention that. Well, not funny ha-ha, but you know. The Senate's just begun an overhaul of New Jersey's criminal code. After four years debate, it's about time! We've been lobbying to include animal cruelty in their revamp, but currently? The penalty depends on a number of criteria: most notably, the evidence and history of the case, and how well or poorly it's been investigated by what few, if any, trained agents an SPCA chapter might employ. It also depends on how a judge interprets one-hundred-year-old statutes that are woefully outdated."

Biting her lip, Peggy frowned. It didn't sound good.

"It's a bit of a political football, and a right mess," he continued. "When the Society for the Prevention of Cruelty to Animals was first conceived, the founders did not foresee how overburdened their system would become, as the states, and their animal populations, grew. The New Jersey State SPCA acknowledges about a dozen, autonomous county SPCA chapters, but has no say in how they run their outfits. It's rather complicated. Some of them are run by law-enforcement officers, some by volunteers, but between the red tape and ferociously differing opinions as to what constitutes animal cruelty and animal rights, you have a recipe for a holy war. Then, you have people, some in very high positions, who still classify animals as property! These charming folks view any penalty, no matter how unconscionably slight, as an attack on individual rights. We have no SPCA chapter in Essex County, so individual towns either contract their local police or volunteer pound. As Farroway's pound, or shelter, as we prefer to be known, we have authority to investigate cases. With sufficient evidence, we can and do approach the court. The penalties vary. Depending on the offense, we can issue fines anywhere from five dollars to two hundred and fifty dollars."

Peggy gaped at him. "Th-that's all?"

"In rare instances, there is jail time, but it's generally commuted to probation or community service. Even when malicious intent is proven, most offenses are considered a misdemeanor in the eyes of the law."

"But-but that's..." Peggy slumped in her chair, at a loss for words.

"Mmn-hmn."

As he poured hot water into their mugs, she noticed his eyes sweep over Lucky's file, laying open in front of her.

He sat down. "You'd like to nail Harrison to the cross, wouldn't you?"

"Don't you?"

He stirred the cocoa. "As I see it, our first responsibility is to help the animal. If, with information and dialogue, we're unable to effect a positive change in the animal's situation, then it's our duty to turn to the legal system, such as it is, for assistance. The real question is; does it do any good to put someone in jail? Does it really help? I'm not so sure. Then again, for some people, the issue of cruelty and abuse is very much cut and dried, and perhaps a bit more personal?"

Peggy was keenly aware of his scrutiny, and she felt her throat close up.

"One marshmallow or two?" he asked, pleasantly.

"Just one," she whispered. "Thank you."

He dropped a marshmallow into her mug and handed it to her. She sat back, cradling it with both hands, quiet.

"Penny for your thought."

"I-I just think it's wrong," she said, "that people do these things and get away with it."

"When it comes to the law, the issues can be complex. For example, it was only two months ago that the laws protecting children in abuse cases were given another look-see, here in New Jersey. In ninety more days, a few more children might actually find sanctuary from what has otherwise been a quagmire of ineffective laws, all but handcuffing social workers." Taking a sip of hot chocolate, he shrugged. "In light of that comparison, there are those who ask, why should anyone be taking up the court's time about stray cats and dogs?"

Peggy put her mug down, a little too hard. "I don't think it's any different, how you treat animals and how you treat people."

"Couldn't agree with you more, but the issue in the court's eyes is not a philosophical one. The reality is that most cruelty cases get tossed out for lack of evidence, or a lack of willing witnesses who'll come forward to testify—never mind the legal loopholes the size of Rhode Island—as well as the expense of prosecuting a case. Here's another example. The law we're trying to amend in Farroway at the moment, is a warden's right to impound an animal for its own protection. It's a sticky wicket. Under Title four, Chapter Twenty-Two, if cruelty or neglect is apparent, that is to say if, in an officer's opinion, the animal's life is in immediate danger, or if the owner is not present, or if an owner is arrested, only then can the animal be taken. If any of those conditions is not met, currently, we cannot forcibly take the animal. Firstly, that's a lot of 'ifs'. Secondly, I'm not certain that impoundment is the answer, either. Best case scenario; we win, but the owner merely goes out and gets another animal. Back to square one. Nothing is solved. Never mind the fact that, for every Lucky we know, there are at least a hundred out there we never even hear about."

Peggy frowned. "Then, what's the answer?"

"Ah!" Terry brightened and snatched up a folder of papers, holding it up like a torch. "The answer is education! Information, with an eye towards prevention as opposed to punishment after the fact! If we can get out into the community and talk to people, real grass roots and such, I believe that's how we can effect real change."

Peggy perused the folder he handed to her and looked over a few papers.

"That is a grant application. A spin of the roulette wheel, as it were. I am quite serious about growing a new building here. May as well dream big! You know," he mused with a prodding smile, "the community programs would be a splendid project for you."

"What? Oh, no, no." Peggy practically shoved the folder back into his hands. "I couldn't do that."

"Why not?"

"Well it's just...I mean, after yesterday?"

"Yesterday doesn't count, only tomorrow."

"I-I can't do things like that..."

"Why not?"

Keep quiet!

Peggy squirmed in her chair and began to stutter. "Be-be-because-I-I-I-"

"What say, we take a breath? Breathe in. That's it. I didn't mean to pressure you. But I would appreciate you explaining to me why you're being so hard on yourself."

Peggy tried to take a deep breath, but a gush of bile kept welling up in her esophagus, threatening to erupt out of her mouth. "It's just, what you want takes a-a kind person..."

"You're not a kind person?"

"No, I-I meant, I mean, it takes a k-k-kind of person. I'm-I'm not that kind of person."

"Ah, and what kind of person is that?"

"I-I don't know, just not...I can't-I can't talk to people like-like Betty or..."

"Like Betty? Well, I should hope not, good heavens!"

"Or you! Y-you talk to people as if you care."

She hadn't meant the words to shoot out quite as sharply as they had. She stiffened with remorse. "I-I didn't mean that the way, the way it..."

Liar!

"I'm sorry."

"It's all right," he replied. "I know what you meant. However, public speaking and its arguably practiced diplomacy aside, I don't expect, nor want, you to be like Betty, Joe, Clara, me, or anyone else, for that matter. We each bring to this job qualities peculiar to who we are, and that includes you. Whether you want to admit it or not, you have certain traits and skills that are unique to you and..."

Peggy shifted in her seat, trying to relieve the terrible cramping in her stomach, closing the notebooks as if the recess bell was ten minutes late in ringing.

"And you're always so quick to run away," he added, taking a sip of his cocoa. "I can't help but wonder why?"

Peggy cast her eyes away, her heart racing.

Careful!

"You know what I think?" he prodded.

There followed such a long pause that she felt compelled to look up at him.

"I think you wish you didn't care as much as you do, because it means you can't ignore things as easily as others do. It's scary to feel that much, isn't it?"

Peggy felt as if she were under a glaring white-hot light. She was afraid to move, afraid to breathe, lest her eyes spill over and betray her.

"I really do believe we can change things, Peggy. One little corner at a time. I say that not only because I believe it, but because I know it to be true. You don't reach my age and not learn a thing or two. Wait, I take that back, I've been to AARP meetings. I daresay there are a few members who make those of us over a certain age look like blithering idiots. But, I digress. What I'm getting at, is...I very much believe in what we're doing, here, and...I believe in you. I'll tell you something else. Whether you believe me or not, it's that very quality you work so hard to hide, that makes you exactly the right kind of person for the job. So there! You're stuck with it. How do you like those apples?"

While the wind rattled the windows, Terry's words rattled her heart. At last, the roiling inside her gut quieted, and she risked a peek up at him. His eyes were gentle and kind.

With effort, she swallowed the lump in her throat. "I'm-I'm sorry."

"For what?"

She shrugged.

"Well, I'm not!" Terry replied, an impish smile playing on his lips. "Truce?"

She nodded eagerly. "Truce."

He looked up at the clock. "Let's call it a day?"

Feeling both relieved and yet oddly unsettled, Peggy packed up her notes and pulled on her coat. When she turned around, Terry held out a small package wrapped in shiny paper and tied with a satin bow.

"Merry Christmas."

Peggy blinked at it in surprise. "But I...I don't have anything for—"

"Not allowed to bribe the boss." He smiled and rocked back on his heels. "Aren't you going to open it?"

Peggy took the box, and gingerly peeled off the wrapping. She lifted the lid and pulled out a silver pendant.

"That's Saint Francis," Terry said. "Saint Francis is the Patron Saint of Animals. You two have a lot in common."

Peggy stared at it, feeling an ache in her heart. So, he had heard all the teasing the crew had dished out, all along!

"Allow me?" He lifted the necklace from her fingers and carefully clasped it around her neck.

She glanced up at him and their eyes met, caught fast by a moment of profound warmth. Gazing into his eyes, Peggy suddenly felt her cheeks flush.

Terry took a faltering step back. "Well...Merry Christmas."

Peggy backed up, too. "M-merry...th-thank you."

Terry searched for his keys across the counter. Peggy cleared her throat and pointed to his hand. He'd been holding them all the time. With an awkward chuckle, he reached to open the office door and the door knob popped off in his hand. He glanced at her.

"It's in your other pocket," she prompted, raising her eyebrows ever so slightly.

He dug into his jacket pocket and pulled out his recorder. "Fix the office door knob," he mumbled into it. "By New Year's, I promise," he assured her. "But just in case, remind me."

"Okay," she laughed.

He reached to shut off the radio.

"Would-would it be all right to leave the radio on for them? They say it helps."

Terry glanced around at the cats and dogs. "They do?"

She stifled a giggle. "I read it in an article in *Dog Days*. They said music...it helps."

"Helps me, too. Good thinking!" He shut the lights out, and then gestured her out the door. "After you."

They strolled through the kennel, checking on the dogs, one last time. He opened the front door, and they both paused on the threshold, looking out at falling snow. The parking lot was already dusted.

"Looks like a white Christmas, after all. Perhaps it bodes well for a happy New Year, too! At the very least, it has to be better than last year, eh?"

Peggy nodded. "Indeed."

Terry grinned, shut off the lights and closed the door behind them.

Thirty seconds later, the great steel door opened again, and Peggy ran back into the office. Gathering up her study folder of notes, she caught sight of her reflection in the window. She looked different, some-how. Maybe, it was the smile on her face. Bing Crosby sang *Silent Night* on the radio, as she touched the St. Francis pendant around her neck.

"Merry Christmas," she whispered to the cats and dogs, before hur-rying out into the snow.

Chapter 23

"Happy friggin' New Year."

The icy wind stung Joe's face, as he kicked the browned Christmas tree free from the fencing. It fell with a crunch of frozen, splintering pine needles, and the dogs promptly peed on it through the fencing. "Jeeze, you killed it already, okay?"

Inside the shelter, everyone bundled about in new scarves and coats, blowing on their hands to keep warm.

"'Scuse me?" Betty snapped into the phone, "No! Givin' us ten puppies from yo'unspayed bitch ain't, I ree-peat, *ain't* no donation!"

"Half-baked boobies," scoffed Clara, tugging on her new silver wig.

In the midst of sorting files, Peggy heard the familiar sputter of the Pinto pulling into the lot, and she looked out the window with a smile. She reached for her pendant and gave it a little rub. In a hurry to finish, she picked up one last file and paused. It was Lucky's. She felt a stab at her heart, but steeling herself, she laid the folder into a box labeled Closed Files. She shoved the box under the counter.

The dogs in the kennel barked, and soon Terry bustled in, setting a Have-A-Hart trap onto the counter. "Happy New Year, folks!"

"Oh, pound it 'til it's putty, ye pasty-faced putz! Me cats're turnin' to popsickles!" Clara growled.

Half out of his parka, Terry felt the chill in the air. "Not again."

"Must have gone out last night," Peggy told him. "Betty has a call in to Mr. Riley."

"Be cheaper to call a preacher," Clara shot back. "And just what are we to do with Miss Nasty there?"

Peggy peered over Clara's shoulder at the oppossum in the trap.

"Not to worry, she's not staying," Terry scanned the log book.

"The park?" Peggy prompted.

"Well, I recognize this little lady. See the notch out of her ear there? Third time trapped under the same house, and what with the owner mentioning rat poison as an easier solution, I thought I might play Jehovah and give her a fighting chance in a more marsupial-friendly zone. It's South Mountain Reservation for her, this time."

Peggy peered closer, and the opossum hissed at her.

"Careful," Terry warned her. "Their teeth are razor sharp, and they've no patience for the likes of us. Which reminds me, we need to have you vaxxed."

"Vaxxed?"

"Rabies vaccination. It's an occupational hazard, dealing with wildlife. Not so much this little lady here, and honestly, outside of a few bat removal calls, there hasn't been a documented domestic rabies case in this state since—well, I can't remember. At least two decades. But, health department recommendations aside, a pre-exposure, preventative vaccination is a good idea as opposed to the God-awful, post-exposure series that you might have heard about—the fourteen shots in the stomach?"

Peggy's eyes widened and she gulped.

"Not to worry!" he chuckled, "The vaccination is a mere three injections, in alternating shoulders, three weeks apart. Very simple and painless." He flipped open a well-worn address book and scribbled on a napkin. "Call up Doc Sanford at the hospital. He handles all of the regulatory nonsense for us. Make an appointment, bring your information: social, etceteras, and he'll set up the vax series for you."

"But, I-I'll be okay. I'll be careful."

"Trust me, no one's more of a chicken than I am when it comes to hospitals and doctors. You've no idea. But, it's a piece of cake, honest injun. Ask Joe. You know what a baby he is. Never even blinked an eye! Bragged about it for weeks. You'll see. Besides, come spring, if I know you, you're going to want to handle all the baby wildlife coming in, and unless you're vaxxed, I wouldn't be able to let you."

Peggy finally took the napkin of instructions from him.

"Oh, by the by," he asked, "did you ever fill out the W-two form and—"

"Um...yes," Peggy folded the paper into her pocket. "I think Betty sent them in to—"

Betty raised her voice to the caller. "You sayin' you come home and found them ten puppies wiff you unspayed bitch, and you axin' *me* how they got there? Don't you sass me, honey! I be one coal-serious mamma jamma! Oh yeah? You come on ovah! I be more n' happy set yo' sorry butt straight!" She slammed down the phone and sneezed three times in a row.

"Ah yes," Terry commiserated. "Another backyard breeder learns the birds and the bees from his dog?"

"I axe you, do it take a rocket scientist?!"

Joe kicked open the door, whacking pine needles off of his pants.

"'Ere comes their poster boy," Clara remarked, "let's ask 'im."

"What?" Joe eyed her. "Don't start, Brunhilda, I'm just lookin' for trouble."

"You and what army, droopy drawers?"

Joe displayed a fist to the old woman, who brusquely flipped him the finger. "Did you see that? Did you see that?" he demanded of Terry.

"Mmn-hmn." Terry searched through his papers. "Where the devil is that file for the wildlife? I just had it."

Peggy handed him a file folder.

"Ah!" he exclaimed. "There we are! Where did you find it?"

"Under W, in the file box?"

"Oh, you mean where it belongs? Point taken. It's simply that I think of a filing cabinet as one more place to lose things, alphabetically." He released the trapped opposum into a cage with a bowl of cat food. "Joe, on your way home, take this little lady up to South Mountain, will you? Close enough to the trash bins at the back of the zoo where she'll have a week's worth of pickings until she gets her footing."

"Uh, ain't that like, against our policy, and the zoo's?"

"A one-time mercy mission. Unless you want to trek down to the Barrens, tonight? In the sleet?"

"Just askin'."

"All right, folks. Gather 'round. Oh, happy nineteen seventy-five, by the way. May it be better than—"

"The last four sodding years?" Clara quipped.

"Ter, it's too late," Joe said. "They made Rocker-feller vice prez. We been hosed."

"Well, at any rate, we have a guest due in today. Our EVC intern… *excuse me*, he's not an intern…" Terry pulled a few napkins from his pockets, reading them. "He's a full-fledged vet and then some. Here we are. Yes, his name is Paul Hayward. *Doctor* Hayward, kapish?"

"Yeah, yeah. What time's the prodigal son showin'?"

"Noonish. So let's have the place spic and span, shall we?"

Peggy glanced at the clock. It was nine-thirty, and due to the holiday catch-up, they were running at least an hour behind with the chores. Not that she was terribly worried; she had become familiar enough with the routine to handle the opening chores herself, with the help of the warden's many cheat sheets tacked up on the walls.

"Now, I think it's fair to say," Terry continued, "that he's going to feel a bit out of his element."

"Odds are with th'ouse on this one," Clara announced, slapping a dollar on the counter.

"So, I want you folks to make him welcome."

"We'll give him a twenty-one gun salute," Joe saluted, then pulled a brand new water pistol from his holster.

"Joe!" Terry snatched it out of his hand. "If I've told you once, I've told you thrice, *no* firearms, plastic or otherwise."

"C'mon, Ter, that's a Christmas present!"

Terry squirted him with it.

"Hey! No fair! I'm unarmed!"

"I will personally break your arm if I catch you with another one, again."

"What good is this badge if we can't back it up with some muscle?"

"Try the muscle between your ears." Terry tossed the water pistol in a drawer and turned for the door.

Betty cupped a hand over the phone. "Just where you think you goin'?"

"Call from the Mayor. I'll be back long before—"

"The Mayor? Did Harrison squeal on us?" asked Joe.

Peggy's stomach lurched. It was the first mention of the man since Christmas Eve. Even Clara looked around, her face creased with concern.

The warden shook his head. "Mr. Harrison is running for city council. I promise you, the last thing he wants is an issue with us, or any scandal for that matter. The Mayor has squirrels in his attic, that's all."

"And bats in his belfry if he think we kin survive on peanuts! How we gonna make next month's rent?" Betty demanded.

"We could always put her out on the corner," Joe gestured to Clara.

Whap! Betty smacked him over the head with a rolled up newspaper. "Ow!"

"I'll sort it out," Terry said, and headed out the door. "No rough-housing, please."

"You wearin' yo' watch?" Betty asked narrowly.

"I'll be back in plenty of time. Promise. Hold the fort!"

At the sound of the front door closing and the valiant chug-chug sputter of the Pinto's engine, Peggy felt a familiar flip-flop in her gut. She peered out the window and fidgeted with her St. Francis pendant, as she watched him drive away. Almost as an afterthought, she pulled out the folded paper from her pocket, and looked over Terry's scribbled instructions for the rabies vaccination. The napkin trembled in her hands.

Dr. Paul Hayward packed the remaining contents of his desk into a moving box. Dressed in a crisp, pale blue shirt and dark tie, he tossed his lab coat into the box. Hearing laughter, he peered out the glass porthole in the door and spotted Dr. Miller, holding court over the interns in what had been, until today, his domain. Miller laughed the loudest at his own story, the first year interns kissing up to him with applause.

Abruptly, Dr. Caldwell rounded the corner, nearly slamming into Paul with the door.

"There you are! All packed and ready to head out? Excellent!" Caldwell rummaged through a shelf and handed pamphlets to Paul. "Here's some info on the world you're about to enter; SPCA, HSUS, PETA, Green-peace—might come in handy. And, by the way, I know how ambitious you are, but I want you to think twice about over-extending yourself with graveyard duty here, while pulling full time hours at the shelter."

"I can handle it." Paul took the booklets, distracted once again with Miller's laughter erupting from the surgical suite.

"I know you can handle it, but the point is to immerse yourself into another discipline, add to your knowledge base, not drive yourself into... Paul?"

The young vet glanced around to his mentor. "Yes."

Dr. Caldwell gave him a long appraising look. "What you're going to learn down there . . . Paul I think you should know that I'm sending you because you *are* the best." He picked up his appointment book and walked out.

Paul looked after him a long moment, then tossed the pamphlets into the box without a second glance.

 Chapter 24

People streamed in and out of the shelter nonstop, despite the fierce wind and vicious cold. It was the shelter's busiest day on record. It should have been a cause to celebrate, but unfortunately, most of the people hadn't come to adopt animals, but to turn them in.

Run off their feet, Betty, Clara and Peggy juggled jangling phones and the influx of confused animals. Peggy glanced at the clock and peered out the window, her St. Francis pendant clutched in her fingers. It was four minutes until noon, and Terry was late.

"What you doin' there, Saint Francis?" Betty snapped. "We got phones ringin'!"

"Maybe w-we should call Mr. Brannan?"

"Who?"

"T-terry."

"How? Smoke signals?"

"On the…that CB thing…or a walkie talkie?"

Betty snatched a walkie-talkie out from under a pile of papers. "You mean this one he nevah bring wiff him?"

"Oh."

Betty spotted a fat little boy pulling a cat from a cage. "Hey! Do I come ovah yo' house and pick up yo' stuff wiffout axin'? NO!"

Clara took the cat from the boy. "Be off with ye, ankle-biter!"

The boy burst into tears. His mother pushed through the crowd and confronted Peggy. "What did you do to him?"

"N-nothing! He took a cat out w-without asking, and…"

"Where's the manager?" the woman called out over her.

Mr. Riley burst in through the office door. Covered with soot, he was hopping mad. "'Eya Girlie! How many times I tell ye? Why don't ye check 'er water?!"

"What? The boiler? Oh no, I-I can't! Th-that's Mr. Brannan's, I mean Terry's job."

Clara pushed Peggy aside. "Don't wag your wrench at her! Iffen you'd fixed that spiteful firebox right the first time, you bunglin' gaffer, it wouldn't've quit to begin with!"

"Why y'ungrateful old wench!" Mr. Riley turned purple, and then burst into rhyme.

> *"A cat in despondency sighed,*
> *and resolved to commit suicide,*
> *he got under the wheels*
> *of nine automobiles,*
> *and after the last one -*
> *he DIED!"*

Clara instantly spat out one of her own.

> *"There once was a geezer named Tucker,*
> *a semi-retired diesel trucker,*
> *he drank like a fish,*
> *chased women, the swish,*
> *a downright, regular ol' ffff-!"*

"I want the manager!" the mother of the boy shrieked.

"You there!" A burly man backed Peggy into the door, waving a summons at her. "What's with this effin' fine you left on my effin' porch, effin' Christmas eve?! My effin' dog was hit by a car, two effin' weeks ago!"

"Oh! I-I'm so sorry!"

"Hey!" Betty pushed between them. "You been warned upteen times 'bout yo' dog runnin' stray and attackin' the mailman! That dog was mean an' dangerous!"

"He's *dead*!"

"Whose fault *that* be?"

"May-maybe we should discount it?" Peggy squeaked. "He-he *is* dead."

The man ripped the summons to shreds and tossed the fluttering paper over them both. "Eff-you, dog catcher!" He yanked the door open and stomped out.

Betty pounced on the CB microphone. "Fo' thozza you on daylight savin' time, *Joe*, the clock on the wall say you be half-past *big* trouble!"

Peggy nearly tugged on her sleeve. "Is there any way he can call Terry?"

Parked outside of Jack's Chinese Take Out and Doughnut Shop, Joe popped a frosted, chocolate doughnut hole in his mouth. His boots propped up on the dash, he giggled over the Mad Magazine in his hands and sang along with the radio. "Sherry, Sheheherree-ee bayabeee." The CB crackled with static. He fiddled with the volume knob. "Sherry baaaaby..."

"...back here...half-past noon...you sorry butt cheeks!" Betty's voice broke up.

Joe checked his watch and spit crumbs. "Shoot!" He keyed the ignition and spun the wheel hard, fishtailing the van up the street.

"This does not bode well," Terry sighed to the caged squirrel on the seat beside him. He checked his watch, while the wind rocked the frigid little Pinto. Stuck in gridlock, he watched workmen sawing a tree that had fallen across the road. Tires squealed behind him. His eyes flicked up into the rear view mirror.

A sleek red, Series III, XKE Jaguar whipped around the corner, the driver apparently not expecting the wall of stopped traffic.

"Lord love a duck!" Terry braced for a rear-end impact.

Braking hard, the Jaguar sloshed gravel, ash and salt into the air, slid to the left and just missed the Pinto's bumper. Terry's heart was in his mouth. He rolled down the window just in time to get a blast of horn in his ear. The Jaguar zipped onto the road's shoulder and sped past the line of stopped cars, cutting off a Parks Department truck.

"I say there!" Terry called after it. Another horn blast and Terry ducked back inside the window, just as the shelter van jumped the curb and sliced off the Pinto's side mirror. It skidded around the bend, following in the Jaguar's tracks.

Terry stared after them for a second. In a snit of frustration, he gunned the Pinto's engine and pulled the wounded car out onto the shoulder, too. Instantly a siren wailed behind him. Terry spotted red and blue flashing lights in the rear view mirror, and a cop waving him to pull over.

"Bloody hell!" He thumped the steering wheel with his palm, and with a sigh, pulled over.

"I'm-I'm sorry, but you have to—you have to talk to the manager!" Peggy's voice broke, trying to out-shout the phones, clanging pipes, barking dogs and the impatient crowd. "He-he should be back any—"

"No, I can't wait! The pet shop won't take it back! I'm a tax-payer, so you have to take it!" The dark-skinned man shoved the large box into Peggy's arms and fled out the door.

"S-sir! You can't just…"

Peggy lifted a flap to peek in the box. Instantly, a Rhode Island Red rooster burst up and out in a shriek of flapping. People screamed and scattered. Peggy did, too. Dropping the box, she ducked under the counter. She heard horns honking and popped her head up to the window.

A red Jaguar and the shelter van barreled down the driveway. Each vied for the right of way, barely missed hitting the firehouse, the warehouse and each other. At the last moment, they both swerved, just missing old Mr. Riley stomping out of the gate. Behind the wheel of the Jaguar was Dr. Paul Hayward!

"Oh no!" Peggy lamented.

The rooster squawked, and with a squeal she grabbed the broom as it dive-bombed past her with a flutter of feathers.

Dr. Hayward yanked on the parking brake and jumped out of the Jaguar. "That was a red light back there, you moron!" he shouted at Joe, then slipped on the ice and landed on his backside.

At the gate, Mr. Riley slapped his knees, wheezing in toothless, helpless laughter.

Slipping and sliding back to his feet, Paul looked down on his muddied coat and ripped, Italian wool slacks. Snatching his medical bag from the car, he slammed the door closed and strode past them through the gate and up the walkway.

He shoved the front door open and, bombarded by the din of barking dogs all around him, fell back against muck-coated fencing. "Dammit!" He launched himself past the runs towards the office and yanked on the door. The doorknob popped off in his hand. "What the…"

He jammed the knob back into place, and then shouldered the door open. He stumbled across the threshold just as a huge rooster flew at him. It collided with him, and together they fell on the floor, wrestling to be free of each other. Feathers fluttered everywhere, and people stampeded over him, screaming.

Clara shielded a fat cat in her arms and shook her fist at him. "Keep that cock away from me pussy!"

Joe barreled through the front door and skidded to a stop before them all. "Aw Jeeze!"

"Don't just stand there!" Paul hollered. "*Do* something!"

Joe reached down and yanked him up by his collar and tossed him into the office, followed by the squawking bird. Slamming the office door, he chased the rooster into a cage.

Paul scrambled to his feet, spitting feathers. "Who's in charge here?"

"He-he'll be back any minute. He promised."

Paul whirled around to find Peggy, standing on a chair and wielding a broom. "Who promised what?"

"Terry...Mr. Brannan. He-he —"

Paul held up a hand. "Just point me to...oh great. Perfect." He examined his cracked watch face.

Peggy gulped. The young vet looked pretty miffed when he saw his watch was broken, and she noticed a tic spasm at the corner of his left eye.

"Which way to my office?" he sighed.

Peggy blinked at him. "Office? This-this is it."

His eyes widened. "This is my office? You can't be serious! It's...it's a pig sty!"

Peggy glanced between the stunned crew members. Were they just going to let him insult them—and Terry—like that? Peggy squared her shoulders. "Doctor, we-we may not look like much, but we-we've got what it takes. Wh-where it's counted. I mean, where it counts!"

"Oh? And where's that?"

His scathing look stripped her of her voice. Peggy looked to the others. Betty nudged Joe. His voice cracked like a teenage boy's.

"Uh...how 'bout a tour?"

"Oh, good. There's more." The vet held up a hand, again. "First, where's your lavatory?"

"The who?"

"The rest room!"

"Oh. The pyros leave their back door unlocked for us."

"Excuse me?"

"Well, see we don't got a john, so we use the firehouse."

Dr. Hayward glanced out the window and across the parking lot to the firehouse, where a number of the firemen still stood in the windows, sipping coffee.

"Don't worry," Clara grinned. "So far it's only a rumor 'bout the peep hole."

Joe sputtered out loud, but stifled it when the vet turned a sharp eye on them.

Peggy still stood on the chair, frozen in place. When his humorless gaze finally rested on her, a small schnauzer poked its head out from under her chair, and barked at him.

"What's that dog doing loose?" he demanded.

"S-sorry." Peggy climbed down and encouraged the dog out from its hiding place. She scooped it into her arms. "He's afraid of the dogs."

"He *is* a dog. And loose dogs in a public office...full of cats, I see, is also not in keeping with health department..." He blinked at Houdini, the ferret, twitching its whiskers at him from his cage. "Are you aware ferrets are now illegal to own as pets in this state?"

Joe snorted another laugh. "Why you think he's behind bars?"

Dr. Hayward leveled him with a dour look. Then, the rooster crowed. With a roll of his eyes, he tossed Joe the doorknob. "Let's start with the dogs."

Joe passed the knob off to Peggy and kicked the door open. He backed up to let the doctor pass him then whispered to the crew, "Jeeze!"

The phones began jangling again, but were ignored. The crew gathered around the door and watched the doctor disdainfully pick his way through the kennel room.

"Well, well, well," Betty sniffed. "Somebody got hisself a *tude!*"

"Prince o' peahens, if you please!" Clara agreed.

"What he think he gonna do, out there, wiffout Terry?"

"Nuke the whole house, what you wanna bet?" Joe hefted up his pants and headed into the kennel.

"Bah. Five'll get you ten 'e's gone in fifteen," Clara said, and laid a dollar on the counter.

Betty rummaged in her purse.

Peggy glared past them to the arrogant vet, already inspecting their dogs. Who did he think he was? She deftly inserted the wayward knob into place and led the schnauzer out into the kennel, closing the door behind her, hard.

Chapter 25

"This dog's been here since September?"

From her crouched position in the run, Peggy bristled at Dr. Hayward's tone as she brushed the little schnauzer in question. "Scooter is-is a sweet dog and—"

"It says here, and I quote; 'not cool with brats.' " He held the cage card out to her so she could read it.

"That-that doesn't mean—"

"I know what it means. I repeat; you're overcrowded."

"Well," Joe shrugged, "technically, yeah, but—"

"Then why is this dog still here? Technically."

"'Cause his number didn't come up. Well, it came up, but he sorta got pardoned on accounta the nuns."

"Pardon—what? What nuns?"

"See, we do a kinda lottery thingee."

"Lottery? What do nuns have to do with it?"

"They're the black hats behind all this, man! Maybe raffle is a better word?" He looked to Peggy, who shrugged.

For a split second the young vet looked baffled, and then his eyes hardened. "I hate to be the one to break it to you people, but this is a pound, not a swap meet! Now, I want a list of all the animals that have been here over seven days. You need at least ten euths in order to free up enough space before—"

Peggy rose to her feet. "You-you have to wait until Terry—I mean, Mr. Brannan—gets back. He's the manager. He makes the decisions here."

Dr. Hayward's lips drew back into a curt smile. "What's your name again?"

"Peggy Dillan. Assistant m-manager," she added with a lift of her chin.

The vet's smile never wavered. "I'm Dr. Hayward, VMD-PhD. VMD, as in Veterinary Medical Doctor. PhD, as in it's my job to make sure this pound complies with state health department regulations."

"This isn't-this isn't a pound!"

"Excuse me?"

"It's a shelter. Th-there's a difference!"

"According to which dictionary?"

Peggy's hands trembled with anger. "You have to wait for the warden. He-he runs things here, not the state and-and not *you*!" With that, she stalked past him right out the front door.

Slam!

The vet stared after her, but only for a second. Tossing Joe the cage card, he strode out the door right after her.

Slam!

The office door creaked open, and Betty and Clara peeked out.

Joe heaved a sigh. "This is gonna be a loooong winter."

Peggy wrestled the hose onto the frozen spigot in front of the runs, with shaking hands. In her dramatic exit she'd forgotten her coat, and the cold wind sliced through her baggy uniform. She heard the front door slam, but her hopes of the vet walking out, as in quitting, were quickly dashed.

"Excuse me," she heard him ask tersely, "Would you mind telling me what the problem is here?"

"Over-pop-population, poverty," she darted a frown at him. "Ignorance. Take your pick."

"I wasn't referring to this facility," he said, evenly.

Peggy wasn't the least bit cold anymore. Her face flushed hot in anger. Then, she heard the Pinto's choking sputter behind him, chugging down the driveway. Let's see you hold on to that smug smile now, you jerk! Terry's back!

Through the Pinto's grimy windshield, Terry spotted the young vet and Peggy toe to toe, glaring at each other. "Uh oh..."

The lot full, Terry had to park down in the gravel driveway. He shouldered his door open and waved. "Hello! So sorry I'm late! The traffic was a bear, you see and…" all at once he spied the red Jaguar… parked sideways in his space…the one clearly marked: Warden. "…and I was regrettably delayed."

The caged squirrel in one hand, he reached out his other to shake the vet's hand with enthusiasm. "So, I see you two have already broken bread, as it were." Their freeze-dried silence fairly shouted above the groaning wind. "Bit chilly, eh? Well, why don't we go inside where it's warmer, relatively speaking."

Peggy brushed past the vet and tossed the gate back smartly behind her.

Thwack!

Dr. Hayward caught it just before it could smack him in the groin. He followed after her and swung it shut hard behind him.

Clang!

Terry watched as both of them opened and slammed the front door in turn.

Bam! Wham! Even the dogs seemed taken aback.

The front door squeaked open, again, only this time it was Joe. He huffed and puffed down the walkway, hefting a large box. "You're late!" he hissed at Terry.

"Yes, my apology. I'm almost afraid to ask. What's in the box?"

"Tonight's supper if I can't get it in a friggin' pen!" Joe snapped.

Terry watched him skid down the gravel towards the cellar. Just as he disappeared under the overhang, Terry heard the muffled but distinct crow of a rooster. The dogs, who'd been watching Joe and his box with rapt interest, swiveled their collective heads toward Terry.

"Don't ask me, I only work here." He had to lift the front gate up to open it. Cyclone Hayward-Dillan had twisted it off of its hinges.

"…Due to failed negotiations, work has been abandoned on the British end of the Channel Tunnel with no indication of when, or if, it will resume. Meanwhile, the U.N. has proclaimed nineteen seventy-five as the start of 'Woman's Year'…"

Terry shut off the crackling radio and glanced over his shoulder. Dr. Hayward and Peggy stood on opposite ends of the room. The office being only six foot square, that still left the two of them within striking distance of each other.

"Well," he smiled. "Here we are. A brand new start to a brand new year."

Silence.

Terry picked up his daybook. "All right. Joe'll have to catch up later. Meantime, I wanted to bring you all up to speed, as it were, on where we stand fiscally. I dropped by Town Hall and well, it seems we're on our own. That's what it boils down to. The mayor's not inclined to sink any more funding into this particular part of town in the foreseeable future. Animal control is simply on back-burner status when schools are losing their lunch programs, so on and so forth. So. We're facing a bit of a challenge and it's up to us to sally our way through this...this..."

"Ree-cession?" Betty raised her brow.

"Depression!" Clara snarled.

"Rough patch," Terry suggested. "Now, I know what you all must be thinking. When are things going to improve? Well, I don't know. And I don't think anyone else does, either. But, what I do believe, is if the five of us put our heads together, we can and will figure out ways to turn lemons into lemonade and—oh excuse me, Doc, I meant the six of us."

The vet shrugged it off. "I'm not a factor for your long term."

"Ah, well, I dare say we can always use advice. Fresh perspective and all that! It would be much appreciated, so please, don't hold back."

"All right. I don't know about your previous help, but if I'm going to be any use at all here, I'm going to need a quiet, sterile place to work."

Clara sputtered a delighted laugh. "It'd take an atom bomb to sterilize anything five kilometers o' here, y'twit!"

Betty chuckled. Across the room, Peggy didn't try to suppress her own smirk.

"Uh, Doc?" Terry said. "I've an idea. Bit of a compromise, but it might be just the thing. Follow me?" The two men walked through the kennel and out the front door.

Surprised, Peggy looked out the window, along with Betty and Clara. They watched Terry lead Dr. Hayward down under the office overhang and towards the cellar. Peggy's smile faded. She felt her insides twist, and then liquefy, draining down into her shoes and right through the floor, leaving her without strength to stand.

"Atom bomb?" she heard Betty remark. "He gonna need somethin' bigger n' that, down there."

Chilled to the bone, Peggy sank down into her chair with a shudder.

Dr. Hayward followed the warden down a gravel driveway and had to duck under the building. They passed Joe, trudging past with an empty box, feathers fluttering behind him.

"I take it we were successful with...?" Terry prompted.

"Bird's lucky Thanksgivin's over."

"You're not considering adopting out a rooster?" Dr. Hayward said.

"No, no, no—" the warden began.

"It shouldn't be kept indoors, either—"

"Well, you see we—"

"—because the chances of it developing upper respiratory—"

"Precisely! How right you are!" Terry interrupted. "It's a real risk, isn't it? Especially this time of year. We don't usually see chickens until after Easter, do we Joe?"

"I'm tellin' ya, it's a bad sign," Joe said.

"Yes, well, swing by the Cider Mill, will you? See if they can use a breeder. Thank you, Joe!" He turned to the vet with a smile. "There's always someone who'll take in the odd cock."

Paul glanced at the warden. For a split second, he wasn't sure if the reference had been solely about the rooster.

The warden pushed on a yellow door. It wouldn't budge. He twisted the knob back and forth. "Sometimes it warps a bit." He leaned back and shouldered it. It creaked open. "We must fix that. After you. Mind your head!"

Paul ducked under a massive steam pipe and a swinging sign dangling at eye level. As he descended the narrow, wooden stairs into the musty cellar, his spirits sank with every step.

In a wooden pen beside the stairs, the rooster ruffled its feathers and eyed him with a warning cluck. Brushing cobwebs from his hair, Dr. Hayward ducked under rag-tied pipes and rotting beams, then looked down at the cracked slate flooring. Against the crumbling wall, a stained, claw-foot tub sat atop a chest of crooked, warped drawers.

"Needs a little paint, here and there," the warden blew dust off of the pipes, "but I always thought it would make a first rate infirmary. Plenty of light." He pointed to a sloping ramp and two, mini French-doors. Latched with only a hook and eye clasp, the wind whistled under a one-inch gap beneath them. "Believe it or not, it's actually warmer down here, thanks to Beula, our goddess of volcanic heating bills."

Paul took in the rusty brown boiler, gurgling in the corner, the floor underneath it stained greasy black with oil. "I'm told that's a firehouse out front?"

"Not to worry. Old Beula's safe, she's just not reliable."

"It looks like a depth charge." Paul tapped it with the toe of his boot and the floor grate fell off, clanging to the floor.

"Och! Watch it!" Mr. Riley's voice startled them both, as he creaked into view from behind the boiler, a wrench between his gums.

"Mr. Riley!" Terry greeted the old man. "Have you met our new vet, Dr. Hayward?"

"Aye sorr, dat I have. An' him proud as a white-washed pig, he was, 'til he met himself comin' n' goin'! How's yer bum, den, lad?" the old man wheezed with laughter and leaned on Terry's arm. "I tink y'might want t'ash yer walkway."

Dr. Hayward rolled his eyes.

"I'll do that," Terry grinned. "Thank you, Mr. Riley. How is our diva, then?"

"How nicely would ye be, if left dry fer thirsty, if ye don't mind me askin'? If I telled ye once, I telled ye a baker's dozen o'more, I have! Check 'er water!"

"As the good Lord is my witness, I promise."

"Whist! Don't be pesterin' HIM none 'bout it! I tink he's got more n' his fair share jest seein' d'place don't fall down 'round yer ears!"

"I'm sure he does. And if you'll be so good as to give our fair lady, Clara, a bit of a wide berth, this afternoon, we might prevent just such a calamity."

"Let's spake it fair, she has her a tongue dat can clip a hedge, she does!"

"I'll have a check for you at the end of day..." The warden said it as if it were a carrot on a stick.

"'Tis our cross to bear den," Mr. Riley acquiesced.

"Thank you, Mr. Riley."

The old handyman hoisted his tool box up the creaky stairs, dust wafting up around him with every step. The boiler clanked and groaned as if in unhappy response to the old man's departure.

"Doc?" Terry pointed out the water gauge. "I'm going to ask you to 'check 'er water' every morning, all right? If it's low, just fill it so that the level is up to this mark here?"

Paul peered at a skull and crossbones drawn in marker alongside the water gauge. He turned a baleful eye to Terry.

The warden smiled. "Any questions so far?"

"Just one. How much do you bribe the inspectors?"

"That implies anyone comes down here to inspect."

Paul peered into the rust-stained tub. "What was this place before? It obviously wasn't designed to be an animal facility."

"You...didn't hear the scuttlebutt from Doc Caldwell?"

"Scuttlebutt?"

"Ah...well, four years ago, animal control used to be two hired goons with an exhaust pipe, garbage bags and...I'm sure you can connect the dots. Until your mentor came along with a Polaroid and a few demands, that is. Placing his own career on the line, he squared off against Town Hall, and single-handedly forced an entire town to do the right—the humane thing. He won his case, saving the day, and the lives of count-less animals. Rather like him not to mention it. Bit of a hero, down here by the tracks."

Paul mulled that over, gazing around the dilapidated space.

The warden cleared his throat. "I know we may not look like much, Doc, but—"

"You've got what it takes where it counts? Yes, she told me. Your... assistant manager."

"Peggy? She said that?"

"Among other things. Look, Mr. Brannan, I can't promise you more than whatever it is I can do within these limitations. But, I'll do what I can while I'm here. Though it just might take an atom bomb..."

"Thank you, Doc. And it's Terry."

The young vet shook his hand. "Paul."

A buzzer startled them both. Terry hit a button over a dusty inter-com. "Yes?"

Betty's voice crackled over the speaker. "Better git up here. Both of you."

"On our way." Terry sighed to the vet, "When it rains, it pours, here." He headed up the stairs.

Half way up the creaky steps, Paul looked back at the space that was going to be his ball and chain for the next six months. Right then and there, he decided he'd maneuver it so that he'd be out in five. Whatever it took; extra nights plus weekends filling in at the EVC. He was not going to be trapped here longer than necessary.

As if reading his thoughts, Beula hissed steam. Paul hurried up the steps.

Bending against the wind, Terry trotted to the van, cross-parked at the gate. Joe and Peggy were both huddled over a stretcher. Hurrying past the barking dogs, he came to a stop, not quite prepared to see the battered form in Peggy's arms. It was Lucky.

Bleeding from lacerations shoulder to tail, the dog also looked thinner than before Christmas. He whimpered pitifully.

"*Jesus.*"

Peggy looked up at him, her eyes brimming with tears.

Dr. Hayward pushed between them all and dropped to his knees. He whipped a stethoscope from his lab coat pocket and listened to the dog's chest.

"Found him by the park," Joe told them. "If I didn't know better, I'd say he was on his way back here. Thought it was faster to come back, the doc bein' here an' all."

Terry clapped Joe lightly on the shoulder, and then knelt down beside Peggy. She looked like she wanted to scream. "I told you so!" was written all over her face. He untied the frayed rope from around Lucky's neck, and stuffed it in his pocket.

His triage finished, Paul stood up, looking from the cellar to the office, as if debating something.

"I can run him up to the EVC," Joe began.

The vet shook his head. "They'll charge you eighty dollars just for walking in the door. I can handle it. It's not as bad as it looks."

"How bad does it have to be?" Peggy croaked. When no answer was forthcoming, she gathered Lucky protectively in her arms and hefted him past the vet, towards the front door.

Joe glanced to Terry, and he nodded. The young man reached the gate before Peggy and opened it for her. He followed her inside.

"Until we can set up the cellar," Terry suggested to Paul, "it might be more sterile in the office. Your call."

Paul held up a hand and followed after Peggy, with Terry close behind.

Chapter 26

The wind rattled the windows. Paul wiped sweat out of his eyes with the back of his gloved hand and felt a twinge in his back. An office counter top was not only a far cry from a proper surgical table, it was a good two feet lower than even a young, healthy back ought to be bent over for more than a few minutes. He'd been stitching the dog for the better part of an arduous hour. With no suitably trained, technical assistance, he might as well have had one hand tied behind his back. Performing surgery in a pound was ridiculous enough. Sterility was no longer an issue, it was a joke. *It'll be a minor miracle if I don't pick up a staph infection,* he brooded. Above all, he wished the girl would quit staring at him.

"More light, please."

Peggy angled the flashlight closer over Lucky's shoulder.

"Abuse, man," she heard Joe whisper. He stood holding up a bottle of Lactated Ringers Solution, looking like a human IV stand. "It's a slam dunk, right?"

Only the clatter of the vet's surgical instruments in a stainless steel dog bowl broke the quiet. She glanced at the young vet's masked face. She couldn't tell if he'd heard Joe or not, but her skin prickled when he refrained from comment. How could he deny it now?

"So, we got him, right?" Joe whispered again. "We got him this time?"

She peered over Lucky's unconscious form to Terry. His brow furrowed, his eyes remained riveted on Dr. Hayward's scissors and their rhythmic clicking. She couldn't read him one way or the other behind his glasses. It was clear, though, that he was very concerned.

Betty approached and leaned close to his ear, whispering, "Call from Mrs. Cruikshank, again."

Terry nodded, but remained quiet.

Peggy clenched her jaw tightly, so as not to scream out loud.

After he tied off the last stitch, Dr. Hayward gingerly removed the IV from Lucky's foreleg. He straightened up slowly, and Peggy watched him

draw six cc's of penicillin into a syringe. He injected Lucky's thigh, then pulled a brown bottle from his medical bag, and filled another syringe.

"He's going to wake up fast. Be ready."

"Yes," Peggy said, and unfolded a clean blanket in her arms.

Dr. Hayward slipped the needle into the dog's vein, untied the rubber tubing from around his elbow and depressed the plunger on the syringe. In about three seconds, Lucky's body flinched, and his eyes fluttered open. Groggily, he lifted his head.

"Okay," Dr. Hayward nodded to Peggy.

She wrapped Lucky in the blanket and gently stroked his ears. "Good boy." He blinked at her, sleepily and thumped his tail.

"Wow. That's mondo cool," Joe said. "Never saw that stuff in action, before."

"He'll sleep it off, tonight," the vet said. "You can offer him some tepid water in about two hours. Hold off on food until morning."

"First rate work, Paul," Terry said, removing his glasses.

"So we got him, right? Right?" Joe reiterated.

Peggy waited for the vet to answer. He peeled off his surgical gloves, dropped them into the trashcan, and then he turned around.

"I can't say beyond a reasonable doubt that it's abuse. The dog's been running stray and—"

"Aw, c'mon," Joe piped up. "Ya gotta be kiddin' me! Ya gotta be!"

"It's a serious charge and—"

"And that's a serious cop out!"

"Joe," Terry interjected quickly. He turned to the vet. "Thank you, Paul. We appreciate what you've done. These cases are—"

"A waste of time!" exclaimed Joe. "What's the point, huh? What's the mother freakin' point of anything?!" He flung his summons book to the floor and stormed out.

Terry followed after him.

"Great," Dr. Hayward muttered, then reached for Lucky, but Peggy stepped in between them. She gently hefted the dog into her arms and turned her back on the vet. Despite the struggle with the dog's limp weight, she kneeled down and eased him under the counter, onto a blanket beside the radiator. When she stood up, she found the vet standing in front of the door, his arms folded across his chest.

"We need to talk," he said.

"Joe, we're going to do what we can, you know that. We always do."

Pacing outside the front gate, Joe fisted tears off of his face. "It's bogus, man and you know it!"

"Joe…"

"We're nuthin' but friggin' dog catchers, and pretendin' we can do jack is nuthin' but pie in the sky!"

"No, it isn't."

"B.S.!"

"Joe, listen to me. Joe?"

"*What?*"

Terry waited until a passing police siren faded away in the gusting wind. "Joe, you know better than anyone what we face here, every day. And every day, you stick it out. Because you, more than anyone else, know why we do." He reached out and rested a hand on the young officer's shoulder. "Kierney's in an hour. Order a pie and a pitcher. All right?"

Joe wiped at his nose with his sleeve. "I hate this place."

"I know."

He strutted away to the van, hefting up his pants. Climbing in, he turned the engine over and steered up the driveway to the street.

Terry watched him turn the corner. He was just about to head back to the office, when a ringing bicycle bell jerked his attention back to the driveway.

A bicycle messenger coasted down to the gate, his cheeks rosy and wind-chapped, and his nose running from the cold. Puffing, he pulled three large manila envelopes from his knapsack.

"Special delivery for a Dr. Hayward? X-rays from the EVC."

"Oh yes, thank you." Terry signed for them and handed the messenger fifty cents.

"Thanks, man."

"Watch yourself on the hill. Wind's picking up."

"Yup."

Reentering the office, Terry was not entirely surprised to be walking into another argument between his new assistant and the new vet.

"…two plus two does not equal five, here!" Paul addressed Peggy's back, following her, as she cleaned up after the surgery. "And not to beat a dead horse, since this case is circumstantial at best—"

"Circum-circumstantial?! So much for an expert opinion!" Peggy brushed past him and stalked out into the kennel, flinging the door closed behind her.

Slam!

Paul barely glanced at Terry as he passed him, following right after her.

Slam!

The door knob dropped to the floor, rolling to rest at Terry's feet.

"Gonna need new hinges, they don't quit that," Betty remarked.

"Pffft. Gonna need a new door!" Clara said.

Terry picked up the doorknob. "Mmn-hmn."

Peggy twisted the sink taps on full blast to drown out the vet's voice. What was taking Terry so long to intervene and save the day? Surely, he wasn't going to let this jerk keep hounding her. Not when the jerk was so obviously wrong!

Paul stepped in front of her. "Are you this rude to everyone, or is it just me? Excuse me, I'm talking to you!"

"At me, you mean!"

"Pardon?"

"That-that white coat doesn't give you license to-to bully people!"

"Bully?"

"You think you can just-just waltz in here and-and…"

"Waltz? Whoa! Whoa! Can we please stay on the subject?"

"Which one?"

"That dog!"

"That dog's name is Lucky, and he's lucky he's not dead! He was beat-beaten within an inch of his life!"

"I can't prove that, and neither can you!"

"I don't have to! It's obvious!"

"Really?! Funny how I missed it, I only happen to be—"

"Suma cum *rude*, right! But you won't do anything about this because you-you'd have to stick your neck out."

"Hey, I'm not going to lose my license here, just so you can prove a point about something you don't know anything about!"

"So, look the other way! What do you care? In six months you won't even be here! You won't have to listen to them cry at night! You'll b-be long gone, charging people eighty dollars just to walk in your door!" Her voice cracked, and she slumped against the sink, having run out of steam. She rubbed her eyes with a shaking wrist.

"Aren't you being just a little emotional about this?" he suggested.

Peggy glared at him. "As much as you are heartless, you jerk." With that, she stalked back to the office, yanking hard on the door. It popped open, revealing Terry crouched on his knees with a screwdriver in hand.

Peggy glared at him, too, then strode past him into the office and resumed cleaning up, opening and slamming drawers. She heard the vet's boots traverse the kennel room and come up behind her.

"I don't know what your problem is," he said, cornering her. "Frankly I don't care, but let's get something straight. Number one, I am not here to right the big bad world out there. Number two; I don't care what you think of me. But, since we're stuck here together for the next six months—five if I play my cards right—the least you can do is extend to me the same courtesy you do the damn dogs!" He snatched up his medical bag and walked out.

Slam!

Terry caught the doorknob before it hit the floor.

Shaking with anger, Peggy ducked down under the counter to sit with Lucky. He licked her hand, but she had a hard time swallowing the lump in her throat. The office was strangely quiet for a few minutes, and then she heard Clara move to the coat rack, and shuffle to the door.

"Another day, another dollar."

"Betty," she heard the warden's voice speak low. "Lock up downstairs if...oh, and, if he's still...would you give him these, please?"

"You won't forget Mrs. Cruikshank?"

"Right. Thank you."

The office door squeaked open and then shut. Wiping her cheek with her sleeve, Peggy looked up from under the counter.

Terry set the kettle on the hot plate and ripped open two packets of cocoa, dumping them into two mugs. He peeked down at her.

"One marshmallow or two?"

Paul pounded on the warped window frame over the rooster's pen. He smacked the joist one last time and bruised his palm. "Dammit!" Quickly, he examined both of his hands. They were shaking.

"Forcin' it only make it worse."

Startled, Paul looked up the darkened cellar stairs. Descending down into the light, Betty handed him the x-ray envelopes. "EVC say you axed for these."

"Yes." Paul opened the envelopes and held each film up to the light. Still hot under the collar, it took him a few seconds to really see them. "Exactly what I thought. You've been on this case for two years. Two years. And there's not been one broken bone."

"Not yet." Betty sat on the stairs and opened a pack of candy cigarettes. "Just 'cause you don't find the match, don't mean the fire ain't been set."

Paul shot her a look and flicked the films up to the light, again.

"Need anythin' else?" she asked.

"Yes. I need it to be six months from now. Correction, five."

"I be wagerin' three."

He glanced at her, not sure if it was a smile he saw in her eyes, or a dare. Tossing the envelopes aside, he returned to wrestle with the window, smacking it again. "Does anything work around here?"

Betty squeezed between the vet and the wall, and pressed gently against two points on either side of the window with her palms. With a gentle push, weight chains rattled and the window slid up easily. Paul eyed her.

She shrugged. "Like I say, maybe you push it too hard."

"All right, I'll bite. How would you have handled it, up there, if she'd talked to you like that?"

"Don't nobody talk to me like that!"

Paul massaged his hand. "Well, there's sure no talking to her!"

"As God is my secret judge, when you get down to it, ain't no talkin' to nobody."

"How does Brannan put up with such anthropomorphic histrionics?"

"If you mean what I think all them syllables mean, well...she be different wiff Terry. She be like one them mutts, up there. They come in and you can only wondah where they been." She offered the pack of cigarettes to him.

He shook his head. "I don't smoke."

"You will."

Paul leaned against the window and closed his eyes, taking a few more deep breaths of cold, sobering air. It was quiet for such a while, that he looked over his shoulder.

Betty was gone, but she'd left the pack of cigarettes on the stairs. It wasn't until Paul picked them up that he discovered they were candy. Smiling wryly, he tossed them beside the x-rays on the counter. The rooster crowed loudly, sending him a foot in the air with fright.

"Christ!" His heart thudding in his chest, he made a grab for the pack of candy cigarettes.

Chapter 27

"*Why* can't we impound him? He's been abused! You know it!"

Peggy paced back and forth, unable to sheath the accusatory tone in her voice.

"What we know and what we *know* are two different things," Terry reminded her. "Without proof, we've no ground to stand on. We have to abide by and work with the rules of the system. One corner at a time, remember?"

That was the last thing Peggy wanted to hear. She turned her back on him and covered Lucky with her own coat. He thumped his tail and snuggled deeper into his blanket. "The stupid system doesn't work. You said so yourself!"

With the toe of his boot, Terry eased a chair closer to her. Heaving a sigh, Peggy sat down, but she wouldn't look at him. She began counting the tick tocks of the clock on the wall.

Terry regarded her a good long moment. They'd been working side-by-side since Christmas, neither one speaking about what had sparked between them, and had remained unspoken, since that night. It had been a difficult act for him to balance. He pushed every thought of her out of his mind every time she entered it, pretending that the moment had never happened at all. Whatever she might have been thinking about it, he could only guess.

She sat before him now, her hands clenched so tightly in her lap, her knuckles were white. His heart went out to her. Despite her near crippling insecurities, she was the one member of his crew he could count on to see past her own nose in a given situation. Betty might be brutally honest, but she wasn't willing to embrace the flip side of a coin. Joe didn't want to see the flip side. And Clara...well, Clara didn't care about the flip side. Peggy was different. Not so easy to finesse, or pin down. She was like a mystery book. One he would have liked to linger over, but one he was ultimately, afraid to open. Not so much for fear of what he might find between the pages, but rather, of what he might want to find of himself between the lines—with her. How could he help her to see the complex situation before them presently, without dashing her hopes completely, for future change?

"Let me ask you something. If God himself were to walk in here right now, what would you suggest he do in this situation?"

"If-if this is the best that God can do, then he ought to be fired!"

Terry waited patiently. He knew that in another moment, having vented her frustration, she'd consider the question, again.

Peggy shifted in her seat. She knew what Terry wanted to hear. He never asked her anything for which he didn't already have the answer. Up until tonight, she had always come around to his point of view. Not to please him. She really could see the validity to any one of his arguments. This time, however, was different. This time she knew that he knew, she was right.

She took a breath. "I'd expect him to do the right thing, no matter what."

"Peggy, I wish things were different, I really do. More than you know. If it were up to me, so help me I'd…" he took a breath. "However, we represent the law and we must work within the boundaries of that law. Dr. Hayward has to play by the same rules, by the way. He's not the enemy."

Peggy shook her head, wrestling with a burning lump in her throat. It was a long time before the warden spoke again. When he did, he sounded tired and sad.

"I know how easy it is to get caught up over a case. When I first started here, every day was a new fight, a battle to be won, between what was right and what was clearly wrong. In the middle were all of these animals, and if we lost even one of them, it was as if we'd failed somehow, as if I'd failed. However, it wasn't long before I discovered that, no matter how hard I worked…" he hunched over his knees. "I fought in the war. Hitler's War. Poland. We were sent in to assist liberating the camps and…" he paused.

Peggy stole a glimpse of his face. Even in the twilight she could see a shadow pass over his eyes.

"Well," he continued, "it dawned on me one day, here in the shelter, that a part of me was still over there, you see, in a displaced sort of way. I was attempting to make right a nightmare not of my own choosing, yet one that I seemed unable to let go of." He looked directly at her. "This isn't just about Lucky, is it?"

Peggy froze, unable to answer him. Outside, the dogs erupted into barking. She dragged her eyes to the window and spotted Mr. Harrison. He strode past the dogs up the walkway, towards the front door.

She turned to face Terry, incredulous. "You...you called him?"

"I had to call him, Peggy. His dog had surgery."

Peggy backed away from him, shaking her head in disbelief.

Harrison opened the office door, brushing past them both. "Let's make this quick, shall we, Warden? I want my own vet to check the patch job done here—without my permission."

"Emergency surgery on a stray dog without tags is done at the discretion of our state-licensed veterinarian. You were contacted as soon as your dog was stabilized and identified."

"I suppose we have to take your word on that," Harrison shot back, pulling out his checkbook.

"Too-too bad they can't talk." Peggy's croaking voice broke the tension.

Harrison looked around at her

Shut up! Who do you think you are?

The moment Harrison's eyes met hers, Peggy's throat clamped shut. She stared back at him, paralyzed, as their cold green depths raked over her slowly. He smiled, ever so slightly.

"Yes, isn't it?"

Peggy felt rooted to the spot.

"That'll be three hundred dollars, Mr. Harrison," she heard Terry's muffled voice from far away.

Harrison's eyes flicked away from Peggy's. "*Three hundred?*"

"Here's a copy of the surgical bill, the medical report for your own veterinarian, along with a summons for your dog being off leash. Again."

"Anything else?"

"Yes. Your dog shows up in this condition again, we'll be settling the issue in court. I'm sure that's something you'd like to avoid, what with county elections coming up this fall."

"Are you threatening me?" smiled Harrison.

"Promising you." Terry held out a form. "He'll need to go straight to your vet. Sign this, please, acknowledging that you've been so advised."

"Small world, isn't it?" Harrison read the form. "I hear you're applying for a grant." Initialing it, he tossed a check onto the counter. "Good luck with that."

He turned to Peggy. "Leash up my dog, please?"

Peggy stood like a post staked in quicksand. She couldn't hear a word the chimerical form above her snarled. She saw his lips moving, but the roar in her head deafened her to anything but the screams wailing all around her.

Run! Hide! Down! Get down!

Terry stepped in between them, knelt down and helped to lift Lucky to his feet, looping a leash around his neck. "Your dog is still drugged, Mr. Harrison." He handed the leash over to the man, but held on to it, until Harrison was forced to look at him. "He needs your help to recover."

Peggy saw a shadow flit across Harrison's face. He jerked the leash out of Terry's hand, and moving past her, in slow motion, he led a wobbly Lucky out of the office. She felt helpless as Lucky looked back at her, before being pulled past Dr. Hayward, leaning against the doorjamb, huddled in his coat.

Above the thick muffled roar in her head, she picked out the front gate opening and closing, then car doors open and slam shut. It was only after the car's engine faded in the distance, that she was able to breathe. She unclenched her balled fists with painful difficulty and she heard the men's voices as if through a fog.

"Get some supplies." The warden extended Harrison's check to the vet.

Paul regarded it. "I think your boiler's out. It spit steam twice then went quiet."

Terry pushed the check into his hand. "Thank you. I think our warranty's still good from this morning."

"Need anything else?"

"Thank you, no. Appreciate it."

Paul pocketed the check, paused a moment at the door, and Peggy met his eyes. He looked as if he was going to say something, but didn't, and walked away.

Behind her, she heard the kettle's metal scrape on the hot plate, and the clinking of two mugs.

"One marshmallow or two?" the warden asked.

Her arms and legs tingled with pins and needles, as if thawing from a winter freeze. Peggy stiffly picked her coat up off of the floor.

"I-I have to go."

"Oh. Well, let me drive you."

"N-no, thank you."

"All right. See you tomorrow, then."

Peggy forced one foot in front of the other, trying not to splinter her frozen legs as she ambulated past him through the kennel and out the front door.

Terry stood at the window until Peggy disappeared around the corner in the drizzling rain. The wind blustered a bit harder at that moment, and it felt as if the cold settled between his shoulders with a heaviness he hadn't felt for a long time. He pulled out his pocket recorder, about to dictate a thought, but sank down in his chair. Pushing the wrong button, he listened absently as his own voice rattled off notes of the week.

"....take another look at the grant apps, September second is final deadline. Ask Joe to take Ethel in for a lube...maybe Fegetti can take another look at the doors before we lose her to Old Man Winter. Remember to fetch the traps from Mrs. Cruikshank's."

"Damn." He listened to the rain a few moments then pushed himself onto his feet. He shut off the lights and stood there in the dark looking at the blanket where Lucky had lain. He pulled the frayed rope from his pocket and stared at it a good long moment. He finally tossed it into his box of papers and walked out.

The bus driver steered the bus to the curb and hauled on the door lever. He regarded Peggy curiously, when she disembarked the bus there in the middle of nowhere and in the pouring rain.

"Ain't no othah bus stop here goin' back."

"Thank you," Peggy said, her voice hoarse.

The bus pulled away from the curb, leaving Peggy beside a dark empty field.

What're you doing? No! Go back!

Peggy didn't listen this time. She couldn't. And, she knew that if she ignored the voices, she'd soon be abandoned, anyway. Sure enough, it came to pass. Silence.

Her hands shaking, she pulled a slip of paper from her pocket, checked a street sign, and headed up the hill in the rain. A half mile later, she turned onto a heavily wooded road and began to check addresses on mailboxes set before modest, suburban homes. Hunkering down in her coat, she continued up the hill. It helped to walk. Heel toe, heel toe. It helped to pound out the buzzing numbness from her bones.

The streets widened, along with a size change in the trees and homes around her. Young naked maples gave way to hundred-foot red oaks flanking both sides of the street, sheltering homes hidden behind evergreens and holly. Street lights too, were replaced with the intermittent glow of Victorian gas lamps. Walking underneath the tall, ornate fixtures, she could hear the soft hissing of gas within the etched glass globes. The glow of light thrown by the flickering, blue-yellow flames was impotent against the deep winter night, yet there was a comfort in their warm hissing. It was as if they were alive and watching over her.

Aside from the groaning creak of the tree limbs in the rising wind, the streets were quiet. There were no car horns, no boom boxes, no sirens up on the mountain roads. Peggy could hear herself think, although she didn't necessarily want to think.

Snatches of Lucky's last look at her kept tugging her forward, like an invisible leash. All at once the whole incident flooded into her mind, as if a berm had been breached. She saw the warden hand Lucky's leash over to that monster. How could he? He'd promised that he'd make it all right! From the very beginning, from her very first day, he'd promised. She felt sucker-punched and stupid for not seeing the swing coming. How could she have allowed herself to believe him? She'd let her guard down, and like everything else, in the end it was always the same. The only thing you could count on was…

She skidded to a stop in a puddle, out of breath, having been nearly at a run for blocks without even realizing it. Overheated, she snatched off her hat and gloves, sweat trickling between her shoulder blades.

Up ahead, a branch snapped loudly and hit the road, echoing sharply in the dark. Shakily, she pulled out the scrap of paper from her pocket, checked a curb address, and then peered across the street to a corner house, behind stone walls. As if pulled against her own free will, she crossed the road and read an inlaid slate on the wall. Harrison.

Peggy looked up to a proud colonial house. Light poured from the windows, illuminating a picture perfect porch. A plastic Christmas wreath still hung on the front door. She stalked the length of the stone wall, until she came abreast to a wooded acreage. She raised herself up on tip toe, and snuck a peek over the wall.

It was difficult to discern anything beyond the throw of the house lights. In a moment, the wind gusted clouds from the face of the moon, just long enough to make out the silhouette of a dog house under a tree. She searched the shadows, but there was no sign of Lucky. Relief flushed her cheeks. Maybe the monster took Lucky to his vet or had him indoors.

She gazed up at the wood-smoke curling above the chimney top. If Lucky hadn't had surgery, would he be out in the dog house, tonight? How long before he would be tossed out there in the cold, alone? Her grip tightened on her St. Francis pendant. She felt a sudden urge to yank it off of her neck. Abruptly, a dog barked next door, and a back porch light engulfed Harrison's yard. Peggy dropped down from the wall and tore down the street, running hard.

Terry tied a last knot of rope through the handle of a trap. Pacing inside the trap, a fat raccoon churred. Perched on the third story roof of Mrs. Cruikshank's century-old Victorian home, Terry blew on his numb fingers, wishing he'd called Joe out to help him. It was hard enough hauling one Hav-A-Hart trap, let alone three, each stuffed with a fifteen pound raccoon inside. The wind had shifted and made maneuvering on the slippery roof a challenge. Terry checked the knots in the guide pulley for the fourth time, then took a moment to rest.

He shook rain off of his jacket, wishing he could shake off a nagging worry. Why did he attempt to bluff Harrison with en passant, when he did? He'd disregarded the rules. Now, he couldn't see the chess board clearly in his mind, anymore. Where was Harrison's Bishop? Where was his own? In an attempt to protect two pawns, he'd been put in check, and in danger of losing the entire game. It was careless. He knew better. Especially when challenging a man like Harrison.

Still, Harrison's biggest weakness lay in his arrogant belief that any game could be won by cheating. This time, all eyes were on the board. The last thing Harrison wanted at this point in the city's election cycle would be a scandal of any sort. He'd do, or not do, just about anything in order to qualify for the next level of play, which was the county seat.

Then again, Harrison might try to discredit them, by raising a rallying cry against the shelter being privately run on the city's coffers.

Terry blew on his cold hands. He did not relish starting World War III with the village schmuck and master manipulator; not if the shelter was caught in the cross fire.

He kneaded his brow, unable to banish from his mind the look of betrayal on Peggy's face. What was it about her that made him step out on a limb like that? At first, he'd thought that it was just her youthful idealism and innocence. It had certainly rekindled the same spark in him. He could remember a time when he didn't need anyone else to inspire him that way, a time when he had passion for so many things. He gazed out across the rooftops. When did everything become so gray?

He wished he'd handled it differently. Even so, he wasn't sure how he could mend things with her, or if he should even try. Like it or not, he could not pretend that right would always vanquish wrong. Not anymore. Perhaps that was the real rub.

The wind gusted, sweeping clouds from the face of the moon, and illuminating the neighborhood's wet rooftops. It was getting late. Terry rubbed his hands together briskly.

"Let's get you goblins inside where it's warm."

Terry bent into the wind, and with a zig-zag pivot across the shingles, he maneuvered the traps to the edge of the roof. He crouched against a chimney and eased the cages over the edge one by one, lowering them toward the ground. Once the third cage tipped over the side, the load dangled heavier than he had anticipated. He stood up to counter balance the weight, when a sudden wind gust tipped him forward. He swung his arms backwards and slipped, dropping down against the roof. Sliding towards the edge, he shot out a hand to grasp the lead rope.

Below him, the cages spun like dizzy pendulums, smacking the house. He could hear the raccoons shrieking. The rope burned his hands, and he knew that if he didn't let go, the raccoons would crash to the ground. Letting go of the pulley, he lurched for the gable, but missed, and fell off of the three-story house.

Chapter 28

Bam! Bam! Bam!

"No! Please no!" Her arms flailing, Peggy wrestled out from under the blanket and another night terror. "No!"

Bam! Bam! Knock! Knock! Knock!

Confused, Peggy panted. Someone was pounding on a door. Her door. Her eyes darting around the well-lit apartment, she saw that there was no one else there. She was in a bed, her bed. She could see that the door was shut and it was locked, from the inside.

Knock! Knock! Knock!

Still in her uniform, Peggy staggered to the door and peered out the peep hole. Fumbling with the many dead bolts and latches, she yanked the door open in surprise. Joe looked up, his face contorted in anguish, tears streaming down his ruddy cheeks.

The wind rattled the windows of the hospital's emergency waiting area so hard, even the nurses at the front desk paused in their work and listened.

Peggy leaned her throbbing head back against the wall. The sickening smells of the hospital reminded her of the EVC. It occurred to her, that they hadn't called Dr. Hayward. She looked across to Joe. Slumped over his knees in a chair, he stared at the waxy floor. Betty gazed blankly at a television cart in the corner, a rerun of *The Honeymooners* on low. They had decided it best not to call on Clara until morning.

Perhaps they should have called Dr. Hayward, Peggy thought, again. On the other hand, what would be the point? Peggy frowned. She really didn't want him there. This was one time she didn't want to hear his expert, medical opinion.

Twisting the St. Francis pendant in her fingers, she tried to remember the last thing she'd said to Terry, but couldn't. What was it that he'd said to her? All she could see was the strained look on his face, when she left, without even saying good night.

It's your fault! You're to blame!

Peggy cringed. It was true. If she'd only just...she heard the squeak of rubber soles on linoleum. A tall doctor with spectacles and two interns approached. Gripping her St. Francis pendant, Peggy studied their faces. Their lack of expressions chilled her to the bone.

"Hello, I'm Doctor Greenberg. Sorry there's no room available. But, I thought you'd like the results sooner than later." The doctor pulled x-rays from a manila envelope, holding them up to the fluorescent ceiling light. "Preliminary x-rays show that Mr. Brannan has a broken left ulna, three rib fractures; here, here and here. His pelvis has also sustained a fracture. You can see it there. The most serious are the three compression fractures of the spine; three thoracic vertebrae; T-six, T-eight, T-ten and one in the lumbar region, L-3."

"You say spine?" Betty breathed. "His back be broke, that what you sayin'?"

"Yes."

Joe sank back down in the chair with no attempt to hide his tears.

"As dire as all of that sounds," Dr. Greenberg added, quickly, "the good news is; there's been no puncturing of any major organs, he's conscious, and he has feeling in his extremities. Those are very positive indications. Having said that, he is by no means out of the woods. Far from it. But, as I said, these are all very encouraging—"

"Can he walk?" Betty interjected.

"At the moment, no."

"Will he?"

"A prognosis at this time would be premature. But, there's every reason to feel encouraged."

"So maybe he can't now, but maybe."

"As I said, it's too soon to say, but there are positive indications all in his favor."

Peggy observed the doctor. He was perched, not really sitting, on the arm of a vinyl sofa. He spoke to them respectfully, but with the same detached demeanor that she'd seen at the EVC. Dr. Hayward shoved his way into her mind. She wondered if all medical schools churned out doctors in the same manner, squadrons of white-coats from conformed molds.

She noticed his foot tapping against the sofa leg. Although his face was placid, his foot twitched as if he was half past in need of a fix. She wondered what he would do if she abruptly screamed and threw a chair through the plate glass window. Would his blank face crack? Would he stop jiggling his stupid foot?

"What now?" Joe sniffled.

"As soon as the medivac arrives, he'll be airlifted to Chicago."

"Chicago?" Joe and Betty echoed in unison.

The doctor checked the chart in his hands. "We've spoken with his sister, Mrs. Irene McGuirk. Being his emergency contact, she's authorized the transfer. I understand she's an RN at Chicago Hope. They've an excellent trauma center and rehab facility out there."

Peggy swallowed hard. "How...how long before..."

"Again, it's too soon to speculate, but he's a strong man, for his age. There's a good chance that he'll pull through this to a full recovery. Let's just get him to where they can best address his injuries, and take it one day at a time."

One corner at a time, Peggy corrected him, silently.

"Yeah," Joe rubbed his sleeve on his wet nose, "but what are we talkin' here? A coupla weeks? A month? Two?"

"I understand how difficult this must be," the doctor began.

"Guesstimated ball-park," Betty said. "He's our boss, and all we got."

The doctor checked the pager buzzing on his hip. "Given no complications, and with the best case scenario playing out, you're looking at a year. Perhaps less, probably more."

Betty sagged, as if deflating. Joe covered his eyes with his hands and wept like a little boy. The doctor's foot finally stopped twitching. He nodded to his interns, and they left, shuffling off, expressionless. He glanced at Peggy. She stared back at him, dry-eyed.

Peggy hesitated outside the ICU unit.

"Are you family?" a nurse on her way out asked her.

"N-no, but…"

"She be family." Betty appeared in the doorway, wiping her nose with a tissue, then she left.

Joe exited next, his eyes puffy and red. "He asked for ya."

The nurse gestured Peggy inside. "Two minutes."

Peggy stepped inside the room. She couldn't see past the machines and the cluster of white coats huddled around the bed. She stood there, wringing her hands. She didn't want to see Terry. She felt rotten for feeling that way, but if she didn't see him, then somewhere in space and time, he would still be all right.

It's all your fault!

She pressed her eyes closed. Yes, yes, but please, don't punish him! Punish me! She flinched, feeling a hand rest on her arm. A nurse with kind eyes peered at her.

"Are you all right?"

Peggy nodded.

"This way," the nurse led her through a wall of blinking, bleeping machines.

Peggy peered down at a man on a gurney obscured by thick padding, his head and neck in metal braces, his puffy face mottled black and blue and purple; a man almost unrecognizable. Almost.

"Let him know you're here," the nurse whispered to her.

Peggy rested her trembling hand on his. It was warm. His eyes opened and focused glassily on hers. His cracked lips moved, but no sound escaped.

"You...you're going to be all right," Peggy whispered hoarsely, "We'll...we'll send whatever you need so...so you can, so you can run things from there."

He grimaced, forcing the words out of his mouth. "...hold the fort. Take over."

"Wh-what?"

"You. I want you to take over."

Peggy drew back. "But, I...I can't. I'm...I'm sorry—" She flinched when his fingers grasped hers in a weak squeeze.

"You're the only one who can," he whispered, and his eyes locked with hers. "Promise."

His grip tightened. It hurt. She nodded. "Okay. Promise."

The doors burst open, and four medivac techs bustled in along with half a dozen aides wrangling more machines on carts.

"It's time, miss," the first nurse said, and stepped in between them.

Terry wouldn't release Peggy's hand. In a flurry of activity, she was nudged back against the wall, and with a last squeeze, he let go, being whisked away out the doors. She stood in the doorway, watching Joe and Betty hurry after him.

The kind nurse approached Peggy, offering her folded clothes. It took a second before Peggy recognized the clothes as Terry's uniform.

"This is what he came in with. And this." She handed Peggy Terry's pocket recorder. "It fell out of his pocket."

Peggy took it from her. "Thank you."

"Are you all right?"

Peggy nodded, but she couldn't feel a thing. She wasn't even aware of having sat down in the chair. Why couldn't she feel anything? She looked up from the recorder in her hands and found herself alone. She wasn't sure how long she'd been sitting there. With a start, she noticed that someone had turned out the lights. She stood up on wobbly knees and backed out of the shadows into the bright hallway. She hurried off in search of Joe and Betty, too afraid to be left behind there in the dark.

Chapter 29

Peggy was late, but she did not hurry down the driveway to the shelter. Jittery from lack of sleep, her mind felt fractured. The wind had howled all night, whipping tree branches against the frosted glass of her windows. Likewise, she had used Terry's voice on the recorder like a whip, punishing herself with every playback, with the reminder that it was all her fault. Staying awake for the rest of the night, she avoided the night terrors, but it was a hollow solace. For the first time in her life, standing before the shelter in the cold light of day, being wide awake was more terrifying than the nightmares that stalked her sleep.

Under the steel-gray sky, the compound was gloomier than ever. The dogs watched her approach without barking. That meant one of two things; they were either all barked out already, or they'd been fed. At the gate, she halted. Next to the fence sat the Pinto, and for a split second her heart leapt with hope. Maybe it had been nothing but a bad dream, after all! Then, she spotted a yellow police tag on the door handle, flapping in the wind.

She rested her hand on the hood. It was cold. Swallowing a lump in her throat, she scanned down the runs to where Lucky had been only a week before. I should have kept running with him, she berated herself. That very first day, when I had the choice. We should have run!

It's not too late! Go! Now! Run!

Peggy covered her ears against the gusting wind. The cold bit at her fingers. She turned to the driveway leading up to the street and the bus stop. If I had, she thought, none of this would have happened. Terry would be up in the office doling out his friendly persuasion...instead of fighting for his life, fifteen hundred miles away.

Peggy bowed her head against the fence. I'm sorry...please, what can I do?"

Hold the fort.

Startled, her eyes snapped open, and she whirled around. It sounded as if Terry was right behind her. The front gate clanked in the wind. She frowned. Despite the bitter cold, she didn't want to go inside. She didn't want to face the crew, not any of it. Not without Terry.

Hold the fort.

Clutching her St. Francis pendant tight in her numb fingers, she cringed in shame. Terry had been the only one who had helped her and believed in her. How could she even think of running away, when he needed her help the most?

At that moment, she made a pact with God. "Please God, she begged, please help him get well. If you do, I *promise* I'll do anything you ask of me, just please, *please* make him better." She imagined shaking God's hand, like she did with Terry that day out in the back. *Deal.*

The wind whistled through the clapboards of the empty mill behind her, rocking the Pinto from side to side. She would have sworn that little Ethel had nodded her assent. Just then, it began to rain.

Clambering to her feet, Peggy drew in a shakey breath, and then opened the front gate. The dogs trotted alongside her in their runs, as she made her way up to the great steel front door. Twisting the knob, she pushed it open. It felt heavier than usual. She thought of the doctor's comment about Terry being a strong man. She certainly didn't feel strong at all. Gathering her resolve, she shoved harder on the door and stepped inside. Right away, she felt the chill in the air.

"Oh no..." She walked towards the office and paused by the silent hot air blower. She laid a hand on the radiator rungs. They were cold. Great. Not ten seconds in the door and there was already a problem! She wasn't sure what to do. Should Joe check the boiler first, or should Betty call Mr. Riley right away? She overheard muffled voices from behind the office door.

"I can't believe he left her in charge!" Dr. Hayward's voice rose above the others. "Look, it's ten a.m. and she's not even here!"

Peggy held her breath. Apparently, they hadn't seen her arrive.

"Whattya want from me?" Joe's voice piped up. "That's what he said!"

"What about seniority? Why don't one of you take the reins!"

"I ain't lookin' for no promotion," she heard Betty declare. "I'm already HNIC and wiff no benefits! I ansah phones and count beans. Other n' that, I don't know the half of what or how he done things, 'round here!"

"Ditto," Joe said. "I just ride shot gun, man! I ain't no paper pusher!"

"Don't look at me!" Clara's voice growled.

"Bulleeve me, we *ain't*."

"Doctah, I don't know what to tell you. If this be what Terry want, then it be what he want! He musta had his reasons."

"Aw, Jeeze, let's face it," Joe whined, "we're Toast City. This is the straw that's gonna break it! Maybe we should just get it over with and shut down!"

"T'isnt an option to shut down, y'balmy palooka." Clara's voice sounded tired.

"I'm tellin' ya, we're kaput!"

"Clara's right," Betty spoke over Joe's protests. "Closin' up shop ain't a option, baby toes, so just can it! You forgettin' we be under contract to the town?"

"Alls I'm sayin', he wasn't in his right mind when he said it. Look, I feel sorry for St. Francis too, but she can't handle this place! Mention the you know what, and she gets the screamin' meemies, for friggsake!"

Peggy's throat tightened with shame. They were right. Then she heard Dr. Hayward respond.

"Look, somebody's going to have to make the decisions around here, and if she's not even responsible enough to come in on time, maybe I should take over until—"

Peggy pushed open the door, startling them all. "Sorry I-I'm late."

She walked past them to hang up her coat and found Terry's jacket hanging on the rack. Momentarily confused, she turned to his empty chair, then looked up, and noticed them all staring at her. Her fingers closed around the cassette recorder in her pocket. Pulling it out, she set it on the counter.

"Last night, I-I was up listening to-to Terry's notes. He talked about a grant application. He showed me the papers, once, but does anyone know anything about it? When is it due?"

Betty slid Terry's box of files across the counter to her. "If it be any-thang important, it be in there. You know that; you filed it."

"Oh. Yes. Right. Thank you. Um...I noticed Beula's out? What should...I mean, someone should call Mr. Riley."

"Done left a message wiff his son. What you want me to tell him when he call back and axe about the last bill? Correction. Bills, as in plural. " She held up the thick folder, "And it be first of the year fo' the rest of 'em, too."

"Oh. Well, um...h-how many other bills are there?"

"Let's puddit diss way," Betty ripped open a pack of candy ciga-rettes, "do you want heat or lights?" The phone rang. "Or phones?" She snatched up the receiver and crossed herself. "Sheltah." In a mo-ment, she shook her head to Joe and Clara, looking relieved. "'Bout time, Mistah Riley. Yes, it be out again; why else would I bothah callin' you?"

Clara rolled her eyes to heaven. "Ministers of grace defend us."

"So? Put on yo' galoshes! What? Oh. Uh-huh. No, not yet. Don't know. Thank you. Yeah, yeah, okay, just git here when you git here." She hung up. "Mistah Riley done heard 'bout Terry from Gus down the hardware store."

"Bad news travels fast," Joe said, staring at his boots.

The other phone rang and everyone jumped in unison. Crossing herself, again, Betty snatched it up. "Sheltah. Yes," she shook her head again to the others. "Ten to six, Monday troo Sunday...where you be co-min' from?"

From behind her, Peggy heard the vet clear his throat. He was the only one who hadn't spoken since she walked into the room. As if taking his cue, Joe rolled his chair over to her.

"Dillan, listen, ya don't gotta do this. The doc here can take over."

"I'll-I'll come in early," Peggy cut him off. "I'll do the kennel room and the runs, so you can-you can do patrols and things ju-just like nor-mal. Betty will do the office like she does, and Clara will take care of the cats and we'll-we'll do everything just like if Terry was here. We'll hold the fort 'til he gets back."

"But, we don't know if—I mean, when—when he's comin' back."

Peggy looked up, sharply.

Joe glanced past her shoulder, then wheeled away from her stare.

Peggy turned around to face the sure culprit of the attempted mu-tiny. Leaning against the back window, Paul Hayward looked back at her. Unlike the others, his eyes looked rested and clear.

"Sorry for your loss."

"He's not dead."

"I meant—"

"He'll be back."

"Yes. Well, until then, you've got issues, here. First, you're over-crowded."

"There wasn't exactly a chance to do anything about it, yesterday!" Peggy snapped.

"Understood. But, what are you going to do about it, today?"

Peggy clenched her jaw tight, before angry words shot out of her mouth. "I-I'll s-sort it out."

The crew looked at her. She averted her eyes. Well, that's what Terry always said. She wondered if the vet had been there long enough to know that, too.

Paul picked up his medical bag. "Well, when you do, I'll be downstairs." He walked out into the kennel.

Feeling her skin flush hot, Peggy watched him walk away. How could he be so cold?

Betty hung up the phone and broke open a fresh bronchial inhaler. "I don't know how much mo' I kin take of these damn phones ringin' off the hook."

A loud jangling from the far wall made everyone jump with fright, especially Peggy.

"Jesus H. Christmas!" Joe knocked Terry's jacket and the coat rack aside, revealing a black wall phone. Snapping up the receiver, he answered it. "Pound."

Her heart in her mouth, Peggy had never seen the black phone before. She looked on as Betty slid the log book over to him and even Clara crept closer, apprehensive.

Joe scribbled into the log book. "Copy that. Affirmative. Roger. Ten-four." He hung up, still writing. "Just a road kill."

Betty and Clara exhaled and sank back into their seats. The desk phone rang then, startling them all over, again.

"As God is my secret judge, this gonna do me in, by noon!" Betty snapped and picked it up. "Sheltah." She listened for a moment, shook her head to the others, then pulled down the Lost and Found notebook. "Nuh-uh. When you last see her?"

Joe re-hung Terry's jacket back up on the coat rack, brushing it off and straightening the lapel. It covered the black wall phone from view.

"I-I didn't know we had three phones," said Peggy.

"That ain't a phone, it's the hot line. Didn't Ter explain the hot line? It's the cops one way shout out to us. See?" he peeled Terry's jacket aside. "It ain't got no dial. Whenever this one rings, no matter what, drop everything you're doin' and answer it. And we gotta say 'pound', not shelter, 'cause to the cops, shelter means the homeless dump, downtown. We're dog catchers to them, and they don't want no confusion when we pick up."

"Why don't they just use the regular phones?"

"Last thing they want in a nine-one-one is to call us and get a busy signal."

"Nine-one-one?"

"Emergencies? HBC's—y'know, hit by cars, house fires, stuff like that. Anytime they get called and there's an animal in the mix. It ever rings and I ain't around, call me up on the CB."

"Does it...does it happen very much?"

"Use t'only happen once a year. Lately, 'cuzza the drugs movin' in, maybe every month now. The first time, they called us to go in after a drug bust down on Gates, to nab the dens' guard dogs. I was like, no way! We ain't armed! But it was either us go in or the cops were gonna shoot the dogs. No jerkin' 'round. So Ter, he says, we're goin' in, all hero-like, okay? So, I get the rabies pole, right? And—"

"Rabies pole?"

"Don't tell me. He didn't show you that, neither? Okay," he reached under the cage bank. "We hardly never gotta use it. Got two in the van and one under here." He pulled out what looked like a fishing net, but without the net. Instead, it had a thick, cabled loop at the end. "This end's the snare and goes 'round the neck, kinda like a lasso, see?" He demonstrated around his own neck.

"Hang 'em high, Howdy Doody," Clara muttered, pulling on her coat.

"You wish." Joe removed the noose, demonstrating the pull cord at the other end of the pole. "This here is how ya control 'em. Push comes to shove, ya take the fight outta them by tightenin' the noose."

Peggy recoiled at that, and his face grew taut and serious.

"Lookit, when they're hurt or scared, or worse, if they're trained attack dogs, they can take your face off. No joke, they can kill ya. It's for your own protection against nut cases." He thumbed to Clara as she tottered out the door with a bag of cat food. "Which is how come we keep one, in here."

Butting out the door, Clara flipped him the finger.

Joe rolled his eyes heavenward. "Terrr..." The second desk phone rang beside him, sending him a foot in the air. "Jeeze!"

Betty leaned over and snatched it up. "Sheltah." She shook her head, again. "Walnut Street. Uh-huh. Where you comin' from?"

Joe exhaled, hand over his heart. "Friggit. I can't hack this." He shoved the pole under the cage bank and headed for the door. He paused, and then looked back to Peggy. "It's day-old free day at Jack's. Ter always had me pick up a box of doughnuts for everybody? Outta petty cash."

It seemed as if he was asking her permission. Peggy managed a shrug. "S-sure."

He looked sheepish all of a sudden. "Lookit, what Ter says goes. So... if you need me, I'll have my ears on. Jack's is just up the road. You know how to use the CB?"

Peggy nodded. "Just press the microphone lever?"

"Ten-Four." Joe zipped his jacket and left, closing the door.

Peggy reached into Terry's box. In surprise, she pulled out a piece of frayed rope. She examined it. It was the rope that had been around Lucky's neck. What was it doing in Terry's box? She certainly hadn't filed it. Without warning, a rising tide of anguish welled up in her. It was all she could do not to break down and sob her heart out, right then and there. Terry had cared very much about Lucky. How could she have accused him of less than that? Her stinging eyes rested on Terry's empty chair. Was he all right? And Lucky...was he all right? She wasn't sure which was worse, finding out or not knowing about either one of them.

She heard the dogs erupt into barking outside and peered out the window. She spotted Mr. Riley, clad in yellow rain slickers and fishing gators, dragging his little red wagon of tools down the driveway. Just then, she remembered that Clara had just gone out and down to the—

Oh no! She tossed the rope back in Terry's box, and dashed out to meet the old handyman before he ran into Clara, and before another phone could ring.

"T'isn't enuff to call me out in diss waither, bein' cruel wet enough fer ducks! And me walkin' all diss way, wit me bunions!"

Water poured from Mr. Riley's rain hat onto Peggy's shoes, as he showed her his afflicted feet. "Now yer wantin' me to swim back against that tide out der t'fetch a cup o'Joe, when I jest near drowned, I did, gettin' here in the first place!"

Peggy closed the front door on the barking dogs. "I'm so sorry, Mr. Riley, it's just that she's…I mean, we're kind of behind down in the, well, downstairs. If you just give her—I mean us—fifteen minutes to get organized, she won't—I mean we—we won't be in your way."

"Now, now," Mr. Riley cooed, "nivver fear, lass, I kin see you're all done in, wid d'likes o'such a down blow, t'be sure. Aye, d'warden were always in d'field when luck were on d'road, he was, oh 'tis a sin! And, him havin' been such a right, decent feller!"

"Yes, he was. I mean is, is!" Peggy corrected herself with alarm.

"I tell ye, and make no mistake, a better feller der nivver was, neidder diss side d'river or dat!"

"No, there never was. I mean is! He is, yes."

"And him bein' a Tan coat, too! You'd nivver know it tho', no! Treated everyone a fair shake, no matter! Nar a truer one to his word, neidder, an' gen'rous to fault, he was! And it were'nt to get on d'good side of our good Lord, neidder! No, he weren't that sart o' man!"

"No, no, he wasn't. I mean yes, he was. Is! He is a-a special man."

"It were cursed luck, I tell ye, d'cruelest luck to fell a decent sart like that!"

"Yes, yes it was—I mean it is—was!"

"Aye, I were dead fond of d'warden, dead fond of him I was!"

"Mr. Riley!" Peggy gasped. "He's not dead!"

"Ho der! What's dat? Who's not dead?"

"Terry! Mr. Brannan! The warden! He's not dead!"

"Och! I should hope not! Tanks be t'God, for he knows what's best in all tings, o'course! What would give ye call to be tinkin' dat he were passed on?"

"I'm sorry, I thought you said—nevermind. Mr. Riley, about the heat…"

"Arra, den! I'm obliged to make it right it fer ye, on account of I'm a man of me word as well, but mark me, yer furnace is more crusty dan d'Queen o' Demon Cats in der, she is!" He wagged a finger at the office door.

Just then the front door opened, and from under her dripping umbrella, Clara spotted him. "No wonder it's colder n'a brass monkey down there! 'Ere you are, flapping your gums up 'ere!"

Mr. Riley reddened. "'At's what I tawt! Der's d'blue rinser! D'clarsy in d'flesh put pishrogues on yer furnace, if ye want to know d'truth of it! Down der puttin' the hex on ol' Beula as we spake!"

"Oh, you blinkin' duffer! Pull your finger out and mend that sleucin' stewpot as you were 'ired to, the first go 'round!"

"Hey, hey, hey!" Joe hurried up the walkway, a box of doughnuts in hand. "I can't leave for five minutes without—what's goin' on?"

"What good's pissin' good brass away on that gastric old tankard?" Clara demanded.

"You talkin' 'bout the boiler or Riley?"

"Oh please," Peggy stepped between them all. "Please, can we call a truce, just this once? Terry needs our help now. He-he needs us to hold the fort!"

The mention of the warden's name caused them all to stop, mid-whine. As she'd seen Terry do so many times before, Peggy attempted to referee, with some of his "friendly persuasion".

"Beula's all we've-we've got, now, and I-I know it would mean so much to him. To Terry. That Mr. Riley's come all-all this way in the freezing rain, to-to-to fix her, again, for him. For free. Which is very generous of you."

Mr. Riley gaped at her. Not about to appear less than the stalwart hero, he swept his dripping hat over his heart, as if it had been his own idea.

"And, Clara?" Peggy's voice squeaked. "You're the one Terry counts on when-when it comes to the cats."

Clara narrowed her eyes. "Who?"

"T-Terry. Mr. Brannan? The warden?"

"Oh, him," Clara nodded, then turned her nose in the air. "For the Commodore, then." With a regal nod to them all, she tottered into the office without another word.

"Arra den," Mr. Riley donned his rain hat with equal decorum. "I've a ronday-voo with you-know-who, below decks." He headed out the front door, without further ado, pulling his squeaky wagon of tools behind him.

Joe blinked at Peggy. "Did hell just freeze over, or what?"

Peggy exhaled in surprise, too. "Maybe it's a good sign?"

"Yeah, right." Joe raised a brow and opened the office door. "Place your bets."

Chapter 30

As the chilly afternoon wore on, Mr. Riley's hammering on the pipes wore on the crew's frazzled nerves. The phones rang constantly, but not a single call had been the one they'd been waiting for, from Chicago. And, they were still in their coats and hats.

"Bloody 'ell, that kettle's a black hole what swallows every ha'penny we got!" Clara griped. "Only one making out is that daft old salt, every fortnight! Be cheaper to buy a boiler and be done with it!"

"Wiff what, green stamps?" Betty ripped a length of paper from the adding machine and studied the numbers.

"I...I think Clara's got a point," Peggy thumbed through Terry's notes. "See here? Terry was planning to buy a new one when you had enough money. How-how many bills need to be paid before you have enough money?"

"Let's puddit diss way. We be on a first name basis wiff small claims court. Wait," Betty leafed through the bills, "we might owe them money, too."

They heard the dogs burst into barking in the kennel, and shortly, Dr. Hayward pushed open the office door. Sooty and rain-soaked, he looked alarmed. "Do you know your handyman uses a Bic lighter to inspect the gas line?"

Joe snorted a laugh. "He'd have to get past the creosote to do any real damage!"

"Oh, now there's a comfort. Well, on the outside chance there's still a building here in the morning," Paul handed Peggy a soggy piece of paper, "this is a list of the items I'll need. They don't have to be brand new, used is all right, as long as nothing's older than two years. Oh. You need more chicken feed, and you owe me lunch. The rooster ate my sandwich."

"Corn and a corned beef. Got it." Joe jotted it down. "Bet, we got any petty cash left?"

"Since when we got any to begin wiff?" Betty updumped paper clips and I.O.U.s from a metal cash box. "The last bet I won paid fo' the cat treats. Lunch be on you, this time."

Joe emptied his pockets on the counter. "Why'd I ask?"

Peggy scanned the vet's long, dripping list. "I-I don't understand. Spec..tro..meter, fleur-o-scope, autoclave...what's all this?"

"Equipment I need. To do my job?"

"Can't-can't you borrow these things from the EVC?"

"It's a hospital, not a lending library."

"But I thought...I thought you came with everything."

"I'm a vet, not a hot dog."

"We'll be the judge of that," Clara remarked and dumped cat litter into the trash.

Joe laughed. "Walked right inta that one, Doc!" The vet's expression wiped the grin right off of his face.

"It's just that..." Peggy held up Betty's adding machine tally. "They can't afford it. They...they can't afford to fix Beula!"

"Heck, we can't even afford lunch," Joe grumbled, counting pennies.

"A moot point, since you're going to need a new roof when your handyman blows this one into Hackensack."

"Can't you just...improvise?" Peggy asked, doing her best to sound polite.

"Again, I'm a vet, not a comic."

"Again," Clara eyed him, "we'll be the judge of that."

Paul folded his arms across his chest. "Just how do you expect me to conduct any kind of routine medical procedures? I don't know what you're used to down here, but I don't do second rate work."

Peggy was in no mood to fence with the young vet. "I–I didn't say you do second-rate work. No one did. After what-what happened, you just show up and expect—"

"I don't expect anything; I'm merely requesting some basic supplies."

"You seem to expect a place that-that can't even afford heat to-to cater to you when—"

"Cater? *Cater*? Since when is it catering to ask for simple everyday supplies to treat animals? I'm just asking for the rudimentary tools to do my job!"

"You know what's h-happened. There's not enough money for any-one to do their jobs!"

Out of breath, Peggy stopped at the exact moment Paul ran out of steam, too.

"Looks like a draw," Clara murmured to Joe and Betty.

Her throat sore, Peggy kneaded her pounding temple. "I don't-I can't-you're just going to have to-to do whatever you do, with what's here."

"And I'm telling you, I'm not comfortable with what's here!" the vet countered.

"Well, I'm sorry, but it's-it's not my job to make you comfortable! This is a shelter, not a country club!" Before the temptation to dump Terry's box of papers over his head overwhelmed what little remained of her self control, Peggy walked out into the kennel. The dogs barked at her, as she stormed all the way to the end, where she slammed the bowls into the sink.

"Country club?" Paul exclaimed. "This place doesn't even have a john!" He tossed the list into the trash. "*Fine.* Waste my time! It's your call."

"Actually, it ain't." Betty opened a pack of candy cigarettes. "If it was, we'd have a toilet. The town only give us twenty thou' a year, and that bag of peanuts gotta covah everythang; salaries, feed, medicine and you."

"But, that's...that's ridiculous."

"Tell us 'bout it."

The pipes clanked dully in the walls, and they all paused to watch wisps of smoke creep up through the floorboards.

"If she's going to play manager, shouldn't she at least be down there to oversee what he's doing?" Paul asked.

"Saint Francis?" Clara chuckled. "Do pigs fly?"

"Pigs...Saint who?"

"Dillan," Joe said low. "She don't go down the cellar."

"Oh? Any particular reason, or is that not in her job description either?"

Joe exchanged a furtive glance with Betty and Clara. "She...just don't go down there. Claustrophobe or somethin'."

"Or something." Paul shot a glance through the doorway to Peggy at the far end of the kennel, loudly scrubbing bowls.

"Say Doc, don't worry 'bout Beula," Joe said. "We got the firehouse right out front and Riley ain't blown us up yet."

"Fine. It's your house. Speaking of which, as I mentioned, it's over-crowded. That's something you can deal with, right now. You need to draw up a list and euthanize a few."

"Yeah, well, see, she was kinda workin' on that when, y'know..."

"You had Saint Francis working on the euthanasia list?"

"Nah, I mean Ter put her in charge of barkin', y'know, marketing. Ads and stuff, so maybe we don't gotta, y'know, nuke 'em as much. Christmas was her first thingee."

"It's January."

"Yeah. Wow. How 'bout that! Time sure flies, huh?"

Paul held up a hand and walked out into the kennel towards Peggy. The crew craned their necks around the door to peek after him.

"Y'know, I'm kinda on the fence about her now," Joe whispered. "She might be Spaz-City, but frig if she don't pull it out of a hat when ya least figger! Sure put his royal Hard Nose City on notice, catch that?"

Clara wrinkled her nose. "I don't like th'odds."

"Okidoke." Betty flipped a quarter in the air. "Who gonna referee this one?"

"I can't hack this." Joe whined at the silent phones. "Ter..."

Peggy heard the vet approach. She knew it was him, because he was the only one who strode with such deliberate intent that his boots squeaked on slate flooring. She had hoped that he'd just stalk out in a huff, but no such luck.

"You know," he said, squaring off with her at the sink, "providing me with medical equipment might not be something that you're required to do. But, you are required to adhere to certain conditions for these animals. That *is* part of your job. I'm not going to say it, again. You're overcrowded. You need to draw up a list."

"In case you didn't notice, th-there hasn't exactly been time to figure things out yet! Next week I'll-I'll put another ad in the paper."

"You don't have a single run free for the weekend, let alone the week ahead! My sole concern is for the animals' health, here and now. Fact of life number one: overcrowding leads to illness. Fact of life number two: you are and have been overcrowded, for some time. Now, I want a list in fifteen minutes, or I'll draw one up myself."

"You will not!"

"Don't make me pull rank."

"Rank?! Th-this isn't the army!"

"My state license supercedes your badge, Officer! You've got two dogs that have most likely got kennel cough, which, by the way, is highly contagious, and since those two are each doubled up with another two dogs, they're guaranteed to have infected both of them, as well! The longer you keep them, the more dogs they'll pass it on to, leaving you with a kennel full of sick dogs that you can't adopt out, ad or no ad!"

Peggy heard a dog cough behind her. Terry had warned her about kennel cough; the doggie version of the common cold. Like the common cold, there was no medicinal cure and no vaccine, yet. It simply had to run its course, and usually did in seven to fourteen days. It could however, lead to secondary infections like bronchitis or pneumonia in puppies and older dogs, killing them. How had she not noticed the coughing?

"We-we could keep them away from the other dogs," she began.

"Where? Down in the cellar?"

Peggy looked up sharply. "I-I guess that would b-be best."

"Really? Well, maybe if you checked up on it, you'd know that the cages are full up down there with eight cats, two possums and a Bantam rooster that shouldn't be down there at all, since it can't be adopted out due to zoning ordinances! Even if you had the space down there, even if I'd okay isolating four ten-year-old, infectious, arguably adoptable dogs, down there for two weeks or more, that's only two runs you're talking about. To get down to a reasonable number of dogs in this kennel, you need to clear out an additional four more runs. As per state guidelines, I suggest you start with the dogs who are sick, and who've been here the longest. Like this one." He lifted a card from the front of a black lab's run, reading it aloud as Joe sauntered up to them. "Female lab mix, eight years-old, never spayed and one that's been here for two months."

"Spats is a sw-sweet dog! She's not even coughing! You can't put her down! There's nothing wrong with her!"

"Is that your diagnosis of that dog?"

"She is a real nice dog, Doc," Joe said. "Labs've got the best chance of gettin' adopted too, more n' any other."

"She's been here two months," the vet repeated.

"Just b-because sh-she's been here f-for—" Peggy stammered. "For God's sake, you're supposed to be a vet! Where's y-your humanity?"

Paul snatched a leash off of the center post and looped it around the dog's neck, leading Spats out of the run.

"I'm-I'm not going to l-l-let you…" Before Peggy got the words out, Paul grasped hold of her wrist and ran her hand under the dog's abdomen.

"What do you feel?"

Aside from the vet's firm grip around her wrist, Peggy felt a curious, thickened bumpiness under the dog's belly, as if it had swallowed small apples. She jerked her hand away.

"That's a helluva mass in there," he said. "I'd need an x-ray to confirm, but judging by the yellow tint to her eyes, I'll wager that along with her lungs and spleen, it's already spread to her liver, which means she most likely has less than two weeks to live."

"What?" Joe gasped and knelt down beside the dog. "You talkin' the Big 'C'? Cancer?" Paul nodded. "Oh, man, I thought she just whelped a litter. I never saw it neither, Doc."

"Cancer?" Peggy gazed at the dog, stunned. "But-but can't you operate on her or…"

"Not at this advanced stage. There's nothing anyone can do. The humane thing would be to put her to sleep, a.s.a.p., before she's in any more discomfort and pain than she's already in."

Peggy dropped to her knees beside the yellow-eyed, dying Spats. She caressed her ears, trying to make sense of it. And Terry…how had Terry missed it?

"There are four others in this kennel with chronic conditions of one variety or another," he continued. "That schnauzer with Cushings and skin tumors that, in a younger dog I'd say might be treatable, but the dog is ten years old and bites children. That old shepherd down at the end has advanced hip displasia. He'll be crippled in eight months. You've got two more geriatric cases, one with cataracts and the other with chronic arthritis and diarrhea, not to mention that dog over there." He pointed to Digger, listless and staring at the front door.

"Digger deserves a second chance m-more than any of them!" Peggy argued. "He was dumped by his own family like garbage. There just hasn't been time to-to…"

"To do what? I believe these are your own notes, here." Dr. Hayward read from the cage card. "'Unless you spend most of every day with him, he is miserable and does nothing but stare at the door.'" He looked at her. "Two months he's been lying in here, caged and miserable. Look at him. Where's your *humanity*?"

He led Spats back to her run, hung up the leash, then without another word, returned to the office, closing the door behind him.

Joe glanced to Peggy. "Look, I'm not sidin' with him, but he's right about the KC. It'll whip through here like frickin' fire. And Spats? Man, if she's got the big "C"...you know it ain't right to keep her sufferin'. And...I know we all wanna help Digger, but..."

Her throat tight, Peggy took six leashes off of the center post and handed them to Joe.

He shifted on his feet. "Look, you ain't never been through this before. Why don't you take off."

Peggy shook her head no. "Take Spats in first."

When Joe walked Spats into the office, Paul opened his medical bag and stretched a pair of latex gloves over his hands. "Anyone coming in?"

"Coast is clear." Betty took both phones off the hook.

"Lock the front and flip the sign on the gate, will ya?" Joe said.

"Want anythang while we be out?" she asked, helping Clara on with her coat.

"Yeah, a new job."

"Doctah?"

Paul shook his head no.

Pausing to pet and whisper to two old cats, one last time, Clara followed Betty out the door.

Paul stood at the window until he saw the women walk through and lock the front gate, turning the sign around to read: Closed. "What about..." he gestured to the kennel.

"She's stayin' out back with the rest of 'em. She don't want them to know what's comin'."

"The dogs?"

"Yeah."

Paul pulled a bottle of T-61 out of his bag, filling a 20cc syringe. Tying a small length of rubber tubing around Spats's foreleg, he paused and glanced to Joe.

"Ready?"

Joe stroked Spats's ears and sighed. "I hate this place."

Slipping the needle into the dog's vein, Paul murmured, "You and me both."

Peggy shivered. She'd walked outside without her coat again. She climbed the concrete steps leading to the back runs. Below her, a half dozen dogs played with a torn tennis ball. The abandoned warehousing hunched all around them, dark and rain-sodden, like waiting vultures. Peggy lifted her face to the leaden sky that was fading into twilight. She cursed the cold and the unfeeling God who allowed innocent animals to be put to death for no other reason than that there were too many of them. Most of all, she cursed God for allowing heartless men like Dr. Hayward and Harrison to walk the earth, while not lifting a finger to keep a man like Terry from falling off a stupid roof.

She heard the grating scrape of the back gate and looked down from her perch above.

Joe and the vet hefted the last of the limp, black garbage bags past the romping, spared dogs, and disappeared under the runs. In a few moments, Peggy could smell the freezer's skunky stench in the wind's updraft. The dogs paused in their play and sniffed the air, too.

Peggy's heart ached. Each one of those plastic bags held an animal that had once purred or wagged its tail, looking only for a kind hand and a smile. How was it, that they each ended up here, unwanted and now dead?

As the men headed back through the gate for the last time, the vet looked up and spotted her. She stared back at him. He averted his eyes and before latching the gate, leaned over to scratch Digger's ears. Sitting apart from the other dogs, Digger watched the vet walk away and follow after Joe. Peggy watched, too, and wiped tears off her cheek.

 Chapter 31

Peggy filed the records of the seven deceased dogs and two cats into the Closed File box. She washed their bowls, cleaned their cages and runs. Fighting the sting of tears, she couldn't believe it. Her first day holding the fort for Terry, and nine animals had been put to sleep.

She was surprised that Dr. Hayward had not put Digger on the euth list. It didn't make her feel all that better, though. If anything, she felt worse. She could no longer look at Digger and not see an unhappy dog, pining for a past that was as dead and gone as those carcass bags in the freezer.

Why then, did Dr. Hayward spare Digger's life? He didn't say, and she didn't ask. She knew it was a temporary stay, at best. If she couldn't find a home for the dog within the next week, Digger would be first on the vet's euth list, the following Friday.

All through the chores, Peggy couldn't keep her mind off of Digger.

While the crew kept busy with phone catch-up, she pulled Terry's Poloroid camera down from the shelf and retreated to the kennel. Squeezing into Digger's run, she took a few photos of his long, sad face. Then she brushed him and whispered soothingly to him, until he dozed off.

It took her less than five minutes to write up an adoption ad for him. She didn't care that the vet had no faith in the ads. She was determined to find Digger a home before the week was up.

The only saving grace to the whole day, had been that she and the good doctor managed to avoid one another entirely, which did not entirely escape the crew's notice.

"Hey, the doc never came up for lunch." Joe looked at the clock. "It's fifteen to closin'. What the frig's he been doin' down there all day long? Ain't got no patients."

"You kin say that, again." Betty blew her nose.

Joe snorted a laugh. "Good one, Bet!"

"Maybe we ain't th'only ones get eat up ovah it, evah think of that?"

"C'mon. The guy's got ice water in his veins. Ya gotta, doin' what he does."

"He spared Diggah."

"Okay, so maybe he's got a slice of heart. So what?"

"Me thinks there's more to that starchy white coat than meets th'eye," Clara said over her clacking knitting needles.

Peggy wiped glue off of her ad mock up, listening to every word.

The office door opened, and the crew whirled back around in their chairs to busy themselves.

Paul walked in and shook sleet off of his coat. "It's locked up below."

Peggy taped a Polaroid of Digger onto the new ad. "Thank you."

"Any word, yet? From Chicago?"

"Not yet."

He walked away to the medicine cabinet and rummaged in the shelves. "I don't suppose you have any aspirin?"

Betty emptied her purse onto the counter. "Baby or full grown?"

"Industrial size."

The kennel dogs erupted into barking.

"Aw Jeeze, it's closin' time!" Joe peered out the fogged window.

"It could be somebody looking to adopt!" Peggy entreated them.

"Cor, we could use a wink and a nod," Clara agreed.

Please, yes! Peggy closed her eyes in prayer. Please, just one shred of good news to tell Terry, when he called! She searched the shelves. "I think we-we need more adoption forms."

"Okay," Joe flipped a quarter in the air, "heads I take it, tails you take it, Saint Francis."

The office door opened, and Joe's quarter hit the floor, clattering loudly in the abruptly silent room. Peggy looked around and gasped.

"Evening," Mr. Harrison said, with a pleasant smile. He walked right past Peggy. "I was just on my way home from a meeting at Town Hall, and thought I'd stop by to offer condolences from the mayor. Discussing budgetary cuts, purely by coincidence, your situation came up. Terrible tragedy. How is he?"

Peggy stared at the man's back, her heart thudding in her chest so hard she was sure that everyone could hear it.

He didn't see you! Run!

Despite the whispering voices in her head urging her to flee, she couldn't move. She couldn't breathe.

"We ain't heard, yet," she heard Joe say above the din.

"Well." Harrison turned to the vet. "I expect you're in charge then?"

"No, Officer Dillan is manager in situ."

Harrison turned and looked at her. "Really? Well." He turned his back on her and addressed the vet, again. "As I said, I just stopped by to offer the mayor's sympathy."

"How is your dog?" she heard the vet ask.

"Better, now."

"Dr. DeGrate mentioned that he'll need suture removal in about ten days. I'm happy to do it."

"You know Dr. DeGrate."

"Trauma's a small world."

"Apparently. Did a fantastic fix for you on Boy, by the way."

His name is Lucky. Peggy opened her lips to speak, but nothing came out.

Shut up! Keep your mouth shut!

"Well," Harrison said, "if you'll excuse me. All the best to your manager from the mayor's office."

After he eddied past her and out the door, Peggy managed to pull in a breath through the skintight constraint of her chest. Her arms and legs burned with the fire of pins and needles, as they thawed. She heard the muffled barking of the dogs in the kennel, and the slam of the front door.

"What wuz that about?" Betty remarked.

"Checkin' us out, whaddyou think?" Joe replied, as he rubbed fog off of the window.

"Didn't offer his own condolences, you'll notice." Clara's voice cut through the thickness in Peggy's head.

"'Cause he ain't sorry!"

Remember that, Peggy counseled herself. Monsters don't care.

"So, Doc! You been keepin' tabs on ol' Lucky, too?" Joe asked.

"Just a professional followup, one vet to another."

"Yeah, right! So, this DeGrate sawbones, what'd he say?"

"There was no indication of secondary infection or reason to suspect complications. The dog was alert and able to walk out on his own."

"Walk out? So Doc DeGrate sent him home?"

"An hour ago."

Joe raised a brow to Betty and Clara. "Uh-huh, uh-huh. Some coinky-dink the jerk stops by, huh?"

"In a pig's eye," Clara spat in the waste basket.

"Hey, Saint Francis. You okay?"

At the window, Peggy felt her nails digging into her palms. It hurt to unclench her fists. Struggling to try and answer Joe, she turned and felt a jolt of surprise to find Paul's eyes on her. He tossed back two aspirins with a swallow of soda.

The crew waited another hour and a half, hoping for a call from Chicago. Even Dr. Hayward hung around, apparently absorbed with some sort of paperwork of his own. At seven-thirty, Betty swiveled around to Peggy.

"We all best head home befo' it starts snowin'."

Peggy kneaded her throbbing temple and nearly asked her for aspirin, but didn't. "Okay. Yes."

"He prob'ly still be in ICU, all doped up. I bet we git word, tomor-rah."

"About what?" Clara asked.

"You're kiddin', right?" Joe sniped, zipping his jacket.

Out of the corner of her eye, Peggy caught Betty nudge him and nod her way. Joe cleared his throat.

"Oh. Hey, Saint Francis, you wanna ride? It's sleetin', out there."

Peggy closed Terry's box of papers. "Oh, thank you, no, I have errands." She donned her coat and followed them all out, surprised to find Paul holding the front door open for her. "Thank you."

One by one, the crew's cars came up the driveway, as Peggy crossed the street to the bus stop. At the corner, Dr. Hayward's Jaguar didn't make it through the light with the others. Stamping her feet in the cold, she noticed that when the light changed green, the Jaguar continued to sit there. When it changed from green to yellow, another car honked at him from behind.

She watched as the Jaguar sped up through the intersection, just as the #21 bus pulled alongside the curb. Had he been sitting there watching her? Why?

He knows!

Peggy's heart thudded hard in her chest. How could he? She climbed aboard the bus but paused to watch his tail lights disappear into the rain.

You can't trust anybody!

I know!

The voices silenced as the bus door whooshed closed behind her.

Thirty-five minutes later, Peggy departed the bus, and it seemed to her that the bus, too, hovered by the curb a moment longer than need be. As if it, and everyone aboard, were scrutinizing her. The driver peered at her through the door glass, as if he knew, too, and did not approve.

Peggy pulled her hat down around her ears and sloshed across the road. The bus ground gears and chugged up the hill. A light rain pattered on the dark roads, underneath groaning, slick-wet trees. She walked briskly, trying to shake off the day's events. She was thankful that they hadn't heard from Terry. From the crew's vote of no-confidence to the euthanizing of seven dogs and two cats, capped off by Dr. Hayward's accusation of her lack of humanity, she couldn't bear to hear the disappointment in Terry's voice, on top of everything else.

Abruptly, Harrison's icy stare shoved its way into her mind. She skidded to a stop.

Go back! Run! Hide!

For a split second, Peggy hesitated. Then, she shuddered No! She picked up her pace. Her shoes pounded hard on the sidewalk, and the houses flew by her in a blur. Still, she couldn't ditch the chill gripping her gut. She strode past the hissing gas lamps and pushed on through the sleet until it turned to snow flurries, unable to shake the montster's eyes on her.

After four blocks, she stopped and bent over her knees, out of breath. Her nose ran and she searched for a tissue in her coat pocket. She raised up and looked across the road to the brightly lit colonial home of Mr. Harrison.

Her heart pounding in her ears, Peggy sneaked across the street. She bent over double and skirted along the stone wall, past the side of the house. Just before the wooded hillside, she stood on tiptoe and peered over the wall into the back yard.

Under the trees sat the dog house, as before. Her eyes strained to see through the darkness. She hovered there, squinting and listening intently, but there was no sign of Lucky.

A car's headlights swept over her. Peggy dropped down and dashed in front of a car whooshing by in the wet snow, causing it to swerve.

A horn honked. Caught in the headlights, she froze.

Run, stupid, run!

Peggy spun around and ran down the street. By the time she'd made it back to Tory Corner, the snow had turned to rain, and she was soaked through. Shaking with cold, she trudged into the lobby of the boarding house and climbed the stairs to her apartment, her legs feeling leaden. There was still so much that she didn't know. She didn't know if Terry would come through this hurdle all right, let alone how she would cope without him. She didn't know if Lucky was all right now, or would be again. All she knew was that they were both inside, somewhere, out of the cold. That would have to be enough for now.

Chapter 32

"Please! I didn't do anything! *No!*"

Peggy woke with a scream. She was on the floor between the bed and the wall, tangled in blankets. Drenched in sweat, she looked around. The lights were still on. She could see there was no one else in the apartment. As she caught her breath, the buzzing roar in her head ebbed, and she became aware of a voice; a radio announcer.

"...calling for the immediate release of POW's still unaccounted for. Meanwhile, in Britain, International Women's year is being launched by Princess Alexandra and Barbara Castle in a series of appearances meant to bring awareness to the issue of women's rights. Weather is next."

She reached out and checked the clock. It was only three a.m. She had barely just fallen asleep! She'd stayed up until one a.m. searching the books that Terry had loaned her, during her Christmas Adoption Event, for information on canine kennel cough. She thought she'd finally worn out her internal task masters. Apparently not. She dropped her head and moaned.

"This isn't just about Lucky, is it?"

Hearing the warden's voice startled her. She cradled her head in her hands and whimpered. Terry, I can't do this!

"You're the only one who can."

She drew in a shaky breath and choked back tears. How could he believe that? I can't even fall asleep without the lights on! What can *I* do? If he only saw me now, cowering in the corner, clammy with fear. If he knew the truth...if he knew...

Her eyes darted to her suitcase. It was still open and ready for a quick escape. She could be on the next bus out of here and be gone in a flash.

"You're always so quick to run away. Why is that?"

Peggy grasped the pendant around her neck. All at once, it was Christmas Day again. It was as if Terry was right there in the room with her, clasping it around her neck. She fisted her eyes, unable to staunch the flow of tears.

In a fit of anger, she swept her books and papers off the bed to the floor. How could she have allowed a man she didn't even know to crawl under her skin so deeply, that she couldn't walk away, even when he wasn't there to stop her? Poised above the abuse cases strewn over the floor, she sighed.

Okay, so what if it isn't just about Lucky? So what? It doesn't change anything. It doesn't change the past, and it sure doesn't change the here and now.

Sniffling, Peggy climbed across the bed that offered her no rest and picked up the books and her notes off of the floor.

"I'm the only who can?" Peggy muttered. "Yeah, right." She picked up the frayed rope that had been around Lucky's neck. She stared at it a good long moment, then sank down on the bed beside Terry's box of files. Without ownership of her own bones and spine, what was she supposed to be able to do, that no one else could do? Especially against a monster like Harrison who was masquerading as a human? Who's kidding who?

She tucked Lucky's rope into her pocket. Maybe I can't do anything to help Lucky, but...

But?

But...a promise is a promise. I'll hold the fort. What else can I do? With reluctance, Peggy set out the files and books across her bed, again. She picked up her pen, sat back against her pillows, and propped her notebook on her knees. She wiped the tears off of her face with her sleeve.

Maybe by the time you come back, Terry, she sniffled, I'll have made it through a day without burning the place down, or being tarred and feathered by your crew.

The wind rattled the window panes, and though she shivered, Peggy ignored it and opened her notebook. "Place your bets..."

"What're you're nuts?" Joe stood with hands on his hips. "You ain't serious with this!"

The crew gazed around at the newspaper-stuffed walls of the kennel room, and the dogs; lounging on dry, newspaper-lined beds, looking down-right comfy.

Peggy stuffed one last wad of newspaper into the north-facing wall, then sat back on her heels. "Terry said it was a good idea at Christmas, remember?"

"And if *you* remember, I told you then it was pistachio nuts! We gotta hose the place twice a day! And with one less uniform to help out, you know how much work this is gonna be? How'm I supposed to patrol three times a day up by Harrison's, on top of all this?"

"I'll do both kennel shifts, if it helps keep the place warmer—and it does, see? Not one draft! The books say their chances of-of staying healthy are better."

"Saint Francis," Betty said, "every wintah them dogs git KC, and ovah-crowdin' just be a fact o'life here."

"Yes, but it says here, in this book," Peggy read aloud from a worn Merck Manual, "under infectious trach-eo-bronchitis of dogs—that's kennel cough—it says; 'environmental factors such as cold, drafts, and high humidity apparently increase susceptibility to the disease'. That's this kennel, perfectly. If we try, maybe we can beat the odds."

"Book, what book?" Joe snatched it out of her hands.

"It's-it's Dr. Hayward's veterinary manual. He leaves it in the office, every night."

"Guy's prob'ly got it memorized."

Betty scanned Peggy's notes. "What's this, here, 'bout doin' laundry?"

"Oh, well, to get their beds dry after hosing them off, I-I sort of... used up all the paper towels."

"You what?!" Joe balked. "That box is supposed to last a month!"

"I-I'll buy more, out of my own pocket! See, I-I already figured it out on Betty's adding machine. If you use blankets and towels, look how much you'd save instead of buying paper towels! I-I've done up another ad ask-asking for old towels and blankets."

"And chicken broth?" Clara read over Betty's shoulder.

"Oh, yes! You know how some of them won't eat because they're depressed or scared; well it says right-right here: 'attempts may be made to stimulate the appetite by giving warm food or by offering several different types of food. Beef gravy, chicken, fish or perhaps raw or cooked red meat or liver.' So I-I thought, what's the next best thing? And I figured...chicken broth. And it worked! Look! Even Digger ate every bite of his food!"

"Fart yeah!" Joe exclaimed. "Dish some out to me, I'll eat it too! Jeeze Louise! What's for dessert?!"

"It also says here: 'Individual persuasion, such as talking to and petting the dog, hand feeding may be necessary by attendants who like dogs and will cater to them as occasion demands'. I-I'm sure they meant to... to include cats in that, too, Clara."

"I daresay," the old woman sniffed, her nose in the air.

"We do a lot of this stuff already!" Joe flipped through the pages. "More than most places!"

"Yes, I-I know. It's just that they need more. Especially one-on-one time. I'll do that, too!"

"I seem to recall only twenty-four hours to a day," Clara admonished.

"And just where we gonna git the bread fo' all this when we gotta put the damn kibble on credit?" Betty asked. "Uh, and what's this, here, 'bout askin' folk to donate a washah 'n dryah?"

"Yeah, right!" Joe sputtered a laugh. "Wait a sec! You serious? Jeeze, screw the laundromat! Why not ask for a new car?"

Clara raised her hand. "I'd like a four-door in blue."

Just then, a dog coughed. Peggy whirled around. "Shhhh!" Holding her breath, she paced the kennel and scrutinized the dogs. A skinny little beagle coughed. "Oh no, not again!"

"This what I be sayin'," Betty said. "It only be a mattah of time."

"Uh boy," Joe sighed. "You know what his royal highness is gonna say, Saint Francis."

Peggy's heart sank. Yes, she knew exactly what Dr. Hayward would say. She leashed the little beagle up and walked him past the crew, straight into the office.

Already an hour late, Paul whipped the Jaguar down the driveway into the parking lot. He claimed his spot along the fence; far enough away from the shelter's entrance and the firehouse exit to avoid any dings or break-ins. He grabbed his coffee and medical bag, jumped out of the car and slammed the door on his coat.

"Damn it!" He keyed the door and upended the coffee down his pressed Italian slacks. "Oh for...perfect. Just *perfect!*"

He slapped the wetness off of his groin. It had been bad enough, having to euthanize some of the shelter's favorite misfits, right after their beloved manager had been crippled. To then have to fill in for that jackass, Miller, on the graveyard shift at the EVC, without benefit of a break, no dinner, or even a shower, while the aforesaid bootlicker traveled in style with Dr. Caldwell to a neuroblastoma seminar up in Syracuse...he was in no mood.

Adding insult to injury, he spent the rest of the night pumping the bloated stomach of a two hundred and fifty pound Saint Bernard. It had left him not only sleep-deprived and smelling like vomit, but feeling like he'd been slam-dunked to the bottom of the barrel of his career.

He unlocked his coat from the door, then took a deep steadying breath. If extra moonlighting at the EVC helped to chip away at the six month contract with the pound, even by two weeks, then it was worth eating crow, every night.

He trudged up the walkway and into the building, vowing to himself with every step that, grief or no grief, rookie or no rookie in charge; he was the veterinarian in charge and would not tolerate another challenge to his authority.

Before shoving the front door open, he steeled himself for the onslaught of barking. It didn't happen. Entering the kennel, he gazed around at the dozing dogs on their padded beds, and stared at newspaper stuffed walls.

The office door flew open, and Peggy rushed towards him, stammering, shoving a dog's file folder into his hand.

"Th-this is B-beetle's record. He's the beagle that came in last week and he's-he's been fine until this morning, I-I swear. It only just start-started an hour ago. He doesn't act sick. Not like the others did, yesterday. And they all ate fine, for the first time! I-I should have asked you first, but it's from your book, here, you see? It's a nutrition plan. I-I put broth in their food, and see? They all ate. Even Beetle! But I isolated him in the office right away, b-because he coughed."

"Good morning."

Peggy took a breath and noticed the vet's haggard appearance. It looked like he hadn't even shaved. "Oh. Yes. Morning. S-sorry, it's just…"

"Beagle, you said?" Dr. Hayward looked over the dog's record.

"Yes."

"With a cough."

"Yes, b-but it's not like the others. It's more like; ack...ack...aaaack," Peggy imitated Beetle's cough, gagging in demonstration.

"How was that, again?"

Peggy gagged and lolled her tongue, dramatically, doing her best to imitate the little beagle as precisely as she could for the vet. "Ack...ack.. aaaack." Looking up, she caught what looked like the hint of a smile in his eyes, but he turned away, reaching for a paper towel from the emtpy dispenser.

"Oh sorry, we're out." She paused, noticing the broad, wet stain down the front of his slacks. She diverted her gaze to his shoes, which were mismatched.

"Yes, I know," Dr. Hayward remarked. He walked past her, to the office.

Peggy gawked at the rip down the rear of his nice wool coat. She clapped a hand over her mouth and followed him into the office.

"Mornin' Doc," Joe called out as they entered.

"Morning Doctah," Betty chimed in.

"Vit'riny," Clara nodded civilly.

They all stared at him with plastered smiles, while looking him up and down.

Paul spotted the beagle underneath the counter on Peggy's coat, beside the radiator. He knelt down, donned his stethoscope, and listened to the dog's chest.

Peggy watched closely, as he opened the dog's mouth, then shone a flashlight into its throat. Beetle pulled away and coughed into a quick, gagging spasm. Paul studied him until the spasm ceased, then ran his hand over its coat, and palpated the abdomen. "Hold his head, will you?" he murmured to Peggy.

Peggy cradled the dog's head in her arms, and Paul inserted a thermometer into its rectum. He placed his other hand over the dog's heart. After a quiet minute, he removed the thermometer and read it. Using hair clippers, he shaved off a patch of fur on the inside of Beetle's leg, swabbed it with alcohol, and then tied a length of tubing around the dog's elbow.

Peggy looked to the crew. They seemed worried, too. She cleared her throat. "Are you-are you putting him to sleep?"

Paul uncapped a syringe with his teeth. "Not yet. Scratch the top of his head. The idea is to distract him."

Peggy scratched the dog between the ears. Paul tapped a swollen vein on the inside of Beetle's foreleg, and then slipped the needle in. He untied the rubber tubing and the syringe filled with blood. When nearly filled, he eased the needle out and handed Peggy a cotton ball. "Hold that, there, please."

Peggy pressed the cotton against the injection site. Paul injected the blood into a rubber-capped glass vial and labeled it.

"Will that tell you if-if he's got kennel cough?" Peggy asked.

"No, but it might confirm my hunch that he's got heartworm."

"Heartworm?" Peggy had prepared herself to hear kennel cough, but heartworm? It sounded horrible and serious.

"Aw jeeze," Joe sighed, and pet the dog. "Poor little guy."

"How-how did he..." Peggy began.

"It's a mosquito-transmitted parasite," Paul explained, "using the dog as its favorite host. A lot of dogs don't show symptoms until winter, when it's often misdiagnosed as kennel cough. By the time the symptoms intensify, they're coughing up blood and generally collapse with congestive heart failure." He nodded to the beagle. "The time frame matches. He's an outdoor hunting dog, the ones most vulnerable. He has all the tell-tale symptoms; dry cough, acute weight loss, listless demeanor, fatigue after mild exercise, and a dull coat. If he's infected, it should show up in the test. If it had been a month ago, the test might have been negative. The antigens don't usually show until seven months after infection. Vets rarely used to see heartworm in the northeast. It's been creeping northward with the warmer winters."

"Oh...well, if-if he has it, then you'll put him to sleep?"

Paul wiped the scopes with alcohol. "The cure is tricky, time-consuming, and not always successful."

"But there's a cure? It's just that there was a couple interested in him, last week. They told Terry they'd come back when his seven days were up, which is tomorrow."

"Did I mention it's expensive?" He turned away to the medicine cabinet.

"Maybe, if they knew there was a cure, they'd help pay for it."

Betty stifled a chuckle. "Honey, they could get a healthy one wiff papers at the pet shop, fo' less!"

"Hypothetically," Paul advised, "even if they want him, and they're willing to pump money into him, they'll have to know the risks. The therapy alone might kill him. We use an arsenic compound to kill the worms, and it's not just a one shot deal. It's going to take a few months. The dog must remain in strict, tight confinement. He's going to have to be carried outside to do his business, and then carried back inside. He's not allowed to walk, play—no activity whatsoever. It also has to be quiet. Any excitement can raise his blood pressure, causing dead worms to break loose before they're absorbed, killing him. And that's just the first phase of therapy. There's a second phase to rid his bloodstream of microfilariae; the live young that can circulate through the blood stream for two years, just waiting for another passing mosquito."

"That'll pass it to another dog. I see." Peggy sighed. Beetle wagged his tail. She pet him, sadly. He would have to be put on the euth list.

"Let me talk to the couple," Paul scribbled in a little notebook. "If they're willing to pay for his adoption up front, and see the whole process through for the duration, even without a guarantee that treatment will be a success, I'll pick up the tab for the treatment."

Peggy looked up, surprised, along with the rest of the crew.

"For now," he continued, "I'll set up a crate for him, downstairs. It'll be quieter and warmer." He pocketed his notebook and gathered the little beagle in his arms.

Peggy climbed to her feet and opened the door for him. "Th-thank you."

"It'll be an interesting case. I've never done a heartworm, before."

The crew watched him carry the beagle through the kennel and out the front door.

"Uh...is it me or did Doc get up on the wrong side of somebody's bed this mornin' and like, turn inta somebody else?" Joe whispered.

Whap!

"Ow!"

"What Terry tell you 'bout gossip?" Betty scolded him. She tossed the rolled up newspaper onto the table, close by, just in case.

"You saw him! You heard him! Who is that guy? C'mon! He ain't never without a frickin' tie tac! And now Doc-let's-nuke-before-they-puke is springin' for heartworm? He musta got some last night is alls I'm sayin', 'cause why else is he in such a Good Samaritan mood and lookin' like an unmade bed?"

"'E's just pushing for a get-out-of-jail card early. Burnin' candle at both ends. Time off for good behavior, more like it." Clara set a dollar on the counter.

While they debated the vet's ulterior motives—and his extracurricular activities—Peggy peered out the window, watching him carry Beetle down under the overhang towards the cellar. She had to suppress a shiver when she heard the cellar door shoved open, but she felt a surging rush of relief, too. There would be no death march of black bags to the freezer, today.

And, interesting case my foot, she thought. You're a closet Beagle Man, Dr. Hayward!

All at once, a tan Mercedes Benz pulled down the driveway and stopped in the middle of the parking lot. A middle-aged woman in a Chanel suit stepped out. Peggy watched her hurry to the passenger side, and lift a fat old Pug out of one of the new child-protective car seats.

"Oh, no," Peggy sighed.

Joe looked out, over her shoulder. "Figures. Get used to it, Saint Francis. Way it is. Clear a coupla runs, they fill right back up." He handed her the turn-in clipboard. "Your turn."

"Right." Peggy took the clipboard. She'd been dreading her first turn-in without Terry, even before his accident. She knew there would come a day when he would have handed her the forms and sent her out to do one herself, but, she'd never imagined that he wouldn't be there to coach her.

Betty smacked Joe with her rolled up newspaper, again.

"Ow! What?!"

"She ain't nevah done a turn-in befo', and that be a Benny out there. She gonna git chewed up and spit out befo' she know what hit her."

"Hey, sooner ya get knocked around, sooner ya tough it up!"

"Do I hafta say it again?"

"Jeeze!" Joe yanked open the door. "Nobody never rode rough-shod for me!"

"That's 'cause we still be waitin' fo' you to grow a pair!"

Joe heaved a sigh. "C'mon, let's go."

Feeling her face redden in embarrassment, Peggy hurried out ahead of him.

"I want to see someone in charge!"

The woman called out to Peggy from the middle of the parking lot, as if she was keeping a safe distance between herself and a plague house.

Peggy walked out to meet her. "May I—may *we* help you?"

Holding the rasping, snorting pug to her bosom, the woman craned her neck past Peggy, towards Joe. "You there! Are you in charge?"

Joe sauntered down the walkway and through the gate. "Nope."

"Who is, then?"

Joe nodded to Peggy. The woman looked her up and down, and Peggy wasn't sure if she read disbelief or disappointment in her eyes.

"Oh. Really? Well, then." Still, the woman turned her attention to Joe. "I have to turn in my dog. My husband and I are moving to Florida."

"Florida?" Peggy wrote that down on the form. "What's his name?"

"Bob."

"Hello Bob," Peggy reached out to pet the Pug.

"His name is Monty!" The woman drew back from Peggy, hugging the dog close.

"I'm sorry?"

"My husband's name is Bob, this is Monty!"

Peggy scrubbed the eraser over the form. "I'm sorry."

"Your dog prefer sleddin' to surfin'?" Joe asked.

"I beg your pardon!" The woman peered down her nose at him.

"What I'm sayin' is, if you and your husband are movin', then why not take him with you?"

"Ex-excuse me," Peggy interrupted. "How-how old is he?"

"I don't think that's any of your business!"

"We-we have to know."

"I think she meant your dog," Joe said.

"I know who she meant! What would my husband's age have to do with anything? He's only eleven!"

"Your husband's eleven?"

The woman rolled her eyes and turned to Peggy. "Monty's only eleven."

"Only!" Joe repeated.

"A very young eleven. He has more energy than most boys your age."

"Lady, he could be the Energizer Bunny, but the fact of life, here, is—"

"You seem to love him very much," Peggy interjected. "And he obviously loves you. I'm sure he'd love to go with you."

"Well, he can't!" the woman blurted out, choking up. "It's a retirement..." she was unable to continue. She dropped her chin over the happy, panting Monty, and kissed him.

Peggy noticed that the woman's heavy pancake makeup was streaked, as if she'd been crying. Her coat was old, too. The buttons were mismatched and the lining looked like it had been repaired more than once. The Bentley that had at first seemed so ostentatious was an older model. The paint was chipped, and dings peppered the doors. The woman's shoe's were worn, too. Clean, but worn.

"I see," Peggy said.

This was usually the point when Terry would have asked where the woman lived, to verify resident status, just before taking the dog in. It wasn't fair. The woman didn't want to turn her dog in. Peggy glanced at Joe. He was quiet. He saw it, too. Peggy turned the clipboard towards the woman, and offered her pen.

"Of course we'll take him in."

The woman blinked rapidly, scanning the form, and the pen trembled in her fingers. "He's been trained by professionals. Sit, stay...ten different commands. A ribboned champion! You won't have any trouble finding a...finding him a..."

"Yes," Peggy voiced what the woman could not bring herself to say. "We'll find him a good home."

Joe nudged her in the ribs and mouthed silently: "Don't tell her that!"

Peggy mouthed back, "Why not?"

The woman signed the form. "He likes chicken. White meat only. Eggs, cottage cheese and blackberries. We have...we had a vine..." her voice choked, again. She abruptly handed the pug to Peggy, turned and trod to her car.

In Peggy's arms, the pug watched his mistress get into the car. When she started the engine, he began to squirm. "Shhh...it's all right." Peggy looped a leash over his neck.

The car backed up, spinning tires on the wet pavement. Monty barked. When the car swerved away up the driveway, without him, the fat little dog writhed wildly in Peggy's arms until she had to set him down. Straining against the leash, he barked frantically after the car, and when it turned the corner he threw his muzzle into the air and howled; a pitiful, raspy, asthmatic wail that set off the rest of the dogs into barking and howling along with him.

Peggy dropped to her knees and tried to console the dog, until the firemen appeared at the rear door of the firehouse, glaring at them.

"Friggit," Joe snapped. "Get him inside before they report us, again!"

Peggy scooped up the squirming dog and hurried him through the gate. Over her shoulder, Monty fought to be heard over the other dogs, barking wildly, his eyes fixed on the spot where he last saw his mistress turn the corner.

Chapter 33

Monty howled for two hours before his raspy voice finally gave out.

Listless, he laid in his bed, refusing food and all attempts to comfort him. Peggy knew what Dr. Hayward was going to say. Monty is another Digger; another eleven-year-old, depressed dog, with asthma, whose odds for adoption were fifty to one.

Maybe if they hadn't taken in four more dogs right after Monty, the little dog might have a ghost of a chance. But, the other dogs were younger, and they now had a full house.

The four turn-ins demoralized Peggy. The shelter was no match against the economy. Three more people had decided to move out of state. The fourth dog was found wandering Bloomfield Avenue, most probably dumped for the same reason. If they needed one more space, little Monty would be placed on the euth list, right alongside Digger. It was so unfair.

Peggy knelt down in the damp run with the dog and pet him. What could she do? Like Terry had said, the animals just kept coming. What would Terry do? She wondered again, why they hadn't heard from Chicago. She could only hope that no news was good news.

A car horn blared from outside in the parking lot. The dogs burst into their deafening chorus, and Peggy clapped her hands over her ears.

Joe kicked open the office door and waved the turn-in clipboard at her. "I told ya we shoulda locked up! C'mon, I'm gonna need help with this one."

"But-but there's no open run!"

"Run? We're gonna need a new friggin' wing!"

"N-new wing?" Peggy scampered after him. "What do you mean?"

Peggy followed Joe out the gate, as a long battered station wagon pulled into a space. Pressed up against the tailgate window were the runny-nosed faces of about seven children, all jockeying for a better view out the fogged windows.

"Joe, w-we can't take in children! Can we?"

"Lookit," he warned her, "we been through this a gazillion times already with Mrs. Pytleski. Whatever you do, don't feel sorry for her!"

"B-but…"

A pinched woman with frayed, russet hair stepped out of the station wagon. Instantly, a two hundred pound, hairy black behemoth of a dog exploded out behind her. His leash tied around her waist, he half-dragged her across the lot.

"Ahhhhhhhh!" Mrs. Pytleski cried out, holding on to the leash for dear life.

"Oh my gosh!" Peggy gasped.

Joe jumped in between them. "Halt!" he ordered the dog. It bared four-inch fangs with a bone-chilling growl. Joe drew a pistol from his holster and aimed.

Peggy ducked.

"Don't shoot! Don't shoot!" the woman wailed.

Too late. Joe pulled the trigger, and a stream of water hit the huge dog's snout. Startled, it stopped in its tracks. Then, it snatched the water pistol out of Joe's hand—and ate it.

Peggy's mouth dropped open. The giant canine crouched, about to jump Joe. Peggy scrambled to her feet, grabbed hold of its leash, and yanked hard.

"No!"

The great black dog turned on her with a growl. Backed against the fence, Peggy shook her fist at it and shouted. "No! Sit!"

To her amazement, the dog lay down and whined, hiding his head under his paws. Peggy couldn't believe it.

"Holy cow! Good goin', Saint Francis!" Joe helped Mrs. Pytleski back up on to her feet and untied the leash from around her waist.

"How you do zat?" the woman exclaimed in a clipped, Slavic accent. "I tell him to sit, he eat da sofa!"

"I-I don't know. He-he must have thought I was going to hurt him." Peggy hid her fist behind her back.

"Hey lookit, if not you, I was gonna!" Joe smacked his own fist into his palm.

Peggy wrung her hands. It had been nothing more than a knee-jerk response to save her own skin. Still, what good was a fist when he could have bitten her hand off? Or, her head?

"Dat's vat last trainer do. He put on bunny suit, but den..." she covered her face in her hands and cried.

"Don't tell me," Joe said. "He ate the guy."

"Almost."

"Bunny suit?" Peggy asked.

"Riot gear," Joe explained. "Thick padding. Supposed to protect the trainers."

"I don't understand," Mrs. Pytleski wiped tears from her face. "Why he lissen ziss time?"

"Beats me, but good thing he did! Jeeze, he's even bigger than last time. What the heck you been feedin' him?"

"Anyzing he vants."

The giant dog peeked up at Peggy from under his great paws, then wagged his broom of a tail.

"Saint Francis," Joe said, "meet Gorgo. Eight-month-old water buffalo."

"Eight months? You mean he's…"

"Still a puppy."

Gorgo woofed at Joe, sending him backwards into the fencing. If she didn't know that Joe was scared to death, it would have been funny. It was then, that Peggy understood the problem. This "puppy" got his way, because he was as big as a house, and everybody was afraid of him! This was no dumb dog! Still, why did he respond to her raised fist and not the trainer's?

"Look at him," Mrs. Pytleski sniffled into a hankie, "he tinks it funny!"

Panting happily, the great dog did indeed look like he was laughing at them.

"Awww, Mrs. P.," Joe said, "don't cry. Lookit, you tried. More than anybody's business!"

Joe explained to Peggy that Mrs. Pytleski and her earnest, moppish brood had come to the shelter six months previously and had adopted the Newfoundland-mixed pup. Mrs. P's husband traveled to Europe, extensively, and both he and his wife felt it would be best to have a dog, both for protection and family companionship.

"Mrs. P. don't like to be alone, right Mrs. P.?"

"Is true!" Mrs. Pytleski blew her nose into a hankie.

How the woman could feel alone with seven children, Peggy couldn't fathom! The woman had adopted the affable Gorgo, and off they went, on their way to happily ever after, only to return again and again, with stories of how he ruled the roost with an estimated IQ greater than that of her eldest child. He'd also tripled in size and weight every month, and had taken to eating major portions of her house.

Those tales convinced Terry and Joe that the dog was ill-suited for Mrs. Pytleski, despite the woman's obvious affection for him. Yet, every time she brought Gorgo back, she'd end up sobbing with remorse and resolved to try another trainer. Off she'd go, wiping away brave tears, dragged back into her car by the oafish dog. So far, he'd flunked out of two obedience schools and was the subject of a formal complaint filed by a third.

"I did try!" Mrs. Pytleski cried. "I do everyzing they tell me. Every time he eat da clothesline, I squirt him vit hose, like dey show me. Den he eat da hose!"

Peggy glanced at the children, still crammed in the back of the car. Their faces grubby with animal cracker crumbs, they were apparently quite used to this scene.

Mrs. Pytleski blew her nose. "Den, he help himself to da garbage. Everybody's garbage. He make himself da Pest of Passaic. Den, he see garbage come first from Fridgidare. He vatch me every time I open Fridgidare door. Pretty soon der nothing left for supper but dog food! Only ting he von't eat."

Joe shook his head. "Mrs. P, you've gone far and above the call of duty. He's just too—"

"Stupit!" Mrs. Pytleski sniffled. "He got goot home vit us. Vee love him. I bring him home because he vass lonely like me. Stupit doggie. He too smart for me."

Peggy regarded Mrs. Pytleski. Here she was, being eaten out of house and home by an unruly dog blacklisted by trainers in three counties, and yet she couldn't bear the thought of turning him in. Still, what more could they do after trying everything? There was nothing to do really, but to take the dog back.

Peggy glanced behind her to the runs. Where on earth would they put him? And for how long? Because, Monty the eleven-year-old pug was one thing. A two hundred pound gorilla of a dog with a penchant for living room furniture as an appetizer was another. The vet would never okay the dog's adoption to anyone else! He'd be put down first.

"You don't need to sign any papers," she heard Joe say, "you gone the distance with this guy."

"Six times. I'm six times crazy! But diss da last. I can't take no more. I'm so sorry." The woman dabbed her nose with her hankie, then paused, looking past them to the runs. "Vat's wrong vit dat one?"

Joe and Peggy followed her gaze around to little Monty, sitting at the end of his run, watching them. Until a moment ago, he'd been depressed and unresponsive.

"Nuthin'," Joe said, "he was dumped by his owner."

"Oh noooooo..." Mrs. Pytleski burst into fresh tears. "Oh, poor baby..." She walked over to Monty's run.

Gorgo jumped up, about to gallop after her, when Peggy again shouted. "Sit!"

Instantly, little Monty sat down, straight and proud in his run. So then, did Gorgo, right in the middle of the parking lot! His eyes were fixed on little Monty. Peggy glanced between them and called out again.

"Down! Lie down!"

Monty laid down, obediently. Gorgo flopped down, too, imitating the little pug.

"Oh my gosh!" Peggy exclaimed. "Look! He's imitating Monty!"

"Vat?" Mrs. Pytleski sniffled.

"Get outta here!" Joe gaped.

"Roll over!" Peggy commanded.

In his run, fat little Monty flopped down and rolled over. Gorgo clumsily followed suit, his eyes riveted on the pug.

"Sit!" Peggy called out. Up Monty sat, with Gorgo mirroring him just a half second later. Both dogs wagged their tails at one another and whined.

"Wow. Monkey see, monkey do!" Joe laughed.

"Maybe diss vat Gorgo need?" Mrs. Pytleski whispered. "A doggie friend to be good influenza?! I take wittle Monty home to teach Gorgo?"

"What a good idea!" Peggy blurted out.

"*What?*" Joe gasped.

"Monty's a trained champion," Peggy reminded him. "It could work!"

"What?" Joe repeated.

"It's worth a try! Joe, we're full up and-and I'm afraid if we don't find a home for them both, today, they're done for."

"Oh, poor wittle Monty!" Mrs. Pytleski wept his name and crouched down to the pug. "Aww, you vant come home vitt us?"

"You off your rocker?" Joe hissed at Peggy. "She's already half-way to bonkers with Bigfoot, over there!"

"Look at them!" Peggy gestured to the two dogs wagging their tails at each other. "What could it hurt?"

"Lookit, even if it works, we're still a run short. We're still gonna hafta put somebody down."

"Who's dat sad sack der?" Mrs. Pytleski asked, pointing behind them.

Joe and Peggy followed her point around to Digger, sitting at the end of his run, watching Gorgo and Monty with sorrowful eyes, the tip of his tail wagging, too.

Peggy looked up to Joe with a smile. He rolled his eyes.

"Aw, Jeeze..."

After cramming Gorgo, little Monty and Digger into Mrs. Pytleski's already overstuffed car, Peggy and Joe waved goodbye to them. As the car back-fired past them, Gorgo stuck his head out the window and woofed one last time at Joe.

"Jeeze!"

Monty jutted his muzzle out from under his new friend and yapped hoarsely at Joe, too.

"Louise!"

Out of the back window, Digger wagged his tail, the arms of seven children wrapped around him.

Feeling a bit smug, Peggy raised her brows to Joe.

"Okay," he admitted, "that was like a trifecta, and against every policy we got. Y'know that, right?"

"All I know is, those are three dogs that Dr. Hayward won't be able to put on the list."

Hearing the gate latch, they both turned. Paul leaned against it, casually. "Funny, I don't recall giving those dogs an exit exam, vaccinations or a health certificate. Do you?"

Looking sheepish, Joe glanced at Peggy. She wrung her hands and gulped. Abruptly the front door opened and Clara hollered. "Call from Chicago!"

Peggy and Joe nearly fell over each other dashing past the vet into the building.

"Lemme talk to him!" Joe made a grab for the phone.

"Git! Git!" Betty smacked him repeatedly with a newspaper and spoke into the receiver. "Sorry, what's that? Yes, I understand...uh-huh..."

"That Ter? C'mon! I wanna talk to him!"

"Shushup!" Betty smacked him, again. "No, not you! Yessum. Uh-huh...uh-huh..." she looked up to Peggy.

Peggy gripped the back of Terry's chair with one hand and her St. Francis pendant in the other. She studied every line in Betty's face. Her heart was beating so fast that she felt light-headed. Please God, please, let him be all right! Let it be good news.

"Uh-huh, well, maybe you wanna talk to Peggy? What's that again? No, no. Uh-huh...I understand, yeah...uh-huh..."

"What, what, what?" Joe insisted.

When Betty's smile turned to a frown, Peggy's stomach twisted into a double knot.

Joe shoved in close to Betty's ear, trying to listen in.

"Uh-huh, uh-huh," Betty nodded, her face solemn. "That be good tho', right? Uh-huh, uh-huh. Well, that be somethin', praise the Lawd. Uh-huh, uh-huh. What do that mean? Uh-huh. Oh yeah, tell me 'bout it. Okay, so do you want us to..." she smacked Joe off of her shoulder with the newspaper. "Okay, no I get it...uh-huh...sounds good." She looked to Peggy again. "You give him our love, okay? We be thinkin' of him and hopin' he git better real...uh-huh...uh-huh. Okidoke. Bye."

"What'd she say?" Joe demanded. "That was Irene, right? Is he okay? I couldn't hear a friggin' thing with that accent of hers!"

"Well," Betty broke open a fresh pack of candy cigarettes. "All told, it be good news."

"Why didn't ya just say so!"

"Be*cause*, tho' he be stable, he still listed as critical."

Peggy felt a stab of fear, because Betty took a moment then, weighing her words; something she never did.

"They done put him in a coma, on account his brain swell up, which happen wiff cases like his, Irene said, that be why she didn't call right off, but the good news be, the swellin' already be comin' down. They gonna wait another forty-eight and if it stay down, then they gonna wake him up. He gonna need a body cast, but the good news be, it look like he gonna walk again. Just gonna be mattah of time. Longer than we maybe hoped, but, that E.R. doctah warned us 'bout that, already. Irene say she gonna call when she can, keep us in the know."

Peggy couldn't remember a thing Betty had said past, "they done put him in a coma."

"How long is longer?" The sound of the vet's voice startled her. He was standing beside her. She hadn't even heard him open the door.

"You know how it be. They nevvah wanna say fo' sure, but Irene think it gonna be a year an' a half. Maybe less. It all gonna depend on him."

"Stable is good."

"Really? Yeah?" Joe looked like he was grasping for a lifeline.

"Yes...considering. Stable is very good."

Clara laid a dollar on the counter. "Odds are with th'ouse on this one. 'E walks in by Christmas."

Peggy held a death grip on Terry's chair, feeling as if she were about to fall off the edge of the world, but she smiled, relieved that not a single bet was placed against Clara's call. Christmas. It seemed so far away. But, it was something to cling to, and maybe, just maybe, like today's happy adoption, it was a sign that things were looking up.

Chapter 34

"We're screwed."

"What?" Peggy jerked her head up from Terry's grant application. "What's happened now?"

"At eight a.m. sharp today, Febu-erry second; Punxsutawney Phil did not, repeat, did *not* see his shadow!" Joe announced.

"No!" Clara gasped.

Betty kissed her crucifix and crossed herself with abject solemnity, clasping her hands in fervent prayer.

"Joe!" Peggy exhaled. "I thought you were going to tell us something terrible!"

"Saint Fran, this is like, the worst news, ever!"

Peggy shook her head, not sure whether to laugh, or smack him with the newspaper. Her first month without Terry had flown by in a frenetic blur. In a valiant attempt to hold the fort for him, she was run off her feet from the moment she unlocked the front door in the morning, until she locked it, each evening. She struggled every hour on the hour just to keep up, and make up, for her vast inexperience. As if to test her, the place sprang new and unexpected challenges at her, daily.

Between the exhausting toll of the chores, trying to keep the animals healthy, adopted, and off of the euth list, Peggy barely closed her eyes before falling into a deep, dreamless sleep. That alone gave her the impetus to continue working herself into the ground the next day and the next; anything to help keep the "screaming meemies" at bay, and to keep her from worrying over Terry, and Lucky, too.

Once a week, Irene called with an update regarding Terry. Since Betty answered the phones, it was usually Betty who held the conversation. Twice, Peggy had been out back hosing the runs and missed the call altogether. Although she never would have admitted it to anyone, Peggy was secretly glad to have missed them. Not knowing meant that Terry was still stable. She was also glad to have Betty as a buffer, because Peggy wasn't at all sure that, if handed the phone, she wouldn't break down sobbing, begging him to come back.

It took a week before the doctors brought Terry out of the induced coma. They kept him heavily sedated and on a respirator for the following two weeks. Twice, Irene's calls were cut short, due to her schedule. Those calls were hard on the crew, but they all coped by diving head first into the work.

Joe's daily patrols around Harrison's neighborhood had turned up no sign of Lucky outside, but gave them no additional information, either. They had not seen nor heard from Harrison, since his late night visit with "condolences" from the mayor. Since working late every evening, Peggy had been unable to sneak past the stone wall around Harrison's house to check for herself. After the temperature fell and a few inches of snow had fallen, the extra bus ride became an iffy prospect with regards to making it back to her apartment before freezing to death.

"Doncha get it?" Joe sat down beside Peggy, jolting her back to the present. "No shadow equals early spring!"

"No shadow? Oh! Groundhog Day. But, an early spring, that's good news, isn't it?"

Joe, Betty and Clara shared an incredulous laugh, then Joe swept Terry's jacket aside on the coat rack. On the other side of the hot line phone, hung the graphic poster; the large photo of a wide-eyed, innocent puppy sitting in front of pile of dead puppies and kittens.

"Every spring, when everybody else is plantin' posies? Guess what we're plantin'!"

Peggy's hand fluttered to her mouth. "Oh no!"

"You think we be overcrowded, now?" Betty blew her nose. "Just the tip of th'iceberg, baby."

"And the ice caps're melting," Clara reminded them.

"But y-you can't just euth puppies and kittens!" Peggy entreated them.

"Why you think I'm always haulin' in all those unspayed studs runnin' around, off leash? Thanks to back yard breeders, guess who gets all the bastard rejects? Beware the Tides of March, all I'm sayin'."

"That's 'Ides of March', y'beefwit," Clara growled.

"Six of one, yada, yada, yada..."

"There must be something we can do!" Peggy insisted.

"It boil down to numbers, Saint Francis." Betty broke open a new inhaler. "You been here long enough to know that."

My God, Peggy balked. How could they? How could Terry? She glanced at the calendar, counting the weeks until spring. Maybe he would be back before spring.

The kennel dogs woofed at the front door opening and closing, and in a moment, Paul ducked his head in the office.

"The boiler's acting out again. It's got water, but it's not putting out any heat, and it sounds as if it's got gas, which I assume is not a good sign."

"Natch," Joe sighed, and checked his watch. "It's only quarter to deep freeze. Why're we sweatin' spring? We ain't never gonna make it to Valentine's Day!"

"Maybe w-we better call Mr. Riley." Peggy flipped through the Rolodex. "It's going down below zero, tonight!"

"And pay him how?" Betty asked. "We done spent the town's check fo' this quarter already!"

"Okay, which bills can we float?"

"Float? Honey, every bill got at least two lead sinkers on 'em. We been overdue wiff half of 'em, since New Year's. I told you."

Peggy bit her lip. Yes, Betty had told her. But, she didn't tell her what to do about it.

"Well, you've got to have heat," Paul said. "Can't you put it on credit?"

Betty sputtered a laugh. "Doctah, they cut up our liberry card, two years ago."

"Oh, bugger it," Clara snapped, over her clacking knitting needles. "Hand me my bag, there, Saint Francis."

Betty stayed Peggy's hands, wagging her finger at Clara. "Oh, no you don't! Only bigger I.O.U. to you is the one the country owe us all after 'Nam!"

"Bah! And, when 'aven't you coughed up brass for bunny food or a chew toy for one o' them curs, out there?" Clara snatched her purse from Peggy and pulled out a large, cameo brooch, then handed it to Joe. "Take it to the pawnshop; tell Neville we need to cover the stewpot's exorcism by that sodden leprechaun again. 'E may take pity."

"I can't hock your family jewels!"

"Oh Clara," Peggy agreed, "they're right, you can't!"

"A one time loan!" Clara waved her away. "It's a bargain at any price, considerin' it were a donation to me, ages ago, for services rendered."

The old woman caught Joe's raised brow and raised her own. "Cat services, if you please!"

"Did I say nuthin'?"

"Then be off with you! Longer you dilly dally, longer me cats be shiverin'!"

Peggy and Betty shared a furtive look but said nothing. Joe sheepishly pocketed the brooch and grabbed his keys.

"I'll have my ears on."

Peggy watched him leave, sauntering by Paul, leaning in the doorway. The dogs jumped to their feet and barked at Joe as he walked through the kennel.

"Shadaaaaap!" Joe flipped the front door closed behind him with his boot.

Peggy watched the vet approach the medicine cabinet. They exchanged brief glances, and then he pulled bottles out of his medical bag and arranged them on the shelves.

"Beetle's had the first Carposolate dosage."

"Oh, thank you." Peggy jotted it down in the record book. "H-how is he?"

"So far, so good."

Peggy waited, but he didn't elaborate any further. When he finished, he closed his bag and headed out the door.

"I'll be downstairs."

Peggy watched him go. Settled down for their morning nap, the dogs did not bark at him.

"Guess we should be grateful he be payin' fo' that medicine," Betty said, returning to her adding machine.

Peggy craned her neck at the window and watched Dr. Hayward walk through the front gate, past the red Jaguar, and on down under the overhang, down to the cellar.

She sat back, a shiver snaking its way down her back. When she heard the door below shove closed, she frowned. Yes, the good doctor was paying for the medicine to make Beetle well, and yes, she was grateful for that. Still, what she really wanted to say was, "Hey, Mr. Moneybags, how can you not feel like a heel, driving around in that fancy sports car of yours, when an old woman is hocking her jewelry, just so we can have heat?"

It wasn't like the shelter's plight was a secret. He had been working there over a month now and had witnessed their "rob Peter to pay Paul" tactics with paying the bills. The shelter leaned worse than the tower of Pisa towards having its doors closed.

Peggy pulled Terry's grant application out of the box, determined to figure out a money-making strategy by day's end. The next calamity might very well put the shelter under, or an old woman out of her house!

Later that afternoon, as the pipes clanked and banged in the walls over the muffled curses of Mr. Riley, Betty counted out the money Joe brought back from the pawnshop.

"That's all of it, then?" Clara sighed.

"Your pal, Neville, said everybody and their grandma's dumpin' this kinda stuff." Joe flopped into his chair and chugged a can of Mountain Dew. "No offense."

Clara looked to Peggy. "It's on you, then."

Peggy set the grant application aside and kneaded her temple. "The deadline's not until September. There's got to be a way to bring in more money, now."

"Like how?" Joe burped. "Hangin' out on the corner with a tin cup?"

"Sporting idea!" Clara shot back. "Put your arse to use for a change!"

"Har, har, har."

Peggy stared at them, more specifically, at the empty soda can Joe twirled idly on the counter like a top. Her heart skipped a beat. "That's it!"

"What's it?" Joe looked at her askance.

Peggy dashed out into the kennel room and pulled an empty dog food can from the garbage can. She rinsed it out, then trotted back into the office. She searched the waste basket and pulled out a brown paper bag, then wrapped the can in it. She took up a black marker and drew pawprints on it, then set it in front of them.

Joe grimaced. "Uh...I was only kiddin', okay?"

"Why not?" Peggy entreated them. "L-like all those other charities! UNICEF, and the Salvation Army? They've got cans in the shops all over town."

"Hold your horses there, Saint Francis! Schleppin' inta the pawnshop and hockin' Brunhilda's dowry was bad enough! Ain't no friggin' way I'm beggin'! Ain't no friggin' way!"

Chapter 35

Clank.

Peggy flinched when Joe slammed her donation can down on the counter in front of Jack, the owner of Jack's Chinese Food and Donut shop. She hung by the doorway and bit her lip.

The immutable Chinaman regarded the can wrapped in glue-stained paper and paw prints affixed to it. "You beggar man, now?"

Joe popped open a soda and thumbed over his shoulder to Peggy. "Her idea."

Jack peered past him to her, with blank reserve. "Who she?"

"Rookie with the City. She thinks we can dodge Chapter Eleven with this Pennies for Puppies schtick."

Peggy's toes curled with embarrassment. She'd stayed up all night, decorating close to a hundred empty dog food cans. To her, they looked silly next to the likes of cans from The Salvation Army and UNICEF.

Jack's was their first stop in the donation can campaign, because it was Joe's favorite shop. In the heavy rush-hour traffic, Joe had filled Peggy in about Jack's colorful history. The nondescript storefront had no sign out front, but everyone in town knew the shop.

Jack's offered the best greasy chow mein, orange chicken, and beef broccoli from 7 a.m. until 7 p.m., seven days a week, alongside twenty varieties of the most delicious, home-made doughnuts anyone had ever tasted. Every Monday was "day-old" day. Handing out day-old pastries to law enforcement was the only legal way Jack could get around the town's health codes. To Jack, the concept of expiration dates was more than just silly—date or no date. To toss food in the trash was utterly un-thinkable. Forty years previously, Jack had fled Communist China as a child of eleven, with his family. After surviving famine, war and a sweat-shop upbringing, he was a man who had pretty much seen everything.

To look at him, one would never suspect a long-suffering past. The man embodied the serenity borne of a Buddhist monk. His smooth,

Pacific face never once betrayed opinion or judgment, outside of a sly twinkle in his eye.

Jack shrugged to Joe. "Where I come from, dogs on menu."

"Aw c'mon, Jack."

"True. Good roasted, with fungi sauce. Must tenderize big ones, but puppies nice and fat."

Peggy's jaw dropped.

Joe grimaced, forcing down a swallow of soda. "Uh, ain't kosher here, Jack, y'know that, right?"

"Here, you feed dogs. Over there, dogs feed you. Different perspective."

"Yeah but, I mean c'mon...a puppy?"

"You eat veal parmesan? White Castle double patty?"

"A cow ain't no way the same thing!"

"Cow sacred in Calcutta."

"Okay, okay, I get it. Just don't tell me they taste like chicken."

Jack's eyes twinkled. "Want something to go? On house. You took in stray cat."

Joe scanned the trays of steaming chicken and beef, looking wary. "Uh...maybe just some chocolate-frosted holes."

Jack bowed his head and opened a glass case of pastries.

Peggy heard a stifled laugh from the back of the tiny shop. Three black youths shared a bear claw. The taller kid studied her, chin in hand. He looked familiar to her. All at once, she heard Terry's voice in her memory, calling out to them to volunteer, as they ran away up the driveway, past she and Lucky, her very first day.

"Yo', Curtis!" Joe waved to the taller boy.

"Yo." Curtis gathered his books and cleared the table. "C'mon, we gonna be tardy."

"Tardy farty, so go," the middle one sassed back.

"You want castigated, you keep it up!"

"You ain't the man!"

"Git yo' gloudos up, now!" Curtis grabbed both boys by their hoods, yanked them up onto their feet, and pushed them towards the exit. When they passed Peggy, the two younger boys "woofed" under their breath.

Curtis called out to Joe. "Stretch back?"

"Not for a while, man," Joe said.

Curtis nodded, then followed the younger boys out. Once the door closed, Peggy overheard Joe and Jack's hushed voices behind her.

"How boss?"

"Had a coupla operations, already. They got him in a body cast, now. We still ain't talked to him, direct-like. His sis gives us the low down. Got his good days and bad days. More bad days."

"Time."

"That's what they say, huh?"

"Because, it true."

Peggy noticed Jack peer over Joe's shoulder at her, again. She averted her eyes.

"Odd job for girl," he said.

"And vice-a-versa. But, she keeps comin' back every day; gotta give her that. Got more moxie than we figured. So, can we leave it?"

Jack set the donation can beside the register with the others. "Penny here, penny there."

"Thanks, man."

Joe joined Peggy at the door, and handed her the bag of chocolate-frosted holes. "This'll cheer us up."

"Th-thank you," Peggy offered a shy little wave. Jack bowed his head to her.

As they walked to the van, Peggy took a bite of one of the balls of fried dough, and her eyes widened in surprise. Moist and thick with deep chocolate and spices; it was delicious!

Joe grinned. "Told ya. He may come from the great wall of Shitzu-shishkabob, but ain't nobody makes better frosted-holes than Jack."

Peggy was pleased that almost every store they visited accepted her donation cans, except for one. The Old Towne Pet Shop on the border of neighboring Verona, rejected the idea. The manager felt that with so many causes, she didn't want to play favorites. Peggy and Joe were ushered from the shop rather quickly. Back in the van, Joe tossed the rejected can aside.

"You know why, doncha? She's one of the reasons we're in business to begin with, and she knows it! Joints like hers are cozy with the puppy mills in the Midwest, that crank out pups like widgets. We call 'em three pees—piss-poor purebreds. Doc Caldwell sees 'em all the time; bum hearts, lopsided ears, bad hips, jeeze, some of 'em even show up dyin' of distemper! Some of the traffickers cheapskate it when it comes to shots and bam, down goes a whole litter. Doc Caldwell's been on the warpath with the mills for like, forever. The big push starts at Christmas, at the malls. And they'll sell a pup to anybody who slaps over a check, right? The pet shops don't give a rat's buttcheeks if the buyer's a douche bag. The shops don't check inta the pups' bloodline, neither." He popped a chocolate hole into his mouth and offered Peggy the bag.

"And, don't get me started 'bout how they don't know nuthin' 'bout the breeds they sell. Take border collies, right? They got the collie thing goin' an people think awww, a little Lassie dog! But, they ain't got a clue that these dogs need a job to do. It's in their blood, okay? They wanna herd sheep, it's what they do. So, the pet shops don't say nuthin', that it's natch for these dogs to nip your ankles, butt you in the back of the knees to get ya to go where they think you oughta go. So, the peeps got kids, right? See where I'm goin' here?"

"The dogs start nipping the kids?"

Joe nodded, spitting crumbs. "Or buttin' 'em and knockin' 'em down. Dog's just tryin' to herd the kids, doin' his job. So, Fido ends up tied outside or dumped on a pound that don't know, neither, and they get euthed 'cause the gazooney in charge thinks they're biters! And, man oh man, the way the mills're messin' the breeds! Half of 'em're nutzoid now. Ya got cockers who, back when TV was black and white, were like, the best family dogs? Now, most of the nippers don't even like kids! And Irish setters? Whooeeee! Talk about fruit loops! Those're dogs needin' some major meds, man! It's cause they all been bred inta the dirt by every Tom, Dick n' Dope who's got a stud and a bitch. They sell 'em to anybody with a buck. Just 'cause junior wants a puppy, ain't no reason to get one! Not if Mom 'n Pop're both workin'! 'Cause then, who's gonna train it? Pup don't learn nuthin', so it grows up with bad habits and then, from March 'til July? We get hit with all those Christmas gifts gone bad." Joe keyed the ignition and revved the engine.

"But I thought...aren't there laws?"

"This is the U.S. of A., Saint Francis. You can sell anything to anybody stupid enough to fork it over! Backyard breedin' is a billion dollar biz. Why should anybody give a crap 'bout breedin' laws, when kids are bought and sold in this country? Don't get me started!"

"People can't sell children!"

"Courts call it foster care. You say potato, I say tomato."

Peggy shifted in her seat and gazed out the window. Joe had a point. The bigger question remained. Was there anything that anyone could do to change any of it?

One corner at a time.

Peggy pressed her eyes shut. Instead of giving her comfort, Terry's voice sounded further away than it had just a few weeks ago. She could only hope that her donation cans might bring in the needed funds to keep moving forward, or at the very least, keep the shelter doors open. How hard could that be?

Chapter 36

"Oh, for cryin' out loud! Who'd steal a friggin' donation can?"

Joe paced in front of the doughnut cases.

Jack shrugged. "Why steal letters off back of Toyota pickup?"

"Well that I get, but what kinda butt-wipe pinches pennies from puppies?"

Peggy gazed out the door to the snow-dusted parking lot. She had a pretty good idea of who had stolen the can. Those kids! Curtis and the other two. It had to have been them! They saw Joe set the can down, and they had laughed at her. Who else would have done such a thing?

For a whole week, Peggy had hurried down to the shelter, hoping to find the fruits of her can and ad campaign sitting on the Shelter's front stoop; perhaps someone left a bag of dog food, a jar or two of chicken broth, maybe even a donation check. But, morning after bitterly cold morning, she found nothing except more bills shoved through the slot in the front door.

She was sure that, after paying for groceries, people would happily drop their loose change in a can to help out the town's dogs and cats. She imagined that they might even stuff a few dollar bills in for good measure.

Peggy couldn't wait to see how much money had been donated to their cause, as they started out in the snow at eleven-thirty in the morning. By noon, she was so discouraged, she was ready to toss the rest of the cans into the town's dumpster. A few cans contained a dollar or so in change, but most held mere pennies, and a total of five had been stolen, including Jack's.

"Got another can?" Jack asked Joe.

"And what, chain it to the counter?"

"No. Nail it."

"Cool. They try to lift it, they can't!"

Jack held up a cleaver. "Then cut off hand."

"Whoa! Jack this is Jersey, not Bangkok!"

"They think twice, next time."

"No crap, but against the law, here, okay?"

"No thieving where I come from."

"No justice, neither."

"Checkmate." Jack's eyes twinkled. He turned to Peggy. "Try, try again, Miss Francis?"

"Only if...if you promise not to chop off anybody's hand."

Jack bowed his head, took the can from Peggy, then handed Joe a bag of day-old frosted holes. "How the boss?"

Joe shrugged. "Same, I guess. We didn't hear nuthin' this week."

Jack dropped a few fresh jelly doughnuts into a bag, tapped a shaker of powdered sugar into it and handed the bag to Peggy.

"Oh," Peggy searched her pockets, "I don't think I have…"

"Keep dollar for doggies. Bring good luck."

"Thank you."

On the snowy ride back to the shelter, Joe drove slowly, unusually subdued and quiet, despite annoying traffic. He didn't even bother to turn on the CB. Peggy didn't voice her suspicions about Curtis and the boys. What was the point? She had no proof. Still, she stewed about it, silently. It wasn't just a slap at her, but at Terry, who'd been nice to them. The stolen can mushroomed Peggy's concern regarding the shelter's growing debts. She could see clearly that securing funds was going to take time. More time than the shelter had to lose.

Long before Joe skidded the van down the shelter's driveway, Peggy's mood had soured. Once again, she had to face the shelter's problems with no idea what to do next. Peering ahead out the windshield, she suddenly sat up straight.

At the runs, sticks in hand, were the same three black kids, playing Keep-Away with the dogs. Before Joe had even come to a complete stop, Peggy hopped out of the van.

"Hey!" she called out over the barking dogs. "G-get away from them!" Startled, the boys looked up.

"We ain't doin' cypher!" said Curtis.

Peggy snatched the stick out of his hand. "What's this?"

"We just regalin' 'em!"

"Teasing them!"

"We don't tease 'em!"

"Just like you-you didn't steal the can, either!"

"Say what?"

"You know what I'm talking about! You stole the can!"

"Can? What can?"

"Yo!" Joe trotted up to them. "What's up?"

The two younger boys took off, running up the driveway.

"Joe, stop them!" Peggy cried.

"Why?"

Curtis turned to Joe. "Hey, Smokey, where you come off accusin' us of stealin'?"

"They stole the can!" Peggy said.

Curtis faced off with Peggy. "Why, 'cause we got black faces?"

"C'mon, Curtis," said Joe, "Ix-nay the color card, okay? That's bogus around here."

"She bogus, man! Accuse us purloinin' yo' garbage can? What we want wiff yo' garbage?"

"It's not about garbage cans and y-you know it!" Peggy raised her voice.

"You teched!" the boy squealed back at her.

"Hey," Joe stepped between them, "watch your mouth, Curtis. You ain't helpin' your case by sassin'."

"Case? Ain't no case! I didn't do nuthin'! My br'ers neither! But whaddoo you care! It be my word agin her badge, right? No mattah what I say!" He pushed past Peggy. "I gonna sue you fo' inculpin', you brachet!" He ran up the driveway.

"What'd he just call you?" Joe asked.

"Joe, stop him! They were at Jack's! They took the donation can!"

"You see them take it?"

"No, but, they were there, who else would do it?"

"It coulda been any scuzz who trucks in there when Jack ain't lookin'. Half the time he's on the phone to his bookie!"

"They're trouble Joe, you saw them t-tease the dogs!"

"Ter always let 'em play fetch with the dogs. Lookit, even if they did it, we can't prove it, so, c'mon, you been here long enough; you know the drill. No evidence, no case."

"Well, then why didn't...why didn't Terry teach them how to...to... to play right?!" She threw the sticks over the fence so hard they splintered against the warehouse. Bristling, she paced the runs. "There should... there should be padlocks on these gates!"

"Uh...if they're gonna nab anything around here, it'll be the battery in the Pinto. But, even they know better."

Peggy whirled around. "Then what am I supposed to do?"

"About?"

Peggy clamped her mouth shut. "Forget it."

"C'mon, fess."

"We're driving stupid cans around town when w-we can't even afford to gas up the van! How are we gonna get through the winter?"

Joe pulled a pack of peanuts from his pocket and tore it open with his teeth. "Like we always do. By the seat of our pants. Lookit, just forget about the pinched cans. Ain't worth th'agida! So what? You'll make more of 'em."

Fists on her hips, Peggy stood irresolute and shaking.

"Lookit, I'll help. C'mon, what's really eatin' ya?"

Peggy felt her face get hot as she struggled with pent up anger. "I told you!"

Don't you raise your voice! Are you looking for trouble!

Abruptly, like steam from a pressure cooker, the words hissed out of her mouth. "No! I can't do this! I told him I can't! How am I supposed to hold the stupid fort if I-I can't even...it's been two months! Two stupid months! And we haven't heard a single, stupid word from him!"

Her words hung in the frosty air and echoed off the walls of the compound.

Joe's mouth hung open.

Peggy kneaded her forehead with numb fingers. "I-I'm sorry."

Joe swallowed the peanuts in his mouth. "No, I hear ya...lookit, I ain't exactly jake with the deep freeze, neither, okay? But...maybe it's like what Irene said, and Jack too. Time, y'know? Maybe he needs...time."

Peggy managed a stiff nod.

Joe ran a hand through his damp hair. "I mean, what do I know? But, ya gotta, y'know...hang in, right? Because, I mean...what else're ya gonna do? Like Ter always says, when push comes to shove...ya deal."

Peggy squirmed in her shoes, as if they, and she, had just shrunk four sizes. "I-I didn't meant to take it out on you."

"Forget about it. Hey, ain't nobody hates this place more n' me."

"I-I don't hate it."

"Oh yeah?" He offered her the bag of peanuts. "Watch it. You said 'we' four times, back there. You ain't careful, you're gonna end up a lifer, like Brunhilda."

"In a pig's eye," Peggy said, and cracked open a peanut shell. "And, you can bet on that."

"Ten-four," Joe grinned and opened the gate for her. "You're catchin' on, Saint Francis!"

❦ ❦ ❦ ❦ ❦ Chapter 37 ❦ ❦ ❦ ❦ ❦

To Peggy's chagrin, while they'd been out "doing the can-can", as Joe referred to their donation can round-ups, Irene had called with an update about Terry.

The doctors anticipated weaning Terry off of the respirator and moving him out of ICU by week's end. At first, Peggy felt guilty about her outburst in the parking lot, as if she'd somehow betrayed not only Terry, but everything that he stood for, as a warden, and as a person. She thought about what Joe had said, and Jack too, about time. She wanted to believe it. Wasn't that what everyone always said about time? That it heals everything? Well...almost everything.

She paid penance for her rebellious tantrum by lugging Terry's box of files home with her on the bus. She hoped to discover somewhere in his papers, the magic solution to the shelter's fiscal woes. She knew just by observation, that he had been elbow deep in them.

She ended up falling asleep across piles of files on her bed, holding on to Lucky's frayed rope collar like a talisman. She hadn't had the strength, or the courage, to make the trek to Harrison's to spy on his yard. Not in the icy snow. She used Joe's patrol reports as an excuse; they were the same, every day, with no sign of Lucky. That too, should have been good news to Peggy. Why then, did it bother her so much?

Everyone else seemed to be so adept at "dealing", as Joe put it. They let it all roll off their backs. Why couldn't she do the same thing?

The next morning, she departed the bus juggling both Terry's box and a grocery bag filled with cans of chicken broth. She noticed that the sky looked nearly as white as the snow-dusted driveway leading down to the shelter. Pinpoints of white sifted down over the warehouse roofs, like confectioner's sugar. She spotted the van parked alongside the warehouse. That could only mean that Joe had nabbed an early morning stray on his patrol. One less run, she thought with a jab of worry.

Her arms full, she butted backwards through the front gate with Terry's box. She slowed when she saw, on the front stoop, a case of dog food, a big box of dog biscuits and two cases of expensive, gourmet cat food.

The great steel door flew open, and she stumbled backwards against the fencing. "Oh!"

"Whoa!" Joe caught the grocery bag before it hit the concrete. "Hey! I thought you weren't gonna spring for all this stuff, no more!"

"I didn't! Well, just the broth, but not all the rest of this! Look!" Peggy gestured to the pet food. "Our first donations! People must have read my ad! They *do* care!"

"Lookit, don't get all wonky over a maybe one time thing, okay? Sometimes when somebody's pet croaks, they give us their leftovers. Maybe that'll be all she wrote, know what I'm sayin'?"

"But, it's dog and cat food! Both pets wouldn't have died at the same time! I think this is a good sign! And, maybe if we play our cards right, maybe it's just the beginning!"

For the first time in as long as she could remember, Peggy felt a surge of real hope. She hurried inside and scoured the cabinets and shelves, taking stock of inventory. Then, she sat down and wrote a new "grocery list" for the next newspaper ad.

"Anothah ad?" Betty asked. "Why not let thissun pay fo' isself, first?"

"Yeah, she's right, Dillan, it's better n' bein' blind-sided by pie in the sky." Joe opened a box of dog biscuits, popping one in his mouth.

"Would you quit eatin' they food!" Betty said, snatching the box.

"Hey!" he snatched them back. "I paid for 'em, I can have one!"

Peggy whirled around. "You bought the dog biscuits?"

Joe gulped and glanced at Betty. She whacked him over the head with his summons book.

"OW! Hey! I didn't say nuthin'!"

Peggy looked between them. "What's going on?"

Betty sighed. "Who cares where it come from?! A gift be a gift!"

"You two bought it all?"

"Just the dog food! Somebody else musta forked over the bucks for that hoity-toity cat chow!"

They all paused a second, then looked around to Clara. The old woman stuck her nose in the air. "Somebody 'ad to give a fig 'bout the cats!"

"So, no one answered the ad..." Peggy began.

"We just thought—you been tryin' so hard," Joe admitted. "I hate always bein' right, but people just don't give a rat's butt."

"That's not exactly true, is it?" Peggy smiled. "Thank you. It was-it was really nice of all of you."

"You started it," Joe shrugged it off. "You and that friggin' soup! And the friggin' donation cans!" He shoved a brace of his own, freshly stamped cans across the counter to her. "Jeeze. Talk about Guilt-Trip City!"

"Don't expect it be a habit!" Betty chided her. "We got bills to pay!"

"No. Of course, not."

"What next morn's sun may bring, forebear t'ask; but count each day that comes by gift of chance, so much to the good," Clara quoted, then added, "Horace. 65 B.C.."

"What the frig's that supposed to mean?" Joe scoffed.

"It's cold as charity out there."

"Amen," Betty laughed.

Hearing the front door open and close, they all peeked out the window. "Coast clear," Joe said. "It's just the doc."

Peggy watched the crew return to their work. She was touched by their foiled attempt to make her feel better. Joe must have snitched about her outburst the day before. Not that it mattered. If nothing else, she learned she wasn't alone in carrying a torch over Terry's MIA status. More importantly, she learned that she wasn't alone in the fort.

Out in the kennel, a few of the dogs woofed, once or twice, before Dr. Hayward opened the office door. He hefted a carrier up onto the counter, stamping snow off of his leather boots. "When are you closing?"

A bit put off, Peggy frowned. "The rent's not overdue for two more weeks! Why would we close?"

"The threat of five-foot snow drifts, by noon?"

Joe swiveled around in his chair. "They said it was gonna miss us!"

"That's not what they said, five minutes ago." Paul removed a slender tabby cat from the carrier and handed it to Clara.

"Who said what's going to miss us?" Peggy asked.

"Sshhhh-ugar!" Joe flipped both the radio and the CB on at once. "Th'one day I'm rockin' to my eight track!"

"Shoulda known," Betty blew her nose. "All them tiny flakes. Sure sign."

"Sign of what?" Peggy asked.

The radio announcer's voice interrupted her. "...with the barometric pressure dropping, should the storm continue along its present track, we can expect between eight and twelve inches of snow across the Tri-State area. Essex and Bergen counties will get the brunt of the storm..."

"Blizzard," Betty, Joe and Clara said, in unison.

"Blizzard?" Peggy exclaimed. She'd been so overworked, she'd not even listened to her own radio.

"Not just a blizzard," Joe piped up, "a friggin' nor'easter! Shhh!"

"...Forecasters expect this storm to intensify over the next several hours and we could see as much as three to four feet of drifting snow, gale force winds and thunderstorms before the front moves up into New England sometime over the next forty-eight hours..."

Betty tossed a quarter on the counter. "My first mind say we git a foot."

Clara slapped down fifty cents. "Two meters."

"Two an' a half feet." Joe dug in his pocket for change.

The radio announcer continued, "The storm looks like it might be stalling twenty-five miles off the coast of Atlantic City; winds are already gusting to seventy miles per hour along the cape. Governor Byrne has called out the national guard in preparation. Flights out of Newark are being canceled, so please call your airline if you're planning to travel. Stay tuned for school closings. If you do not have to travel, don't. Chains will be required after three p.m. for the mountain roads."

"National Guard?" Peggy repeated. "Do we have chains?"

"Only for the doors during summer riots," Joe told her.

"Riots?"

"Sooo," Dr. Hayward reiterated, "when are you going to close?"

"Well, what about the animals?"

"They got water, food and a roof over their heads," Joe said. "We're the ones in deep doo-doo if we don't hit the roads before the plows do!" He pulled on his jacket. "C'mon, Saint Francis, call it."

Surprised to find the whole crew waiting for her to make the decision, she nodded. "Okay. Yes."

"Joe, can you take Clara and me?" Betty asked. "I don't trust the roads."

"Ain't the roads ya gotta worry about. The van's tires are bald, and the brakes are crap. We'll be bobsleddin' through Bloomfield, for sure."

Peggy buttoned up her coat, biting her lip. Was Terry worried about the storm? Had he even heard about it? Would he be worried about the animals? About her? And what about Lucky? Joe hadn't had a chance to patrol, yet. She peered out the window, fidgeting with her pendant.

Behind her, she heard Paul packing his medical bag, and he asked, "When do they stop running the buses?"

For a split second, she wondered why he cared about the buses, with his Jaguar right out front.

"Buses? Forget about it!" Joe scoffed. "They ain't never gonna make it up the...oh! Hey! Right! C'mon, Saint Francis, you're hitchin' with us. No way the twenty-one is makin' it up to Tory Corner."

"Th-thank you." Peggy glanced at the vet, but he was rummaging in the medicine cabinet, his back turned to her.

"Yo' Doc, we got room for one more," Joe said.

"Thanks, I'm covered."

"Yeah, right! In that Matchbox of yours? Hope you got a shovel, flares, and some candy bars with you, man."

"I've got Triple A and American Express."

Clara turned to Betty. "Can I ride with him?"

"Maybe we should all take the train," Betty suggested. "You know how bad it gets."

"Y'kiddin'? Be quicker to walk." Joe opened the door for them. "C'mon, let's make tracks. We got less than fifteen before they'll close the turnpike." As they all filed out, he raised a warning finger to Clara. "One crack about my drivin' and I tie you to the hood, I swear."

"You ever hear 'bout the Donner Party?" she countered.

"What do we do in the morning?" Peggy asked. "About the snow?"

"Town plows the lot," said Joe. "Only perk in sharin' the driveway with the pyros, 'cause otherwise, we'd be under ice 'til June."

Peggy reached out a worried hand over the radiator, just to make sure Beula hadn't heard the news and croaked, just to spite them. "But what if…"

Betty ushered her out, "We been through storms before. They gonna be fine."

Peggy had to take their word for it. The kennel was balmy, the dogs fed and half-asleep. She turned the volume up on the radio over the cabinet until she heard the soft strains of Vivaldi. She looked around one last time, feeling like a protective parent.

Joe stuck his head back in the front door. "Yo! Let's go!"

"Coming." Peggy walked through the kennel and paused once more in the doorway. For the first time, she didn't want to leave the shelter and all of its problems. She wanted to weather the storm with the animals. She reluctantly flipped off the light switch, and then closed and locked the door.

"All aboard!" Joe threw his weight against the side door of the van and slid it open.

While Betty helped Clara up into the passenger seat, Peggy watched Dr. Hayward brush two inches of snow off of his sleek red Jaguar. He jumped into the sports car and with a muffled, clacketty-clack of chains on his tires, drove up the driveway and out of sight. Of course, Peggy rolled her eyes. She should have guessed he'd think of chains!

Getting situated in the back of the van was no easy feat. A standing cage stood right behind the driver's seat. The rest of the van's interior was littered with animal carriers, traps, empty cans of Fix-a-Flat and a box of empty donation cans. There was one additional bucket seat behind the standing cage, propped up with boxes. Peggy insisted that Betty take it, then squatted on a bucket behind the passenger seat, where Clara tied herself in with the broken seat belt.

Joe fired up the engine, flipped a switch, and the van's rooftop emergency light popped on; flashing yellow rays swept the compound as they revolved.

"You git stopped, I won't lie!" Betty warned him and strapped herself in. "You already been pulled ovah fo' flashin' that thing!"

"The Gov is callin' out the National Guard. That's emergency mode, sister!"

"This ain't no official emergency vee-hickle!"

"Hey, you wanna get broadsided by a salt shaker or a snow plow? They see us first this way! And FYI, that ain't no cherry top, up there, but sunshine yellow. We ain't breakin' no law. I say we head up the hill first and drop Brunhilda. The rest'll be all down hill. Game?"

"Go slow."

"Chill out! I am one with this machine! Okay, hold onto your hats." He threw the clutch into reverse.

Betty crossed herself, Clara crossed her legs against the dashboard, and Peggy crossed her fingers, holding on for dear life. Joe stepped on the gas and the van fishtailed up the driveway, towards the street.

"Look out!" Peggy cried.

"Holy Crap!" A dump truck blared its horn, and Joe whipped the wheel around, sending them swerving around the #21 bus, and into the opposing traffic lanes. Peggy was sure she saw her regular bus driver in the window, wide-eyed and swearing.

Joe skidded the van around oncoming cars, then muscled into a lane of slow moving traffic. "Get outta the way!"

Angry motorists honked horns at him.

"Up yours with a rubber hose!" he hollered out the window.

"You supposed to pump the brakes on ice!" Betty hollered.

"The tires are bald, what's the point?"

"Just slow down!"

"I can always pull over, whoever wants to walk!"

They all raised their hands.

Joe swerved around the corner and clipped a mailbox, sending Peggy rolling to the back of the van.

An hour later, the van chugged in idle, stuck behind gridlock traffic at the bottom of the mountain roads. It gently rocked in the rising wind. Peggy silently thanked the gods of snow removal cut-backs for the traffic. At least now, Joe couldn't reach the speed limit, let alone "double-nickel" over it.

"Did I call it, or what?" he griped. "Soon as they close th'exits to the Turnpike, every bozo with wheels alla sudden's gotta go somewheres."

The van's engine sputtered and stalled.

"Crap." Joe turned the key and pumped the gas pedal. "C'mon...c'mon, sweetheart."

Peggy rubbed the fogged window with her sleeve. The roads were already rutted with snow. "Is that plow up there, stuck?"

"As God is my witness, we be lucky to git up this hill befo' March," Betty grumbled.

Eventually, more and more cars gave up their efforts to climb the mountain roads. Joe managed to cleave a way between retreating vehicles to take on Eagle Rock in first gear. It worked. But, by the time the van slid onto Clara's Mountain Road, the snow had accumulated another two and a half inches.

"Watch it," Betty directed. "Clara's driveway be third down on left, 'round the bend."

"I know, I know. Wait! Where's the bend? Aw, jeeze. Friggin' plows!"

Peggy held her breath.

Ruts left by the few vehicles able to commandeer snow this fast and heavy made it impossible for the van to steer in any way resembling a straight path. As they swerved around the bend, Peggy spotted a bicyclist struggling his way towards them in the tire ruts.

"Look out!"

"Marone!" Joe pumped the brakes and fought the wheel. The van spun around and missed the cyclist, but slid toward a row of parked cars. The engine sputtered and stalled.

"Crap!" Joe stomped on the clutch and shifted into reverse. With the crunch of grinding gears, the van bucked and skidded with a whump-bump, into the pile of plowed snow that blocked Clara's driveway.

Breathless, they all sat listening to the scrape, scrape, scrape of the wiper blades on the windshield. The bicyclist teetered past unsteadily, but managed to shake his fist at them.

Joe rolled his window down and leaned out. "Ya friggin' space cadet! I shoulda hit ya!"

Betty whapped him over the head with a rolled up newspaper.

"OW! Hey! I missed him, didn't I?" He ground the ignition, over and over, but the van's engine would not turn over. "Aww, friggit! What now?"

Peggy peered over his shoulder at the dashboard. "What does that red light mean?"

Joe thumped the steering wheel. "Double crap!"

"Clara, honey?" Betty sighed, "How'd you like company tonight? I'll cook."

Clara opened her scrunched eyes. "We're not dead?"

"Close, but no cigar."

Peggy gazed up at Clara's three-story, Victorian home. It perched majestically on a small hill, embraced by half an acre of old-growth woods. At least 150-years-old, it had earned the wear of three genera-tions of ownership.

With a great deal of slipping and sliding, they all managed to climb the snow-encrusted stone stairs, ascending the hill to the house. Enter-ing a glassed-in porch, they stomped clumps of snow off of their shoes and pants.

Clara patted herself down. "Where're me keys?"

"Oh for…" Joe stifled a curse. "If you left 'em at the shelter, you're walkin' back to get 'em!"

"Joe!" Betty snapped. "She left her bag in the van. Go get it."

"Why me?" Joe stomped out of the porch, muttering under his breath.

"And, straighten out that fool parkin' job, while you at it!"

"With what, a forklift? Anything else while I'm at it? Coffee? Tea? A friggin' sleigh ride?"

On the road below, a young boy in a snow-suit pulled his friend on a round, aluminum snow-saucer. The rider scooped up a ball of snow and threw it. Thwack! Wet snow splattered Joe on the back of the neck. He let out a girlish yelp, slipped and fell face first into the snow.

Clara whooped with delight and applauded from the porch.

Joe staggered to his feet, scooped up a handful of snow and wound up to pitch it at her.

"Joseph Thomas Wozniak!" Betty shook her fist at him. "Do I hafta come down there?"

Pouting, Joe dropped the snowball. He stomped down the rest of the steps to the van, smacking snow off of his jacket. "I catch pneumonia it's on your head!"

Watching from the frosted windows of the enclosed porch, Peggy crossed her fingers. What would they do if Clara'd left her purse at the shelter? Even Betty mumbled a silent prayer. After a tense moment, Joe emerged, holding up Clara's carpet bag, triumphantly.

"Oh, thank you," Peggy exhaled in relief.

"Amen!" Betty kissed her crucifix.

"Don't dawdle, then, Yeti!" Clara hollered down to Joe. "It's monkey freezin' up 'ere!"

Chapter 38

"Coats in the closet, if y'please."

Clara opened a handsome, cherry-wood door beside an exquisitely carved staircase that climbed elegantly up to the vaulted heights of the three-story home.

Peggy stood in the foyer and gazed around, in awe.

A massive mahogany grandfather clock stood beside the stairs; four, pinecone-shaped iron weights hung on long brass chains, and a polished brass pendulum beat out the time in deep rhythmic tick-tocks. The clock face harkened back to days long past, when the solar and lunar cycles were important to those living off of the land. Planting cycles had been painstakingly painted on three different wheels of the clock face, depicting the seasons and moon phases. A suit of armor guarded the second landing. Peggy wondered what it might be protecting on the floors above.

Peeking into each ground-floor room was like peering into the past. A "gathering room" welcomed visitors to the right of the foyer hall. A stone fireplace on its far wall was flanked with floor to ceiling bookcases. Tucked into a corner sat an upright piano. Wool carpet runners spread over chestnut-hued hardwood floors, under leaded stained-glass windows. Heavy mantles of carved wood topped the fireplaces. Pocket doors hidden within the walls could be closed to separate the rooms. Clara was dwarfed in the enormous house. She reminded Peggy of a little gnome in the woods, tottering about under flowered wallpaper that rose up to twenty-foot ceilings above her head.

Within the century-old atmosphere, Peggy could still pick out the scent of three generations worth of home-cooked meals, the romantic fragrance of faded roses, and—Peggy's face soured—the unmistakable odor of a house full of cats.

It took a few minutes for her eyes to adjust to the dim interior of the old house. When they did, she saw cats of every color, size, shape, and

breed. They were everywhere! Cats lounged on top of and under tables, sofas and chairs, and scampered about, playing.

"'Ellooooo me babies!" Clara called out.

A twangy chorus of meowing filled the air, as felines dashed out from every corner and poured down the long, winding staircase in a kitty waterfall, to welcome their benefactor home. Clara cooed to them all, as they circled her sagging stockings.

Joe nudged Peggy. "Welcome to the Cat House."

"All right then, who's peckish?" Clara asked.

"Me!"

"I were addressin' the cats."

"Lemme help git these kitties fed," Betty offered, as she hung up their coats. "Joe, go clean the cat boxes."

"Hey, I'm a guest, here!"

"You wanna eat? Chip in wiff chores."

"I drove!"

"*Need* I say more?"

"Litter's in the bins by the boxes, thank you!" Clara called out as she shuffled away, the cats ferrying underfoot.

While Joe stomped up the stairs, Peggy followed the two women, trying to avoid treading on tails, down the hall into a vast airy kitchen. She was again, captivated.

Tall, double-hung windows wrapped around the entire kitchen, giving the illusion of a glass wall. Each window was framed with velvet green, winter drapes hung over lace insets. Delicate daisy flower wallpaper ran from the crown molding down to the wainscoting that finished at the dark wide-planked flooring. A rustic, flagstone fireplace to Peggy's left framed a double cast-iron stove. A stainless steel side-by-side refrigerator occupied an alcove on the far right side of the stove, directly opposite a double porcelain sink built into mahogany cabinetry. A magnificent glass-fronted kitchen hutch commanded the right side wall of the kitchen entrance, shielding a narrow, arched doorway. That doorway led to a smaller wooden staircase that wound tightly upwards, out of sight. To the right of the alcove, tucked in between six floor-to-ceiling cupboards, peeked a walk-in pantry with a "cooling" air shaft that ran all the way up to the roof. Situated under a long rectangular Tiffany ceiling lamp, a rough-hewn, Douglas fir table surrounded by eight chairs, dominated the center of the room. It was a kitchen fit for a queen.

While Clara and Betty fussed over an electric can opener, Peggy peered out the frosty windows to a luxuriant wooded acreage. The snow fell so thickly, it was difficult to discern just how far back the property stretched. Through the white haze, she could make out a white gazebo and canes of bare-root roses around a frozen fountain and pond. The soft, yellow glow of lights from a neighbor's house shimmered through a thick stand of conifers, separating the properties.

How beautiful, Peggy thought, and how peaceful it must be to sit out there, winter or not, in the serene quiet. What a difference between Clara's house and the boarding house where she stayed. The boarding house was unsettled by the intrusive blare of car horns and sirens, and where the drone of televisions often masked late night arguments easily heard through the thin walls.

"Peggy? Set these six bowls over there for those new rogues what 'aven't learnt to share." Clara indicated three lanky orange cats trying to pry their way into the garbage pail. "And, 'ere's the list of who gets what, and who won't eat next to who."

"Okay."

It took the better part of an hour to feed, medicate, then finally clean up after Clara's army of felines. Once done, the cats disappeared into the woodwork like slinky shadows. A few tubby tabbies remained, insisting they were still hungry.

"Oh, get out of it, y'beggars," Clara chuckled. They ignored her feigned scolding and rolled over at her feet, batting at the hem of her dress.

Betty opened the refrigerator. "What you in the mood fo' tonight, Clara, honey?"

"What I'm in the mood for and what we got, is another bag o' chips. Pull out that lentil-mushroom loaf and the gravy, there. There's a few taters in the bin and a bunch of carrots and broccoli left, I think."

Joe trudged in with a yard-sized garbage bag filled with soiled litter. "Hey, Croft, a suggestion? You feed them too much."

"Not through kitchen." Clara waved him back out.

"The back door's right there."

"We eat in 'ere!"

"So do *they*." He pointed to the tabbies up on the table, licking plates.

"Joe, just take it out the front and walk it 'round the back," Betty said.

Joe stomped out, whining. "But, it's right *there*."

"I never seen such a baby-toes in all my life as that boy," Betty lifted a cat off the table and deposited it on the floor.

"They're all alike. Need a boot in the arse 'til the testes descend," said Clara.

"Yeah, well, it be a wonder he don't git his old man's boot, more n' he do."

"'E's of age, of 'is own mind."

Then they fell quiet. Peggy sponged the table. Whatever it was they were mum about, they knew plenty about it. She couldn't help but remember her very first sight of Joe, and the black and blue shiner he'd hidden under sunglasses.

A tap on the window pane jerked their attention up. Joe stood at the glass with two large icicles stuck in his mouth, like walrus tusks. He barked, scaring cats off of their window seats.

"This what I be talkin' 'bout," Betty said, then hollered at him through the glass. "Do somethin' useful and shovel the walk!" She yanked the shade down before he could protest.

While Clara and Betty pared potatoes, seemingly occupied and confabbing between themselves, Peggy wandered into the gathering room. Two comfy, well worn claw-foot sofas embraced the fireplace. Large pots of Aspidistras screened the windows, their elegantly tapered, dark green leaves contrasted nicely against burgundy drapes. The bookshelves were semi-bare, and held more record albums than books. She ran her fingers along the collection, pulling out Tommy Dorsey, Benny Goodman, The Andrews Sisters, Maria Callas, Enrico Caruso, Debussy, Tchaikovsky, Gershwin. It was a treasure trove of first pressed recordings. Between the bookcases was a round table with an old rosewood Victrola on a lace doily.

The front door opened, and Joe blustered in, stamping snow off of his boots. He flopped onto the high-back boot bench and pulled them off. "Some pad, huh? Her and her gazillion cats."

Betty poked her head into the hallway. "Joe, go bring in some wood fo' the fire."

"I just came in! C'mon, it's Ant-frickin'arctica, out there!" He held up his sodden socks. "Have mercy, c'mon!"

"Bettah haul butt, befo' the snow's up to yo' butt crack."

"I can help," Peggy offered.

"Leave him do it! He need th'exercise, all them holes and dog biscuits he eat, all day long!"

"I get frostbite, it's on your head!" Joe trudged out the door.

"Yo' head's on yo' head!"

Clara shuffled to the stairs, cats in her wake. "I'm goin' to change."

"Okay," Betty said, "But don't you go fixin' up no beds. Peggy and me kin do that aftah suppah."

"All right." Clara gestured to the Victrola and a box of records under the table. "Those seventy-eights, over there, those are th'ones for your church. Go ahead and take what you want."

"You sure? I mean, you wanna git riddah all of 'em?"

The old woman stood with her hand on the bannister, looking down at the box. She seemed to struggle with something and then nodded. "Things, things, things...they just clutter up our brains and make us stupid." She turned and walked up the stairs.

Peggy's eye was caught by a bank of framed photographs on the wall under the staircase. Most showed off a strapping man in uniform, with a diminutive blonde beauty at his side. She smiled up at him with unabashed adoration. In a couple of pictures, twin teenage boys flanked the couple.

"That be her husband," Betty pointed out. "He was a exporter, somethin' like that. Those be her boys. Lost 'em all in World War Two. They be travellin' troo Burma when the war broke out. They tried to git back home but got caught there when the Japanese invaded. He bein' American, they killed him, her boys too. She escaped inta the jungle, wanderin' 'roun, tryin' to stay alive. She found orphans hidin' out. 'Bout dozen of 'em, and fo' a whole year they hid in the jungles and on farms, just one step aheada the Japanese. Met othahs on the run, like her. Some were nuns, all wiff kids in tow, but they had to go they own way, so's not to git caught. She be one of the lucky ones git rescued by American and Chinese troops. She nearly died. Got beriberi. But, she seen to it all them kids got adopted, before she come back. Got wrote up in all the papers. Big wigs threw this big thang—a hero dinner. In New York City. But she nevah went. Nevah returned no calls, letters from the govenah, even the President. After bit, the calls n' letters, they stopped. Those seventy-eight's be her husband's record collection."

Peggy looked back over her shoulder to the records on the shelves. "Why is she getting rid of them?"

"She be donatin' 'em to my church. I'm goin' to try and put 'em on cassette fo' her first, 'cause all them books an' records? They all she got left. 'Cept fo' this house. Few pieces of furniture. And her cats. She been sellin' things off here and there to git by and keep the house. Everythang else she done sold off, years back, to help the shelter git off the ground. But, hush, 'cause we ain't supposed to know nuthin' 'bout that."

Peggy returned to the photographs and spotted the cameo pinned to young Clara's blouse, the one she had Joe hock at the pawn shop. She knew, now, the sacrifice she'd made, all the while not letting on. She stepped back into the gathering room and tried to imagine the house alive with laughter and music. She could almost see Clara's husband and sons clustered around the piano, singing those old songs, while Clara played, her face aglow with love and happiness.

The front door burst open, and a blast of frigid air pushed Joe across the threshold. The lounging cats scattered, as he juggled the load of wood and tried to shut the door with a booted foot.

"Close the door! The cats'll git out!" Betty called out.

"Would serve 'em right!" Joe finally butted the heavy door closed, and staggered to the fireplace, dropping logs into a copper bin beside the hearth.

Betty inspected the load. "Two mo' like that set her up troo the weekend."

"They abolished slavery, y'know!"

"And you be payin' penance fo' it, Miracle Whip, now git! Suppah be ready."

The door was so heavy and so well made that there was no way to slam it, but that didn't stop Joe from trying.

"See what I be sayin'?" Betty said to Peggy. "Baby Toes." A bubbling hiss from the kitchen sent them both running towards the stove.

Peggy couldn't remember the last time that she'd had a home-cooked meal. After a day at the shelter, she was often much too tired to cook for herself. Peanut butter and jelly toast or a can of soup most often served as supper. She'd never had a vegetarian dinner before. It seemed that, like Betty, Clara was a vegetarian, too.

"Humanitarian, if you please," Clara corrected her, with great sincerity.

The steaming legume-mushroom loaf, smothered in a mushroom gravy, thick mashed potatoes and seasoned vegetables that Betty and Clara had prepared was so delicious, she had two helpings, and if she wasn't so shy, she would have asked for thirds. Even "gimme a burger-with" Joe scarfed his down and licked his plate clean with no complaint!

After cleaning up the kitchen, the crew gathered around the blazing fire Joe had built. It wasn't even nine o'clock when the warmth had lulled Joe, Clara, and her hundred cats to sleep. Clara snored lightly on the divan nearest the fire, curled up in her shawl. Joe lay in a heap on the wool rug, in front of the fire, cats snuggled up against him. He too, snored lightly. The young man and the old woman's snores, in tenor and soprano, along with the crackling of the fire and the purring cats, created a bizarre harmony with the wail of the wind outside.

Against her will, Peggy's eyes drooped. She cradled a ceramic mug of hot cocoa in her hands and fought the urge to sleep. For a split second, she thought of the animals back at the shelter and hoped that they, too, were warm and comfortably sleepy. Betty sat next to her on the davenport, sharing a quilt. A fat, black cat purred on Peggy's lap, kneading the blanket, as Betty reminisced.

"...I took his drinkin', his gamblin', his cheatin'...but the day he raised his hand to me, that be the day I up and left."

Peggy studied the woman's handsome, nut-brown face in the firelight. Her heavy lidded eyes were sunken, and it wasn't hard to imagine the years of turmoil they'd seen. But in their deep black depths, Peggy could not read one way or the other if there were any regrets.

"Friends thought I was crazy stupid fo' walkin' out," Betty admitted. "Said, 'whatchoo doin' girl? It parta bein' married!' Parta bein' married? Since when it be expected we be punchin' bags fo' some numb-nuts who can't even aim his piss wiffout a map and die-rections?"

Peggy sputtered a laugh and snuffed a bit of cocoa up her nose.

"Parta bein' married," Betty snorted with disdain. "Where we git fool ideas like that?"

Peggy wiped her nose with a napkin and shrugged. "I guess-I guess they get passed down like an old guilt. Quilt," she corrected herself. "I meant *quilt*."

"Mmn-hmn," Betty nodded, "I think you got it right wiff yo' first mind. You know."

It was the way she'd said those last two words that made Peggy flick her eyes up.

Betty raised a brow at her. "Please, ain't like two plus two don't make four, here, like Doctah DoRight always be sayin'. Why else you git so eat up ovah that Lucky dog?"

Peggy chose her words, carefully. "It's just that...just because it's a dog, it seems people don't think it matters, as much. I think it does."

Betty sat back, the flames of the fire reflected in her eyes. "I guess sometime it take bein' treated like one, to learn that, uh-huh; it do, too, mattah."

Peggy couldn't help but wonder, why does it always have to come to that?

Chapter 39

It was still snowing when Peggy woke up.

She and Betty had shared one of the many rooms on the second floor of Clara's vast house. Both women were too unnerved by the fierce wind rattling the windows to wait out the storm alone in their own room. They chose the yellow room at the top of the stairs, boasting framed magazine covers on the walls. Most of the covers depicted sunny meadows bursting with daisies and sunflowers, the perfect talisman against the raging blizzard outside. Twin beds weighted with down comforters flanked a tall, empty armoire. Joe had elected to sleep on the davenport by the fire with the cats, where he could keep the logs blazing.

Peggy raised up on one elbow and peered out the window framed thickly with wet snow. The whole world had been cloaked in a great white marshmallow comforter. Mounded tree limbs bent under the wet weight of the snow, hanging down over soft, rolling white drifts. Except for roof peaks jutting up here and there, Peggy could barely make out where the sky ended and the horizon began.

She yawned, still tired. Although the wind had shaken the house violently all evening long, it hadn't been the storm that had kept her awake.

Deep into the night, listening to Betty breathing in sleep, Peggy thought about their conversation. The vulnerability she'd felt was much like being strip-searched. Worse, it was as if Betty had lifted her mask and had found absolutely no one underneath. What could she have said in response to Betty's rather obvious invitation to open up about her past? How could she share, though, under the circumstances?

The scent of coffee teased her back to the present. Rolling over, she expected to see Betty slumbering away, but instead, surveyed a perfectly made bed. She was up, already! Throwing off the comforter, Peggy pulled on her socks, made her bed, and ducked into the half-bath in the hall. The water in the bowl sink was cold, but she did her best to wash off the night's disquietude.

"Hope evvybody be hungry." Betty scraped oatmeal out of a large pot into bowls on the counter. "Do you believe it still snowin'?!"

"It's winter, what's the surprise?" Clara asked, picking up kitty bowls off of the floor.

"That you still got power!"

Peggy hung back in the doorway, wondering if Betty had discussed their little chat with Clara, but neither woman seemed to pay her any mind.

"Here," Clara handed Peggy a bottle of orange juice. "The glasses're in the cupboard there."

"If Joe axe fo' any help out there, tell him we got chores, in here. Don't take any of his belly achin'," Betty advised her.

"Okay." Peggy felt relieved. It was to be business as usual, then. They didn't poke their noses into each other's business, she reminded herself. What could Betty know, anyway?

"I thought the roof gonna come off, last night," Betty said. "I had half mind to wake you up and hide us both down cellar. Cinnamon?"

Peggy gulped. "Th-thank you." She heard a scraping sound from outside and looked out the back windows to find Joe attempting to shovel a path through the swirling white curtain of snow. "W-we'll be able to get to the shelter, won't we?"

"Be lucky we git out the door. Town plowed the van in."

Joe pushed the back door open, shaking off snow. "Jeee-*eeze* it's freakin' freezin' out there!"

"Joe!" Betty chided him, "You trackin' in snow!"

"Hullo! It's winter!"

On the counter, a black dial phone jangled. Clara answered it. "'Ello? 'Ello?" She smacked the phone receiver against the breadbox and tried again. "Anybody out there?"

"The phone company know she still got that?" asked Joe.

"Git a mop and clean the floor," Betty said.

"What am I, the janitor, now?" Joe headed for alcove.

Clara handed the phone to Betty. "Maybe you can make this blower work."

Betty spoke into the phone. "Hello? Hello Onetta...uh-huh. That be real nice, yes. Okidoke, thank you." She hung up. "Onetta's boys comin' ovah to dig us out."

"They outta prison already?" Joe taunted, slopping a mop across the floor.

"Those boys are activists! Heroes, not felons!" Clara declared.

Joe leaned in to Peggy. "What would you call two coconuts who write the Capital and say, if Uncle Sam don't stop buildin' nuke plants, they're gonna take matters inta their own hands, then they go and sign their names and put their return address on the envelope?"

"Brave is the word comes to mind!" Clara insisted.

"Dumb is what pops inta mine."

Peggy smiled, but looked out the window at the drifts of snow, her mind drifting to Terry. Was there snow in Chicago? Would he be worried about them? About the shelter? And what about the animals?

Betty handed her a milk jug. "Quit your worryin'. Dogs ain't goin' nowhere. And they ain't gonna starve, way you been feedin' 'em."

Peggy didn't tell Betty that she wasn't worried about the shelter dogs, exactly. She was worried about Lucky. Was he safely inside, out of the storm?

By the time Onetta's two sons, Frank and Jesse, had arrived and shoveled the van free of four-foot drifts, it was ten-thirty and still snowing. With matching goatees and Dead Head tattoos on opposite arms, they finished the job wearing only thin white tee shirts. When they were done, they jump-started the van. Peggy watched from the porch, bundled and ready to go.

Joe hauled himself up the slippery front steps. "They're almost done."

Peggy stamped her numb toes. "Thank goodness!"

"Yeah, well, we might not be goin' any place, real fast, dependin' on the mess the town left everybody below." Joe ducked his head in Clara's front door. "Yo! Rock n' Roll in five!"

"So, when do you think you'll be able to go back out on patrol?"

Joe laughed. "What year is this?" He opened the front door again. "I said *yo*!"

"No need to shout, mutton head, I'm not deaf!" Clara traipsed out onto the porch swaddled in wool scarves over a heavy, wool pea coat, pinned from collar to hem, with protest buttons.

Joe looked askance at her. "Oh, give it up, wouldja? You think all that hippie stuff matters, no more?"

"We impeached Nixon!" Clara declared.

"That was different. He was a dope."

"Leave her be," Betty said, and bustled onto the porch. "Some folk give a diddly 'bout world mattahs."

"Whatever." Joe was about to pull the big door closed, when Clara stayed his hand.

"Got the keys this time?" she asked.

"It's your house!"

"A simple yes or no, will do!"

"Keys be in yo' purse, dear," Betty said.

"Got the records?" Clara asked.

Betty pointed to the box by the door. Clara nodded to Joe, and he pulled the great oak door closed.

All at once Frank, or Jesse, Peggy wasn't sure which was which, raised a snow shovel and waved it.

"They're done!"

"Dyn-o-mite! Let's go sleddin'." Joe hefted the box into his arms.

Clara offered Peggy her arm. "Quarter says you go down on your keister, first."

Peggy giggled and took Clara's arm. The two followed Joe and Betty down the ash-dusted steps. Remarkably, nobody fell. Just as they'd made it down to the street, Frank and Jesse's pickup truck fishtailed out of sight, honking their horn as they turned the corner. They were lucky that Frank and Jesse had come along. Peggy saw that all of the snow on Clara's road had been plowed into the driveways and smack up against stranded cars.

"Let's split before the friggin' plows come back," Joe said, and climbed into the idling van. He pressed his foot on the gas and revved the engine.

"Do I hafta say it?" Betty said, strapping herself in. "Go slow."

"Hey, I got us here, didn't I?"

Peggy closed her eyes and braced herself when Joe released the emergency brake, spinning the van into the first skid of the day.

"Turn left!" Betty hollered. "Wait! It's a yellow light!"

"Too late!" Joe spun the steering wheel. The van skidded sideways around a snow plow being towed by a flatbed truck, onto what Peggy assumed was a two-way street. It was not.

"Joe?"

"Cheese crap!" Joe gunned the gas, swerving in between three stuck cars and a buried mailbox. Snow cascaded onto their windshield from a passing Volkswagen Bug's wheels. Briefly blinded, they bounced over the median, towards a brownstone church, it's freshly plowed parking lot guarded by an ice-encrusted chain strung across the entrance.

"Look out, that's my church!" Betty shrieked. "Don't you dare snuff my church!"

"I see it! I see it!" Joe cried, and wrestled the steering wheel so the van pointed at the parking lot. They hit the snow-packed curb and catapulted up and over the sidewalk.

Whack! The van snapped the chain in front of the lot, and they sailed onto the icy macadam. Joe stood up on the brakes, sending the van into a full 360 degree tail spin for what seemed like a day and a half, before it finally slid to a stop.

Betty snatched a flattened pastry box from the floor and smacked Joe over the head.

"Hey!" Joe protested. "I missed it, didn't I?"

Peggy picked herself up off of the floor and peered out the window. The van had stopped just short of crashing into a cottage rectory attached to a brownstone Revolutionary War-era church. A delicate grove of bare dogwood trees stuck up through the drifts, like match sticks, beside an historic marker and a fenced-in cemetery.

"Clara?" Betty asked, "want to come in and use the rest room?"

"Too late now, " Clara said.

"Aw, jeeze, you didn't!" Joe whined.

Betty smacked Joe over the head, again. "You wait here and keep this toboggan warm."

"Yeah, well, FYI, we're runnin' on empty again."

"We-we're out of gas?" Peggy piped up.

"Joe, what Terry tell you 'bout keepin' the tank filled in wintah?" Betty scolded.

"Ter didn't make me fork over my own moola! I been floatin' this can, since New Year's!"

"Joe?" Peggy grasped hold of the van's side door and shoved hard. "I might have a couple of dollars in my—" The door slid aside too quickly, and she toppled out onto the slush with a yelp.

Joe was beside her in less than ten seconds. "Omigosh! Y'okay?" He helped her up, but her feet slid out from underneath her. She grabbed the side of the van, while Joe did his best to keep his own footing and her from falling down.

"Y'okay?" Joe panted.

"I'm okay," Peggy said.

Betty got out, skated over to Joe and smacked him over the head.

"Ow! What was that for?!"

"Git yo' butt behind that wheel and keep this tin can warm!" Betty snapped, and helped Clara down. "Saint Francis, can you git the box?"

"Okay."

"You better hurry up, or we'll be walkin' back!" Joe warned them.

Peggy muscled the box of records out of the van and followed Betty and Clara towards the rectory door. Despite the plowing, there were spots where she stepped into knee-deep snow. Betty inserted a key into the side door and pushed it open.

"Off to the Ladies!" Clara called out, and headed towards an alcove.

Peggy stumbled over the rectory threshold, plopped her box down on a long, stainless steel table in the center of a large, very modern kitchen.

"C'mon n' warm yo'seff ovah here," Betty waved Peggy to join her over a circular, cast-iron heating grate in the floor. Peggy stepped over the grate and closed her eyes in rapture as eddies of warmth enveloped her shoes. The smell of steamy, wet wool filled her nose and she had to shift her feet, as her thin soles got too hot on the grating.

"Here," Betty pushed a chair under her. "Take off yo' shoes 'n socks and let 'em dry."

As grateful as she was for the chance to warm up, Peggy glanced out the window towards the van, idling sluggishly in the snow. "Should we tell Joe?"

"He fo'evvah be exaggeratin'." Betty removed her own socks and wiggled her toes over the grate. "Ah, that be a whole lotta bettah. Clara, honey? You all right, in there?"

"'Aven't fallen in, yet!" came the old woman's reply from behind a closed door in the alcove.

Peggy surveyed the room and noticed a clock above the sinks. It was already eleven a.m.. Her stomach knotted, when Betty leaned back in the chair and closed her eyes with a contented sigh. Peggy tried not to think of the dogs waiting inside their runs, anxious by now, to go outside.

Clara finally came out of the alcove and Peggy pulled on her damp socks, ready to go.

"Where you think you be goin'?" Betty asked. "You socks still wet! Set yo'seff down."

Clara pulled up a chair, sat down, and began peeling off her stockings.

"What if...what if the heat went out, last night?" Peggy began.

"All the snow on that tin roof and yo' newspapah be plenty insulation. They be fine. And speakin' of roofs, praise be to you, Clara, honey, I think the pastor be able to redo the church tower this summah, wiff the extra penny those records gonna fetch. You sure, now?"

"Die is cast. Might fetch enough to fix them upper windows, too."

"Gonna need anothah rummage sale or two, for that job. Them windows be hundred years old, if they be a day."

Peggy listened, perplexed. Was the church using charity money to remodel? Wasn't that illegal? Or at least, unethical?

"Y-you're allowed to do that?" she asked. "I mean, I thought the money you make was supposed to go to charity?"

"It all be fo' charity, honey. Got a wait list two miles long who gits the dough. Church only keep a bitty percent out of donations, puddit in the bank, then 'bout evvy two years, we git 'nuff to do a fix of our own. Gotta take care of the Lawd's house, too." She gestured around the kitchen. "Where you think all this come from? The Pope? Shoulda seen this here place, fifteen years ago. Puh! Was close to bein' razed. It was the community dollahs saved it."

Peggy's eyes widened, and she saw the gleaming new appliances clearly, now, as Betty's words sunk in. "You got all this from-from rummage sales?"

"And bake sales, raffles, bingo night, dance socials, car wash; you name it, we'll sell it. We done wait 'til Sears had one of them no sales-tax day. They threw in the dishwashah on accounta we helped out the manager wiff one of his fave charity events. Did a booth and baked two-hundred cupcakes. Sometime, it pay off big. Y'know, you scratch my back, I scratch yours."

Peggy's heart pounded and her mind raced. It felt as if a veil had lifted from her eyes.

Chapter 40

Peggy didn't hear Joe complaining about waiting so long out in the cold. She didn't even flinch when he hit the brakes, skidded through a four-way intersection, and side-swiped a road block in front of the railroad tracks. She barely noticed.

Her head swam with images of the rectory's new appliances and the promise of a new roof. She laughed to herself. How could I have been so blind? An ad, a flyer, or a donation can, in and of itself, was little more than a shingle hung out on a fence; a tin cup on the corner! The shelter sat down by the railroad tracks in the shadow of empty, abandoned factories, serving as little more than a dumping ground for the community's unwanted animals. How much time had she wasted, waiting for people to offer them help, instead of the other way around?

As much as she had determined to push thoughts of Terry out of her mind, it was as if he'd sat down right next to her and whispered in her ear.

"What's the answer? Education! Involvement! One corner at a time."

Or, as Betty had put it, "you scratch my back; I scratch yours." Like the church reaching out to its parishioners, the shelter needed to reach out and offer people something more than just catching stray dogs. Despite her fatigue, the snow, the cold and the pile of waiting, overdue bills, Peggy couldn't wait to get to the shelter.

By the time the van reached the firehouse, it was past noon. Slipping down the narrow, slick, driveway the van's engine coughed, choked, then stalled.

"We're outta gas!" Joe cried as he stood up on the brakes—with no response. "And the brakes are shot!"

He pumped the brake pedal hard and swore as the van shot down the driveway. It lunged, skidding sideways into the open lot and accelerated fast towards the runs where the dogs were barking.

Everyone shrieked and ducked, except Peggy. "Joe stop this van or-or you're fired!"

Grabbing hold of the emergency brake, Joe yanked it upright. Instantly, the van spun around and careened backwards towards the runs. At the last second, due to the slight upgrade, the van lost its forward momentum and eased up to the drifted snow against the fencing. Joe's shaking hands still clutched the wheel.

"Everone okay?" Peggy asked.

Hearing applause, she glanced out the window. Dr. Hayward was leaning against the front door to the shelter, clapping his hands with wry appreciation. WHAP! Betty whacked Joe over the head with the pastry box, and this time he didn't protest. Ghostly pale, he stared back at a dog looking in his window.

Her feet planted firmly against the dashboard, Clara looked at him, too. "Y'owe me a fiver, fly boy."

Peggy eased out onto the slippery drive, under light snow flurries. Four feet of crusty snow-pack had been plowed up against the warehouse fences and the mill wall. Unlike the lot, the front walkway had not been shoveled, so she had a hard time helping both Betty and Clara through the drifts to the front door. Halfway there, she stopped and looked around, alarmed.

"Someone stole the Pinto!"

"Fat chance." Joe pointed to an antennae sticking up out of a sooty snow-bank running the length of the warehousing. "She'll be buried 'til March, courtesy of the town plow. Guess it don't matter since she won't run 'til May Day, anyhow.

"Oh."

Peggy didn't know why she felt so relieved. The car was useless to them, but seeing its antennae sticking up like a snorkel through the drifts, assured her that somehow, Terry too, would still be hanging on.

As they reached the front door, she noticed that the vet's eyes, although a bit sunken, looked amused.

"You ever consider a career in Nascar?" he asked Joe.

"Yeah, how'd ya guess?"

"Just a hunch."

"It was either that or astronaut, but I get dizzy on the merry-go-round."

Paul nodded, as Joe, Betty and Clara stomped snow off their boots and headed inside. Then he looked down on Peggy. "I almost called a search party."

"They would have needed sled dogs. Thank you for t-taking care of the dogs," she gestured to the dogs outside. He pulled a pink receipt from his lab coat pocket and handed it to her. Peggy blinked at it. "You're billing us?"

"It's a fine from the town. For not shoveling the walk."

"What? B-but they're the ones who plowed the lot!"

"Apparently, the walkway is the shelter's responsibility. They said it should have been cleared in time for public hours, and that the manager is aware of that."

It was then that she noticed a parking space had been neatly shoveled out of the mountain of plowed snowdrift beside the firehouse. The vet's sports car was tucked into it, safely out of the way of falling icicles from the firehouse roof.

He held the door open for her, without apology. "Tomorrow's Friday. The kennel's full, again. We'll need to talk."

Folding the receipt into her pocket, she raised her chin. "Yes. Five o'clock—at the meeting." With that, she headed inside.

"Meeting? What meeting?"

At five minutes before five, Paul shoved the warped cellar door closed and padlocked it. "Five o'clock meeting," he muttered to himself.

He crunched over the snow in the dark, carefully trudging up the slope towards the entrance, using his medical bag for ballast. The storm was over, having moved on to wreak havoc up through New England, but it left behind bitter cold, and an icy mess. Powdery snow blew across the roofs of the warehouses like white sea spray, illuminated by the solitary pole lamp at the end of the runs. With relief, he saw that the town plow had not returned after having plowed the Jaguar in, twice, during its afternoon sweeps. It had taken the young vet forty-five minutes to clear each onslaught of snow away, to the amusement of the firefighters watching at their windows.

"Five more months," he consoled himself under his breath, and pushed through the gate. "Four, if I can function without sleep."

On entering the kennel, he stomped snow off of his boots, then walked up and down the runs, observing the dogs, as they finished their evening meal. He sighed, noting that every run was full. Why did he have to go to loggerheads with her, every week, over the issue? He glanced at his watch, took a breath, and headed for the office.

Joe cleared his throat loudly when the vet walked in. Hunched over her notebook, Peggy glanced up at the clock and then put her pen down. She swiveled around in Terry's chair. Paul stood in the doorway, arms folded across his chest. The entire crew had apparently been waiting for her.

"I-I've drawn up a list of things that need attention. First, is the van. Those brakes have to be fixed, and it needs to pass inspection."

Joe snorted Mountain Dew up his nose with a laugh. "Rottsa ruck!"

"I'm serious. If it's impounded, how will you do patrols? We can't risk it. It's got to be road worthy and legal. The second fix is repairing the cracks in the cinderblock."

As if in agreement, the pipes in the walls clanked and banged. They all held their breaths.

"And we need a new boiler," she added. "The dollars spent having Mr. Riley patch it every other week, could be put towards other things, like new chute doors and a new roof."

"That be all honky-dory," Betty said with a polite nod. "But, we be broke!"

"Th-that has to change, too. With one more ad in the Recycler I think—"

"Excuse me," Paul interrupted, "but you have a more pressing problem here than remodeling. You have X number of spaces that fill up, every Friday. Need I remind you what happens when—"

"No please! I-I will get to that. It's the last item on the agenda. In the meantime, I intend to finish the grant so that the shelter can expand and maybe get you the equipment you asked for."

"Grant?"

"Expand?" Betty coughed up her tea.

"No offense, Saint Francis," Joe burped, "but you're talkin' long shots, here! Even Ter said the grant's a spin of the roulette wheel."

Paul glanced at his watch, again. "Look, not to beat a dead horse, but…"

Clara looked him up and down. "You don't like horses, do you?"

"Forget about expanding," he continued, "you can't ɼay your bills, now. It's simple economics. You talk about putting ads in the paper.

That's like putting a Bandaid on a pumping artery. And a grant is like a tourniquet, you have to apply it at just the right time. Not to beat…" he glanced at Clara, "…not to rain on any parades, the warden was right. It's a long shot, in the future. How do you propose to deal with your immediate needs, here and now?"

"Bartering," Peggy smiled.

"Bartering," repeated Paul, with just enough emphasis to make it sound silly to her.

"Betty's church was able to-to redo the entire rectory, just by holding rummage and bake sales and-and doing favors for Sears."

"Favors? For Sears?" Paul shook his head as if to clear it. "Look, even if there's anyone out there still alive who remembers bartering—"

"Me grandad got me mum for a sack of taters and a hog," Clara declared.

"Got her cheap, huh?" Joe remarked.

Paul sighed. "As of January first, I do believe the year to be nineteen seventy-five, in a cash and carry society, minus the push to plastic. Outside of peeling road kill out of pot holes, or chasing stray dogs while half the town is pissing away their welfare checks at the corner bar, what can you possibly offer this community in return?" Peggy glanced at his medical bag, then up at him with another little lift of her chin.

His eyes widened with alarm.

Chapter 41

FREE VET EXAM TODAY

The cardboard sign flapped over the front gate in the cold wind. Adorned with pink and red paper hearts, it also said: Happy Valentine's Day.

"Is this normal, Doctor?" The middle-aged woman vaccillated between addled cat owner to flirty cougar.

Bent over an ornery orange tabby cat that did not appreciate a thermometer stuck in its rectum, Paul spit cat hair out of his mouth. The folding card table serving as exam table tilted sideways on the uneven, trampled snow, threatening to dump the cat and his pile of health forms to the slushy ground. He slipped the thermometer out of the cat's rear end, wiped it on his sleeve and read it.

"No," he finally answered the woman. He replaced the cat into the woman's carrier and was about to take a sip from a styrofoam cup. The block of ice that used to be his hot coffee smacked his teeth.

"I knew it! You feel it, too!" The woman place a gloved hand on his arm, in a caressing move of familiarity. Paul deftly withdrew his arm and checked his watch. He looked up the line of waiting people and pets that snaked up the driveway. It was noon. He'd been standing out in the bitter cold since eight in the morning.

Despite the bitter cold and treacherous driving conditions, the turnout had taken him by surprise, since the crew had only had a day and a half to create the crude flyers, and staple them to telephone poles all across town. He watched Peggy as she moved up the line of waiting pet owners, taking down their names and pet issues on a clipboard.

"Well," the cat's owner said, "what do I do? I have spent a fortune on cat food. He just won't eat! Doctor?" She stepped in front of him, blocking his view of Peggy. "Doctor?"

"Hmn?" He dragged his attention back to the woman. "Well, for starters, stop cooking for your cat."

"But, he won't eat anything else. And then, I have no one else to cook for!" The woman smiled coyly. "Once he tasted my cooking, he fell in love."

"Put down a good quality cat food, and if he doesn't eat it—"

"He *won't* eat it."

"Not if you keep serving him chicken parmigiana, he won't."

"'Scuse me," the next man in line complained, "I'm freezin' here, can you hurry it up?"

"Wait your turn!" the woman scolded him, then batted her eyes at Paul. "Maybe if you made a house call, you could see for yourself."

"Ma'am," Paul blew on his numb hands, "I don't need to make a house call to know that your cat is fat because you're indulging him. Offer him cat food and cat food only. When he gets hungry enough, he'll eat it. Give a call to your regular veterinarian and ask for their feline dietary guidelines. They'll be happy to help."

"You're sending me to my own vet? Why am I here?"

"For the free exam?"

"Well! I guess you get what you pay for!" The woman lifted her cat carrier and strode away in a huff.

"About time!" the next man in line shouted after her and set his sweater-clad Yorkie on the table. "If y'ask me, she was lookin' for more of a puss-puss exam, know what I'm sayin?"

Just then the van skidded down the driveway, blocking the woman's exit.

"Look out!" Joe hollered out the window. "I can't stop! Yo!"

The woman leaned on her horn. Joe leaned on his horn. All the horn honking set off the shelter's dogs to barking within the building, which incited all the dogs in line to bark, too. The resulting melee was so loud it brought the firemen to their windows.

Peggy darted in between the line of waiting people and pets to the vehicles. "Joe let her pass!"

Keeping an eye on the ruckus, Paul gave up trying to listen to the Yorkie's chest with his stethoscope, and handed the dog to its owner, having to shout. "I said, he's got a bit of a heart murmur, I suggest you make an appointment to see your vet."

"I stood in line for 'see your own vet'? I coulda saved myself th'trouble of standin' out here in the frickin' cold?!"

Honk! Honk! Honk!

"Sir, I...what?"

No one could hear a thing over the battle of the horns. Paul gave up and stood with his arms folded across his chest, and watched the frackas unfold, as the Yorkie owner complained loudly to the people behind him in line.

"Joe!" Peggy rapped on the van's hood. "Get out of her way before the firemen call the cops!"

"I got the righta way here!" he hollered, then threw the van in reverse and swerved aside. The woman continued leaning on her horn, scattering people right and left.

Peggy hopped up on the van's bumper, reached in through the window and yanked the keys out of the ignition. "You're not even supposed to be driving this thing!"

"And I'm supposed to patrol, how?"

"Quietly! Under the radar! That's a failed inspection sticker on the windshield!"

"This is the thanks I get for riskin' my life for this place!" He released the parking brake and coasted down to park beside the drift-buried Pinto.

Peggy raised a timid wave to the firemen. "S-sorry!" She then hurried over to Paul, still watching, and waiting, for the Yorkie owner to either give up his tirade, or let him finish his exam.

"An hour! I been standin' here a freezin' hour and this is what you tell me?" the man yelled at him.

"Is-is there a problem?" asked Peggy.

Paul handed her his clipboard of forms. "Yes. The vet needs a break or you'll be taking him to the hospital for frostbite, as well as a ruptured bladder." With that, he strode towards the firehouse.

"The sign there says free vet exam!" the Yorkie man snapped at Peggy. "He says my dog's got a heart problem, but he wont do nuthin' for it!"

"Well, he-he can't, you see."

"What is this? He ain't a real vet?"

"Oh he's a vet, it's just, I mean he could if...see, we don't have the money to do anything more than a free exam. We don't have the equipment or-or the medicines to treat any illnesses or conditions."

"Yeah? You shoulda put that on your sign! Free vet, but don't expect bupkes! The three B's maybe should hear about this!!"

"The three what?"

"Better Business Bureau!" the man hollered at her and walked away with his dog.

"But-but we're nonprofit!"

"Good heavens, people are something, aren't they?" the next man in line said to Peggy, with an apologetic smile. "Well, don't worry, I appreciate what you're doing, here." He pointed to his name on her clipboard. "That's me. And, this is Sam."

"Thank you," Peggy exhaled with gratitude. "Hello, Sam." She stroked the handsome spaniel mix, then glanced to the firehouse. For the first time, she hoped that Paul hadn't continued walking right out their front door, running for the hills.

"Your vet, is he new? Looks rather young."

"He's one of the best from the EVC. Up the hill?"

"Ah yes. Smart outfit. Helped us out when Sam here stepped on a broken bottle, last summer. This is new, what you're doing, down here."

"Yes, we hope it might help if people knew what a shelter does." She extended a flyer to him. "And, what we need."

"Ah! Good thinking. Good business!" He tapped a finger alongside his temple with a little wink. "Give a little to get a little. Capital. We adopted Sam, here, from you people, about two years ago, now. We couldn't be happier. Where's your manager, by the way? Mr. Brannan? He'll remember Sam."

Peggy's stomach flip-flopped on hearing Terry's name. "Oh, he's-he's away right now, on medical leave. I'm sure you're right; he'd remember Sam."

"Sorry to hear that. Nice man. He'll be back, though?"

Peggy's first impulse was to say yes, but she couldn't get the words out. To her relief, Paul appeared again, exiting the firehouse. "Here comes the vet. He'll be able to give you an exam. I mean Sam. An exam."

"Well, on behalf of the neighborhood, thank you." The man tipped his hat to her, dropping a dollar bill into her donation can.

Peggy suddenly wanted to throw her arms around the man, bury her face in his nice coat, and sob. "Thank you," she managed to croak over the lump in her throat. She walked away, not even looking up as she passed Paul.

Huddled in his overcoat, Paul watched Peggy retreat back to the waiting line of people. Something about the way she walked and wiped her cheeks, caused him to pause.

"Good afternoon, Doctor!" Sam's owner smiled and extended a hand.

"Afternoon." Paul shook the man's hand and knelt beside the handsome dog. "What seems to be the problem?"

"Oh, no problem. Just thought I'd bring Sam down for a visit. He almost ended his days here at the shelter awhile back. My wife and I adopted him just after we'd pulled through a difficult patch of our own. It was fate, and I believe it's good to revisit where one has been, from time to time, to truly appreciate how far one has come, wouldn't you say?"

Paul scratched the dog's ears. "I suppose so." He donned his stethoscope, listened to Sam's chest, then looked in his ears, eyes, and mouth and then palpated the dog's abdomen.

He asked all of the usual questions regarding the dog's habits, all the while searching for the tell-tale sign that Sam remembered the shelter. He thought that maybe the dog would react to the scent of it, the sounds, maybe display a hint of the fear of past confinement. However, he saw nothing in Sam's behavior that would suggest such a memory. Paul observed only love and adoration for the man who had rescued him from the place. Did the dog not remember, or did it no longer matter to the dog, because he was loved now and in a good home?

"He appears to be in excellent health. You might want to consider a senior wellness screening with your regular vet."

"Thank you, Doctor, we will! Have a good evening. Come on Sam, let's go home." The man enunciated the last phrase with a warm smile, then tipped his hat to Paul, and led his dog up the driveway.

Paul watched them walk away. The man tipped his hat, again, to Peggy. She knelt down and patted Sam's head.

A stout woman in a quilted parka stepped up to the table, with a boy of about five, toting a cardboard pet carrier. "We got this guinea pig off a guy in his school, yesterday, and we wanna know if it's okay."

Paul opened the top of the carrier and looked down on a long-haired, white guinea pig. Twitching its whiskers, it looked up at him from a mass of shredded toilet paper.

"Well, he looks all right. Clear eyes, nose. Is he eating? Good. He looks alert. You might want to put wood chips and a towel or some sort of blanket in there for him if you take him out in the cold like this."

"We didn't think we'd be standing out here in the freezing cold for over two hours!" the woman said, sourly.

"Look at it this way," Paul said with a polite smile. "This is probably the warmest its going to be today, the sun will be going down and along with it, the temperature." He pointed to the line of people that went clear up to the street. "You might still be waiting back there with all those people. But, now you're here. Look how far you've come."

The woman looked him up and down. "Is that supposed to make me feel better?"

By five o'clock, Dr. Hayward had seen every person that had braved the cold and waited in line. Peggy couldn't have been happier with the turn out. Miraculously, there were no more unpleasant outbursts. As a matter of fact, Peggy noticed that there were quite a number of women who were more than willing to wait, once they got a good look at the handsome vet. A few of them went so far as to ask her if he made house calls.

As the last woman skidded her car away up the icy driveway, Peggy approached Paul. Shivering, he handed her a pile of paperwork and the donation can, before clearing the table.

"How much did we get in donations?" Peggy opened the can and counted out four dollars and sixty cents. "Oh."

"You didn't really expect a windfall, did you? Most of these people hadn't seen a vet in years. If ever. And, it was a freebie, remember?"

"Well..." Peggy managed to shrug it off. "It's a start."

"A start? You're lucky nobody was armed."

"Yo, Doc!" Joe picked up the last of the litter blowing around the lot and dragged the garbage bag up to them. "Score any dates? I spied some ladies workin' their wares."

Folding the table legs, Paul looked up from under lowered brows.

"Whoa!" Joe laughed. "You look like you been hauled in a trawl there, Doc!"

Peggy stifled a smirk. It was true. His lab coat was filthy, stained with assorted exudates, fluids, and animal hair. His Italian wool slacks had ripped at the knees after kneeling on the icy macadam all day long, and his face was splattered and scratched.

"How many freeloaders you see, Doc?"

"I lost count after I lost feeling in my fingers."

Joe nodded to the papers in Peggy's hands and opened the garbage bag. "Wanna file those?"

Peggy held the papers close, protective. "This isn't garbage! These names and addresses are going to change our future!"

"How you figger?"

"Instead of handing out flyers willy-nilly, we can mail them out every week, tell people about what we need and maybe people will send in donations after what we did for them, today!"

"We?" Paul repeated.

"You, I-I meant, you."

"Uh, Saint Francis?" Joe opened the bag wider for her to see. It was stuffed full of her crumpled flyers. "Happy Valentine's Day."

Chapter 42

Munching Betty's homemade Valentine's Day cookies, Peggy perused Dr. Hayward's medical notes, while the crew wrapped up chores. Aside from varying heart and respiration rates, she noticed a consistent pattern of common ailments: ear shaking (mites), bad breath (dental issues), and scratching (flea related dermatitis).

However, there was one pattern in particular that turned up in the stats, repeatedly. "Look at how many of these cats and dogs haven't been fixed!" she said aloud.

"You sound surprised," Paul said, as he jotted down an inventory of the medicine cabinet. "Just so you know, I counseled them all on the health benefits of neutering, for all the good it'll do."

"Well, now that you've told them, maybe they will."

"Will what?"

"Spay and neuter their pets?"

The vet looked at her over his shoulder, as if at a child. She heard the rest of the crew chuckle, too. She frowned at them.

"Why not?"

"Saint Fran," Joe popped the cap off of a Mountain Dew. "It's like this; peeps who don't snip Rover 'n Tom don't for a reason. They'll tell ya it's a sin."

"Unnatural," Betty corrected him.

"Fiddlesticks," Clara growled, "it's because there's no law what says they 'ave to."

"No, it's 'cause it cost too much!" Betty said, and raised an accusatory brow to the vet.

Paul refrained from comment and turned back to the cabinet. Peggy wondered if his silence meant that he knew it to be true. Her eyes rested on the gruesome poster on the wall beside him, the image of a pile of dead kittens and puppies. It wasn't just a poster to her, now. She knew, first-hand, the grim reality of pet overpopulation and dreaded the coming spring, when the shelter could see the slaughter come to pass.

"M-maybe we should tell them about what happens to the puppies and kittens when they don't spay and neuter," she ventured. "Maybe they'd take it more seriously."

Joe laughed. "Oh, yeah, right, that'll win us brownie points!"

"If people won't neuter their own pets to protect them against certain forms of cancer," the vet interjected, "which is the best reason I can imagine to do it, they're certainly not going to do it for the greater good of population control."

Peggy tried not to feel discouraged by their consensus. She felt sure that if people knew that they were part of the problem, that they would do something about it. It was just common sense! She wrote a note to herself to make another flyer about the statistics of overpopulation, maybe with a picture of the poster on it. If anything might sway opinion, that graphic picture might! It sure opened her eyes! She was just beginning to feel encouraged about this new project, when Betty pushed a stack of invoices in front of her.

"Hate to be a party poop, but what you wanna do 'bout these?"

"I don't suppose there are any valentines hidden in there?" With an irrational skip of her heart, Peggy hoped that there might be a card or message from Terry, although she felt rather silly immediately after she'd said it.

"Valentines? Ain't likely."

"We...we haven't heard from Irene yet, have we?"

"I imagine they still be diggin' out from undah ten feeta snow. Done got socked worse than we did. We don't hear by tomorrah, I'll call."

"I got a Valentine." Joe pulled a pink invoice from his pocket. "From Fegetti's. Feel the love. Hey, what you still doin' here, Doc? Don't you got a date?"

Peggy glanced at Paul, just as he tossed a bemused look over his shoulder at Joe.

Betty snatched the invoice out of Joe's hand. "What this fo'?"

"Chill out! Just an estimate on the van's brakes. Best deal we could get. We still owe him for a set of tires and the Pinto's lube last summer."

"Add it to the pile?" Betty asked Peggy.

Peggy looked over the estimate, her eyes popping. "F-four hundred dollars?! Where are we going to get four hundred dollars, on top of all of these other bills?"

"We could always stick up a gas station," Joe suggested. "They're th'only ones makin' a buck these days."

"Feudal Bastards!" Clara raised her fist to heaven. "What about all that lip service they served up 'bout looking into sun power?"

"Soon as they figger out how to make a gazillion dollars on ol' Sol, and keep the rest of us in the dark they will, bulleeve me. Then we'll be payin' just to open the shades every day, just you watch."

Peggy leafed through the bills, feeling as if she was grasping at straws. "Well, maybe...maybe people will send in money after what we did for them today."

Paul shot her a dry look.

"I mean," she stammered, "I meant—what *you* did for them. Maybe they'll donate to our cause, seeing we're in need?"

Betty sighed to Clara. "Remembah when you was that young?"

"No."

"But, why not?" Peggy entreated them. "I mean if-if we keep it up? People will see what we're trying to do, and they'll want to help out."

"What do you mean by 'keep it up'?" Paul asked. "Not to beat a..." He stopped when skewered by Clara's narrowed eye. "...not to put a damper on things, but I don't see how my standing out in subzero weather giving free exams to half the town is going to help pay your bills. If anything, it's going to get me into hot water with vets from here to the Water Gap, for prostitution."

"You're working for a nonprofit," Peggy reminded him.

"My peers are not."

Betty opened a pack of candy cigarettes. "Saint Francis, I know you be holdin' tight to the fat man 'gainst the hole in a doughnut, but the doctah's got a point. What we gonna do now 'bout these here bills that was due last month?"

Peggy hadn't a clue what Betty meant by half of what she'd said, but she understood the question, and didn't have an answer. "Well, which bills are more important?"

Betty held them out to her like a flush of cards. "Pick a bill, any bill."

"Hey, you said we gotta have the van runnin," Joe piped up. Without the Pinto, we gotta have wheels!"

The pipes clanked and thunked in the walls. They all held their breaths.

"And that's anothah thang," Betty whispered, "we gotta start a boiler repair fund. Terry kept sayin' we gotta, and now we *gotta*, 'cause we done wore out our sympathy card wiff Mistah Riley."

Peggy skimmed through the bills, then gazed out the window, stymied. What to do? She felt as buried as the Pinto out there in the snow drift, and about as useless. Slowly she focused on the buried car, feeling a stab of annoyance. What was the point of having a busted car that only ran sporadically at best for six months out of the year? It was little better than a pile of scrap metal junk. Dimly, the memory of the junkyards by the turnpike that she and Terry had driven past on the way to Charlie's place, pushed into her mind.

"What if-what if we trade the Pinto in for the brake job on the van?" she heard herself say aloud.

"Yeah, right!" Joe snickered. "Her radiator's cracked, transmission's shot, she ain't passed inspection in three years. Jeeze! The demolition derby won't even take her!"

"Th-that's what I mean. Why keep it around? Why not sell it for parts, for scrap metal, to one of those junk yards off the turnpike?"

Joe sat up in his chair, the smile wiped from his face. He looked between Betty and Clara. "But Ethel is, well she's Ter's car. I mean, not his, but...y'know."

Peggy cast her eyes to the floor and then took a breath. "But, he's not here and we need the money, *now*."

"What'll we do if the van bites it, in the meantime?" Joe argued.

"If it broke down, tonight, could we get the Pinto up and running, tomorrow?"

"Sheesh. Not without a magic wand and a thousand bucks."

"You have to have an emergency vehicle," Paul spoke up. "What if you get a call for an HBC?"

"What's wrong with your buggy?" Clara asked.

"Thankfully, it's just a two-seater."

"Joe," Peggy entreated him, "we're sort of stuck. And it's just sitting out there rusting under the snow."

Joe looked to Betty, who shrugged.

"She gotta point. Either that, or you pay them bills."

"Fine!" Joe sighed. "But, I want it on record I ain't happy 'bout it."

"When you evah happy 'bout diddly?"

"Betty," Peggy asked, "could you call around and see who might take Ethel? So, Joe? You said that for four hundred, Fegetti's will fix the van's brakes, right? Joe?"

Joe squirmed in his chair. "Uh...well...this probably ain't the best time to bring it up, but she's also been gulpin' two quarts of oil a day. I'd take her to AA, but I think she's a lost cause."

"An oil leak, too? What'll that cost?"

"This ain't gonna work," Betty tossed her candy Camels aside. "What boob we gonna find dumb enough to think that hunka junk be worth the tow, let alone a grand!"

Peggy thought hard. "Maybe we can pay for the brakes with an IOU for the Pinto money, and ask Fegetti for the oil leak on loan?"

Joe barked a humorless laugh. "I show up at Fegetti's without a check, they're gonna put a boot on the van, sic their mangy dog on me, and hold us both hostage 'til somebody pays up from last time."

Peggy blinked at him a second. "Dog? They have a dog?"

"They whistle, it comes, I'm guessin' it's a dog. Could be Sasquatch. It's freakin' bigger than Gorgo. Dirty, mangy, stinkin'...why?"

Peggy slowly smiled and turned her eyes to the vet. The crew looked at him, too.

Paul looked between them and then he rolled his eyes. "Hell."

Chapter 43

The van hit a patch of crusted snow and popped over the curb, aimed for Fegetti's Auto Works across the meridan. Flying into the repair lot, it sideswiped the gas pump, and only stopped when it plowed headlong into a drift of snow, just in front of the shop's roll up doors. Old Man Fegetti, who stood beside the doors, calmy wiped his oil-soaked hands on a grimy rag.

The van's side door slid open with a slam and Paul jumped out, steaming mad. "Throwing a clutch into reverse at forty miles per hour is not downshifting!"

"Brake check?" Fegetti asked, grinning toothlessly.

Paul yanked open the passenger door. "Ask her." He tossed his overcoat inside.

Peggy stepped down. "Why are you so upset?"

"Why aren't you? We nearly made the six o'clock news on that turn!"

"I already bobsledded to and from Clara's house in a blizzard. Trust me. This was a cakewalk."

"Right." Paul yanked his lab coat closed and buttoned it with cold, stiff fingers, as if it could steel him against the chilly indignity of being lent out like a candy-striper.

"Doc, I swear that stop sign wasn't there yesterday." Joe leaned back and crossed his feet on the dashboard.

Paul snatched his medical bag off of the floor, and then slammed the door shut.

Peggy stepped up to the grizzled mechanic. "Hello, Mr. Fegetti. I-I understand we owe you a bit of money and, well, we-we have a proposition for you."

"That the same thing as a check?" Fegetti waved to Joe, who half-heartedly waved back.

Peggy made her impassioned pitch to the garage owner, reading from a crib sheet in her trembling hands, while Paul waited, shivering in the cold.

"Free vetting?" Fegetti exclaimed.

"Free exams," Paul clarified, and stuffed his stethoscope in his pocket. "Not including what the dog might need in medications after examination."

Fegetti grasped Paul's hand and pumped it up and down. "You have yourself a deal there, young man."

Paul looked down at his now grease-blackened hand. With a barely contained grimace, he yanked out a handkerchief and made a big show of trying to wipe his hand clean.

Peggy ignored him. "Th-thank you!" she gushed to the mechanic.

"Thank *you*!" Fegetti grinned. He gestured to Paul's nicely pressed and starched lab coat. "Might wanna stow your doctor coat, though. My dog gets kinda nervous 'round you fellas."

"Think I'll keep it on, thanks." Paul gave up trying to wipe the grease off and reached in through the van's passenger window. He withdrew, holding a muzzle. "Is your dog inside?"

"If you stow your whites, you won't need that. Ain't big enough, anyway."

"It's an extra large. They don't come any bigger."

Fegetti shrugged. He put his fingers, grease and all, into his mouth and whistled in the direction of the garage.

Peggy thought it odd that Joe wasn't right there telling Fegetti what the van needed in so far as repairs. She looked behind her and saw him frantically rolling up her window and locking the doors.

All at once, a monstrous shaggy black dog leapt over a pile of tires with a blood-curtling snarl and charged right at Paul.

"Oh my gosh!" Peggy squealed and hopped up onto the hood.

"Holy mother of—" Paul dropped to the ground and rolled under the van.

The mammoth dog circled the van around and around, barking viciously, clearly trying to get at the trapped vet.

"Call him off! Call him off!" Paul hollered.

"Won't do no good now, son," Fegetti called out, "he'd sooner take my arm off at the elbow!"

"Joe!" Peggy shouted through the windshield, "do something!"

Joe threw on the emergency lights and leaned on the horn. The devil beast of a dog howled along with the horn and then crouched down to squeeze under the bumper.

Oil dripping over his face, Paul kicked at the undercarriage, and shouted over the horn honking. "You're making it worse!"

"Don't take it personal," Fegetti called out to him. "Ain't a vet can get near the bugger. Have to knock him out with a shot just to give him his shots! I tried to warn you! It's your uniform!"

Peggy sat up. Uniform? Whites! She hung upside down over the hood and called out to Paul, underneath the bumper. "Take it off! Your lab coat! Take it off! He thinks you're a vet!"

"I *am* a vet!"

"Well, he wants to *kill* the vet!"

"Son of a..." Paul wrestled off his lab coat, hitting his head on the van's muffler. "Goddammit!" Bunching the coat in a ball, he waited for the dog to snap at him, again, then tossed the coat straight at the dog's open jaws.

The dog snatched it and with wild snarls, ripped it to shreds in a matter of seconds.

"Keeerist!" Paul breathed, wide-eyed.

Fegetti leaned down and waved to Paul. "He'll be okay now. You can come out."

"I'm going to need more assurance than that!"

"I don't sell no insurance."

"No, I mean—hey!" Paul kicked the undercarriage again. "Wozniak! Don't you have a pole in there? Isn't this your damn job?"

Peggy looked to Joe through the windshield. Pale, Joe shook his head no.

"I'm tellin' you," Fegetti insisted, "he'll be like a pup, now, you can all come out." He leaned down and offered the vet a hand. Paul hesitated, but then grasped the man's arm. Scuttling out from under the van, he saw the gargantuan dog drag what was left of his lab coat over the snow like a dead antelope.

Fegetti whistled again. The dog spit buttons and sauntered towards them.

Paul backed up against the van, but the mechanic was right. The huge dog ignored him, and sidled up to Fegetti, panting happily.

Fegetti patted the great dog's rump and grinned at Paul. "Told ya. C'mon, make friends."

"He just tried to kill me."

"No he didn't. Just the vet. Now, you're nobody special."

The dog looked up at Paul and wagged its great fan of a tail. He nosed his hesitant hand, until the vet patted it's massive, greasy head.

"What is it? I mean, the breed?"

"You're the vet; you tell me. Picked him up as a pup off the tracks, few years back. Maybe a gorilla mix." Fegetti threw his head back and laughed.

Joe opened his driver's side door and snuck a foot out. The other foot followed shortly afterward, and then the rest of his body. He peeked around the rear bumper.

Paul caught sight of him. "Thanks for the backup, Officer."

Joe stepped into view, sans his shades. He was wearing a nondescript raincoat that hid his badge and utility belt. "Hey, no offense, but I ain't stupid!"

Peggy slid down from the hood. Taking a hint from Joe, she removed and pocketed her badge. The dog loped over to her and wagged his tail. "What's his name?"

Fegetti grinned. "Tiny."

While Joe supervised Fegetti in hoisting the van up on the lift, Peggy and Paul walked Tiny, the canine behemoth, into the garage office. Paul decided that the best way to approach examining the dog, was to remain on the left side of cautious. He pulled out a vial of small yellow tablets from his bag and shook out one in his palm.

"This is Acepromazine," he told Peggy. "It's a mild sedative." He slipped the tablet in a spoonful of canned dog food. "Help me lay out the tarp, please."

Peggy helped the vet unfold and set down a canvas tarp. He arranged a tray of clippers, a few tubes of ointments, and the scopes from his medical bag.

Fifteen minutes after gobbling up the treat, Tiny lay down on the tarp and heaved a sigh, ready for a nap.

"Can you give me a hand?" Paul asked.

"M-me?"

"No, your shadow."

"S-sorry. Yes. Of course."

He handed her a pair of latex gloves, then took a breath. "He should be fine, but let's make it quick. I don't trust those pills thirty minutes past a hundred and fifty pounds."

Peggy stretched on the gloves and knelt beside the dog, opposite Paul. He rested his hand on the dog's chest and checked his watch. "I'll have to forego listening to his heart and lungs on this visit, since what's left of my stethoscope is scattered halfway across the damn parking lot. Hand me that tube of KY jelly, please."

Peggy handed him the blue and white tube, and watched as Dr. Hayward squeezed the gel over a thermometer and inserted it in the dog's rectum. Tiny didn't move.

"Squeeze a bit on the clipper blades, please, then open that notebook and take notes, all right?"

"Yes." Peggy coated the clipper blades and opened his small black notebook. She noticed that it was neatly indexed, and had a section devoted to the shelter's animals. She had to admit that no matter what she might think of Paul as a person, he was very thorough as a vet of record.

"Follow the format on the preceding page. Date, time, location. Jot this down: male Newfie-Mastiff mix." He lifted the dogs tail. "Neutered." He lifted the dog's lips with a gloved finger and looked at its teeth. "About four years old. Gums pink. Cap refill normal." He removed the thermometer and read it. "Temp one hundred one. Normal."

Peggy jotted everything that he said in the notebook, hoping that she was spelling the words right.

Paul wiped the thermometer with a swab of alcohol and handed it to her. "Put it in the zippered pocket on the front, please."

By then, Tiny's eyes were half-closed.

"Dog is most likely not on any medications. The ace is knocking him down fast."

Peggy jotted that down, too.

Paul switched on the electric clippers and paused a moment. The dog did not react to the buzzing. Satisfied, Paul carefully shaved off greasy, matted knots from the dog's fur. Snoozing comfortably, Tiny even rolled over so that the vet could get at the tighter coils on his belly.

"He needs regular brushing, if not grooming."

"Should I write that down?"

Paul shrugged. "Why not? Be good for a dog like this to get daily handling. No indication of mange or external parasites. But, I'm going to do a scraping to be sure. In the side pocket of my bag there's a blue plastic case. Take out a slide and the scraper. Be careful not to slice your glove."

Peggy found the case and handed him the slide and what looked like a slim butter knife.

"Hold his foreleg up for me."

Peggy held the dog's leg and watched Paul gently scrape the skin under the dog's armpit and smear the slide.

"Hand me another slide and one of the plastic slip cases."

She handed him the items, and he carefully pressed the slides together, sealed them in the plastic, and handed them to her again.

"Use the marker there and write on it: Tiny Fegetti, parasite check. Mange check. Date it. And, hand me the ear scope—that one there—that's right."

Peggy handed him the heavy instrument, then marked the slide package. She watched as he looked into each of Tiny's ears.

"There's a mild yeast infection in each ear canal. Can you hold his ear open for me—like this. And, hold this basin under it."

Peggy followed his lead and held Tiny's ear upright, positioning a small bowl underneath, as he rubber-syringed saline solution into each ear, then swabbed out a dark, waxy exudate with cotton watting.

"Hand me that tube, there. Thank you. This is an antibiotic that will help rid him of the infection." He squeezed a bit of ointment into each of Tiny's ears, then opened the dog's enormous mouth. "He's got a lot of tartar. See that crusting, here and here? The red and inflamed gums? He needs some meaty bones to chew. That would help keep the plaque and tartar in check."

Paul rummaged in his medical bag and pulled out a steel dental pic and scraper. "Hold his jaw open, will you?"

Peggy gently held Tiny's toothy jaws open, while the dog snored loudly.

Paul picked over the dog's teeth a good fifteen minutes, wiping plaque on squares of gauze. Finished, he rubbed the gums with peroxide wipes.

At last, he pulled out two small vials and syringes from his bag. "Write the vax lots down for me, will you? One is distemper, the other rabies."

While he swabbed the dog's shoulder and rump with alcohol, Peggy jotted down the vial numbers into the notebook.

After injecting the dog, he inserted the syringes partway in a red plastic box, and snapped off the needles. Handing her a small brass tag, he said, "Jot that number down beside the rabies vax lot number and attach it to his collar, please." As she did so, he filled out a form. "This paperwork is for the garage. They ought to keep it somewhere for reference in case Tiny tries to kill anybody else, they'll have proof he's not rabid."

Peggy stifled a smile and noticed that Paul glanced at her with a wry smile of his own.

He scraped the skin between Tiny's toes onto a few more slides, then used another scope to peer into his eyes. "Eyes clear," he intoned. He palpated Tiny's abdomen and lymph glands, making the dog scratch in the air, as if being tickled. "No masses or growths on palpation. Lymph glands normal."

He then pulled out a prescription pad from his bag, just as Fegetti appeared in the doorway.

"Well, looky there!" Fegetti kneeled down to rub his dog's belly. The dopey dog thumped his tail, lazily. "Hey, you old bear, you look as good a new dog, as there is!"

"He has a mild yeast infection in both ears. This prescription should clear it up in seven to ten days. You'll need to keep his ears wiped out. They're prone. Here's a jar of ear wipes."

"Thank you. Well, then," Fegetti rose and took down the bikini calendar over his desk, "when can we expect you, next?"

"Next?"

"Yes sir, I see here we still have few bills in the arrears."

"Oh, yes," Peggy swallowed a gulp. "Those..."

Paul closed his medical bag with a snap. "How many is a few?"

"Let's see here," Fegetti tallied a few invoices. "Winter of nineteen seventy-two through the spring of seventy-three."

Paul turned a dark eye on Peggy. "A year's worth of bills?"

Peggy wrung her hands. "Um..."

"Tell you what," Fegetti suggested. "If you can take care of those mitts of his when he needs it—already broke four nail clippers. Too big and thick. I got a sand grinder might work. And every month he kinda needs his butt cheeks squeezed for them boy glands? You don't wanna know the stink it makes!"

It was all Peggy could do to keep a straight face. She didn't dare look at Paul.

To her utter surprise and relief, he did not challenge the deal, and it was agreed that he would stop by once a month to attend to Tiny's not so tiny issues. His wiping Tiny's butt would eventually wipe the shelter's slate clean.

Fegetti stamped the pink invoices "Paid in Full", and then shook Paul's hand.

Paul looked at his hand, a new swath of black grease matching the first.

"Next time, son," Fegetti said in parting, "just leave the uniform behind."

When they arrived back at the shelter, Joe couldn't resist sailing the van down the slick driveway at top speed. Before Peggy could stop him, he stomped on the brakes, sending the van into a side skid right up to the runs, where it stopped sharply, bouncing back down on the rear tires.

Once again, Paul jumped out and shoved the sliding door closed, hard.

"Do that again, I will tie you to the tracks out there, just in time for the five-fifteen!" With that, he stormed into the building.

"Joe..." Peggy sighed.

"I had to make sure they worked!"

Peggy hopped out of the van and paused, gazing at the empty parking spot in the snow bank, where the Pinto used to sit. "Looks like the tow truck picked Ethel up."

"I'm sure glad we didn't pass her on the way back," Joe said, then stared at his boots. "Thanks, Dillan."

Peggy smiled. "Yes, well...just...just don't mention it to Dr. Hayward, yet."

Joe mulled that over. "How many free vet visits you figure we got before Fegetti can get her to pass inspection?"

"Well, we've got the good doctor 'til June."

"Cool."

They headed for the gate and stopped in their tracks, confronted with two cases of dog food and a fifty pound bag of cat litter on the stoop. An attached note fluttered in the wind.

Peggy hurried up to it and read the note aloud. "'To the shelter; maybe this will help.' Oh!" The wind blew an enclosed check into the air. She chased after it and snatched it before it slipped into the slushy gutter. "It's from that nice man and his dog Sam! From the free vet exam. It's a donation check for twenty-five dollars!"

"Hul-lo!" Betty blinked at the stamped, paid invoice from Fegetti's in one hand and the donation check in the other. She looked over her glasses at Peggy, surprise in her eyes. "What's the catch?"

"No catch!" Peggy said, excitedly. "It's just proof that-that bartering works!"

"Not quite," Paul interjected. "The shelter owes me a stethoscope and a new lab coat. However, there's nothing here that you have to offer that I want."

"Oh...well, here," Peggy took the check from Betty and offered it to him. "Will this help pay for a new one?"

Paul eyed the check in her hand, but made no move for it. "Thank you, but that won't quite cover the tax."

"You shoulda seen it, Bet," Joe jumped in, "dog takes one look at him in his whites? Like a wolf, goes right for his throat! I mean, killer loco, okay?"

"Speaking of which, where were you and the rabies pole, Officer?" Paul asked pointedly, and turned away from the check still outstretched in Peggy's hand. He opened the medicine cabinet.

"With all due respect, Doc, Fegetti warned ya. You two were the mopes jumped inta harm's way!"

Betty snatched the check out of Peggy's outstretched hand, shrugged at the vet's turned back, then winked at Peggy, and dropped the check into the cash box.

Peggy shrugged, too, and addressed Paul's back. "Well, I sure learned a lot, today. I mean, minus the damage to your-your listening thing."

"You mean my two hundred dollar stethoscope?"

Peggy cleared her throat. "Um, yes but aside from that, bartering works."

"It only worked because the garage has a dog nobody in the state can get near with a ten foot pole."

"Aha!" Joe regaled him. "See? I was right."

"Well," Peggy acceded, "the van's fixed, and we got these donations, too, and you can't call that on account of Tiny's reputation. That stuff on our stoop, and that check is all because of-of..."

"Bartering, yes, so you said," Paul said, without turning around.

"Mostly, it was because of what you did," Peggy said.

Paul faced her. "It's my job."

"Well..." she turned back to Terry's box of papers. "I-I better get back to this."

Paul noted the crew's smiles, then returned to stocking his medical bag.

Joe popped open a soda. "Ya know Doc, I think we all learned a lesson today."

"I'm afraid to ask."

"Serious, man. You guys in the white coats? You can be seen comin' from a mile away!"

Peggy laughed along with everyone else. Paul looked at her and said, "They say the craziest usually can."

"That so?" Peggy rejoined. "Don't they also say it takes one to know one?"

Joe coughed up soda and pounded the counter in laughter.

"That's two points for Saint Francis!" Clara chortled.

"She got you there, Doctah!" Betty tossed the vet a pack of candy cigarettes.

The dogs in the kennel erupted into barking.

"Awww, c'mon," Joe moaned, and checked the clock. "Can't people read? Dillan, ya gotta start lockin' that door!"

"I'm off duty, as of an hour ago," Paul warned Peggy, and closed his medical bag.

"Maybe it's another donation!" Peggy swiveled around to look out the window, just as the office door opened. Instantly, the expressions of the crew sent a chill down her spine, and wiped the smile from her face.

"Evening," Mr. Harrison said, and closed the door behind him.

Chapter 44

Peggy felt as if she was suddenly balancing on a wire, with no net beneath her. As Harrison passed her, she felt herself freeze cold, and pressed her eyes closed against his caustic presence.

"Imagine my surprise," Mr. Harrison said genially to Dr. Hayward. "There I was, driving down Main Street, and on every corner I see your flyer, for a free vet exam, was it? I hear you caused traffic jams."

"It was a decent turnout. How's *your* dog?"

"Fine, though I'm surprised you'd ask, given your numerous patrols up in my neighborhood, lately."

"Ya wouldn't bulleeve th'infractions I turn up, up there," Joe said with an even tone.

Harrison smiled. "Speaking of which, I thought I'd pass along a heads-up. I said to the mayor this morning, 'Frank,' I said, 'are you really going to cite them for defacing the town? After all, what's a few flyers in the gutters? I'm sure they'll clean it up, and I'm sure they won't do it again, once they find out it's a misdemeanor offense.'"

Peggy wondered if Harrison's threat was apparent to everyone else. Surely, they heard it!

"Although admirable, Dr. Hayward, when you're just starting out and have your career to think about, I'm sure you don't want to be making enemies of your fellows at the AAHA."

"I'm not worried about it," Paul replied.

Harrison glanced around the office. "The town really ought to make it more feasible for you contract hires to provide decent services. But, times being what they are, what can you do besides trying to hold on to what you have, right? That's the other thing. I'm sure you don't want to worry your manager unnecessarily about run-ins with Town Hall. I understand he's been having a rough go of it."

"He be one step closah to fine, every day." Betty glowered at him.

"Well, I know you're probably close to closing. So, I'll say good night."

Harrison turned and walked out the door. When she heard the front door close, Peggy felt the pins and needles in her limbs begin to dissipate. She shook out her hands and wrung them vigorously, then paced back and forth in front of the window, watching as his car drove away.

"Damn," she heard Betty mutter. "We gotta take down all them flyers, but quick!"

"B.S.!" Joe retorted. "He's just bluffin'."

"Havin' the town cite us fo' defacin' public property ain't no bluff!"

"I'm tellin' ya, he was just blowin' smoke! Cite us? Gimme a friggin' break! Everybody and their brother posts flyers all over, all the friggin' time! They gonna cite every jocko with a garage sale? Since when the town give a crap? He's just yankin' our chain."

"Why?"

"'Cause he's a dick!"

"Watch your mouth," Clara grumbled.

"Aw, c'mon, what would you call him, then?"

"No need t'use foul language! Just say what's what! The bastard's all mouth and no trousers!"

"I ain't so sure he ain't," Betty argued. "Got his mitts in everybody's pie. He could make us trouble, if he want to."

"I still say he's bluffin'," Joe muttered.

When her head cleared, Peggy noticed that Paul was studying her.

"Are you okay?" he asked, in a confidential tone.

Peggy unclenched her fists, with difficulty. "Yes," she croaked. She dragged her eyes back down to Terry's box of papers.

"Well, see you tomorrow, then. Good night."

Peggy watched him leave, and then noticed everyone watching her. They abruptly found something important to do.

"C'mon Dillan, let's go! Before this slush freezes, again!" Joe called out from the van, idling by the snow-packed fence.

It had begun to drizzle by the time Peggy closed and locked the front door. Her stomach was still tied up in painful knots and her head ached. Worse, she felt humiliated, as if she'd been cut off at the knees. She had been rendered mute and useless, but this time, with a marked and frightening difference. She'd had no help. Where had her protectors been hiding? And why? Had they abandoned her for good? They were usually so quick with an order, a slap or a tongue-lashing. And now, after it had all blown over, she was left without a word of direction. Then again, she concluded, what better punishment for her disobedience, than to be left stranded?

It had been hard to meet the crew's eyes as they performed their rote closing tasks. They had no idea what was going on in her head, but she had a sneaking suspicion that they noticed her fright in Harrison's presence. Paul had sensed something, and she wondered how he interpreted it. Did he see the monster hiding in the shadows? He'd asked about her welfare, but quickly resumed his "business as usual" demeanor, as if he didn't care, one way or the other. If she thought about it long enough, Dr. Hayward wasn't one to let his guard down, either.

Making her way down the walk to the front gate, Peggy replayed what she could remember about Harrison's visit in her head, in fits and starts. The lack of substansive information about Lucky, outside of the curt response Harrison gave Paul, chilled her heart. How was Lucky, really?

Of more concern, was the question of how the shelter was supposed to move ahead with her ideas of bartering out Dr. Hayward's services, if Harrison intended to use Town Hall and the AAHA as disincentives? They had been stopped in their tracks before they'd even reached the corner. She wasn't sure what they could do without Paul's participation.

The most confusing thing about it, was why Harrison cared? He had his dog back. The shelter could not prove wrongdoing. Why then, was he, as Joe had so succinctly put it, "yanking their chain"?

Half-way down the walk, she saw Paul waiting at the gate. He held it open for her.

"Listen," he said. "Putting aside I nearly bought the farm today, you may be on to something with this bartering idea. In exchange for my services, you could conceivably get a few things taken care of, around here. I'd like to suggest a place to start. My office downstairs. I know you're concerned about the boiler, but there's a leak in the water pipes down there that's going to be a major problem if you don't catch it, now. I only suggest it, because, if you really want to make use of me, then I need a space that's workable. Think about it."

Peggy glanced at the Pinto's empty parking space, unable to fess up about having already bartered him out for the next three months. "Yes. I-I will."

"One more thing." He gestured to the notebook clutched in her hands. "Add an RSVP stipulation at the bottom of your next flyer. You need some sort of crowd control. And, have another flyer done up to hand out about the benefits of spaying and neutering. Kill two birds with..." he paused, as Clara tottered past him with narrowed eyes. "...or you might say, a bird in the hand, two in the bush."

"Next flyer?" Peggy repeated. "You mean, you'd do another free vet exam? B-but what about what-what he said?"

"Let's just say I don't like being told what I can or can't do. By anyone. You shouldn't, either."

Peggy averted her eyes. When he didn't walk away or step out of her way, she was forced to look up, held fast by his eyes. She felt compelled to nod in agreement.

"Good." He turned and walked towards his Jaguar.

The van's horn honked, and Joe hollered. "Yo! Saint Francis, let's gooooooo!"

After dropping Betty and Clara off, Joe pulled the van alongside the curb by Peggy's boarding house.

"Thanks, Joe." Peggy gathered her notebook and papers into her arms.

"Listen, don't let Harrison rattle ya. I'm tellin' ya, we got his number."

"Oh," Peggy frowned. "Was it that obvious?"

Joe ripped open a bag of peanuts. "Hey, the effer can freeze a bottle of rat gut at twenty paces. But, don't sweat it. Like I said, we got his number."

"And, he's got ours. He knows we're watching."

"So what? Patrolling's my job. He don't like it, he can kiss my sweet summons book. I say, screw him, let's do a drive-by right now!"

"No, Joe, don't make him-make him mad. He might take it out on Lucky."

"Dillan, lookit, I don't wanna say nuthin', but bottom line, we ain't got no control over it, y'know?"

"I know."

He offered her some peanuts. "Tell you what, though. Startin' tomorrow, I'll mix up patrol times, y'know, poker it up so it ain't so obvious."

"Thanks."

"Hey, like I said, it's my job, right?"

"Yeah, right." Peggy took a couple peanuts and got out. She sprinted through the rain up to her building. At the lobby door she paused and watched the van drive away around the corner. Pocketing her keys, she popped the peanuts in her mouth and headed back down the steps towards the bus stop.

Peggy was relieved to have had a different bus driver; one who would not question her sanity with his eyes, when she asked, yet again, to be let off in the middle of nowhere in the rain. Once the bus turned the corner, she hiked up the hill. Much of the blizzard's snow had melted, leaving only fast-shrinking, sooty snow mounds against sagging wooden fences and curbsides.

By nine p.m. the streets were quiet, as Peggy passed the hissing gas lamps that bordered Upper Farroway. The cold-blue light of televisions flickered in house windows. Towering above her wet, slushing footsteps, the bare tree branches clacked in the moaning wind.

At last, she came to a familiar corner and hid behind a tree. Breathless, she peered across the street to Harrison's house, then looked up and down the deserted road. No one else would be out on a rainy night like this, but still, she felt on edge, almost giddy, as if she were being watched. Taking a breath, she darted across the road and crept along the stone wall, to its midpoint. Standing on tip-toe, she peered into the yard.

In the dark, Peggy spotted the dog house under the trees. She could make out the outline of the same water bowl, but couldn't tell if it was full of ice, water or if it was empty. Then, she noticed the stake with a chain attached, and the chain seemed to be loosely coiled in front of the house. With a start, she heard the sound of the chain clink, and then saw it move an inch or so, inside the dog house.

Lucky was in the dog house!

Peggy listened to the rain patter on the roof of the dog house and felt her heart smolder in anger. The lamps in the Harrison household spread light on the frozen ground, just out of reach of Lucky, in more ways than one. Peggy felt a bitter resentment burn her throat, but there was nothing she could do. Harrison was within the law. It didn't matter that Lucky lay out there alone, in the cold night. The dog had shelter, water, and food, and in the law's eyes, that was enough.

All at once, Lucky barked. Peggy dropped down off the wall. He couldn't have seen her! She felt the wind at her back. He must have picked up her scent! She heard the chain drag out of the dog house, and then Lucky barked, again, louder and more insistent.

The back porch light switched on and flooded the yard. Peggy ducked and tore across the street. What she hadn't seen was the shadowy silhouette of someone in the flickering television glow behind a second-story window.

"Noooo!"

Peggy screamed and yanked her broom-handle club from under her pillow. She swung it in front of her face in a desperate attempt to fend off her attacker. The thick fog around her dissipated quickly, taking with it the shadows and echoes of voices shrieking at her.

Run! Run!

Gulping hot, salty tears, Peggy blinked herself awake. The room was just as she'd left it when she'd fallen asleep. She sat up and leaned over her knees to catch her breath. She could hear the rain drumming on the dumpster below. The same rain that would be hammering on the roof of Lucky's dog house, right now, she thought bitterly. Her eyes fell on Lucky's file folder, the papers strewn across the foot of the bed. She shoved them aside, feeling a surge of anger. She got up. Marching into the kitchenette, she splashed water on her face, repeatedly. She hung over the sink and stared at the water flowing down the drain. If only one could open up a cork in the head, and let all the putrefying, liquid filth inside gush out and pour down into the sewer, maybe people wouldn't need those stupid blue TV lights at night, or drugs, or drink, or a stupid broom handle club tucked under the pillow, in order to sleep at night. She pounded the faucet closed with her fist. Damn that monster to hell.

Still shaking, she hoisted Terry's box of papers onto the little table and sat down. She rummaged inside the box, shoving files aside until she found the one she'd been looking for, a worn folder with a faded, torn label: Harrison. She opened it, and a folded napkin fell out. She caught it before it fluttered to the floor. As if it were spun glass, she handled it gingerly, staring at Terry's hasty handwriting: Look at Harrison BG.

She pressed her eyes closed. BG. Background. It had to be. But what background? She'd been going over and over this scribble for months, and was no closer to a solution than Terry had been. What was behind what he'd jotted down in the folder? Wasn't Harrison's background a matter of public record? Terry had already looked into Harrison's company, Allude Steel Inc., located on Watchung Avenue in East Farroway. It was a parts manufacturing company, legitimate as far as anyone knew. It just didn't seem to be Harrison's focus. Politics was his game, and that's where the real money came into play. Peggy read that he married old money, which brought the sort of connections that only old money can buy. Again, a matter of public knowledge. His education was nondescript, if one didn't count his stint at Stanford. A university graduate in business law, with no special honors or distinctions, Harrison, outside of his wife's social pedigree, weighed in as little more than ho-hum average.

She reached into the box again, and pulled out the frayed rope that had been tied around Lucky's neck. She studied it with a frown. Why had Harrison come down to the shelter last night, really? Why did he bother tipping them off that he knew about Joe's patrols? The shelter was no threat to him, especially without Terry. Yet, Harrison had gone out of his way to suggest punitive action against the shelter from the mayor's office, twice now. And this last time, he'd made a point to warn the vet. Why? Maybe Joe was right. He was rattling their chains, simply because he could.

Why does it rattle you so much?

Peggy shook off a familiar shudder, with annoyance, this time.

Well, well, well. Come out of hiding, have we?

She gritted her teeth. Why? Because, she admitted to herself, she got the distinct feeling that Harrison was doing it to rattle her chain, specifically. But, the more niggling question was, why?

She worried and fiddled with the frayed rope in her fingers and wished she could ask Terry about it. She wasn't even sure what she'd ask. Not that he'd have the answer, either but...

She sighed. It was going to be quite some time before Terry was well enough to entertain questions, nevermind help her answer any of them.

With effort, she pushed thoughts of Terry aside. He couldn't help them, now.

She set the rope aside, too, despite the nagging feeling that she was so close to unraveling its secret. Until they caught some sort of infraction, there was nothing that she could do. For now, she had a bigger responsibility, to hold the fort. A fort full of animals that needed help.

Overcome with weariness, but still too shook up to sleep, she perused Terry's grant proposal for the tenth time. She hoped that she had time to figure it all out by the September deadline. She was determined to file it for him. What if they didn't win? What would they do then? She couldn't very well barter for a brand new building.

Or could she?

Peggy sat back and thought about Paul's offer. The gesture had taken her completely by surprise. Why this sudden interest in helping them? True, he was to get an office out of the deal, but, why would he care, since he was only contracted with them until June? Was the timing of his offer merely a coincidence? Or, was it a knee-jerk response to Harrison's cloaked threat towards him? She couldn't help but notice that there was something similar in the haughty demeanor between the two men.

Another shudder ran down her spine. It wasn't an easy one to shake off. She set a pot of water on the stove and lit a match, igniting a blue flame. She had to figure out how best to maximize the vet's impromptu offer. Maybe if Paul wrote the grant, she thought as she pulled a mug from the shelf, and he presented it himself, to whoever judged those sorts of things, they'd have a better chance at winning. If nothing else, she reasoned, people tended to listen to the vet when he talked. Especially women, she mused, dropping a tea bag into the mug. She smiled to herself, wondering how many of those women at the free vet exam day, would have paid a fee to sit out there in the freezing cold just to listen to him talk, with or without a pet!

A rush of adrenaline hit her, prickling her skin from head to toe. She flung open Terry's well-thumbed grant folder and rifled through the papers. On the sixth page, there it was, a half-composed letter from Terry to the Ronde Foundation:

"We are applying for this grant in the hopes that it will help us to create an education center on behalf of the community, and an outreach source for the advancement of animal welfare."

Education center. Terry wanted more than to just keep the shelter afloat, and he wanted more than just a new building. Hadn't he belabored his desire to build a bridge out into the community, to the future?

Free vet exam? She'd been thinking much too small! She staggered to her feet and rushed into the other room, snatching Terry's recorder off of her nightstand. She pressed the record button.

"Talk to Betty, because we're going to need a lot more flyers!" She picked up the broom handle and thrust it, like a fencing foil, at the bed, using the recorder as a shield. "En guard, Harr-Harri...Mr. Dickweed!" She paused in mid-thrust and depressed the record button, again. "Um... better ask the good doctor how he feels about crowds."

Chapter 45

"Crowds? Why? Are you planning a public hanging?" Paul fixed Peggy with a wary gaze.

"Not yet," Peggy replied, trying to sound casual. "I-I'm thinking if we start now, advertising with flyers all over town, then…"

"Time out!" Betty swivelled around in her chair. "You forgettin' The Man's song n' dance 'bout littering?"

"No. But, see, this time, we-we'll leave flyers inside the shops, not stapled to telephone poles. We can leave piles of them by checkout registers, and maybe ask to put some in windows. That way, he can't complain."

"Piles of 'em?" Betty repeated, her fingers poised over the adding machine. "Just how many you talkin'?"

"Oh. Well," Peggy squirmed, "maybe two or three hundred."

"You wanna piggy-back three hundred flyahs onta the church program order? Gratis?"

"It-it doesn't have to be all at once. Maybe a hundred a week?"

Betty cast a cagey glance at the vet. "Pastor got a few cats."

"How many's a few?" Paul countered.

"Do it mattah?"

Paul kneaded his brow. "I suppose not for three hundred flyers."

Betty raised her nose in the air. "Then I'll axe."

"So, what are we hawkin' now, a circus?" Joe asked Peggy.

"Look," Paul interjected quickly, "I agreed to work free vet exams, but I draw the line at working with clowns."

"Too late for that now," Clara reminded him.

"Not a circus, a presentation." Peggy handed Paul a thick folder of papers. "I was…well, I thought, what if you brought your free vet exam to a whole lot of people, all at once, except without all the animals?"

"A vet exam, but with no animals to examine."

"If you had a-a talk, instead. If you talked about the benefits of spaying and neutering, and maybe showed some pictures."

"Pictures?"

"Gross!" Joe wrinkled his nose.

"Not those kind of pictures," Peggy held up copies of medical charts on dogs and cats. "These kind, you know, like in your books? And, then you could hand out a-a brochure of information at the end."

"Where'd you get all these?" the vet murmured, leafing through her papers.

"The library."

"Brochures?" Betty repeated. "Three hundred flyers and now brochures?"

"Why would anyone stand out in sub-zero weather out there just to hear me spout off factoids without benefit of having their pets examined?" Paul asked.

"Oh! Not out there," Peggy pointed out past the driveway to the streets beyond. "Out there!"

"Just how 'out there' are you talking?"

"Out in the community!" She fished for a list from the folders in Paul's hands. "If you go to the country club up the hill and other places like-like the Elks club, and The Rotary. Oh! And the new mall up in Livingston, that was written up in the papers? The Upper Farroway Garden club, the YMCA; there's lots of places! Maybe you could give a few talks at each place, with a different topic each time, like a public service kind of thing, you know? Like McGruff, the Crime Dog?" Peggy was talking so fast, she had to pause to take a breath.

"McGruff, the who?"

"It's-it's for kids."

"And this gonna help pay the bills how?" Betty asked.

"If Dr. Hayward tells them what we do here, that-that spaying and neutering's a good idea, and what happens when you don't, he could even show them the poster there on the wall, to prove it!"

They all looked at the poster on the wall.

"I assume that's when you send in the clowns?" Paul asked.

"No, that's when you would bring out a dog or a cat, maybe both, like-like mascots, and then you tell them some happy endings!"

"Happy endings?"

"Yes, like Beetle? The Heartworm beagle? You could tell them about the couple who are waiting to adopt him, or tell them about Gorgo, Monty, and Digger! And, when they hear about how some of them get a second chance after...y'know. And how things could be for them if people only...if they only..."

Paul regarded her, then the thick folder of papers in hand. "This is a lot of information."

"Yes, I'm sorry, I-I wanted to get it all together first, so maybe you could look it over on the weekend?"

"I have plans this weekend. Joe? Where's a place the three of us can sit down and spread this out over a bite to eat tonight?"

"Us?" Joe repeated.

"Tonight?" Peggy echoed.

Paul gestured to the calendar. "It's the end of February. If not now, when? And if it involves the transport of mascots, then it's going to require transportation."

Peggy and Joe looked to Betty and Clara.

"Go for it." Betty shrugged. "We can lock up."

Almost at the same moment, Peggy and Joe checked their pockets, with a glance to the empty petty cash box.

"On me tonight," Paul added, pulling on his coat.

"That's cool, Doc. Thanks." Joe nudged Peggy.

"Yes, thank you."

"How 'bout Kierney's, Doc? On Valley Road. Aint too swank, but..."

"Do they have draft?"

"Does a bear you know what in the woods?"

Paul held up a hand. "All I need to know. I'll lock up downstairs." He handed the papers back to Peggy, grabbed his medical bag, and walked out the door.

The crew listened to the dogs woof half-heartedly, as he strode through the kennel.

"Well. I'da lost that bet!" Betty said, after the front door closed.

"Chap's a bugger to 'andicap," Clara agreed, with a sigh.

Joe nudged Peggy, again. "Lucky I'm third wheel, huh?"

"Hmn? Oh." Peggy laughed, self-consciously. "Yeah."

"Three of us can fit in the van," Joe said, holding open the gate.

"No, then you would have to drive us all the way back here. I'll just follow you," Paul said, and unlocked the Jag.

Peggy stood between the two vehicles, not knowing which one to get into. Joe jumped into the van. Paul slid into the Jaguar. Both engines started.

"Yo'! Saint Francis!" Joe called out, "Waitin' for the bus?"

"Sorry!" Peggy stumbled over sooty slush and hopped in the van.

"Whattya wanna bet he's got heated seats?" Joe blew on his hands and revved the engine. Frigid air from the vents blasted their faces and damp feet. He rolled down the window and shook a fist at the sky. "Three weeks and you're history, Old Man Winter!"

Peggy strapped herself into the seat. Three weeks! She couldn't believe there were only three more weeks left until the spring equinox. It felt like only yesterday that she'd walked down the driveway for the first time in the bitter cold of early winter. Then again, sometimes it felt as if it was a very long time ago.

Peggy waved to Betty, who stood in the office window. She had hoped to hang around the office a bit longer, waiting for the call from Irene, in hopes that Terry might be feeling well enough to speak to them, this time. She felt so sure that he would approve of her idea, and she wanted to tell him, herself. For the first time, she felt a little surge of pride over her work. She couldn't wait for Terry's approval, though, because an offer from the vet was not one to take lightly. She felt she had to jump at the chance, in case he changed his mind, and before spring turned to summer, when his contract ended and they lost his services.

Joe gunned the gas and cut across two lanes of traffic to shoot into a parking lot beside an old two-story, Tudor tavern. He squealed into a space by a stone wall along a frozen brook. The Jaguar continued on past the van, further back into the lot, tucking out of sight under the bare trees.

"What's the point in having a car," Joe said to Peggy, "if ya hafta worry about it gettin' dinged everywhere ya go?"

Peggy's stomach flip-flopped now that they'd arrived. She was moments away from sitting in front of Paul and presenting her ideas.

As they approached the tavern, she spied a plaque beside the doorway that detailed Kierney's history. Set back from the road, surrounded by conifers, the revolutionary pub stood beside the stone-walled, picturesque Toneys Brook. According to the sign, Kierney's had burned down

once and had been painstakingly restored by its third-generation family owners.

"What a cute doggie door." Peggy pointed to a miniature replica of the main door in the cornice, complete with a brass knocker and it's own entrance lantern.

"That ain't a doggie door," Joe grinned. "That's the leprechauns' entrance."

"Really?"

Hunkered down in his overcoat, Paul trotted up to them.

Peggy pointed to the mini door. "Look! They have a door for leprechauns! Maybe it's a good sign."

"Show me a pot of gold on the other side; that would be a good sign."

"Looks like we got ourselves an unbeliever," Joe laughed and pulled open the main door.

Once inside, Peggy felt like she might become a believer. Warm and welcoming, the place fairly brimmed with laughter, overflowing with people toasting and singing along with a fiddle player, in front of a great stone fireplace. Woolen rugs hugged the wood-plank flooring beneath walls adorned with framed clan shields, sheep shearing tools, and poems written by some of Ireland's favorite poets from centuries past.

Just beyond the entryway spread the dark oval bar beneath a hanging, wooden rack for glassware and mugs. Wooden booths jutted out from the walls, and here and there stuffed chairs and hassocks squatted around chess tables. Behind the bar, shelves sprouted all the way to the ceiling, crammed with tins, crocks and boxes containing spices, tobacco, and crackers. Beside the fireplace crouched a tree-stump table set for one, with a flickering candle and a full whiskey glass.

Joe nudged Peggy. "Guess who that's for?"

"Really?"

"Glass is always kept full."

Over the crackling fire hung a black iron kettle, exhaling a delectably spicey aroma. Adorning the walls all around it hung coats of arms, crossed swords and paintings of the Irish countryside and cobblestone towns, the names of which Peggy couldn't pronounce, let alone read, the language being unfamiliar.

A man clad in a long apron swung the kettle forward, lifted the lid and stirred it, to enthusiastic chants from throughout the room.

"Maireann croí éadrom i bhfad!"

"What are they saying?" Peggy asked Joe.

"Somethin' like, 'live long an' prosper', in Irish."

"'A light heart lives long,'" Paul corrected.

"You speak Mick, Doc?"

"Gaelic, and no." He pointed to a framed needlepoint over the archway, the English translation underneath.

"What I said!" Joe agreed. "They're cookin' up hot toddies. It's kinda tradition."

"What are they celebrating?" Peggy asked.

"That it ain't Monday."

A red-haired girl in a green plaid skirt, her arm tucked with menus, greeted them. "Only seventeen nights, now, 'til Saint Paddy's Day! Join us for a brew, a bite, or both?"

"Both! Set us up, Bridget, Doc's orders!"

They followed Bridget into another large, crowded room with another stone fireplace, and Peggy couldn't help but notice women's heads turn as the good-looking Dr. Hayward passed by. She wondered if he noticed.

Bridget sat them at a table beside the crackling fireplace, and Peggy surreptitiously studied the young vet as he looked around, clearly sizing up the place. When he took off his overcoat, she noticed that he was not wearing his doctor's whites, just a sleek jacket and tie. When he removed his jacket, and unknotted his tie, he suddenly looked like a different person. Peggy was grateful that Joe was with them. She couldn't imagine being alone in a pub, or anywhere else, with Dr. Paul Hayward, VMD-PhD. She wondered about the plans he'd mentioned earlier, and whether or not they involved a girlfriend, and what his girlfriend might look like. Was she blonde and brown-eyed, like him? No doubt, she was rich and beautiful. A far cry from herself. She felt her face flush with embarrassment, just thinking about it.

"Mike'll be with ye in a shake." Bridget handed them the menus and as soon as she turned away, Joe leaned closer and spoke in a hushed shout above the crowd.

"Whole family hustles here. Grandparents, kids, all of 'em. In the kitchen, behind the bar or waitin' tables. There's been dirt that way, way back, somebody was in the Irish mob, high-tailin' it over here to ditch the clinker."

"So it's a real pub, not a knock off." Paul sounded impressed.

"The real deal. I'm a Pole-lock, okay? But, I dig it. Cops hang here, all the time. Ter's fave place, too. He always got the Philly Cheesesteak and a Bass ale. The cheesesteak ain't Irish, but it's good."

Peggy smiled to herself. She could picture Terry here, by the fire, sipping an ale. Terry, more than anyone else, would appreciate the leprechauns' entrance.

"I'm surprised they serve Fish and Chips," Paul murmured, looking over the menu, "that's not Irish either; it's English."

"Irish, English, what's the diff?" Joe shrugged.

"About a thousand years of history, give or take a few wars."

"Okay, so I kinda get it, if I was a shamrock I'd be pissed too, them fruitcakes scammin' my turf, but why the frig are the Micks killin' each other over there?"

"Religion's a powerful divider."

"Ain't that supposed to be th'other way around? Jeeze, it's the same friggin' God!"

"I think it's a little more complicated than that."

"Whatever. Alls I know is, nobody can make a better brewsky than the Micks. Except for maybe the Krauts."

"Joe!" Peggy exclaimed.

"It's true!"

Paul nodded. "We do make the better beer."

"No way! You're a Kraut?" Joe gaped. "Hayward—that don't sound German!"

"It's not. English. My mother's maiden name. My father's side is German."

"Oh. So you...wait. If it's your mom's name...how does that work? Your mom didn't marry your pop or—"

"Joe!" Peggy gasped.

"Past life," Paul deflected the question by studying the menu, again. "What are you having, Joe?"

"I might have to flip a coin. It's all good."

Peggy studied Paul, her curiosity piqued. If Hayward was his mother's name, then what was his father's name? And why wasn't he named after his father? It made sense to her, in a perfectly stereotypical way, that Paul was part German. He was so precise, so disciplined so...suddenly he looked up and caught her staring at him. To her relief, a ruddy-faced, whiskered waiter approached them and bowed politely.

"Evenin' all."

"Yo' there Mike," Joe grinned. "How's it hangin'?"

"Low an' to the right, m'friend," the man replied with a thick Kilarney accent and clapped Joe's back. "Long time, no? Ye're not steppin' out on us, air ye?"

"Nah. Been super friggin' busy, and ya heard about Ter?"

"Aye, it's a sin, a sin. He's healin' up, tho', is he?"

"On the road, they say."

"Praise God. Well, 'til we see him again, we're happy t'ave ye back. What'll it be, then?"

"The usual for me. Shepherd's pie. And maybe tonight, what the heck, gimme a Heinie. Doc?"

"I'll have the beef stew and a draft. Bass."

"Fine choice," Mike said and looked to Peggy.

She smiled. "The Philly cheesesteak."

"An' t'drink?"

"Oh, just water, thank you."

"Get outta here!" Joe chastised her. "This is Kierneys! It's Friday! Hey Mike, y'know what? Bring us all a hot toddy. I mean, if that's okay, Doc! Ya gotta try one; it's tradition!"

Before Peggy could argue, Paul nodded. "Sure. A round of toddies for the table."

Mike bowed his head. "Bridget'll be back wi' chips."

Joe scoffed at Peggy. "I can't buleeve you'd order water! What're you a Puritan or somethin'?"

"No, no, it's just that I-I don't drink."

"A toddy ain't a real drink. It's like grog or somethin'. Anyhow, it's Friday. And..." Joe drummed his fingers on the table. "It's the end of freakin' February, man! Time to celebrate! Wait! How you say that in Irish?" He turned his chair around and listened to the chanters being served the first of the kettle's toddies.

"Let me see your proposal, again," Paul said to Peggy.

"Oh! Yes." She handed him her notebook and wrung her hands under the table as he looked it over. Halfway through, he paused.

"This idea about going into the schools is admirable, but with the economy the way it is, I doubt they'll have money to spare to pay you. It's a lot of time and effort without any real return."

"Well, maybe not in cash, but it's a way to get the information out there. You-you went to school and somebody taught you. If kids learn from people like you, maybe they'll remember and maybe teach their kids, and then their kids will teach theirs and..." she shrugged, "...well, may-maybe someday it'll make a difference."

"That's a lot of maybes."

"Maybe."

"Then again, one corner at a time?"

Startled, Peggy looked up. She'd been so used to hearing Terry say that phrase, that it sounded suddenly foreign, when voiced by Paul. And yet, the words sounded fresh and new, too, charged with possibility. "Well, yes."

"Okay," he said, and set the folders aside. "I'll take it on, under one condition. I handle all the medical aspects of the topics, but you talk about how it relates to the shelter."

"M-me? Oh, but I-I thought you would handle it all. I-I can't..."

"Peggy, it's your project. How badly do you want it?"

Peggy blinked at him a second. She'd never heard him call her by name before. It sounded equally foreign on his tongue, like someone else's name. She squirmed in her shoes, but he wouldn't release her from his gaze, waiting for an answer.

"Okay," she heard her own voice croak aloud.

"Good."

Mike appeared through the chanting crowd and set down three steaming mugs.

Joe turned back around to them. "I think I got it!" He lifted a mug in toast. "Marianne's bedroom is fat!"

Chapter 46

By nine p.m., Kierney's had filled up to bursting, and as per tradition, if you had a glass in hand, you were free to stay as long as you could sit or stand, unaided.

On her third mug of the richly-spiced, whiskey toddy, Peggy could honestly say that Kierney's boasted the best craic, this side of the tracks. She would have toasted this fact along with the rest of the raucous crowd on this matter, but she couldn't feel her tongue anymore.

Joe had started the round of toasts in honor of the absent Terry, and then Paul toasted Terry's speedy recovery, and then a group at an adjoining table who knew Terry, toasted him. Pretty soon the whole room went round robin toasting Terry, followed by toasts for his sister Irene, the city of Chicago, and anyone and everyone who ever spent time in a hospital. The besotted crowd toasted birthdays, anniversaries, divorces, bankruptcies and two recent prison releases. Then the toasts erupted into passionate sonnets to the Blarney stone, songs sung to the House Leprechaun, proud exaltations to the forefathers of Eire, and tearful toasts to mothers and their mother's mothers, up and down the Hudson river and beyond.

It was somewhere in between the sonnets that Peggy noticed her head felt lighter than a balloon. With every sip, she felt her nervousness melt away into the crowd's laughter. All gone. Poof! Like magic! The Philly Cheesesteak was scrumptious, too! Steaming with thick, melting cheese oozing over thinly sliced, juicy steak on a buttered, fire-toasted roll, Peggy had never tasted anything so perfect!

She gazed around the room, feeling full, warm and something else—something she'd never felt before. Contentment. That was it. She felt content to just sit amidst all the revelry. Perhaps it was because everyone seemed so happy. Happy, happy, happy! Maybe if she asked, she could live there, instead of Vida's boarding house. She would learn to cook kettles of toddies for all these wonderful, singing, laughing, happy people.

"Like it?"

Peggy had trouble dragging her blurry eyes away from the singing crowd and focusing on this person who seemed to be speaking to her. He looked an awful lot like Dr. Paul J. Hayward, MDV...DMV...Dph... hpd...what did all those letters stand for?

"I said, did you like it?" the blurry, handsome guy said, a bit louder.

Peggy raised her empty mug. "Delishush."

"I meant the cheese steak."

"That, too." Peggy hiccupped and pressed her napkin to her mouth; not so much to be polite, but so that her jaw wouldn't drop and hit the table. Somehow a screw must have come loose, because she couldn't seem to keep her mouth closed without assistance. She reached up and wiggled her jaw back and forth with concentrated concern.

Paul leaned back in his chair and called out to Mike the waiter. "I think we could use that coffee now!"

"Y'okay there, Saint Francis?" Joe asked.

"I can't feel my face."

"Better make that espresso," Paul amended.

"Lass isn't used t'fine whiskey." Mike smiled and carried their mugs away. Peggy wondered why he was moving in slow motion.

"Peggy? Peggy?"

Peggy heard her name and tried to uncross her eyes. There were two Dr. Haywards looking at her, rather queerly.

"Uh oh," she heard Joe say. "Looks like we got ourselves a light weight!"

"We've got ourselves an underweight," Paul said.

"I don't box," Peggy told them, with the utmost sincerity.

"Round two." Paul held a cup under her nose. It had magically appeared out of nowhere.

"How did you do that?" she asked, and sniffed the cup. "I don't like coffee."

"That's all right, you won't taste a thing. Take a sip."

Peggy took a sip. He was right. She couldn't taste it. It was nice and warm, though.

Paul waved to Mike in the shimmering crowd. "Check, please!"

Peggy didn't want to appear rude, so she waved too, tilting backwards in her chair. Suddenly she was falling into a well.

"Whoa!" Paul caught her before her head hit the stone wall. "You weren't kidding when you said you didn't drink!"

"Whew," Joe said, shaking his head clear. "She ain't the only one feelin' good. I'm kinda buzzed."

Paul flipped open his wallet. "Listen, have a couple cups of Java, I'll get her home, come back and pick you up."

"Nah, it's okay, I'm cool. Think I'll hang, tho', get me a cheesesteak to sop up the last two toddies. Mike can always give me a lift. It's cool."

"You sure?"

"Affirmateevo, Doc, thanks. Gimme time to catch up with my buds."

"Okay. I better get her home before her stomach catches up with her hippocampus."

"Her what catches her what?"

"Never mind. Here, you better finish this coffee."

Peggy could barely follow their conversation. She could hardly hear them over the fuzzy hum of the room, and her head was stuffed too full of itchy wool. She squinted at the good doctor. Really, he was quite handsome, wasn't he? Like a prince, or an angel. Yes, that was it. An angel. His sandy blonde hair was back-lit by the flames, crowning his head with a bright, glorious halo spinning just like the table tops all around her.

"Beautiful," she mumbled. The beautiful "angel" scribbled his signature on the piece of paper that Mike held out to him.

Paul turned his attention to Peggy. Chin in hand, she was smiling at him, a strange expression on her face. Maybe it was the alcohol, but her face had softened, erasing the perpetual worry lines etched in her forehead. He'd never noticed before, how delicate her features were, without all that tension.

She gazed at him with large, liquid eyes. They held a childlike vulnerability that Paul suspected would embarrass her, if she were sober. It was disconcerting to him. Her lips moved. He leaned in and shouted above the crowd's drunken laughter. "What?"

"When did you die?"

He blinked at her, then pocketed his wallet. "Long time ago." He stood up and eased her chair back. "Can you walk?"

"Where are we going?"

"Back to Terra Firma."

"She gonna be okay?" Joe asked.

"Until she wakes up, tomorrow morning. Whoa, hold on there!"

Peggy swayed sideways towards a throng of willing, open arms at the bar. Paul grabbed her waist and steadied her. "Here," he draped her other arm across his shoulders. "Lean on me."

"But, you're dead!"

"Maybe, but I'm the best bet you have of getting out of here alive, tonight."

"I'll have to judge your trustment." Peggy hiccupped.

Paul led her through the crowd and out the door.

Jostling over slushy ruts, Paul guided Peggy across the lot to the Jag. He propped her against the car, out of breath. "Still with me?"

"If you'd parked closer, we'd be there by now," Peggy said.

"That's debatable." Paul unlocked her door, easing her backwards into the seat.

"You know," she slurred, sincerely, "no matter what anybody says, I'm sorry you're dead."

He nodded. "Me, too."

He latched her seat belt and locked her door, and then jumped into the driver's seat. Inserting the key, he revved the engine, while he blew on his cold hands. "It'll just take a second to warm up."

"Why are you driving in circles?"

He leaned her head back against the headrest. "Try to sit upright. It might help."

She giggled at him.

"What's so funny?"

"Oh, my gosh! You do have butt warmers!"

Paul threw the clutch into reverse. "Hold on to your lunch."

"I said hold on!"

Carrying Peggy over his shoulder, Paul slipped on the icy walkway when she saluted a mailbox. "What're you doing?"

"That sholdier, there, deserves some reshpect."

"Save it for Veteran's Day, would you please!" Paul grabbed hold of the mailbox and shifted her center of gravity. That she was hanging nearly upside down behind him, waving at passersby, did not help. After getting her settled, he aimed for the lobby doors. Tripping up the steps, he stumbled and fell against them.

"Sorry!" He eased Peggy down and leaned her against the building. He was breathing hard and chided himself silently for eschewing the gym, lately. "This is it, right?"

Peggy rested a hand on the bronze and glass lobby door. "The Pearly Gates?"

"Could be. You said I was dead. Maybe you're right. Probably happened back there at the curb when we fell the first time. Check there tomorrow, to see if someone plants a cross and some flowers. Come on, up you go."

He hoisted her over his shoulder again and backed through the lobby doors with a grunt. Turning, he came face-to-face with a churlish woman in a greasy apron, wielding a mop.

"Evening," Paul said, then addressed Peggy's rear end. "Which apartment did you say?" An incomprehensible mumble sounded from behind him. "What?" He turned around so Peggy faced the scowling charwoman. "Do you recognize her?"

"Vida!" Peggy threw her arms out as if to hug the stubby woman.

"Hey, hey, hey!" Paul staggered to keep his balance.

"You're here, too?" He heard her say to the woman, with great compassion. "He is a forgiving God!" He turned back around.

The pink curlers on the super's head bounced in indignation. "Whatta I tell you 'bout no mens!"

"Look, she's a bit under the weather. I'm just dropping her off. She said she's in apartment three D? Please, my back begs you."

The super pointed up the stairs.

"Of course it is," Paul groaned and staggered towards the stairs.

"You no stay. You're a man!"

"Not tonight, I'm not."

Peggy's voice trailed behind him. "Heaven could use some paint."

"Say goodnight to the folks, Gracie." Paul plodded up the steps.

Cresting the third floor landing, Paul eased Peggy down to her feet and leaned her against her apartment door. "Okay, here you are."

"Where's that?" Peggy hiccupped and listed sideways.

Paul steadied her. "Hangover Central." He took in the bank of locks. "Is there something behind this door I should know about?"

"Gosh, I hope not."

He waggled his fingers at her. "Keys?"

"Key. One. Pocket."

"For the record, I'm just after your key." Paul struggled to keep her sagging form upright, while he searched her pockets. She giggled, apparently ticklish. "Laugh, clown, laugh," he said, "because tomorrow you're going to wish you had died and gone to heaven."

Paul searched one coat pocket and found it had a hole in it. He reached into the other pocket but found only some tissues. He grimaced. "Tell me these are clean."

"They were this morning."

"Charming." Paul was flummoxed. He could hear the distinct jangle of keys. Perhaps, inside her coat? He began to unbutton it and spotted a ring of keys attached to her belt loop.

"Hey!" Peggy clutched her coat closed.

"I thought you said you only had one key!"

"One key. Three-D."

"Give 'em here," Paul sighed and reached out to unfasten the clip.

Peggy slapped his hand, sloppily. "I hardly know you, dead man!"

"I'm only after the key for the door, not your chastity belt!"

"Says you."

"Scout's honor."

"I'll do it." Peggy hiccupped and fumbled with the key ring. "Boy Scout. Ha."

"For your information, I led my troop out of the Great Swamp for a medal. Have some respect."

"Respect is earned."

He regarded her steadily. "Yes, it is."

She held his eyes a moment longer, then dropped the keys in his hand.

He tried several before he hit pay dirt. He opened the door, hoisted her over his shoulder and carried her inside.

"Got enough lights on? There's an energy crisis, y'know."

"Yesh."

He aimed for the rumpled bed and tossed her onto the blankets. In the momentum, he followed suit, and they both wound up in a heap, sinking slowly into the accomodating mattress.

He untangled himself from her coat and raised up on his elbow. He saw that she was out cold. He rolled off the bed and stretched his spasming back, with a groan. Smoothing a hand through his hair, he took in the cramped digs. There was little to look at, and nothing personal save for the stacks of library books, which encircled her bed. He perused the titles: cat books, dog books, books on animal behavior, health, and nutrition.

On her nightstand were more books: *Abuse and The Law. Childhood Abuse. Surviving Abuse.*

He glanced to Peggy's sleeping form on the bed, then picked up a book and leafed through it. He noticed that corners of many pages had been turned down, and sections had been highlighted in yellow marker. He checked and found that they were not library books. She owned them.

The wind howled outside and drew Paul to the window. Frozen clotheslines were strung from windows below, flapping about in the wind like jump ropes. Below them gaped the open maw of a rusty dumptser.

He looked back to Peggy. Softly breathing, she was deeply asleep. He set the book back on her night stand and squared it the way he'd found it. He didn't want her to think he'd been prying. Pulling her shoes off, he lifted her legs and then covered her with the blanket. One last look at her, and he headed to the door, shutting off the lights. He tripped the door's lock from the inside, and made sure it had latched, before he headed down the hallway.

Chapter 47

March blew in like a lion, roaring right through Peggy's head.

A gust of wind howled and shook the window panes, rousing her enough to raise her two-ton eyelids to half-mast. She had no idea where she was, and what's more, she didn't care. She was more afraid to move her head, lest it snap clean off her shoulders and fall to the floor with a shattering crash.

As her vision cleared, she saw the bare walls of an apartment reflecting the dawn. Dully, she discerned that she was in her apartment. It was morning. The last thing she remembered was drinking a toddy amidst a very loud crowd. But, how'd she get back here? Beneath the pounding ache within her skull, bits of memory, like puzzle pieces, gathered themselves into an almost cohesive picture. Toasts to a leprechaun, a roaring fireplace, an angel, a head of pink curlers, and a key lumbered out of her consciousness. Wait...an angel?

Her eyes popped open. Paul! She smacked her forehead. "Ouch," she groaned. Oh my gosh, did he really carry her up three flights? She searched her memory, and sure enough, an upside down journey replayed itself with cruel clarity. Criminey!

She sat up, her head following after her with a ten-second delay. She groaned, again. How could anyone in their right mind ever become an alcoholic when it felt this lousy? Her temples pounded painfully, and she would have testified on the Blarney stone, the Bible and her own still warm corpse that she'd been hit repeatedly with Kierney's toddy kettle. What was left of her brain felt like sloppy, wet cement slowly solidifying between her ears. Her mouth tasted sour, her tongue was as raspy as cracked leather, and the thought of food made her instantly gag.

Peggy catapulted to the bathroom in a queasy panic. She dropped to her knees over the toilet and breathed rapidly, fighting dizziness. The sickening roil in her gut passed, but the pain in her head did not. Blindly, she groped for the medicine cabinet, but stopped cold, confronted by her visage in the mirror.

Her eyes were bloodshot and swollen. Her hair was so frazzled she looked like she'd stuck her finger in a socket. Dangling from her chin was a crusty yellow mass of melted cheese that completed the ghastly mug shot. Her outside looked like her insides felt. She almost slapped her forehead again, when it dawned on her that this was Paul's last image of her!

Swaying to the kitchen, she searched the counter for a clean mug and paused at the table. Her keys glinted in the early morning sun. She jerked her head up. When the room stopped spinning, she noticed that the light was off. Carefully inspecting the whole apartment, she saw that *all* the lights were off. She'd spent the entire night alone in the dark, without suffering a single nightmare. She sank into a chair and held her breath.

Silence. No whispers, no recriminations.

Maybe that's why people drink, Peggy thought. To keep the voices appeased. Or, at the very least, quieted.

A bubble of queasiness eddied inside her and she cradled her head in her hands. Silence versus hangover. Not a good enough trade-off, she decided. Once the nausea passed, she picked up her keys and studied them. So, the good doctor Paul J. Hayward had indeed been inside her apartment!

She peered around and felt her toes curl. What did he make of the stark, dingy place? The things he must be thinking about her! She dropped her head into her hands and imagined the laugh that he would have with the crew about the entire episode.

Standing up, she toured the room, each bleak detail raining embarrassment on her. When she reached her nightstand, she stopped. Something wasn't right. Where was her notebook? She shoved books aside, furiously looking for it, and that's when she discovered that Terry's recorder was gone, too! Panic welled up. Where were they?

Late, Peggy bent against the blustery wind and wobbled down the driveway to the shelter. She skidded to a stop. Tar-paper flapped across the office roof, where shingles should have been. Jagged planks of green fiberglass had been stripped off of the runs' roofing, too, and scattered like broken glass around the driveway.

"Oh no!"

The dogs burst into barking, as she trotted past the crew's cars and through the front gate. She cupped her hands over her ears, barely muffling the painful noise.

When she opened the office door, Joe, Clara and Betty all twisted around in their seats to greet her. They were all smiling really big.

"Well, well, well," Joe smirked, "look what the cat dragged in! Quick! How many fingers am I holdin' up?"

"What happened to the roof?" Peggy began, and then gasped. Her notebook and Terry's recorder were on the counter in front of her chair. She pounced on them. "Oh, thank God! I thought-I thought I'd lost them! I couldn't remember, I mean, when I woke up, they weren't there." She hugged them tightly to her chest. "I didn't know where I'd left them."

"Don't thank me, Saint Francis." Joe thumbed toward the back of the room. "Thank the white knight, there."

Peggy reluctantly peered over her shoulder.

Casually leaning against the back window, Paul sipped his coffee. "Morning."

"Good morning." Peggy eased her hat off of her head and ran a trembling hand through her hair. "Thank you."

The phone rang, and Peggy cringed. The jangle pierced her teeth. With shaky knees, she eased down into her chair.

While Betty dealt with the caller, Joe pulled out a small bag of ice cubes from the mini-fridge and plopped it in front of her. "Better light-foot it today, Miss Boll Weevil."

Peggy lowered her head against the ice bag. "Ten-four, good buddy."

Joe stuck out his hand to Clara. "Told ya. Nuthin' but a rookie."

Clara handed Joe a dollar. "First wager I'm 'appy to lose."

A small dark bottle was then set down in front of Peggy's face. She squinted up. Paul, sans halo, peered down at her. He nodded to the bottle. "Some 'hair of the dog that bit you.' It's Bitters. Put it in tomato juice; it'll help. When you feel better, brief me on which of the, um, two dozen topics you introduced last night that you want to present for our first talk."

Peggy managed a weak nod. "Okay."

He left then, easing the door closed behind him.

"Any way you kin keep 'em fo' awhile? See, we just not set up yet," Betty's conversation caught Peggy's attention, "to fostah kittens!"

"Punxie Phil was right!" Joe wailed. "Man, oh man, we're boned!"

While Joe hovered by Betty's ear and listened in on the phone call, Clara tottered over to Peggy and poured the bitters into a bottle of V-8 juice, and then handed it to her.

"Bottom's up, doctor's orders."

Peggy eased up on to her elbow, took a sip, and grimaced. "Oh, I'm sure he gave you all an earful."

"Doctor Tight Zipper? Never breathed a word. When does 'e ever? Now the Pillsbury Dough Boy there, on th'other 'and," Clara gestured to Joe. "'ad 'imself a right time of it about the saint's night out. Nay then, don't fret. 'Be thou chaste as ice, as pure as snow, thou shalt not escape calumny. We might as well get thee to a nunnery!'" She tittered. "Apologies to The Bard."

And to the vet, Peggy added, silently. She felt a little jab of remorse for having tarred and feathered him, prematurely. She sipped the bitters and tomato juice, and listened to the pipes clanking in the walls. Soon, she felt a modicum of warmth rising up, from below.

Unlike her lingering hangover, the wind ceased its whipping of the compound, but not until it had ripped off nearly half of the shelter's roofing. With rain forecasted later in the week, Peggy decided they should try and piece together what was left of the fiberglass, to shield the dogs.

All morning, her throbbing headache was a constant companion. Despite it, she helped Joe collect scraps of the shredded green planks from the lot and taped them together with gray duct tape. It looked awful—so shanty-town—but it was all they had on hand to make the repair.

Peggy steadied the the ladder for Joe and tried not to think of Terry up on Mrs. Cruikshank's roof. She had a sneaking suspicion it was on Joe's mind, too, since he had roped himself to the security light pole with double knots and a bungee cord.

A sudden gust of wind howled through the empty warehousing. Peggy gripped the ladder and held it tight.

"Joe, be careful!"

"You bet," he called out, and hammered a plank with renewed energy.

The kennel roof was made of tin and had weathered the wind storm, fairly well. Joe pointed out a few rusty spots that needed patching. The office roof had sustained the most damage. About a third of the shingles and half of the tar paper had been stripped off.

Paul was unable to assist them, as he and Clara had been inundated with incoming kittens. It was all Betty could do to keep up with the calls. Just as Punxatawney Phil had predicted, spring had sprung early, and the Kitten Tsunami had begun.

Over the next few days, Betty would receive over a dozen more kitten calls, most litters being borne of feral cats in garages. She would coach the callers to bottle feed their "orphans", stalling for time, but Peggy knew they needed more help.

"Maybe, they'll foster them to weaning, if we ask, nicely?"

"Please!" Betty sputtered a laugh. "Come the first two a.m. feedin', it be ovah, and we be gittin' 'em all!"

"We oughta sue Gobbler's Corner!" Joe griped, bottle-feeding a squirming kitten.

"T'ain't the groundhog's fault!" Clara said, wiping formula off of the muzzles of two kittens in her lap. "It's sun spots what causes boom n' bust like this."

"Sun spots? We ain't seen the sun in three months!"

"Clara's right." Betty lined a box with soft towels. "Hor'scope say Mercury be in trine with Uranus, and that do not bode well."

"Hey, ain't nobody in trine with nuthin' a mine, okay?"

"Baby, it be astrological. Don't flattah yo'self."

Peggy hovered by Clara, watching her feed the kittens. One sneezed milk from its nose, and the old woman patted its back with her fingers until it burped. Then, she handed the kitten and bottle to Peggy.

"'Ere, might as well learn, now. We got three more comin' in."

"Oh, but I've never —"

"They chew rather than suck at it, and 'alf the time it goes up their wee conks. Be gentle, be patient and you'll get the 'ang of it."

As nervous as she was, Peggy was instantly smitten. She'd never seen anything so adorable as those kittens. And just as Clara predicted, the mewing ball of fluff sneezed formula out its nose.

"Poor little thing doesn't even seem to like it!" Peggy worried.

"They know it isn't the titty. Can't fool a cat, eh, what?" Clara cooed to the kitten and wiped its face with a damp cloth.

"Can't fool a cat," Joe scoffed. "How'd they survive as a species bein' so stupid?"

"You tell me, homo stupidus."

"Hey watch it!" Joe hefted up his pants and puffed out his chest. "Somebody might get the wrong idea!"

"Not likely!"

"And not from yo' swaggle-butt!" Betty sputtered a laugh.

From Clara, Peggy learned how to keep the kittens warm with a hot water bottle wrapped in a towel, and how to massage their rear ends with a warm, damp cloth to help them urinate and defecate, as a mother cat would do. Otherwise, she learned, they might become septic and die. As much as Peggy loved caring for the kittens, she knew that the clock was ticking against them; if even a third of the litters came in at the same rate as the calls, there would be no choice but to euthanize a large proportion of them.

"I've got the topic for the first talk!" Peggy told Paul, the instant he walked in the door for afternoon rounds.

He set a carrier of kittens on the counter. "'How To Kill a Vet In Six Months Or Less?' I'm not dead yet, by the way."

"I see that. I mean, I know that. I-I thought the topic should be 'Pet Overpopulation and You!'"

"Sounds like a sex-ed class," Joe laughed.

"Better late than never," Paul murmured, and checked over the other boxes of kittens.

"And, here's the mockup for the brochure. I figure we can have it ready to drop off by the end of the week." Peggy held the paper out for him to look at.

Betty peeked over Peggy's shoulder. "Where's the picture?"

"I think Joe might be right about it being too depressing," Peggy said, and covered up the graphic poster on the wall with Terry's jacket.

"No, I mean..." Betty looked at the vet.

"What?" Peggy followed her gaze to Paul. Betty wiggled her eye brows at the young vet, and Peggy felt her face flush hot. "Oh!"

Paul turned and looked at her. "'Oh,' what?"

In a dark brown suit and tie, Paul braved the bitter cold, posing in front of the outside dog runs while Peggy fumbled a roll of film into an instamatic camera. Just as she raised the camera to her eye, she was stopped by Betty.

"The doctah don't look like a doctah!"

"That's because he's just a vet," Joe corrected her.

Paul rolled his eyes. "Thanks."

"No, they're right," Peggy murmured. Something wasn't clicking. It wasn't just that his hair had grown out a bit. Yes, it had softened his ordinarily preppie demeanor, but that wasn't it. It wasn't the suit. He wore a jacket and tie every day. He was always immaculate. All it once it dawned on her. "Wait!"

Peggy darted inside the shelter, and in a moment, trotted back out with the vet's white lab coat and his brand new stethoscope. She ran them over to him. "Now, you'll look like a doctor!"

"Isn't this rather cliché?" he said, pulling on the lab coat.

"Trust me, baby," Betty told him, "the ladies like a uniform."

"I was told these pictures were for a seminar, not a calendar."

For a split second, Peggy considered that.

"Forget it," he said, quickly. "I draw the line at Chippendales."

"Hey, Doc!" Joe laughed, "if it turns out, you could maybe have a second career!"

"That's assuming I ever have a first one."

"Maybe he should have a dog beside him," Peggy suggested.

"Maybe 'e should 'old a box of kittens," Clara said.

"Maybe it should be a grown cat and a puppy," Joe said.

"Maybe you should take the picture before the vet freezes to death and you end up using it for his obituary!" Paul called out.

"I know!" Peggy decided. "Let's just put all the dogs out in the runs behind him!" She hurried back inside the building and began raising the guillotine doors.

"'E's got to 'ave a cat, too!" Clara insisted. "Equal representation!"

In the end, she shot a whole roll of Paul standing in front of the dogs in their runs, doing his best to keep hold of Clara's favorite tabby cat, Silver, in his arms. Peggy knew that she had the perfect shot with the very first click of the camera's shutter. She just got a kick out of seeing the vet put on the spot, squirming, his nose red and runny. It almost made up for him seeing her in all her overhung glory.

Chapter 48

Any one of the photos of Dr. Hayward would have sufficed. He came off confident, professional, and very handsome, in every single shot. He was, as Betty declared, "some kinda fool looker". Peggy noticed it, too, and it wasn't just the uniform.

Paul had been genetically blessed, she decided. Tall, with broad shoulders and a tapered waist, he looked like one of those cowboy models on billboards, except that he was younger and he shaved. He had the same high cheekbones and chiseled chin, the same wide-set, large brown eyes framed with perfectly shaped brows, brooding under a healthy head of tousled, sandy hair. Betty was right, Peggy smiled to herself. The ladies were going to love him!

Betty slipped the brochure mockup into the church's bulletin order. They would run off a hundred at a time, in exchange for Dr. Hayward's examination of half a dozen stray cats on church property, all of which had just had litters. By promising to find all the kittens homes, Peggy got the church's office staff to type up, then bulk mail query letters, along with the brochures, to prospective clubs. While she waited for responses, she and the crew scrambled to keep from drowning in the rising tide of the Kitty Tsunami.

The office had run out of cage space, in short shrift. To Peggy's surprise, Paul asked Joe to scrounge up a few feet of scrap wood and chicken wire from the lumber yard, so that they could at least outfit Beula's cave with a few more pens. He did the work himself.

By Friday, Betty could no longer put off six people, who'd wanted to turn in litters. Thankfully, five of the litters came with mom-cats.

"More n' likely, they were owned cats what found better grub at the neighbor's," Clara told Peggy. "But, now that they've whelped, they've been given the boot."

The sixth litter was borne of a feral mother, and no amount of explaining to the caller that the kittens needed to be left where they were found, would deter the people from wanting the kittens out of their garage.

"Sounds like they 'bout a week old," Betty said, after she hung up the phone. "On they way here now."

"Short straw," Joe sighed and held up five straws in a closed fist.

They all pulled one each, and to Peggy's relief, she did not draw the shortest. Betty did.

"Damn if this be th'only thang I evah win! A month of no sleep!"

The intercom buzzed. Joe hit the reply button. "Yo' Doc."

"Do you have wire cutters up there?" Paul's voice sounded tired.

"In the van, yeah. Need 'em now?"

"No, right now I need a drink."

"Got a Mountain Dew up here with your name on it."

"Pair it with a coffee chaser, you're on. Leave the cutters out."

"Copy that. Over and out."

"He gonna be ready?" asked Betty.

"I swear," Joe replied, "he's got HUD approved pens down there. They gotta stack, break down, do this, do that. You'd think he was buildin' the freakin' Ark."

"Might have to," Betty sighed, going over the log book. "Lookit this incomin'. And we ain't even got past Saint Paddy's Day!"

"Will we have enough room?" Peggy asked, bottle-feeding two kittens in her lap.

Joe burst out laughing, but clammed up when he saw her face. "Oh. You're serious, again. Lookit, let's just keep 'em all downstairs, then we don't gotta see it when he hasta off 'em all."

"Joe!"

"I'm just sayin'! It's a fact o' life. 'Sides, it ain't like it phases him!"

"Wouldn't bet on it," Betty said.

"Bah. You'll notice 'e never places a wager," Clara noted.

"He don't gamble; so what?" Joe shrugged.

"When a surgeon 'eals, what is 'e? 'E's a miracle worker, a winner. When 'e can't, 'e's nobbut a cutter, a loser. Our Doctor Dandy's the sort what doesn't like to lose."

"Whatever. Like I said before, guy's gotta have ice water in his veins to do what he does sometimes, alls I'm sayin'."

"Just 'cause he do his job wiffout bellyachin' 'bout it like some baby toes," Betty pointed out, "don't mean he ain't wigged-out by it."

Peggy thought about that. Was Clara right? If she looked at it fairly, Paul didn't come in every day looking to put animals down, even though that's the way it had seemed to her, at first. Maybe what irked her had something to do with the sense of coldness about him that Joe referred to. Still, she concurred with Clara's conclusion that the vet's cold distance might be the only way he could do his job. Either way, Paul was not as he appeared at first glance.

"Is there anything else about him, I mean about-about the kittens we need to take care of before closing?"

"Not without a million bucks," Joe said and popped open a soda can. "Look, I wasn't gonna say nuthin' 'til after noon patrol, but I tooled by Harrison's this morn, and guess what? Lucky's back in the dog house."

"In this monkey-brass cold?" Clara exclaimed.

Betty blew her nose. "Please, you ain't surprised?"

"Pfft. Not by a long chalk."

Peggy hung her head. She wished that she had the same ice water in her veins that protected Paul. Maybe it would be easier to do her job, too, and sleep at night.

"I hated to havta tell ya," Joe sighed. "I mean, it ain't like he's suf-ferin' or nuthin'. He's got blankets in there, food and water, too. All jake with the law. But, he's on a chain this time."

Peggy couldn't very well tell Joe that she already knew, and that up until the Kitten Tsunami, she'd been spying on Lucky herself, nearly every night that it didn't snow.

"I'm keepin' my eyes peeled, don't worry," Joe assured her.

"Thank you."

"Hey, that's another thing! We ain't heard from Irene this week again. What gives?"

"If I don't by Sunday," Betty said, "I'll call. Probably ain't no news worth the toll."

"I know, but it sucks when we don't hear, y'know?"

Peggy walked over to the window and tugged on her St. Francis pendant. She'd noticed that the calls from Irene had become rather sporadic. True, the news tended to be the same. Terry was doing as best as could be expected; he had his good days and not so good days. As upbeat as the crew tried to be after every call, Peggy noticed that they, too, seemed a bit let down. They didn't make a big deal of it, but they had yet to speak with Terry, directly.

It was quiet a moment, as they all sat with their own thoughts. Clara frowned. "Terry who?"

Joe sighed. "Are we gonna have to put you away?"

Peggy couldn't help but see the irony in Clara's comment. Week by week, it had become more difficult not to ask that same question, herself. Everyone understood that Terry's rehab must be tough, but as the weeks turned into months, she felt more unsettled about the silence. It was almost as if he'd abandoned them.

Betty sent Terry a care package of cards, regularly, and Peggy always added a report on the shelter, with as many glowing terms as possible. As always, Irene told them how much he appreciated hearing from them, but there was never any answer from him, directly. They had all agreed not to ask him questions or put him in a position whereby he might worry about the shelter, and possibly jeopardize his health. However, as the weeks passed, the silent gulf between Farroway and Chicago had grown and fed Peggy's fears that he was never coming back.

The dogs woofed in the kennel room, and Peggy turned away from the window.

Paul entered the office and shook dampness off of his coat. "Do you have an ETA on those last litters? I have to leave by six."

"I done wrote it down here, somewhere..." Betty searched the log entries. "They said they be here befo' closin'."

"Got a hot date, Doc?" Joe grinned. Peggy glanced up at that.

The vet rummaged through the medicine cabinet. "If you mean lavaging another bloated Saint Bernard, then yes, I have another hot date with a real gasser."

"That sucks!" Joe wrinkled his nose. "EVC's been haulin' you in for a lotta graveyard shifts, lately. Who's slackin'?"

Paul didn't answer right away. He seemed to choose his words with care. "Just filling in for the head surgeon while he attends conferences with Dr. Caldwell."

"Wait, I thought you were head cutter."

"Not official. And, not while I'm here."

"So, after punchin' the clock with us, you pull an all-nighter, up there? When do you get any shuteye?"

"I don't."

"Jeeze, that ain't cool."

"Just part of the job."

"Man, how do you skate through the day?"

"I've no idea. Toss me a Mountain Dew, will you?"

Joe reached under the counter and pulled a soda from the mini-fridge. "This's the last one. Naw, you take it Doc; we still owe ya for the last case." He tossed the can to the vet.

"Which we'll pay you back for," Peggy said, "after-after the first donations from the talks."

Paul turned to her. "Any calls yet?"

Peggy tried to sound nonchalant. "Not yet."

"All the litters spoken for, this weekend?"

"Unless we get more, after this one coming in."

"Only one I know 'bout," Betty piped up, scanning the log book.

"How are you stocked for formula?" Paul asked.

Peggy checked a chart on the wall. "We have enough to get us through Monday."

"What about after that?"

"Joe? Is it too soon to hit on the donation cans?"

"How'd ya think I paid for the cat food?"

The phone rang. Betty crossed herself and answered it. "Sheltah."

Poised over Terry's grant application with two kittens in her lap, Peggy held her breath. Paul pulled up a chair beside her.

"I know it's the last thing anyone wants to do," he said, "but it may be time to consider..." Peggy pulled her kittens close. "Look," he sighed, "you're stretched to the max, here. Everyone's fostering at least two litters, and even if you bring them to weaning, how will you find homes for all of them?"

"Yes!" Betty swiveled around in her chair, her eyes bright. "Yes, I think they be free to give a talk at the country club! How much we charge? Well, uh..."

Paul snatched the pen out of Peggy's hand and scribbled a note on the back of an overdue bill, then held it up to Betty.

"Two hundred fifty dollahs!" Betty exclaimed. She cleared her throat and lowered her voice. "Two hundred fifty dollahs. Thass right. Uh-huh. Lemme check." She cupped a hand over the receiver. "When you be free?"

"Today!" Peggy blurted out.

"It's five o'clock!" Paul exclaimed.

"Tomorrow?"

"Monday."

"How's Monday sound?" Betty said into the phone and looked to Peggy. "Noon?" Peggy nodded and looked to Paul for confirmation. He nodded.

"Noon Monday look fine," Betty said into the phone. "Uh-huh. Lemme take down yo' particulars."

Paul wrote himself a note, and then addressed Peggy. "Sorry to jump in like that, but I know someone on the entertainment committee, and they can afford to pay you."

"Done!" Betty hung up. "Hot damn!"

"Two hundred fifty smackeroos!" Joe exhaled. "That'll cover us this month, right?"

Breathless with excitement, Peggy leaned over and scanned Betty's ledger. "It'll pay the feed bill with enough left over to get more Esbilac for the kittens, and to do the laundry for the next three months!"

"Whew!" Joe sank back into his chair. "One more load of laundry at my place, and my ol' man woulda crowned me!"

Peggy turned to Paul. "Can we wait on...you know," she nuzzled a kitten. "....just until we start these talks. It could make all the difference. I can handle another litter. You've checked them all over. They're all healthy, and since we're fostering, it's not really overcrowding."

"No, just employee exhaustion."

"We're-we're fine, right?" Peggy looked around to the others. They exchanged glances.

"Well, me COACOA fellowes just might foster a few more," Clara offered.

"I'll hit up Bible study," Betty volunteered, and turned to answer the ringing phone.

Joe rolled his eyes to heaven. "I'll trade ya one more load of laundry for a litter."

"Thank you!" Peggy exhaled with relief. "I'll take the rest."

"Just out of curiosity," Paul asked her, "how do you plan to juggle round the clock bottle feeding, your work, and still be ready for the seminar on Monday?" He nodded to the counter strewn with her papers. "That's a lot of homework."

"Well, I'll..." she gestured to the others. "We'll figure it out."

"Okay. You're the ones who'll be sleep-deprived for the next six weeks."

Peggy shrugged with a little smile. "Just part of the job."

Betty hung up the phone, looking dour. "We got two more litters comin'."

Paul packed up his medical bag. "I'm on graveyard all weekend at the EVC. Just in case you need to revisit the issue," he added, and handed her a business card. "This is the private line."

"Thank you, but we won't."

Both phones rang at once, and everyone swiveled to look askance at them.

Paul handed Peggy his half-finished can of Mountain Dew. "You're never going to make it until Monday."

Betty cursed and picked up both phones, one at each ear. "Sheltah." She listened a moment, and then sneezed three times in a row.

Joe pulled Clara's dollar out of his pocket and handed it back to her. "Forget it. This is my last George Washington, and we're outta paper towels, again."

Paul raised a brow to Peggy and walked out through the kennel room.

She grimaced and dug in her pocket. She tossed Joe a quarter. "Place the bet."

Juggling a litter of kittens in her lap, Clara giggled. "Odds're with th'ouse."

Chapter 49

Hearing a chuckle beside her, Peggy jerked her head up, momentarily disoriented. "What?"

"I said, did you get any sleep at all, this weekend?" Paul asked.

"Oh. Yes. Why?" It was the second time she'd nodded off while he had been talking, and they hadn't even cleared the driveway, yet.

"Just asking."

Peggy pinched herself to try and keep her bleary eyes open. She wasn't about to admit that, for a second back there, she had no idea who he was or what she was doing in his car. It irked her that Paul had somehow managed to look rested after an entire weekend of graveyard shifts at the EVC. Then again, he must have been able to sleep during the day. She was envious.

As it turned out, soon after Paul had left on Friday, four more litters of kittens were brought in before the crew unplugged the phones in self-defense and locked up. Peggy was determined to see that none of the kittens were put to sleep, so she took a good number of them home. Joe helped her sneak them in after Vida had left her post.

At first, staying awake was no problem. Peggy's nerves over preparing her half of the "Pet Overpopulation And You" presentation kept her working late into the night. The constant mewing and merry-go-round kitten feedings inspired her to live up to the expected calibre of Dr. Paul J. Hayward's presentation. But, by midnight on Saturday, she was hooked on black Oolong tea and used the stove's timer to remain conscious.

The kittens' feeding ritual took two and a half hours, followed by a thorough cleaning, then another eleven minutes to re-fill all the hot water bottles. This left Peggy with nineteen minutes to work on the presentation, before the cycle started all over again. Thankfully, the alarm kept her on track, but Monday morning arrived way too soon.

For their very first out-of-shelter program, Paul had waved transport via the shelter van. Peggy had to admit that the Jag was a far cry from chugging along in the van. It was an even further leap from bumping shotgun in the dear old Pinto, she thought, with a wistful tug at her heart. Peggy didn't have much memory of her first trip in the sports car, except for the oily scent of leather and the heated seats. She felt her eyelids droop and pinched herself, again. If allowed to, she could quite easily nap for the next hundred years.

Paul switched on the radio, and tuned the dial to WNEW FM. *Teach Your Children* by Crosby, Stills and Nash filled the interior. If Terry were the driver, he'd have whistled along with it, even if he didn't know the tune. With a start, she realized that she hadn't even thought to send word to him about the talks! She reached for her St. Francis pendant. The whole idea had come about so fast, it hadn't occurred to her that perhaps she ought to ask permission. Then again, they hadn't yet even spoken with Terry, since the accident! What would he say, she wondered, if he was asked about it? No? Perhaps, it was best not to mention it. He might worry. Rightfully so, she thought, and kneaded her brow.

Peggy knew they were heading to high-brow country. She tried to contain her stomach, which was flip-flopping at an annoying rate. She balanced her notebook and a carrier of sleeping kittens in her lap. In less than twenty minutes, she would be standing before the upper crust of Uppah Farroway's elite, and for the life of her she couldn't remember a single word of her presentation. The vet seemed ill at ease, too, but Peggy didn't know if it was due to the talk, in general, or sharing the bill with her, in particular.

"Are you nervous?" Paul asked.

"Hmn? Oh...no. Well, yes, a little. I've never really done this before."

"It'll be a cakewalk, as you say."

"Have you? Done this before?"

"Half of our qualifying exams are oral, before university faculty and practicing veterinarians. Then, I had to present my PhD dissertation. To prepare for it, I took on extra TA work, filling in with a few lectures to get over the jitters. In my last year at Rutgers, I subbed for a couple of adjuncts, as a kind of warm-up for the firing squad."

"Did it help?"

"No. But it's true what they say. It helps if you picture them all naked."

"Oh!" Peggy felt her face flush. "I'll have to remember that."

Tucked away down a winding, tree-lined entrance, The Upper Farroway Country Club was not as imposing as Peggy had expected. Situated beside a lush golf course, it reminded Peggy of the EVC. The white colonial building held court at the head of a sweeping, circular drive. Red-jacketed valets scurried down the steps to greet members that arrived in gleaming Bentleys and Lincoln Town Cars. The manicured grounds sported winter browns and grays, but Peggy could imagine the hundred or so rose canes that flanked the cobblestone walkway, in brilliant summer bloom.

Paul steered the Jaguar along the stone steps, pulled the parking brake, and got out. A valet opened Peggy's door and she scooted out, juggling her notes and the cat carrier.

"Thank you."

The vet opened his wallet to a second valet, showing him a card. The man tipped his cap and hopped in the driver's seat. He drove the sports car around the corner of the building to a heated and gold-plated parking garage, no doubt. Paul took the carrier and gestured for Peggy to follow him up the steps.

A uniformed doorman tipped his cap to them and opened the etched glass entrance door. "Good afternoon, Doctor."

"Afternoon."

Peggy realized then, that the doorman must know the young vet, since he was not wearing a lab coat. Once inside, Peggy felt instantly ill at ease. The club interior was much grander than it appeared from the outside. An elegant white staircase, adjacent to the entrance vestibule, swept upwards to a second level. A lofty, tiered chandelier hovered over a round mahogany table with the largest vase of fresh flowers she had ever seen. Great oil paintings of polo, golf and cricket matches graced the walls.

A smartly suited maître d' greeted them. "Doctor, so good to see you. I understand you're presenting a seminar this afternoon."

"Yes, along with Officer Dillan."

To hear Paul refer to her as "officer" in other than his usual challenging tone surprised Peggy. She'd all but forgotten that she was an officer of the court. Overwhelmed by the sumptuous decor, she suddenly wished she had worn something other than her uniform. Despite her attire, the maître d's courtesy never faltered.

"Lovely to meet you, Officer Dillan. May I take your coat?"

"Th-thank you." Her cheeks reddened when she saw the plethora of patch jobs on her coat lining. The man either did not notice or chose not to. He folded her coat over his arm, the lining tastefully hidden.

"We've prepared the Striker room for you, Doctor," said the maître d'. "I hope that will be satisfactory."

At first, Paul frowned, but then he nodded. "That'll be fine. Thank you, Daniel."

Paul led Peggy down a warmly-lit hallway, over a thick wool tapestry runner to a doorway, under an engraved, slate plaque that read: The Striker Room.

Peggy blanched when she spotted nearly two hundred chairs set up in the large, chilly room. "Oh, my gosh. I-I didn't picture this many people."

"The other rooms are probably booked. We'll be lucky if a dozen people show up. They only had Friday and Saturday to get the word out."

Peggy breathed a sigh of relief. A dozen was much easier to swallow than two hundred. On a wooden stage framed with royal blue drapes, a microphone and a lamp had been affixed to a podium. Beside it stood a claw-foot table, with an overhead projector sitting on top.

"Good. I can use that," Paul said, and skipped up the stairs. He flipped a switch on the projector, and it lit up. "Have you ever used one of these before?"

"N-no."

"It's easy." He looked around. "There must be a screen in the back." He followed the projector's extension cord and ducked behind the wing drapes. He found a switch on the wall and flipped it. The upstage drapes glided apart, revealing a small movie screen. "Perfect. Do you have any photos or charts?"

"No, I-I didn't think of that."

"Testing..." Paul tapped the microphone, and Peggy heard a corresponding little thump-thump from the back of the room. "I don't think we'll need this, but..." He gestured to the far right side of the stage. "Why don't you set yourself up, over there. When I'm done with my spiel, I'll introduce you, and you can come out and take over."

Peggy managed a little nod, wondering if she should tell him now that she might not make it past the introduction, never mind cross the stage without throwing up over the front row, just before fainting in a swan dive, straight into the orchestra pit.

"How would you like to be introduced?" he called out.

"I'm sorry?"

"Officer Dillan? Manager of the Farroway Animal Shelter?"

"Okay."

"Which one?"

"Oh. Um, either one is-is fine." She didn't want to admit that she'd rather not be introduced by name at all. She'd rather make a nice clean getaway, before anyone became the wiser. "Wh-what about you?"

"I'll just introduce myself. Most of them know me, anyway."

Well, that answers that question, Peggy thought. Paul was a regular. It didn't surprise her. She suspected that the country club's understated elegance mirrored its membership, each with a pedigree borne of very old money. One didn't have to show off one's wealth, in a place like this. It was understood. That proud reserve described Paul, perfectly. He embodied a deep-seated knowledege of his own worth but didn't flaunt it. Other than his Jag, that is.

Peggy took her place behind the curtain and set up a folding wooden chair. She peeked inside the carrier at the kittens. They were curled up in a tangle of paws and tails, asleep. She wished she could crawl inside and hide with them.

"Is everything to your satisfaction, Doctor?" Hearing the maître d's voice, Peggy pulled the curtain aside. "We'll be directing the members to be seated in about ten minutes, if that's all right?"

"That'll be fine. Thank you, Daniel."

Ten minutes. Peggy gulped and opened up her notebook. Papers fluttered to the floor. She snatched them up and scrambled to put them back into some semblance of order. She glanced across the stage to Paul. He positioned a colorful graph on the overhead projector. He didn't seem a bit nervous. Not like he had been in the car. Then again, why should he be nervous? He knew this material cold, and what better way to promote his burgeoning career than to trot out in front of the local gentry? It was a smart maneuver. With only three and a half more months of indentured servitude to the shelter, a young man of his talents and background had a world of options open to him.

Peggy dragged her attention back to her notes and tried to ignore the swarm of butterflies barnstorming her stomach. Before long, she heard the hall doors creak open to a murmuring flow of voices. Chairs squeaked as people sat, and it sure sounded like more than a dozen people. She peeked around the drapes and nearly gasped out loud. There were easily a hundred people! Most of them were women dressed in spring suits, fur wraps and hats.

"Oh God..." Peggy breathed. She looked across the stage to Paul. The maître d' was introducing him to an older couple with drinks in their hands. As they talked, a beautiful blonde draped in a fur stole, slinked up to Paul and kissed him on the cheek.

All at once, Peggy was wide awake. She, a bedraggled dogcatcher, was about to stand up in front of the uppah class, and tell them to spay their bitches! She remembered Paul's comment, about picturing everyone naked. She closed her eyes and tried. It wasn't helping. She ducked back behind the drapes. Good gosh, she chided herself. What on earth made her think that she could do this? What if she really did trip and fall down on the stage? What if she fainted? What if—?

"Ready?"

Peggy jumped, with a little gasp.

"Sorry!" Paul said, peering behind the drapes. "You okay?"

"No, no, I mean, yes."

"A Deb Ball Committee just let out. I think Daniel had something to do with corralling them all in here. He insisted on introducing me."

"Deb ball?"

"Debutante. Daughters of the Ladies Who Lunch. They're planning the inevitable coming out party in May. It's the society page's version of the 4-H club." He peered at her. "Are you all right?"

"I-I don't know if I can do this."

"What?"

"I-I mean...who am I? Why should they listen to me?"

"Maybe because you have something to say?"

"Look at me. I'm-I'm dog poop from the tracks and-and they're..."

"First off, this isn't about you. It's about the shelter, remember?"

Behind him, the maître d' ascended the stage steps and stood in front of the podium. "Ladies and gentlemen..."

Paul faced Peggy directly. "Look, this is your party. You either do this or not. Make up your mind. What's it going to be?"

Peggy couldn't believe the detached tone of his voice and was unable to swallow the sudden lump in her throat. In the background, she heard the maître d' wax on.

"...it is my pleasure to welcome you to our new Luncheon Seminar Series. We are delighted to have as our first speaker, a doctor of veterinary medicine who practices the art of healing right here in our fine township. Many of you, I'm sure, will recognize him as the youngest grandson of one of our most esteemed founders, and son of our former director."

"Yes or no?" Paul shrugged.

"...honored with academic achievements befitting a scholar, we have no doubt that a burgeoning career will follow in his stead. Won't you please welcome; Dr. Paul J. Striker, VMD-PhD."

Peggy glanced up at Paul, but he either ignored or didn't hear Daniel's misnomer. He waited for her answer.

"Yes," she finally heard herself croak.

She couldn't be sure, but for a split second, he looked relieved. With a curt nod, he donned his lab coat and strode across the stage, to the sound of appreciative applause from the audience.

Chapter 50

"Thank you, Daniel," Paul's voice sounded rich and deep through the speakers on either side of the auditorium. "And, thank you all for attending this, the first in what will hopefully be a series of informative lectures."

Peggy gulped when he glanced towards her, in the shadows of the wing curtains.

"Unless I fall flat on my face up here," he added, "which is a distinct possibility. If so, ask for your money back."

Peggy heard the audience laugh. They sounded friendly, enough. Still, her knees quivered. As he introduced himself further as a graduate of the school of Veterinary Medicine at Pennsylvania State University, she wondered why he didn't correct Daniel, by sharing his real name. By then, Daniel reached the wings, and then leaned in and whispered to her.

"Dr. Striker insisted that he introduce you himself."

"His-his name is Dr. Hayward," she whispered back.

The maître d' smiled, as if she were a child. "Not in this room, he's not."

Peggy remembered the plaque above the doorway, and all it once it dawned on her. She looked out at Paul, speaking to the crowd, and thought about the night at Kierney's, and Joe's confusion over Paul's last name, when he admitted to being half German. She wondered too, why he went by his mother's last name, while here at the Country Club everyone referred to him as Dr. Striker?

She heard more laughter. Paul was seated at the overhead projector, cracking a joke while correcting upside down charts on the screen. She glanced at the audience and saw attentive faces with genuine smiles. Well, that was another thing she'd been wrong about. She'd assumed that Paul's public speaking ability would mirror his dry, detached rapport with the shelter crew. In the spotlight, before his own kind, he was a man transformed. He was relaxed, candid, and a quick-witted speaker, with an absolute command of the room. She wondered if he was picturing the crowd naked.

With a slight shudder, she took in the audience. Aside from a few men, the crowd was predominately comprised of well-heeled, middle-aged women, accompanied by their debutante daughters, all sleekly decked out in their spring finest. Like exotic birds, they perched on the edges of their seats, listening to the vet with sparkling eyes. She wondered if they were picturing *him* naked and felt her cheeks blush.

"...of the Farroway Animal Shelter, Officer Peggy Dillan."

Peggy heard applause and realized with a start that Paul had just introduced her. He waved to her.

She gathered her notebook and the kitten carrier and stumbled forward. Papers drifted out of her hands onto the stage, but she kept her eyes glued to the podium and Paul. He seemed relieved when she finally reached him. He took the carrier from her and set it on the table. Peggy gripped the podium to steady herself and then cleared her throat. She was startled to hear the sound projected forward at her, from the back of the auditorium.

"Sorry," she murmured, and heard her nervousness ricochet swiftly back to her.

Paul picked her notes up off of the stage and handed them to her.

"Th-thank you." She felt a rush of warmth when he momentarily rested his hand on her shoulder and watched him walk into the wings.

She perused the jumble of papers with shaking hands until she found the first page. Looking up to the audience she suddenly went blank; were they picturing *her* naked?

When she finally spoke, her voice shook worse than her hands. Statistics of animal overpopulation spit off of her tongue like buckshot. "...the non-neutering of pet cats and dogs re-results in an overpopulation of kittens and pup-puppies in the spring, both wild and-and-not so wild. Not wild. Dumb-I mean—dom-domestic. It is estimated that approx-approximately t-ten kittens and puppies is, I mean are-are euthanized for every one that is bored. I mean bred."

She overheard a collective, sympathetic murmuring from the audience and risked a glance up. Paul had lifted one of the hungry, mewing kittens from inside the carrier and held it against his chest. He gently pulled another one out.

"Ohhhhhh....." cooed women from all around the room.

Peggy paused. What was she rambling on about? Overpopulation wasn't about facts and figures! It was about those helpless kittens in Paul's embrace; kittens who had done nothing wrong, except to be borne into a cold, overcrowded world. Their frightened mewing drew Peggy towards them.

"They're hungry," she said, and took one of them from Paul.

Paul drew out two bottles of formula from his bag and handed one to her. The audience sighed in unison.

Peggy's kitten squirmed and fought the bottle nipple. "It's always a wrestling match. They know I'm not mom."

Soft laughter rippled around the room.

"Where's their mother?" A statuesque woman in a pink Chanel suit spoke from the second row.

"We don't know. Joe—Officer Wozniak—found them behind the Acme market, in the dumpster."

The audience tsk-tsked.

"How could someone do such a thing?" a woman in a mink jacket asked.

"I don't know. But...it happens a lot. We have six more litters back at the shelter and-and it's all because of unspayed, un-neutered pets. I couldn't believe how many, at first, but over ninety-percent of them get put to sleep, every spring."

The audience recoiled and members began conversing ardently.

Peggy glanced to Paul. With a discreet nod of his head, he gestured her to the front of the stage and walked the carrier down to the prosce-nium. Peggy followed his lead, and they both sat down, dangling their feet over the edge. They offered the bottles to their kittens, again, and this time the squirming felines closed their eyes and suckled, lustily.

Some of the women surged forward to get a closer look.

"How can you do it? Put them to sleep, I mean?" a woman in a flow-ered hat asked.

Peggy looked to Paul, but he said nothing, clearly waiting for her answer the question. "Well, we-we don't want to, but...we only have so much room and…"

Paul's kitten sneezed formula all over his face, which drew titters of laughter and another wave of "awwwws." The pretty young blonde woman stepped up and handed the vet a lacy hankie.

"Thanks, Susan."

"What about finding them homes?" Susan asked.

"Are you offering yours?" Paul countered, wiping his face.

"Anytime." She raised her perfectly arched brows.

"We're always looking for help, Miss," Peggy suggested. "You know, volunteers." She was sure that wasn't what the woman had in mind, but Peggy said it anyway.

"Foster homes are always appreciated," Paul concurred. "But, it requires round-the-clock commitment. With most people's busy schedules, it often isn't feasable. It's a serious commitment."

"I'm willing," Susan pursed her lips, coyly.

Paul stifled a wry smile. "You say that now, but when they wake you up at midnight, again at two, then again at four, and in between you've only gotten half an hour of sleep because there are six of them. And it's not just about feeding them. Just like with kids, it's about spit up and wiping their butts...believe me, the romance fades fast."

Many of the older matrons nodded their heads and laughed.

"Anyone who thinks they're up to the task," Paul added, "I'm sure Officer Dillan would be happy to work something out. And she was being conservative, by the way. Most of the animals that the shelter euthanizes are both the direct and indirect result of pet overpopulation. I can attest to that, because I'm the bad guy who puts them down."

This admission sobered the audience. Peggy glanced at Paul. He had made no attempt to soft-soap his role.

"What about the law?" asked one of the few men in the crowd. "Can't anything be done, legally?"

Once again, Paul turned to Peggy. She sat there a good long moment. Lucky sprang to mind, and Terry, too. "There's...there's no law in Essex County saying you have to spay your cat and dog. Would it help? I'm not sure. Maybe. But, the law can only do so much. And maybe it isn't so much about the law, but what people do or don't do when it comes to just doing the right thing. I'm still trying to figure it out. I just know that these kittens, all the animals...they have no choice, no voice in any of it. But, we do. We can speak for them, and we can do the right thing. Law or no law."

Peggy took a deep breath. It occurred to her that she'd been talking to the crowd without her notes, unaware of her fear, unaware of herself. Had she touched on all the points she'd labored so hard over? She wasn't sure. She found Paul's eyes on her. They were unguarded, for once, and what she saw in their depths startled her.

The pretty Susan insinuated herself between them then, and asked, "May I hold it?"

"Hmn? Oh, sure." Paul hopped down off of the stage and offered her the kitten.

"How do you-oh! Oh!" Susan squealed, trying to keep hold of the kitten squirming in her hands. "Can you help me, Doctor?"

Half a dozen other women requested to hold a kitten. It wasn't long before Peggy and Paul were engulfed by the crowd and inundated with questions. In the midst of conversations, laughter, and mewing kittens, their eyes met again, and they shared a smile.

During the ride back to the shelter, conversation was lively, now that the event was over and was a huge success.

"C'mon, she didn't really say that!" Paul laughed.

"Her exact quote was; 'How can you work in a place like that? It's like Auschwitz.'"

"Well, from her point of view, you have to admit, it looks like a prison and it's where animals are put to death."

"Hardly the same thing! And to quote you; 'two plus two does not equal five.'"

He turned a wry eye to her. She raised her brow in return.

"Okay," he acquiesced, "but I'm sure she didn't mean it the way it came off. Chalk it up to Waspish, bad taste."

"I'm glad you said it, not me."

The young woman in question was Susan. After Paul had handed her the kitten, she had tried to monopolize his attention for the better part of the afternoon. Peggy had been more annoyed than she cared to admit, especially when Susan cornered her and asked rather transparent questions about how she liked working with Dr. Striker. Peggy had nearly corrected the girl, but she didn't, because she wasn't sure, anymore, who this new Paul was, that stood beside her today.

"Do you honestly think she was saying it, just to be crude?" Paul asked.

"I don't know. They're your people, you tell me."

"My people! Care to define that?"

"I don't-I don't know how to say it and not insult you."

"You can't insult me. I thought you figured that out, already."

"That!" Peggy pointed out with a little laugh. "That's what I'm talking about. You can't be insulted by someone like-like me because we're from different sides of the tracks."

"Are you saying I'm class conscious?"

"Are you saying you're not?"

"What's your evidence, Officer?"

"Oh well, look at the car you drive!"

"Because I drive a Jag I'm the enemy?"

"I didn't say enemy. You did."

"That's the implication. What if I told you it was leased or that it's used?"

"I don't think I'd believe you."

"Okay, you'd be right, but that's not the point."

"Oh ho!" Peggy laughed.

"You're making assumptions about me because of the car I drive? Who's class conscious now?"

"Hey, I'm not the one with a banquet room named after me!"

Paul's smile slipped and he fell quiet a moment. When he spoke again, his voice was tense. "It was named after my father. Not me. It has nothing to do with me."

Peggy glanced at him. Whatever the beef was concerning his family name, it was serious enough to darken his mood in an instant. He shifted in his seat, as if shoving something off of his shoulders. "Just because I have money, that makes me a snob?"

"I-I didn't say that."

"That's the inference."

"Well, I didn't mean—"

"Maybe you're a snob about money. C'mon, Miss Holier Than Thou."

"I just meant that-that if I had money, I wouldn't…" she stopped herself.

"If you had money…*what*?"

She shook her head. "Never mind."

"You're not getting away with that. Finish what you were saying. If you had money, you wouldn't…"

"Well, I wouldn't waste it on-on stuff, just trying to prove I was better than everybody else, you know, with cars and furs and clubs. I mean, instead of-of people trying to prove they're so important because they *have* it, why not do something important *with* it?"

Paul turned the car down the driveway and into the shelter parking lot, sliding the Jag alongside the fence, in his coveted spot, and shut off the engine.

Peggy squirmed in her seat. "When I said 'you', I didn't mean..."

"The hell you didn't. But, like I said before, you can't insult me, so let's cut the bull. You don't have to have money to do something important. Maybe the real question is, what's stopping *you*?" With that, he got out of the car.

Peggy sat there a second, feeling stung. He had some nerve! Who was he to challenge her, when he couldn't reconcile the beef he had with his own name! When she got out of the car, she found him waiting for her at the gate, a smug look on his face. She carted the kitten carrier to him, mulling over a comeback, but then she remembered that he didn't care what she thought of him.

"Just out of curiosity..." he said, and pulled out an envelope from his coat pocket. "If you did have the money, what would you do with it, first?"

"I-I don't know, why?"

"Well you better think about it, because, let's see..." he opened the envelope and pulled out checks. "In addition to the two hundred and fifty dollar speaking fee, here's a check made out to the Farroway animal shelter for seventy-five dollars." He pulled out another one. "This one is made out to the kittens for fifty dollars, and here's another one for twenty dollars made out to the veterinarian. Hmn, always good to know one's worth."

Peggy gawked at all of the checks in his hands.

"And last but not least," he held a check in front of her face. "Here's one from Ms. Susan 'How-can-you-work-in-a-place-like-Auschwitz' Brewster, for one hundred and fifty dollars. Now, what was it you were saying about class?"

Peggy twisted her mouth into a repentant smile. Poker-faced, Paul Hayward slash Striker opened the gate for her.

Chapter 51

There was no time to celebrate.

Inundated with five more kitten litters, they were all run off of their feet. Most frustrating for Peggy, was that Paul politely declined three foster offers from the club, based solely on the members' lifestyles. To his credit, he had weighed the offers, carefully. Two came from career women with a daily commute to Manhattan, and one came from a woman he classified as a trophy wife; a woman on the boards of more action committees than the country club membership combined. Simple arithmetic precluded any of these women from foster duty, since none of them had the hours free to properly care for week-old kittens, round-the-clock.

Peggy knew that Paul was right in his assessment, but it left the sleep-deprived crew scrambling to keep from drowning under the tide. And, she refused to call in his mercy euth card.

Betty smuggled three more litters home with her, while Clara had already pawned off six to her COACOA group, and took on two more, herself. Even Joe took a litter home with him every night, despite arguments with his father. No one was getting any sleep, especially Peggy. She had to wait until seven o'clock every night, either hitching a ride with Joe on his last patrol, or accepting a ride with Paul on his way to the EVC; all just to avoid Vida and her mop, standing sentry in the lobby.

Once she was able to sneak the litters into her apartment, Peggy was up all night with them, and only fifteen minute cat naps snuck in between feedings. She had to be dressed and out at the curb by five-thirty a.m. to catch a ride with Joe and avoid Vida's morning stakeout at the lobby mailboxes.

Those patrols with Joe were difficult, since poor Lucky was outside, whether rain or shine, sun or stars. There was nothing she could do about it, and it infuriated her. Peggy's only consolation was that she could see for herself that he was being fed and had water.

Despite the long hours, the sleepless nights, and her concern for Lucky, Peggy felt invigorated by the success of her grassroots efforts on the shelter's behalf. The presentation at the country club was an immense validation that she was on the right track. The donation checks seemed to prove that community outreach was the answer. There followed, too, a number of donated goods left at the front gate. Every few days, a case or two of cat food showed up, along with cat toys, kitty litter, and even cans of dog food! Peggy could see a light, maybe not quite at the end of the tunnel, but definitely a light in the distance. And, it wasn't a train intent on running her down! It was the light of hope, that they might actually be able to effect change, just as Terry had imagined it.

Perhaps, Peggy thought, there might even be a way that she could effect legal change for Lucky someday, with similar outreach. She wasn't exactly sure how that might come about, but it remained a secret mission, tucked carefully away in the back of her mind.

As grateful as she was for the donations, Peggy knew that what the shelter needed most, were extra hands, if they were to buck the statewide statistics regarding springtime euthanasias.

"No pressure, Saint Francis," Joe warned her, "but we're on the heels of puppy season, next."

"Puppies." Peggy squelched a rising alarm. So swamped with kittens, she'd forgotten completely about the inevitable puppies!

"Yup, and right on their tails comes all the Easter bunnies and chick-chicks that ain't cute, no more."

"Bunnies?" Peggy's head reeled in horror at the prospect.

"I'm tellin' ya. You think it's bad now?"

The office door opened, and Paul ducked his head in. He nodded towards the window. "Hope you all didn't mothball your chains."

The crew groaned in unison. It had begun to snow, again.

"Jeeze Louise," Joe griped, "when's Ol' Man Winter gonna take a friggin' hike?"

"When he done killed us all, dead." Betty blew her nose, while packing up her carriers of kittens.

Peggy confronted the calendar. "Well, he only has ten more days to finish us off, and then it's officially spring. Anyone hear the weather report?"

"A Ouija board would be more accurate," Clara chortled.

"Where you hidin' yours?" Joe switched the radio station from Sly and the Family Stone to the news.

"...North Vietnamese troops in an attack on Ban Me Thuaot, in South Vietnam. Unconfirmed reports cite thousands fleeing in the wake of this latest offensive with growing concern over the numbers of refugees flooding the borders of..."

"Surprise, surprise..." Joe twisted the dial to another station.

"...arrested, protesting the groundbreaking that began yesterday on the Trans-Alaska pipeline. Environmentalists haven't given up their attempts to halt the construction and have filed another..."

"Yeah, yeah, yeah," Joe mumbled, twisting the dial again. "Rottsa ruck. They'll charge us a dollar a gallon to pay for that pipe, you watch. Shh! Here we go."

"...light dusting of snow already reported at Newark Airport with a possible accumulation of up to an inch in the outer-lying suburbs. Temperature's going to remain above freezing tonight, inching up a few degrees by morning to turn all of this to rain, with a high reaching forty-six degrees, by afternoon."

"Whew, we're skatin' by, this time."

Paul looked over all of the kittens. "Any sneezing or mattery eyes?"

Peggy showed him her notes. "They all check out fine."

"All spoken for tonight?"

"Yes. I'm taking these four. Clara's got those three."

"Celie at the church takin' two and I got these three," Betty said.

"I'm takin' three," said Joe, "or, is it four? I'm losing track." He started counting on his fingers.

"Not to be the black hat here," Paul interrupted.

"Why spoil a perfect record?" Clara asked.

"Thank you. But, there's no more room, downstairs. I've got three litters weaned, but you're full, up here. One more turn in..." He looked pointedly at Peggy.

She frowned. What could they do? One more litter, and...the phone rang, and everyone froze.

"It be aftah six," Betty whispered after the third ring.

Peggy sighed. "We'll just have a box of them waiting for us at the gate tomorrow morning, and it's snowing."

"Hey!" Joe yelped. "It could be Ter!"

"Lawd!" Betty grabbed at the phone. "Hello? Sheltah."

Peggy's hand fluttered to her St. Francis pendant. She couldn't believe she hadn't even thought of the possibility that it might be a call from Irene.

"Yes, it is," Betty glanced around to them, shaking her head no. "Mmn-hmn. What's that?" All at once, she waved to Paul and Peggy both, pointing to the calendar. "You wanna vet talk at the school? When? Tomorrah?! I dunno, lemme axe." Betty cupped a hand over the phone receiver. "They regular assembly got the flu. They need a sub."

"Yes!" Peggy exclaimed.

"Tomorrow?" Paul repeated. "A school? Private, yes?"

Peggy waved to Betty. "Yes, tell them yes."

"It is a private school?" the vet repeated.

Betty shook her head no and spoke into the phone. "Tommorah be fine. Eight o'clock?"

"Wait a minute! I haven't anything prepared for a—"

"We can repeat the country club talk," Peggy entreated him.

"We don't even know if it's kindergarten or—"

"Interview?" Betty shushed them. "Fo' what? Oh. I see. Wiff Mistah Franklin? Uh-huh. I see." She looked to Paul and cupped a hand over the receiver. "You need a interview wiff the principal, first."

"Interview? What for?"

"Say yes!" Peggy insisted.

"Then you gots to sign some papers," Betty relayed, listening to the caller.

"Whoa, whoa," Paul held up a hand. "Papers? What papers?"

"Just say yes!" Peggy hissed.

"Signin' off on stuff so you kin go talk in the classes," Betty repeated. "Uh-huh...one at nine, anothah one at ten, then eleven."

"Classes," Paul enunciated, "as in plural? I thought they said assembly, as in singular?"

"Uh-huh. Not enough subs...yeah, it be goin' 'round. Lemme write this down. Go 'head. Uh-huh. I get it. Security wise...sure. Bettah to keep the kids in class, in smallah numbahs, uh-huh."

"Security?" Paul repeated. "What kind of school is this?"

"The high school," Betty whispered to them both.

"That's great!" Peggy said. "It's a chance to ask for volunteers!"

"Volunteers? It sounds like we might need bodyguards!" Paul said.

"Yes, ma'am, that be fine," Betty said into the phone.

Paul threw his hands in the air.

"Hold on, lemme axe. They wanna know how much it gonna cost."

"It's already costing me my better judgment!" Paul replied.

"I don't know," Peggy thought hard. "Ask them...what can they afford?"

"Ask them what they have set aside for special programs," Paul said.

"How much you got?" Betty asked the caller, and scribbled on the back of a bill, then held it up to them.

"Tell me that's missing a zero," Paul said.

"It's okay," Peggy interjected, "we'll do it!"

"Works fo' us," Betty said into the phone.

"What!" Paul faced Peggy. "Twenty dollars? It'll cost us twenty dollars in gas just to get there!"

"Shhh!" Betty wagged her finger at him, and returned to the caller. "Say that again? Uh-huh. Where you at? Irvington Ave."

"Uh-oh..." Joe swiveled around.

"Uh-oh? What do you mean uh-oh?" Paul demanded.

"Depends on the cross street." Joe peeked over Betty's shoulder. In another second, he stood and pointed to the map on the wall.

Paul blanched and turned to Peggy. "You might want to reconsider this one."

"Why?"

He slapped a hand onto the map and glowered at her.

Peggy shook her head, feeling confused. "You're saying it's somewhere near that big orange section? So?"

"Right next to the big red section marked Newark!"

"Be on the safe side?" Joe suggested, "Take one of the Rotties along, and an attack Dobie to protect the Rottie."

"It's just a school!" Peggy admonished them. "And, a paid talk is a paid talk!"

"Filling in all day, for six substitute teachers, for twenty dollars?" Paul argued, "That's not being paid, that's a joke! And, a room full of teens bussed in from the projects is not on a par with a country club full of paid members. Don't give me that look, you know what I mean."

Betty hung up the phone and handed Peggy the note. "It all set, this here, th'info."

"They called us," Peggy reminded them. "I don't think the school would have called if-if it wasn't an okay thing. They're kids, not criminals."

"Oh? I'm willing to wager they don't pair these kids with guidance counselors, but with parole officers."

"Who's being judgmental now? Just because some kids have had it tough, doesn't mean they're bad. Blame the adults! They're the ones who've screwed things up. The kids are the victims, here."

"I'll wager Newark's police log begs to differ."

"It's Irvington, not Newark, and even if it was, we need help. We'll never make it through spring without having to euthanize dozens of kittens...and bunnies! The school's the only other place that's called back so far."

Hands on his hips, Paul shook his head and sighed. "Fine. It's your call."

"Thank you."

"Psst." Joe drew Paul off to the side. Pulling his water pistol out of a drawer, he said, "Might wanna pack some heat."

"Joe!" Betty snapped, and slammed the drawer closed.

"Just in case!"

"I'll just in case yo' head!"

Peggy frowned at Paul. "I don't understand what the big deal is. It's a school. They're just kids. What can they do?" She nonchalantly popped open a soda. "Look, if-if you get nervous? Just picture them in diapers."

Paul folded his arms across his chest. "Diapers."

"Works for me." Peggy had to press her lips together to keep her smile under wraps.

Chapter 52

"You forgot your lab coat."

Peggy could tell that preparations for this impromptu school talk had kept Paul awake most of the night, too. Dark circles hung below his brooding brown eyes. He wore a chocolate-brown sport coat over jeans, and for the first time since she'd met him, he wasn't wearing a tie.

"I didn't forget it." He revved the Jag's engine and skidded the tires up the wet driveway. A light rainfall accompanied them, as they turned south and bumped over the railroad tracks.

"You're not going to wear it?"

"Not if I want to walk out of that school alive."

"I don't understand. You're a doctor. They'll respect a doctor."

"You're talking about seventeen-year-olds with chips, the size of dump trucks, on their shoulders. I wear that lab coat, and like any pen of incubator chicks spotting the odd one out, their first instinct will be to peck me to death. And, you might want to hide that badge."

"Why?"

"The firemen need a police escort whenever there's a call, down there."

"But, we're guests!"

"Invited by the principal, not the inmates."

"I'm still in a uniform."

"Without the badge, you're a girl in uniform. I'm betting on hormones versus chips on shoulders. Give me credit for knowing what I'm talking about, for once, okay?"

To placate him, Peggy pocketed her badge, only because he seemed truly unsettled about this trip into the projects, almost as uneasy as she had felt about facing the mink-laden cougar tribunal, up the hill. But, kids're different, she thought smugly. They get it. He'll see.

"I'll start with the diverse career opportunities that can be found in medicine," he went on, "they'll hook into that—like being a pharmacist; it's a way to legally make money selling drugs."

Peggy rolled her eyes, but refrained from comment.

"Then, I'll bring up the idea of applying community hours toward college credit as a kind of bait for volunteers, again, assuming any of these kids aren't going straight into juvie after school detention. Then you can take it from there."

"To where? Lock up?"

"If the ankle-bracelet fits."

Peggy crinkled her brow at him, but let it go. She turned her focus to her half of the presentation. She intended to get right to what a volunteer could do at the shelter, by describing the crew's needs at the moment: fostering kittens and, soon, puppies.

As they drove through increasingly beaten-down neighborhoods, she was sure that the kids' attitudes towards them would be much more positive than Paul's assumptions of their class. Regardless, she counted on the kittens to soothe the lion's share of his projected, and rather judgmental, teenage angst.

Washington Street School crouched in the center of a block of halted redevelopment. While the rest of the country rioted over desegregation, schools in New Jersey had already acclimatized many years prior, sparing communities the racial violence erupting in other cities, like Boston. However, the economy had dealt such a heavy blow to the education system, the schools around Newark were left especially vulnerable to cutbacks, closings and subsequent overcrowding. Caught in the middle were the students. Bussed miles away into over-burdened schools already strapped for resources and decent teachers, the students faced an unremitting battle of "catch-up" to an already lowered, national average. The resulting inequity had begun to take its toll.

Winter-denuded oak trees abutted the concrete walk leading to the school entrance. According to the plaque by the stairs, the school dated back to 1931. A two-story, brick goliath inspired by the architecture of some of New England's finest ivy-league, private schools, it had seen better days. A central bell tower held a clock that lagged behind Greenwich time by three hours and twenty-two minutes all year long, even during daylight savings time. It was a mystery that no one could figure out. What used to be grassy grounds had, within the last ten years, been reduced to plots of bare dirt and litter, beside a parking lot in sore need of grading.

Paul circled around and around the lot until a space opened up near the police car guarding the exit. When they got out of the Jag, he locked it, and Peggy's side, too. He pulled on her handle, just to be sure.

As they walked past the police car, he said, "Tell me again about how they're just kids?"

Peggy contained a sigh and hoped he didn't notice the smell of fresh paint slapped on the stairwell—over the faint swatch of graffiti expletives it almost, but not quite, deleted.

Once inside the building, Peggy's nose was assaulted with heavy odors of waxed linoleum and the same industrial pine cleaner that the shelter used. It barely masked the musty scent of gym clothes and mildewed lockers...and something else. Peggy could smell the almost palpable odor of confinement, and then she noticed the exit doors were chained shut.

So did Paul. "We make it out of here without needing to file a police report, you owe me."

Peggy crossed her fingers behind her back and said a little prayer. Please let this go well!

They entered a brightly-lit office that buzzed with activity. Bespeckled women bustled about, some answering phones, some whose fingers flew over clacking typewriters, some hovered over metal cabinets, pulling out or stuffing files. All work ceased when they saw the box of kittens in Peggy's arms. The women gathered around, chattering. Oh how cute! Did you ever? Oh, my goodness! Exactly like the women at the country club.

A heavyset black woman, glasses resting on the shelf of her bosom, noticed the time and exclaimed, "Oh! Come with me!"

Peggy and Paul followed her to a frosted-glass door, on which she rapped a few times, then peeked within the room. "Mr. Franklin? The town vet is here to see you."

"Come in," a deep voice called out.

They walked into the small office, and a tall black man, dressed in a tailored gray suit, held out his hand.

"Welcome to Washington Street School," The principal gestured for them to take a chair. Paul made sure Peggy was seated first, before taking the one next to her.

"Thank you for coming on such short notice, and I know it's way out of your jurisdiction. Your program interests us, as we're always looking for ways to involve our students in the community. With shrinking budgets, the first things tossed out are the very things that we feel make a measurable difference in whether or not a student remains involved and committed to becoming a viable member of this community. Softball, the science club, drama club, phys-ed, the music programs—without these activities, students have no outlets, and they're prey to unsavory influences, like gangs and drugs. Despite the stats, the state continues to slash our budget. If we don't close the gap, we're going to lose these kids. That's not an option for me. The closing of the community center this year was a blow. It was the last place in walking distance to play the hoops, tennis, hang with a Big Brother, or score a new skill from a trained job counselor. At least eighty-percent of the latch-key student body now has nowhere to go after school, except to a corner hangout, where it's only a matter of time before they meet up with trouble. Our students deserve better. Our community deserves better. I read your brochure, now tell me plain. What is your proposal?"

Peggy glanced at Paul. He, too, seemed impressed with the man's organized, thoughtful introduction. He looked back at her with the same polite deference he showed her at the Country Club. Despite that the principal had been addressing the vet, she cleared her throat.

"I-I think we're in the same boat. Your students need after school programs, and we need extra hands. Maybe we can help each other."

"Such as?"

"Well, we thought, what about volunteer experience for credit?"

Franklin mulled that over. "Grade point average, or future college credit?"

"Either one," Paul offered. "I'd also be open to mentoring the right student, in exchange for a certain amount of volunteer hours."

Peggy looked at him, surprised.

"At least for the duration of my tenure at the shelter," he added, as an afterthought.

"That's a generous offer." The principal handed them each a folder of papers. "My only concern is liability. We can't afford a lawsuit, frivolous or not. If you can sign off on this waiver for today, absolving the school of any and all legal ramifications, then have the students' guardians sign releases to authorize any volunteering, it'll make our superintendent happy, and I think we can move forward."

Paul scanned the papers. He nodded and then handed them to Peggy. After she read them, they signed.

"Miss Harper?" Franklin called out into the office. A diminutive gray-haired woman appeared in the doorway. "Miss Harper will be your escort and take you from class to class. Just a few ground rules. Without a teacher present, students are not to leave the room at any time during your presentation, the talks must be kept to under thirty-five minutes to allow for class changes, and if there is any question, all classrooms are equipped with intercoms and panic buttons. But, after having put the fear of God into them this morning, I'm confident you'll have no trouble."

Paul cleared his throat. "Panic buttons?"

"Thank you," Peggy spoke up quickly, avoiding Paul's eyes.

The vet needn't have worried. They were an instant hit with the students, or rather, the kittens were, especially when the first one out of the carrier urinated all over his shirt. Peggy laughed along with the students. Everything was going to be just fine.

Comprised predominantly of black students, some classes were peppered with a few Irish, Polish and Italian kids, whose families hadn't yet taken flight over the tracks. If there was any friction between the culture clubs, Peggy didn't see it in the presence of those helpless kittens. The biggest surprise turned out to be the tender, almost timid reactions from the football jocks. The hulking young men and their tough-guy attitudes melted at the sight of the tiny kitten claws, and how they compared to their massive hands. Not surprisingly, the girls all wanted to bottle feed the kittens, especially when it meant getting the proper instruction from the good-looking vet.

In contrast with the country club, the presentations to the students followed no formal structure. The uninhibited, curious minds of the students made that impossible. Their questions leapt from one to the next in rapid succession; their interactions were spontaneous and challenging, unfolding differently with each class.

Since the kittens garnered most of the attention, Peggy talked about them, first. Students readily shared stories of their own pets, past and present, lost and found. Peggy listened with keen interest, finding in their disparate cultures a common thread of caring and attachment to cherished pets. In each class, Paul managed to interject a few pet care facts in the chaos, but he didn't press it.

"Are you a vet, too?" a girl asked Peggy.

"She be a dogcatcher, douche bag!" a lanky boy in a basketball jersey exclaimed, and the class laughed until their teacher, Miss Lipowitz, and Miss Harper both clapped their hands for quiet.

"No," Peggy glanced at Paul. "I'm not a vet, but I'm not a dog catcher either. I'm-I'm a warden. An animal warden."

"That's a cop!" the lanky boy said, suspicion creeping into his voice. A few of his friends hissed and thumped desk lids.

Out of the corner of her eye, Peggy caught Paul leaning back against the teacher's desk, surreptitiously feeling around underneath for the panic button.

"Yes," Peggy spoke up over the disruption, "but-but I'm not a people cop, I'm a cop for animals."

"Why you do that?"

"Because they can't call nine-one-one?"

The students laughed, again.

Peggy shrugged. "I guess you might say my job is to-to make sure that the animals are treated right and kept safe from harm." She hesitated, then pulled her badge out of her pocket, and pinned it back on. "That's why I-I wear this badge. To remind myself of that."

The lanky guy in the back nodded. "It's cool."

Paul stopped looking for the panic button, about then, and started listening, as Peggy answered questions as to how and why she became "an animal cop". She talked about her harrowing first day at the shelter, being lost and trying to help Lucky. He noticed that she didn't mention Harrison, but he saw those clenched fists of hers, again. He laughed along with the students when she shared some of her biggest mishaps, like the day she accidentally let all the dogs loose. He fell quiet along with them, when she admitted to her distress over the issue of overcrowding, and how her own error resulted in many more dogs having to be put to sleep, than might have been, otherwise. She talked about what she hoped for the shelter's future and introduced how the students could help.

Leaning against a window, Paul studied her as one might study a cheetah in the wild. You had to look closely in the shadows, to discern the spots and see her true beauty. The classroom's fluorescent lights glistened on her auburn hair, which today was tied with a plain green ribbon behind her neck; simple, yet elegant on her. Her eyes were full of life, as she talked to the students, and her smile was genuine and generous. Exasperating as she was at times, he had to admit that this girl, in a dog catcher's uniform, had more substance than most of the women he knew.

Abruptly an arm shot up in front of his face, startling him.

Miss Lipowitz nodded to the pitch-skinned, broad-shouldered bruiser in a hooded sweatshirt. "Lawrence?"

"Yeah, so what you gotta do to be a vet?"

Paul ran a hand through his hair and moved to the front of the class. "Well, about eight more years of school for starters." The class erupted into groans. "That's just an estimate, by the way!" He nearly had to shout over the protests. "It can happen in less, depending on your course of study."

Peggy stifled a smile, as she watched Paul doing his ivy-league best to make another decade of school sound not only enticing, but exciting to students already chomping on the bit for graduation day. She listened to him downplay the extensive math and chemistry requirements that he called "a weeding-out hurdle" and focus, instead, on the varied and truly interesting job credits available to them at hospitals, aquariums and zoos.

"And, working at the town pound is another way to do that."

"How much all that gonna cost?" Lawrence interrupted.

"That depends."

"How much it cost *you*?"

Paul hesitated. "Well, it didn't. My education was paid for."

"Daddy Warbucks!" one kid in the back coughed into his hands, and the class broke out into hoots and whistling. Miss Harper and Miss Lipowitz clapped their hands.

"People!"

Peggy couldn't help but grin. Let's see you country-club your way out of this one, rich boy!

"Hold on, hold on," Paul laughed and spoke up over the students. "It wasn't exactly a free ride! I busted my butt for six years. It'd be a helluva lot easier for some of you than it was for me, and that's the truth! You want to know how much it might cost if you paid for it in cash? Anywhere from one-hundred to five-hundred-thousand dollars, depending on your course of study."

The students really whooped, then, and even Peggy gaped at him. Did he just say half a million dollars?

"Most of you sitting here, today, are eligible for a helluva gift basket of financial aid and scholarships, unlike this Wonder Bread boy," he pointed to himself. "It's a fact. I didn't have anywhere near the same advantages you do."

"Oh boo, hoo, hoo!" one stout jock challenged amidst more hoots.

"Okay, cards on the table. I come from money. That fact alone makes me ineligible for any financial aid, no hardship scholarships, nothing."

"So what?" a boy with a voluminous afro exclaimed. "You just said you got the bread!"

"Not when you're disinherited," Paul replied.

"Dissed by who?" the boy asked.

"Disinherited. Cut off from the family coffer. I had to find a way to pay for my own education with no help from dear old dad, and no help from the state. I had two choices. I could join the military, or apply for a double degree program; that is, get my VMD, that's the vet degree, and at the same time pursue a PhD in research. This took about eight years to complete. It's highly competitive, and you have to keep your grade point average up above the rest. But if you do, your education is paid for, courtesy of pharmaceutical and research labs. Their hope is that you'll join their rank and file in research, of course, but..." he shrugged. "That's up to you. The point is, there are options. There are people out there and programs in place that can help you get to wherever you want to go. Depends on how badly you want it. For me, that meant if I wanted something more than pushing papers around in a cubicle, where I'm bored every day and hating my life, I had to make it happen, myself. So I did. I may be starting out with zero cushion, but the future is wide open. Better than that, I get to be my own boss. Every day is different, and I get to cut things up and play with bones and guts, all day. It's great."

"Eeeeewwww!" the girls squealed over the boys laughter.

"Righteous," Lawrence nodded, duly impressed.

Peggy was astonished. She thought back to her indictment of his wealthy background just the day before, and wondered why hadn't he corrected her.

"Yo', what you do to git dis-riched?" another boy asked.

"Tyrone!" Miss Lipowitz scolded.

"It's all right," Paul said, picking up a mewing kitten from the carrier. "I got into some trouble, and it cost me. One day, I woke up and decided I didn't want to end up where I was headed, so I took steps to change my life, and here I am. So, keep your noses clean and in the books, and you too can..." he held out the kitten to Peggy, "...one day get urinated on by all kinds of mammals."

The students laughed as Paul used his jacket lapel to wipe fresh urine from his shirt front.

"Let's thank the town shelter for their time!" Miss Lipowitz called out. "If you take your seats, we'll hand out information for you to take home for your parents to look over. Remember, they must be signed by a guardian and returned to the principal's office to be considered for the volunteer program and extra credit."

Peggy handed out forms and flyers to the students as they headed out to their next class.

"I can't believe how well this is going!" Miss Harper tittered. "We haven't had to call security even once!"

"I should have placed a bet," Paul conceded.

Peggy smiled at him, brimming with questions herself. "Me, too."

❦ ❦ ❦ ❦ ❦ ❦ Chapter 53 ❦ ❦ ❦ ❦ ❦ ❦

At two-fifteen, Miss Harper guided Peggy and Paul down yet another hallway to the last class of the day.

"It's one of the remedial classes," she confided in hushed tones. "These are the students who are most in danger of flunking out and not graduating. Mr. Crenshaw rules with an iron fist, so don't worry, they won't look crosswise at you, or else!"

Miss Harper opened the door, and Peggy instinctively ducked, as a paperback book zipped past her face and smacked the wall beside her.

"Hello?" Miss Harper called out over students' hoots and jeers. "Oh, dear!" She withdrew and trotted around the corner.

Paul looked to Peggy. "Is she coming back?"

"Yo! What's in the box?" a boy's voice called out from within the classroom.

Paul peered in the doorway. "Mr. Crenshaw?"

"Takin' a piss," another student announced, eliciting raucous laughter around him.

"Oh." He turned to Peggy. "We should probably wait 'til he gets back."

"What's in the box?"

Peggy stepped across the doorway with the carrier. The boys in the class whistled with appreciation.

"Look out, it be the pussy cops!" a kid called out from the back.

Paul stepped up beside Peggy. "Okay, down fellas!"

"What's - in - the box?" the hooded boy repeated.

"Wanna see?" Peggy offered.

"Wait—" Paul began, but before he could dissuade her, half the class engulfed them in one simultaneous wave of movement, sending Paul backwards against the blackboard.

Dwarfed by the tall, heavy-set teenagers, Peggy lifted the box flaps to reveal the tiny, sleeping kittens.

"Whazzat, a boxxa turds?" a stout kid asked.

"They be cats, fool!" his buddy chided him.

"Cats? We got rats bigger n' dat!"

"Dem's baby cats, nigger!"

"Jones!" a voice bellowed from the doorway. The students collided with each other, scrambling for their seats.

Mr. Crenshaw, a dark and smoldering man, shut the door behind Miss Harper with barely the click of the door latch. His deeply-furrowed frown threatened to rupture his mocha face in half; his eyes pressed the students down into their chairs from twenty feet away.

"What did you say?" he growled to the offending student.

"Dem's baby cats, bro," a repentant Jones intoned. "Sir."

Mr. Crenshaw swooped the paperback book up off of the floor without taking his eyes off the students, then held it up. "Whose?"

Silence.

Peggy could hear her own heart thumping in her ears. Taking a shaky breath, she reached out for the book. "Um...thank you. I-I must have dropped it."

Crenshaw looked at her, momentarily confused. So did Paul. Whether out of politeness, professional courtesy, or complete and utter disbelief, neither man challenged her. Peggy mustered a smile and pocketed the book.

Mr. Crenshaw extended his hand to Paul. "Welcome, Doctor."

"Paul. This is Officer Dillan, the shelter manager," he said, emphasizing the word "Officer" a bit more than Peggy thought necessary.

Mr. Crenshaw extended his hand to Peggy, searching her eyes. Peggy shook his meaty hand without flinching.

"This is Officer Dillan and Dr. Paul," Crenshaw told the class, as if they hadn't already heard the introductions. "We're pleased to have them here as our guests."

The class applauded politely. If lacking enthusiasm, they were at least on cue.

"Please," Crenshaw gestured to Peggy. "Continue." He stepped aside, his eyes riveted on the students.

Peggy reached into the carrier, the tension in the room so taut, her arms buzzed with it. How on earth could she break the ice with students buried under that man's glacial stare? She held up a tabby kitten.

"Th-this is one of the many kittens brought to us at the shelter. He's only about three weeks old. We have two litters here. You can hold one, if you like."

The students glanced to Crenshaw under lowered heads. Only when he nodded brusquely, did they dare to move. One by one, row by row, they stood up and filed past the desk and looked in the box, as if they were at a funeral, looking into a casket.

Peggy glanced to Paul and saw that he shared her concern over the atmosphere in the class. Once the students had all returned to their seats, Paul clapped his hands together abruptly, startling her and Crenshaw.

"So! Anyone have any questions about being a vet?" he asked. The students remained mute. "C'mon, you've got to wonder what makes anyone want to stick thermometers up animals' butts!"

A couple of students chuckled and, thankfully, Mr. Crenshaw nodded his permission for their questions.

One light-skinned kid by the windows raised his hand. "Money."

Before Paul could respond, the kid named Jones raised his hand and said, "Yeah, that right, why else y'all charge eighty dollahs fo' just walkin' in the door?" He looked around at his buddies. "That don't include no exam, no shots, no drugs, no nuthin'. Just fo' walkin' in the door, shhhh...."

"Jones..." Crenshaw growled in warning, but Paul held up his hand.

"No, it's okay. It's a legitimate question." He sat on the edge of Crenshaw's desk. "Sounds like you've had an experience that wasn't all that satisfactory."

"Yeah, you kin say that," the student muttered. "Some nig...some fool let our dog out the gate, thinkin' they gonna rob us. Stupid dog go and git hisself hit by a car. Took him to the ee-mergency place and they say it gonna cost two G's to save his life. And that diddin' include two mo' operations on his legs. Who got that kinda bread, man? They want ten puh-cent up front, too. Shhhh-oot. So my ol' man told 'em to put him out his mis'ry. And now, just 'cause we ain't got ten puh-cent of nuthin', my dog's dead."

Paul did not counter the student's sucker-punch by explaining what it takes to run an animal hospital like the EVC. Instead, he sat and listened as a few more students related their own stories of having had a pet, or having found an injured animal, then seeking help and being confronted with the choice of keeping their pet alive or doing without food that week. The conversation segued into similar complaints about human medicine, where run-ins with HMOs and the endless bureaucracy fairly dwarfed the stories about their pets. Not once did Paul attempt to defend himself, or the medical profession, even when the comments became accusatory in nature, suggesting greedy doctors who lived lavishly. Every time Mr. Crenshaw made a move to intercede, Paul raised his hand in a respectful request to allow the students to continue. After thirty minutes, the students were talked out, and the room fell into awkward silence.

Glowering, Crenshaw looked like he was about to chastise the class, when Peggy stepped forward.

"You're right. All of you. It's-it's a crime that people can't get the help they need when their animals are sick or hurt. Or, their families. It's not right. You have no way of knowing, but Dr. Hayward works long hours with us at the shelter. Longer than he's supposed to. He takes care of all the medical needs of our animals, and-and I don't know how he's doing it, because we don't have the money to pay for any of the medicine he's using. We can't even afford to pay him. But somehow, the medicine is there when we need it. He gives free vet exams to people who bring their pets to the shelter, and I-I'm not saying that any of this makes all the rest of it okay, it's just that he's not the enemy. I know how hard it is. There are so many people that don't care, but maybe someday, if more people stand up, it doesn't have to be that way. If we all work together to change things, maybe things will get better...one corner at a time."

For a moment, all she could hear, besides the clock ticking on the wall, was the plaintive mewing of the other kittens in the carrier. Abruptly the three o'clock bell jangled.

Crenshaw clapped his hands in an effort to elicit applause, but the students were half-hearted, at best.

Peggy handed out a couple of flyers, as they filed out, and that's when she spotted a lone teen at the back of the class. Chin in hand, he stared at her. He looked familiar, and all of a sudden she remembered. Curtis!

Having caught her eye, he crooked his books under his arm and walked out of the classroom. For a split second, Peggy just stood there. Then forcing one foot after the other, she followed him.

The halls were jammed with jostling students, and it took her a minute to pick Curtis out of the crush. He was already halfway down

the hall, when she called out to him. "Excuse me! Wait! Please, I-I want
to talk with you!"

Weaving away between his peers, the boy never looked back. He
walked out of the building, past the guard untangling the chains from
the doors.

School traffic snarled the streets in gridlock. Between the snow flurries, waiting parents, crossing guards, both school and public buses all
vying for the right of way on double-parked streets, the Jaguar sat six
cars deep at a stand still. With only one way out, around the demolition
of a crumbling community center, each car had to wait for a light, which
only let just one car make the turn before turning red, again.

Peggy regarded the boarded-up windows and coats of graffiti splattered across the deserted building, now being crushed under the weight
of a bulldozer. Fences snapped and whipped defensively at the relentless
plow, dust exhaling from shaking walls like last breaths.

She glanced at Paul. He seemed far away, lost in thought. She didn't
tell him about Curtis. However she may have deserved the boy's rebuke,
she felt that the vet had not deserved to be so maligned by the class, just
because he wore a white coat...and drove a Jag.

"I'm-I'm sorry about the way they-they just don't understand," she
began.

"You know how much a capsule of Ampicillin costs?" he murmured.
"Ten cents. Ten cents is our cost at the EVC, and we charge thirty-two
dollars for an average, per milligram, ten day prescription. Two pills a
day at ten cents a pill adds up to thirty dollars profit. Twenty-eight ninety-nine, if you count the five cent vial we buy in bulk and tack on two
extra dollars for."

"You don't make the rules about what to charge."

"But, I know about it."

He said nothing more after that. Half an hour later, when the Jag
zipped down the driveway into the shelter lot, Peggy felt as if they'd been
away for a week. The place looked strangely unfamiliar to her all of a sudden, although she could see that nothing had changed since they'd left
that morning. The duct-taped run roofing had not blown off, as of yet.
The early morning rain had eaten away a bit more of the hard-packed
snow drifts, but outside of that, it all looked the same, and yet, different.

Getting out of the car, Peggy spotted a fifty-pound bag of dog food and a crate of chicken broth at the gate. She hurried over to it and plucked off the attached note. It was written on country club stationary. She read it aloud, hoping to cheer Paul.

"Look at this! 'For the dogs, ruff-ruff love, Susan'. Oh! Sorry. Th-this is...I guess it was for you." She handed the note to Paul, feeling her cheeks blush with embarrassment. "Bless the Ladies Who Lunch! You were...you were right."

Paul read the note. "About what?"

"About your side of the tracks."

Paul crumpled the note. "I slept with her. And, not to get a fifty-pound bag of dog food, in case you wondered."

"I-I don't. Didn't."

For an awkward moment they both just stood there, the fast-fading light of day draping the warehouses around them in deepening shadow.

Paul eased the kitten box out of her hands. "You were right about those kids, today. And you were right about the Ladies Who Lunch. Don't let a checkbook, or a book tossed at your head, change your mind about the things that you know." With that, he headed down under the office overhang towards the cellar.

Peggy looked after him, her heart tumbling in confusion. She wasn't sure if she should feel better or worse, for what he said. She listened to the crunching of his boots on the gravel, the shoving creak of the warped cellar door, as it was pushed opened and yanked shut again. A chunk of ice broke off of the roof gutter and crashed down through the fencing onto the concrete runs, shattering like glass.

She pulled the paperback book out of her pocket and looked at it: *Catch 22* by Joseph Heller. She opened the cover, but there was no name, just a library card with the due date stamped on it: January 1st. It was overdue. The wind picked up and a familiar, distant honking caught her ear. She looked up to the sky.

A small flock of Canadian geese winged over the abandoned warehousing in a tattered V formation, returning north. It startled her. Wasn't it just a little while ago they had flown south for the winter?

It was officially spring. It should have cheered her, but it didn't. She looked towards the cellar, unable to shake off the chill. Backing away from it, she headed into the shelter.

Chapter 54

"How can you be so cold?!"

Joe's accusation was made more hurtful when he shielded the fat, yelping puppies in his arms from her, as if she was the enemy!

Peggy kneaded her pounding brow, feeling so sapped and tired, that she could barely think straight. While she and Paul had been out talking to ten half-dozing members of the Kiwanis club about the benefits of spaying and neutering pets, the shelter had not only been inundated with another four litters of kittens, but two litters of eight unwanted puppies each!

Peggy looked over her shoulder to Paul, where he leaned against the back window, waiting for her decision. He glanced at his watch. She sighed. She didn't have to look at the clock. No matter what time it was, it was high noon with guns ablazing. The shelter had reached critical mass. They were out of space and out of time.

"I-I don't mean to be," she began. "It's just…"

"There's gotta be somethin' else we can do!" Joe held up a fat puppy, and whimpered right along with it. "Lookit his widdle face!"

Peggy bit her lip. The talk at the school had not garnered the instant extra hands that she had counted on. The red tape of liability write offs might take another week or two to get sorted through the school system, but she needed help, now. She turned back to Paul.

"What if I advertise free shots and vet care for any adopted kitten or puppy for the next two months, after adoption?"

"It would take ten people coming down in the next five minutes, adopting at least two apiece, and you'd still be short hands to juggle the rest, tonight. I don't think there's any getting around it, this time."

He'd said it quietly and without rancor. The worst part about it was that Peggy knew he was right. He was about to say something else to her but lifted his gaze past her shoulder, his attention on something outside.

Peggy turned and saw a lone, hooded figure shuffling down the driveway, in the stiff wind and light rain.

"I don't see a box," Betty said, crunching a candy cigarette.

"Do we see a gun?" Joe asked.

Reaching the front gate, the figure unzipped the hoodie and shook off the rain. It was Curtis.

Peggy hurried out the office door.

When Peggy opened the front gate, Curtis crouched before the runs. He watched the dogs alternately barking at him and howling at a passing police car siren. When she latched the gate behind her, he stood up but didn't acknowledge her. She stood beside him in the drizzling rain and waited until the siren faded away into the distance. Soon the dogs quieted down.

"I'm-I'm sorry I thought you stole the donation can. I'm sorry for the hurtful things I said to you," she said, finally.

It was a good long moment before Curtis responded. "That dog need a bath," he jerked his head to a skinny shepherd in the end run. "Y'all need to pay mo' 'tention to 'em. They be lookin' pediculus."

Peggy had no idea what pediculus meant, but she was pretty sure it wasn't a compliment. "Yes, we're-we're short-handed. We could use some help. Would you be interested?"

Curtis raised his chin. "Maybe."

"Thank you."

"I said maybe."

They stood in the drizzle, observing the dogs in silence. Then, Curtis pulled a donation can out of his pocket and handed it to her. It was heavy, full of coins.

"From the liberry."

"Thank you."

"Y'welcome."

From her coat pocket, Peggy extracted *Catch 22* and offered it to him. He took it. "Thank you."

"You're welcome."

Curtis saved the day. Even though he was the only one to volunteer at first, he had two brothers, two adult cousins with college-age children, and a nurturing and able grandmother. They were all living under one roof, and all willing to foster a few litters. Paul coached them, and they learned quickly.

His weary grandmother, Wanda, had burst into tears of gratitude for Curtis finding something that interested him, instead of trouble. She explained to Peggy that his mother was in jail, serving time for possession of crack cocaine. No one had seen his abusive father since before the youngest, Ramone, had been born, and Wanda's biggest worry was the toll it had all taken on Curtis.

"It be a wondah the boy ain't hit the streets befo' this, what he been troo," she told Peggy. "Boy got mo' brains than most. Don't axe me where it come from. Ain't my side. Ain't his daddy's side, neither. Gift from the Good Lawd, hisself, A-men, thank you, Jesus! But, mo' n' brains, boy got *mind*. Damn fool school don't know what to do wiff mind like that! And mind wiffout die-rection ain't nuthin' but trouble!"

Curtis took the bus from school, arriving at the shelter, every day at 3:30 p.m., Monday through Friday. He also came in at eight, every Saturday morning, staying all the way through to closing. Peggy suspected that Curtis would have shown up on Sunday too, if it hadn't been for Sunday school, church, and the mandatory, sit-down dinner at his aunt's.

Soon, it became clear that Wanda had not been exaggerating about the boy's intelligence. Aside from his strangely prolific vocabulary, he exhibited a profound manner of integrating new information and skill sets in such abstract ways, at times, that one might think he was either a savant, or mad. He accomplished most tasks more efficiently, and in less time, than the seasoned crew, and wound up picking up the slack for them.

Peggy noticed that Curtis spent every lunch break, reading a book. Every day, he came in with a new word. Sometimes Peggy had to wait the entire day to find out what the word was going to be, because Curtis only used a word in its proper context. Regardless, nine times out of ten, she hadn't a clue as to the meaning of the word, and it forced her to look it up in the dictionary on the second shelf.

For the life of her, she couldn't figure out why Curtis had been placed in the remedial class at school. It made no sense. He was obviously bright, a voracious reader, and a quick study. Maybe, his grandmother was right; damn fool schools don't know what to do with kids who possess "mind".

One afternoon, after Curtis had been playing fetch with the dogs in the back yard, Peggy found a well-thumbed copy of Familiar Quotations under the maple tree. It was an anthology of famous quotes from Aristotle to Emile Zola. It seemed like such an odd book for a fifteen-year-old boy to be reading, let alone a boy from the projects. But little about Curtis was typical. Peggy figured that he'd more than likely picked it up after listening to Clara's daily quotes from her vast memory-cache of historic notables. On more than one occasion, he was able to match quotes with Clara over an issue, which impressed the old woman to no end.

"Little basket's a Rhodes in the makin'!" she predicted.

Beyond welcoming Curtis's help, Betty remained strangely reserved with the boy. "Crack baby, nuthin' more n' a baby addict," she sniffed without apology.

There was just no reasoning with her about it. Joe often cajoled her about her holier-than-thou contradictions, but to no avail. This attitude confounded Peggy. Here was the best role model of a mother figure this boy would ever have, aside from his grandmother; Betty was an honest, hard-working woman involved with her parish, and who commanded everyone's respect when it came to issues of right and wrong. Yet, she remained a closed door to him.

Happily, this was not to be the case, for long.

During one rare, quiet lunch hour, as Peggy worked on research for Terry's grant, she noticed Curtis take a seat opposite Joe and Betty, at the end of the counter, to eat his peanut butter and jelly sandwich. She watched Curtis watch Betty agonize over the weekly reconciling of the ledger books. He watched her fingers flit over the adding machine keys, as she struggled to come up with the same tally, at least once.

After the sixth try, she tossed her pencil aside.

Curtis pointed to one of her tallies. "It be veracious that third time."

Betty peered at him over her glasses. "S'cuse me?"

"Third time be right."

"And just how you know that?"

"You didn't make no mistake that time. First time, you punched in five sixty-five insteada sixty-five five, and you done that four times more in that column, there. Second time, you figgered first column right, but misconstrue haff way troo that second column, and y'inverted three othah numbahs. Third time, you done just mix up so many numbahs

I quit countin'. Fourth and fifth time, you juxtapose numbah six evvy time it be nine, and the sixth time, I don't know what you be doin', 'cause the numbahs you punch in wasn't even on the page."

Joe spit crumbs in a snort of laughter.

"Shush up!" Betty glanced at the ledger, then back to Curtis. From where he sat, the ledger was upside down. She picked through the two columns, again, with a polite interrupt from Curtis, whenever she made an error. Sure enough, with his help, the tally finally added up.

"Jeeze," Joe said to Curtis. "Which six numbers you see winning to-night's lottery?" Later, after having witnessed Curtis single-handedly fix the books for Betty, Joe took Peggy aside. "How 'bout I take Curtis on an out-reach program for some off-track betting?"

"Have you lost your marbles?"

"Have you seen what he can do with racin' forms?"

"Tell me he doesn't actually bet on them."

"Nah, it's like a hobby with him, like crosswords. But, I'm tellin' ya. I ain't never seen nobody can handicap like this kid! He's like, zen with numbers. Lookit, I'd place the bets."

"Try these numbers: five for him, in juvie, and ten in the slammer for you."

"Nobody has to know!"

"You got a sound-proof head?" Betty interjected. "What parta illegal you ain't hearin'?"

"I'm just sayin'! We could get a new boiler!"

"We could get closed down!" Peggy exclaimed. "We're supposed to be keeping him out of trouble, not taking lessons from him on how to get into it! He's not to set one foot off this property until driven home, straight home, you hear? No side trips, no horses, no numbers, no gambling of any kind, and no taking him on patrols, either! Consider him our biggest liability and biggest hope to get Grade A for Community Service from the mayor by summer. I intend to get a lot more out of Town Hall, than just a new boiler."

"Ace is wild," Clara declared.

Peggy sighed as dollar bills were slapped down onto the counter. "You know, those three dollars could buy two rolls of paper towels."

"Where you think petty cash come from, all this time?" Betty asked.

As for Paul, he accepted Curtis, from day one, as his assistant. It was clear the boy wanted to work with the vet, and they were a perfect match. Like Paul, Curtis was an intensely focused individual, taking pride in being above average in every task undertaken. Peggy wasn't sure who sported the better poker face, though. This was tested when Paul brought in a lab coat for Curtis. Peggy knew he must have been bristling with excitement, but Curtis thanked Paul politely and donned it as if he'd been born to wear it.

Peggy had to smile to herself. If there was anyone who was going to be able to match wits with Paul, she was willing to bet that it was this young man from the tenements. Sure enough, there were many times when Paul surreptitiously slipped into the office, to pull the dictionary from the shelf, thumb through it, and then head back downstairs.

Curtis and Peggy never spoke again about their misunderstanding. Peggy drafted a letter for all the shop vendors, giving him permission to both remove and replace the donation cans. There developed between them an unspoken, almost intuitive communication, during the course of the day. He always seemed to know what she might need or require to be done, sometimes before it had even occurred to her. Soon, he was indispensable to everyone, and Peggy credited his help, more than any other factor, in saving as many of the spring litters that they did.

Joe missed his first St. Patrick's day celebration at Kierney's, and he let everybody know he was not happy about it.

Too swamped with fostering puppies and kittens, and with a growing schedule of seminar bookings, Peggy and the crew nearly missed the date altogether, which would have suited Clara, just fine. Still, Betty brought in shamrock cookies to appease Joe, and Peggy noticed that Clara had two of the green-sugared shortbreads, without complaint.

Although it was officially spring, and only two days before Easter, Peggy swore you'd never know it by the weather. Winter temperatures held on tenaciously, barely reaching freezing each day, and the wind howled out of the northwest, rattling the windows so hard, she joined Betty in daily prayer for the patched roof.

With Curtis's help, Peggy and Paul were freed up to accept three more talks: the Rotary club, The Elks and The Farroway Garden Club, all generated by word of mouth from their very first talk at the Country Club.

It became routine to find a box or two of donated items left by the gate, at least once a week, along with a few donation checks sent in the mail. Things were definitely looking up.

Paul blustered into the office one frigid afternoon, shaking off the cold and damp from his overcoat. "Greenhouse effect, my ass."

"I'm tellin' ya, we're headin' into another ice age," Joe said. "Nobody listens to me."

"How's the boiler holding up?" Peggy asked.

"Better than I am." Paul opened the medicine cabinet. "I'm going to need some help tomorrow with first round vaxes on the kittens and pups." He turned to Peggy, as if expecting her to offer.

"Oh. Well, I'm sure Curtis would like t-to learn how to do that."

Paul turned back to the cabinet. "We'll have to get his guardian's permission."

"Of course. I'll ask his grandmother."

"So Doc," Joe popped open a soda, "how's the boy wonder doin'?"

"He's a good kid. Has a good head on his shoulders. If he keeps his nose to the books and doesn't screw up his life by...well, you know..."

Betty swiveled around in her chair with narrowed eyes. "Become a dope head or baby daddy befo' he graduate?"

"I didn't say that."

"Puh! You much too white to git away wiff it, but I can say it."

"Because you're black?"

"No, 'cause it be true. And Doctah, the term be African-American, now."

"Please, call me Dr. Caucasian."

"Pfft!" Clara dismissed him with a wave. "We've other names suit you, so much more than 'alf."

"If they make it outta high school drug free and baby free," Betty said, "be a chance they make it outta the projects. Odds ain't on they side, but..."

"I predict better things ahead for Curtis," Paul insisted. "He can do the Times crossword puzzle upside down and without the dictionary."

"That ain't impressive, that's weird," Joe said.

"He's got the hands of a surgeon," Paul continued as he restocked his medical bag. "And he's got the mindset. Focused, steady. I think he's got a natural instinct for diagnostics. He picked up on Fritz's hookworm, before I suspected the need for a test."

"Maybe he could be our next intern," Joe said.

Paul turned around at that. Peggy looked up, too. Almost at once, they both looked at the calendar, and then at each other. On Monday, it would be the first of April.

Paul averted his eyes. "Wouldn't put it past him. He really ought to be skipped two grades ahead, as it is."

"Maybe y'all should tell the school principal," Betty suggested.

Paul once again glanced at Peggy. "We should."

Peggy nodded. "Yes."

He returned to the medicine cabinet and Peggy became acutely aware of the clock ticking on the wall. Summer was just around the corner, and with it, Paul's six-month contract with the shelter would come to an end.

Chapter 55

"Blimey, there is a God!" Clara declared.

Despite the fog and rain on Easter afternoon, a crowd descended on the shelter, every single person looking to adopt an animal.

Peggy could have cried for joy. A number of country club members had apparently read her Easter Adoption Ad in the Chronicle. It had cost her a week's pay. Four couples were attracted by the free two-month veterinary service, which accompanied any adoption. Even more of a surprise, three students from Washington Street School showed up with their parents—including Lawrence, the hulking football jock—asking to volunteer.

All in all, Easter weekend was a success, and as word spread, the following week was busy, in spite of ferociously windy, cold mornings. Even on Thursday, when it rained and the wind gusted at fifty miles per hour, ripping off more of the fiberglass roofing, people ventured down to the shelter.

The best news, however, came at the end of the day, when Irene called.

Terry had been moved to another wing of the rehab facility/nursing home, she said, and was scheduled to begin therapy the following week. He'd had a rough three weeks with a bronchial infection, the doctors fearing it might turn to pneumonia. Exhausted, he was finally on the mend and ready for rehab. Irene hadn't wanted to worry the crew, she explained, and that was why they hadn't heard from her for so long. Irene signed off, with the good news that things were looking up for her brother.

As soon as she hung up the phone, Betty burst into a rant. "I want my bad news up front, not post-dated, dammit!"

Although Betty was miffed about being kept out of the loop, Peggy was grateful that they didn't know about Terry's brush with pneumonia. It would have worried them sick. All she felt, now, was a huge sense of relief. Terry was going to be all right; he was on the mend and in good hands. That's all she needed to know. She felt free to focus her full attention on steering the shelter forward for him.

Peggy and Paul's speaking calendar was filling up. They accepted engagements from all over town. They kept to their first topic, overpopulation, as concurrent cries concerning human overpopulation reverberated all around them, in the news media. The often violent public battles over abortion, welfare, and poverty had been usurping the fallout from the end of the American involvement in the Vietnam War with both sides villified on the evening news, and on talk radio.

Their seminars were charged with spillover from the same headlines, and more than once they were forced into playing referee to a spirited debate between audience members. Word spread about the talks being nothing less than entertaining, and before long, they were asked back to speak at places they'd already appeared, creating a new pressure to come up with additional program content, often on the fly. Lunch time became a harried affair of greasy pizza or Jack's two-item special take out, juggled between chores and foster feedings.

Betty appointed herself as their secretary and used her no-nonsense style to its fullest advantage in the negotiation of their fees. Along with more frequent talks came more frequent goods left at the gate, and increasing numbers of donation checks sent in the mail. Peggy set up a separate savings account for the shelter to take in the donations, using proceeds to pay off the shelter's outstanding debts, one invoice at a time.

Joe acted as chauffeur on the occasions when they brought a dog along as mascot, and Peggy could tell that he got a kick out of being the official-looking presence in the back of auditoriums. He polished his boots and badge, and decked himself out in full utility belt accessories to better play the part, just in case the public debates escalated beyond name calling.

Happily, Peggy and Paul did not suffer a lack of material to structure their talks. Peggy knew precisely the issues that she wanted to tackle and present to the public, using her own trial by fire initiation as a guide: *Proper Care of Pets. Responsible Pet Ownership. Adoption versus Puppy Mills.*

Chipping away at the ignorance, which Peggy felt was the biggest obstacle to change, became a big raison d'être for her. Every morning she sprang out of bed energized and excited to get to work. There was no question in her mind that the more information people had, the more problems would diminish and eventually disappear, altogether. Peggy had never felt so sure of anything before in her life, with one glaring exception.

Joe's patrols had garnered no change concerning Lucky's situation. The essence of his report was always the same: Lucky was routinely sighted in Harrison's yard with food, water and what appeared to be a blanket inside the dog house. Even though his reports concurred with Paul's opinion that, being an outdoor dog, Lucky could ride out the early spring's lingering cold better than most of the shelter's dogs, Peggy was not as satisfied.

She sat before the office window in Terry's green vinyl chair, and stared out at the pouring rain. Her pen was poised over her note pad, where she'd written only one word: Abuse.

All at once, Betty whooped and tossed coils of adding machine tape in the air. "Halleluiah, we be debt free!"

"What?" Peggy swiveled around, and Betty held out a tally to her. "Oh my gosh!"

"Whahoo!" Joe shook a can of Mountain Dew and popped it open with a spray of fizz over their heads.

"Hey, hey, hey!" Paul shielded a cat with his lab coat. "That's the last can we've got!"

"Next case is on me, Doc!"

Paul shook soda out of his hair and turned to Peggy. "Congratulations!"

Peggy exhaled with a big smile. "Thank you."

"Now don't be goin' and buyin' the store, but we also got ourselfs a little surplus," Betty told her.

"I vote for the run roofing!" Joe blurted out.

"Might want to hit the plumbing first," Paul suggested and pulled a candy cigarette from a new pack of candy Camel's, then tossed the pack to Betty. "I've done what I can, but that boiler's never going to make it through another winter."

"Told you you'd get hooked," Betty smirked.

"Careful Doc, next stop is the real smoke," Joe cautioned him.

The candy dangling from his lips, Paul nodded with what looked like weary acknowledgment.

"Fair do's then, ante up all!" Clara demanded.

Joe slapped down a dollar bill. "Damn, Doc, you had me."

Betty snatched Joe's dollar, but then had to turn it over to Curtis, who then stuck his hand out to Paul. With a resigned sigh, the young vet forked over a five dollar bill to his protégé.

"You too?!" Peggy's brows shot up. "I don't believe it!"

"Me either," Paul admitted. "Never bet against the house."

Peggy returned his smile, and when his lingered a moment longer on her, she averted her eyes and reached up to make sure the St. Francis pendant was still around her neck.

"Okay kiddies," Joe drummed on the counter, "I say we up the ante this time, and set th'odds for The Easter Parade. All proceeds go to the New Boiler Fund."

"We just got through Easter," Peggy reminded him. Betty, Joe, and Clara shared what sounded like a knowing laugh. "What-what's so funny? We adopted out all the puppies and kittens."

"Get out your umbrella, Saint Francis," Joe warbled off key. "Whenever it rains it rains...guess! Not pennies, but..."

Clara set a dollar bill on the counter. "Memorial Day."

Betty pursed her lips and tapped a pencil against her chin. Curtis whispered in her ear. She circled the calendar. "May Day."

Joe dug into his pocket. "Okay, Croft, I'll see your Memorial Day and raise you another week."

"I don't understand," Peggy began.

"Look around. You notice anything missing? Clue number one: one plus one equals a gazillion? Who goes hoppin' down the bunny trail?"

"Bunnies!" Peggy winced and hung her head.

Paul sighed. "And all the foul fowl."

"How soon?" Peggy moaned from behind her hands.

Betty blew her nose. "In 'bout three weeks, maybe four at th'outside, cute little thumpah be grown into a fifteen-pound buck wiff a temper. And the cute ugly ducklings be grown inta horny geese won't let nobody in they baff tubs, and all them fuzzy chicks be crowin' at dawn."

"How many?"

"Let's put it this way," Joe said, "we could have KFC twice a day from oh, 'bout May first 'til th'end of summer and still have some wings left over for the holidays. Remember Big Red? The Rooster we traded for that litter of kittens up at Glenn Erin Egg farm, last month? Easter baby gone bad, for sure. If we were smart, we'd get a butcher block out back and—"

"Joe!"

"What's the diff, the doc offin' 'em or maybe makin' good use of 'em?"

"Can't we give them to the egg farm?"

"We're lucky if Glenn don't end up suin' us for pawnin' off el pollo diablo on him."

"Aside from Glenn Erin farm," Paul interjected, "there's the issue of zoning laws. I don't see the point in keeping chicks and ducks. You can't adopt them out. The rabbits, maybe. They're legitimately kept as pets."

"Then, why do the pet shops sell the chicks if…" Peggy began.

"It ain't against the law to sell 'em," Joe said, "just to keep 'em in town."

"That doesn't make any sense."

"Welcome to Capitalism, USA!"

"You won't nevah see 'em in the shops any othah time of year," Betty concurred. "Just Easter. Git 'em dirt cheap from breeders in Pennsylvania."

"Forget the Quakers, try Bayonne!" Joe snorted. "Hutches on rooftops like friggin' skyscrapers. It's big business, man. Especially with Ricans. All legal, too. The lucky ones end up here, the rest of the rabbits are sold off to schmucks skinnin' 'em for their pelts or python food, or dumped in the woods. The chickens end up as Sunday supper. The ducks're tossed in the ponds up in Verona Park where they get picked off by fox and bobcats. Ter tried to spread 'em out up Sussex county, but we're losin' the farms now to strip malls and McDonald's."

"'Ow's that for irony," Clara remarked.

"How much wildlife do you see down here?" Paul asked.

"We could repopulate Mars," Joe said.

"Ree-populate?" Betty ventured.

"Yeah. Where you think we came from?"

Betty shook her head, as if to clear it. Curtis handed her a fresh pack of candy cigarettes.

Paul shrugged. "Okay, round three. I assume you're all vaccinated against rabies?"

Curtis raised his hand and shook his head no.

"Doc Sanford takes care of us," Joe nodded. "Except for Curtis, we're all good. You got vaxxed, right Saint Francis? Yo'! Dillan!"

Peggy turned to Paul. "Isn't Curtis underage? And, why would he need it, if it's just baby wildlife?"

"I wanna work wiff the ferine," Curtis said.

For a split second, even Dr. Hayward VMD-PhD looked unsure about what Curtis had just said. "Right. Well, I'll need to talk to the Health Department and your guardian." He turned to Peggy. "To answer your question, a litter can carry it through the dam. I'm especially concerned about skunk and raccoon kits, and I want to make it clear, under no circumstances does anyone touch a bat without thick gloves, goggles, a mask. *And* my supervision, period. We clear?"

"Yes," Peggy agreed. She chewed the inside of her lip and worried the St. Francis pendant between her fingers.

"I ain't afraid to get innoculated," Curtis told Peggy.

"No need to be," Paul said. "It's not like the post-exposure series you may have heard about. The fourteen injections in the stomach? That is why anyone who handles wildlife needs to be vaxxed, because if you're not, and you get bitten, you'll be going down that road. So don't touch any wildlife, Curtis, until we get you cleared. Once we get permission, the vax is just three shots in opposite shoulders; one injection, once a week."

"Copesthetic."

"What's your policy on releasing wildlife?" Paul asked Joe.

"Well, Ter tried not to release in the reservations except in emergency or special cases, 'cause it ain't fair for 'em to just get dumped in a strange place with no skills and in some other critter's turf. We got a few peeps bordering the reservation who help us out, doin' it real slow like. But when we get slammed, we foster 'em 'til they're weaned, then call on Cedar Creek Refuge down in the Barrens. Mrs. Woodfield's got a rad rehab program. The critters come and go when they're ready."

"Sounds good." Paul glanced to the calendar, and then turned to Peggy. "It's been an early spring. Better hope it's not a long one, too."

"Yes." Peggy noticed the crew place another bet, behind him.

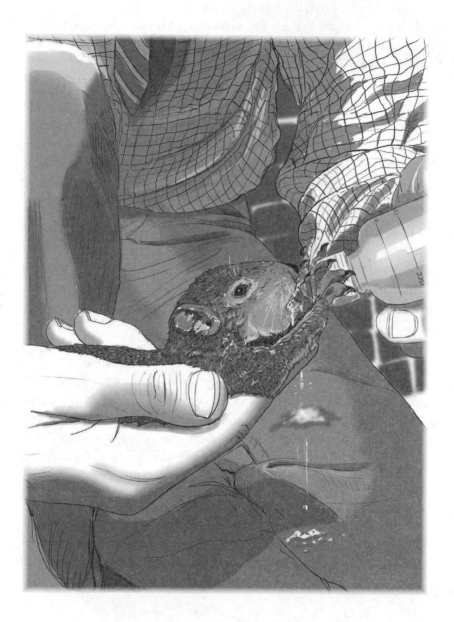

Chapter 56

"Aw, man, we're doomed! This is the worst friggin' spring ever!"

Joe stumbled in the office door with a wail, his arms laden with another litter of squirrels. He searched the countertop for some space, to no avail.

Peggy sank into Terry's chair, exhausted. For five straight weeks, the entire crew put in fourteen-hour days. A veritable zoo of squirrels, robins, raccoons, opossum, rabbits and pigeons flooded the shelter, while record floods soaked the towns of Wayne Township, just north of the EVC. Peggy considered asking the vet to build an Ark.

Just as Old Man Winter lost his icy grip on blustery April, Joe's "Easter Fallout" began in earnest. Half-grown chicks, ducks and a noisy flock of guinea hens invaded the shelter, and much to Paul's chagrin, he was saddled with another fledgling Bantam rooster. Joe named it Rocky G, after Rocky Gracziano, the boxer, because it sparred with everything from its own shadow to the broom. Its weekly attempts at escape left shredded curtains, collapsed shelves, and frazzled humans in his wake. Paul thought hard about tranquilizing him, and Joe, who did most of the chasing, was all for it.

"Why doncha?!" Joe had cried one morning, crawling out from under the counter, spitting feathers.

"Because I'm afraid I'll kill him!" Paul had retorted, and Peggy got the distinct impression that he didn't mean it would be accidental.

Peggy and the crew forged ahead as the shelter transitioned into an increasingly bustling, but organized place of business. Permission was secured for Curtis to receive the rabies vaccination, enabling him to take on a good portion of wildlife fostering with Joe. Lawrence chose to foster the puppies and his buddy Willie took on the domestic fowl. Curtis's brother, Ramone, mastered the kennel chores and exercised the dogs out in the back yard, with his friend Lewis.

Between coordinating all of the foster care, adoption campaigns, and bi-weekly seminars, Peggy pushed herself ever harder, mainly because she witnessed the rewards in a steady increase of donations, both in goods and cash.

Peggy and Paul rotated two main seminars. For the first, Peggy chose the chicks and ducklings as mascots, and Paul lectured on the consequences of keeping them as indoor pets versus on a farm, where they could roam freely and stay healthy. For the second presentation, Peggy spoke about the perils facing captive-bred animals that were released into the wild, and they brought along the baby bunnies and squirrels for those talks.

Though the Easter Fallout babies were ambassadors to the cause, they took up precious cage space. Every day was a juggle of shifting priorities, peppered with crises of incoming and outgoing animals. Paul released Beetle, the heartworm beagle, two weeks earlier than he had planned, just to free up one more cage. Within minutes, it was filled with wild baby rabbits. The ducklings had at first been kept down in "Beula's Room," swimming in the tub and bedding down with hens in a double-decker pen beside the old boiler, but it wasn't long before they had all outgrown their accommodations.

Taking advantage of warm drizzly afternoons, Curtis, Ramone, Lawrence and Joe solved one space issue by setting up plastic wading pools in the back yard, for the waterfowl. However, with the addition of a small flock of domestic geese, even that solution proved short-lived.

Once May blossomed, Paul suggested to Peggy that outdoor pens and hutches be built out in the yard, too, as well as in the storage room under the back runs. Armed with donation checks to purchase materials, she turned the young men loose to tackle the project before cages burst.

Late at night, bleary-eyed, Peggy delved into additional research. She hunted for places willing to take in their fowl brood before the vet dropped them all off to the Colonel, himself. She managed to squeeze in half a dozen more "Free Vet Exam" days in the parking lots of area pet stores, including the one that had initially refused her donation cans in the beginning. In exchange for free vet service for their animal inventory, the shop owners were eager to comply.

"Now that's what I call prid quo-pro, Dillan!" Joe congratulated her with a high-five.

Despite the additional work and late hours, Peggy never once heard Paul complain. Then again, she had thought to herself, why should he? He only had eight weeks left at the shelter. After that, none of this Easter Fallout, pet overpopulation, euthanasia, nor the shelter itself, would be his problem. She had to admit that his departure had been looming in her mind for some time. They had all been working seamlessly together, and the thought of losing him now, was unthinkable.

Taking a brief break, Peggy sat back in Terry's chair and listened absently to the radio in the background.

"...despite the message of peace and brotherhood, music from the likes of Stevie Wonder and the supporting turnout of one hundred twenty-five thousand attendees in Washington, the final toll of the Human Kindness Concert event is ironic, if not disastrous; over five hundred robberies, six hundred injuries and one hundred fifty people treated at area hospitals. Due to the unprecedented chaos and violence reported, officials are now questioning the consequences of another such event, especially given next year's bi-centennial. Out of Saigon; as U.S. military helicopters complete the evacuation of fifteen hundred Americans marking the end of the thirty year war, South Vietnam has officially surrendered to Hanoi. Meanwhile, sources out of Phnom Penh have reported forced evacuations as Cambodia falls to the Khmer Rouge. Communication was cut off to the city April seventeenth, but rumors of mass murder and internment camps have persisted, as well as reports of thousands fleeing the violence in make shift boats. Out of Washington; the one hundred forty-one billion dollar price tag for the war..."

"Bah, so much for Human Kindness Day!" Clara growled.

"Ha!" Joe scoffed, and twisted the radio dial until he heard Rock n' Roll. "Think it was gonna change nuthin'?"

Peggy studied the calendar. May seventeenth. It was barely a week after the aforementioned Human Kindness Day debacle in the nation's capital, and what had changed? She pushed it out of her mind and pulled out her list of the wild and domestic fowl ready to be transported down to New Brunswick. She'd managed to track down Rancho Rabbit, a new, domestic rabbit rescue, in Middlesex County. Their only stipulation; the rabbits had to be neutered.

Paul had taken on the challenge without blinking an eye. Neutering rabbits was another first, hence, another notch on his belt of experience. Apparently he'd consulted with Dr. Caldwell at the EVC and performed the surgeries there during his graveyard shifts. As expected, every rabbit came through just fine.

The chickens and guinea hens were accepted by egg farms up in Sussex, as well, especially when offered a free vet visit to their coops from Dr. Hayward. When it came to the geese and ducks, it was the young vet himself who suggested a call to the Ag school down at Rutgers University, to split the burden of numbers. To everyone's relief, Paul's contact owed him a favor, and so the shelter was given permission to bring their final Easter overflow down to live on their behavioral study pond at the animal science work station.

Joe wheeled his chair over to Peggy. "Ya got Rocky G. on the list, right?"

"He was first on mine," Paul remarked, as he packed his medical bag.

Betty said, "If he ain't the demon seed of chickens, I don't know th'devil from dust!"

Peggy chewed on her pencil, worried about their Bantam bad boy's placement. His recent molting into full blown breeding mode had taken a dark turn overnight, and he mutated into a scary yellow-eyed devil-bird, with a penchant for attacking men.

"They're so sweet when they're chicks," she reminisced aloud. "The wildlife, too. What happens to all that sweetness, as they get older?"

"They grow a pair," Clara remarked, and then frowned at Joe. "You're all alike."

Joe leaned in to Peggy, and whispered, "Can we give her away, too?"

"I heard that," Clara called out over her shoulder.

"But you can't hear the friggin' phone?"

"I'm all set," Paul closed the cabinet doors. "We'd better hit the road. Curtis, I couldn't have gotten all this together without you. You too, Lawrence."

Curtis fisted his palm and bowed with humble Kung Fu respect, while Lawrence high-fived Paul. Joe hefted a couple carriers out the door, as Peggy performed one more head count. Being that the van was not air conditioned, she was relieved that it was a cool morning for their trip, before the onset of the muggy, summer heat.

Paul climbed into the back of the van and sat with the cages, while Peggy sat up front beside Joe. In her lap, she held two additional carriers. Travelling down the Garden State Parkway, Peggy relaxed for the first time in months and gazed at the passing scenery: apartment buildings, car dealerships and strip malls eventually gave way to fallow fields and woods, and then pastures green with clover, timothy, alfalfa, and the first shoots of corn.

She rolled her window down and closed her eyes, breathing deep gulps of the sweetly-scented meadows. She felt as if she, herself, was being released from a cage. Soon, her spirit felt as light as the puffed clouds above them. This was the garden state that she'd heard so much about, and had longed to find.

Even Joe, listening happily to the truckers over his CB unit, seemed to unwind behind the wheel, as the traffic fanned out behind them.

Crouched just behind Peggy, Paul looked out over the passing landscape, too. Every now and again his glance fell on Peggy's half-turned face as she looked out of the window. Her hair pulled back in a casual braid, he was struck, again, by how pretty she could look, in that offbeat, unassuming way of hers. Wisps of hair blew back from her face as she looked out over the countryside. Her rapt expression and contented smile made Paul wonder if this was her first time touring this part of the state. He could have started a conversation, but he didn't want to disturb her communion. Instead, he leaned back into the sunshine streaming through the window and closed his eyes. He was grateful for the breather, and the lush scent of fresh-mown fields.

The AJ Egg farm gladly took in all of the guinea hens. They believed that the introduction of exotic, pickled quail eggs might be the perfect addition to their product line. It was a thrill for Peggy to watch the guinea hens, after being released into a thirty-foot round chicken-wire pen. The owner told her that his sons would move it around certain times of the day, in an adjacent pasture, so the hens could scratch and dig. It was such a far cry from the cramped hutch in the shelter's back yard.

The Tilden Chicken Farm had agreed to take on the shelter's chickens and Rocky G., since their own Bantam Randy had lost interest in his hens. The old rooster had taken to sunning himself on their porch for most of the day, not even bothering to crow at dawn. The family felt it might be time for a bit of new blood. To Peggy's relief, the family planned to let the old rooster spend his days pretty much any way he wanted, as he'd served them and their hens, very well.

After Paul gave the farm's nesting coops a look-see, he praised the family on their pasture-raised chickens.

"Well," Mrs. Tilden shrugged, "when chickens are happy, they lay more and better eggs."

Peggy released the shelter's brood chickens into a large aviary adjacent to the pastured coops, so that the chickens could get used to their new environs. It didn't take long before the hens were scratching and digging as if they'd been hatched and raised, right there.

"All right, how about that big Bantam, then?" Mr. Tilden said.

"You sure?" Joe asked. "He can be a handful."

"Oh, he'll settle in," Mr. Tilden insisted.

Even Paul hesitated. But, it must have been the fear of being saddled with the bird that finally overtook his own conscience, because he nodded to Joe, and the two young men hauled Rocky G.'s cage out of the van and set it down beside the aviary.

The rooster snatched at Paul's tie through the wire, emitting a sinister garble of angry clucks gurgling in his craw.

"Good lookin' feller," Mr. Tilden admired the bird. "Knows it too, I reckon." Before they could stop him, he opened the cage door.

The rooster sprang out in a flurry of ruffled feathers. Looking twice his size, he crowed loudly. Even the Tilden's big Holstein cow stopped chewing her cud and looked over the fence at the bird.

Mrs. Tilden reached into her apron pockets and tossed out a handful of cracked corn. In the flash of an eye, a dozen hens flitted to the corn from all corners of the adjacent field. Startled, Rocky G. flapped his wings, but he surprised the humans by promptly scratching for corn among his new harem. He didn't even notice Randy, the Tilden's retired rooster, when he shoved his old comb into the mix.

"Whew," Joe whispered to Peggy and Paul. "I'da lost that bet."

"You and me both," Paul admitted.

 Chapter 57

The van backfired down a dirt road toward their next stop—The Ensminger's Dairy Farm.

Although Peggy had liked both fowl farms, she especially liked the dairy farm. The warm, rich, sweet bovine scent enveloped her like a comforter, as opposed to the chicken coops, which smelled a mite sour. Even though she preferred the slow, soft-eyed cows, she felt that she could be very happy living on either farm. The idea of working out in the open, tilling her own garden, walking Lucky along the streams...

She sighed at the thought of the dog, again. It had been awhile. Spring fostering had kept her so busy, she'd barely thought of him, and that bothered her. She watched the farmer's two German shepherds romp through the barnyards, while Paul and Joe released the last group of hens into the coops.

How happy Lucky would be here, she thought, and the idea tugged at her heart. How she would love to see him unchained, free to run and play. She wondered if anyone ever played with Lucky, even though she was fairly certain of the answer. Part of her wished she could simply kidnap him and bring him to a farm like this one, so he could know happiness, if only for one sunny afternoon. Would Harrison even notice his dog missing? With concentrated effort, she pushed thoughts of both out of her mind. What was the point in torturing herself?

The agricultural school at Rutgers University was their last stop. It was located further south, outside of Jamesburg in New Brunswick, about a stone's throw from a tributary of the Raritan River. Being more southerly, the weather was a bit warmer. The old poplars on campus had already greened out, towering over white dogwoods, blooming in profusion along grassy meadows dotted with grazing sheep and horses. As they approached the campus, Peggy caught sight of gas lamps, like the

ones in Upper Farroway, lining cobbled paths around the brick buildings, festooned with banners for upcoming graduation ceremonies. Everywhere, silken flags emblazoned with a Scarlet Knight waved in the
breeze.

"So Doc, this is your old stompin' grounds!" Joe called out. "Sweet."

"Yeah," Paul murmured, looking out the windows.

"I thought you went to school in Pennsylvania," Peggy said.

"I did. Completed my undergrad here first. Pre-vet."

"So, were you like, a rah-rah frat boy?" Joe prodded.

Paul half-laughed. "Not exactly."

Peggy spied on him through the side-view mirror, as he contemplat-
ed the campus. She could hear him softly humming a tune to himself.

"That your school song?" Joe asked.

"On The Banks Of The Old Raritan."

Peggy tried to picture Paul in a college fraternity. It was difficult
enough to picture him as a student. She couldn't imagine what it must
have been like, pursuing two degrees at the same time, then graduating
two years early—with honors, no less.

More so, she wondered about his closely-guarded past. He never
mentioned it, again, after that class talk where he'd admitted to the
students about "getting into trouble". She wondered what kind of
trouble he'd gotten into, that his family felt they had to disinherit him.
A drunken frat party? He hardly seemed the type. Watching him, it
was clear that he had a fondness for the university. He pointed out the
window.

"Make a left up ahead. See that spot? That's where they used to drag
Princeton's cannon every year, beginning all the way back to eighteen
seventy-five."

"Jeeze," Joe laughed, "you guys been rivals forever!"

"Over what?" Peggy asked.

"The whole 'mine's bigger than yours' contest," Paul admitted. "Every commencement day, the Princeton campus fired their prize cannon
in a pompous ceremony, so, of course, one year, the Rutgers football
team went down and stole it the night before. They painted it red and
displayed it right here in the courtyard. A real coup. Anyway, Rutgers
bragged about it, the Princeton robes demanded it back; Rutgers complied, and then stole it, again, next commencement eve. This went on
every year until Princeton got fed up and cemented the damn thing into

the ground. To this day, the week before Princeton's ceremony, Rutgers seniors go commando down there to paint the cannon red."

"Wow," Joe mused, "we're talkin' a hundred year war!"

"Right in our own back yard."

"Maybe it'll start a trend," Peggy murmured. "I mean, instead of cannon balls, people will settle their gripes with paint balls."

Joe laughed. "Yeah, right. Keep dreamin', Saint Francis."

"Pull in over there, I just have to find a phone." Paul pointed to modest brick buildings facing the courtyard. Joe maneuvered the van into a space, in front of a plaque that read: Voorhees Mall.

While Paul took a moment to check over the animals, Peggy got out and stretched her legs. Between blooming pink and white dogwood trees, she spotted a large, dark statue of a man dressed in what looked like Shakespearean clothing, covered with a green patina. It was surrounded by footpaths radiating outward to colonial style, brick buildings.

Joe got out and slammed the door. "Cool digs, huh?"

"Yes." Peggy studied the statue.

Paul hopped out of the van, papers in hand, and joined them. "That's "Willie the Silent", speaking of wars. It's a very special statue."

"What's so special about it?" Joe asked.

"Prince William, somewhere around the fifteen hundreds, led the Dutch rebellion, setting off the Eighty Years War. It was a gift to commemorate Rutgers' Dutch roots."

Joe shrugged. "So?"

"Oh, well, they say it's...enchanted."

"Whaaat?" With a dubious smirk, Joe crinkled his brow.

"Enchanted?" Peggy's curiosity was piqued.

"Oh yeah," Paul said. "They take it very seriously around here, the Scarlet Knights. Legend has it, Willie the Silent, whistles whenever a virgin passes by."

"Oh." Peggy blushed.

"Get outta here!" Joe laughed.

Paul rested a hand over his heart. "Truth."

"The statue whistles."

"Whenever a virgin walks by."

"Wait." Joe's brows knitted together. "Then, how come he's called Willie the Silent?"

Paul flashed a smile and walked away into the building. Joe looked perplexed another second, then he honked like a seal in laughter and elbowed Peggy. "Get it? Huh? Get it?"

Her cheeks hot, Peggy rolled her eyes, not sure if she should be embarrassed to get it or not get it.

In a few minutes, Paul returned and pointed down a service road. "Okay. Down that drive." As they walked back, he started whistling *On the banks of the Old Raritan.*

Peggy turned a narrowed eye to him, but he either didn't notice or chose not to. Joe snickered and nudged her, as she climbed back into the van. Paul remained poker-faced and continued to whistle, as Joe backed the van away from Willie the Silent.

Maneuvering down a few paths, Joe parked the van in front of corrals and livestock barns. Peggy got out and looked up the hill, where an ivy-covered, brick building flanked by imposing red oaks, held court over a large pond.

While Paul dealt with paperwork and talked with the supervising stockmen, Peggy wandered over to a wooden fence sprouting up out of the thistle beside the pond. In the adjacent meadow, a small flock of thickly-wooled sheep grazed. The sheep's muzzles and legs were black and their wool grayish, instead of the creamy white she'd always imagined. Reaching gingerly through the fencing to a browsing ewe, she was surprised to find its coat was coarse and greasy, instead of soft and fluffy.

The sun warmed her face, and Peggy breathed in the pungent scent of murky pond water, while she watched iridescent blue dragon flies flit above the water lilies.

"Nice, huh?" Joe said, and draped his arms over the splintered fence. "Ter loved this place. Used any excuse to come down here."

Peggy smiled. Of course, she thought, letting the thought of Terry waft over her with the breeze. She could picture him at the fence, gazing out across the water, just as they were, now.

The last that they'd heard from Irene, Terry had begun the most difficult phase of the therapy, and although making progress, he was often exhausted and in a great deal of pain by day's end. As always, Irene forwarded his love and appreciation for the crew's updates. But, there was never a personal message to her. That last phone call had been almost three weeks ago.

Betty continued to send him updates in cards, having everyone sign them before the mailman picked up their outgoing mail on Fridays. But, just as they had weaned the kittens and puppies off of bottle feeding, Peggy couldn't help but feel as if they, too, were being weaned off of Terry.

It had taken all this time, but Peggy found that she could think of him without the eviscerating sense of abandonment that had nearly crippled her in the beginning. Having been so absorbed in "holding the fort", the jagged edges of guilt had worn away and begun to scab over into the first rough patches of acceptance. She could see him, now, smiling at this fence with the sun on his face, and it didn't hurt nearly as much as it used to.

She looked at Joe and wondered if he still missed Terry as much. The pond reflected in his aviators, so she couldn't see his eyes. He exhaled a long sigh.

"Man oh man...this is the life. What in the frig we doin' poundin' pavement in Tin Can Alley, huh?"

Peggy half-laughed and shook her head. "I don't know."

"Okay," Paul's voice called out, and he waved to them.

Joe grinned at her. "This is the best part. You're gonna love this."

They rejoined Paul at the van and assisted in hauling out the goose and duck cages. It didn't help that the fowl were nearly full grown, and unused to travelling. Fat Denny, the big Chinese goose, thrashed inside of the cage, inciting his female flock to do the same, while Peggy, Joe, and Paul wrestled to keep from falling down under the sheer weight of them. Huffing and puffing, Peggy eased her side of the cages down at the water's edge, and unhooked her cramped fingers from the wire.

"Let's let them calm down first," Paul tossed off his lab coat, and wiped perspiration from his face.

"You fed 'em too much, Dillan!" Joe groaned, slowly straightening his back.

Shading her eyes with both hands, Peggy gazed out over the green-brown water, rippling in the breeze. "What a nice home for them."

"Canard Heaven," Paul agreed.

"Those are different." Peggy pointed out a few brightly colored, crested ducks that skirted the edge of the banks among wild mallards.

"They're wood ducks."

A few blackbirds with red patches on their wings, like the ones she'd seen with Terry in the dying Meadowlands, darted in and out of the cattail rushes, balancing on the sword-like stalks like trapeze artists. "What're those birds there?"

"Red-winged blackbirds. Marsh birds."

"Turtle!" Joe called out, and pointed to a muddy brown shell and head poking up from the reeds. "He's a big sucker."

"Looks like a snapper."

"Did you learn about the wildlife here?" Peggy asked.

"Just enough to get me in trouble. Oh, you mean the animals," Paul added with a wry smile. "No. I got hooked on birding at camp in the Poconos, every summer."

"Nice," Joe commiserated.

"Yeah." Paul picked up a pebble and skipped it across the rippling water. It sank three quarters of the way across the pond.

"Good one, Doc!" Joe said, and tried one of his own. It plopped a few feet from the bank. "Jeeze. I'm outta shape."

As Joe tried over and over to get a pebble to skip more than a foot, Peggy studied Paul. He sat on a boulder, the breeze brushing his hair from his eyes. Minutes ago, he'd been cracking jokes, but now, he seemed to fold inward, contemplative and unapproachable. Sunlight sparkling on the water, rippled in reflection on his face; illuminating a young man deep in thought.

It reminded her of the times she observed Terry gazing out the back window, his eyes following a flock of geese as they flew south, towards a horizon that only they—and he—could see.

"Counting the days?" she murmured aloud. Startled, Paul looked at her. "Sorry. I didn't mean to...I mean...well, it's almost summer."

He looked away with a small shrug.

Peggy wished that she'd kept her mouth shut. She knew better than to cast into his private waters, but, she was bothered that he hadn't answered her question.

Honk! Fat Denny broke the quiet, poking his bill on the cage wire, his interest fixed on the water.

Joe laughed. "I think we got a thumbs up from the peanut gallery, Doc."

The ducks and geese had calmed, and quacked amongst themselves. Paul slipped off of the boulder and nodded to Joe and Peggy. "Let's do it."

Together, they lifted the cage doors. For a split second, none of the fowl moved. Fat Denny poked his neck out first, and then with a rush, they plowed into each other in a mad plunge into the water, splashing and honking wildly.

"Boooorn Free," Joe sang off key, his arms open wide, "as free as the wind blows..."

"Will they be able to fend for themselves?" Peggy asked Paul.

"They get some feed from the school initially, but they tend to adapt fast. The school'll collect any eggs to keep the population in check. They're good study, for both the Ag side, and as a behavioral comparison with the wild natives. But we—I mean, you, have to make sure not to make this a regular dumping ground, or you'll wear out a thin welcome. It's lucky they have a study going."

"'Til there's a law, man," Joe shrugged.

"Keep pressing the town for an ordinance against selling farm fowl at Easter, and keep up the education talks in the schools." He picked up a cage and walked it to the van.

Peggy watched him walk away and thought to herself, I have to get used to this—watching him walk away—back to the EVC, back to his own world, and this is what it will look like. Then again, she thought with a skip of her heart, the EVC was only twenty minutes from the shelter. What if she could arrange to borrow Paul once or twice a week, for the out-of-shelter talks, just like they'd borrowed him for the past five months? Surely, as much as Paul was looking forward to getting back to his career, surely this might be something that he'd consider! Especially if it was only once or twice a week? If they paid him? That way, they could continue on as they were—almost.

She wondered who their next intern would be. Maybe Paul would even take it upon himself to train the new intern; maybe he would stay on, just a bit longer. Her spirits brightened suddenly, thinking about the options.

Joe tried skipping one more pebble across the water, but it bounced once and hit Fat Denny's broad, feathered butt. The goose honked loudly and flapped up in the air about a foot, splashing down into the water, scattering the others.

"Sorry 'bout that, buddy!" He joined Peggy. "Didn't I tell ya you'd love it? Man, I envy the doc. Bein' down here, every day. Can y'imagine?"

"It must have been nice."

"Yeah. No, I meant when he splits with us. To come down here after Memorial Day? To head up a new bio-somethin'-somethin'-research-somethin' whatever department. And that's just one of the offers he got."

Peggy looked at him blankly. Seeing her expression, he looked over his aviator shades at her.

"What? Didn't he tell ya? There's like, a biddin' war over him."

Peggy's heart stop skipping and sank like a stone. "No. H-he didn't mention that. Next week? It's only May. He's with us until June."

Joe peered at her. "Where you been? He's been pullin' double duty up at the EVC, shavin' off time from his deal with us. You knew that, right?"

Peggy suddenly felt as if she'd been sucker-punched. "Oh. Right. Right." Too embarrassed to admit that she was clueless, Peggy stared out across the water. No wonder Paul had never complained about the long hours. He'd been bartering for his freedom!

"I don't know how he did it," Joe added, folding the collapsible cages, "but, it was smart, that's for sure. Doc Caldwell says he's the youngest to nab this kinda offer. Six figures to start! Man, I shoulda studied harder. Or graduated."

Peggy watched the ducks and geese floating around, inspecting their new home, an hour and a half away from the rat race and a dead end street. She bent over and picked up the last cage. With leaden legs, she reluctantly walked it to the van, under gathering clouds.

On the return trip, Paul manned the wheel and listened to traffic reports. Leaning against a pile of tarps in the back, Joe had fallen asleep with his mouth open and snoring.

Peggy vowed not to say a thing about what Joe had told her. First, because she was hurt that Paul hadn't told her about it, himself. Secondly, she was mad. How could he just walk away without so much as a word to her, after everything that they'd been through? She felt as if she'd been slapped, even though the offense was only in her mind. It wasn't as if Paul was quitting. It wasn't as if his entire tenure hadn't been temporary, right from the start. He'd been assigned for six months, only. Yes, he was leaving a month early, but it was within his right to do so, and apparently sanctioned by the EVC. During his many rants, whenever he made cracks like, "five more months", she didn't realize then, that he meant it. Maybe it was wishful thinking on her part, that his growing involvement with the shelter, and his interest in her programs had meant something more to him than just punching a time clock. Maybe she was mad, not just because he didn't tell her, but because she'd come to depend on him, more than she cared to admit.

It's your fault! You can't trust anyone! You know that!

Peggy nearly gasped aloud. For a long time, her warning voices had lain dormant, but now, with the imminent danger of having to fend for herself again, they'd reawakened.

It is my fault, she acquiesced. I knew this day was coming. I didn't want to deal with it. I need to let go and move on. But, how? Her internal, backseat critics fell silent. It didn't surprise her. She'd become used to their fickle presence, of late. She thought hard. Well, what would Terry do? The answer came so easily, it seemed silly. He'd call the EVC and ask for another intern. Yes. I'll call the EVC and arrange for his replacement. Crisis solved.

She felt better for the decision, but couldn't quite ditch the hurt she felt.

"Listen," Paul said abruptly, and turned down the radio. "I know it's been wild lately, and if I'm tired, you must be, well, I can't imagine, because I have never, in the past five months seen you take a day off."

"Oh, well, I-I can't, you know that."

"Why not?"

"After five months you have to ask?"

"The place wouldn't fall down if you took a day off. Last time I heard, seven days a week without overtime is considered against the law, at least in some states."

"You did, too."

"Only these last couple of weeks."

"Well, you know it's the only way to keep the place together."

"No, I don't know that. The place would run fine without you—"

"Thanks a lot."

"—for two days a week!" he finished his sentence with a pointed tone. "And, it's a *compliment*, by the way. I'm not suggesting you abandon ship. Just lift the anchor, now and then. You've managed to get a sinking vessel not only back on an even keel, but sea-worthy. The crew can sail her just fine, now. You've done a good job."

Peggy stared at her folded hands in her lap, feeling as if she was back in school, sitting outside the principal's office.

"You know what the burn-out rate is for your job?" he asked, finally. "One year. You may need to last longer than that."

Peggy jerked her head up and glared at him. "He'll be back."

"Have you spoken to him?"

She clamped her mouth shut and looked out the window, her skin prickling with anger. She knew full well what he was suggesting, and she didn't want to hear it, not from him, and certainly not now, when he was the one abandoning ship.

"Terry will be back," she said through clenched teeth.

"Peggy, all I'm saying is, whatever happens, take some time out for you. You need to do that, because...right now, you're all they've got. The crew needs their captain ready for battle. And you can't do that if you're burned out."

Feeling a stab at her conscience, Peggy realized she was behaving like a petulant child. Paul wasn't deliberately trying to hurt her. Whatever his reasons for not divulging his plans to her, he was now kindly laying the groundwork for his own departure, weaning her off of him just exactly the same way they'd weaned the orphaned animals, just as she suspected Terry had been weaning her off needing him, too. The only snag had been one of her own doing. Her voices were right. It was her own fault. She'd let down her guard. She'd become attached.

"Thank you," she said, finally. "I'll take some time off."

"Good."

It was quiet a few moments, and then Peggy took a breath. "What about you? Are you going to take time off before you put on a six-figure suit?" When he glanced at her, she shrugged. "Joe told me."

"Oh..." he said, and shifted in his seat. "It depends. I...I haven't decided which of the offers I'm taking. I've been weighing the pros and cons of each, and there's a lot to think about."

There. You see? She scolded herself. No conspiracy. No betrayal. No ambush. He's just a guy confused about his future, too. "Well, I'm sure you'll pick the right one."

He glanced at her. "In the end, it's really not up to me."

"With your credentials? I'd think you could do anything you want."

"There are only so many opportunities and a lot of talented graduates."

"What-what offers have you had?"

He didn't answer her right away. "There's a surgical post at AMC, in Washington and one up in Buffalo. Both are top notch, and I'd be heading trauma centers. A lot of admin desk work. But then there's the vet school, UC Davis, in California, with a huge research department. They've expressed an offer that's pretty tempting, along with a couple others."

"Cal-California...?" Peggy repeated, feebly. Good gosh. She thought New Brunswick was a far throw. But D.C.? Buffalo? California? What did he leave out, Africa?

"It's a hell of an opportunity, but there're drawbacks, too. A research position, it'll be even more desk work than New Brunswick. On the other hand, it's twice the money Rutgers is offering. And, it'd be a big change."

Peggy thought about that. "Maybe change is what you're looking for."

He was quiet a long moment. "Maybe. Listen, I want to ask a favor. Not that you were planning one, but, I don't want a party or anything, okay? For my last day, I mean. Which is next week, by the way. I'd just appreciate it if you didn't. And, Caldwell's going to be expecting your call about the possibility of picking a replacement."

"I was-I was planning on doing that," she fibbed.

"Good."

After the silence between them stretched into miles, he turned up the volume on the radio, listening again to traffic reports. Peggy couldn't help but notice that he pushed the van's engine just over the speed limit. Not enough to draw radar attention, but enough to cut short the trip by about fifteen minutes.

Peggy watched the countryside slowly blur into beige and brown subdivisions, then scab over into two-story residential neighborhoods, which in turn collapsed into strip malls and used car lots, that metastasized into the industrial desolation along the turnpike.

Clouds had overcast the sky as they approached the rusted outskirts of Newark, and she felt herself sinking back into the gray, wondering who in their right mind wouldn't choose Rutgers and its beauty, over such urban sprawl? Better yet, if given the choice, who wouldn't flee it all for sunny California? If she had a choice, she would. She rolled the window up, shutting out the noxious, oily odor of diesel. The van skirted around acres of industrial waste, which ran headlong into the worn out tenements and foreclosed shops, that had become all too familiar to her; the downtrodden, beaten path that led the way back to the shelter.

Chapter 58

"Whaddoo you mean we can't have no party?" Betty demanded. "Who do he think he is?"

It was the Wednesday before Memorial Day weekend, and flags were up all over town, flapping in defiance of the forecast calling for thunderstorms. Peggy felt just as turbulent inside, as the atmospheric pressure, outside.

"He-he just doesn't want a party. I promised."

"Perhaps we're all the party 'e can stand," Clara suggested.

"That bites," Joe pouted. "He's always out partyin'! He just don't wanna party with us."

Whap! Betty smacked Joe over the head with the newspaper. "What you been told 'bout gossip?"

"Ow! Hey, can I help it I hear things out there? People got loose lips, okay?"

"What-what gossip?" Peggy tried to sound nonchalant.

"Fer once, the toad's not 'alf-baked," Clara informed them. "I've got it on 'igh authority, the plebe's been seen at some swishy-posh soirées of late."

"Told ya!" Joe sneered.

"Well, we should respect his wishes," Peggy said, finally.

"I still say it sucks."

"He didn't say nuthin' 'bout a present," Betty pointed out.

Joe sat up. "That's right! Screw him! We'll get him a friggin' present!"

Peggy smiled, despite her own inner tug of war. Aside from not having the heart to nix their enthusiasm, it bothered her to hear about the young vet's escapades around town. She didn't know why it should. It only made sense that he would rub elbows with his own kind. What she couldn't figure out, though, was when he'd found the time!

She forced the aching, vaccuous feeling in her chest back down. She just had to get through these next two days. All she wanted from the good doctor, now, was a letter of recommendation from said Dr. Paul Hayward, VMD-PhD. She planned to attach it to Terry's grant application. Paul had promised to deliver the letter to her, by Friday—just before he flew the coop.

Over the next forty-eight hours, the shelter broke its own record in successful adoptions, so Peggy did not have to broach the euthanasia bugaboo on Paul's last day. They had also received enough donations to make a few repairs to the place. Peggy should have felt ecstatic. After all of the chaotic days, the sleepless nights, not to mention the sweat, blood and many, many tears, the shelter had not only survived the winter, it had begun to regenerate up out of the ashes of misfortune. Better times were ahead. But still, Peggy felt let down by Paul's departure.

At eight o'clock, Friday night, she sat before the front window, gazing down towards the dreaded cellar. Paul still hadn't come up. She shivered and felt herself fold inward under the weight of a half-forgotten, yet ever-present shame. Paul had long since dropped his cloaked invitations to "come downstairs" and check out this, that, or any number of the projects that he'd set up for the shelter. He must have wondered about her litany of excuses. She couldn't remember when exactly, but one day, the invitations stopped, much like the country's many invitations to Clara for a hero's banquet, after the great war. Except, that I am no hero, Peggy reminded herself and stared at her shoes, feeling miserable.

"Here he comes," Joe said, over her shoulder.

Peggy jerked her head up to the window. Curtis and Paul appeared from under the overhang. Peggy ducked away and tried to calm her racing heart. Before long, she heard the front door open and close. Over the woofing dogs in the kennel, she heard Paul give Curtis a few last pointers, as they examined the dogs for the last time together.

At last, Paul opened the office door. The crew bent over their work, appearing busy. Peggy looked up from the grant application. "And the verdict is?"

"Looks good out there. Curtis is giving Balzac his last dose of Dichlorvos. You might see a few round worms in his stool, over the next day or so, but that should be it."

"Thank you."

Joe stretched to his feet. "Toodles ready to go downstairs with his bro's?"

Paul pulled out a churring young raccoon from a cage and examined a bald spot on its tail. "Yes. Scab fell off. He'll fuzz out."

"I'll take him down, Doc."

"Hang there for a few, will you? Make sure there's no scrapping?"

"Ten-four." Joe placed the kit in a carrier and walked out past Curtis, who was drying off his hands. "Hey, man."

"Yo."

Peggy watched Dr. Hayward and his protégé examine the office cats, one final time. Curtis had never mentioned it, but Peggy could tell that Paul's departure was not easy for him. He'd not come in with a new word for three days, and his proud, placid face seemed long and drawn.

All too soon, the rounds were finished, and Paul turned to face her.

"Well, that's it." He handed her his notebook. "You're supposed to hand this in to Caldwell, along with your review."

Peggy handled his notebook as if it was made of glass. "Yes, I have an appointment with him, tomorrow."

"Any idea who our new medicine man gonna be?" Betty asked.

"Caldwell keeps that pretty close to the vest," Paul replied, "but ultimately, it's up to your manager, here."

Peggy smiled feebly. "I don't know why. How am I supposed to know who to pick?"

"He'll cull the herd, but he wants you in on the final top three, because you're going to have to live with the guy."

"Good point," Betty said. "Could end up bein' a match from hell. We done lucked out wiff you, that be a fact."

Paul and Peggy shared a wry smile. He closed his medical bag with a snap.

"Okay. To recap; the dogs are all up to date with vaxes, boosters, and worming. Trudy is putting weight on both front paws, so she's good to go for adoption. Just tell any prospective owner she's got terrier acne issues that might flare up across her back from time to time, and she'll need follow up with a vet for a pow-wow on allergy meds. Jake's ears are clear, but let any adopter know that he's prone to yeast infections. Curbing sugar and yeast in his diet, it can easily be kept under control. Boris is ready for adoption, too. That laceration's healed up well."

He turned to Curtis. "You'll want to work with him when it comes to commands. An adopter needs to know how to control a dog that large, and one who tends to want to be the boss."

Then, he addressed Clara. "As always, the cats are in great shape. Our burn victim, here, is going to need a special home after what she's been through." He pet a partly bald, shy black cat through the cage bars. "She should go to an indoor-only household. Calypso's going to need eye drops for another week, both eyes BID, then just a squeeze of Lacrilube once a day after that for about a week or two. You'll know. If you wouldn't mind, let Curtis practice once and again so he doesn't lose his touch?"

Clara nodded. "Not likely that. 'E's got the gift, but o'course."

Paul rested a hand on Curtis's shoulder. "Any last questions?" Curtis shook his head no and shifted his eyes to the floor.

The buzzer sounded. Betty sniffled into a tissue and hit the button. "Yeah?"

"Doc?" Joe's voice sounded worried, over the intercom.

"Yeah, Joe."

"Can you take a look at this down here a sec?"

"Everything okay?"

"I just think you oughta check it out."

"On my way." Paul snatched up his medical bag and hurried out the door. Peggy watched him go, the plastered smile on her face fading.

Paul trotted past the runs and headed down under the overhang. He ran his day's itinerary over again, in his head. What had he overlooked? Had he jumped the gun reintroducing the raccoon kit? He ruled that out. They were litter mates. Outside of a hissy fit, he didn't expect any real issues. The opossum's facial lacerations had healed, and he'd removed the stitches, leaving virtually no scar. The squirrels, wild rabbits and the songbirds were ready for release at the refuge, as well. What had he missed?

He ducked under the Low Duck Head sign and stopped short. Someone was leaning against the doorjamb. His eyes adjusted to the shadows and he saw it was Joe, a cocky grin on his face and a screwdriver in his hand.

Paul heard the crunch of gravel behind him and looked over his shoulder. The entire crew approached and ducked under the overhang. Peggy brought up the rear.

"Okay, what's up?" he said, cautiously. He glanced at Peggy, who stood with her hands behind her back, a sure sign that she was nervous. She wasn't looking at him, though, she was looking beyond him. He followed her sightline and swiveled around to look at the cellar door. For a moment he was confused, but then realized something new had been added to the door. A polished, bronze plaque, and it was inscribed:

The Paul J. Hayward, VMD-PhD Surgical Unit. In honorarium.

Paul blinked back his astonishment. From behind him, he heard the slow build of applause. He turned, and a flash went off. Peggy lowered the Polaroid camera and busied herself with removing the picture.

Betty shoved her way to the front and embraced Paul in a bear hug. "C'mere, you!"

Joe clapped him on the back with a snorting laugh. "Gotcha!"

Clara grasped hold of his tie and pulled him down to her eye level, and then gave him a peck on the cheek. "God speed, vit'riny."

Curtis bowed, Kung-Fu style.

Paul looked past him to Peggy. "You promised."

"You said no party. You never said anything about dedicating a wing after you."

Joe handed him a bottle of Irish whiskey wrapped in green ribbon. "Maryann's bedroom is fat, man! Salute!"

It took Paul a moment, but he finally found his voice. "If you think I'm wasting this on christening this place, forget it." He raised the bottle of whiskey in toast, and directed his gaze to Peggy. "To the shelter and her crew. Let's party."

The radio in the office blared rock n' roll. Over Dixie cups of Irish whiskey, Mountain Dew and chocolate-frosted doughnut holes, the crew regaled Paul with their favorite "Doc Hayward" memories. Peggy popped off Polaroid photos as they each acted out the stories, quoting and imitating him, mercilessly.

Peggy noticed that Paul laughed the hardest of them all. More than once, she caught him looking her way, and she made sure to smile for him. It wasn't easy. How on earth were they going to cope without him? Even with a new intern, it would not be the same, and she knew it. Would the new vet agree to partner with her out there in the community? Would he even be any good at it? Could he charm the Ladies Who Lunch, even half as well? Who was she going to turn to when…

"…apology."

Peggy looked up from the photo in her hand, and found Paul smiling at her over his Dixie cup. "Sorry?"

Betty lifted the camera from her lap and pointed it at them. "Say cheese!"

Peggy caught Paul holding up two fingers behind her head, just as the flash went off.

"That be the one!" Betty laughed.

As the crew carried on over the photos, Paul sat beside Peggy. "As I was saying, before we were so rudely interrupted, I owe you an apology. You really pulled it off."

"Well, it was their suggestion. When I told them you didn't want a party…"

"No, I meant managing the shelter. It's because of you, this place survived. You even beat the euthanasia stats. I didn't think you could do it, but you did."

"Well…then I owe you an apology, too. I thought all you cared about were the stats. Every day you showed up, I hoped you'd quit. But you never did."

"I never quit. Hope you don't." He peered at her closely, without apology.

Peggy could barely breathe under his scrutiny. He leaned closer, and the music seemed to muffle around them, for what seemed like an eternity, and then he handed her a napkin.

"You've got icing on your chin."

Another flashbulb popped, and Peggy snatched the napkin from him. "I'm surprised you told me," she said, feeling her cheeks blush, as she wiped at her chin.

"I almost didn't."

"So Doc," Joe said, waving a wet Polaroid picture dry, "what's your fave shelter memory?"

Paul's eyes darted to Peggy. "That's a tough one. But, I'd have to say… my first day."

"Ya kiddin' me? That was like, nutszoid!"

"Yes, it was."

"I best git Curtis home," Betty said with a reluctant pout.

Paul stood. "I have to get going, too."

"Aw, c'mon, Doc! It's early, man!" Joe beseeched him.

"I've got an exit interview with the EVC."

"Bummer! So, where ya off to after that?"

"I haven't decided yet. Depends."

"That's the kinda probs ya want, though, right?"

From the corner of the room came a resounding burp. They all turned to find Clara in the corner, with the bottle, a tipsy smile on her face. "I beg pardon."

Joe rolled his eyes, then helped Clara to her feet. "C'mon, Bubbles, time to call it a night."

"Pfft. In my day, we'd see the sun come up!"

"In your day, the dinosaurs were still here."

"Take my arm, Missus Croft?" Curtis offered, with a gentleman's bow.

"Thank you, young man," Clara patted his arm, dressing Joe down with a frown. "Why can't you be more like your brother, here?"

"Dillan..."Joe whined to Peggy.

Peggy folded her arms across her chest and spoke with the authority of a mother hen. "Thirty-five miles per hour, straight home, and wait there until he gets in the door."

"Yes'm," Curtis assured Peggy.

"Thanks, Curtis."

"Ha. Ha." Joe retorted. "I get it."

As the trio passed Paul, Clara stopped. She looked him up and down. "'A true professor can nivver distinguish himself more n' encouraging a clever pupil, for the true comets are among 'em in the stars.' Linnaeus, if you please."

"I'll remember that, Clara," Paul said.

"Weren't talkin' to you." Clara thumbed to Peggy and Curtis. "To them."

"Of course," Paul laughed.

Curtis bowed deeply to him. "Fulgurate, Sifu." His head held high, he walked out without another word.

Joe looked to Paul. "What'd he just say to you?"

"I have no idea."

Joe shook Paul's hand. "Fleas on ya', Doc."

"Back at 'cha, Napper."

"C'mon, Brunhilda, get your broom, let's go."

"God bless!" Betty sniffled and stuffed a pack of candy Camels into his lab coat pocket. Blowing her nose, she hurried out.

The crew walked out through the dim, quiet kennel of dozing dogs and after the front door closed, Paul turned to Peggy.

"So."

"So." Peggy echoed and looked at her shoes.

"Any final questions?"

"No."

"Mind if I ask you one?"

"Sure."

"Why won't you go downstairs?"

Peggy stared at him, caught between the emphatic tick-tocks of the clock on the wall.

"You had that plaque put on the door for me," he said, "but you never once came down to see what I was doing. I could have been conducting whacked-out, gruesome experiments for all you knew."

"I-I trusted you."

"Bull. You don't trust anybody, least of all me."

"What? I-I can't-I don't believe you're…"

"What are you afraid of?"

Peggy's mouth clamped shut, and a shiver coursed down her spine.

"Is it me?" Paul asked, finally. "Were you…are you afraid of me?"

"N-no."

"No?" He moved towards her.

Peggy backed up and bumped into the cages. "No!"

"I don't think you're being straight with me, or yourself."

By this time, he was standing close enough for her to smell the day's chores on his skin. She moved away, stammering. "Who-who do you… you don't know what you're…"

"Let's cut to the chase. I know why you won't go down in the cellar."

Peggy couldn't look at him, trying to push her words out without gasping. "Then why did you ask?"

"Because, I wondered if you'd be honest."

"If I'd be…how-how dare…you don't know anything about-about me!"

"Enough to know that I've been on both ends of the same whip you've been on. Both ends. You know what I'm talking about, don't you?"

"No, I-I don't," she whispered hoarsely.

"I think you do." He leaned in closer to her. "We both know that until you walk down those stairs—face it, once and for all—you'll be running and hiding for the rest of your life from every son of a bitch who picks up your scent, and they will. They'll keep hounding you, until you figure out that you're the one holding the whip. Nobody else. Now, you can either face it or keep flagellating yourself like some twisted martyr or—"

Abruptly, Peggy shoved him away, her face hot. "Get out!"

Paul stood his ground. "The place between where you were a minute ago, and where you are, right now, that's where you need to be. That's where there's nothing to be afraid of, anymore."

"Get out." Peggy's voice cracked.

He pulled an envelope from his jacket pocket and tossed it on the counter. "The letter of recommendation for the grant. For the shelter. That, you earned."

He picked up his medical bag and paused at the door, as if debating something, then finally pulled a small card from his pocket. He set it on top of the letter. "This, will help earn the rest." He turned, and left.

Peggy's heart hammered in her chest so hard, her whole body shook. She heard the Jag shoot up the driveway and zoom off, the sound of its departure stabbing her, deeply. She massaged her sternum to ease the pain, but it didn't help. She paced the cluttered office, so full of laughter just a few minutes ago, feeling as if she'd been struck. All that remained now was to shatter, like glass, all over the floor. But, it didn't happen. He hadn't hit her hard enough. She was certain that he knew it, too.

A surge of anger rushed her, and swinging her arm she swept her books and files off the counter to the floor. She stood over the mess, panting. How could he? How could he be so cruel? She paced back and forth through the papers, but she couldn't out run the stinging shame at her heels. Damn him! Damn him to hell!

What are you afraid of?

Peggy stopped at the back window and covered her face in her hands.

She wasn't sure what hurt the most; that he said what did, or that he was right. At last, she sank to the floor among the papers. Reluctantly, she picked through them, and found the card Paul had left for her. It was a business card for the Stillwater Family Counseling Center.

Anguish crawled up her throat until it breached the levee of her defenses. She hung her head and wept in great, heaving gasps.

Chapter 59

Crash!

"What?" Peggy jolted awake, blinded by searing hot sunlight glaring in through the open window. She squinted through puffy eyes at her surroundings. She hadn't woken in abject terror or confusion, but instead, knew exactly where she was; it was a shift in her pattern, of late. She took in familiar details of her room: the open windows, the locked door, Terry's recorder on her night stand beside the bed, the closet door hanging open, and the lights were still on.

Crash!

She rubbed her eyes and peered out her bedroom window, just in time to see a beer bottle lobbed over the fence into the dumpster with another crash. Cheers and laughter erupted above the incessant pounding of Disco Tex and the Sex-O-lettes emanating from someone's boom box. The neighbor's Memorial Day disco-barbecue had begun.

Peggy sat back on her bed with weary annoyance. She'd barely fallen asleep. The apartment had already begun to heat up, and that, after barely cooling off. She dragged herself up and into the bathroom to run a cool shower. Without a fan, it was the only relief to be had. She stood under the water and leaned her face into the stream. Worse come to worse, she thought, she could always camp out in the shower to escape the heat.

What are you afraid of?

Her eyes popped open and a searing shiver ripped down her spine. She slapped the faucet off. Breathe, just breathe, she coached herself. No more tears, no more! She pounded the shower wall with her fist. No more! She almost gagged, trying to swallow the painful lump in her throat. Once upon a time, she'd been quite adept at shoving it all back down, but lately, it was nothing short of exhausting. It took a few moments, but finally, the buzzing in her head subsided.

With time, Dr. Paul J. Hayward's PhD voice would subside, too, fading from memory, just like Terry's.

Peggy cradled her head in her hands. After all this time, the thought of Terry still twisted her heart. Why couldn't she let go? He had! It had been five months without so much as a peep from him.

Crash! Laughter. Crash! Crash! The sound of beer bottles smashing into the dumpster grew to an irritating crescendo.

She roughly wiped her nose, then yanked a towel off the rack, and dried herself off. She had no choice. There was no one to help her, anymore. She had to press on.

Expected at the EVC at noon, Peggy was meeting Dr. Caldwell before his own Memorial Day Bash, to discuss the next externship with the shelter. She'd been told there were three candidates to choose from, and as acting manager, she would make the final decision. If there was ever a time she needed to feel in control, it was today.

She reached in the closet and pulled out a gingham sundress and crinoline slip she'd picked up at the Good Will for two dollars. Squiggling into it, she used a hanger to zip up the back. She looked in the bathroom mirror and paused. Having lived in her uniform for six months, she'd forgotten what she looked like out of it. Although it was a different costume, it looked like the same girl, staring back at her. Even so, she wanted to go to the meeting looking like something other than a smelly dog catcher.

The St. Francis medal around her neck glinted in the sunlight. It looked out of place all of a sudden, as if it belonged to someone else.

What are you afraid of?

Peggy gripped the sink, knocking soap to the floor. It took several deep breaths to steady herself and shove Paul's parting words out of her mind. He won't be there, she reminded herself. He'll be long gone, off to wherever it was that he had chosen as his next stop on the way to his deification.

She heaved herself away from the sink and, despite the heat, pulled on a white cotton sweater over her exposed shoulders and arms. She paused before the mirror, one more time. After a long, considering moment, she unclasped the St. Francis pendant from around her neck and left it on the sink.

She wiped her eyes dry, snatched up a folder marked "Review of Dr. Paul J. Hayward, VMD," and headed out the door.

By nine a.m., the temperature had already reached ninety degrees in town. Flags hung limp in the steamy, breezeless afternoon, and with the few remaining shops closed for the holiday weekend, the deserted streets lay prostrate under the glaring sun.

If one lived in Uppah Farroway, the day promised to be a perfect summer kick off. Live jazz quartets scatted in gazebos amidst a backdrop of croquet and tennis matches. A delectable, hickory-smoked haze hung over the trees, as steak kabobs sizzled on grills alongside roasted corn and glazed halibut. Glasses clinked in the hands of linen-frocked guests beside hosted bars serving up Sea Breezes, Cape Cods, and chilled Chardonnay.

If one lived down in the valley, it was still Memorial Day, but of a decidedly different flavor. Sunbaked two and three-story walk-ups cooked in the heat-wave. Fans perched in windows and people either camped out on fire escapes, or if they were fortunate enough to have one, on shaded porches. Men and women nursed pitchers of lemonade and six packs of beer, while kids hosed each other off on parched lawns.

For those without a back yard or porch, the best bet to escape the heat was to pack a cooler full of fried chicken and potato salad, load down the station wagon and head for the shore—to Asbury Park, or to Atlantic City. If you had extra cash and a couple of teenagers, Seaside Heights and its colorfully salty, crowded boardwalk was a popular destination. Due to soaring gas prices, most valley residents opted for the next best thing: tailgate parties in community parks, where burgers and hot dogs caught fire in eruptions of lighter fluid. White boys in white tee shirts, pitched soft balls alongside crusty Italian men rolling Bocce balls. Puerto Rican kids swung stick-ball bats in back alleys, and the black kids opened fire hydrants to cool off.

Music blared everywhere. The Beach Boys, The Four Seasons and The Temptations crooned over battery-operated boom boxes, the new stereo-on-steroids craze that perched proudly on picnic tables in Brookdale, Watchung, Nishuane, and Clairmont Memorial parks. Nat King Cole's *Hazy, Crazy Days of Summer* aired continually over car radios; a perfect holiday anthem. The music almost drowned out the crash of beer bottles in garbage cans, across town.

Well, almost. Peggy flinched at the sound of shattering glass and hailed the bus, anxious to escape the radiating heat of the brick buildings. With a blast of hot air brakes, the bus pulled alongside the curb. Peggy climbed aboard and paused in disbelief. It was hotter inside the bus than on the street, and the heat was on!

"Don't axe," the bus driver lamented, and wiped sweat from his face with a handkerchief.

Peggy dabbed perspiration off of her own forehead with the sleeve of her sweater. "The Emergency Veterinary Clinic, please."

The bus driver peered around her, as if he expected to see a dog. "Two dollah."

Peggy opened a small, white purse and deposited two dollars into the fare box, then with downcast eyes, she walked past sweaty riders in muscle shirts and cut offs. Despite the heat, she felt much too self-conscious under their curious stares, to remove her sweater.

After a suffocating, sluggish, thirty-five-minute ride into West Hills, Peggy wobbled through the overheated bus to disembark. The bus driver mopped his brow and opened the door for her.

"Stay cool."

Peggy felt as if she might swoon, right then and there. Her damp dress clung to her back, but she mustered a feeble smile. "You, too."

She staggered down the steps, and the bus chugged away in a puff of sooty exhaust. Behind her, the EVC glared white under the blazing sun. She shielded her eyes. Images of Terry, Lucky, and her first meeting with Paul simmered in her mind. She gazed at the hospital, struck by how much smaller it seemed to her, now.

A live drumroll and crash of cymbals punctuated laughter behind the blue haze of barbecue smoke drifting over the packed parking lot. She peered through the hemlocks bordering the road. Party guests gathered around a small stage under the trees, and a live band began riffing a medley of popular hits. It was another EVC bash, no expenses spared. Early, Peggy hid behind the trees and observed the crowd for a good long while.

What are you afraid of?

All at once, Peggy felt dizzy and swayed on her feet. She bent over and inhaled slow, deep breaths, just like Terry had coached her that first time so long ago. I can do this, she told herself. Paul won't be here. All I have to do, is hand in my review of him, pick a new extern, and then I can leave.

The dizziness ebbed, and Peggy straightened up, even though her knees still felt a bit wobbly. She mopped her forehead and with concentrated effort, forced one foot after another, up the walk towards the hospital's entrance.

If nothing else, she cheered herself, it would be cool in there.

"Could it be any hotter?" Dr. Caldwell dabbed at his brow with squares of cotton gauze. "Transformer blew somewhere in town. Seems these new A/C units pull too much power. We've got an emergency crew on it, right now, trying to figure out how to turn the damn things back on. Please, sit down! May I take your sweater?"

"No! I-I mean, thank you, no, I'm fine!" Peggy pulled her sweater close about her neck.

He swept papers off of a chair and sat down opposite her. "Hate to be in such a rush, but let's get to it before something else melts down! The candidate I wanted to discuss with you…well, let's be frank. The one I'm hoping you'll give the slot to is Dr. Miller."

Peggy stared at the file folder in his hand. "Dr. Miller?"

"He's a fourth year, and his eyes are set on head of surgery, here at the EVC. I feel that a stint at the shelter will be a good rounding-out of his education, and then we could simply segue the second candidate into the slot at the end of Dr. Miller's term, if you like. I can spare Dr. Miller for three months full time, six if part time."

It took a great deal of effort for Peggy to keep her face from falling as low as her heart had sunk. She remembered Dr. Miller. He was the intern who'd talked so disparagingly about the shelter back in November, when she and Terry brought Lucky in for help.

"The second candidate," Dr. Caldwell continued, "needs no extra sell from me, his prior record speaks for itself." He handed her a second folder. "Of course, the decision is entirely up to you. Did you happen to bring Dr. Hayward's review?"

"Yes, yes." Peggy handed him her folder. "But I-I thought there were three candidates you wanted me to choose from."

"I'm sorry, didn't I mention? It's been a circus around here. As I'm about to possibly lose not one, but two of my top surgeons, I had to withdraw the third offer or I'd be short staffed. My fault, I apologize. If you want, I can call up another hospital and see what I can do."

"Thank you, it's all right, I'm sure that your choices are..." Peggy paused over the second folder. "Oh I-I think there's been a mixup."

"Pardon?"

"You gave me Dr. Hayward's hospital record."

"Yes."

"I...I don't understand."

Caldwell looked perplexed. "Well, he's...Dr. Hayward is the second candidate."

"Dr. Hayward?"

"Didn't you...didn't you know about this?"

"He said he had other offers."

"Yes, but he turned them all down. All except for the offer to head up surgery here at the EVC. Contingent on whether or not he gets the full time position with the shelter."

Peggy grappled with his words, trying to make sense of them.

"Say, do you need a glass of water? This heat is draining."

"No, no, thank you." Peggy gave the doctor a tremulous smile.

"He never said anything?" prodded Caldwell.

Peggy shook her head no.

Caldwell appeard equally flummoxed. "I see." He pulled on a pair of glasses and began to read Peggy's five month evaluation of Dr. Paul J. Hayward, VMD-PhD.

Peggy stared at Paul's folder in her hands. Whatever possessed him to turn down multiple, high paying positions in favor of another stint at the shelter?

What are you afraid of?

Peggy winced inwardly, her head swimming in utter confusion. Had Paul deliberately goaded her into rejecting him outright, last night? Why? It made no sense! Dr. Caldwell said that he'd applied for the position. If so, then why would he challenge her to a fight, the night before she was to choose? Why hadn't he said anything to her in the first place? And why, when he had worked so hard to cut short his tenure, would he eschew all the opportunities waiting for him, only to apply for a permanent position at the "town pound"?

She looked at Dr. Miller's folder in her other hand. To be fair, she opened it. Dr. Caldwell wouldn't have offered Miller's services if he wasn't confident about his abilities. On paper, Dr. Miller seemed to be an entirely different person than the one she'd met back in November.

He came off as another smart, talented vet with honors under his belt. He was not as honored a vet as Paul, but she could see why Dr. Caldwell had picked Dr. Miller out of his corral of talent.

Although Dr. Miller measured up on paper, Peggy couldn't forget his rather arrogant, boorish attitude upon their meeting. She paused, feeling a flush of heat under her collar. If she were honest with herself, that was exactly what she'd thought of Paul when she'd first met him. Feeing foolish and flooded with misgivings, she glanced up at Dr. Caldwell, as he perused her review of his protégé. She suddenly wished she could rewrite it.

Dr. Caldwell finally sat back in his chair and looked at her over his glasses. "I guess you've made your choice."

"Tie a yellow ribbon 'round the old oak tree, it's been three long years, do you still want me?"

Tony Orlando and Dawn's hit single rollicked in the background as a reminder that, despite the barbecue haze and iced-tea laughter, it was Memorial Day Weekend, a time to remember those lost and still missing after the war.

A DJ spun records on the portable dance floor, while the band took a break. It was so muggy and hot though, that no one wanted to dance. Scattered under the trees, festooned with party lights, grills sizzled under chicken, burgers and franks. The air hung thick with delicious aromas. Behind the hosted bar, three bartenders perspired over blenders and martini shakers as they served the thirsty guests.

Peering outside the back door of the hospital, Peggy finally stepped out into the party, unsure if she'd be able to pick the young vet out of the crowd. Every guest wore white.

Soaked through with perspiration, Peggy felt foolish in her wilted red gingham party dress and sweater buttoned to the neck. Short-shorts, tube tops and a great deal of tanned cleavage made their season debut, here. Peggy pulled her sweater tighter and wandered around. She was about to give up, when she spotted him, sitting alone at a small table under a birch tree near the brook. He nursed a bottle of beer, looking haggard and unhappy.

Peggy was tempted to hop the next bus and flee out of town, but gathering her nerve, she stepped into the scorching sun. Aware of heads turning, she crossed the sundrenched yard. She hoped that by the time she reached the table, she'd know what to say to him, and that he would not embarrass her in front of the crowd. Between her jangled nerves and the searing heat, her courage all but melted away when her shadow fell across him, and Paul looked up at her.

Just then, the clinic's back door opened, and Dr. Caldwell rang a cow bell. "Roster is up!" Cheers erupted, as the wave of interns and guests rushed to the posted lists.

Paul stood up and faced Peggy, about to say something, when Dr. Miller strode up to them and cut in.

"Crazy son of a bitch!" Miller whipped off his sunglasses. "Hayward, what the hell are you doing?"

Paul drained the last of his Heineken and tossed it in a waste basket. "Having a beer. Aren't you supposed to be assisting Caldwell?"

Miller looked Paul up and down, disappointment dripping from his eyes. "He gave me and my surgical team the day off to celebrate."

Peggy squinted at Paul and noticed that even his cool, halcyon smile had wilted. Still, his voice was gracious as he addressed the young man.

"Congratulations."

Miller took a sip from a martini. "Not that I'm ungrateful. You've spared me the half year incarceration, but I don't get it. You maneuver an early out, and then pull this? Why are you throwing it all away?"

"Throwing what away?"

"Everything the rest of us have to beg, borrow, and steal just to get close enough to whiff. Come off it, Hayward. No way you'd turn down the AMC and USC, let alone helming this bridge, just to euth dog shit, unless…" his eyes flickered, "unless it was part of a bigger deal. What'd Caldwell promise you? First pick of the juicy government contracts when you wrap at the pound?"

Perspiration stung Peggy's eyes. She looked at Paul. Government contracts? What was Miller talking about?

"I have to apply like everybody else," Paul replied, evenly.

"Except you're not everybody else." Miller took another sip of his martini. "Are you…Dr. Striker?"

Paul flinched and then shot a look at Peggy. Miller turned his attention to her, too, and scoured her from head to toe. "Well, never let it be said the man has bad taste. I don't believe we've had the pleasure. Dr. David Miller."

"We've already met," Peggy murmured. The rising temperature between the two men made her nervous. She wished he'd just leave, so she and Paul could sit down in the shade and talk. And, she was so terribly thirsty. A wavy shimmer of heat undulated off of everything. Woven into the haze of charcoal smoke, solid objects shifted into ethereal ghosts. She blinked at Dr. Miller, as he, too, undulated in the heat. She reached for the table's edge.

"That's not possible," Miller smiled at her. "How could I forget meeting a fox like you?"

"Save it, Miller," Paul sighed, sounding irritated. "This is Officer Peggy Dillan, manager of the Farroway Animal Shelter."

Miller did a double take. "Oh, now I get it..." A smile teased at the corner of his lips, and he turned to Paul. "One last *slummer* fling?"

With one quick swing, Paul's fist socked Miller squarely on the jaw. The thwack of connection was followed by stunned silence, as the crowd swiveled, all eyes on them. Peggy watched the scene unfold in slow motion, hot air rushing through her head. Miller staggered backwards, and then he crashed into a table. Glasses shattered, and the table upended onto the grass.

Paul stood over him with clenched fists. Peggy thought she saw the downed vet smile, just as a heavy curtain of darkness enveloped her.

Darkness gave way to a spidery brightness. Peggy felt a heavy thumping pulse in her bones. Men's muffled voices drifted in and out...and a form hovered over her, struggling to come into focus.

"Pick up...pick up the pieces...pick up the pieces..."

"What?" Peggy heard her own voice croak.

"Can you hear me? Wake up." The voice was familiar.

The shadow slapped her hands, and she flailed her arms at it. "No! Please!" Hands closed around her wrists.

"It's okay. You're all right. Wake up."

Peggy fought the constraint, as the buzzing hum in her head receded into the pounding beat of music. She blinked, and the shadowy form sharpened into Paul.

He took in a deep breath and then released her wrists. "Okay?"

She became aware that she was in an office, on a cot. A fan pivoted back and forth across her. She felt something cold and wet behind her neck and tried to get up.

"Whoa, not so fast." Paul pulled an ice pack out from under her neck and applied it to her forehead. With his free hand, he held a glass to her lips. "Take a sip."

Peggy did and wrinkled her nose. "Ugh...salty."

"It's Ringers. You're dehydrated. Take another sip."

Someone knocked on the door, and Paul stood, blocking her view. She heard Dr. Caldwell's voice.

"Paramedics on the horn."

"She's all right, it was just the heat."

"A word, please."

"Yes." Paul glanced back to Peggy. "Keep the ice against your temple. Two more sips of the Ringers." He followed Caldwell out the door.

Still feeling woozy, Peggy tried to piece together the minutes before darkness had overtaken her. She remembered the suffocating heat, sweat pouring down her back under the sweater, and parching thirst. Then Paul swung a fist at her—no, not at her, at someone else...Miller. He hit Miller with his fist and knocked him to the ground.

A shiver ferried up her spine, as a motor kicked in and cold air blew downward, through vents in the ceiling. She reached to tug her sweater closer, but discovered, with a frightening start, that she was not wearing it.

The door opened and Paul stepped back into the room. Peggy hugged herself in an attempt to hide herself and the scars that crisscrossed her shoulders and back; scars she'd hidden under the missing sweater.

Paul gently pulled her sweater out from behind her head and offered it to her. It took her a moment to take it from him. He sat down in the chair opposite her and shut off the fan. Except for the pounding disco outside and the soft, cool air through the vents, it was quiet.

"You okay?" he asked.

"I'm-I'm sorry," she whispered.

"For what? That out there? That had nothing to do with you. I took the bait and I know better. If anything, I owe you an apology. Make that two. One for last night."

Clutching her sweater against herself, Peggy couldn't look at him. At last, she cleared her throat. "Maybe...maybe you were right."

"It wasn't my place. That makes me wrong." He pulled two folders off of the desk. "Caldwell suggests you take a look at these two candidates from Cornell. He could arrange a six month externship with either of them."

"But I-I already signed your contract."

"He won't hold you to it."

"I don't understand...are you withdrawing your offer?"

"Caldwell is. He was going to pay my two-year contract, but, with me looking at a year's probation, if you choose me, it'll be on the shelter's dime, not his. Miller's already been given the senior surgical slot, Caldwell won't renege on that and he shouldn't. Look, I don't know these two guys from Cornell, but they're more than qualified."

"Probation? But...you're not an intern."

He averted his eyes. "It has to do with a pact I made with Caldwell, a long time ago." He offered her the other folders. "You ought to look at these guys."

"I don't need to look at other candidates."

"Peggy..."

"I made my decision. I want you. To-to be the shelter's vet."

"You sure?"

She met his familiar, unwavering gaze head on. "Are you?"

The muffled sound of laughter and bass thumping the walls punctuated the standoff between them.

"Why did you turn down those other offers?" she asked. He averted his eyes and massaged his hand. She searched his face, trying to read him, when suddenly, something dawned on her. "What are *you* afraid of?"

His eyes flicked to her. Clearly, he hadn't expected her to turn the table on him. "It occurred to me, that signing on to be a desk jockey and answering to a bunch of suits might not be the smartest move on my part, since I...don't exactly play well with others." He paused a moment. When he finally spoke again, he sounded tired. "There isn't much that scares me, anymore...except maybe the guy looking back at me in the mirror, every morning. I...spent some time in juvie. For assault. Long story. Long time ago. Reader's Digest version; Caldwell saved my ass...my life. I owe him." He looked at her. "On the flip side, what we—you and I—started, has potential in the long run, to turn into something substantial. And, being it's my name on the new wing, down there, maybe I have a problem with somebody else moving in and taking credit for it. But, this isn't about me. You have to do what's best for you and the shelter."

"Is it too late to add an arbitration clause to the contract?"

He suppressed the barest hint of a smile. "With respect to world peace, it's probably not a bad idea."

"When can you start?"

Chapter 60

"I don't know why I'm even here."

Peggy gave the counselor a shrug. With a quick sweep of her eyes, she took in the small, dim office of the Stillwater Counseling Center. The walls were adorned with a pastel blue paper and dainty bluebells in bud. All the shades were drawn. A few tulip-shaped lamps glowed warmly on tables in strategic corners. A copper desktop water fountain gurgled beside her. It was all meant to be calming, but Peggy felt vaguely disconcerted. The narrow closet door, just behind the counselor, stood open a crack; its interior dark, from where she sat.

"Why not start at the beginning?" The pretty counselor sat across from Peggy and balanced a note pad on her knee. The woman had introduced herself as Margaret. She sported a shag haircut and wore delicate pearl earrings. Her face was unlined, yet she embodied the serene air of age-old wisdom. Peggy felt the weight of Margaret's penetrating blue eyes.

"The be-beginning of what?" Peggy asked.

"Whatever brought you here."

"Paul gave me your business card."

"Paul?"

"Dr. Hayward." Peggy showed her the card.

"Oh, so your doctor referred you?"

"No, he's a vet. At the shelter?" Peggy shrugged. "I thought you...he seems to know this place."

"Oh. So, he's a veteran at the homeless shelter, downtown?"

"No! No! A *veterinarian*. He—*we* work at the animal shelter. I'm usually in uniform. This is my first day off."

"So, you're new there."

"Um, I've been there since Thanksgiving."

"Since Thanksgiving? That was seven months ago. And this is your first day off?"

"Well, there's so much to do!"

"Even God took a day off!" Margaret smiled.

"I'm-I know, but I'm not God."

"That's a relief, isn't it?"

"Umm...I guess so." Peggy frowned, again wondering why she was there.

"I'm not, either." Margaret smiled. "So. Dr. Hayward hasn't given you a day off since Thanksgiving."

"No, no, no! He's not my boss. He's in Chicago."

"Dr. Hayward's in Chicago?"

"No, Terry's in Chicago. The warden. He's on medical leave. He put me in charge."

"So, you're the boss."

"I-I guess. I mean, yes, I'm in charge."

"That's a big responsibility for someone so new."

"Yes."

It was quiet for such a long time, that Peggy glanced up at her. Chin in hand, Margaret waited, studying her.

"You said Dr. Hayward gave you our card."

"Yes."

"Why do you think he did that?"

"He-he picked a fight with me, on his last day. I got mad and asked him to leave.

"What was the fight about?"

"H-he accused me of being afraid! Afraid of him."

"Are you?"

"No."

Margaret gazed at her another long moment. All at once, Peggy was aware of her knee jiggling up and down. It took a concentrated effort to keep it still.

"Why would he think you're afraid of him?" Margaret asked, finally.

"Maybe, because he was locked up for assault."

"That would do it for me, I think."

"But, I didn't even know about all that, until after he decked Miller at the party, yesterday. Besides, he was just a kid wh-when that happened."

"Miller?"

"No, Paul. Dr. Hayward. When he was thrown in juvie. Miller's just a jerk."

"Oh. So, you're not afraid of *him*."

"Miller? No."

"I meant Paul."

"No."

"Even though he has a history of violence."

"He's not...he's not..."

"Violent?"

"Right. I mean, no."

"How do you know?"

Keep your mouth shut!

Peggy jumped, startled. Her knee began jiggling again. She had to cross her legs to stop it. "Well, I-I think I'd know the difference."

"You would?" Margaret prodded. "How?"

"Because...well, you can tell."

"How would you, though, if you're new, and don't know his history?"

"It's not a history...I mean, I don't know what his history is, but it's not like that. I mean, he-he's not…"

"He's not what?"

It's a trick! Keep quiet!

"What? I'm sorry, I didn't...what was the question?"

Margaret peered at her a moment. "He's not what?"

"V-vi-violent."

"So, you're *not* afraid of him."

"No."

"What are you afraid of?"

Peggy looked up sharply. "Nothing."

"Really? I never met anyone who wasn't afraid of *something*, before. What's your secret?"

Peggy clamped her jaw shut, tight. "I don't have any. I mean, I don't have one."

"Wow. Almost everyone I've met has at least one. You must be a saint!"

Peggy felt hot under her collar. "Why are you-are you trying to make me mad?"

"Are you?"

"No!"

"You said it made you mad, when Dr. Hayward accused you of being afraid."

"Well, yes."

"Does feeling afraid make you mad?"

You better keep your mouth shut!

"Look, I-I didn't come here to talk about me!"

"Why did you come here?"

"I told you. He gave me your card. Why do you keep-why are you-I just don't want to end up in a another fight with him, anymore, that's all!"

Shutup!

"But, you're not afraid of him."

"No!"

"What is it you're afraid of, then?"

"I don't know! *Nothing!*"

"Nothing?"

Shut-up!

"What? No! I just told you, I'm not!"

"You're not? Then, why did he give you the card?"

Shutup! Just shutup!

"Why don't you shutup and just leave me alone!" Peggy's shout richocheted off the walls, and she found herself on her feet with her fists raised. Instantly, she jerked them behind her back, trembling from head to toe. "I'm-I'm sorry! I didn't mean you, I—I meant..."

Margaret nodded. "I know."

Peggy's knees suddenly gave out and she flopped back down into the chair.

"Keeping all that stuff bottled up takes an awful lot of energy, doesn't it?" Margaret said kindly, then smiled. "Ready for round two?"

"No."

"Liar."

Peggy jerked her head up. It was Margaret who'd said it, gently, but clear as day, her eyes reflecting a deep-seated understanding of something that Peggy couldn't quite grasp.

"I take it that's what the voices in your head call you, in between floggings?" Margaret asked, finally.

Peggy's mouth felt suddenly dry.

Margaret sat back in her chair. "Now, do you still have no idea why you're here, or are you ready to talk about it?"

"This...this is abuse."

The women of the Uppah Farroway Women's club gasped collectively, their manicured and gloved hands fluttering to blood-red painted mouths. The image projected onto the screen showed the bleeding, pus-weeping lacerations that crisscrossed a dog's boney back. The poor creature hung his head in abject terror, looking at the camera with sorrowful eyes.

Peggy turned slightly away from the microphone to clear the catch in her own throat. "And abuse comes in many forms."

Seated at the overhead projector, Paul switched out the photo for another. A half-bald cat looked up at the camera, its exposed skin red and oozing, scalded from burns, its left eye swollen shut.

More moans and exclamations of shock erupted from the audience.

Peggy winced, too, even though she was familiar with the image. She heard a woman somewhere in the second row openly weep.

"I'm sorry. I know these pictures are hard to look at. But, I don't know what's worse, seeing their suffering, or the fear in their eyes, when we try to help them. It's even harder to hear the statistics—the reasons why people do it. One study says this, another that. Some blame poverty, some blame ignorance, some blame drugs and alchohol, some even blame the rise in violence on TV, but the truth is, we're all to blame."

Peggy took a moment to collect her thoughts, then looked up again to the crowd. "We arrogantly walk our dogs off leash where, in the blink of an eye, they could chase a squirrel into the street, in front of a car, or attack another dog, a cat, the mailman, our neighbors, all in a heroic effort to protect us—their family, their pack. We declaw our cats, and then let them outside where they can't defend themselves or even escape danger by climbing a tree. We allow our unspayed cats and dogs to roam free, causing a crisis of overpopulation in shelters that requires weekly, sometimes daily euthanasias, nationwide. We're too busy to take the time to train our dogs. Instead, we chain them outside, all day and all night in all sorts of weather, alone, where they pine away in loneliness. These social pack animals want and need companionship, a companionship that we deny, because we find it inconvenient. They mess up our house, our clothes, our stuff. We walk past stray cats and dogs picking through garbage on city streets, while kids throw snowballs at them and don't even think twice about it, because, well, it's just a dog.

"We allow the wholesale breeding and sale of puppies in Midwest 'puppy mills', without caring about the ruination of the breeds from irresponsible breeders trying to make a buck, never mind the conditions of the animals' housing and resultant health issues, because we all want a Yorkie, Chihuahua or Golden Lab for under a hundred dollars. We bet on greyhounds confined in cages from birth, allowed no social interaction, and then when they've outlived their usefulness on the track, we allow the owners to kill them. We allow our legislators to define animals as property, to do with as we see fit—and we—as a society allow our courts to classify such cruelties, as you've seen evidence of here, today, as a misdemeanor. We say nothing. We do nothing. There is no one else to blame."

Peggy's voice wavered. The audience barely stirred. She took a shaky breath. "Above all, we are to blame, because we know where it all begins. It's no secret, anymore. The studies are out. It's public knowledge. It all begins the moment a hand is raised in anger. Most especially, against a child. A seed is planted at that moment, and a vicious cycle takes root. When we do nothing to protect that child in harm's way, we foster a legacy of abuse that's handed down, like an heirloom, from one child to the next, creating generations of hurt, anger and loss. Every single photograph of animal abuse that you saw here, today, can be traced back to a child having been subjected to hurtful, humiliating, soul-killing neglect and abuse."

Unable to swallow the lump in her throat, she glanced to Paul.

He'd been listening, raptly, but started, when he heard a cough in the audience. Then it seemed to dawn on him, that she needed him. He cleared his throat and stood up.

"I think Officer Dillan makes an important point about responsibility. As a veterinarian, I am at the end of the line in this runaway train of societal failure. I can only try my best to stitch the animals back together. But the deeper wounds, the scars that you may never see, they're the ones that I can't make better. And what's frustrating, is that it need never have happened to begin with. The issue of abuse—no matter if it's animal, mineral or vegetable—it's everyone's problem. And it's one that can only be solved with education, involvement, and compassion. Any questions?"

Not a hand was raised until Peggy raised her own.

"I-I have a question." She looked out to the audience. "How many of you would sign a vet's petition, calling for stronger laws that-that might help put a stop to what you saw up on the screen today?"

"Petition?" Paul repeated.

Peggy raised her hand high. With an expanding wave of murmurs, one-by-one, hands rose, until a sea of them filled the auditorium.

Chapter 61

"Rebellion to tyrants is obedience to God!" Clara cried, shaking a fist at the ceiling like a zealot. "Thomas Jefferson!" she quoted to Paul. "Your forefathers knew sommat about revolution!"

Peggy lifted her chin at Paul. "Told you they'd vote for it."

He leaned in to her and lowered his voice. "Didn't Joe say the FBI has a file on her?"

"Where *is* Joe?" Peggy asked Betty. She knew full well he'd vote for a petition, too.

"He be half-past hot water, he don't git his sorry butt in gear. It be aftah noon!"

"Miss Peggy, which law you wanna metamorphose first?" Curtis asked.

"Impounding a dog for its own protection on our own call."

Betty chortled aloud and broke open a fresh pack of candy cigarettes. "Terry done been aftah that fo' years!"

"Yes, I know," Peggy smiled.

"Then you also know," Paul said, "that there's a reason it's not a slam dunk on the books. Hackles are raised when you start making noise about regulating anything people consider to be their rights."

"Where does it say anyone has the right to beat up a dog?"

"Wherever an animal is considered personal property, and there are a hell of a lot of places and people that still think that way. You're talking search and seizure, without the search. We had a little war over that with her people, two hundred years ago?" he thumbed at Clara.

"We gave that 'un to you, by the way," Clara sniffed with a haughty air. "Too much trouble, you lot."

"I'm not saying seizure without the search part," Peggy countered. "It's just, if the symptoms can be cited as prob-probably abuse..."

"Probable."

"Probable abuse. And, that if we even suspect it, then whether or not the owner is present, if there's enough circum-circum…"

"Circumstantial."

"Circumstantial evidence. Then, we should have the right, the duty to protect the animal."

"It's going to take more than regurgitating what's already been on the books to change a statute."

"Yes, but now it's a law here in Jersey, that says children can be taken from a siutation, even if its just suspected they're in danger. Don't you see? It's the same thing. There was a law on the books, but there was no way to uphold that law, only just a couple months ago."

"Catch twenty-two," Curtis murmured.

"Exactly."

"But animals are not children. Hell, in certain religious circles, they're not even considered on a par with humans," Paul said.

"I should say not!" Clara declared. "Damned little ankle-biters! The scourge of Mother Earth's woes!"

"For the record, I was referring to the animals."

"What if a whole community disagrees with that philosophy?" argued Peggy.

"Mine or society's?"

"'Scuse me, ain't no policy of my Lawd!" Betty huffed.

"What if a whole town, what if a whole county gets behind a petition saying that animals ought to be on a par with humans?" Peggy argued. "At least when it comes to protecting them? And, what if a judge agrees?"

"That's a lot of ifs," Paul conceded. "Either way, challenging the law is going to ruffle a few feathers. You know that, don't you?"

Peggy knew exactly to whom he was referring. Just the thought of going up against that monster, Harrison, sent a thrill of a shudder searing down her spine. She shook it off. "Maybe it should. Wh-what could he say about a law meant to protect abused animals, w-without compromising his image in the eyes of the whole town?"

"If he's elected to Town Council? A *lot*."

"I say yay." Betty held up her hand.

"Yay, and I raise you a dare," Clara tittered.

"Condign!" Curtis said.

"I take that as a yay?" Paul ventured. Curtis nodded.

"We don't gotta wait for baby toes," Betty blew her nose. "He's for anythang that'll legally let him slap somebody wiff a fine."

Peggy raised a brow to Paul. He acquiesced with a shrug.

"Just one suggestion. You might want to hold off in presenting anything to the town officially, until after you hear about the grant. You can't afford to be blind-sided by anyone with an agenda. Speaking of which..." he pulled a list from his pocket and handed it to her.

"Oh please, not a euth list already! I know we're crowded, but—"

"It's not a euth list. It's my wish-list from back in January. I thought I'd put in a request first, before funds get divvied up when you win the grant."

"Ain't that countin' chicks befo' they hatch?" Betty suggested.

Paul pulled out his wallet and laid a dollar on the counter. "I'll wager it's a sure thing."

"I say!" Clara tittered gleefully. "Joker is wild!"

"Doctah," Betty counseled him, "might wanna start yo' downhill slide wiff a quarter."

"I'll stand by George Washington." He winked at Peggy.

Peggy felt a rush of warmth inside that took her by surprise.

"Oh, well, th-they're right," she stammered. "Save your dollar. It's already a done deal. The day you signed up for another go-round with us, the crew decided that if we win the grant, the first check goes to setting up your own surgical suite, for real."

Paul looked to Betty. She nodded with a smug grin.

"Oh. Thank you," he said, finally. "Wait a second. What's the catch?"

"Catch? Why would you think there's a catch?" Peggy feigned insult, but Paul folded his arms across his chest and narrowed his eyes at her. She fidgeted in her chair. "There's no catch! It just makes sense. If we have our own surgery, then we could do spays and—"

"Whoa, whoa, whoa! *We?*"

"Well, you, and Curtis can be your assistant! See, I was thinking that people might be more inclined to adopt if they don't have to pay extra later for...wait! That's it! Why should we wait for the grant to come through? What if we put an adoption ad in the papers right now, offering a free spay or neuter for any animal adopted?"

"Tabling the fact that I have no surgical suite down there, you're asking me to neuter every animal that walks in this door? For *free?*"

"No, just the ones who walk out. And if-if we raise the adoption fee from twenty dollars to-to forty-five let's say, it's less than fifty, then that would give us extra money. I don't think an adopter would mind the raise, because the spay would be done for them, for free. By any comparison, it's a huge savings!"

"And I'd be thumbing my nose at fellow vets whose bread and butter revolves around getting paid to do those surgeries!"

"But, that's just it! At least forty percent of the animals adopted from shelters don't get neutered right now, no matter if they've got a contract like ours saying they have to or not. Those are only the ones we know about. We can't police it. Not really. With those numbers, hospitals can't claim we'd be taking away the bulk of their business." Peggy gestured to the kennel. "And this is the result. We get the brunt of those numbers and their litters. If it was state law, that all pets have to be neutered before adoption, how many less euths would we—would you have to do?"

"Forty-five dollars you say?" Clara considered it. "Cor, if they're shellin' out that sort o'lolly, you can be morally certain they won't be cheese-pairin' when it come to keepin' 'em, proper like."

"Again, you don't have the facility for it, now," Paul countered. "Where do you expect me to operate?"

Peggy took a breath. "On your graveyard shifts up at the EVC?" Paul passed a hand over his eyes and sighed.

Betty offered him the pack of candy cigarettes. "What the hay, you don't git no sleep as it be, now."

He tore open the pack of candy. "No promises, but I'll talk to Caldwell."

Peggy could have thrown her arms around his neck and kissed him. Her cheeks flushed hot at the thought, and she smiled from ear to ear, grateful to have him on her side and back at the fort.

Neither one of them had broached Memorial Day, his brawl, her scars, or their respective pasts. It was as if their tête-a-tête had never happened. It was an odd truce, a secret pact: "I won't ask, if you don't". Once a week, however, Peggy made the trek to Stillwater Counseling. She couldn't determine whether or not it was helping, but she and Paul managed to sidestep each other's mine fields during the day. That alone was worth the sliding fee. Still, every time Paul said "I'll be downstairs," Peggy couldn't look him in the eye. It remained the big elephant in the room.

As for the rest of the crew, they had been at once surprised, happy, and relieved at Paul's return. For one thing, they didn't have to suffer the "agida" of breaking in another green horn, as Joe had put it.

At first concerned with bearing the brunt of his salary, when Betty learned that it amounted to minimum wage only, she thanked Jesus for returning what she considered to be the back half of the shelter's cash cow into the byre.

To a casual onlooker, the imperturbable Curtis might have seemed unfazed upon finding his mentor back at work. With the exception of a very deep bow to his "sifu", he never said a word about it. More than once, however, Peggy caught the apprentice smiling to himself as he looked up words in his pocket medical dictionary, before hurrying downstairs.

With respect to Paul, Peggy didn't discuss the vet's deal, except to repeat what he'd said to her; he had made the decision with the belief that the shelter was a good investment in the long run. Joe, Betty, and Clara had laughed so hard when they heard that, they each needed a trip to the firehouse toilet.

As happy as they were about having him back, the moment Paul had left the room that first day back at the fort, Joe and Betty had groaned when Clara stuck out her hand, chortling, "Fair do's!"

"I can't believe you made book on him, like that!" Peggy had exclaimed.

Counting her winnings, Clara winked at her. "Insider tip."

"What do you mean?"

Joe swiveled around in his chair. "Hey, does Ter know 'bout the doc?"

"I-I don't know," Peggy admitted. Apparently, from the expressions on the crew's faces at the time, they hadn't thought to send word to Chicago, either.

"He musta known 'bout it," Betty declared, "'cause he be th'one hired Doctah DoRight in the first place."

"Yeah, 'cause Ter n' Caldwell are like this," Joe held up two crossed fingers.

Peggy felt a pang of guilt and consternation at the same time. It had been two weeks since Irene's last call and update. If he'd known about the deal, if he'd had anything to do with Caldwell's initial offer, why wouldn't Terry have let the crew know? Why wouldn't he have sent word to her? At the time, she had felt a bit irritated. On the one hand, she felt bad about not consulting Terry. It wasn't the first time she'd forgotten to consider Terry's opinion on a decision, but it was the first time that it bothered her. On the other hand, she was tired of second-guessing herself. At least, not in a way that made her feel like a rebellious child for not having consulted "Daddy" before inviting the boy next door over to help her with homework. What helped distract her from this uncomfortable notion, was the more curious tidbit that had burrowed its way up into her consciousness. That "insider tip" Clara had mentioned.

"Terry who?" Clara asked finally.

"Don't start," Joe sighed.

"It's moot, anyhow," Betty shrugged. "Deed be done."

"Still," Peggy acquiesced, "either way, we should let him know."

"I'll drop him a note, tonight. If we don't hear nuthin' by tomorrah, I'll call Irene, anyhow."

Joe flipped a coin. "Okay, two-to-one the doc quits before the fourth of Juuu-ly."

"Say what?" Betty squealed. "Labor Day, baby, Labor Day. Clara?"

"Pfft," The old woman dismissed them both. "Full term." She laid a dollar on the counter.

"No way! If maggot season don't get to him," Joe declared with a giggle, "the cockroaches will!"

"Hey, he just got back!" Peggy had laughed in disbelief. "Let's not give him any second thoughts!"

Outside, the dogs suddenly burst into barking, bringing Peggy back to the present. She'd been hard at work on the grant proposal and had taken a brief break, as her thoughts once again had drifted to Terry. She glanced out the open window. The van coasted down the driveway into the parking lot. "It's just Joe."

Betty glanced at the clock. "'Bout time! What gonna be his alibi, this time?"

"'E were prob'ly hiding out in the flicker palace to keep cool," Clara shrugged.

"Can you hold his head still, please?" Paul asked Clara, as he swabbed a tabby cat's ears clean with gauze.

"Not when he smells them curs, out there!"

With June's warm up, the crew kept the office door and windows open, along with the guillotine chutes in the kennel, which allowed cross airflow and unrestricted access to the breezy outdoor runs for the dogs. The drawback came with the endless scramble to shut the office door before the dogs charged inside and their barking upset the cats.

"Speaking of," Paul said to Peggy, "I saw an A/C unit out back in the storage room. Might be a good idea to put it up before July?"

"Then, you didn't git a good goggle at it," Betty said, as she tallied the ledger.

"*Hush* you bloody curs!" Clara hissed, trying to hold on to the squirming cat.

Frowning with concentration over her work, Peggy reached out a foot and flipped the office door shut, just as the dogs charged inside, barking riotously. The sound of the front gate clanging shut barely registered with her. She even managed to tune out the barking dogs and she didn't bother to look up when the office door opened, and Joe staggered in.

"That the biggest kitty litter you could git?" Betty chastised him.

"It's thirty pounds!" Joe snapped.

"You pick up the dog food?"

"Yes, *and* the kitty chow, *and* the newspapers *and* the rice! What the frig we still usin' BJ for, if I keep havin' to pinch hit?"

"Coulda got this cheaper at the Acme."

"And drive ten minutes the other direction, wastin' gas, when I'm already passin' the Shopwell?"

"Nevah mind that, when you gonna git that A/C unit up? Befo' hell freeze ovah, I hope?"

"Yes! Jeeze, don't I always get it up?"

"No comment," Clara said.

Peggy barely noticed when Joe tossed a yellow ticket onto the counter, until Betty snatched it up and hollered.

"*What* is this? You run a stop sign again?"

"Can I help it when I step on the brakes, nuthin' happens?"

"Because you ride 'em like a damn fool cowboy!"

"Brakes?" Peggy looked up at her own reflection in his aviator shades. "What do you mean the brakes? We just got them fixed!"

"Five months ago!" Joe yanked off his jacket and tossed it at the coat rack. It missed and hit the floor. He swiped at the perspiration on his forehead with his sleeve.

Paul looked around to Peggy. "He's driving without brakes?"

"What else is new?" Clara chimed in.

"If a certain monster finds out," Peggy said, "we could lose our insurance!"

"Which we only just got!" Betty reminded them.

"Insurance?" Paul repeated. "For Christ's sake, he could kill somebody!"

Joe slapped the summons book down hard on the counter, sending papers fluttering to the floor. "Thanks for being so freakin' worried about me, out there! Thanks a lot!"

He stormed out and slammed the door. The dogs exploded into barking in the kennel, but Peggy didn't hear Joe's usual "shaddap" in kind. She looked to Betty and Clara. They sat and stared at the door.

"What the hell was that about?" Paul asked.

"Ain't 'bout no brakes," Betty raised a brow to Clara, with a nod to the calendar. Clara noted the date and with a nod of her own, lifted the cat off the counter and put it into a cage.

Peggy got up and walked out into the kennel room, closing the door behind her.

Joe hauled on a guillotine cable with a rough yank, and it jammed in the tracks with a screech. He kicked at the door, again and again.

Peggy called out over the barking dogs. "Joe?"

Hearing her voice, Joe stumbled over the gutter and dropped his sunglasses. He snatched them up, but not before Peggy caught sight of a fresh black and blue shiner over his puffy left eye. Fumbling with the sunglasses, he was unable to cover it. He gave up and slumped against the fencing. He covered his face with his arm and shook with the force of his tears.

Peggy tossed dog biscuits out through the chutes and closed the dogs outside, as quickly as she could. After the room quieted, she walked up to Joe. "What happened?"

"The same ol' shit!" Joe blurted out. "He says he's goin' to his meetings, I find out he ain't. Every freakin' Memorial Day, it's the same freakin' thing! Six years Chris is gone. What's the point, huh? He's gone, man! He's gone! But I'm here! I'm his son, too, ain't I?" His voice cracked and he sank down to the floor.

Peggy knelt down beside him. In a moment she reached out a hand and rested it on his shoulder, then sat with him until his shoulders stopped shaking, and he was cried out.

Upon returning to the office, Betty and Clara looked up from their work, their expressions of concern speaking volumes. She found Paul back against the rear window, his hands deep in the pockets of his lab coat, his eyes hooded and drawn. She couldn't imagine the ladies would betray Joe's confidence, since they'd never once discussed Joe's past with her, but something in Paul's demeanor told her that he somehow knew, too.

"He-he needs a place to stay," she said. "My building has no vacancy. Does anybody have any ideas?"

Clara creaked to her feet. "Cor, if the bin lid's up to flitting, 'e can park 'is keister in the west wing of me 'ouse. I can't find it anymore, anyway."

Peggy watched then, as the old woman tottered down between the runs to the end of the kennel, where Joe sat on an upturned bucket, staring at the floor. Although Peggy couldn't hear what was said between them, when Clara patted his shoulder, he leaned into her and wept some more.

"Ain't that poetic justice?" Betty murmured to Peggy. "Maybe this be the straw that git his butt in gear. Ain't the first time he come in here like this, but praise Jesus, maybe it be the last."

Still staring at the floor, Paul cleared his throat and spoke up. "Between now and my shift at the EVC, I can help move him."

"That'll mean a lot to him," Peggy said.

Together they walked out into the kennel. When Joe saw them approach, he rubbed his nose on his sleeve. As he got up, he donned his aviator shades. "Yo', what's up?"

The front door opened then, and Curtis bustled in, calling out over the barking dogs outside. "Heads up. Y'all got company. A suit."

"I'll take it," Peggy said quickly. "Curtis, could you help Clara with the cats?"

"Yes'm."

"Joe, why don't you make a list of what you need from your place and we'll help you move, tonight."

Joe adjusted his shades and ran a trembling hand through his hair. "Cool."

"Speakin' of," Clara said, "get that frosty machine in the window before the dog days, eh?"

"Nag, nag, nag." He hefted up his pants and tried his very best to swagger back to the office, hauling on guillotine door cables as he went, letting the breeze back inside.

No sooner had he closed the office door behind him, when the front door opened and the dogs dashed into the kennel through the chutes, barking wildly.

Peggy clapped her hands over her ears and turned just as Harrison stepped over the threshold.

Chapter 62

Peggy found herself standing between Harrison and the office, with Paul, Betty and Clara directly behind her. Like a cornered animal, she stared at the man, wide awake; every sense on high alert.

Harrison stared back, his hawk-like eyes sizing her up. Six months ago, she would have wilted right then and there, but now, surrounded by her crew—her friends—Peggy refused to cower. It took great effort, but she deliberately folded her arms across her chest and noticed that his expression betrayed irritation.

When it became apparent that she wasn't going to liquefy into a quivering mass at his feet, he deflected his piercing gaze to Paul. Inwardly, Peggy sagged with relief, and when the familiar icy numbness began to thread its way up her legs, she fought it, focusing her attention on her own breathing, slow and steady.

"Dr. Hayward?" Harrison called out loudly over the dogs. "I'm surprised to find you, here." He looked about the noisy kennel, as if to elicit an invitation away from the noise. No one offered one, forcing him to continue to shout. "I came down to meet the new vet!"

"That would be me," Paul leaned against the center pole, blocking the man's way into the heart of the shelter.

"Really? Is this a permanent post?"

"That wouldn't be up to me."

"I would have thought your sights to be set higher."

"What..." Peggy's voice croaked out of her, and she cleared her throat. "What do you want?"

Talking back? Now you're going to get it!

Her courage was sucked out of her, as Harrison swiveled around to face her. She scrambled to remember what Margaret had taught her. Recite the alphabet and times tables, and it will distract you and help you remain grounded. Taking a deep breath, she recited in her head: A is for action. She held on tightly to the run fencing. Two times two is four.

B is for breathe. She struggled, but inhaled a breath. Two times three is six. C is for courage...

It felt like forever, before Harrison pulled his eyes from her and addressed Paul. "I've just come from a council meeting, and it seems there's been some tongue wagging about photos of a violent, graphic nature being shown around town, upsetting people."

"Good. Then we did our job." Paul shrugged.

"Oh?"

"Yes. Abuse is upsetting. Or it *should* be."

Under the flickering fluorescent light, Peggy focused her attention on Harrison's face, to see it as a collection of separate, small, harmless elements: a nose, two bloodshot eyes, two ears, a mole above his thin lips, and beads of perspiration glistening across his forehead. Peggy blinked at that. It was hot in there, for sure, but not that hot. Why was he sweating so much?

Shutup! Don't ask questions! You looking for trouble?

D is for dare, Peggy recited over the warning voices. Two times four is eight. E is for...

"How's Lucky?" Paul asked, point-blank.

Two times five is...

"Who?" Harrison rejoined.

F is for fibber. Two times six is twelve...

"Your dog."

"His name is Boy. Why is it, you people can't seem to remember?"

"H is for Harrison. Why can't you remember to take him in, at night?" Peggy's voice hissed out of her like steam from a pressure cooker.

Everyone gaped at her.

"Excuse me?" Harrison narrowed his eyes. "How would *you* know we don't?"

Peggy froze. What-what came after two times—what was it? Two times what is what?

Shutup!

"Mr. Harrison," Paul interjected, "If the town council has any question about our seminars, they can speak to me, directly. For your—and their—information, the photos used are forensic and part of an invited, educational program."

Harrison kept his eyes on Peggy, but said to Paul, "That doesn't address the questionable violation of privacy with a public exhibition of such graphic material."

Peggy began to perspire. She couldn't remember the next letter of the alphabet.

"The cases chosen for the *seminar*," Paul said, emphasizing the word, "are mine. They are a matter of public record, the names expunged and the cases settled in the courts."

Harrison's lips drew back in a polite smile. "I was referring to the photos of alleged animal abuse, Dr. Striker."

Peggy held her breath.

A dark cloud occluded Paul's eyes. "The name is Hayward," he said, flatly. "On my diplomas and in the courts."

Peggy took a faltering step back. The atmosphere had become charged, and she felt a heavy curtain of darkness begin to descend over her, just as it had that suffocating, blistering day at the EVC when Paul swung his arm back and...

"It's after closing." Joe's voice ricocheted off of the cinderblock walls. He stood sentry in the office doorway, hands on hips. Peggy latched onto his image like a lifeline. His polished brass badge glinted in the flickering fluorescent light, and his fingers rested on a holstered firearm on his hip.

Clara stepped forward and lifted her chin at Harrison. With an impish twinkle in her eye, she chirped, "Pop goes the weasel!"

Harrison looked between them all and raised his hands in feigned surrender. "Just passing on the council's concerns, not looking to join the debris field, Dr...*Hayward*." He turned to go, but slowed as he passed Peggy. His eyes raked her up and down before walking out the door, leaving it wide open.

Joe stalked past her to the door and slammed it shut. In one fluid move, he drew his pistol and pulled the trigger. A stream of water splashed down the door.

"Christ!" Paul exclaimed. "He could've nailed you for even brandishing that!"

"It's a water pistol!" Clara reminded them.

"It's implied threat."

"This is our house!" Joe shot back. "*He's* the implied threat! We got a right to protect ourselves. And, what's he jackin' off with the Dr. Striker crapola? What's his beef with you?"

"I wear white." Paul glanced to Peggy. "Forget it. Water under the bridge."

Through the ebb tide of roaring between her ears, Peggy heard the snarl of Harrison's car engine as it drove away. Sooner than expected, painful pins and needles tingled in her legs and arms. The rampant beating of her heart eased into a flutter, then slowed to a regular rhythm.

"Bridge?" Joe repeated. "What bridge?"

Peggy felt a gnarled hand on her arm and flinched. It was Clara.

"Best move on with it," the old woman said, and then turned to Paul. "And 'elp Billy the Kid there get moved, before 'e squirts 'is own eye out."

"Gotta clear out the van, first," Joe said and holstered his pistol.

"Hold it, Dick Tracy!" Betty bellowed and marched up to him. She yanked the water pistol out of the holster and wagged it at him. "You flash this, again, I'm gonna whoop you upside the head wiff it!"

"That's the thanks I get for savin' the day," Joe whined.

"C'mon, Starsky," Paul opened the door. He paused on the threshold and looked back to Peggy. His eyes searched hers. "We're okay to call it a day?" Peggy swallowed hard and nodded. "Okay. Lock this behind me and don't open it for anyone, until we come back."

He shut the door, and she could hear him rattle the doorknob on the other side. When she didn't move, Betty sashayed past her and slid the deadbolt into place.

"What wuz that all about?"

Peggy wiped the sweat off of her face and stared at the door, unable to wipe the image of Harrison's own sweaty forehead, and his lurid, scouring look, out of her mind. She opened her mouth, and was surprised that words came out, instead of vomit. "I-I'm not sure."

Perched in front of the office window, Peggy held a cold can of soda against her forehead.

"Don't fret about it," Clara said over her clacking knitting needles.

Peggy glanced up, then back out the window. "I can't help it. He's a monster."

"I was referrin' to your young cockeral."

"Paul?"

"'E's been 'round the block and knows which end's up, mark me. 'Specially when it come to bottom feeders like Mr. Magsman. 'E can do for 'imself in a scrap."

"Another insider tip?"

After a few moments of clacking knitting needles, Clara finally answered her. "Me Cat n' Cat Owner's Aid members got eyes and ears in 'igh places. Our Dr. Do Right does indeed 'ave 'imself a first rate pedigree. 'Course 'e were born to it. Old money. Sure it burns Mr. Magsman, and make no mistake, for the good doctor comes by 'is silver spoon, honest-like. Well, at least 'e's heir to it. 'Is sire's a right robber baron. Munitions, mostly. Now, word 'as it, 'is pater were never 'ome, what you call a globe trotter, and when 'e were 'ome, 'e dallied with workin' birds down in the projects. Tenements 'e owned, no less! As for 'is mum, third generation DAR. Proper lady, but you can only feign not to see billy-o for so long, as th'actress said to the bishop!"

Clara wiggled her brows at her for emphasis.

"You mean she had to..." Peggy pieced it together. "...see no evil, hear no evil?"

"Those were'nt the only rumors," Clara nodded. "There were never any public rows, but more n'once 'is mum showed up at 'ospital late at night—nasty bruises—claimed she fell down the stairs. Nurse phoned social services, on account she 'ad the cockeral with 'er, o'course. Right ugly scandal. Scruffy divorce. Caught in the middle? Young Dr. Dandy. 'E were the best and brightest up until 'e come of age, as they say, when all 'ell broke loose. 'E were only twelve when 'is own pater disowned him, because the lad testified against 'im during the divorce. 'Is mum stayed mum 'til she passed on. Now, some say that's the straw what broke the lad. Or, maybe th'apple doesn't fall far from the tree."

Clara shrugged. "Like 'is old pater in some respects, they say. Belly full of piss n' vinegar. In and outta borstal, or what you yanks refer to as reformatory, 'til 'e were sixteen. Pfft! 'Twas only matter of time before push came to shove. Prit'near killed one of the Big Brothers assigned to 'im, just for trying to straighten 'im out. It were all 'ushed up, of course. Would've been all over the papers, 'cepting 'is family owned most of 'em, at the time. Palms got the grease, to be sure. It weren't for the lad's sake, no, but rather the family moniker. That might've been th'end of it and 'im, and lips are sealed on the seconds, but seems it were a judge turned 'im over to Sir George Caldwell. Keeps it on the 'ush-'ush, does our Dr. Caldwell, but 'e funds a trust through the EVC. A home for wayward rapscallions, 'aving been one 'imself during depression. 'E were quick to see the scamp's mother wit. As for the lad, whether twas the scare of near takin' a life or, maybe just providence that somebody gave a tinker's dither about 'im, 'e turned full circus, after that. Night to day. I mean to say, a proper, pushing choir boy. Even changed 'is name to 'is mum's, cut the cord to 'is pater outright. Seems 'e come out trumps, or you might say," she grinned at Peggy. "Worth the wager. That's the scuttlebutt, any road. Quote me, I'll deny it, of course."

Peggy sat back, as the jigsaw puzzle pieces of Paul's secret life fell neatly into place. No wonder Margaret had grilled her so mercilessly about him. No wonder. As a therapist, she somehow knew. Peggy shuddered. What else did she know? She reached into Terry's old box of papers, and pulled out the frayed rope collar, Lucky's file and Terry's napkin note that said: "Look into Harrison BG".

"Clara," Peggy murmured, "what sort of scuttlebutt have you heard about Mr. Harrison?"

"Pfft! Everything what opens and shuts! But, you don't think a greasy by-blow like 'im wouldn't be right sharpish 'bout covering 'is tracks? Remember, 'e's a magsman—a politician; 'one that would circumvent God'. Shakespeare, if you please. T'isn't many of 'is green-welly brigade willin' to blow the gaff on 'im, I wager. Not when 'e keeps their larders full-stocked. Not much to be said for the likes of 'im."

Peggy was not surprised. What was it going to take to shake that monster's cast-iron countenance, in order to make a difference for poor Lucky?

You know.

Peggy shot a glance to Clara, hoping she hadn't heard. Clara measured a knit sweater against a shaved cat, her attention wholly on her task. Peggy pulled her knees up to her chest and wrapped her arms around them. No. I don't know, she protested silently. Still, she made a mental note to ask Margaret about it and shuddered, aiming an irritable frown at her own reflection in the window.

Chapter 63

"Okay, don't flip out! But, guess who called!" Joe panted, out of breath.

Peggy and Paul had only just arrived back from their last high school seminar for the school year, when Joe barreled out of the gate and across the lot to meet them, clearly agitated.

"Oh no," Peggy slammed the car door closed. "What does that monster want, now?"

She'd barely slept all week preparing and presenting seminars with Paul in the rush before graduation commencements. They had not only continued to present the abuse seminar, but Peggy took additional steps to promote it. She'd placed ads in a dozen area newspapers and pursued signatures and accommodation letters from shop owners around town. She knew full well that Harrison would get wind of it.

Paul eased a cat carrier on the hood of the Jag. "I wouldn't worry about it."

"Monster?" Joe repeated. "You mean Harrison?"

"What did he threaten us with now?" Peggy studied Joe's face. After weeks of raw steak compresses and Clara's alchemic nursing, his black eye had almost faded.

"Harrison didn't call. Doc's right, he knows we got his number, he ain't gonna stir up nuthin'."

"Then, who?"

"C'mon, guess!" Joe squealed, and snatched the carrier off the Jag's hood, escorting her towards the gate. Paul winced and quickly bent over his car, examining the paint.

"I don't know," Peggy began.

"Duh!" Joe apparently couldn't contain himself a second longer. He opened his arms wide and shouted. "Ter! Ter called us!!"

Peggy's heart thudded in her chest so hard she was sure even the firemen heard it. In a purely reflexive move, her hand reached for the St.

Francis pendant around her neck, and then remembered that she hadn't worn it since Memorial Day.

Paul joined them. "You heard from Terry?"

"Lookit her face, Doc, she don't believe it neither! Swear to God! Not his doctor, not Irene. Ter! Himself; in the flesh! Well, sorta. C'mon!" He ushered she and Paul through the front gate. "Bet's bouncin' off the walls!"

"It was right aftah you two left," Betty sounded almost apologetic. "Not more n' ten minutes!"

"He sounded fantabulouso! Didn't he, Bet? And guess what? He's outta the body cast." He turned to Clara. "That's a deuce ya owe me!"

"He done be graduated to braces," Betty went on, "and they got him on a walkah half an hour, three-four times a day. When he ain't bein' made to treadmill or bench press with them legs, he be in a wheelchair, but the good news be, he gonna be outta that hospital and home wiff Irene, by end of the week!"

Clara thrust her hand out to Joe. "That's a fiver, you owe me."

"You don't even know who we're talkin' about!"

Clara lifted her chin. "A bet's a bet, mister."

Joe waved her off and babbled again to Peggy. "It was like he was standin' right where you are, no kiddin'. Sounded just like himself. Oh, and guess what else? He didn't know about the doc. Yo' Doc! We told him how you stayed on, and he was like, 'Indeed?' Y'know how he always says, right? Indeed? Then he goes, 'Splendid', like he does, y'know? Splendid!"

Paul closed the medicine cabinet doors and turned to Peggy. "You didn't tell him?"

"I-I didn't think I had to, I mean, I was sure he had something to do with it."

"With my deal? Why would he?"

"I-I don't know." Peggy tried to grab hold of at least one thought buzzing around in her head. They were like hornets swarming for attack. She didn't know why, either, but her cheeks hurt from smiling.

Paul regarded her a second, then bestowed his own smile on the crew. "Well, it's great news."

"You said it, man!" Joe agreed. "It's as good as it gets! He didn't stay on long. He sounded tired. Didn't he sound tired to you, Bet?"

"Well, what you expect?" Betty turned to Peggy. "I told him, Lawd, Lawd, you was gonna spit teeth, missin' this here call!"

"Did he-did he say anything else?" Peggy asked.

"We was so fool tore up to hear his voice, truth be told, we wasn't sure what to say or not say. We told him how good things was goin', kept it nice and positive."

"But, we didn't let on it was too good," Joe jumped in, "'cause we didn't want him to feel like, y'know, outta sight, outta mind, like."

"Who?" Clara asked.

Joe heaved a sigh. "I want my dough back."

"It's just a question. Who are y'yammerin' on about?"

"You can remember the names of a hundred cats, but you can't remember Ter?"

"The warden, dear," Betty reminded Clara. "We be talkin' 'bout the warden."

"Oh, him! Where's he been?"

"Doc," Joe rolled his eyes. "You got any meds for that?"

Paul chuckled, but Peggy noticed that he glanced her way, again. She felt she ought to say something of a celebratory nature, but only one question pressed against her lips.

"Did he-did he say anything about-about when he's coming back?"

Joe clapped a hand against his forehead. "Jeeze Louise. We were so flipped out hearin' his voice, we didn't think about it."

The phone rang.

"I didn't even think to axe!" Betty admitted. "He'da told us. He knows we been waitin' on him all this time." She answered the phone. "Sheltah. Uh-huh. Six o'clock."

Peggy still wore a smile, but for the first time, she wasn't sure anymore if she could say that she'd "been waitin' on him all this time". She looked up at the calendar on the wall. It was the end of June. Terry would have mentioned coming back, if he'd been planning on it, any time soon. Gazing at his empty chair, she felt vaguely disconcerted. She couldn't see him sitting there anymore, the way she used to, when trying to comfort herself. His ghost had disappeared somewhere along the way, and she tried to remember when it had departed. She couldn't.

"Did he want me to call back?" she asked, at last.

"I dunno," Joe shrugged. "Hey, Bet? Did Ter want her to call him back?"

Betty hung up the phone. "Hmn? He didn't say nuthin' 'bout it. It be a real short call, 'cuz he wuz real tired, like Joe say."

Both phones rang at once and Betty swiveled around to work.

"I'm gonna swing by the station and check out a bite report." Joe donned his shades and swooped up the summons book off the counter. He headed out the door, and the dogs lept up from napping to bark at him. "Shadaaaaap!"

Clara counted her winnings and resumed cleaning kitty boxes.

Peggy rested her hands on the back of Terry's chair. She thought back to Joe and Betty's recap of the call from Terry. As if a breeze had winnowed over her soul, she felt a stir inside her—a shift, of sorts. What would happen, if Terry returned? So much had changed. Could she go back to the way it had been before? She'd held the fort for the warden, just as she'd promised, but at some point, it had become *her* fort. Her eyes came to rest on the thick grant folder and piles of petition signatures she'd gathered. She felt a sigh escape her lips. For now, Terry had his own mountain to climb. And, so did she. She and the crew had made it to base camp on that mountain. They'd survived winter. Things were looking up. Terry was on the mend. And Harrison, for whatever reason, had ceased harrassing them about the seminars. Only two more months until the grant deadline. She couldn't think of a better way to honor Terry's fight, than to plant his flag at the summit of this mountain, the one that he'd begun to build, by winning the grant for him.

Peggy sat down in Terry's chair and, with a steady hand, opened the grant folder to continue her work. It was a few minutes later that Paul sat down next to her and popped open a Mountain Dew.

"Everything okay?" he asked.

"Sure."

"And?"

"And what?"

"You want to circle around, one more time? What's on your mind?"

"Why do think anything's on my mind?"

"Oh, I don't know. Maybe, because for the past ten minutes you've been reading a piece of paper that's upside down."

Peggy righted the paper. "I'm channeling Curtis."

"C'mon. What's bugging you?"

"I-I'm worried about this stupid grant. I feel like I've been jumping through hoops. How does the town expect us to do what we do on the peanuts they toss us?"

"They don't. You know that already. C'mon, Peg, from here on out, it's just about keeping it together until he gets back."

She mustered a smile for him. "Yes."

"You worried about that?"

"About what?"

"Once more on the merry-go-round? Terry. Are you worried about him coming back?"

She averted her eyes. "He-he didn't say anything about it."

Paul pulled out another soda from the mini-fridge and wiped off the condensation with his handkerchief before setting it in front of her. "That's not what I asked you."

The phones rang.

"You think he might not?" Paul asked.

She shrugged. "I don't know."

"Would it bother you, if he didn't?"

"Doctah?" Betty called out. "It's th'EVC on line one. Need a update on the pyo you did last night?"

"I'll take it downstairs."

Peggy averted her eyes when he got up. She heard him walk out into the kennel, then out the front door. From her place at the window, she saw him head past the runs and disappear under the overhang. She listened until she heard the warped shove of the cellar door open and close behind him, and felt her spirits sink like a stone.

What are you afraid of?

She scrunched her eyes closed, too tired to work Margaret's timestable trick. Please, leave me alone. I'm tired. Tired of worrying, tired of trying, tired of feeling, tired of pretending that there's nothing wrong.

Mercifully, her inner enforcer took the hint for once and remained silent.

She dragged her attention away from the window and forced it back down to the papers in front of her. But, she couldn't concentrate. Paul's question nagged at her. Would it bother her if Terry didn't come back? She hadn't actually thought about it in those terms. She hadn't dared to, before. Now, maybe the question itself was moot. Was that what Paul was getting at?

She kneaded her eyes with her palms and took a long slow swig of the soda that he placed before her. Maybe he was right, in what he'd said to her back in May, on their drive back from New Brunswick. The worst was over. She wanted so much to believe that. And why not? They had steered the place through the worst of times, it was true. All they had to do, now, as far as she could see, was to sail the shelter safely through the summer. How hard could that be?

Chapter 64

"We're doomed!" Joe wailed. "Ain't no way we're gonna make it to the Fourth! We're gonna fry!"

Summer had officially arrived. Old Sol scorched the Tri-State area with a roasting blast of ninety degrees during the day, and a steamy eighty-five degrees at night. June had been unusually mild and rainy. But, now July loomed hot and sticky, and there was no question; summertime meant to make New Jersey pay for having paved over the woods and meadowlands.

To Peggy's subsequent horror, Joe hadn't been kidding about the season's bug infestation. From mosquitoes to cockroaches to maggots, Peggy considered bathing in DEET. Road kill pick-up became a skin-crawling affair, and they heard no end to the complaints from Joe. Even Dr. Hayward's stalwart reserve wavered when he had to minister to strays so infected with maggots that Peggy begged him to euthanize the animals as an act of mercy. How he managed to pull every one of the animals through their gruesome ordeals without losing his lunch was nothing short of astounding to her.

The cockroach numbers alone were the stuff of very bad dreams. Although Peggy always thought they were nocturnal creepy-crawlies, she found the beetles scuttling among the book shelves, and inside drawers and cabinets, in broad daylight! Due to the toxic danger, they could not spray insecticides around the animals, so Joe took on a loony determination to eradicate them into extinction, armed with only a fly swatter. He collected their smashed carcasses in an empty pickle jar, then challenged the crew to a cockroach count by summer's end. No one took him up on it.

"Is this thing even on?" Joe whined and pounded on the old A/C unit, lodged in the back window.

"Oh, quit makin' heavy weather of it," Clara growled. "What do you think folks did before th'invention of the Frigidaire?"

"They *died*!"

"Touch that thermostat you be dead, mistah!" Betty hollered. "It be set at seventy-eight fo' reason!"

"This is two hundred-percent sweatshop city, man! I can't hack it!"

"That unit's all we got and it already be on borrowed time."

Peggy fanned herself with a file folder. "I wish we could lower the thermostat, Joe, but Betty's right. The motor can't handle it, and we can't afford a new one."

Since the schools had let out for the summer, and with most of the county away on vacation, the out-of-shelter talks had fallen off the calendar, along with donations. At first, Peggy had worried that Harrison might have had something to do with the dwindling bookings. However, Clara's COACOA "eyes and ears" collected no scuttlebutt suggesting this was the case. It was just the ebb and flow of the season. At the moment, it was mostly ebb. Taking a hard look at the shelter's finances, Peggy knew that they needed to tighten their belts.

Perched on its makeshift shelf, braced with scraps of wood and duct tape, the little A/C unit vibrated, loudly, with an incessant buzzing that grated on everyone's nerves. A junkyard find, it was not only obsolete, it was technically illegal. It wasn't made for windows, in the first place. And, to run it any cooler was to risk burning out the old motor, which would surely start a fire and burn down the shelter. Unfortunately, the model had been discontinued, so there were no replacement parts to be had.

The shelter couldn't afford a new unit, because not only would walls need to be knocked out and new standard size windows installed, but the entire building would need to be rewired to support the larger BTUs. Peggy had no choice but to play it safe and keep the obsolete little unit at a setting closer to Bora Bora balmy. It was better than being hotter than hell.

"We better win that friggin' grant," Joe pressed a can of soda against his forehead. "I can't hack this."

"Quit your belly-achin'," Betty scolded him, "and go soak yo' head."

"Maybe that's a good idea Joe," Peggy agreed. "Go out back and help the guys cool off the dogs in the wading pool."

"Forget it!" Joe balked. "I just saw Jaws, man, I'm afraid to take a bath!"

"That explains the stink in here," Clara sniffed.

"Ha. Ha."

Peggy was sure that Joe's refusal to sacrifice his official image, by wearing his full uniform, including a vest, long-sleeved shirt, ranger boots and utility belt, didn't help matters, even if it meant keeling over with heat stroke.

Betty, on the other hand, wore flouncy, seersucker skirts and blouses, and Clara had taken to wearing a white linen tunic over cotton safari slacks and sandals. Paul still wore a tie every day, but even he was wearing short-sleeved white shirts. He only donned his lab coat for the public.

Despite Joe's constant complaints about the heat, Peggy never said a word about his being over-dressed because she, too, wore long sleeves and kept her collar buttoned to the neck. She was grateful no one questioned her about it, either.

By noon the day before the Fourth, most of Jersey had fled to the beaches. Since the holiday fell on Friday, it gave everyone a three-day weekend. Not a soul came down to the shelter. Even the phones were quiet.

"Don't let it fool ya," Joe warned Peggy. "When the first backyard cherry-bombs go off, we'll be swamped."

"Cherry bombs?"

"Startin' around six is when every dope with a stash of pinched gunpowder comes outta the wood work, and it's like friggin' 'Nam between here and Nishuane Park. There's a couple legits. Y'got Bloomfield, there in the park, which is pretty boss, then up the college off Mountain, in their football field. Hey, where's th'other one, Bet? Oh yeah, th'one over in Watchung. That's a biggie. The rest are all home grown, and I swear they get bigger every year. And there's always some bozos take their dogs to see the sparks, right? So we end up gettin' calls to find Rover and Puss-Puss when they freak out. Jeeze, the Fourth happens every year, howzzit nobody figgers to leave Rover home and just pop him a couple doggie downers?"

"Gee, I never thought of that, either," Peggy admitted.

"You don't count. Until your first year in, you're still a rookie."

"Say what?" Betty exclaimed. "First week workin' wiff you, I think her dues be paid in full!"

"Do we have enough medicine for all the dogs?" Peggy asked. "And what about the cats? Do they get some, too?"

"Wuuulllll..." Joe exchanged a glance with Betty. "Not exactly. I mean, you know the score. We can't afford all that dope."

"Then, what do you do?"

Joe exchanged another furtive glance with Betty.

"Oh fer cripes sake," Clara exclaimed, "what's the big whoop-dee-doo? We put beer in the feed!"

Peggy raised her brows. "You get the dogs drunk?"

"Just enough to take the chill off," Joe assured her. "It's okay, we got it down to a science. See, wine ain't no good for dogs—somethin' 'bout grapes—but beer...hops...that's okay. Not every day! We ain't pushers. Once a year it don't hurt to curb their 'tudes, y'know?"

"Helps me git ovah," Betty admitted.

"Yeah, and for the cats? We just leave the radio and A/C runnin' all night. Can't hear friggin' nuthin' over that hunka junk!"

Peggy buried her face in her hands. "I don't suppose Paul knows about this?"

"Uh...we were kinda hopin' you could maybe ask him to pinch us a keg from somewheres. Hob-nobbin' with the snobs up the hill, he's got connections, right?"

Peggy peeked at Joe through her fingers in disbelief.

Peggy did ask Paul when he came up for air, that afternoon. She figured that she'd better, before he got wind of the plan, first. He closed his eyes in disbelief, too.

"It's easier just to sedate them with medication."

"Well, it's the cost," Peggy said. "We're kind of strapped. Joe says it can get pretty bad with the noise around the neighborhood."

Paul seemed to debate it. "Let me see what I can do. What about you?"

"Me? I-I don't need medication."

"I meant, what are your plans for the Fourth; are you going to be around?"

"Oh. Yes. I think I should be, just in case. You?"

He looked around the kennel and then sighed. "Looks like another hot date night."

As it turned out, Paul managed to talk Dr. Caldwell into fronting the shelter enough tranquilizers for all of the dogs and cats, in exchange for taking in an abandoned dog with a broken leg. All in all, it was easy enough to dose the animals with an early four o'clock meal. Peggy, Curtis and Lawrence monitored the animals under Paul's instructions, and to Peggy's relief, the dogs and cats grew sleepy by five p.m., so much so, that Peggy let the entire crew go early, so they could enjoy the fireworks up at the college. Peggy remained behind with Paul, to keep an eye on the animals.

The fireworks began in earnest around seven p.m., with the explosive booms of cherry bombs blowing out garbage cans down the street. From within the shelter, the sound was muffled, and with the radio turned on in the kennel, the dozing dogs didn't seem to care. At eight-thirty, Paul looked around, satisfied.

"It's been a long day. What do you say we take a break?" He tossed her the keys, and headed for the front door. "C'mon, we can probably catch at least one of the shows from the trestle."

"Okay." Peggy was glad for the break and followed him outside into the hazy night. Hearing firecrackers sputter down the street, she felt grateful to have someone, especially a confident young man, to walk with up the dark driveway. She followed Paul and climbed over the old trestle, above the train tracks, where they had an unobstructed view of the sky over the rooftops.

"Oh!" Peggy ducked at the detonation of blue rockets that exploded in the sky above the storefronts. Bright red streamers popped and cascaded down in a crackling rain of light. Rapid-fire missles launched upwards in red flashes, then burst into a sparkling, red, white and blue American flag that hung suspended before them, like a blazing curtain, until it fizzled out with staccato pops—and a doozy of an explosion that nearly knocked her off of her feet. Somewhere down the street, she heard the faint strains of *Stars And Stripes Forever*, played on a flute, and in the dark sky, green streamers and blinding white "screamers" shot up into the clouds. Twice, jolting claps echoed off of the buildings behind them.

"Are you sure the animals are all right?" Peggy asked, clapping her hands against her ears.

"Relax!" Paul offered her a square of pink bubble gum. "They're not caring about jack, right now."

"Since when do you chew bubble gum?"

"Since going cold turkey with the damn candy Camels, before I end up on Marlboro's, for real."

Peggy ripped off a chunk of the gum and popped it in her mouth. "Ooooh! Look at that one!"

A succession of red, white and blue cluster rockets streaked in a dozen directions, scattering in a glittering fire fall. Paul saluted and blew a big, pink bubble that popped almost as loud. Peggy tried to blow a bubble, but her tongue kept ripping the gum.

"You have to ply it, first," Paul unwrapped another piece. "Here, you don't have enough."

Peggy tossed it in her mouth and chewed furiously, as a massive orange star shattered the sky. Nearby rooftop party-goers jumped up and down, tooting party horns.

"Look at that!"

"Whoohoo!" Paul applauded, then turned back to her, more interested in her bubble gum tutorial. "Okay. How to blow a perfect bubble one-o-one. Chew it up nice and soft. Good. Now, flatten it out with your tongue, yeah, now anchor the edges against your teeth. Next, picture you're sticking your tongue into a balloon…easy…now start to blow. Not too fast, take it slow, nice n' easy, that's it, yeah, don't stop, more, more…oh yeeeah! Just like that!" He chuckled. "If anyone happens to be listening, they're calling the cops right about now."

Peggy sputtered a laugh.

"Don't lose it!" Paul laughed along with her. "C'mon, we're reaching critical mass, here. Nice…nice."

Peggy blew out a large pink bubble.

"Now," Paul instructed, "you can do one of two things, you can try to get the whole thing in your mouth before it pops or…"

Pop! The gum bubble burst all over Peggy's face.

"…or you can wear it home." Paul laughed. "Lucky you."

Lucky. Peggy's smile stiffened. So did Paul's.

Behind them the fireworks erupted in a discharge of frenzied blasts, as all three towns set off their finales within seconds of each other. A fountain of fire rose up from behind the trees and a wall of color dwarfed the cheering, rooftop partiers in a crescendo of detonations. With three bright flashes and three sonic-delayed booms, it was all over. Gunpowder smoke drifted in foggy, eddied layers all around them, and left the shadowed, abandoned shop fronts resembling a deserted combat zone.

"I-I forgot all about him," Peggy said, at last. "The noise...he must be terrified." She picked at her face, pulling off bits of bubble gum, feeling suddenly ridiculous.

"He'll be okay." Paul held out his palm as a receptacle for the gum.

"I didn't even think of him!"

"Why would you?"

"Why would I? How can you say that? After we've been talking all over town about-about..."

"He's a past case, Peg. When are you going to learn that it doesn't pay to get hung up on one case, when you've got a full kennel, back there, that needs you just as much, if not more? Their time is ticking away, every day a little closer to a body bag in the freezer. I know you don't like to give up, and it's admirable, but what Terry told you when you started, is still true. Lucky was not the first abuse case they've seen here, and he won't be the last.

"How do you-how do you know what he told me?"

"He told me what he told you."

"Oh." She searched his face. "You said...you just said 'abuse case.'"

Paul diverted his gaze off into the smokey distance. "Yes, well, without proof, I can't swear to it, but off the record, if I thought I could nail the son of a bitch, I would." His expression turned to granite. "Listen," he said, finally. "The noise is pretty much over. And, in his neighborhood, there won't be a lot of fireworks." A whistling homemade firecracker whirred like an incoming missile, causing them both to duck. "It'll be quiet up his way."

"How do you know where he lives?"

"Same way you do. The address is on file."

"Oh. Right." Peggy darted a glance up the hill. "Maybe, we should drive by."

"And do what?"

"See if he's okay."

"Drive by Harrison's house. After hours. In a non-official vehicle. I'm thinking that doesn't include knocking on his door and asking permission to spy over the wall into his yard. If he catches you skulking around; just one phone call, and the police could cite you for harassment.

Or stalking. Or both. Without a complaint from a neighbor, without a summons, you've no right to go near that man's property and infer there's a problem. It's asking for trouble. And, I don't think I have to tell you that Harrison's just the kind of schmuck who'd be happy to make sure you get it, too. Up to your neck. Speaking of which, come here."

He reached out and gently picked a piece of gum off of her cheek.

Peggy held very still. She didn't dare tell him that up until a month ago, she'd been skulking around up by Harrison's almost every night.

"Look," he said, "as professionals, we can only do what we're permitted to do, not necessarily what we want to do. That's the bitch with responsibility."

Peggy raised her brow. "You get that off of a Celestial Seasonings box?"

He blew one last bubble and popped it in his mouth. "Bazooka wrapper." He offered her another piece.

She smiled half-heartedly and shook her head no.

They quietly walked back to the shelter through the murky smoke of spent Roman candles. Peggy hoped that Paul was right about Lucky, because she knew he was right about there being a kennel full of animals needing their help, especially if they were going to make it through the rest of the summer.

Chapter 65

"It's the freakin' Dog Days of August, man, we're doomed!"

Joe pitched the screwdriver to the floor and flopped down on his butt, rocking back and forth with his head in his hands.

Peggy peered into the guts of the dismantled A/C unit that Joe had been trying to jump-start for the past two hours. It was only ten o'clock in the morning, and the outdoor thermometer already registered ninety-three degrees in the shade of the silver maple tree.

"We need this like a bear wiff a sore head!" Betty snapped.

Peggy knit her brows together in concentration. What to do? They'd skated through July, more or less. The day after the Fourth, the shelter had breached full capacity. As Paul had promised, the sedated dogs and cats had fared just fine during the fireworks, but not so the neighborhood dogs and cats. When he and Peggy had returned to the shelter, that night, they fielded a rush of calls from panicked owners whose dogs were jumping fences and dashing down the highways, or cats stuck in trees or on rooftops yeowling for help. In an attempt to prevent a late night euthanasia session of their own dogs, Peggy called Joe and Betty back to the shelter, and the four drove around town, all night, trying to match up as many of the calls to wandering pets as they could, before morning.

It took weeks of juggling space and cross-referencing the Lost and Found ads to reunite pets with owners. They were so busy during most of July, that Peggy didn't have the luxury of time to worry about Lucky, Terry, or very much else, outside of keeping free space in the shelter, and keeping that space cool. With the guillotine doors kept up, the kennel remained tolerable, due to all the cinderblock and slate flooring, and the silver maple tree shading the back runs.

The office, however, was a square box with only two small windows, the front facing east and the back facing west, the overhang socked in by the old mill, under full sun, all day long.

Peggy looked at the forlorn little A/C unit, her shirt clinging to her sweaty back. "Oh please, can't you fix it?"

"I look like a magician?" Joe shot back.

Betty groaned. "What we gonna do?"

"How 'bout defect to Canada?" Joe said. "I'm tellin' ya, Saint Fran, we oughta just pull the plug, right now, 'cause August in Newark? It's like roastin' in hell with the lid stapled on!"

Peggy kneaded her brow. Joe was right. They were in for it.

As August began its blistering march forward, beating the heat was made increasingly more difficult to accomplish, especially for the "economically challenged". Unemployed men, in stained undershirts, loitered around corner bars or parks, hiding beer cans in paper bags and complaining about the lack of jobs and their women. Women sat on stoops with their feet in pans of cold water, complaining about hoodlum kids and their men. Those stuck in sweltering apartment buildings lay awake on their fire escapes, at night, dreaming of escape. The only people moving about in the roasting afternoons were the ice cream vendors, lugging their carts up and down the neighborhood streets. In town, there was no escaping the scorching heat.

Peggy stood with the crew before the broken A/C unit, close to throwing in the towel.

"Ma-rone!" Joe smacked it with his palm. "Freakin' machines! Brunhilda's right. They're tryin' to kill us off."

"One mo' month, baby," Betty begged it, her hands clasped in prayer. "That's all we be askin'."

Joe picked up a wrench and tried once more, but wrenched his finger. "OW! Friggit. That's it. I'm callin' it." He stepped away from the unit. "Time of death: ten o' four a.m."

"Well, you tried," Peggy sighed. "I guess we'll have to get by with fans."

"Dillan, we'll never make it to fall with a fan."

"Fall?" Betty exclaimed. "We ain't makin' it to *night* fall!"

"The cats'll be cooked by noon!" Clara said.

Peggy wiped her sweaty forehead with her sleeve. "Betty, remind me, what would it cost to get a new one?"

"Got it right here." Betty pulled a folder down from the shelf and handed it to her. "Same dance last year, except now it gonna cost more."

"Three thousand dollars!" Peggy sank into Terry's chair. "How would we ever pay for this?"

"Charge it!" Joe said. "That's what everybody else with no dough is doin'!"

"In Septembah," Betty said, "when you and the doctah start your talks, again, we could catch up."

"Catch up? We'd have to win the lottery!" Peggy said. "What if nobody books us in the fall? What if Beula croaks? What if the roof finally fails? "

"Oh, what if the moon curdles to cheese and the sun explodes?" Clara said, with an exasperated tone. "What ifs are only good for scarin' worry warts into their belly buttons! Maybe it's time for some blind faith, Saint Francis!"

"Too late, they've disbanded." Paul squeezed past a standing fan in the doorway and joined them to examine the busted unit. "Looks like it's time for last rights."

"You're too late," Joe tossed the wrench. "It's gone to hell."

"And we be stone right behind it, we don't figger somethin' quick." Betty declared. "It gonna take at least a week to find a contractor ain't gonna flake out on us, maybe two to grease the permit office, then they gonna take they time to bust walls by the hour, and boom! There goes anothah week, maybe two."

"By then, it's September," Peggy noted.

"We'll be maggot meat, by then!" Joe cried.

Paul shrugged. "What if we do the work ourselves?" Peggy and the crew stared at him.

"You been sniffin' ether, down there, Doc?" Joe asked.

"C'mon, between you, me, and the guys, we can knock out a wall and put in a window."

"What about the wiring? I get shocked just flippin' the CB on, in the morning."

"Riley's a handyman, he'll know about electricity."

"Just enough to fry us!"

"How much harder can it be than keeping the boiler from exploding and taking out half the state, this winter?" Paul looked to Peggy. "I'm sure we can do it in a week. It'll be a good test run for what has to happen downstairs anyway, when you win that grant."

Peggy proffered a wilted smile. "It's really nice of you to offer, but everyone is already so busy."

"I'm not being nice. You can't go through August like this. I can't, I'll tell you that much. Neither can the cats."

Peggy observed the cats. They were panting. She looked to the crew, all damp with perspiration and looking miserable. "Okay. Well...Betty, what if we offer Mr. Riley the three hundred we've got left in the account, then put the rest on the new credit card until we start generating some cash, again. It's a risk, but let's do it."

"Fricken A, I second it! Let's do it!" Joe cried.

"Amen," Betty agreed.

"How do we keep me cats cool, 'til then?" Clara asked.

Paul studied the room a moment. "Keep the office door open, set up a box fan in the front window, on reverse, to pull in the cooler kennel air. Point two standing fans at both banks of cat cages, hang ice bags on each cage, with catch pails underneath for the run off. Keep rotating the ice bags in the freezer out back. Once it's time to break walls, we'll take the cats downstairs; it's cooler, down there. I'll have Curtis and Lawrence start setting it up, now. I prescribe wet bandanas around our own necks and lots of fluids." He opened his wallet. "Let's start with a cooler of stout, and some root beer for my homies."

"Now, you're talkin'!" Joe climbed to his feet.

Paul handed him a twenty. "Make it stretch to next payday, please."

After relocating the cats downstairs to Beula's cave, Paul, Curtis and Lawrence removed the glass window from the office wall with the help of crowbars and two bars of soap.

Sporting goggles and a hard hat, and with the crew safely on the kennel side of the office door, Joe hauled back with a mallet and took a hulking swing at the window frame.

Wham! Wood splintered and dry wall crumbled to the floor.

"Righteous," Lawrence said.

"Oh man, that was sweet!" Joe laughed. "Anybody else wanna whack?"

Clara raised her hand.

Between them, the four young men had the window prepped to the new dimension specs, by mid-afternoon. They removed most of the drywall surrounding it, and exposed the wiring. This was no mean feat, since the temperature had reached a blistering ninety-nine degrees by three p.m.. The humidity weighed in at ninety-percent, making it feel at least twenty degrees hotter.

Peggy kept the ice bags rotated in front of the fans, now aimed at the working men. This presented a new and unexpected challenge—trying not to gawk at Paul, who had stripped to the waist early on in the demolition and was, essentially, half-naked.

The taut, toned vet took turns swinging the mallet at the walls, rivulets of sweat running between his muscled shoulders and down his drywall-dusted, bare chest. With sunlight splashed over his shoulders, he reminded Peggy of marble statues she'd seen in picture books. He'd tied a wet bandana across his forehead, and Peggy tried to focus her eyes on that whenever he spoke to her. She'd concentrated so hard on not looking at him, that several times she had to ask him to repeat what he'd said.

Once Paul had gone shirtless, Curtis followed suit, with an iced bandana around his neck. Although his deep cocoa skin was beautiful, his was the gawky, rake-thin frame of a teenage boy, not the chiseled physique of a man. Since Peggy did not feel the desperate need to look away whenever Curtis spoke to her, she knew that her painful shyness had more to do with Paul, rather than just the fact two young men had removed their shirts.

True to form, Joe remained in full uniform, complete with hard hat and goggles. He was soaked through in less than ten minutes, but Peggy knew that he would rather have been found dead and mummified, than out of that uniform. She made doubly sure that he had plenty of water and Gatorade. She transferred pitchers of it from the outside freezer to the unplugged, mini office fridge. Eventually, they had to shut the power to the freezer out back, as well, and Peggy prayed that it wouldn't be for more than a few hours, acutely aware of the bagged road kill underneath the bags of ice. There were still two more days until garbage pickup!

The men took a lunch break at one-thirty, in the back yard. They joined the dogs in the wading pool and had a water fight with the hoses. Peggy used her own paycheck to order sandwiches from the deli, along with six packs of beer and soda. She ate her lunch in front of the fans in the office and listened to the crew's laughter and conversations outside. She had no trouble, as all that was left between the office and the outdoors, by then, was one layer of drywall and a gaping hole where the window had once been.

She'd never seen the interior of a wall exposed before. The lattice work of boards and braces that held the building together reminded her of a skeleton. Wires dangled like veins and arteries. The building seemed fragile to her, like a patient in a hospital. She thought of Terry.

Frowning, she realized she hadn't even thought of asking Terry about punching holes in his walls. She pondered that a moment, then raised a bottle of root beer in toast to Terry's chair.

"Deed be done." She took a long, slow swallow of it, and then burped loudly. "You have a problem with that, you'll have to call me and tell me yourself."

"Peggy?"

Peggy jumped.

Betty peered in the doorway. "Who you talkin' to?"

"Oh, nobody. Just me. Thinking. Out loud."

Betty eyed the root beer in her hand. "I was gonna say, you ain't drinkin', this early?"

"No, no." Peggy half-laughed. "Not yet, anyway."

Betty regarded the gaping hole in the wall. "Maybe we boff should."

Clara tottered in and surveyed the room. "Boys. Pfft! They can take things apart, all right, but where are they come time to sort the fright?"

"Searchin' the trash fo' th'instructions! Speakin' of," Betty glanced out the front window. "Batten down the hatches. Here come Mr. Riley, now."

Peggy peered out the window.

Togged out in baggy shorts under a wide-brim Panama hat, Mr. Riley hobbled down the driveway, lugging his little red wagon of tools behind him. The dogs woofed at him, briefly, but it was even too hot for them to exert any more energy than that. Peggy heard his grizzled falsetto from half-way across the parking lot, as he crooned loud enough to draw the firemen to their windows.

> *"Summer's here, so pour th'ale,*
> *sail away on th'back of a whale,*
> *go fishin' an' swimmin'*
> *wit bow-legged women,*
> *an' bless the tail kept outta jail!"*

"Oh, please, God," Peggy begged. "Have mercy." Behind her, Clara had already begun muttering retaliatory insults, when Peggy corralled her. "Clara? How'd you like to place a wager?"

Clara eyed Peggy, like a wily cat. "What're the odds?"

Chapter 66

Mr. Riley shuffled into the building, bidding a hearty heidy-ho to the dogs. He came to a halt in the office doorway, when he spotted Clara scowling at him from across the dusty room. He looked his nemesis up and down, in a condescending manner, and then he turned to Peggy.

"T'ought yer ice box was busted," he remarked.

Clara glowered at him, and Peggy swore she could see steam hissing from her ears, but Clara kept her lips tightly pressed, and a dollar bill tightly clenched in her hand, behind her back.

"Yes," Peggy spoke up fast and led the wiry man to the exposed wall. "The A/C unit. It's broken. We need your help."

Mr. Riley blinked at the gaping hole punched out of the wall. "What'd ye do, blast it to Watchung?"

"No, no, we took it out. We have to put in a new window to install a new unit."

"Aye, aye. Sure'n there was pishrogues on it, I'll have to dekko a right. Good hap ye tinkled me, make no mistake."

Peggy couldn't decipher a thing he said, and glanced to Betty for translation.

Betty sighed. "He say he suspect a fairy hex, so he'll have to inspect it, good thing you phoned."

"Fairy hex?"

Betty jerked her chin towards Clara. "Don't axe."

"Oh," Peggy turned to Mr. Riley. "Will it take very long?"

"If dis job don't see me out, t'isn't day, yet."

Peggy glanced to Betty. Betty shook her head no.

"Pfft!" Clara rolled her eyes to Peggy and muttered under her breath. "'E'll never make old bones of it!"

Betty headed off Peggy's questioning glance with a wave of her hands. Let it go.

Mr. Riley seemed to have heard more than he let on. While rummaging in his tool box, he sang another limerick to himself, just loud enough to be overheard:

"A widder whose singular vice,
was t'keep 'er late 'usband on ice,
said "'Tis been 'ard since I lost 'im - I'll never defrost 'im!
Cold comfort, but cheap at the price!"

Clara dumped the contents of a litter box in the waste basket, and sang one of her own, also just loud enough for the firemen to hear:

"A lechy, northumbrian druid,
'is gray matter filthy and lewd,
awoke from a trance
with 'is 'ands in 'is -"

"Clara?" Peggy broke in, "care to up the ante?" She handed the old woman a six pack of Mountain Dew and pointed to the door. "What do you wanna bet the men can't finish before we run out of soda?"

"What men?" Clara shot back. "I see no *men*, here."

"Let's go check out back, then, dear." Betty ushered Clara out the door.

Peggy turned to address Mr. Riley and gasped, as he fired up a blow torch - whoosh! The flame shot clean to the wall and singed the boards.

"Mr. Riley! What are you doing?"

"What's 'at?" he shouted behind his iron welder's mask. "Oh, tanks be to God, I'm very well indeed, I am!"

"Holy Christ!" Paul exclaimed from the doorway, his shout shifting the old man's attention—and the blow torch—away from the wall. "Mr. Riley? What can I do to help?"

Peggy sagged against the counter, in relief.

Through his fogged mask, the old man looked Paul's half-naked body up and down. "Bless us n' save us, Harry, what've we here, a bit o' bouzzie Quality, an' in the buff, noo?"

"Paul," the young vet corrected.

"What's 'at?"

"The name's Paul!"

"I kin see it's a wall, Harry. Colleen, here, already made that plain!"

"He calls everyone Harry," Peggy told him.

Joe, Curtis and Lawrence skidded to a stop in the doorway, and spotting the smoking boards behind Mr. Riley, Joe squealed.

"Except for girls," she added.

Paul lifted the blow torch from the old man's hands. "Just tell me what to do."

Riley snatched it right back. "Aye, den, Harry! You'll be takin' orders from dis Harry here!" He handed the torch to Joe. "He's done up smart an' proper like for de job, he is!"

"With all due respect Mr. Riley, I'm more than able to help," Paul began.

"Dats right, avick!" Riley wagged the torch at him. "Lesson lairned. Be said by me, ye don't look a boy to men's work. Now, twill do ye no harm to remember, Harry, tis de work praises de man! Y'canna goo 'round like a Sleiveen an' plaise yer father. An' one more ting; y'know what I'm goin' to tell ye, now, Harry, don't ye? Notting is aisy as it looks; ever'ting takes longer than y'expect, an' if anyting kin goo wrong, it will, at de worst possible moment. Dat's Spuds Law! So now, git to de west o' me, gorsoon, an' stay out of it, 'til dis here Harry asks after yer arse."

Joe grinned at Paul, lowered his goggles and fired up the blow torch.

"Yes, sir." Paul grit his teeth and stepped back behind Mr. Riley, who was already shouting orders at Joe.

"What're ye playin' at der, Harry? Yer makin' a bollicksing bags of it, y'are! Jaysus! A bigger bollox nivir put 'is arm troo a coat! Let the corner boys have at it, then!" Riley tossed tools to Curtis and Lawrence. "God help us an' save us, at least they kin handle a spanner!"

Paul glanced over his shoulder to Peggy. Wordlessly, she handed him a beer.

Three days later, on Sunday, precisely at three p.m., when the thermometer outside the office read ninety-seven degrees, Peggy and the crew crossed their fingers. Mr. Riley stepped up and flipped the switch on a brand new Sears air conditioner, set in a brand new window. The unit hummed to life with a soft purr, and in a moment, cool air blew out of the vents. Nothing flickered, nothing smoked, and nothing caught fire.

"Go m-beannuighe Dia air bhur n-obair!" The old man cried, affixing a little Irish flag to the unit.

"God save the Queen!" Clara countered, and set an even bigger English flag on the unit.

"Leave it to a cat to begrudge a king!" Mr. Riley declared, with indignation.

"A barbarian crowned t'isn't royalty in civilized corners!" Clara snapped.

"Clara? We-we had a bet!" Peggy interceded. "Mr. Riley, thank you for all your help."

"Tink you've boxed the compass on it, then, have ye?" Mr. Riley faced off with Clara. "I tink it high time, then, to give ye a piece o' me mind, I do!"

"Careful there, praitie, you've not much of it left!"

"Why, y'narky Rossie ye!" Mr. Riley hollered. He took a deep breath and spat out a limerick:

> *"There once was a cranky ol' broad,*
> *a snooty society fraud,*
> *in company I'm told*
> *she was awful cold,*
> *but not when y'nipped her alone, by Gawd!*

Clara waggled her hips at him:

> *"There once was sodder from Kent*
> *who 'ad a peculiar bent.*
> *'e collected the turds*
> *of lice-ridden birds*
> *an' 'ad 'em for lunch during Lent!"*

"Clara! Mr. Riley, please!" Peggy implored them, but three days of pent-up insults had festered in their vacuum-sealed silence, and there was no stopping the steam blast, now.

"That's enough!" Paul's voice boomed above the octegenarians' scrabble. He tossed Mr. Riley a jar of nuts and bolts, and rattled off a pointed limerick of his own:

> *"The plumber presented his bill*
> *to the vet who gave him a pill.*

His tongue corroded,
his rear end exploded
and they found his nuts in Brazil!"

He yanked on his lab coat and delivered the next one to Clara, tossing her the wig that had fallen onto the floor during her tirade:

"The widow of a corp'rate raider
tried the ire of all who way-laid her.
'Til the demanding itch
of this cranky old bitch
so annoyed a crusader he spayed her!"

Slack-jawed, both Mr. Riley and Clara gaped at the young vet. The rest of the crew tried hard not to laugh, and Peggy had to clap a hand over her mouth to stifle her own.

"Now, either kiss and make up, bury the hatchet or so help me, I will," Paul warned them.

Rooted to the spot, the two elders exchanged a glance. Now that Paul was dressed in his hospital whites, he apparently commanded a modicum of respect, because Riley gummed his chin up to his nose at Clara, and although her eyes glinted at him with a dangerous spark, neither took the bait from the other.

"'Tis corking, all Sir Garnet," Clara acquiesced finally, with a nod to the new A/C unit. "Well done."

Coddled by the old woman's compliment, Mr. Riley removed his hat. "Much obliged, I am, to be sure." Then, his eyes twinkled. "Arrah now, no kiss den?"

"And, pigs might fly!" Clara exclaimed.

"Good enough!" Paul interceded and hefted Mr. Riley's tool chest onto the little red wagon.

"Some Vitamin G for the road, Mr. Riley?" Joe handed the old man a bottle of Guinness and ushered him towards the front door.

Clara swung the office door shut behind them. Bam! "That's a tenner you owe me," she growled to Peggy in passing.

Peggy dropped into Terry's chair with weary relief. Paul pulled up a stool and held out two bottles, one of Guinness and the other root beer. Debating, Peggy finally reached for the soda.

"You owe me, too," he said, popping the caps off.

"Name it."

"Next year, we install one of those units down in the...in my surgical suite."

"Deal."

They clinked bottles. Taking a long swallow of the root beer, Peggy closed her eyes and drank in the cool air with a contented sigh.

With the phones ringing and the boys laughing and talking behind her, she didn't hear the horn honking outside. She didn't see the inconsiderate driver swerve around Joe and Mr. Riley and park in front of the no parking sign. She didn't see who got out of the car. If she had, she might have chosen the bottle of Guinness.

Chapter 67

"I've come to report my dog missing."

Peggy swiveled around in Terry's chair and her smile froze.

Mr. Harrison, clad in a pastel-lime leisure suit, stood in the doorway, his expression dour. He did not remove his sunglasses. Joe was just behind him in the doorway, looking ashen.

"What?" Peggy almost choked when Harrison looked at her. Seeing her reflection in the man's sunglasses, she felt like a fly facing a praying mantis.

Run! Hide!

The floor began to dissolve under her feet, when she dug her fingernails into her palms, to jerk herself back to the present. No! You will *not* take me down there, again! Breathlessly, she coached herself: A is for am. I am at the shelter. I am surrounded by dogs and people who care. I am safe. I am in charge. Two times two is four. B is for brave. The bastard can't touch me here!

Raising herself up to her full height, she spoke, again. "Missing? H-how is that even possible when you had him chained?" Harrison raised an eyebrow at her, and her mouth went dry. She realized in an instant, that she'd given herself away. Betty eased up beside her, holding the Lost and Found notebook. Peggy took it and gripped it tightly to keep her hands from shaking.

"When he go missing?" Joe's voice piped up behind her.

"Somewhere around the holiday. The Fourth."

"Of *July*?" Paul's voice sounded sharp, beside her.

"W-what?" Peggy gasped and looked to Joe.

For a second, he looked as if he'd been sucker-punched. He snatched up the log book. "You're only reporting it, now?"

Harrison seemed annoyed by this. "Our maid claimed she fed him the night of the Fourth, swore up and down on her Bible that everything was fine. The next day he was gone."

"It's August fourteenth!" Paul said sharply.

Harrison cocked his head at them and pushed the silence right up to the edge of discomfort. "As I was about to explain, I was in Europe on a junket. I never got the message. Which is why I'm here *now*, having only just arrived back in town last night."

He aimed his sunglasses at Peggy and lowered them ever so slightly, to peer at her over the rims. "You haven't seen him, have you?"

Peggy felt as if she were being leered at through venetian blinds by a Peeping Tom. But, there was something off kilter about him. Why was this brazen man suddenly so coy?

Keep quiet! You asking for trouble?

"No?" His flat, dead eyes searched hers, one more breathless moment. "I didn't think so. Or you would have called me, right? Sure, you would have." He pushed his sunglasses back in place and turned his attention to the crew. "I'm here to file an official report. I assume you still perform that function?"

Joe stepped forward. "Was he wearing a collar?"

Harrison checked his watch, again. "Don't you have his description on file?"

"Yeah, but we gotta update it, now, okay? Fill this in here."

While Joe took the report, Peggy's mind bent backwards through a gathering fog. She fought to remember, to remain lucid. Lucky was chained. She saw it! So did Joe! How did he get loose?

Don't ask questions! You know what happens!

I can't think! Please! She grasped hold of Terry's chair and concentrated, hard. Two times three is six. C is for courage. Two times four is eight.

"If that's all," Harrison held out a business card to Joe. "My secretary knows how to reach me. If you find him." He headed for the door.

"It's a shame!" Peggy heard her own voice slice through the silence.

Harrison turned. "Excuse me?"

Peggy expelled the words like bitter seeds. "Th-that your secretary couldn't reach you for over a month!"

For a moment, Harrison just stared at her. Then, he shrugged. "But, we can put a man on the moon, right?" With that, he left.

Over the roar in her head, Peggy heard the dogs dash out underneath the guillotine doors and continue barking at him, all the way to the front gate. Her head spinning, she turned to the window, while the crew's conversation erupted behind her.

"Who wuz that honkey?" Lawrence asked Curtis.

"Mephistopheles."

"Son-of-a-baby-kissin'-pila-puke!" Joe slammed the logbook on the counter in disgust. "How the frig did Lucky get loose, hooked to that friggin' chain?"

"Maybe his maid done turn him loose outta pity," Betty suggested.

"When did you see him last?" Paul asked Joe.

"Jeeze, a while back. We been so nuts, here, with the programs and tryin' to keep ahead of the euths...I'm sorry, it's my fault Lucky fell through the cracks."

"N-no," Peggy said hoarsely. "It's my fault."

"It's nobody's fault," she heard Paul say.

She peered out the window, trying to see into Harrison's car windows. Where was his wife and children? Did he leave them at home? Afraid they might spill the beans, this time? All at once, she felt pain and looked at her palms. She'd clenched her fists so tightly, her fingernails had cut into her flesh. Shaking, she sucked on the blood. She heard the crew behind her, manning the phones in a search for Lucky.

"This be the Farroway sheltah," Betty said. "Listen, you git a dog in there, look back to last month, okay? Lemme read off his M.O...."

"Hey man, this is Joe over at the shelter...yeah, hey, you get a dog over your way, last month? Big white fella with rust patches over his..."

"Peg?"

Peggy looked up. Paul stood beside her.

"How many signatures do you have on that petition so far?" he asked.

With effort, she cleared her throat. "Not enough."

Clara sidled up and offered them a swig from her flask. "Gonna need more than a packet of John Hancocks to 'ang that Magsman out t'dry."

Joe hung up the phone and snatched up keys. "I'll have my ears on." He paused at the door and looked back at Peggy. "We're gonna find him."

Peggy nodded and blinked back hot stinging tears.

"You all right?" Paul asked, low.

At first she nodded, then she swiped the wetness from her cheeks. "No. No, I'm not."

The crew searched all month. Every day. Every night.

Joe hit the road patrolling at six a.m. each morning, and combed the streets until well after midnight. He was an officer on a mission. Each day, he checked at Jack's Chinese Doughnut Shop, the Claremont Diner, Frank's Deli, Tony's Pizzeria, Fegetti's Auto Repair Shop, Woody's Soda Fountain, Finn's Tobacco Emporium, Tim O'Malley's Newsstand, and the bowling alley.

Unable to sleep, Peggy joined him in the evenings. They searched from the railroad tracks through the shop districts, all the way up all three mountain roads. They routinely swung by Kierney's, checking in with Mike and the wait staff. They even hung out at the police station, now that Joe had a bona fide reason to be there, checking for stray dog complaints.

Curtis and Lawrence hit the street on foot, garnering help from friends and family.

Clara put word out to her COACOA cohorts, a first for the cattish clan, on behalf of "an enemy cur".

Using snapshots of Lucky that they'd kept on file, Betty made up a flyer and had her church run off copies, then posted them over town. "Let's see that butt wipe complain 'bout this!" she huffed, and tacked a flyer to the telephone pole at the top of the driveway.

What tormented Peggy most, were the HBC, or road kill calls, from the police station. Each time Joe hurried out, she knew that he was just as afraid of what he might find out on the street. Every time his voice crackled over the CB static, announcing "possum pancake" or even "incoming for the doc", she breathed a sigh of relief that it wasn't Lucky. But, her heart still ached with worry, because it meant that the dog was still out there, somewhere.

Betty received numerous calls about dogs matching Lucky's description, but it was always another dog, or they'd just missed spotting the runaway, leaving them to wonder if it really had been Lucky.

As the days stretched into weeks, Peggy began to feel as if they were chasing their own tails. Although no one had voiced the notion, when the broiling, dog days of August came to a close, the odds of finding Lucky had dwindled to a long shot.

Peggy knew that no one felt worse about it than Paul. Although he didn't talk about it with her, it was clear that the whole episode had unsettled him in a big way, and yet it hadn't entirely surprised her. Curtis told her that Paul spent most every lunch hour scouring the lost and found ads from papers as far away as Morristown. Only Peggy knew why it bothered Paul, as much as it did.

Harrison phoned twice a week to ask about their progress. Peggy felt sure it was just to irritate them.

"Maybe somebody took the poor mutt in," Betty suggested. "You did, remembah?"

"I hope so," Peggy said, and meant it, with all her heart. It would be the best thing that could ever happen to Lucky, under the circumstances. It would solve almost everything. And yet, she remembered back to the day she had walked in the shelter with Lucky, and she heard Terry's voice, as clearly as if he'd spoken to her that very morning. *"Take Lucky away, and Harrison just goes out and gets another dog, and we're back to square one."*

Peggy shivered. Autumn was just around the corner. With it came falling temperatures, rain, and then snow. They didn't have much time.

Chapter 68

A yellow leaf fluttered past Peggy's face and settled on the brown grass, like a sail boat come to rest on the sand.

The silver maple tree swayed, its corn-yellow and pea-green, diaphanous leaves quivering under the October sky. Early afternoon shadows had crept up, nearly enveloping her. She checked her watch. It was only three o'clock, but the sun was already about to dip below the warehouse roofs. She felt a familiar chill embrace her heart.

Despite valiant and dedicated search efforts, there had been no sign of Lucky. Joe felt awful about it and blamed himself for letting Lucky's status fall through the cracks. He patrolled the streets for most of the day, but without a lead, it had become harder to justify the costs in time, man power and gasoline prices over one dog.

Peggy sat down on the back steps, tired. She'd been in the throes of not only preparing and presenting new seminars for the schools but finishing the grant application. By the eve of the September deadline, she found herself working round-the-clock, forced to relinquish her involvement in the search for Lucky. She made the deadline, and the crew threw her an impromptu pizza party when she returned from dropping the papers off at Town Hall. She suspected it was Paul's doing, in an effort to cheer her up, more than it was to celebrate the tossing of their hat into the ring.

Still, every night, she set a bowl of dog food out by the old dumpster in the empty lot, where she'd found Lucky. She hoped that he might seek her out somehow, all the while praying that Betty was right; that a kind stranger had taken him in, and he was safe somewhere, happy and loved.

She pulled the recorder from her pocket and pressed the on button. "Call Sacred Heart, one last time, and ask if they've seen Lucky."

She shut off the recorder and gazed up at the falling leaves. Mr. Harrison had not appeared in their doorway again, and his calls had

ceased. It bothered her. Why hadn't he tried to adopt another dog to kick around?

From under the overhang, she heard the shoving creak of the cellar door. Paul crested the the steps in unlaced desert boots, a stained shirt accented by a rumpled tie he hadn't bothered to knot, topped by his wrinkled lab coat. He unbuttoned it, as he sat down next to her.

Peggy stifled a smile. "All dressed up and nowhere to go."

He pulled a crumpled pack of candy cigarettes from his pocket. "Those that live in glass houses…"

Peggy shook maple seeds out of her hair. "I thought you quit."

"I never quit. How quickly thou forget-eth." He offered her one of two that were left.

"You're a bad influence."

He pulled the last one out of the pack with his lips. "Thank you for noticing." He crumpled the empty packet and tossed it into the garbage can. A whirling "heliocopter" seed descended in front of him. He reached out and grabbed it. "Need any help, up top?"

"Just waiting on Joe. He got a call and rushed out."

Paul looked at her. "The odds that it would be Lucky…"

"I know."

Paul fell quiet and massaged his hands.

"It's not your fault, y'know," Peggy said, finally.

"It's not yours, either." He brushed maple seeds off of his jeans and looked off to the gathering clouds. "We both could have gone to check on him that night, and missed him by five minutes, or a day. We have no way of knowing when Lucky took off. Was Harrison even telling the truth? We may never know. You can only do so much, Peg. The rest of it—well, you know the drill, by now."

"You mean, let it go." The wind rustled the leaves in the tree. She wrapped her arms around her knees. "You're right. And, you were right that night, too. I'm going to call it tomorrow, close the case."

"I didn't expect a white flag. Not from you."

She was quiet a long moment. "Sometimes, it doesn't pay to care."

Paul reached out and gently brushed maple seeds from her hair. "I never said you shouldn't care."

She looked up at him and was startled by the tenderness she saw in his eyes. It washed over her gently, and the walls, fences and the foils between them fell, leaving them disarmed. Tears welled up in her eyes, and he brushed her cheek with the back of his hand. It was the gentlest touch she had ever felt.

The crisp, cool autumn air sent leaves and whirly-bird seeds cascading down around them as they sat, suspended in time. Peggy was afraid to move, for fear of breaking the spell. Paul took her clenched hand and slowly uncurled her fingers, weaving his own between them. Held fast by his eyes, Peggy didn't resist. As he drew closer to her, she began to tremble, and when he hovered near her lips…

…the van's horn honked, yanking her out of the moment. She looked at Paul, who reluctantly extricated his fingers from hers. The van screeched to a halt, up front, and they got up and scrambled down the steps.

Paul held the gate open for her, but her shirt sleeve got caught on the latch. "Go," she told him. "I'll catch up." She watched him go and then yanked on her shirt. "Let go! Let me go!" She yanked at it until she ripped it loose, and then stumbled on up the gravel driveway.

Finally reaching the top of the incline, she shaded her eyes from the van's bright emergency light, sweeping the walls around her.

"Don't tell me you found him?" she heard Paul call out to Joe.

"Better n' that!" Joe jumped out of the van, but instead of opening the rear doors for Paul, he leaned against them, folding his arms and fixing them with a big, wide grin on his face.

Another door slammed on the passenger side.

Peggy was confused. If it wasn't Lucky, then why…what…who was that? A bent shape moved jerkily between the strobe lighting and oscillating shadows. She drew in a breath and stared.

Limping into the light, Terry leaned on a cane. He looked up and waved.

"I'll be damned!" Paul laughed and extended his hand to him.

Thinner, his hair a bit grayer, Terry shook the vet's hand. "I say, what have they done to you?" His voice sounded whiskey warm.

"You look great! When did you get in?"

"I get the call, right?" Joe babbled. "And I friggin' can't buleeeeve it, I almost busted a gut, but he goes, 'let's surprise everybody', and I'm like, you shittin' me?"

Both Paul and Joe turned to follow Terry's sightline to Peggy.

As if in a trance, she walked through the revolving emergency lights until she stood before him.

Terry beheld her, like one might upon seeing land, again, after a long ocean voyage. "Hello, Saint Francis."

Peggy swallowed the ache in her throat. "Welcome back, Warden."

Terry lowered the copy of Peggy's grant proposal and looked at her from over a new pair of rimless reading glasses. "What can I say? Well done!"

Her cheeks flushed. "Thank you."

Everyone was still reeling at his return. Betty honked into a handkerchief, unable to quell her happy tears for over an hour. Clara's response on seeing him walk through the door had been a cranky squint of her eye and one question:

"Who are you, again?"

"See what we been dealin' with?" Joe regaled him.

"Your purple hearts are on order," he chuckled.

Of all their reactions, it was Peggy's that had both touched and puzzled him the most. She seemed genuinely glad to see him, and yet, he caught her regarding him from a distance; like a wild thing that had been set free, struggling to remember the hand that had fed it. One thing he noticed right away, was that Dr. Hayward sat close to her. Closer than she'd ever allowed anyone, before.

Terry finally set the papers aside and appraised her. "I am overwhelmed with what you've accomplished. Truly, splendid."

"I had help." She glanced to Paul. "Paul—Dr. Hayward—had so much to do with the success of helping us survive."

"Don't let her snow you," Paul chimed in. "I might have dotted an 'i' or crossed a 't', here and there, but the ideas were hers, start to finish."

"But, I couldn't have done it without his-his constant criticism!" She sputtered a laugh. Paul clapped a hand over her mouth.

Terry's brows shot up. She now allowed human touch. Wonderful!

Paul spoke over her squirming. "Constructive criticism, by the way, which she never listened to! And, did I mention stubborn? Never took a break, never came up for air, nights, weekends, I think the library should start charging her rent!"

Peggy pried Paul's hand away. "He still won't tell me how he got the EVC to sign off on the—"

"Indentured servitude?" Paul added to Terry, "Side bar; this one owes me until the cows come home."

Terry looked between them, smiling with amusement. "I can only imagine."

"You have to thank Betty, too," Peggy said. "She crunched the numbers for us."

"Pullleeese!" Betty waved her away and gestured to Curtis. "Mistah Mensa here been cookin' the books. Any audits? See him."

Curtis fisted his right palm and bowed to Betty with respect, Wing Chun style.

"Curtis also handled all the donation cans," Peggy added, "while single-handedly weaning half of Farroway's wildlife. Lawrence is our top dog trainer, Ramone and Lewis have been our right and left hands, and Joe…"

Joe stood up and saluted.

"Joe has been chauffer, bouncer, detective, roofer, and Mr. Riley's apprentice!"

"Don't get me started!" Joe rolled his eyes and flopped back down in his chair.

"And without Clara and her COACOA members," Peggy said, "I don't know what we would have done during the Kitten Tsunami."

"Somebody 'ad to give a rat's arse 'bout the cats!" Clara declared.

"It was a friggin' miracle we didn't bite it, ten times over," Joe admitted. "Mainly cuz, the doc's right, Dillan is stubborn; man you are. Admit it! It's true. She just wouldn't quit!"

"You wouldn't let me!" Peggy glanced at Paul, again.

"She's a bad influence." Paul shrugged to Terry.

"I daresay!" Terry chuckled.

"Hey, a toast!" Joe raised a can of Mountain Dew in the air. "Welcome back, chief!"

They all cheered and clinked soda pop cans all around. Terry smiled to himself, when Paul nudged Peggy with a wink. He also noted how she blushed and glanced up at him, as if self-conscious.

For the next hour, the crew fell over one another, deluging him with all of the stories; the night the wind nearly blew the roof to Connecticut, the battle of the blizzard and the boiler, the SRO vet exams, the bartering, the summer of hellfire, and finally, reluctantly, they broached the subject of Lucky.

Peggy looked up to Terry—and saw his smile slip for the first time since his return. It seemed to her that it might have been the only news that he hadn't already known about.

"Where does it stand now?" he asked her.

She sighed. "Square one."

He looked over the folder and pursed his lips, the way he used to, when deep in thought.

"We're kinda hopin' that Bet's right," Joe said. "Y'know, that somebody took him in."

"Our biggest thorn is handling Harrison," Paul said, and glanced to her, again. "He hasn't shown up for over a month, but I'm sure he'll be back."

"It's only a matter of time," Terry murmured.

"That's our opinion."

"Peggy?"

"You-you know how I feel about it."

Terry nodded.

"There's gotta be somethin' more we can do," Joe prodded. "Can't you talk to the mayor? This guy makes it to City Council, we're boned."

Peggy studied Terry's face with a gnawing unease; he didn't seem as sure about the matter as he had been just ten months ago. Or, was it that she just lost the skill of interpretation, like with any language, by virtue of nonuse? Searching his eyes, she tried to ferret out an inkling of what lurked in their watery-blue depths, but it remained out of reach. What had changed? For a moment, it was almost as if she didn't know him. And yet, there he sat, as familiar as yesterday. She didn't know how to reconcile the two: Terry past and Terry present.

Terry diverted his gaze to Lucky's file. "As far as Harrison making City Council, you can only cross that bridge when and if it comes to pass. To approach the mayor with accusations without solid evidence, you might as well smack a hornet's nest with a stick. It might serve you better to leave well enough alone, at this point. Harrison might not come back. It's possible that he's grown bored with the game."

Peggy's skin prickled. It was his use of the word 'you' as opposed to 'we'. It almost sounded deliberate. "Or, maybe he's looking for better sport, somewhere else," she reminded him.

"Perhaps. However, until you hear from him..." He shifted in his chair and winced. Glancing up at the clock, he said, "Well, much as I might want to, I can't quite wait up for the cows to come home, yet."

"Jumpin' Jehosiphat, why didn't you say so!" Betty scolded him.

When he attempted to stand up, everyone scrambled to their feet, reaching out as if to catch him, except for Peggy.

"I'm fine." Terry avoided their helping hands. "Not to worry. I've got it. I'm sure you all must be ready to call it a day, too."

With a shameful tug at her heart, Peggy realized that they'd spent the whole evening talking about themselves, never once asking him about his ten month ordeal. Gracious as always, he did not mention it, himself.

They donned jackets and walked out the front door, the crew still barraging Terry with stories, as he limped down the walkway. Paul gestured Peggy out the front door, then he closed and locked it.

At the gate, Betty hugged Terry. "We be back?"

Everyone paused, waiting for his answer. Terry hesitated, ever so briefly. Peggy's heart thudded when he glanced her way. He held up his cane to his crew and smiled. "In spirit. Absolutely."

"Okay then, lissen up mistah," Betty wagged her finger at him, "'cuz I gonna say it only once! I don't wanna see yo' face before noon tomor-rah, if that! We kin manage!"

"I have no doubt."

"I mean it!"

"Of course."

"Don't make me git on yo' case!"

"Wouldn't dream of it." Terry kissed her cheek.

"Don't think that gonna cut you no slack, neither."

"I'd be disappointed if it did."

"Bettah know it."

Terry offered a handshake to Lawrence. "Good to meet a true dog talker."

"Wull Jeeze," Joe laughed. "Look at 'im. He says jump, I say how high!"

"It all be 'bout the love, man," Lawrence said.

"Indeed." Terry turned to Curtis. "Words fail me, to finally count you among the flock."

"Apotheosized," Curits bowed, then climbed into Betty's car.

Terry glanced at Betty.

"Dictionary still be on the second shelf," she reminded him.

Joe draped an arm over Terry's shoulder, in confidence. "Y'know he can pick the Trifecta, eight outta ten times?"

"Which you haven't taken advantage of, due to the many restrictions concerning minors."

"Natch!" Joe shifted under Peggy's raised brow. "Just sayin'! For future reference. Four more years, he's legal."

Terry leaned down to Clara. "Thank you for keeping them all in line."

Clara blinked at him. "Have we met?"

"Ya see? Ya see what we been saddled with?" Joe whined.

"The Good Lord never gives us more than we can handle."

Betty eyed Joe up and down. "And then some."

"Hardee har-har," Joe opened the van's passenger door for Terry. "Hey man, since when you turn religious?"

"Since signing up for Medicare."

"Hey! Yo! Y'comin' Dillan?"

Still at the gate, Peggy stood between the van and the Jaguar. She looked to Paul. "Well I...it's kind of out of the way for you, Joe, isn't it?"

"Get outta here! C'mon, the chief's back!"

Paul shrugged to Peggy. "Go on, catch up."

Peggy smiled at him and headed for the van. Joe slid open the side door for her, and she climbed in.

"Are you sure you're all right, back there?" Terry asked from the passenger seat."

"Yes. Yes, thank you." She peered out the window and watched Joe toss Paul a salute, before he climbed in and turned the ignition key, revving the engine.

"By the way," Terry ventured. "Where's Ethel?"

Joe snorted a laugh, backing the van up from the fence. "Two more visits to Fegetti and Tiny from the doc, she's outta hock!"

Joe hit the gas pedal and burned rubber with a squeal of tires. Peggy gazed out the rear windows, as they bumped up the driveway. Paul was still leaning against the front gate, watching them drive away.

"So how 'bout a round at Kierney's to celebrate?" Joe suggested, easing the van to a stop light. "I wanna see Mike's face when you walk in!"

"Rain check," Terry patted his shoulder. "I'm still on a few meds."

"Right-sorry man, that's cool! Well, you name the day. My treat."

"It's a date." Terry tried to turn around and address Peggy. "So!"

She was sitting on an upturned bucket right behind him, and leaned into the light, so he could see her. "Hmn?"

"I'm glad to see that you and Paul finally broke bread."

"Oh, yes well, he's-he's done a lot for us."

In turning to talk to her, he winced and reached for his back.

"Are you all right?" Peggy asked.

"Whattsa matter?" Joe turned to Terry, worried.

"Nothing at all. I'm fine. Just a touch stiff, yet." Terry smiled at them both.

"I can flip the beacon and have ya at St. Mary's, in ten minutes flat."

"Yes, and that ride alone might put me back in traction."

Joe snorted a laugh. "Man, it's good t'have ya back! We missed ya! Didn't we Dillan?"

"Yes. Yes."

Finally the light changed, and Joe put the van in gear.

"You mention the doc and her breakin' bread? I swear, it was like pullin' teeth sometimes, though, right, Dillan? But we broke him in. He's kinda turned out to be an okay guy. Did we tell ya 'bout the time we got the van's brakes fixed?"

"Yes," Terry chuckled.

"You remember Fegetti's ape of a dog?"

"Tiny."

"Right!" As Joe relayed the story of Paul's impromptu heroics again, for the third time, Terry caught sight of Peggy in the side mirror, her face skirting in and out of the passing street lamps; looking preoccupied, quiet.

Joe pulled the van alongside the curb outside Peggy's building.

Terry rolled down the window as she got out. "Looks different."

Peggy looked around at her building. "Does it?" She tried to see it through his eyes. When she turned back around to him, she noticed his gaze settle briefly around her neck, where once she wore the St. Francis pendant he'd given her. Her hand fluttered to her throat, with a flash of guilt. She backed away from the van with a little wave. "So, we'll see you tomorrow?"

"Yes. Good night."

Peggy started up the walkway, buttoning her collar. She stopped and trotted back to the van. "I-I forgot." She reached into her coat pocket, pulled out the recorder, and handed it to him. "To give it back to you."

Terry looked perplexed for a second. "Oh. Ah, yes! Thank you. You might have to remind me how to use it."

"Sure." Peggy hesitated, wanting to tell Terry how happy she was to see him, but the words got stuck in her throat. "Good-good night." She turned and hurried into her building. From behind the lobby door, she watched the van drive away.

What's wrong with me, Peggy berated herself, staring after the tail lights. This is the moment we've all been wishing and hoping for, for nearly a year! Terry has come back! Why can't I feel anything?

She shivered and noticed that her hands were ice cold. She shoved them into her pockets. Pressing her eyes closed, she allowed herself to be whisked back to the steps, with Paul. In a moment, she could feel the back of his hand brushing her cheek, his fingers entwined with hers, his breath warm on her lips. All at once, she couldn't swallow the lump in her throat, and she opened her eyes. How could she feel so numb, so thrilled, and so ashamed, all at the same time?

And, of all the changes Terry could have noticed, why did it have to be the St. Francis pendant, clearly missing from around her neck?

Chapter 69

"I remember now why we had a second vehicle," Terry greeted Peggy, having to raise his voice over the barking dogs, as he limped into the office.

"Good morning," Peggy smiled.

Following him was Joe, juggling a pastry box. He turned and hollered at the dogs. "Shaddaaaaap!" Stuffing a cruller in his mouth, he handed the box to Peggy. "For the record, I stopped at every red light for old time's sake. Bet's gonna pick up Brunhilda."

"Okay." Peggy noticed Terry wince as he eased himself into his chair. "Are you-are you all right?"

His eyes flicked to her neck. She wished, now, that she hadn't worn the St. Francis pendant outside of her collar. It was such an obvious, and belated, gesture.

"When will the Pinto will be road-worthy, again?" he asked. "As I recall, when last we parted, the state police had a bounty on her hood."

"Mr. Fegetti says there's some sort of hold up with fuel pumps at the manufacturer. I'll give him another call and—I mean—do you want to call him?"

"No, no. I'll catch up with him later. How about a nice cup of cocoa?"

"Oh, we ran out of cocoa awhile ago. We've been drinking tea."

"Tea it is, then! I'd fetch it myself, but..." Terry patted his leg in apology.

"I'll get it!" Peggy scrambled to her feet and lifted the kettle off the hot plate. She stumbled over the kennel threshold in her hurry and nearly dropped it.

"Careful there! We don't need any more casualties!" Terry called out.

"I'm okay!" Peggy trotted the kettle down to the sink and flipped open the tap with trembling hands.

God, what's wrong with me? She berated herself, listening to the familiar sound of Terry's voice, as he bantered with Joe in the office. Until yesterday, it had been just a memory. Hearing it in real time threw her mind into a tailspin, careening from the past to the present, while her feelings hung on for dear life. In his presence, she felt like the quivery child who'd been more bedraggled than the scruffy dog she'd brought to the shelter. But, she wasn't that girl, anymore. So, why did she feel so confused?

She pressed her eyes closed and tried to lose herself in the sound of the pounding water in the kettle. Unbidden, she was on the back steps, again, maple seeds whirling over her. She felt the tenderness in Paul's touch when he brushed her cheek with the back of his fingers. She could feel his warm breath on her lips.

Cold water gushed over her hand. She slapped the tap off and poured out some of the water. As she carried the kettle back to the office, her mind raced. What was Paul thinking this morning? What would he say to her? What should she say to him? And, what, if anything, should she discuss with Terry on his first day back?

"What kind of tea would you like?" she asked as she set the kettle on the hot plate and dialed it to boil. "There's chamomile, mint, English breakfast."

Terry sat with the log book in his lap, absorbed in it. "Hmn? Oh. Whatever you're going to have."

"Chamomile sound all right?"

"Chamomile it is!"

Peggy reached for cups on the shelf. She couldn't find Terry's old mug. With a pin-prick of panic, she pushed mugs aside. What had happened to it? She couldn't remember the last time she'd seen it. She searched the medicine cabinet and, at last, found it behind the coat rack, covered in a thick layer of dust. Relieved, she snatched it up and wiped it clean.

"I don't know how ya drink that dishwater!" Joe said, with a gulp from a can of Tab.

"Have you ever tried it?" Terry replied, in his old familiar defense of her choice.

"Yeah, right! I look like a hippie to you?"

"No, Joe, I think it's safe to say you haven't changed one iota." Terry tossed an impish smile to him.

"Got that right!" Joe sputtered crumbs. "Now the doc…he's lookin' like he might go hippie, any day now."

"Joe!" Peggy chided him, "He's hardly a hippie."

"Hey, it starts with the long hair, okay? Before ya know it, it's love beads and Commune-City, I'm tellin' ya."

"I have to say," Terry chuckled. "It is Paul who's changed the most."

Peggy dropped tea bags into the mugs, and although she smiled, she felt a bit stung. She thought she'd come a long way from the first day they'd met.

The dogs erupted into barking. Her heart skipped a beat as she caught a glimpse of the Jaguar out the window, pulling down the driveway into a parking space.

"Speakin' of the doc," Joe glanced at his watch. "What's he doin' in, so early?"

"I'm looking forward to your talks," Terry said to Peggy. "I hear you're quite a team."

"We just…it's-it's nothing really, we just stand up and talk."

"Do you remember when I first suggested it? You fairly dashed out of here, convinced you couldn't do it."

Peggy heard the front gate open and close. "Um, yes I do remember."

"When are you going out again?"

"Going out?"

"With Paul? To your next seminar?"

"I-I'm not sure. Friday, I think."

"Bet has 'em booked almost every day." Joe looked over the calendar.

"Well, I'm looking forward to it," Terry said.

Peggy heard the front door open and close. "Oh, well, I don't know if…I'll have to check with the people who, you know…to see if you can…I mean, ask if it's all right." The moment she said it, she wished she hadn't. Terry looked perplexed.

"I'll sit in the back. You won't even know I'm there."

The phone rang, and Peggy quickly reached past Terry for it, but Joe snatched it up, waving her off.

"I got it. Shelter." The other phone rang. "Hold on a sec?" He swiveled around in his chair. "Jeeze, buckle up, here we go." He snatched up the other phone receiver. "Shelter. Yeah. Uh-huh. Can you describe him for me?"

"Peggy?"

As Joe answered one ringing phone after another, Peggy looked up to find Terry peering at her, concern in his eyes. He looked as if he was about to ask her a question, but the office door opened, and Paul walked in.

"Morning!" Paul said with a cheerful smile.

"Morning." Terry looked him up and down with surprise.

So did Peggy. "Hi."

His hair was still damp and slicked back. A wave of aftershave enveloped her as he passed, burning her nose. His lab coat had been starched and pressed, and he wore brand new Italian slacks, a new button-down Oxford shirt, tie, and tie pin. He looked like he'd just arrived for a job interview and didn't once look back at her.

"How was your first night back? I can imagine how strange it must feel," he said as he unpacked his medical bag into the medicine cabinet. "I mean, the changes."

"What do ya mean there ain't no such place as Walnut street?" Joe cried into the phone. "I'm sittin' here, lookin' at our return address on the freakin' oil bill! Okay, mister? Hear me out. Put the beer down, pick up the phone book and look it up!"

"Then again," Terry mused, "it's almost as if I never left. I was just saying to Peggy, that I'd love to sit in on one of your seminars."

"Great. We've got the Rotary, again, on Friday."

"Ah! Jeff's a character, isn't he?"

"Tell me about it. He always shows up with a list of questions that put me right back to my qualifying days."

"He wanted to be a vet. Knows just enough to get it all wrong. What's your topic?"

Paul closed the cabinet doors, and for the first time, looked at Peggy. "Are we still going ahead with spay and neuter, this one out?"

"If-if that's okay."

"Your call."

"Joe filled me in about the spay-neuter clinic you two are planning," Terry began.

"Oh, well!" Peggy fidgited in her chair. "It's j-just an idea."

She glanced up to find Paul peering at her, now, his brow knitted. Amidst ringing phones, the tea kettle whistled. She lurched past Paul to shut off the hot plate, just as Terry turned to do it. They collided.

"Oh! I'm sorry!"

"We seem to be a bit out of sync!" Terry chuckled.

"Yes." Peggy poured water in the cups.

Terry offered Paul his mug. "Tea?"

"I had coffee on the way in, thanks."

"Well, a spay-neuter clinic sound's like a splendid idea."

"It's just in the planning stages, right now," Paul sat on the edge of the counter. "But, we figured we ought to start early, before next spring's flood, so to speak. We're planning to introduce a policy requiring all adoptions to be spayed or neutered before they leave the shelter, and although we know it might be a tough pill to swallow at first, we..."

Peggy wondered if Terry was counting the number of "we" references Paul made, too, but found that he was smiling with gracious enthusiasm, like always.

"...we've also been debating an approach to the legislature with regards to a statewide, ballot initiative next year."

"That's ambitious."

"We think it's an issue ripe for public support."

Joe hung up the phone and snatched up his keys. "I got three stray calls. Two dogs, one up on Eagle Rock, one up on South Mountain. Probably the same bugger makin' tracks all through the picnic parks, oh yeah, and Taffy's on top of the Dairy Queen roof, again."

"Taffy?" Terry looked perplexed.

"You remember, that big coon cat that lives next door to the place? The con figured out how to get pity handouts by pretendin' she's stuck, up there?"

"Well, I'm sure you'll straighten her out."

"It's Rita, her owner, we gotta straighten out." He donned his shades and flipped the CB unit's on switch. It flashed and zapped him with a shock. "Ow!"

"Ah...that I remember."

"Ha, ha!" He turned to Peggy. "We need anything out there?" Then, as if catching himself, he stammered to Terry. "I mean, y'know, supplies or-or..."

With apparent deference, Terry looked to Peggy.

She cleared her throat. "I-I don't think so."

"Ten-four. I'll have my ears on." He zipped up his jacket and headed out the door.

"So. What's on the agenda today?" Paul asked.

"Well," Terry ventured and turned to Peggy. "How about a peek at what you two have been up to, down in the...in Beula's nether region?"

Peggy exchanged an awkward glance with Paul. "Oh well, that's all Paul's—Dr. Hayward's—work. Down-down there."

"I had help," Paul said, finally. "Lawrence and Curtis have been a godsend, and believe it or not, Mr. Riley straighened out the wiring without burning us down."

"A minor miracle, no doubt!" He grasped his cane. "Care to give me a tour?"

"Sure," Paul opened the door for him.

"Peggy?"

"I-I can't. I ought to stay up here. Betty isn't…"

"Of course! What am I thinking?" Terry demurred.

Peggy smiled, but averted her eyes. Her smile faded, too, when he closed the door behind them. She felt off balance, sitting beside Terry's chair, instead of in it. She couldn't see out the window, but she could trace the steps of the two men, by the direction of the dogs' barking, as they walked down under the overhang to the cellar.

"I must say," Terry looked around at the transformed cellar space, with genuine admiration, "you've made a right good job of it!"

"We're light years away from where we want to be, but, depending on how this year goes, we were talking about maybe knocking through that wall to the freezer's suite of rooms out there. Of course, it's just something we were batting around. Y'know, ideas."

"Splendid ideas," Terry assured him. "I hadn't imagined a medical annex in there. How do you envision the space?"

"Well, if we, that is, you, incorporate the entire footprint, you could have a workable surgery, as well as a recovery room, plus quarantine. I realize it's ambitious, like you said, but that would give us a full service facility."

"It's a mite closer to sterile than what you were handed a year ago!"

Paul laughed lightly. "Yeah."

"There's nothing wrong with ambitious," Terry reminded him, "especially when it's one for all and…" He silently nodded the rest of the adage along with Paul. Looking around, he asked, "Does Peggy ever assist you?"

Paul's smile slipped. "No, Curtis does. Smart as a whip, that kid, he's aiming for pre-vet, after graduating. Peg's got enough on her plate just keeping it together, upstairs."

"Indeed."

"Look, I hope it doesn't seem like…"

"Like you've accomplished the impossible? You have. And in just ten months. I hardly recognize the place." He looked out the little French doors, as leaves drifted down to the yard. "Damned if it isn't true what they say. About time? You hear it ad nauseam when you're a lad. 'Slow down, enjoy your youth, time flies, blink and your life is half over, make the most of it.' Or my all time favorite: Time Heals All. It does, doesn't it? It's rather sobering, too. We all think we're so…necessary. Then, one morning we wake to find the world gets on quite nicely without us. At first, it can be a bit of a shock. Then again, it's rather freeing. Without having to endure a fall, I rather recommend it." He toed Beula's grate. "But, I digress. Truth is, I've been stalling, afraid to ask how you've been getting on with our problem child."

Paul took a breath. "We've had our ups and downs, and there were times I almost drop-kicked her from here to Nyack, but she's…really come into her own. She's…a special girl."

Terry chuckled, and clapped him on the back. "I was talking about the boiler."

Perched on the edge of her chair, Peggy wondered what in heaven's name Terry and Paul could be talking about for the better part of an hour, down there. She grasped her St. Francis pendant tightly and tried to ignore the flip-flopping of her stomach.

"Is it true 'bout you, Miss Peggy?"

Peggy was pulled out of her musing by Curtis. He, Betty and Clara had arrived and were busy making room for Terry in the office. At the moment, they were packing retired case folders into boxes.

Curtis held out Lucky's file to her, his brow pinched in a frown. "You done give up on Lucky?"

"Well, it's been a long time, and I think-I think it's time to move on. There are so many animals we need to find homes for and…"

Curtis averted his eyes, clearly disappointed. It surprised her. She would have thought that Paul's pragmatism had rubbed off on him.

"How could you forgit 'bout him?" he asked.

"I haven't, Curtis. Believe me. It's just…well, sometimes we have to let go. Tell you what, I'll hold on to it a while longer, how's that?"

Curtis hesitated, then handed her the file. "How long?"

Peggy thought about that. "Thanksgiving. That's when I found him. That'll be a year. That sound fair?"

Curtis shifted on his feet. Finally, he nodded. "Thank you." He picked up a box marked "retired" and then turned for the door, just as Terry came in. They bumped into each other.

"So sorry about that, Curtis! I always seem to be underfoot!"

"Copesthetic." Curtis hefted the box out the door.

Betty cupped a hand over the phone receiver. "You come up them stairs by yo'self?!"

"Happily, I am no longer in need of a spotter—just a bit of exercise," Terry eased himself into his chair, grimacing.

"Are you all right?" Peggy asked. He nodded, but she studied his face, weighing how much she ought to press him. "So, what-what do you think?"

"Of the cellar?"

Peggy swallowed and then nodded.

"I like it. Smart use of space. And, the annex idea? Splendid. I hear it was yours."

"Everyone pitched ideas."

"He said you'd say that," Terry smiled. "He's a good man. Not that I told you so, but, I told you so." He reached for the log book, inhaling sharply.

"Terry?" Peggy reached out to him, but he waved her away.

"I'm fine. Just a spasm."

"I saw that!" Betty wagged her finger at him. "What I tell you 'bout overdoin'!" She depressed the mic on the CB unit. "Joe! Where you be at?"

Static crackled over the unit. "How many times I gotta tell ya, it's 'what's your twenty'!"

"Git yo' tail back here RFN or I gonna give you twenty, all right!"

"Ter okay?" Joe's voice sounded concerned.

"Nothing a pie and a pitcher wouldn't put right," Terry called out.

"Don't lissen to him!" Betty replied into the mic. "You know how he be!"

"On my way."

"There!" Betty declared with a proud toss of her head.

"Nag, nag, nag!" Terry scoffed, genially, and perused the log book.

Before Betty could retort, the phone rang. "Sheltah."

Terry glanced over his glasses to Peggy. "I am fine, Miss Worry Wort. A creak and twinge, now and again. Much like being in a new house. Things have to settle. Now then, back to our muttons. What have we spinning on the plate today?"

Peggy pulled out her notebook and slid Lucky's file inside. "Just the feed delivery, this afternoon. And, we promised to look into the squirrel problem up on Mr. Greeley's property. The estate up against the reservation?"

"I don't see it..." Terry scanned the log book.

"Oh, we keep appointments in this notebook, now," Peggy paused, realizing that she'd just told the owner of the company, that his employees had changed the way he did business while he was out of town. "I mean, we still use it for notes."

"Ah!" Terry looked over the new appointment book. "I see. You keep appointments separate from calls. Now that's what I call organization! Smashing."

The office door opened, and Paul walked in, notebook in hand. "What are we doing for lunch?"

Peggy darted a glance to Terry.

He jerked a thumb towards Betty. "I daresay the boss may be sending me home."

"Need a ride?" Paul asked.

"Joe's on his way." With what looked like a covert glance to Betty over his shoulder, he lowered his voice. "I need to nip round to chambers, catch the mayor up." He laid a forefinger against his lips. "Shhh!"

Peggy regarded him with a little jab of surprise. The mayor's office? Why hadn't he mentioned it her? More to the point, why hadn't he invited her along? Shelter business was her business, wasn't it?

"You want to grab a bite at the diner?" Paul asked. "Peg?"

"Well, I'm not sure if..." she looked to Terry.

"No reason you two can't pop out," Terry said.

"Maybe-maybe we should talk about the mayor?"

"Hmn? What about?"

"Well, whatever you think we should talk about."

"Oh, I thought you had something specific in mind. No, you two go get lunch. Unless there's something pressing?"

"Well no, not-not pressing...no."

"Do take lunch, then. I daresay, how often does one ever get a chance, around here, without being interrupted by one daft problem or another?"

From the parking lot, the van's horn tapped, *Shave and a Haircut, Two Bits,* announcing Joe's arrival.

"Speak of the devil." Terry leaned towards the window, this time, eliciting an audible groan of pain.

"Maybe, you're over-over doing it," Peggy stammered. "I can cover, here. M-maybe you should just go home?"

"I'm fine," Terry grimaced.

"Tell you what," Paul pulled a memo pad from his pocket. "Why don't you two stay, talk about what you need to talk about, and I'll pick-up lunch? I can be back in fifteen minutes, if we use Jack's. Terry?"

Terry held up a hand. "I'm fine! Besides, I promised Joe a beer at Kierney's."

Peggy, once again, felt a jab. He hadn't even thought of inviting her to join them?

"Peg?" Paul prodded.

"Hmn? I'm-I'm all right."

"You have to eat. On me. What do you want?"

"Oh, I don't know. Anything."

"Salad anything, sandwich anything, or burger anything?"

"Anything-anything. It doesn't matter."

"Honestly," Terry intervened, "I do wish you'd both go to lunch."

The dogs burst into barking in the kennel. "ShaaDAAAAAAAAAP!" Joe kicked open the office door, accompanied by Curtis. "Get out your umbrellies; it's gonna rain."

"What do you want for lunch?" Paul asked, searching for his keys.

"Gimme a burger-with. And some fries...oooh! Make 'em chili-cheese, with onions."

"Curtis?"

"Got my PBJ, thank you, Doctah."

"Mrs. Croft?" Paul looked to Clara, who'd been knitting in the corner.

She eyed them all. "Milk of Magnesia, if this ring around the rosie you three dervishes been dancin', keeps up."

The list between his teeth, Paul donned his coat. "Going once, twice..."

"Betty?" Terry asked.

"Sheltah." On the phone, Betty held up a bag lunch.

"Ah, yes," Terry smiled, with a tap to his forehead. "I forgot. Our vegetarian."

Betty abruptly spun around, her hand cupped over the receiver. "Mistah Harrison! He want to speak wiff the manager."

Awkwardly, they all glanced between Peggy and Terry. Peggy gestured for Terry take the phone. He took the receiver from Betty.

"Hello. Yes it is. Very well, thank you, and you?"

At the door, Paul had stopped mid-stride to listen to the conversation.

"Yes, so I've been informed. Yes." Terry looked out the front window as he spoke, his back to the room. "Not at the moment. I'll take a look-see, then ring you up. Well, there is the issue of the seven day legal hold, mmn-hmn. Yes, it might require a few days to...no, that won't be necessary, I'll ring you when...mmn-hmn...what is the number where you can you be reached?"

Peggy already had Lucky's file open in her lap, rifling through the papers. She placed Harrison's business card down in front of Terry. He picked it up.

"Yes, we have it. Very good. Yes. We'll be in touch. Thank you." Terry hung up the phone, turning to face the crew. "Mr. Harrison will be out of town for a few weeks, but when he returns, he'll be stopping by to look at our dogs."

"He knew you were back!" Joe pounded the counter with his fist and whirled to Peggy. "What did I tell ya! Ambush City! Well, he can stop by every friggin' day from now 'til freakin' Doomsday, he ain't gettin' one of our dogs!"

"Ovah my coal-sweet carcass!" Betty declared, as she broke open a new inhaler.

"Ter, it's a slam-dunk no!" Joe insisted.

"We can't just hand ovah anothah dog to that banjo!" Betty agreed. "Wiff his record?"

"Record of what?" Paul interjected, and glanced to Peggy, too. "No matter what we might assume, the man's complied with every citation, he's paid every fine, every medical bill, every time his dog came through here."

"But, lookit how many times that sweet mutt done end up here! Turn the damn file ovah to the court, see what the judge say!"

"Without proof of wrongdoing, you could look like the bad guys, over at Town Hall."

"Hey!" Joe jumped in again, "Bottom line, we got the right to refuse to adopt to any Tom, Dick n' schmuck, remember?" Joe pointed to the handmade sign on the wall, declaring just that, verbatim.

Terry adjusted his glasses and peered at it. "Ah. Nice touch."

"So, we're covered!" Joe declared and swung his boots up onto the counter. "He ain't got no rights, here."

"Not exactly," Paul spoke up. "He has the right to sue, remember?"

"Let him try!"

"Can you afford a lawyer? I bet he can."

"'E wouldn't need a solicitor," Clara pointed out. "Town would serve us notice."

"And," Paul pointed out, "he's just the kind of schmuck to make sure the town would do it, too!"

"I don't give a rat's butt hole! That dickweed ain't gettin' one of our dogs!" Joe snapped, and the room fell quiet.

Peggy studied Terry. As when she first met him, he had calmly listened to the crew work it out amongst themselves. Only this time, there was a marked difference. His patient expression had been replaced with one of concern, and he looked tired. He looked at her.

"Peggy?"

All eyes turned to her. She ran her hand over Lucky's folder in her lap and took a breath. "You know how I feel about it."

"Yes. What I'm asking is, what do you think might be done to deal with it?"

Peggy felt her skin prickle at his paternal tone, but she was not about to let it show. She thought hard. "We can use the adoption screening process as we would with anyone else. We can take down his request, ask for his references, we can say none of the animals we have are ready for adoption, or are right for him, but that we'll keep him in mind."

"That's just stone-wallin' a con!" Joe argued, "walkin' him 'round on a rope!"

"Yes," Terry said. "And, what happens when you give a crook enough rope?"

"He hangs himself, but Ter, this guy ain't just a dimestore clepto, he's a weasel. And, he covers his tracks, man."

"It doesn't matter. What Peggy is suggesting, is using what is available to you, to either deflect or trap said weasel. For the time being, until you can trap him, use it to deflect him."

"Okay, so," Joe reasoned, "no matter which dog he chooses, we find a reason why it won't be a good match."

"Catch twenty-two," Curtis murmured.

"Check mate," Terry conceded.

"So, you tellin' us to lie?" Betty queried.

"Not at all. How many times have you steered someone away from an animal that you know in your heart of hearts is the wrong match, even when the person is not..."

"Not the devil incarnate?" Clara suggested.

Terry smiled. "You're not fibbing, you're merely more particular about the matches on the days Mr. Harrison comes trolling. Perhaps you notice that the dog he's interested in barks a lot. Perhaps it has a history of aggression that you need to look into."

"What if he picks out a slap-happy dog?" Joe countered.

"Maybe Happy be too in yo' face," Betty suggested. "Got some of that aggression goin' on."

"Mad dog," Clara offered.

"Bad dog!" Betty grinned. "Bad 'tude, out from behind bars."

"And, if it's a quiet one," Joe chimed in, "it's maybe depressed-like. Maybe he's got med issues."

"That's walking a thin line," Paul joined in. "He'll eventually figure it out. And, I won't fake medical records."

"You don't gotta fake nuthin', Doc, I get it. See it's maybe you ain't handy to sign off on the adoption, or do the exam, you're in surgery, you don't got the right papers, or whatever."

"Soon as we git wind which one he put his evil-eye on," Betty said, "we adopt that one out pronto to somebody bettah suited or put it in quarantine just f'observation, mind you, so you won't be tellin' no white lie, neither."

"Worse to worse, we foster it, like th'underground railroad." Joe nudged Betty. "You remember that, right?" Betty rolled up a newspaper in warning. "What? What'd I say?"

"I don't think it will get that far," Terry interrupted. "I think Peggy's analogy of the sidestep is enough. You are merely using the same loop holes in the law that he skirts around, to your advantage. You hold the deck of cards."

"He'll figure it out," Paul said.

"What you're hoping is that he does figure it out and, as Peggy suggested the other day, he moves on in search of easier sport."

The room fell quiet. Peggy looked between them, then allowed her eyes to settle on Terry. That the rest of the crew seemed satisfied did not surprise her, but that Terry appeared fine with it, bothered her.

"But, that's no answer," she blurted out. "It doesn't stop him. He just goes somewhere else and gets another dog. You said so, yourself! Remember?"

Even she was surprised at the sharpness of her tone. When Terry turned his gaze on her, she suddenly felt like he was standing on the other side of an invisible fence.

He nodded, finally. "But, it won't be on your watch. Not on your corner."

Peggy regarded him, unable to conceal the disappointment she felt inside.

"Well, from our cornah to the Lawd's ear!" Betty broke the uneasy silence. "We gonna hafta spread the good news to othah kennels. By time we troo, he be runnin' into brick walls where evah he go, then!"

"That could get dicey." Paul shook his head. "I think we need to tread carefully because, bottom line," he looked directly at Peggy, "we have a reputation to think of, now."

"Doc," Joe spoke up, "with all due respect and all that BS, how can ya lookit that guy and not see a pattern?"

"Doesn't matter what I see. What we need, is hard evidence to convince a judge to charge the man with Title Four, Chapter Twenty-Two. Because that's the only way you're going to get him. *Legally.*"

"Pfft," Clara quoted; "'A judge is nobbut a referee between lawyers, and lawyers is the trouble with law and goverment.'"

"Epicurus," Curtis noted. Clara nodded, pleased.

"And a jury's nuthin' more n' twelve schmoes putzin' around tryin' to figger who's got the best lawyer," Joe shrugged. "And, you can quote me on it."

"And this from the "G" wearin' the badge!" Betty chided him.

"Harrison's not just any schmoe," Paul added. "He's connected to players out there, and he certainly knows his way around the court system. Enough to tie us in red tape until our account's emptied. And, that I think he'd do just for sport. This is more than just about getting another dog."

Peggy felt eyes on her and looked up, to find Terry regarding her from across the room.

Chapter 70

To everyone's relief, especially Peggy's, Harrison did not show up. The situation at the shelter had become difficult enough without his interference.

It wasn't long before Peggy noticed that hers was not the only poise that had been shaken by Terry's return. After establishing a rapport with one another over the course of ten months, the crew now found themselves having to redefine their roles. It wasn't an easy adjustment for anyone. The dynamics shifted like the winds of the changing seasons. Often, the crew appeared confused as to whom to turn with a question, and when anyone asked for the manager, they appeared stymied, altogether.

No one felt more confused about it all, than Peggy. She'd taken to coming in an hour earlier in the mornings, just because it was quiet; there were no phones, no crew, no tension. She told herself it was so she could concentrate on her work, but more often than not, she just sat in Terry's chair and stared out the window, tugging on her St. Francis pendant. That was another thing; when Terry was around, she wore the pendant on the outside of her shirt. When Paul was around, she kept it tucked inside, out of sight. She felt like a liar to both men, with no real sense as to whom she now owed her allegiance.

Somewhere between the wavering moment on the back steps with Paul, and the surreal moment when Terry walked back into their lives, she had lost her footing. Since neither man had made a move to clear the air with her, she had no clue as to how to reconcile her feelings, and so avoided time alone with either of them, in self-defense.

Tension mounted when Terry not only invited himself to their out-of-shelter talks, he acted as chauffeur. The seating arrangements in the newly repaired Pinto didn't help. Paul insisted that she sit up front with Terry. On the return trip, when Peggy tried to take her turn in the back, Paul wouldn't allow it. It seemed to her that he was actually trying to push her and Terry together. She wasn't sure what irritated her more, that he insisted, or that she complied, without discussion.

The seminar trips should have been fun! For heaven's sake, she scolded herself, over and over. Terry was back! What is wrong with me? Isn't this what I'd wished and prayed for? To hear his voice, in real time, to see him sitting in his chair, smiling that warm, impish smile at me?

She pressed her eyes closed and thought back to the twilight evening on the stairs with Paul. Surely, she hadn't imagined it? Why hadn't he said anything about it to her? Why hadn't he tried to reignite that moment with her?

Peggy sighed. If she was honest with herself, the most confusing aspect of all, was the niggling dilemma of whether or not she even wanted him to rekindle the spark. With Terry around, she didn't. And yet, Terry seemed either to forget, or maybe he wanted to forget, their own lost moment, last Christmas, allowing it to lie undisturbed in memory, until it too, faded away.

It would have been kinder, she thought, had they both just slapped her and been done with it.

Peggy frowned at the calendar. It was already Halloween. Four weeks had passed since Terry's return, and yet it felt as if it had only been four minutes; the tumult inside her heart still twirling in confusion. Halloween, she thought, wryly. How appropriate. Ghouls and ghosts ferrying forth to haunt all the foolish mortals pretending not to fear their own shadows. She wanted to peel the calendar pages back to the way things were before. But...before when? Which date would she have preferred to have missed? When she was on the run, scared and alone? When she worried herself sick over a dog she could not help? When Terry disappeared, dropping the world in her lap to sort out?

Shame on you!

Like a rogue wave, guilt smacked her from behind, washing over her, and filling her mouth with a vile taste. She blinked at the ceiling, grappling with tears. Yes. Shame on me. Because I do, I do wish I could rewind the clock, to the moment just before Terry came back, rewind to the night on the steps with Paul. She wanted to slow it all down until Terry's return was somewhere off in the distance.

Deep inside, another part of her wanted to yank those calendar pages back to January second, to take that ride home with Terry, before the accident ever happened. What might have blossomed between them? Where might they all be, right now? Would that moment on the back steps with Paul have never evolved?

And yet, it had. How could she deny that it had? How could he? Something did happen out there. Some buried part of her had awakened, as if from a deep slumber. In the passage of time without Terry, she had also found a voice of her own. She knew that somehow, she needed to come to terms with it all, otherwise it would become obvious to Terry that something was terribly amiss with his assistant manager.

Searching the watermark stains on the ceiling for a recognizable pattern, she suspected that he already knew.

"Ten-seventeen!" Joe's voice crackled between bursts of static over the CB unit. "—er! —illan! —irty four! —ome back!"

Peggy lifted her head from the stack of newspapers. She'd been scanning lost and found pet ads all morning, as the kennel filled up again with strays, due to the onset of cold, wet weather.

"Did he just say ten-seventeen or thirty-four?"

Betty depressed the mic lever. "Joe, come back, you be breakin' up."

Static buzzed over the CB unit. "—twenty-five the doc?"

"What did he say?" Peggy asked.

"'E never says naught worth a pair of fetid dingo kidneys," Clara remarked, brushing a gray angora cat in her lap.

"Try channel fourteen."

Betty twisted the knob back and forth, trying to hear in between the popping, hissing static. "It's all gobble-dee-gook."

"—Doc...rollin'...ell...im...four." The hissing static cut Joe's voice off.

A spark zapped Betty's fingers. "Ow!" Betty yelped. "Damn gizmo bit me!"

"It's shorting again." Peggy pounced on the unit, twisted wires and depressed the microphone lever. "Base to Napper Joe, you're motor boating. Copy? Come back? Are you rolling with an HBC? Come back yes or no?"

A burst of static, then Joe's voice, but it was cut off. "—O."

"That be a no," Betty said.

Peggy depressed the mic lever and said, "Copy that. Is it a bandaid?"

A hissing moment passed. "—ess."

"That be a yes," Betty confirmed and pressed the wall intercom button. "Doctah?"

Paul's voice intercut the bursts of CB static. "Yes?"

"Injury incomin'," Betty told him. "No othah info. Fifteen at the outside."

"Got it."

Peggy switched channels and twisted the squelch on the CB unit trying to hear Joe's fading voice. "Napper, come back? Ten-twenty?"

"—ssing —ock —eer —chung."

"He's up Eagle Rock way," Betty murmured. "By Watchung. 'Long the reservation."

"That's what, ten minutes?" Peggy looked at the clock.

"Give or take, minus traffic."

"Eight if he runs the lights," Clara said and laid down a dollar.

Betty raised her a dollar. "Five, if he fly down Mountain in neutral."

Being only ten-thirty in the morning, Peggy suspected that there wouldn't be much traffic on the streets. However, it was Friday and it was Halloween. She pressed the microphone lever.

"That's a big ten-four Napper. Keep eyes peeled. Drive the key and don't feed the bears! Out."

There was another burst of static, and although all three women strained to hear, they couldn't make out what Joe might or might not have said.

"He gone behind Eagle Rock," Betty looked at the map on the wall. "Should we ring Terry ovah the mayor's office?"

"Oh." Once again, Peggy had forgotten about informing Terry of a 10-17 when he was off site. "Well, he should be back any minute. It's not an HBC, and it can't be all that serious or Joe'd have Paul meet him up at the EVC for x-rays. If it's like the last two yesterday, they can handle it until Terry shows up. Curtis and Lawrence'll be here by two-thirty today. We should be fine."

"Need me to do anythang?"

"We're all caught up I think, right?"

"Seem as like."

"I'll bring the dogs in." Peggy headed out the office door.

Walking the length of the kennel, Peggy set biscuits into bowls and made sure that there were open runs. Both emergencies that Joe had rushed in the day before involved cats, not dogs. In the morning, two cats were strung up by their necks by a group of boys in the park, and then they were stoned. A jogger chased off the boys and held the two cats up so that they wouldn't strangle, while she screamed for help. It was providence that Joe had been returning from patrol, at that moment, and took the short cut through the park.

Outside of being traumatized, Paul found that the cats suffered no permanent physical damage. The whole incident had upset everyone, especially Peggy. She sent Joe out to try and track down the kids, before she succumbed to the urge to hunt them down herself. So embroiled was she, over the incident, she neglected to inform Terry about sending Joe out on the bounty hunt, when he returned from Town Hall.

It wasn't the first time she'd failed to inform him about shelter matters. She wasn't used to having to confer, let alone defer to him, and she couldn't help but feel dressed down, being relegated back to employee status. Truth be told, she'd begun to resent it, and the guilt she felt needled her, all day long.

She peered up through the small, dusty windows above the front runs, to the sky. At least it wasn't going to rain. The trick-or-treaters would have a good goblin run, tonight. She had let the dogs stay outside longer than usual in hopes they'd tire themselves out, running back and forth. They missed their extended exercise out in the back with Curtis and Lawrence, now that the two were back in school.

She hauled on cables to lift the metal guillotine doors up on their squeaking tracks, one by one, and observed each dog trot inside. She studied their behaviors and the overall look of their health to report in the daily log. The dogs wolfed down the treats, and she paused here and there to pet them through the fences.

She wondered about what Terry was doing at Town Hall. He hadn't talked with her about it. Again. She tried to shove the feeling of unease from her gut, but couldn't. Again. Something had been going on, and she wasn't being let in on it. Again. Not that it was any of her business. Not anymore. Terry was not obligated to include her in his business dealings. But, she felt let down that he didn't. Or, that he didn't trust her enough to include her.

Her thoughts drifted to Paul. The calendar pages had clearly turned back with him, all the way back to the days they barely spoke to one another. He remained sequestered down in the...she shuddered and bowed her head. She couldn't really blame him. Every time they had a moment alone, she made sure it wasn't for long. She felt so unsettled in his presence, she used any distraction to avoid him. And she still had not set foot on those stairs.

An abrupt squeal of tires, and the van's horn honks startled her to her feet. She snatched a leash off of the center post, and raced out the front door.

As she trotted down the walkway, she saw Joe swerve the van so that its nose pointed into the warehouse fence, and the rear doors faced the gate. At the same moment, she spotted Terry in the Pinto, zipping down the driveway into the lot, too.

Joe jumped out of the van without switching off the revolving yellow emergency light. "It's bad, Doc."

"I thought you said it wasn't an HBC!" Paul called out, as he crested the gravel drive with a blanket under his arm.

Peggy hurried out of the gate towards the van's rear doors. "Sorry, we couldn't make out what you were saying."

"Hold off, both of ya!" Joe intercepted them. "We're gonna need the pole!"

"What've you got there, Joe?" Terry asked, as he limped towards them.

Joe eased the doors open. A wild, vicious snarling and the sickening stench of skunk pushed them all backwards.

Peggy peered into the van's interior, to the standing cage. A large, filthy animal attacked the bars of the cage, barking, spittle flying. She gasped.

"*Lucky?*"

Terry looked on, disbelief darkening his countenance. "Good Lord."

"That's...that's not the same dog," Paul said, "it can't be..." He took a cautious step closer. The dog attacked the bars in a frenzy of snarling. "Christ..."

"Watch it, Doc." Joe eased out a noosed rabies pole from a wall brace in the van.

Peggy took a step closer. "Lucky, it's me."

"Stay back!" Paul shot his arm out in front of her, just as the dog lunged, snapping at her from behind the cage.

"Found him caught under a fence," Joe said. "Cops wanted to shoot him."

"Shoot him?" Peggy exclaimed. "He's just scared! Something's happened to him."

"Run in with a skunk, for one thing," Joe agreed.

"He didn't bite you, did he?" Paul asked.

"Tried, but no cigar. I poled him 'til the cops cut the fence."

"He's scared," Peggy repeated.

"He means business," Paul retorted.

"Did you notice any bite wounds on him?" Terry asked.

"Y'kiddin'?" Joe balked. "It was all I could do to dodge those jaws and keep the cops from blastin' him."

Paul crouched down and peered into the shadowy cage. "We'd have to shave him to be sure, anyway."

"Tell me some S.O.B.'s been trainin' him for dog fightin'?" Joe suggested.

"Oh God!" Peggy whispered.

"I don't think so," Paul said, "there'd be some indication—recent scarring, bald patches, especially around the muzzle, ears and neck. But, I don't see any. Where you say you picked him up?"

"Reservation. Cops got calls from rezzies up there 'bout a wolf runnin' down deer. I think he's the dog we've been chasin' tails over, for the past few weeks."

"Do we know if he's bitten anybody?"

"I got some buds lookin' it up at the station," Joe admitted with a sheepish look to Peggy.

Peggy felt her cheeks flush hot in anger. "If he did bite anybody, he was defending himself!"

"I had to check, Saint Fran," Joe said. "Lookit him."

Paul looked up at Terry. "Harrison needs to be notified."

Terry nodded. "I'll take care of it."

"What? *No!*" Peggy blurted out.

"We have to, Peggy, you know that, it's a liability issue," Terry reminded her.

"Why do you think Lucky's in this condition in the first place!" she shot back.

"No one is taking this dog, anywhere," Paul clarified, "until we find out whether or not he's been vaxxed against rabies. That's what we need to get from Harrison, right off."

"Rabies?" Peggy repeated.

"What do we know about his vax record?" Paul asked.

"W-we don't. I mean, he's got no license with Farroway."

"I don't believe he ever received one, here?" Terry looked to Joe.

"Nope. Harrison always picked him up, took him to a vet out of our jurisdiction. He maybe got one in another township."

"Without a tag number to trace..." Terry sighed. "We'll have to contact the state and go through their records."

"Can't you call that other sawbones, DeGrate?" Joe asked Paul. "The one he took him to, last time."

"DeGrate says he changes vets more than a humaniac."

Peggy looked between them, with rising frustration. "Why are we even talking about rabies? There is no way Lucky has rabies!"

"I want everyone to take a good look at that dog," Paul said in a sharp voice. "He's either exhibiting classic rabid behavior, right now, or he's gone feral. Either way, he's a real danger to the public. And us."

At that moment, Lucky stopped barking and cowered in the rear corner of the cage. Peggy could see him trembling, from ears to tail. This only seemed to deepen Paul's concern. Joe too, looked somber. She looked to Terry.

He nodded to Paul. "I agree."

"He's scared!" Peggy entreated them. "All he needs is rest, some quiet, and food. He's practically starved. Look at him! God only knows what he's been through! He might have broken bones, or an internal injury. Pain would make him lash out like that, too!"

She knew that Paul would have to concede that point. He seemed to mull it over. He pulled a pair of latex gloves from his pocket and stretched them over his hands. "Either way, I can't bring him to the EVC like this." He pulled two more pair of gloves from his bag and tossed them to Joe and Terry. "I assume you're all up to date on your boosters?"

"Natch," Joe said, pulling on the gloves.

Terry nodded, then paused, and turned to Peggy. For a moment, it seemed as if he was reluctant to ask, but he did. "Peggy, you were vaccinated back in December, wasn't it? About the same time you filled out your paperwork?"

Peggy felt her face flush. She turned to Paul. "I can't believe you're thinking it's rabies! You said yourself there hasn't been a case of canine rabies since nineteen fifty-six!"

Paul held out a pair of gloves to her. "You also know the stats on rabies in skunks, and what that might mean if Lucky's unvaxxed, and if that skunk bit him. Until we're sure, we have to err on the side of caution."

He paused when she didn't take the gloves from him right away. "You are vaxxed, right?" he asked, point blank.

Terry moved a step towards Peggy and demanded, "Peggy?"

Peggy felt as if she was the only one defending Lucky. "He could just as easily been sprayed by the skunk and that's all! It happens all the time! How many do we deal with every month? We get dozens of calls like that."

"Peggy!" Terry's authoritative tone rooted her to the spot. "This is a safety issue. If you haven't been vaccinated, you're putting yourself and the rest of the crew at risk."

"I don't need a lecture!"

"Apparently, that is debatable!" Terry's eyes were stern. "I asked you a question. Were you vaccinated in December, as you were asked?"

Peggy swallowed hard and shook her head no.

Paul stepped between them and handed Peggy a surgical mask. "Get behind the gate, please. Without a vax, that request is not debatable."

Contrite, Peggy took the mask and gloves and walked away to the gate.

Terry watched her slip behind the gate, and it took him a moment to collect himself. He finally took a breath and turned to Joe and Paul. "I'll get the second pole."

"Not this time, Chief," Paul asserted, as he rummaged in his medical bag. "Dog saw you limp up. He knows you're the weak link. You'll be the first one he goes after."

Terry regarded Lucky in the rear of the cage, baring teeth at him. It was hard to believe, that this once shy, sweet dog, could have been driven to a state of ferocity so complete, that he'd revert to a feral state, where every human was now the enemy, not just the one man who'd mistreated him. Could it be true? Was it any more believable that he could be rabid? Despite his disappointment in her having lied to him, deep inside, he felt Peggy was probably right, and he suspected that Paul felt she was right, too. However, he couldn't argue the vet's cautionary stand.

He nodded to Paul. "Tell me what you need."

Paul handed him a face mask and the blanket, then lowered his voice. "I don't care how you do it, just keep her behind the gate. Deck her if you have to...or I will."

Terry stifled a small smile. "Understood." He limped off to join Peggy behind the gate.

Paul pulled a bottle of Nembutal from his bag and filled a syringe. "Joe? You think you can pole him, one more time? I just need a two second, clear shot at his rump."

"Place your bets," Joe muttered, then yanked on thick, elbow-length leather guards over the latex gloves. He called out to Terry. "Ter? For Christmas? A frickin' bunny suit."

"Burlap or leather?"

"Monogrammed!"

"Deal."

Peggy shivered in the cold, unable to look at Terry as he joined her behind the gate.

"Why don't you go inside where it's warm," he suggested.

"I-I'm fine." Simmering with guilty frustration, she kept her eyes on Lucky in the back of the cage, sure that if he was just given the chance to calm down, he'd be all right. And yet...was she wrong about that, too? All at once, she felt as if she'd landed right back on her first day at the shelter, only this time, she deserved to be sacked. She'd never felt so small before. To have been dressed down by Terry in such a stern manner had pierced her to the core. All of her exemplary work over the course of the past ten months fizzled into thin air. The shame she felt was visceral. How could she possibly explain it to him? Or Paul?

She watched Joe ease a green stretcher out of the back of the van. He handed it to Paul, who crouched behind it, using it as a shield. Balanced on the balls of his feet, like a track runner, he took a breath, then nodded to Joe.

Joe crossed himself and held the pole in plain sight of Lucky. He kept his other arm shielded from sight behind his back. Poised and stealthy, Joe flowed like water towards the cage, his voice calm and reassuring, without a trace of agenda.

"Hey there, Lucky, it's me! How's it goin'? What happened, huh, Lucky?"

Peggy noticed that Joe kept repeating their name for the dog, and she suspected that he was trying to jog Lucky's memory, back to a time when he had been cared for with kindness. Peggy peered into the cage shadows. Lucky stared Joe down, his lips quivering, drawn back in a taut, warning snarl.

"I'm just here to help ya, Lucky, okay? Good boy. Everything's gonna be okay now, Lucky, good boy, you're okay, now, Lucky..."

Peggy glanced to Paul. Despite cold gusts of wind, perspiration glistened across his forehead. Taut and focused, he barely breathed, his eyes barely visible above the stretcher.

"Goooood boy," Joe cooed, "yeah, who did this to ya, huh, Lucky? Not me, I'm your bud, Lucky, that's right, and you're a good boy, Lucky, and we're gonna help ya, now, okay?"

As Joe inched closer to the cage, Peggy noticed that he was directing the dog's attention to his free left hand by easing it out from behind his back, deliberately.

Peggy watched as Lucky's hunted stare followed Joe's left hand, as it came closer and closer to the left side of the cage. Growls rumbling in the dog's throat intensified with Joe's approach. Then, Joe leaned his body to the left as well, appearing to descend toward the left hand side of the cage. Lucky's body mirrored Joe's lean, and the dog's focus zeroed in on Joe's free hand.

Peggy held her breath, as Joe inched his right, pole-hand up and out of the dog's eye line.

Abruptly, Joe stood straight up in front of the left side of the cage. Lucky lunged at that side, barking. Joe flipped open the latch on the right side, and using the barred, cage door as a shield, thrust the pole into the cage, just as Lucky jerked his head around, in surprise.

Joe looped the noose over Lucky's head, and then let go of the cage door to tighten the noose. Lucky leaped from the cage. Lassoed, the dog fell onto the floor of the van and thrashed like a swordfish on a boat deck.

Paul lit forward onto his feet, but Lucky fought so wildly, he couldn't get close enough to inject him. "Hold him! Hold him!"

"I'm tryin'!"

Hearing the dog's gasps, Peggy cried out. "He's choking!"

"He's all right," Terry assured her, "they've got to hold him or someone will get hurt."

"Shit! Watch it!" Joe lost his footing and wheeled into the van door. The dog launched into the air off of the tail gate, in an attempt to dive over Paul, but collided with him, instead. The two pitched onto the macadam with a whump, with Paul pinned underneath the stretcher, the syringe knocked out of his hand.

Peggy snatched the blanket from Terry and burst through the gate.

"Peggy!" Terry shouted and ran after her.

Peggy tossed the blanket over Lucky. Blinded, the dog writhed on top of the stretcher, knocking both she and Joe down to the asphalt.

Terry yanked a second rabies pole from the van, and just as Lucky threw off the blanket, he looped the dog about the neck, and pulled it taut. Joe scrambled to his knees, but neither he nor Terry had the leverage to pull the dog off of Paul, now caught up in the blanket, too.

Spotting the syringe on the driveway, Peggy snatched it up and jabbed the needle into the Lucky's thigh, depressing the plunger. Lucky yelped and fought the poles, but only for a brief moment, more. He swayed, gurgled in his throat, and then his legs buckled beneath him.

"Paul!" Terry called out. "Move!"

Paul shoved upwards, then rolled out from under the stretcher, whipped the blanket off and yanked the syringe out of Lucky's thigh.

"Okay, let up!" he panted to Joe and Terry.

The men released the nooses and Lucky slipped down to the ground, semi-conscious. Paul jammed the stethoscope in his ears and listened to the dog's chest, pulling back its eyelids, and checking refill time on its gums with his gloved finger.

The front door flew open, and Betty trotted down to the gate with the first aid kit. "Lawd Lawd! Everybody all right?"

"Stay behind the gate!" Terry called out. He grasped hold of Peggy's hands, turning them over, checking her forearms. "Did he get you?"

"No. Is he all right?" Peggy slipped from Terry's grasp, and fell to her knees beside Lucky.

"Don't touch him!" Paul snapped, yanking off his stethoscope. "What in hell were you thinking? You could have been bitten!"

"I'm sorry, but he could have bitten you!"

"You all right, Paul?" Terry hovered, looking concerned.

Paul checked himself over. "Yes."

"Joe?" Terry called out.

"I'm cool!" Joe dusted himself off. His trousers were torn, his knee scraped. "I did this on the lot, wasn't him."

Terry gestured to Betty. "Some peroxide and bandage on that, if you would. Joe, stay back until that's fully covered."

"Roger."

Betty squeezed through the gate to Joe and wet down a wad of cotton batting with hydrogen peroxide and pressed it to Joe's knees, with a wince of empathy. "Ouch, ouch, ouch, ouch!"

Biting her lip, Peggy brushed tears off of her face. She watched Paul gently secure Lucky's tongue to his lower jaw with a strip of gauze, fitting a muzzle over his snout.

"He's okay," he said to her.

Terry returned to them. "What do you need?"

"I'll want x-rays," Paul told him.

"Right. Betty?" Terry called out, "ring up Doc Caldwell and fill him in? Tell him they're on their way."

"Have them clear a room QP," Paul said. "Quarantine Protocol."

"Okidoke," Betty replied and hurried through the gate.

"Also," Terry called after her, "put in a call to the Health Department, will you? Don't mention this, yet, just ask them for their rabies stats."

"Tell 'em we be doin' a survey, and you just want a update."

"You're three moves ahead of me, as always."

"But, we know what the stats are," Peggy began.

"Listen to me, carefully," Terry said to her. "For Lucky's sake, we need to err on the side of caution when it comes to a police report of a vicious dog, because if there's a single question, it could mean serious consequences for him."

Peggy's heart wrenched with shame at his tone. She saw Paul run his gloved hands against the dog's fur.

"I don't see any bites," he said. "We'll shave him up at the clinic. Okay," he grasped hold of the stretcher. "On three. One, two, threeee--easy! Got it?"

"I'm cool." Joe helped Paul set the stretcher inside the van.

Paul jumped in after it. "I'll tie him down. Let's go."

Joe slammed the doors shut, then scrambled up into the driver's seat. He rolled down the window and leaned out, lowering his voice to Terry. "What about Harrison?"

Terry took in a deep breath. "Let's see what's what, first."

Without a word, Joe donned his aviators, and flipped on the emergency light. He backed the van up and headed up the driveway.

Peggy watched them drive away, then noticed the firemen draped over their back stoop railing, looking on. She wondered how long they'd been watching without lending a hand. All at once, she felt the chilly wind through her shirt. She turned back around and found Terry holding the gate open for her. His expression was calm, but unyielding.

Chapter 71

"I said I'm sorry! I'm sorry I didn't get the shot! Why-why are we even talking about that, when Lucky is hurt?"

"Because it's your responsibility as an officer," Terry interrupted.

"Please don't tell me what my responsibility is," Peggy shot back, "I know what it is! But, what good is it, what good is this stupid piece of tin," she yanked off her badge, "when we have no real way to protect a dog who we know has been abused to the point of-of-this-this-stupid…" Her words skidded to a stop in the bottleneck of her anger, and she threw the badge into the waste basket.

Terry calmly poured hot water into four mugs, and squirted a stream of Hershey's syrup into each one. He looked around to Peggy.

"One marshmallow or two?"

Peggy clamped her mouth shut, before she spit teeth at him and told him exactly what he could do with the whole bag of marshmallows. She stalked to the back window.

Terry took her silence on the chin and directed his question to the other two ladies.

Betty held up one finger. He dropped a marshmallow into her mug, and then turned to Clara. The old woman held up a silver flask. He smiled and poured a jigger of the contents into her mug.

Betty cleared her throat. Clara nodded to Terry, and he poured a jigger into Betty's mug, too. Clara then thumbed his attention to Peggy, standing stiff and tense at the back window.

Terry mulled the situation over, but poured two jiggers of the flask into his own mug, instead. He retrieved Peggy's badge out of the garbage and set it down on the window sill in front of her.

Peggy refused to look at the badge or him. "I don't want it. It's useless."

"You're right, of course," Terry said. "This tin star, in and of itself, has little value, beyond the abstract concept of law and order that we assign to it. But, I tend to think that what it represents best is the integrity and passion of those who are brave enough to wear it, and uphold what it stands for, even when facing Goliath."

"How does that help Lucky, now?"

"We have a police report, now. Combined with previous enquiries, it just might be enough to—"

"Might?" Peggy exclaimed. "You and I both know Lucky's never going to see his day in court! We're the ones chasing our tails, while that man gets off scott free."

"If you'll just calm down, I promise, I won't call him until we have more information."

"Please stop telling me to calm down. And I don't want any more of your promises!"

The moment the words shot out of her mouth, she regretted them, which only made her madder. She clammed up and turned back to the window. She could hear the ladies get up from their chairs and pull on their coats. In a moment, she heard the office door creak open, then close. She stared out the window and watched the wind tug the last of the maple's stubborn leaves off of its uppermost branch. Eventually, the quiet became unbearable.

"I'm sorry. I didn't mean that," she sighed.

"Apology accepted," Terry replied. "But, I'm still grounding you."

"Grounding me?" Peggy whirled on him. "I'm not a child!"

"Then stop behaving like one."

Peggy was startled. He hadn't said it in anger, but that made it worse. There was no mistaking the fatherly disappointment in his voice, and the undertone that said he was not kidding.

"I'm grounding you, firstly," he continued, "for not getting vaxxed, as you'd promised me you would, ten months ago, and secondly, for lying about it. Speaking of which, there's also the matter of a couple of...inconsistencies regarding your employment application form that's come to light, of late."

In the most casual manner, he presented her with a copy of the form, along with two official-looking letters. "According to the social security number you gave me, you're a seventy-five year old woman from the Chelsea Street Convalescent Center, in New York City. Who died. Two years ago."

Peggy gawked at the papers in his hand. He pulled her chair out
from under the counter, and then set the papers, and her mug of cocoa,
in front of it.

"Let's have a chat, shall we?" He eased into his chair and waited for
her to sit down. Peggy stared at the letters on the counter. It took her a
moment, but she sank into the chair.

"I'm surprised it caught up with you as quickly as it did," he said.
"Allow me to take that back. I'm surprised it caught up with you at all.
They must actually be reading the documents crossing their desks, these
days...either that, or you pulled the unlucky draw for a spot check."

Mute, Peggy stared guiltily at her shoes.

"You want the law to do something for Lucky," he added, "yet, you
yourself have been hiding from the law for...how long?"

"I wasn't, I-I ran away, that's all."

"That's all? You've been registered as a missing minor from the foster care system in New York, for nearly three and a half years."

"I'm eighteen, now."

"But, you weren't last November, when I engaged you, when you
said that you were twenty-two." He held up another letter. "And, according to this, you're not officially eighteen, until Monday."

Peggy swallowed, hard. "I...I have my reasons."

"No doubt."

"If you-if you knew why, you'd understand."

"Most certainly."

"I had no other choice...they'd just send me back to..." she trailed
off, her throat cramping painfully.

"Where had you been hiding before you showed up on our door-
step?"

It took her a moment before she could speak. "Here and there."

"Same place where you learned about the helpful, insulating qualities of newspaper?"

Peggy had a difficult time keeping her lower lip from trembling.

Terry handed her a box of tissues. "Why didn't you go to a shelter
and report it? Report the people who...who hurt you, to the authorities?
That is why you ran away, isn't it?"

Peggy looked up at him, her eyes blurry with tears. "I did. They just
kept bringing me back."

The clock ticked time between them in the quiet.

"Well," Terry said at last. "Things have changed in the state of New Jersey, as of January. But, of course, you knew that." He handed the letters to her. "I didn't see these. Unless you don't take care of it, first thing Monday morning."

Peggy nodded and blew her nose.

He flipped open his day book and wrote on a piece of paper. "Dr. Caldwell's wife, Maria, will be expecting your call. She'll know exactly who to speak to at which agency and can intercede on your behalf, if necessary, although as of midnight on Sunday, no one can tell you what to do. Not in New Jersey, at any rate. Not anymore." He sat back and stirred his cocoa. "Now. About the rabies vax..."

"I would have had to fill out a form. You end up in enough hospitals...you figure out how it works. If they'd checked...they'd have found out I was only...they would have sent me back."

"Well, they can't, now. You know that."

It sounded more like a question to her than a statement. She shifted in her seat.

"Peggy," he began, "to continue working here—"

"I promise I'll get it."

"I don't want your promises, either."

Peggy bowed her head and nodded.

Terry raised his mug to hers. "To no more promises, then?"

With a sheepish attempt at a smile, she clinked her mug against his.

He drained the last of the spiked chocolate and sighed. "Now then, what do we do about Mr. Harrison?"

Moved to hear him use the word "we" again, Peggy wiped at fresh tears. "Is murder still illegal?"

"Generally speaking, yes. Although there have been rumors to the contrary, regarding certain neighborhoods to the left of Hoboken." He paused. "You-you didn't murder anyone, did you?"

Peggy sputtered hot chocolate up her nose. "Not yet."

"Just checking."

Masked and gloved, Peggy stood behind the front gate beside Terry, trying not to appear anxious, while Joe parked the van. When he hopped out, he hurried to the vehicle's rear doors.

"What is our verdict?" Terry asked.

"We lucked out. No surprises. Yet."

Peggy craned her neck, trying to see past the doors and Joe. Paul was inside, and he and Joe unlatched the stretcher from the floor.

The moment he hopped off of the tail gate, Paul slapped his forehead. "Dammit! I left the x-rays. Can we have them messengered? I'll pay for it. I left them on the desk."

"Consider it done," Terry said.

"The films were clean, CBC, BUN and blood chems all within normal count," Paul gestured for the blanket Peggy held. "You can come out from behind the gate and drop the masks. But, keep the gloves on."

Peggy lowered her mask and approached the van with caution. She gasped at the sight of Lucky, who was shaved nearly bald. His ribs protruded prominently through pinkish-white skin, as he lay shivering. A muzzle was laced securely around his snout.

"Is he going to be all right?" she asked.

Hearing her voice, the groggy dog tried to lift its head and whimpered. Before anyone could stop her, Peggy flew to his side and gathered him in her arms. "Shhhh…it's all right…I'm right here." Lucky thumped his tail.

"I take it we're no longer suspecting rabies," Terry said, at last.

Paul covered Lucky with the blanket. "Barring a FAT from Trenton, I can't guarantee we're one hundred percent in the clear, but without any other evidence? I have to say no, his behavior is not consistent with furious rabies. This…this right here." He indicated the affectionate, calm demeanor of Lucky in Peggy's arms. "This wouldn't be happening. They don't switch back and forth, in late stage. He'd be in the throes of violent convulsions, by now."

Peggy stroked Lucky's ears. He tried to give her his paw, but it was strapped down, so his head lobbed against her, and he tried to lick her hand, despite the muzzle.

"Doc offered him water?" Joe added. "He lapped it up. No problem. He'da flipped out he had hydrophobia, right Doc? And we tried loud noises, still nada."

"Could the sedation be masking?" asked Terry.

"We'd see some other symptomatic behavior, a blue funk, maybe, lethargy. But, it's not like they can do a three-sixty. The sedation suppressed his fight or flight response. Once he realized we weren't going to hurt him, his demeanor changed."

"What about the smell of skunk?"

"Could be that, like Peg said; starving, he went after one, got a squirt in the face and just ran off, as Mother Nature intended. His stomach and bowels are empty, so we know he didn't eat it. I'd wager he hasn't eaten in almost two weeks. That's not to say we shouldn't exercise precautions. If I'm wrong, two to three days from now we'll know for sure, because he'll be dead."

Peggy looked up sharply.

Paul met her eyes. "Say your prayers I'm right, or you're in for one hell of a post-exposure ride."

Joe whistled under his breath. Peggy looked down at Lucky, and her fear evaporated. The dog looked up at her with a calm, sleepy expression.

The front door opened. Bundled in her coat-sweater, Betty bustled down to the gate. "Harrison be on his way!"

"What?" Joe exclaimed.

"Goddammit!" Paul yanked off his stethoscope. "This dog can't be released, yet!"

"Which is what you're going to tell him," Terry allowed, in a calm voice. "Since we have the initial police report, you're able to place him under quarantine, yes?"

"But, I can't enforce it. Not if the dog didn't bite anyone."

"We're counting on the words 'police' and 'quarantine' being enough. Oh and...you're in the clear, by the way, in case—you know—you were worried about the legality of not ringing the owner first, before treating him." Terry smiled that innocent smile of his and loaded the Poloroid camera with fresh film.

Peggy stifled her own smile, as Paul tried to backpeddle.

"Yes. Right." He folded the stethoscope into his medical bag. "I wasn't, but thanks." With a flash, Terry snapped a picture of Lucky.

"Ter, if we coulda kept him and bought some more time, why did ya call?" Joe asked.

"He didn't, I did," Peggy said.

Paul and Joe both looked shocked. "You on drugs?" Joe squealed.

"We've no choice. With a police report, he'll find out. They'll call him. And, if we haven't contacted him, he'll have a grievance against us. Better to make the first move. I-I left the message with his secretary."

"What Peggy left out," Terry said, waving the snapshot dry, "is that we might be able to use this turn of events to our advantage. Seeing Lucky in this condition, coupled with our previous enquiry, along with Peggy's stack of petitions, might equal..."

"Impoundment?" Paul prompted.

"It's a stretch, but as good a test case as any."

"And, if he calls your bluff?" Joe asked.

"We're making book on it ending, right here," Terry said. "Having set his sites on city controller, come next election, he may want to be rid of the whole matter, entirely, seeing the dog as a public liability."

"But, the dog didn't bite anyone," Paul reiterated. "If he presses it…"

"How long before he gets here?" Peggy asked.

Stamping her feet, Betty shivered. "He be comin' from Newark. Traffic? Twenny minutes, half-hour."

"Oh, Betty," Terry entreated, "do us a favor, will you? Lucky's x-rays are still up at the EVC. Have a messenger send them down. Might be too late, tonight. First thing in the morning?"

Paul nodded. "Thank you."

"Bettah git him inside befo' the trick or treaters start showin' up," Betty advised, and then trotted up the walkway into the building.

"Yeah!" Joe grinned. "Maybe we bag the boogeyman, tonight."

Peggy glanced at Terry. He didn't cloak the caution in his eyes for her benefit.

"Let's get him downstairs where it's warm," Paul said.

Peggy eased herself out from under Lucky. "Is the muzzle still necessary?" Half asleep, Lucky thumped his tail, again.

Paul stroked the dog's ears, then removed the muzzle.

Peggy smiled, hoping that her repentent gratitude showed. "Thank you."

Hesitant, he returned her smile. Turning to Joe, he grasped the stretcher. "On three. One. Two. Three." He and Joe lifted the stretcher and walked it past the runs.

Terry limped alongside, spotting Lucky.

Peggy followed after them, but stopped when they headed down the gravel drive towards the cellar.

As the men ducked under the office overhang, she saw Terry throw a glance over his shoulder in her direction. Averting her eyes, Peggy turned away, and hugging herself against the rising wind, she headed up to the front gate—unable to look back.

Chapter 72

"Quarantine!"

"Mr. Harrison," Terry explained, "it's for your protection as well as your dog's."

"You think I don't see what's going on here?" Harrison interrupted him. "What are you trying to pull?"

"Pull?" Terry repeated. He stood between Paul and Joe, flanked by Curtis, all of whom stood in front of Lucky's pen, at the bottom of the cellar stairs.

"Mr. Harrison, all we're interested in is what's best for Lucky."

"I am that dog's owner, and what's best is not up to you, but me."

"I don't agree," Paul interjected.

"I'll just bet you don't. Nice cushy piece of change, with this one. You see your student loans decreasing by a zero or two?"

"The cumulative fines in your case, alone, could slash the state deficit by at least half that much."

"Gentlemen," Terry began, but Harrison cut him off.

"Did my dog bite anyone?"

"We have no substantiated reports of bites, as of yet," Terry said.

"Substantiated? As of yet? Are you projecting forward into the future, now? Since there are no bite reports, there're no grounds for quarantine other than you people trying to collect a fat fee for your sorry little operation here. Justify your existence, eh?"

"Mr. Harrison, if you'll just listen—"

"No, *you* listen! I have the right to take my dog out of impound!"

"No one is questioning your rights, Mr. Harrison."

"When was your dog vaccinated last?" Paul moved a step closer to Harrison.

"I don't remember."

"Why doesn't that surprise me?"

"Mr. Harrison," Terry interceded, "as I'm sure you understand, without a vaccination record within the past year, we must assume non-vaccination and take the necessary safety precautions."

"That dog is my property."

"And, if you take him out of this facility," Paul returned to the debate, "you are potentially exposing yourself, your family and anyone who comes into contact with you, to the possibility of infection with rabies."

"Rabies?" Harrison repeated, with an incredulous laugh.

Terry was surprised that Paul was playing the rabies card. The young vet continued, unruffled. "Health department regulations stipulate that any suspected rabies case be quarantined at an approved, county facility, or in lieu of available facilities, a state-licensed, animal control facility."

"You want me to believe that dog has hydrophobia?" Harrison laughed, again.

"Hydrophobia lyssaria, to be precise." Paul handed him his notebook. "If you'll read my initial observations, you'll note that the dog smelled of skunk and displayed behavior symptomatic of infectious, stage-two rabies."

Harrison pointed at Lucky, now hunched and cowering in the rear corner of the pen. "That is not a dog with rabies."

"I'm sorry, which vet school did you say you graduated from?"

Harrison's smile iced over. "Stanford Law."

Paul met his serve and lobbed one of his own. "Well, apparently you missed the MCATS while cramming for the bar, which I hear you haven't as yet passed in this state, so FYI; that dog is heavily sedated. And, since there are three main symptomatic stages to rabies; depending on the form it takes, whether furious-encephalitic or paralytic, two separate behavioral models may emerge that a layman, least of all a desk jockey, may not recognize."

"And which form has he got? Allegedly?"

"Without a fluorescent antibody test, there's no way to be certain. The best anyone can do is keep the dog under observation for clinical evaluation and hope that the symptoms will prove to be nothing more than a neurological disorder, a bacterial infection, or the possibility that due to starvation and neglect," Paul over-emphasized the two words, "he's reverted back to a feral state, i.e., a fear biter."

"You said he didn't bite anyone."

"He tried to bite me, the control officer, and four police officers who wanted to shoot him."

"Under quarrantine," Terry chimed in, "he can be observed in a secure environment."

"For how long?"

"Ten days is the average hold time after first display of symptoms," Paul explained, "because if infected, death is certain within that time frame. After ten days, he will be deemed negative for the disease."

"Why wait? Give him the test!"

"To do that, I'd have to euthanize him, sever his head and ship it to Trenton for analysis."

Checkmate, Terry noted. Paul had said it with such cold detachment, it even gave Harrison pause. "Mr. Harrison, I understand that you want to do what's best for your dog."

"I have a documented record of each and every call I have made," Harrison said between his teeth, "along with every accusation made by that scrawny bitch, upstairs, you had masquerading as the law, in your absence."

Paul tossed his notebook aside and took a step at Harrison. "We wouldn't even be having this conversation had you given a rat's ass about that dog!"

"Gentlemen," Terry interjected, "we all want what's best for Lucky— I mean Boy, excuse me, and if emotions run high, it's because we all feel strongly about trying to help a dog who's been—"

"Been what?" Harrison demanded.

"Given this dog's condition and unpredictable behavior, I will not —" Paul began, but Harrison interrupted him.

"He won't be unpredictable with me!" Harrison dove between them and flung open the pen door. He thrust his arm in and startled the dog. Confused and scared, Lucky bit down hard on his hand. It happened so fast, even Harrison didn't react at first.

Paul yanked Harrison out of the pen. "Curtis, the Betadine!"

Joe shut and latched the pen door, as Paul shoved Harrison to the tub and wrestled the man's bleeding hand under a running faucet.

"Bloody hell. How bad is it?" Terry asked.

Curtis uncapped the iodine solution. "Betadine, Doctah."

"Fill a twenty cc syringe," Paul barked.

"Mother of God!" Harrison cried out, as searing pain registered in his hand. His face flushed red with anger, and he jerked towards the pen and his dog.

"Hey!" Joe bellowed.

Paul jerked Harrison backwards, hard, and forced his hand back under the gushing water. "Move again, so help me Christ, I'll bite your arm off myself! Curtis, time me out at fifteen minutes."

"Yes, Doctah."

It was the first time Terry had ever seen Harrison appear shaken. The man hung over the tub, his eyes fixated on his own blood raining down the drain.

Terry punched the intercom button. "Peggy?"

"Yes?" Her voice sounded anxious.

He ran a reluctant hand through his hair. "Peggy, ring up Dr. Sanford; call his private line. It's in the rolodex, under Mercy General. Tell him we have an emergency."

"What's happened? Is Lucky—"

"Let me know when you reach him, will you? Out." He punched the intercom without waiting for her answer. "Joe, bring the car around and ring Bob, over at HOD. Fill him in."

"On it." Joe took the stairs two at a time.

"*This* is why I advised against taking that dog out of here," Paul hissed, as he scrubbed Harrison's hand with liquid soap and a brush. "*This* is why we have goddamned regulations!"

"Twenty cc's." Curtis handed Paul the syringe.

Paul readied it against a bite wound between Harrison's knuckles. "Somebody, get a chair for this man."

"I don't need a chair!" Harrison snapped.

"That's what you think," Paul said, as he depressed the plunger of iodine.

"*Son of a bitch!*" Harrison cried out, and then his knees buckled. He slumped against the tub.

Terry unfolded a chair behind him. "Mr. Harrison, sit down."

Harrison sank in the chair, shaking his head, vigorously. "Son of a bitch, son of a bitch..." he whispered, his head resting against the cold rim of the tub.

"Breathe deep, Mr. Harrison, that's it, slow and easy. Under these circumstances, perhaps you can better appreciate the seriousness of the situation. It's now a public safety issue. Perhaps the best option, at this point, is to sign your dog over to us. I assure you, with your signature on this form, you will in no way be liable if he has, or does, bite anyone else."

Harrison looked blearily at the papers Terry held in front of him. After a moment, he looked up. "Absolutely not."

"Refill." Paul tossed the syringe to Curtis, then bent over Harrison. "Listen to me. The dog has officially bitten someone. He is now under quarantine by my order, pursuant to health department regulations. If you have a problem with that, you can call their offices Monday morning and explain how you disregarded a state-licensed veterinarian's specific instructions, jeopardizing not only your own safety, but the safety of said veterinarian, and the entire crew of the facility designated for quarantine! And, I'm more than happy to testify to that in court!"

Curtis handed the loaded syringe back to him. Paul inserted it directly into the wound, this time. Harrison bowed his head against the tub, his face contorted in a fierce grimace.

"Mr. Harrison," Terry hovered over him. "Do yourself a favor. Sign the form." His head still bowed, Harrison's shoulders quivered. "Mr. Harrison, would you like a drink of water?" Then Terry heard it; a gutteral, cackling sound. The man was laughing!

Harrison looked up at him with mirthful eyes. "Water? Not if I've got hydrophobia." His head bowed, again, in a fit of giggling. Then, he looked up, dark and ominous, his smile evaporating like smoke. "I want that dog put down and tested for rabies."

The thunder of silence was broken only by the sound of the water tumbling into the tub. Terry took a breath. "That won't be necessary."

"In less than five days," Paul interrupted, "I'll know if we need to confirm with a FAT test."

"Wait five days before I even know if I've been infected with rabies?" Harrison guffawed. "I don't think so!"

"If your dog was vaccinated, there's no need to destroy him. His vax will offer him immunity. If he hasn't been vaxxed and he's been infected, we'll know in less than five days, because once the virus is present in the saliva, the animal succumbs within that time frame. At that time you can start the post-exposure prophylaxis while the test is performed in Trenton to confirm."

"Do the test."

"Are you listening to me? There's no need to start either the PEP or FAT if your dog does not progress to the acute stage within the next five days, because that means he has not been infected, and therefore you will not have been infected! Either way, prophylaxis is one hundred percent effective when administered even as late as a twenty day mark."

"That's all very informative, but I'm not willing to risk my health, my family's, nor yours," he said to Terry, then to each of them in turn, with a broad smile, "or yours, or yours. The dog is my property. It bit me. Put it down. Do the test."

"Fifteen minutes," Curtis announced.

Paul jerked Harrison's hand out of the water, and wrapped it in a towel. "Keep it above your shoulder."

Terry heard a car door slam. "Mr. Harrison, I'll be taking you to the hospital. Dr. Sanford is a trauma expert, and is authorized to administer the PEP series."

"Not until I know it's warranted!" Harrison retorted, pulling away from Paul. "Which is why I want that dog put down. Now!"

"The hell it is, you bastard!" Paul shot back.

"Mr. Harrison," Terry stepped between them. "Putting your dog down now serves no other purpose, but to prove a point. You've made it. If you will reconsider the vet's suggestion of a five to ten day wait period, which is all it will take to be certain and something you can confirm with Dr. Sanford in just a few moments..." he offered the man Lucky's case file, "I will make this entire incident, including the police reports, go away, and you can consider the matter closed in plenty of time for upcoming elections."

Harrison looked from the file to Terry and his eyes iced over. "Bite me." He turned to Paul. "I am the legal owner of that dog. It bit me. It might be rabid. Put that dog down."

"It's going to have to wait 'til tomorrow. I don't have the right forms."

"I said I want that dog tested, now!" Harrison pounded his good fist on the pen, and Lucky cowered in the corner.

Terry stepped up to Harrison, nose to nose, his voice sharp as a rapier. "I'm going to say this once. You have two choices; take the lift we're offering you to hospital at our expense, to a board certified health practitioner for the start of post-exposure prophylaxis—exposure that you brought upon yourself in front of witnesses—or you wait the twenty-four hours this facility needs to work out health department protocol for a case not seen since nineteen fifty-six. Take your pick, because nothing else, I repeat *nothing* happens to that dog until every 'i' is dotted and every 't' is crossed, in goddamn triplicate if necessary, to satisfy the town. So, you can either accept this offer, or you can stand there and bleed to death, I don't give a damn! The choice is yours! You've got ten seconds to make it."

Perhaps it was the implied threat of the cane clenched in Terry's fist and raised at face level, but Harrison seemed to reconsider his position.

"Then, let's go," he hissed, and brushed past Paul towards the stairs. As his shadow passed over Lucky, the dog cowered ever lower in the pen, his whole body trembling.

Half way up the steps, Harrison stopped.

Terry looked up and saw Peggy standing on the threshold of the cellar door. He could see her trembling, and she gripped the doorjamb like it was a life preserver. For a split second, he wondered if she would faint, but something hardened on her face, and her eyes narrowed. She looked ready to lunge with the slightest provocation, and it crossed his mind that she might shove Harrison down the stairs.

"Peggy, Mr. Harrison needs to go to the hospital," Terry called out and pushed a reluctant Harrison from behind. As they reached the top of the stairs, Peggy remained rooted to the cellar door. "Peggy?" Terry intoned.

After a long, searing look from Harrison, she stepped back and let the men by. She stared at Harrison as he stalked past her, her fists clenched. She flinched, when Terry rested a hand on her shoulder. She swallowed hard and took a breath. "Lucky..."

"He's fine. I'll be back as soon as I can. And, Peggy?"

Peggy dragged her eyes away from the van, where Joe had opened the passenger door for Harrison, and looked to Terry. His eyes searched hers.

"Hold the fort."

Peggy managed to nod, and watched him limp up the gravel drive and climb in the back of the van. Joe gunned the engine and drove up to the street. The van's flashing yellow light swept across her face and momentarily blinded her. When the van disappeared from sight, she rubbed her arms. Feeling came back, and the vice grip around her chest loosened enough for her to breathe.

From the cellar below, she heard Curtis's voice. "You ain't gonna put him down, right? Doctah?"

Paul didn't answer him, and Peggy squeezed her eyes shut. When she opened them, the inky darkness had already begun to seep up the stairway, relentlessly pursuing her with caustic acrimony, threatening to grab hold of her ankles and drag her down, down, down, to a place where no one could hear her scream. Stumbling, she whirled around and staggered up the gravel drive. She heard the distant, screaming voices, commanding her to run. So she did. She ran as fast as her numb legs would carry her around to the front gate and into the safety of the shelter.

 **Chapter 73**

Terry didn't return to the shelter until after nine p.m.. He was not surprised to find the crew's vehicles still in the lot, the light on in the office, and Peggy's silhouette in the window.

While he'd waited at the busy hospital with Harrison, Joe had ferried Mrs. Harrison down to the shelter's lot for their car, then escorted her back to the hospital. With Sanford still tied up in surgery, Terry used the delay to pick up the Pinto at Fegetti's. By the time Terry had returned to the hospital, Harrison had been seen and had already left.

He turned off the Pinto's engine, sat back, and sighed. He would have liked to have sat there forever, in the nether world between what had passed and what was to come, but with a grunt, he pushed himself out of the car, and headed towards the front gate.

Halfway across the lot, he noticed a cloud of smoke curling up from under the shadowed overhang. He limped down and discovered Paul perched on the stone wall, his arms dangling over his knees, a half-smoked cigarette between his lips.

Terry sat next to him. "Those will kill you, you know."

"Not nearly quick enough."

Terry pulled two ales out of his jacket pockets and offered him one. Paul looked at the bottle. "It's going to take more than one."

"Hold that thought." Terry slapped the bottle caps off, using the stone wall, and hearing the crunch of boots on gravel, he looked up to see Joe coming their way.

Joe waved. "Sorry I had to bale; got another stray call."

"Understood," Terry offered Joe his bottle.

Joe shook his head no. "Just tell me ya dumped the schmuck in the river."

"That would be polluting."

"Not in the Hudson, it ain't."

"How's Peggy?"

"How ya think? Been on the phone to Trenton since you left."

Terry glanced at Paul. The young vet blew a series of smoke rings upward, into the underside of the office floor above their heads.

"I've been on hold for three hours with six different departments," Peggy tossed her pencil aside when the three men entered the office. "And no one seems to know who to talk to or who to call!"

"It's after hours," Terry said. "You won't reach anyone who can make a decision."

Peggy hung up the phone and kneaded her brow with both hands. She noticed the quiet and looked up. Everyone was exchanging furtive glances with each other and avoiding her eyes completely. Paul looked grim as he leaned against the back window.

"As I'm sure you've guessed," Terry sank into his chair, "we have a dilemma." He pulled a manila envelope from his inside jacket pocket, and handed it to Peggy.

She withdrew copies of x-ray films and a sheaf of papers. Seeing the official town seals at the top of the papers, she felt an icy hand grip her heart. The x-rays were dorsal and lateral views of Harrison's hand.

"What die-lemma?" Curtis asked. "Whole thang be transpicuous. "Turkey stuck his mitt in aftah Doctah Hayward told him not to! It be his besettin' sin."

"It's a bit more complicated, now," Paul murmured.

"What be complicated?" Betty asked.

Finished reading, Peggy met Terry's eyes over the papers. He looked somber.

"It seems," he sighed, "Harrison got an order cosigned at the hospital, authorizing euthanasia, specifically in order to expedite the rabies test in Trenton."

"Say what!" Betty exclaimed. "Sanford's supposed t'be on our side!"

"Sanford was indisposed. Apparently, Harrison managed to convince the on call physician to..." Terry removed his glasses, his voice trailing off.

Betty filled in the blanks. "He just called our bluff, is what you be sayin.'"

Terry stowed his glasses in their case and leaned back in his chair, quiet.

Joe punched the medicine cabinet. "It's bogus, man!"

"Y'ain't gonna let that honkey git away wiff dis?" Curtis asked Peggy. "Is non compos mentis! Just 'cause he git some paper inked? It ain't right! You can't!"

"Curtis..." Paul admonished him. "Let it go."

"Let it go? You the vet! Euthanize dat mo'fo who put Lucky in this die-lemma! Gimme da stuff; I do it myseff!"

"Curtis, that's enough! If you can't control yourself, then go home and cool off until you can!"

"Lucky didn't do nuthin' but protect hisself! You know it!" He turned to Peggy. "*You* know it!"

"Curtis!" Paul barked.

The boy launched himself out of the chair and flung open the office door. He took off in a dead run through the kennel. Drowsy dogs lifted their heads.

"Aw Jeeze," Joe started out after him. "Curtis!"

"Let him go," Peggy said.

Curtis slammed the front door so hard it bounced back open. "He's young," Terry said to Paul. "He doesn't understand."

"Yes, he does," Peggy spoke up. "And what's more, he's right."

"Peg, we all did everything we could," Paul said.

"Except get Lucky away from that man. Ten days. That's all he needs. Why can't we get the court to—"

"The court will rule in Harrison's favor."

"Why? It's not that cut and dried!"

"It is for me. Those papers in your hand give me no choice."

"There's always a choice. Just don't do it! Don't put him down! Wait the ten days!"

"Don't ask me to break the law, because I can't! Not even for..." he stopped himself and looked away.

"Let's all take a breath," Terry said. "For now, it is officially after hours, and so a twelve hour delay will not be considered dragging our feet, nor endangering Mr. Harrison any more than he's already done so, himself. That much we can afford in wiggle room. In the morning we can appeal to the authorities."

"This is my fault," Peggy said, and shook her head in disbelief.

"It's no one's fault. As Paul said, everyone has done everything humanly possible—"

"It *is* my fault! I should have walked out with Lucky back when I had the chance! But, because I listened to you, because I trusted you, that dog has suffered unspeakably, and now is going to be killed just for defending himself against the man who beat the living shit out of him!"

"Peggy!" Terry's voice was sharp.

"What?" Peggy glared at him.

An awkward silence enveloped the room.

"It's late," Terry said, finally. "Let's all go home, get some rest, and regroup tomorrow." Peggy leapt up from her chair. "Peggy, one moment, please."

She stopped but didn't turn around.

"Paul," Terry said, "hang on a tic, downstairs, would you?"

"Sure."

Peggy caught his hesitation at the doorway. He seemed about to say something to her, but then he left.

"I can hang, too," Joe said.

"Get some rest. You've gone above and beyond the call."

Joe reluctantly nodded. Betty helped Clara on with her jacket and gathered up their belongings. As Clara passed Peggy, the old woman patted her shoulder gently.

Listening to their footsteps, Terry waited until he heard the kennel door shut. With the toe of his boot, he edged Peggy's chair closer to her.

Her jaw clenched tighter than her fists, she dropped stiffly into the chair and folded her arms across her chest. It pained him to see her so inimical, no matter how warranted. "You could have, you know. Left. At any time. You still can. You're under no obligation to stay. But if you run away now, after everything you've accomplished…"

"You're the one who ran away."

She'd said it so quietly, he almost didn't hear her.

"I beg pardon?"

Her face screwed up into such anguish, he was taken aback. And then, words erupted out of her like sour milk from a busted carton.

"Who are you to lecture me about running away? For ten months, you just left us here, drowning! You never even called, not once in ten months!" She stood up, shoving the chair backwards, raining nearly a year's worth of pent-up frustration, fear, guilt and angst onto Terry. "And, then, you just show up? As if I'm supposed to just step aside and go on like nothing ever happened? I'm the one who stayed, Terry! I'm the one who cleaned up the mess you left behind! I *stayed*! So, don't talk to me about running away, like I'm the coward!"

Terry took it all in. "I know that I left you here with a lot on your plate, but I'm not sorry for placing it all in your hands. And yes, despite everything, you stayed. Why?"

"Because, nobody else in their right mind would have!"

He didn't know whether to smile or take offense. He waited, knowing that she would eventually rethink her answer, and she did. She stopped pacing at the back window and sighed.

"I stayed, because you asked me to."

"Well I did so, trusting that you could, and would, rise to the occasion. And you did. I was right. So there."

She didn't turn around.

"It can't have been easy for you," he conceded. "To have the old general back, barking orders as if he still ruled the roost."

She shrugged. "It's your shelter."

"No, it's not. Any more than it's yours. At best, we're-we're temporary caretakers, Peggy. We do what we can, help as many as we can along the way, then pass the torch to anyone willing to carry it even further than we have. As for the issue of trust...I appreciate that you placed your trust in me. Having said that...it's not about trusting me, or anyone else to know what's best in a situation. It's about trusting yourself to know."

He studied her, standing at the window, her back to him. "I know that right now, you feel you've misplaced that trust, not only with me, but the system, perhaps the whole world. However, as far as Lucky is concerned, we don't have to do anything for twelve hours. I might have one more card up my sleeve yet to play."

Peggy sighed. "Another bluff?"

"Sometimes, it's all about the bluff."

She expelled a wry laugh, with a dispirited shake of her head. "Do you expect me to make book on that?"

"No. But I'd like you to trust, not me, but yourself, to know that I intend to make certain Lucky will come out of this all right. Will you do that?"

Peggy shook her head again, her eyes on the floor. It took another moment, but she shrugged. "Fine."

"Promise?"

"We agreed, no more promises."

"Yes, we did, but I trust that you are a young lady of your word. I also trust that, no matter what comes to pass, you can handle anything."

As Peggy listened to Terry's words of confidence, she was thrown back to the first day they'd met. He had looked at her with such intensity then, she'd felt she might drown in the watery blue depths of his eyes. It was as if he could see into her soul, and for the first time in her life, she'd experienced hope. She wanted so much to believe him. Looking into those eyes, now, all she could see was her own vulnerability reflected back at her.

"How can you be so sure?" she whispered.

He smiled. "I just am."

Peggy's throat tightened. She tried to staunch the flow of tears, but the dam had broken. She wiped her palm across her damp cheeks, and reached for the box of tissues, but it was empty.

Terry offered her his handkerchief. Repentent, she took it and blew her nose.

"Why don't you go home, get some sleep," he said, gently. "And, brush up on your poker. I'm going to need you, and that feisty spunk of yours, tomorrow." He looked at her closely. "Can I count on you?"

Peggy sniffed, and they exchanged a searching look. He held out his hand to her. Swallowing hard, she grasped it, and they shook on it.

"Splendid! Now, would you help this creaky old man out of his chair?" Peggy helped him up, and then he let go of her hand. He removed her coat from the coat rack and held it open for her. She slipped her arms in and buttoned it up, carefully, over her St. Francis pendant.

Outside, Peggy was surprised to find the crew, minus Paul, still loitering around the lot. Terry held the gate open for her and called out to Joe. "Can you give Peggy a lift?"

Joe saluted. "Y'got it."

Terry whispered to Peggy, "Tomorrow, you might want to make peace with Paul. This has been a bit of a rough patch for him, and I don't expect it will get any easier, any time soon. He needs everyone's support in this matter. Especially yours."

Peggy wasn't sure how she felt about that and wiped her nose with his handkerchief. Finished, she offered it back to him. He cocked his head at her, smiling that kind smile of his, and in a rush of warmth, she wanted to tell him how sorry she was for the miserable things she'd said to him. She wanted to throw her arms around his neck and confess that she was so very glad he was back, that she did trust him, and that she loved him. But, she didn't.

"Yo! Saint Francis!" Joe called out

"Okay," she whispered to Terry.

"Good Girl."

She offered him her bravest smile, then headed to the van.

Terry waved as the van backed up, but Peggy didn't see him. He watched until it turned onto the street, disappearing from sight. He stood there a few moments and listened to sirens until they too, faded in the distance. With a grunt of discomfort, he reached through the open window of the Pinto, pulled out a six pack of Guinness stout, and then limped down towards the cellar.

Joe, Peggy and Clara rode in silence. Peggy was sure none of them wanted to talk about it. She sure didn't. She looked at Joe's profile in the dark interior. He looked especially down in the mouth. She knew he still berated himself for "dropping the ball" over Lucky, in the first place. But, it wasn't his fault. Like Paul said, it wasn't anyone's fault. Not even hers.

As she gazed out the window at the passing hoards of trick-or-treaters, she listened absently to the radio; the news report mirroring their dour moods. Newscasters attacked Governor Byrne's unfulfilled promises and bemoaned the continued tanking of New Jersey's economy, the increasing numbers of MIA stats in Vietnam, and the growing apathy of the general public.

Along with the bad news, her doubts slowly began to erode Terry's call to confidence, and now she struggled with the promise she'd made to him, one she really wasn't sure she could fulfill. How did he manage to finesse her, again? Darn him and his friendly persuasion! As if in response, she heard his voice tiptoe into her mind.

"I know that no matter what comes to pass, I trust that you can handle anything."

She rested her head against the window. Can I? If Paul puts Lucky down, tomorrow, could I handle that? She pressed her eyes closed. Could I ever forgive him, or Terry, if Lucky doesn't come out of this, all right?

She opened her eyes and watched the Halloween revelers. They rushed headlong through mounds of autumn leaves, eddying on sidewalks and along gutters. Kids of all ages swung their orange plastic pumpkins, overflowing with candy; witches, ghosts, black cats, white sharks, skeletons, ballerinas, and baseball players.

"Pull in there," Clara piped up, her voice shaking Peggy's reverie. They pulled into Vinnie's Market. "We need milk, bread, and eggs."

"Awww," Joe whined. "It's gonna be mobbed with brats."

"Want breakfast in the morning?"

"Sheesh!" Joe hopped out. "Saint Francis? You need anything?"

Peggy smiled. "I don't think you'll find what I need on any shelf."

"Copy that, all right."

While Joe went into the store, Peggy watched children cross the road with their parents. She wondered who are all these people were, really. Behind their masks, were they pretending to be their alter-egos? A pair of twins, dressed up as dice, skipped past a walking banana, a walking coffin, and a little boy with bandaged arms and a cast on his leg. He hobbled on crutches, laughing with a boy who might have been his brother, swathed in mummy wrapping. Behind them, a man who was probably their father, was dressed as a doctor. He walked arm-in-arm with a woman in a nurse's uniform. They were all having a very good time.

Suddenly, she wondered, were Harrison's kids out trick-or-treating? Did Mrs. Harrison escort them through the neighborhood, or did he? What costumes would they be wearing? What sort of masks hid their faces? Would Harrison wear a mask? Huh, she thought, he didn't need a mask. He wore one in real life. How else could he manage to fool everyone in town?

Peggy frowned. Surely, a man like Harrison didn't reserve all of his rage just for the family dog. Surely, someone, somewhere, must have noticed something off about him and his whole family.

Peggy sat up straight, feeling wide awake.

"Clara? What...what sort of scuttlebutt have you heard...about Mrs. Harrison...and the children..."

"You know what else pisses me off about her?" Paul took a long swig from the ale bottle. "The way she looks at you, and you know what she's thinking; you can see it on her face. She won't say it, but you know she's thinking it: 'You're wrong.'"

Sitting on the cold slate floor, propped up against Lucky's pen, he drained the last of the bottle and dropped it into the trash bin. It clinked on top of three empties. Behind him, Lucky snored.

One step above him on the stairs, Terry took another sip of ale and listened as Paul vented.

"And you know the worst part? Ninety-nine-point-ninety-nine percent of the time, she's right. And she knows it. You can see the 'I told you so', right there on her lips. But, she won't say that, either." He burped. "That's when I wanna belt her. Christ, what's wrong with me?"

Terry chuckled, rolling a bottle cap between his fingers. "Sounds like love to me."

"If it was, she'd have come down those stairs, by now. First case I couldn't cure."

"She's the only one who can do that. And, she will. When she's had enough of the cage."

Paul was quiet a moment. "She's in love with you, y'know."

"No, she's not," Terry said. "She was lost and needed a kind word from someone. It happened to be me. That's all. And, I think I gave her enough bad news today to smash that particular paternal bond to smithereens. I'll consider myself blessed, if she hasn't lumped me in with Harrison by this time, tomorrow night. She's trying to sort it all out, like the rest of us. With the added handicap of being young. You see that, don't you?"

"I keep thinking...any day, now, she'll be out of diapers."

"Might help to think of her as a late bloomer. Let her get used to casting her own shadow for awhile." He tossed the bottle cap into the waste basket. "She has enormous potential. And, she has a hell of a lot of respect for you."

Paul ran a hand through his hair. "Not after tonight."

"You underestimate yourself, and her, if you believe that. You know, you two are more alike than perhaps you'd care to admit."

"If I was sober, I'd be offended."

"If you were sober, you'd probably agree with me."

Lucky stretched and yawned. He looked briefly at the two men, and then settled his muzzle down on his paws with a sigh.

Terry broke the troubled silence. "Off the record? What are the chances that dog has rabies?"

"Zero to none, on or off the goddamn record. Like someone else we know...he's been traumatized." Paul shook his head. "One thing I regret. That I didn't nail the son of a bitch from the start, evidence or no evidence."

"It's that very quality that made me request you as the shelter's vet. You've got the balls to use your head, rather than your fist." When Paul glanced up at him, Terry noted the vestiges of disgrace in his eyes. "That's not an easy lesson to learn." He popped the cap off of the last beer bottle. "I'd like to hold off at least forty-eight hours."

"Unless you're planning to pull an elephant out of a hat, we're just treading water, here."

"I'd like to try and see what I can do. One more thing, off the record. Why did you stay on? I would have lost that bet."

Paul plucked the bottle out of Terry's hand and took a long swallow. He burped, again. "I must have been drunk."

"For a whole year?"

"I wish."

"You know, I'm going to need you stone cold sober tomorrow."

"Too late, now." Paul handed him the half-empty bottle and groaned, climbing to his feet.

"Perhaps you shouldn't drive home."

"I've just spent another Friday night in a boiler room with a butt-naked dog and a dog catcher. I'm not nearly drunk enough." He picked up his medical bag. "No offense."

"None taken," Terry smiled. "Still, I can give you a lift."

"I ate a pound of chocolate frosted holes, half a box of dog biscuits, and six packs of candy cigarettes before you plied me with warm beer. I'll be up 'til dawn, but I'm fine." Paul glanced at his watch. "You're not staying, are you?"

"Just a few loose ends to catch up. Get some sleep. You'll need it, come tomorrow."

"Thanks a lot."

"'Night." Climbing the stairs, Paul raised a hand of farewell over his shoulder.

Terry took another swallow of ale and looked at Lucky. The dog thumped his tail and yawned again. After a moment of serious consideration, Terry unlatched the pen door, then reached in and offered his hand.

Lucky sniffed his hand, then licked it, and rolled over to expose his belly for a rub. Terry obliged him. "You are one big elephant."

Lucky thumped his tail, again. As he sat there, petting the dog, Terry's smile slipped away. A vague, but familiar, sadness drifted down around him. This wasn't going to be easy. He pulled the recorder from his pocket and fumbled with the buttons.

"All right...down to brass tacks..."

Chapter 74

Rapping on the door.

Silence.

Shhhhhh! It's still there. Look! The light along the bottom of the door - see there - the shadow, tiptoeing past.

It knows I'm here.

Yes!

Far away…dogs barking…menacing laughter…frightened crying…and water…water flushing through pipes that swayed on chains, above her.

From down the hall, the crying drains into screams.

Keep quiet. Stay still.

Footsteps creak the floorboards on the ceiling…following the water flow and the pipes

Stay perfectly still…don't move…

A sinister shadow flits across the hall further down in the dank catacombs…a door creaks…is it opening or closing? Please no…please…

The foot fall on the floor above pauses, as if it heard her. It turns back…

Keep your mouth shut…don't breathe…

Please! Please, someone help, it's coming!

The door looms taller…stretching with agonized, warped creaking, twisting, writhing. And, then it stops.

Silence.

The metal doorknob squeaks, turning. Help me, please help me!

What are you afraid of?

What? Wait! Who are you?

Bam! The door slams back on its hinges.

Blinding light and wild, wailing screams rush forward.

Flailing her arms against the shadows, Peggy gasped in silent shrieks, no air left in her lungs. Her calves seared with cramps, as she kicked against the tangle of blankets. The bedside lamp crashed to the floor, the shattered light bulb plunging the room into darkness.

Choking and gagging for air, she pounded the window panes with her fists, until a blood curdling scream erupted from deep within her.

"NOOOOOOO!"

Crash! Her fists shattered the window and glass shards sprayed her shoulders and face. Thrusting her head out into the night, Peggy gulped for air, as if just spewed from an ocean riptide. Fully awake now, she hung halfway out her broken window and stared downward into the jaws of the dumpsters below.

Her head spinning, she drew back inside, nicking her arm on jagged glass. She caught sight of her fractured reflection in the splintered pane. Her eyes bulged in panic. Scrambling away from her visage, she fell out of bed, entangling her legs in the sheets. Caught like an animal, she covered her face with shaking hands and whimpered.

What are you afraid of?

"No!" She clapped her hands over her ears and rocked back and forth. "A is for angel! Two times two is four. You can't hurt me anymore! B is for begone! Two times three is six. There are no more whipping sticks! C is for calm! Two times four is eight! I control my own fate!" She ripped away the sheets from her legs, stood and yelled into the room. "D is for dawn! Two times five is ten! I will not let you hurt me, again!" Contempt gushed up her throat and exploded into a vehement chant. "I'm awake! I'm safe! I'm in control! I'm awake! I'm safe! I'm in control!"

What are you afraid of?

"Shutup!" A surge of anger flooded her. She lunged at the bed and tore the blankets off. "Leave me alone!" The voices sneered at her. She yanked the mattress off and hurled it across the room. Laughter echoed off the walls. "I said leave me alone!" She grasped hold of the box spring and hauled it off of the iron frame. She flung it with such force, it knocked the kitchen table over. She searched wildly for something else to throw, then stopped dead, and let out a shriek of rage.

"E is for enough! *No more! Enough!*"

Pounding sounded on the ceiling above her and through the walls.

She shook her fist. "Enough! I've had enough!" Snatching up her badge, her coat, and Lucky's folder, Peggy ran out her door.

Rounding the corner of the firehouse Peggy skidded to a stop at the top of the driveway, having run five blocks. In her haste, she'd jumped on the wrong bus and gotten off at the wrong stop. Lightheaded, she leaned over her knees.

A bicycle bell startled her, and she looked up to see a messenger swerving alongside the curb.

"Special Delivery for Farroway shelter?" the winded cyclist asked. Peggy nodded. "Far out. Third time I been around. Dweeb wanted these, but his name ain't on the list. You are?"

"Peggy. Peggy Dillan."

The guy checked off her name, and then pulled four large envelopes from his pack. "Sign by the X."

Peggy signed the forms and glanced at her watch. It was just seven a.m.. "You-you said somebody is here?"

"Yeah. He's pretty ticked off. But he ain't on the list."

Peggy dug in her pocket and offered him fifty cents.

"Thanks." He flashed her a peace sign and took off, back up the street.

Tucking the envelopes under arm, Peggy trotted down the driveway, then halted. Harrison's dark Mercedes was parked by the front gate. A shudder skated down her spine.

The cellar door was open! She scanned the parking lot for any familiar cars. It was empty. She was the first one of the crew to arrive. Why was that monster here? And, how did he get the cellar door open? Her heart thudded in her chest. Lucky!

Forcing one foot in front of the other, her pace quickened, until she broke into a run down the gravel slope towards the cellar. She slid under the Duck Head sign, grabbed hold of the cellar door and flung it aside.

The cellar stairs dove downward, and from the murkiness below she heard Harrison's voice, angry and threatening.

What are you afraid of?

Her heart hammering in her throat, Peggy shot out a hand and grasped hold of the bannister, then swung her foot forward down onto the first step. In spite of the scorching current of fear that shot through her body, muffling her hearing, and numbing her limbs, she forced herself down another step. Then another.

She began to hum. "Two times one is two. I will not let him hurt you!" Lucky! Lucky where are you?

What do you think you're doing! No!! Don't go down there!

Two times two is four…you…he…I…will not hurt us, anymore! Wait. How does it go again?

Save yourself! Go back!

Halfway down, Peggy cast a dizzy glance back over her shoulder; a thick fog spiraled between her and the door. Her escape was cut off!

Run! Hide!

Cold and numb, she ignored the voices. Her legs belonged to someone else; someone who couldn't—no, wouldn't—let anyone hurt Lucky. She would not abandon him!

Peggy continued to descend through the shadows that writhed around and through her, trying to confuse her, the line between real and unreal dissipating with every step down into the abyss.

Hand over clammy hand, Peggy pulled herself down the bannister. After an eternity, her foot touched the slate floor. Instantly, she found herself in the grips of ataxia. Somewhere above her head a light flickered, and through the fog, she caught sight of the source of the raging fury.

Quaking with dread, Peggy gaped at the monster madly bellowing by the wall. It's back to her, the deranged monster gesticulated in ferocious spasms, while it railed into a phone.

A phone? Peggy shook off a wave of dizziness, trying to make sense of what she saw, trying to remember where she'd seen the spectre before—in the night, in the dreams—oh, why couldn't she wake up?

Slam! The wind blew the cellar door shut and Peggy collapsed against the stairs. "No!"

Too late! Too late!

The malevolent chimera turned and saw her. She cowered, as it hung up the phone and slithered towards her.

The phone? A yellow phone. Peggy stared at it, feeling confused. Something isn't right. This isn't how the dream goes. Yes, it was a phone, like the one in the office, but…the office, she remembered, with a breathless start, in the shelter…but, how could she be in the shelter, and in the dream at the same time?

The spectre snaked through the fog towards her, shaking a fist at her. "…trying to pull? Where's my…where's…warden?"

Peggy couldn't make sense of the words, the roar in her head was deafening. This isn't right. This isn't how it goes, she panted. Frantically, she pinched her palms. Wake up, I want to wake up, help me wake up!

"Where is he?" the monster roared at her, spittle hitting her face.

She reached behind her and felt the stairs solid and very real digging into her back. In a rush of panic, she remembered Lucky. She had to save Lucky! Where is he? Through the fog, her eyes discerned a pen. She saw Lucky's blanket but, the pen was empty! Her eyes darted around.

"Lucky?" she croaked. "Lucky!"

Shutup you stupid filth! Or he'll kill you!

"Where is he?" the spectre bellowed.

Expecting a blow, Peggy cowered.

"Where is the manager?" it shrieked.

Manager?

Peggy opened her eyes.

In a fit of rage, the ogre gestured wildly, bumping its head on an overhead light. Light and shadow bounced around, illuminating every corner of the room. Peggy looked around in confusion. This was no cave, no bottomless pit of hell! It was just a room. And, what was hulking before her was no banshee, it was a man.

Harrison.

He snatched up a paper from the counter and waved it at her. "What is this, and where is my dog? Where is the manager? Answer me!"

She tried to speak, but nothing came out of her mouth. She searched the room, hoping for rescue, and suddenly she heard a voice—a kind voice—cresting the waves of panic, rising above the fury crashing into her.

"I'd like you to trust, not me, but yourself...promise?"

Terry's words. Her promise. All at once, she could see Terry standing at the back window in the office, his eyes on the barrier of warehouses, his heart peering past them to a hidden horizon, and the possibilities beyond.

Peggy focused on the piece of paper being thrust at her face. Title 4, Chapter 22; SPCA Claim To Impound, and at the bottom of the brief legal document, was Terry's signature.

Harrison was still yelling at her. "If you think you're going to get away with this, you are mistaken. There is no evidence, no criteria for

this confiscation and no right to impound. I'll bring your entire person-
nel up on charges!"

"I'm going to need to count on you tomorrow...can I do that?"

Peggy gawked at the veins throbbing in Harrison's neck, his face
twisted and seething with anger. And, then she saw it, the faint, fading
bruise just under his eye.

"I will close this place down tomorrow, and if you think I can't, I'll
see your manager in jail before that dog's head is halfway to Trenton!"

Clara? What's the scuttlebutt you hear about...? As Peggy's mind
bent back to her ride home with Joe and Clara, last night, Harrison
wavered into a man dressed as a surgeon for Halloween, following two
kids in bandages. A doctor...like Paul. She closed her eyes to see him
more clearly. She heard him say: *"Until you walk down those stairs, face
your fears, once and for all, you'll be running and hiding for the rest of
your life from every son-of-a-bitch who picks up your scent, and they will
because they know what I know. You're the one holding the whip, no one
else."*

"Are you listening to me?" Harrison towered over her, and waved
the form in her face. "You pathetic, stupid bitch, you have no idea who
you're dealing with, do you?"

Opening her eyes, she saw herself in the sweat-slicked face of the
man. Those were not the eyes of a monster; they belonged to someone
wildly afraid. Like her. She could smell it—cold, raw fear. She noticed
the beads of perspiration on his upper lip. His trembling lips. Pulling
herself up to her feet, she squared her shoulders.

"Yes, yes I do," she breathed, "I-I know exactly who I am dealing
with. And-and I know what you're afraid of."

With all the strength she had left in her, she held up the large, manila envelope of x-rays. "So-so does the hospital, where they've seen the
bruises and broken bones of your children, all these years. Tell me, how
do you sleep at night, next to her?"

Harrison stared at her, sweat dripping into his eyes.

With every word forced out of her mouth, Peggy's voice grew steadi-
er, stronger. "How many times have you and your children 'run into the
door', or-or 'fallen down the stairs'? How long have you been covering
for her? What do you think Town Hall will do when they find out that
you not only didn't stop her from beating your children, but you gave
your wife a defenseless dog to beat on, too?"

Harrison's eyes flickered and he backed up a step away from her. Checkmate.

"Sign the form," she hissed. She yanked a pen from her pocket and held it out to him. Her hand was steady. He finally snatched it, and his own hands shaking, smoothed out the papers on the counter.

She heard pounding, then, becoming loud and insistent. It was coming from above them, on the cellar door. She remembered the wind slamming it shut. She heard her name being called, but she kept her eyes on Harrison, until he signed the form. She could hear footsteps running on gravel, and the back gate's rusted hinges scraping open.

She knew Harrison could hear it, too.

Finished, he tossed the pen on the counter, then narrowed his eyes at her, looking dark, and dangerous.

As if in a peace offering, she held out the manila envelope of x-rays to him. He ripped them in half and flung them to the floor. Just then, Paul burst through the French doors, followed by Joe. They skidded to a stop on the ramp.

"What the hell's going on?" Paul stammered.

Peggy held up the signed papers. "He was just leaving," she said, her voice hoarse.

Harrison dragged his eyes off of her and turned for the stairs.

Peggy took another breath and forced his name out of her mouth. "Mr. Harrison? One more thing." He stopped. She reached into her pocket and pulled out a well-worn business card, lowering her voice. "None of this happened, unless you take care of this, Monday morning. The counselors at Stillwater will be expecting your call."

Harrison unclenched his fist to take it from her, but she didn't let go of it right away. His eyes flicked to hers.

"Your lifestyle has just changed," she whispered. "It doesn't include owning a pet. I trust we have an understanding."

Harrison yanked the card from her fingers, and then ascended the stairs. With a violent shove, he shouldered the cellar door open.

Peggy listened to the crunch of his shoes on the gravel, as if over so many brittle bones. She heard his car door slam and the engine roar. There was an angry horn honk exchange, and she heard the familiar chugging muffler of Betty's Buick entering the lot. Once she heard the squeal of tires up out of the driveway, she knew Harrison was finally gone.

Her knees buckled and she collapsed to the stairs, trembling from head to toe.

"Peg?" Instantly, Paul was at her side, checking her over. "What the hell happened, down here?"

"She okay?" Joe fretted. "If he touched her, I swear to God I'll…"

"I-I'm okay," Peggy handed Joe the form. "We got it. The transfer of ownership."

"What? How?"

With a shaking hand, Peggy picked up a torn x-ray from the floor, and handed it to Paul. "You're going to need to reorder Lucky's x-rays." Puzzled, he looked at her. She shrugged. "Terry was-he was right. Sometimes it's all about the bluff."

Paul suddenly noticed the empty pen and yanked aside the blankets. "Where's Lucky?"

Peggy looked up, sharply. "I thought…you don't have him?"

"Why would I have him?"

"You-you didn't take him to the EVC?"

"Joe?" Paul began.

"Don't look at me! I left before you!"

"Terry must have him," Paul murmured. "He said he had some loose ends to tie up."

"I swung by his place on the way in, but he musta left already…wait a sec," Joe said, leafing through the paperwork on the counter. "What's all this? Ter wrote a letter to the mayor?"

Betty tripped down the stairs, nearly colliding with Joe. "Lawd, oh Lawd, tell me he ain't done killed the dog!" She stopped and gawked at Peggy. "Hel-lo…?"

"Y'all didn't do it, did you?" Curtis pushed past them. He saw the empty pen and turned a questioning face to Peggy. Clara picked her way carefully down the steps.

"Why're me cats still locked up top? Cor, what's all this, then?" she said on finding Peggy at the bottom of the stairs.

"Hey, hey, hey!" Joe jabbered, " Listen to this! 'I, Terrence Brannan, do hereby take full responsibility for the impound of…yada yada…dog belonging to…yada yada…and in no way did any of the shelter's employees or Officer Dillan take any part in…' his smile slipped and he trailed off as he read on, his eyes growing wide. "…what the…holy motherfrickin' crap!" Pale, he looked to Peggy, then to the empty pen.

She followed his sight line, and something in the empty pen caught her eye. She peeled a blanket aside, revealing Terry's recorder, with a sticky note attached, bearing the words: For Peggy. She stared at it, dumbstruck. So did everyone else. She picked it up, then looked to Joe.

"Marone," Joe exhaled. "Now, that's what I call a bluff!"

Paul looked from the impound form, to Terry's recorder in Peggy's hands. "No."

"Mary Francis, Lawd love a duck," Betty hooted. "Yes!"

Curtis snapped to attention, slammed his fist into his chest and then towards heaven. "Powah to the people!" He turned to Paul. "This mean that basilisk gonna hafta git the shots now, right?"

"Harrison?" Betty reiterated.

"The fourteen shots in the gut?" Curtis nodded.

Joe clapped a hand over his mouth to stifle a snort. "Holy shit!"

Paul sputtered a laugh, incredulous at first, then before long, he was doubled over with laughter, unable to stop.

"Lady Justice is served!" Clara declared. Chin high, she held out her hand. "Fair do's!"

"Aw, jeeeeeeeeze, I give up!" Joe tossed her his badge.

Betty handed the old woman her purse, and then removed her earrings and her watch. "I know bettah. I know bettah!"

In a moment, they were all laughing and talking at once. Except for Peggy. Dazed, she walked up the little ramp and through the French doors, leaving the cellar behind.

She wandered into the backyard, and the breaking dawn. The ground was cold and hard underfoot, but it was solid, it was real, and that was enough. Her arms and legs still tingled, but they didn't hurt, anymore.

She sank down on the back steps, and with trembling fingers, pressed the play button on Terry's recorder. After a few bumps, clicks and the shuffle of handling, Terry's voice emitted from the little speaker clearly. It was almost as if he was sitting right beside her.

"All right, down to brass tacks...whomever finds this...Lucky is safe. He's with me. You'll find my signature on the impound form on the counter. I am taking full responsibility for this decision, and I've stated as much in a letter addressed to the mayor, which you'll find on the counter as well. It absolves all of you, the doc, the entire shelter from my actions, should you ever need it. This leaves Harrison two choices; be eaten up alive worrying about coming down with rabies for the next two years, or suffer the agony of fourteen shots in the belly along with some very nasty side effects, just to make sure he doesn't. Either way, serves him right. Bottom line, he will never be able to hurt Lucky, again. That's a promise you can bank on."

She held the recorder closer to her ear, hearing Lucky yawn in the background. "I'm hoping that you're the one who finds this first, Peggy. Knowing you, I should have made book on it. For the record, we both know that Lucky's not the first case, nor will he be the last. One corner at a time, remember? For now, my friend and I are off to take a very belated vacation and see what might be waiting over the horizon. Peggy, tell Joe to hang tough, and make me proud. Tell Betty to keep everyone in line, as only she can. And Clara? The Birthday Honors are hers, now. Oh, and tell the good doc to get a haircut."

Peggy heard him clear his throat. "Saint Francis..." He paused, and she heard a little catch in his voice when he continued, "...the fort is yours. I trust that it couldn't be in better hands."

From that point, the tape was blank. Peggy heard a far off honking and looked up. A tattered flock of Canadian geese soared above the bare branches of the silver maple. In the early winter chill, she watched them continue over the abandoned warehouses, heading south into open skies, following the sun on a morning as bright as the smile on her tear-streaked face.

"You must 'ave endings, in order to 'ave beginings."
- Clara Croft

"Ar scáth a chéile a mhaireann na daoine."
Under the shelter of each other, people survive.
- Mr. Riley

ABOUT THE AUTHOR

Ms. Conroy spent ten years on the stage, starring in comedies, musicals and dramas in award-winning regional theaters such as the acclaimed Center Stage, the Capitol Cafe Theatre, the Cable Car Playhouse as well as radio station KCSN's old time radio recreation show *THIRTY MINUTES TO CURTAIN*. In between theatrical appearances, Ms. Conroy lent her speaking talents to The Bronx Zoo (The New York Zoological Association) and Turtle Back Zoo as a public lecturer for their animal education out reach programs. Her passion for animal welfare led to her involvement with a New Jersey animal shelter, where she worked as an animal control officer, and as a nurse at local animal hospitals and emergency clinics.

She later attended New York University, and was placed in the prestigious Tisch School of the Arts where she graduated with honors and an impressive portfolio of work. She wrote and directed ten short films, one of which was titled *SHELTER*, a film based on a particular incident during her shelter days. *SHELTER* won multiple awards both nationally and internationally, including the Arthur Chisholm Humanitarian Award.

After the release of *SHELTER*, Ms. Conroy won the national NEA/ AFI writing competition, and a grant to make another multiple award-winning half-hour film, *DADDY'S GIRL*. This project took her to Los Angeles where she fulfilled another lifelong dream. She was recruited by the Walt Disney Company as an assistant animator and story board artist, where she helped to develop feature films, before moving on to share her expertise with other studios. Working with directors Stevie Wermers-Skelton and Kevin Deters, Ms. Conroy wrote the short film *THE BALLAD OF NESSIE,* based on Ms. Wermers student film, and which was subsequently released with the *WINNIE THE POOH* film in the summer of 2011, then published as a Little Golden Book (under the pseudonym Kieran Lachlan).

Today, Ms. Conroy's dream is to use her public speaking skills and profits from the sale of her own books and art work to create a network of progressive education programs in both animal and women's shelters across the country, in hopes of bettering the odds and futures for battered animals, women and children; with the express goal of rendering the need for such facilities as obsolete within her lifetime.

Ms. Conroy begins this new crossroads in her life with the publication of *SHELTER–LOST AND FOUND,* as her first step towards making that dream a reality. She resides on a ranch in California where she can be found writing and sketching in between chores; caring for a thirty year-old retired movie horse, a cantankerous pet Holstein cow, two African Pygmy goats, a duck that thinks it's human, a dog that thinks it's a coyote, two kooky cats, two noisy love birds, and a canyon of protected wildlife—including mountain lions, bobcats, coyotes, owls, hawks, deer, rabbits and rattlesnakes.